KU-637-576

Elias Khoury

Gate of the Sun

Bab El Shams

TRANSLATED FROM THE ARABIC
BY
Humphrey Davies

Harvill *Secker*
LONDON

Published by Harvill Secker, 2005

2 4 6 8 10 9 7 5 3 1

© Elias Khoury, 1998
English translation © Humphrey Davies, 2005

Elias Khoury has asserted his right under the Copyright, Designs and Patents Act
1988 to be identified as the author of this work

Maps drawn by Reginald Piggott

This book is sold subject to the condition that it shall not, by way of trade or
otherwise, be lent, resold, hired out, or otherwise circulated without the publisher's
prior consent in any form of binding or cover other than that in which it is published
and without a similar condition including this condition being imposed on the
subsequent purchaser

First published with the title *Bâb al-Chams* by Dâr-al-Adâb, Beirut, 1998

First published in Great Britain in 2005 by
HARVILL SECKER
Random House, 20 Vauxhall Bridge Road, London SW1V 2SA

Random House Australia (Pty) Limited
20 Alfred Street, Milsons Point, Sydney, New South Wales 2061, Australia

Random House New Zealand Limited
18 Poland Road, Glenfield, Auckland 10, New Zealand

Random House South Africa (Pty) Limited
Isle of Houghton, Corner Boundary Road & Carse O'Gowrie, Houghton 2198, South Africa

The Random House Group Limited Reg. No. 954009
www.randomhouse.co.uk

A CIP catalogue record for this book is available from the British Library

The Koranic quotes in this volume are taken from *The Koran Interpreted*,
translated with an introduction by Arthur J. Arberry.
(Oxford, 1998.)

ISBN 1 84343 103 3

This book has been selected to receive financial assistance from English PEN's
Writers in Translation programme, supported by

Bloomberg

www.englishpen.org/writersintranslation

Papers used by Random House are natural, recyclable products made from wood
grown in sustainable forests; the manufacturing processes conform to the
environmental regulations of the country of origin

Typeset in Perpetua by Palimpsest Book Production Limited, Polmont, Stirlingshire
Printed and bound in Great Britain by William Clowes Ltd, Beccles, Suffolk

TRANSLATOR'S NOTE

There are many different approaches to the spelling of Arabic names in
Latin characters, and no one system works perfectly in all contexts. In
most cases here I have used spellings that approach the actual Palestinian
pronunciation and that non-Arab readers should find at least somewhat
familiar and pronounceable. By the same token I have avoided those that
invoke formal literary ("Classical") Arabic or an academic transcription.
I did this on the one hand so as not to betray the Palestinian specificity
of the characters and places occurring in the book and on the other hand
so that readers would not be jolted into an inappropriately pedantic
world. Examples are "El Kweikat" rather than "Al-Kuwaykat", "Sileiman"
rather than "Sulayman", "El Ghabsiyyeh" rather than "Al-Ghabisiyyah",
"Ein El Zeitoun" rather than "'Ayn al-Zaytun," "Saleema" rather than
"Salima" etc. I could have gone further ("Likwikat" for "El Kweikat",
"Libriwwi" for "El Bruwweh") but tried to stay within a range where the
underlying forms were still decodable to those who know Arabic.

The exception that proves this rule is the epigraph about Shaykh Al
Junayd. To be consistent, I should have written "Sheikh El Juneid". But
the passage is not consistent, linguistically or literarily, with the rest of
the book. It invokes a different world — that of classical Arabic and the
pre-modern literary tradition; hence the more formal spelling. Similarly,
when names of Classical poets are mentioned elsewhere in the book (for
example Imru' Al Qays), I have used the Classical forms.

H. D.

He said, God be pleased with him:

Shaykh Al Junayd set out on a journey of devotion and while travelling was overtaken by thirst. He found a well that was too deep to draw water from, so he took off his girdle, lowered it into the well until it reached the water, and set about raising and lowering it and squeezing it into his mouth. A dervish appeared and asked him, "Why do it so? Tell the water to rise, and drink with your hands!" and the dervish approached the edge of the well and said to the water, "Rise, with God's permission," and it rose and the shaykh and the dervish drank. Afterwards the shaykh turned to the dervish and said, "Who are you?" "One of God's creatures," he replied. "Who is your shaykh?" asked Al Junayd. "My shaykh is Al Junayd, though I have yet to set eyes on him," replied the man. "Then how did you attain these powers?" asked the shaykh. "Through my faith in my shaykh," replied the man.

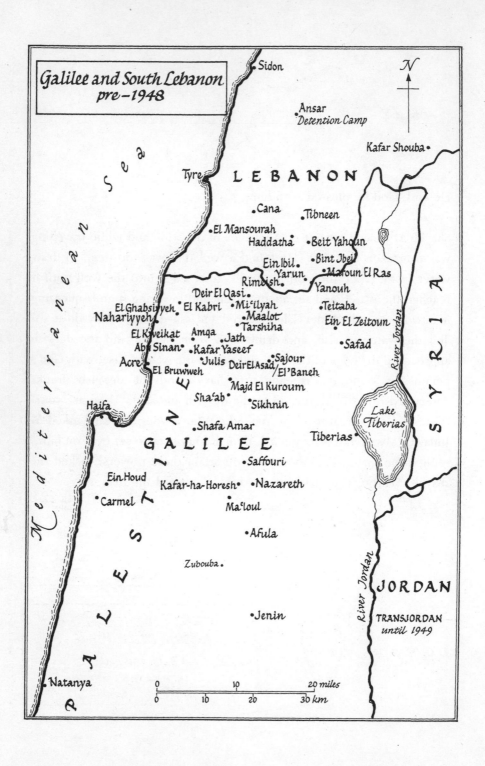

Galilee and South Lebanon
pre–1948

N

Sidon

Ansar
Detention Camp

Kafar Shouba•

Tyre   L E B A N O N

•Cana   •Tibneen

•El Mansourah   •Beit Yahoun
Haddatha•
Ein Ibil•   •Bint Ibeil
Yarun•   •Maroun El Ras
Rimeish•   Yanouh

Deir El Qasi•
El Ghabsiyyeh•   •El Kabri   •Mi'ilyah   •Teitaba
Nahariyyeh•   •Maalot   •Ein El Zeitoun
El Kweikat•   Amqa•   Jath•   •Tarshiha
Abu Sinan•   •Kafar Yaseef   •Safad
Acre•   Julis•   •Sajour
•El Bruwweh   Deir El Asad•   /El'Baneh
Sha'ab•   •Majd El Kuroum
Haifa   •Sikhnin

•Shafa Amar   G A L I L E E

•Saffouri   Tiberias•   Lake
Tiberias

Ein Houd•   Kafar-ha-Horesh•   •Nazareth
•Carmel   •Ma'loul

•Afula

Zubouba•

•Jenin

Mediterranean Sea

P A L E S T I N E

River Jordan

S Y R I A

River Jordan

J O R D A N
TRANSJORDAN
until 1949

•Natanya

0   10   20 miles
0   10   20   30 km

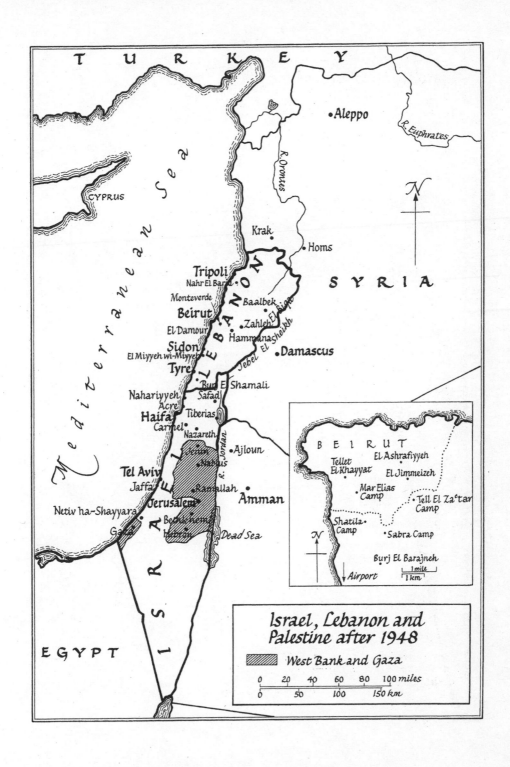

Israel, Lebanon and
Palestine after 1948

⧄⧄⧄ West Bank and Gaza

Part One

GALILEE HOSPITAL

Umm Hassan is dead.

I saw everyone racing through the alleys of the camp and heard the sound of weeping. Everyone was coming out of their houses, bent over to catch their tears, running.

Nabeelah, Mahmoud El Qasimi's wife, our mother, was dead. We called her "Mother" because everyone born in Shatila camp fell from their mother's guts into her hands.

I too had fallen into her hands, and I too ran the day she died.

Umm Hassan came from El Kweikat, her village in Galilee, to become the only midwife in Shatila – a woman of uncertain age and without children. I only knew her when she was old, with stooped shoulders, a face full of wrinkles and creases, large eyes shining in a white square, and a white cloth covering her white hair.

Our neighbour Sana', the wife of Kareem El Jashi the *kunafa*-seller, said Umm Hassan dropped in on her the night before last and told her her death was coming.

"I heard its voice, daughter. Death whispers and its voice is soft."

Speaking in her half-Bedouin accent, she told Sana' about the messenger of death.

"The messenger came in the morning and told me to get ready."

And she told Sana' how she wanted to be prepared for burial.

"She took me by the hand," said Sana', "led me to her house, opened her brown wooden box and showed me the white silk shroud. She told me she would bathe before she went to sleep: 'I'll die pure, and I want only you to wash me.'"

Umm Hassan is dead.

Everyone knew that this Monday morning, 20 October 1995, was the time set for Nabeelah, Fatimah's daughter, to meet death.

Everyone awoke and waited, but no-one was brave enough to go to her house to discover she was dead. Umm Hassan had told everyone, and everyone believed her.

Only I was taken by surprise.

I stayed with you till 11.00 at night, and then, exhausted, I went to my room, and slept. It was night, the camp was asleep, and no-one told me.

But everyone else knew.

No-one would have doubted Umm Hassan because she always told the truth. Hadn't she been the only one to weep on the morning of 5 June 1967? Everyone was dancing in the streets, anticipating going home to Palestine, but she wept. She told everyone she met that she'd decided to wear mourning. Everyone laughed and said Umm Hassan had gone mad. Throughout the six long days of the war, she never opened the windows of her house; on the seventh out she came to wipe away everyone's tears. She said she knew Palestine would never "come back" till all of us had died.

In her long life, Umm Hassan had buried her four children one after the other. They would come to her borne on planks, their clothes covered in blood. All she had left was a son called Naji, who lived in America. Though Naji wasn't her real son, none the less he was: she'd picked him up from beneath an olive tree on the El Kabri–Tarshiha road and fed him from her dry breasts, then returned him to his mother when they reached the village of Cana, in Lebanon.

Umm Hassan died today.

No-one dared go into her house. About twenty women gathered to wait, then Sana' came and knocked on the door, but no-one opened it. She pushed it, it opened, she went in and ran to the bedroom. Umm Hassan was sleeping, her head covered with her white scarf. Sana' went over and took her by the shoulders, and the chill of death flowed into the hands of the *kunafa*-seller's wife, who screamed. The women entered, the weeping began, and everyone raced to the house.

I too would like to run with the others, go in with them, see Umm Hassan sleeping her eternal sleep and breathe in the smell of olives that clung to her small house.

But I didn't weep.

For three months I've been incapable of reacting. Only this man floating above his bed makes me feel the thrill of being alive. For three months he's been laid out on his bed in Galilee Hospital, where I work as a doctor, or where I pretend that I'm a doctor. I sit next to him, and I try. Is he dead or alive? I don't know – am I helping or tormenting him? Should I tell him stories or listen to him?

For three months I've been in this room.

Today Umm Hassan died, and I want him to know, but he doesn't hear. I want him to come with me to her funeral, but he won't get up.

They said he fell into a coma.

An explosion in the brain causing permanent damage. A man lies in front of me, and I have no idea what to do. I just try not to let him rot while he's still alive, because I'm sure he's asleep, not dead.

But what difference does it make?

Is it true what Umm Hassan said about a sleeper being like a dead man – that the sleeper's soul leaves his body only to return when he wakes, but that the dead man's soul leaves and doesn't come back? Where is the soul of Yunis, son of Ibraheem, son of Sileiman El Asadi? Has it left him for a distant place, or is it hovering above us in the hospital room, asking me not to go because the man lies in distant darknesses, afraid of the silence?

I swear I've no idea.

On her first visit Umm Hassan said that Yunis was in torment. She said he was in a different place from us.

"So what should I do?" I asked.

"Do what he tells you," she answered.

"But he doesn't speak," I said.

"Oh yes, he does," she said, "and it's up to you to hear his voice."

And I don't hear it, I swear I don't, but I'm stuck to this chair, and I talk and talk.

Tell me, man, what should I do?

I sit by your side and listen to the sound of weeping coming through the window of your room. Can't you hear it?

Everyone else is weeping, so why don't you?

It's become our habit to look out for occasions to weep, for tears are backed up behind our eyes. Umm Hassan has burst open our reservoir of tears, so why don't you stand up and weep?

Hey, you!

How am I supposed to talk to you, or with you or about you?

Should I tell you stories you already know, or be silent and let you go wherever it is you go? I come close to you, walking on tiptoe so as not to wake you, and then I laugh at myself because all I want is to wake you. I need one thing – one thing, dear God: that this man, drowning in his own eyes, should get up, should open his eyes and say something.

But I'm lying.

Did you know you've turned me into a liar?

I say I want one thing, but I want thousands of things. I lie, God take pity on you, on me and on your poor mother. Yes, we forgot your mother. You told me all your stories, and you never told me how your mother died. You told about the death of your blind father and how you slipped into Galilee and attended his funeral. You stood on the hill above the village of Deir El Asad, seeing but unseen, weeping and not weeping.

At the time I believed you. I believed that intuition had led you to your house there, hours before he died.

But now I don't.

At the time I was bewitched by your story. Now the spell is broken, and I no longer believe.

But your mother?

Why didn't you say anything about her death?

Is your mother dead?

Do you remember the story of the icon of the Virgin Mary?

We were living through the civil war in Lebanon, and you were saying that war shouldn't be like that. You even advised me, when I came back from Beijing as a doctor, not to take part in the war, and asked me to go with you to Palestine.

"But you don't go to fight, Yunis my friend. You go because of your wife."

You gave me a long lecture about the meaning of war and then said something about the picture of the Virgin Mary in your house, and that was when I asked you if your mother was Christian and how the sheikh of the village of Ein El Zeitoun could have married a Christian woman. You explained that she wasn't a Christian but loved the Virgin and used to put her picture under her pillow, and that she'd made you love the Virgin too because she was the mistress of all the world's women and because her picture was beautiful – a woman bending her head over her son, born swaddled in his shroud.

"And what did the sheikh think?" I asked you.

It was then that you explained to me that your father the sheikh was blind, and that he never saw the picture at all.

When did Naheeleh tell you of your mother's death?

Why don't you tell me? Is it because your wife said your mother had asked to be buried with the picture and this caused a problem in the village?

Why do you sleep like that and not answer?

You sleep like sleep itself. You sleep in sleep, and drown. The doctor said you had a blood clot on the brain, were clinically dead, and there was no hope. I ordered him to get out of my way and refused to believe him.

I see you in front of me and can do nothing.

I hold conversations with you, and I tell you stories. I'll tell you everything. What do you say – I'll make tea, and we'll sit on the low chairs in front of your house and tell tales! You used to laugh at me because I don't smoke. You used to smoke your cigarette right to the end, chewing on the butt hanging between your lips and sucking in the smoke.

Now here I am. I close the door of your room. I sit next to you. I light a cigarette, draw the smoke deep into my lungs, and I tell you tales. And you don't answer.

Why don't you talk to me?

The tea's gone cold, and I'm tired. You're immersed in the process of breathing and don't care.

Please don't believe them.

Do you remember the day when you came to me and said that everyone was sick of you, and I couldn't dispel the sadness from your round white face? What was I supposed to say? Should I have said your day had passed, or hadn't yet come? You'd have been even more upset, and I couldn't lie to you. So I'm sad too, and my sadness is a deep breach in my soul that I can't repair, but I swear I don't want you to die.

Why did you lie to me?

Why did you tell me after the mourners had left that Naheeleh's death didn't matter, because a woman only dies if her man stops loving her, and Naheeleh hadn't died, because you still loved her?

"She's here," you said, and you pointed at your eyes, wide open to show their dark grey. I was never able to identify the colour of your eyes — when I asked you, you would say that Naheeleh didn't know what colour they were either, and that at Bab El Shams she used to ask you about the colours of things.

You lied to me.

You convinced me that Naheeleh hadn't died, and didn't finish the sentence. At the time I didn't take in what you'd said; I thought they were the beautiful words an old lover uses to heal his love — but death was in the other half of the sentence, because a man dies when his woman stops loving him, and you're dying because Naheeleh stopped loving you when she died.

So here you are, drowsing.

Dear God, what drowsiness is this? And why do I feel a deathly drowsiness when I'm near you? I lean back in the chair and sleep. When I get up in the middle of the night, I feel pain all over my body.

I come close to you, I see the air roiling around you, and I see that place I haven't visited. I'd decided to go; everyone goes, so why not me? I'd go and have a look. I'd go and anchor the landmarks in my eyes. You used to tell me that you knew the sites because they were engraved on your eyes like indelible landmarks.

Where are the landmarks, my friend? How shall I know the road, and who will guide me?

You told me about the caves dug out of the rocks. Is it true that you used to meet her there? Or were you lying to me? You said they were called Bab El Shams – Gate of the Sun – and smiled and said you didn't mean the Shams I was in love with, or that terrible massacre at El Miyyeh wi-Miyyeh camp, where they killed her.

You told me I didn't love Shams and should forget her: "If you loved her, you'd avenge her. It can't be love, son. You love a woman who doesn't love you, and that's an impossibility."

You don't understand. How can I avenge a woman who was killed because of another man?

"So she didn't love you," you said.

"She did but in her own way," I answered.

"Love has a thousand doors. But one-sided love isn't a door, it's a delusion."

I didn't tell you then that your love for Naheeleh may have been a delusion too, because you only met her on journeys that resembled dreams.

I draw close to tell you that the moon is full. In El Ghabsiyyeh, we love the moon, and we fear it. When it's full, we don't sleep.

Get up and look at the moon.

You didn't tell me about your mother, but I'm going to tell you about mine. The truth is, I don't know much about her – she disappeared. They said she'd gone to her people in Amman, and when I was in Jordan in 1970 I looked for her, but that's another tale I'll tell you later.

I told you about my mother, and I'm going to tell you again. When you were telling me about Bab El Shams, you used to say that stories are like wine: they mature in the telling. Does that mean that the telling of a story is like the jar it's kept in? You used to tell the stories of Naheeleh over and over again, your eyes shining with the same desire.

"She cast a spell on me, that woman," you'd say.

But I know that the spellbinder was you – how else did you persuade Naheeleh to put up with you, reeking with the stink of travel?

My mother used to wake me while it was still night in the camp and whisper to me, and I'd get up and see the moon in its fullness, and not go back to sleep.

The woman from El Kweikat said we were mad: "Ghabsiyyeh people are crazy, because they're afraid of the moon." But we weren't afraid — though in fact, yes, we did stay awake all night. My mother wouldn't let me sleep. She'd tie a black scarf around her head and ask me to look at the face of the moon so I could see my dead father's face.

"Do you see him?" she'd ask.

I'd say that I saw him, though I swear I didn't. But now, can you believe it, now, after years and years, when I look at the face of the moon, I see my father's face, stained with blood. My mother said they killed him, left him in a heap at the door and went off. She said he fell in a heap as though he wasn't a man but a sack, and when she went over to him, she didn't see him. They took him and buried him in secret in the Martyrs' Cemetery. "Look at your father and tell him what you want."

I used to look and not see, but I wouldn't say. Now I see, but what am I supposed to say?

Get up, man, and look at the face of the moon. Do you see your wife? Do you see my father? Certainly you will never see my mother, and even if you see her, you will never know her. Even I have forgotten her, forgotten her voice and her tears. The only thing I remember is the taste of the dough she used to make in the clay oven in front of our house. She would put red pepper, oil, cumin and onions on a piece of dough and bake it. Then she'd make tea and eat, and I'd eat with her, and we'd look at the moon. That burning taste overwhelms my tongue and my eyes, and I drink tea and look at the moon, and I see.

My mother told me that in my father's village they didn't sleep. When the moon grew round and sat on the dish of the sky, the whole village would wake up, and the blind singer would sit in the square and play his one-stringed fiddle, singing to the night as though he was weeping. And I am weeping with drowsiness, and the taste of the hot pepper, and what seem to be dreams.

The moon is full, my swimmer in white sheets. Get up and look and drink tea with me. Or didn't you people in Ein El Zeitoun get up when the moon was full?

But you're not from Ein El Zeitoun. Well, you are from Ein El Zeitoun, but your blind father moved to Deir El Asad after the village was massacred in 1948.

You were born in Ein El Zeitoun, and they called you Yunis. You told me your blind father named you Yunis — Jonah — because, like Jonah, you'd vanquished death.

You didn't tell me about your mother; it was Amna who told me. She claimed to be your cousin on your father's side and had come to help you put the house to rights. She was also beautiful. Why did you get angry with me that day? I swear I didn't mean anything by it. I smiled — and you glowered, went out of the house and left me with her.

You came into your house, and you saw me sitting with Amna, who was giving me some water. She told me she knew everything about me because you'd told her, and she asked me to watch out for you because she couldn't always come from Ein El Hilweh camp to Shatila. I smiled at you and winked, and from that day on I never saw Amna at your house again. I swear I didn't mean anything. Well, I did mean something, but when all's said and done you're a man, so you shouldn't get angry. People are like that, they've been that way since Adam, God grant him peace, and people betray the ones they love; they betray them and they regret it; they betray them because they love them, so what's the problem?

It's a terrible thing. Why did you tell Amna to stop visiting you? Was it because she loved you? I know — when I see a woman in love, I know. She overflows with love and becomes soft and undulating. Not men. Men are to be pitied because they don't know that softness that floods and leavens the muscles.

Amna loved you, but you refused to marry her. She told me about it, just as she told me other things she made me swear I'd never mention in front of you. I'm released from my oath now because you can't hear, and even if you could there'd be nothing you could do. All you could say is that Amna was a liar and end the conversation.

Amna told me your whole story.

She told me about your father.

She said that Sheikh Ibraheem, son of Salim, son of Sileiman El Asadi, was in his forties when he married, and that for twenty years his wife kept giving birth to children who'd die a few days later because she was stricken with a nameless disease. Her nipples would get inflamed and collapse when the children started to nurse and they'd die of hunger. Then you were born. You alone, Amna told me, were able to bite on a breast without a nipple. You would bite and suck, and your mother would scream with the pain. So you were saved from death.

I didn't believe Amna, because the story seems impossible. Why didn't your mother get medicine for her breasts? And why did the children die? Why didn't your father take the children to the village women to nurse?

I didn't believe Amna, but you confirmed what she said, which made me doubt it even more. You said that for the rest of her life your mother used to remind you of the pain she'd suffered when she was suckling you. And when I asked you why your father didn't marry another woman, you put up your hand as though you didn't want me to raise that question — because your people, you told me, "marry only one woman and one time, and that's the way it's been from the beginning".

I imagined a savage child and saw a big head and two lips gobbling a woman's breasts, and the woman weeping.

Then you told me that the problem wasn't because there were no nipples. Your brothers and sisters died because they had a mysterious disease, which was transferred to them from their mother's inflamed breasts.

I see you now, and I see that child, and I see its big head, its face within the flood of light pouring onto its lips. I see your mother writhing in pain and pleasure as she feels your lips grabbing at the milk. I can almost hear her sighs and see the pleasure fermenting in her drowsy, heavy eyes. I see you, and I see your death, and I see the end.

Don't tell me you're going to die, please don't. Not death. Umm Hassan told me not to be afraid, and I'm not. She asked me to stay with you because no-one would dare to break into the hospital to find me — even Umm Hassan believed I've turned your death into a hiding place for myself. Even Umm Hassan didn't understand that it's your death I'm trying to prevent, not my own. I'm not afraid of them, and anyway what do I have to do with Shams's death? Plus it's not right that that story should get in the way of yours, which is mythic.

I know you'll say, "Phooey to myths!" and I agree, but I beg you, don't die. For my sake, for your sake, so that they don't find me.

I'm lost, I swear. I'm lost and I'm afraid and I'm in despair and I'm wavering and I'm fidgety and I've remembered and I've forgotten.

I spend most of my time in your room. I finish my work at the hospital and I come back to you. I sit by your side, I bathe you, massage you, put scent on you, sprinkle powder on you and rub your body with ointment. I cover you and make sure you're asleep, and I talk to you. People think I'm talking to myself, like a madman. With you I've discovered many selves within myself, selves with whom I maintain an eternal dialogue.

The thing is, I read in a book whose title I no longer remember that people in comas can have their consciousness restored by being talked to. Dr Amjad said this was impossible. I know that what I read isn't scientific, but I try, I try to rouse you with words, so why don't you answer me? Just one word would be enough.

You're either incapable of speaking, or you don't want to, or you don't know how to.

Which means you have to listen. I know you're sick of my stories because they're your own stories that I'm telling you; I'm giving you back what I took from you. I tell them, and I see the shadow of a smile on your closed lips.

Do you hear my voice?

Do you see my words as shadows?

I'm tired of talking too. I stop, and then the words come. They come like sweat oozing from my pores, and, rather than hearing my voice, I hear yours coming from my throat.

I sit next to you in silence. I listen to the rasp of your breathing, and I feel the tremor of tears, but I don't weep. I say, "That's it, I won't go into your room again. What am I doing here? Nothing."

I sit with death and keep it company. It's difficult keeping death company, father. You yourself told me about the three corpses in the olive grove. Please don't forget – you're a runaway, and a runaway doesn't forget. Do you remember what happened when you got to Ein El Hilweh camp after you were released from prison? Do you remember how you fired your gun into the air and insulted everyone and they arrested you? When they'd set up tents that the wind blew through from both sides, you said to them, "We're not refugees. We're fugitives and nothing more. We fight and kill and are killed, but we're not refugees." You told the people that "refugee" meant something specific, and that the road to the villages of Galilee was open. You had a beard and were filthy – that's what the police report from Sidon says – and you were carrying your rifle in your hand and talking like a madman. The Lebanese officer wrote in his report that you were crazy and let you go. You listened in disbelief, but he bit his lip and winked before ordering you out of the police post. That day you screamed that you'd never leave gaol without your rifle, so they forced you out. And you forced your way back in at night and got your rifle back, as well as three other rifles from the guard post. With those rifles you began.

I don't want the beginning now. I want to tell you that fugitives never sleep. You told me how you used to sleep with one eye closed and the other one open.

Where's your open eye so that you can see me?

I went over to you, opened your eyes and saw the whites. God, how white they were! I know you saw me searching for you because in those two white eyes I saw all your shadows. Didn't you tell me about a man walking with his shadows on those distant roads? In your eyes I see the image of a man who neither lives nor dies.

Why don't you die?

No, please don't die! What shall I do after you die? Remain hiding in the hospital? Leave the country?

Please, no! Death scares me.

Have you forgotten the olive grove, and that woman, and the three men?

You told me that the woman scared you. "All those wars and I was never scared. But that woman, my God! She made my knees go weak and my face twitch. A woman sleeping beneath an olive tree. I went up to her. She was covered by her long hair. I bent over, moved the hair aside and found that the woman was rigid with death, her hair covering a small child that slept curled up on top of her. That was the first time I saw death. I stood back and lit a cigarette and sat in the sun, and there, behind a rock, I saw three men had been dumped."

You were with them and had no way of escaping, because that day the Israeli machine guns were cutting down anyone who "slipped over", which is what the men had done and what you were returning from doing. You told me you lived on olives for a week. You'd break them with sticks, steep them in water and eat their bitterness. "Olives aren't really bitter – their bitterness coats your mouth and lips, but they're soft, and you have to drink water after each one."

You couldn't dig a grave. You dug with your hands because you'd left your rifle buried in a cave three hours away from Deir El Asad. You dug, but you couldn't make a grave that would take the four of them. You dug a little grave for the child but then had second thoughts: was it right to separate it from its mother? In the end you didn't bury any of them; you broke off olive branches, covered the bodies and decided to come back later with a pickaxe to dig them a grave. You covered them with olive branches and continued on your way to Lebanon. And all the many times you went back to Deir El Asad, you never found a trace of them.

I'm with you now, and it's night. The electricity's off, the candle trembles with your shadows, and you don't open your eyes.

Open your eyes and tell me, have you forgotten my name? I'm Dr Khaleel. You told me I was just like your first son, Ibraheem, who died. Think of me as your son who didn't die. Why don't you open one eye and look at me? You're sick, father. I'm going to call you "father", I'm not going to call you by your name any more.

What is your name?

In the camp they call you Abu Salim, in Ein El Zeitoun Abu Ibraheem, on long-distance missions Abu Salih, in Bab El Shams Yunis, in Deir El Asad "the man", and in the Western Sector Izz El Din. Your names are many, and I don't know what to call you.

The first time we met, you were called Abu Salim – though I'm not sure of this because I don't remember the first time, and you don't either. "Remember," you said to me, "you were alone in the boys' camp." My mother had gone to Jordan and left me with my grandmother. I was nine years old. I remember that she'd left me a piece of white paper on which she'd scrawled things I couldn't read, because my mother didn't know how to read or write. I remember her dimly now. I remember a frightened woman hugging me, looking suspiciously at everyone, saying that they were going to kill us like they killed my father. I was afraid of her eyes; her eyes had something deep in them that I couldn't look at. Fear, father, sleeps in the eyes, and in the eyes of that woman who was my mother I saw a cold fear I couldn't rid myself of till I looked into the eyes of Shams.

I know you'll laugh and say I didn't love Shams and ask me to call you

Abu Salim, because Salim – "He who was saved" – was saved from death, and we're not allowed to die.

You used to call Naheeleh Umm Salim – Mother of Salim – telling her, in the cave or beneath the olive tree, that she should use the name of her second son, who'd become her first.

To tell you the truth, I don't know the truth any more, because you didn't tell me your story properly – it came out like this, in snatches. I wanted you to tell it all to me, but I didn't dare ask you to. "Didn't dare" isn't accurate. It would be better to say that I didn't feel capable of asking you, or couldn't find an opportunity, or didn't realise the importance of the story, or whatever.

The moon is full, father.

I call you my father, but you're not my father. You said your hope was that Salim would become a doctor, but the circumstances – military rule, the curfew, poverty . . .

So he wasn't able to complete his studies and became a mechanic, and now he's got a garage in Deir El Asad and speaks Hebrew and English.

You said to me, "Doctor, you're like my son. I picked you out when you were nine and I loved you, and I asked them at the boys' camp if I could take care of you, and you became my son. You've lost your parents, and I've lost my children. Come and be a son to me."

You took to referring to me as "my son, Dr Khaleel", though I'm not a doctor, as you know. Three months of training in China doesn't make you a doctor. You appointed me doctor to the camp and asked me to change my name the way the fedayeen do, but I didn't change my name, and the fedayeen left on the Greek ships, and the only ones left here were you and me. The war ended, and I was no longer a doctor. In fact Dr Amjad, the Director of the hospital, asked me to work as a nurse. How could anybody accept that, going from doctor to nurse? I said no, but you came to my house, rebuked me and told me to report to the hospital immediately.

When you spoke, you'd open your eyes as wide as eyes can go. The words would come out of your eyes, and your voice would rise and I'd say nothing. I'd steal glances at your eyes, opened to the furthest limits of the earth.

In the office at the boys' camp, you'd stand touching the globe and spinning it and spinning it and then order it to stop. When the little ball stopped turning, you'd extend a finger and say, "That's Acre. Here's Tyre. The plain runs to here, and these are the villages of Acre District. Here's Ein El Zeitoun, and here's Deir El Asad, and here's El Bruwweh, and here's El Ghabsiyyeh, and here's El Kabri, and here's Tarshiha, and here's Bab El Shams. We, lads, are from Ein El Zeitoun. Ein El Zeitoun is a little place, and the mountain surrounds it and protects it. Ein El Zeitoun is the most beautiful village, but they destroyed it in 1948. They bulldozed it after blowing up the houses, so we left it for Deir El Asad. But me, I founded a village in a place no-one knows, a village in the rocks where the sun enters and sleeps."

Dr Amjad said he wasn't sure. The doctor said, and I say too, that you hear sounds but don't know what they are. Do the sounds enter your consciousness, or do they simply remain sounds?

The doctor said you don't see, and I didn't ask him what that means. Does it mean you're in blackness, and is the blackness a colour? Or do you exist in an absence of colour? What does "absence of colour" mean? Do you see that frightening blend of white and black that we call grey? If you don't see colours, that means you're not in blackness but in a place we don't know. Aren't you afraid of what you don't know?

You said you didn't fear death and that you felt fear only once, when you were living with the dead in the olive grove. And you said that men die because they're afraid, and that fear is what is down below.

Are you "down below"? And what do you see?

"It's a matter of arithmetic," you told me. "We feel fear because we live in illusion, since life is a long dream. People fear death, but they ought to be scared of what goes before being born. Before they were born, they were in eternal darkness. But it's an illusion. The illusion makes us think that the living inherit the lives of all others. That's why history was invented. I'm not an intellectual, but I know that history is a trick to make people believe they've been alive since the beginning and that they're the heirs of the dead, which is an illusion. People aren't heirs, and they don't have a history or anything like that, and life is a passage between two deaths, and I'm not afraid of the second death because I was afraid of the first."

"But history isn't an illusion," I answered. "And if it were, what would it be for?"

"What would what be for?"

"Why would we fight and die? Doesn't Palestine deserve our deaths? You're the one who taught me history, and now you tell me history is a ruse to evade death!"

You laughed at me then and told me that your father, the blind sheikh, used to talk that way, and "we ought to learn from them". I don't know if this discussion took place on a single occasion because we didn't have discussions; we'd just talk, and you wouldn't finish your sentences but would jump from one word to another without paying attention to cause and effect. But you laughed. When you laughed, it was like you were exploding from within yourself. Your laughter used to surprise me because I was convinced that heroes didn't laugh. I used to look at the photos of the martyrs hanging on the walls in the camp, and they weren't laughing. Their faces were frowning and closed, as though they held death prisoner within themselves.

But not you.

You were a hero, and you laughed at heroes, and the little folds that extend from the corners of your eyes created a space for the smiles and the laughter. You were a laughing hero – but all the same I wasn't convinced by you and your father's theories about death and history.

You answered by saying that what was worth dying for was what we wanted to live for.

"Palestine isn't an issue. Well, all right, in some sense it is, but it isn't really, because the land doesn't move from its place. That land will remain, and the question isn't who will hold it, because it's an illusion to think that land can be held. No-one can hold land when he's going to end up buried in it. It's the land that holds the person and takes him to itself. I didn't fight, my friend, for the land or for history. I fought for the sake of a woman I loved."

I can't recall what you said now. What you said was simple, transparent and fluent. You speak as though you aren't speaking, and I speak as though I am. But I remember what you said about smells. We were sitting in front of the hospital drinking tea, and it was the time of false spring. That year, spring arrived in February. The sun broke through the winter and tricked the earth, and yellow, white and blue flowers emerged shyly from the rubble. That day you taught me how to smell nature. You put your glass of tea aside, stood up and filled your lungs with air and the smell. You held the smell in your chest till your face started to turn red. When you sat down again and had a sip of tea and talked about the thyme and the jasmine and the columbine and the wildflowers, you said she was like the seasons. With each season she would come to your cave with a new smell. She would let down her long black hair, and the scents of flowers and herbs would fill the air. You said you were always enchanted by the new smells, as though she'd become a different woman.

"A woman, son, is always new. Her smell tells you about her. A woman is the smell of the world, and when I was with her I learned to fill my lungs with the smell of the land."

That was when I understood what you'd said to me about her death: Naheeleh hadn't died because her smell was in your lungs. But Umm Hassan has died. Don't you want to come with me to her funeral? Everyone is gathering at her house, except for her son Naji, who's in America, as you know. I have to go. I want to carry Umm Hassan's bier, and I will fear no-one.

Please get up. We'll go to Umm Hassan's funeral, and then you can go back to your children and die with them. Go, die with them, as Umm Hassan suggested, and set me free.

Do you remember Umm Hassan?

Umm Hassan was my professor of medicine. I was in the hospital when a pregnant woman was brought in; I'd never seen a woman give birth before. In China they'd taught me how to bandage wounds and do simple operations; that was what was called "field medicine". But they didn't teach me real medicine.

The woman was writhing in front of me, and I could do nothing. Then I remembered Umm Hassan, and I sent for her and she came. She managed the delivery and taught me everything. As she helped the woman, she explained everything to me like a doctor training a student. From then on I knew what to do, and I became sure enough of myself to attend births. But the credit is hers. Umm Hassan was the only certified midwife in El Kweikat; she had British documents to prove it.

I can see her now.

She's putting the basin she was carrying on her head and bending over to pick up babies in the olive grove. In reality, she picked up only Naji, who became her son. I told you the story, remember? They were travelling inside Palestine because, having been driven out of El Kweikat, they got lost in the fields and stopped on the outskirts of Deir El Asad, and then they were driven from there, so they went to Tarshiha, which the Israeli planes came and burned, so they found themselves on the road to southern Lebanon, where Cana was their first stop. And on that road, a woman named Sarah El Khateeb gave birth to a child with Umm Hassan at her side. Everyone was running, carrying their bundles on their heads, and Sarah threw herself down under a tree writhing in pain. Umm Hassan washed the baby with hot water, wrapped him in old clothes and gave him to his mother.

Everyone walked on that "last journey", as the people of the villages of Galilee referred to their collective exodus to Lebanon. But it wasn't their last journey. In fact it was the start of wanderings in the wilderness whose end only God knows.

On that last journey, as Umm Hassan was walking with her basin on her head and her four children and her husband and her brothers and their wives and children around her, she saw a bundle of old clothes discarded under an olive tree, and she realised they were the same clothes she'd used to wrap Sarah's baby in. She bent down, picked up the child, put him in the basin on her head and named him Naji, "Rescued". She offered him her dry breasts, then fed him sesame paste mixed with water. At the village of Cana, where they stopped for the first time, the boy's mother came, weeping and asking for her child back. Umm Hassan refused, but in the end, when she saw the milk bursting from the mother's breasts and spotting her dress, she gave him to her.

Umm Hassan said she'd named him Naji and his mother didn't have the right to change his name. Sarah agreed, took the boy, offered him her breast and went away.

"Naji's my only surviving child," said Umm Hassan. "He writes to me from America, God bless him. He's become a professor at the best university, and I send him olive oil."

I see her walking and picking up babies and putting them in the basin on her head. It's as though she'd picked me up, as though I was Naji, as though the taste of the sesame mixed with water still lingered in my mouth, as though . . . I don't know. I swear I don't know. Umm Hassan died this morning, and we have to bury her before the noon prayer, and you sleep as if unaware of what Umm Hassan's death means for me, and for you, and for the people of the camp.

Umm Hassan told me everything about Palestine. I asked her before she set off to visit her brother in El Kweikat, or what's left of it, to pass by El Ghabsiyyeh and tie a strip of cloth on a branch of the lotus tree near the mosque for me. I told her that my father had sworn an oath to do this and that he'd died before he could carry it out, but he'd passed it on to my mother, and my mother had passed it on to me before going to her people in Amman. I hadn't been, and I didn't dare to ask you to do it. I was afraid you'd make fun of me and of my father's superstitions. I asked Umm Hassan to say a short prayer in the mosque and hang the piece of black cloth on the tree and light a candle for me.

When she returned, she gave me a branch heavy with oranges and told me she'd gone to the mosque and prayed.

"Is a mosque defiled if they put animals in it?"

Umm Hassan didn't ask herself that question. She went into the mosque at El Ghabsiyyeh, which had been taken over by cows, drove them out, made her ablutions and prayed. Then she went out to the lotus tree, hung a black ribbon on it and lit two candles.

She said the tree was covered with pieces of cloth.

"I don't know, son. Your village is deserted. The roads have disappeared, and the houses aren't demolished but collapsing and nearly in ruins. I don't know why houses go like that when their people abandon them. An abandoned house is like an abandoned woman; it hunches over itself as though it's falling down. There's no sign of life in your village, but the lotus tree is there, and the mosque is there, and cloths cover the branches, and melted candles are spread about near the tree."

Umm Hassan said she'd been afraid of the tree when they told her about my uncle, Sheikh Azeez Yunis, and how he'd been found dead beneath it, but when she got close to it she felt awe, and she knelt and wept and lit the candles.

She said she heard the rustling of the branches, full of the souls of the dead. "The souls of the dead live in trees," she said. "We have to return and shake the trees so the souls fall and find peace in their graves."

I cut an orange from the branch so that I could taste Palestine, but

Umm Hassan yelled, "No! It's not for eating, it's Palestine." I was ashamed of myself and hung the branch on the wall of the sitting room in my house, and when you came to visit me and saw the mouldy fruit, you yelled, "What's that smell?" And I told you the story and watched you explode in anger.

"You should have eaten the oranges," you told me.

"But Umm Hassan stopped me and said they were from the homeland."

"Umm Hassan's senile," you answered. "You should have eaten the oranges, because the homeland is something we have to eat, not let it eat us. We have to eat the oranges of Palestine, and we have to eat Palestine and Galilee."

It came to me then that you were right, but the oranges were going bad. You went to the wall and pulled off the branch, and I took it from your hand and stood there confused, not knowing what to do with that bunch of decay.

"What are you going to do?" you asked.

"Bury it," I said.

"Why bury it?" you asked.

"I'm not going to throw it away, because it's from the homeland."

You took the branch and threw it in the rubbish.

"What a scandal!" you said. "What are these old women's superstitions? Before hanging the homeland up on the wall, it'd be better to knock down the wall and leave. We have to eat every orange in the world and not be afraid, because the homeland isn't oranges. The homeland is us."

Umm Hassan is waiting. Won't you come with me? I'm in a hurry, so I won't tell you what she did in El Kweikat.

Get up, man. God, you're impossible. The woman's dead, and everyone's at her house. I can hear them weeping through the walls. You hear nothing.

You're not coming? Okay, I'll go on my own. But tell me, why do you look like that – like a little baby swathed in white? For the last three months I've been watching you getting younger. My God, if you could see yourself before you die. It's a shame you don't know what's going on, a shame you can't see how a man doesn't die but goes back to where he came from. I used to think the poets were lying when they said that a man returns to his mother's womb. But now I swear they weren't: a man becomes a baby again before he dies. Only babies die; all death is the death of babies – babies searching for their mothers' wombs, curling up like foetuses. And here you are, turning back into a baby and curling up on yourself, and you can't see. If only you could.

I can't hear you properly. Why are you mumbling? Why are you moving your left hand? You want me to tell you about Naheeleh? You already know the story, and no, I won't tell it again. Do you think of yourself as the hero in a love story? Why have you forgotten your other heroic roles? Or maybe they weren't so heroic. You told me, "Everyone thinks that the fighters are heroes, but that's not true. People fight the way they breathe or eat or go to the lavatory. War is nothing special. All you need to be a fighter is to fight. Being a hero is something else; heroism doesn't exist, and even courage isn't anything special. A brave man can turn into a coward, and a coward can turn into a brave man. The important thing is . . ." You paused there.

I didn't ask what the important thing was. I knew what your reply would be, and I didn't want to hear it again. And now you want me to tell you some stories? No, I won't tell stories, not today. Today I'm busy. Have pity on me; get up and release me, please release me. I'm tired.

I'm tired of everything. I'm tired of your sickness and of how sad you look, I'm tired of the baby's round face suspended above your neck, I'm tired of praying for you.

Did you know that I pray?

My grandmother used to say that praying means laying down words like a carpet on the ground. I lay down my words so that you can walk on them.

Why don't you stand up?

Once upon a time there was a baby.

No, you don't like the story about Naji. You told me Naji was a dog because after everything Umm Hassan had done for him, he went off to America and left her poor and abandoned.

I see a frown on your face and black spots in your closed eyes. Okay, we won't start the story with Umm Hassan or Naji or America. I'll tell you another one.

Back to the beginning.

Do you remember when you used to say, "Back to the beginning!" and stamp your foot? Do you remember what you did after Abdel Nasser resigned in '67? People gathered in the alley of the camp and wept; it was night, and humid, and they were like ghosts weeping in the darkness. You stood in their midst and spat on the ground and said, "Back to the beginning!"

And after 1970, when you'd returned safely to the camp from the slaughter in the forests of Jerash and Ajloun, you said to the woman who came to ask you about her son, "Back to the beginning!" and left.

And after the Israelis went into Beirut, and after each new thing that happened, you'd spit as though you were wiping out the past, and you'd say, "Back to the beginning!"

So, you want the beginning.

In the beginning they didn't say, "Once upon a time;" they said something else. In the beginning they said, "Once upon a time, there was — or there wasn't." Do you know why they said that? When I first read this expression in a book about ancient Arabic literature, it took me by surprise. Because, in the beginning, they didn't lie. They didn't know anything, but they didn't lie. They left things vague, preferring to use that "or" which makes things that were as though they weren't, and things that weren't as though they were. That way the story is put on the same footing as life, because a story is a life that didn't happen, and a life is a story that didn't get told.

Do you like this story?

It isn't real, you'll say, but I don't know any real stories, because my mother left me and went away before she could finish the story. And the stories I know myself, you know too.

Your eyes are alight with memories, and they're asking for the story's beginning.

The story's beginning says that you were like a dead man, and there was no hope of reviving you. Dr Amjad told me, "There's no hope" – but I wasn't convinced and decided to try to treat you by talking to you.

Once upon a time, a long time ago, in days of yore, there was – or there wasn't – a young man called Yunis.

No. I have to start from the place you don't know, meaning from here, from the end, because the story can only start from its ending. I don't want it to be for you the way it was for me: I never knew the ends of stories because I'd fall asleep before my mother got to them.

You, however, are going to know the story starting with the ending.

The ending says that it was 9.00 in the evening. I was sitting on the balcony of my house in the heat and humidity of August drinking a glass of arak. There's nothing like arak in the summer, because it makes you burn hotter than the night. I'd taken to medicating my sorrow and fear with arak every night.

I was drinking on the balcony and eating a salted tomato and pistachios when I heard a violent banging on the door. Opening it, I discovered Amna, her face emerging from the shadows. All I could understand of what she said was that you were in hospital. I thought you'd died, God forbid. Amna told me how you'd fainted and fallen to the ground like a piece of wood. I listened, waiting for her to say you'd died. I wasn't sad. I felt a space emptying in my heart, and I wasn't upset. I asked where you were. I tried to get through the door to go to you, but Amna wouldn't let me by. She stood rooted to the spot and talked.

I tried to get out, but she blocked the door with her hand as though she wanted to stop me.

She said it had started the previous night, when you'd become unable to speak. She'd gone to visit you, and when she'd arrived at your house she'd found you wandering around the place and muttering. She'd asked you what was wrong and you'd answered, but your tongue couldn't form words.

"That's when I realised," Amna said. She ran to the hospital and told them, but nobody came. The nurse said she would send someone to look for Dr Amjad, but Dr Amjad didn't come.

"I stayed with him the whole night. Do you know what that means? He was wandering around his house and wouldn't settle down. He'd raise his left hand and speak loudly but you couldn't understand him. I tried to calm him. I made him sit down and had him drink a glass of aniseed tea. I led him to his bedroom, but when he saw the bed he started to run about and rave, and I ran about after him. He opened the front door and tried to go out. Look at my shoulder, my body's covered in bruises. No, he didn't hit me, but he was as strong as a bull, and I was running about after him and crying."

"Okay, okay, Amna" — and I tried to get past her so I could go to the hospital, but she blocked the way with her hand.

She said she'd been alone with you and you'd scared her, and that she'd knelt in front of you and beat her chest with her fist, and that you'd . . . She said you'd quietened down when you saw her kneeling in front of you. You'd looked at her as though you didn't understand, then you'd fallen to the ground.

When she said you'd fallen, I pushed my way between her hand and the door and went out.

Amna walked behind me, panting and talking, but I didn't listen. And at the hospital door she said that doctors were bastards and that I was one too and had no pity in my heart and that she'd waited for them to come, alone with you.

I went into the hospital and ran to the nurses' room so I could put on my white gown and go to you. Amna ran after me and said God would never forgive us. Then she disappeared.

You're cross with Amna because she doesn't come to visit you. Don't be angry with her. She doesn't know that you hear and feel and are sad. She was convinced you'd died, so why should she come?

Who is Amna Abd El Rahman?

Is she a relative of yours, as you told me? Were you in love with her? Why didn't you talk about her?

The fact is, master, you have to tell me something about your women. You're a man surrounded by women, and there's something strange in your round white face that inspires love; it's the face of a man who is loved. You always described yourself as a lover, but I think you hid your lovers. You only spoke about one woman, and even that one you only talked about a little. Piecing the tale together and arranging your scattered sentences, I turned it into a story. But you only mentioned love incidentally. You jumped over the essential story as though it was a pool and you were afraid of drowning. Once I plucked up my courage and asked you where you made love with Naheeleh. I didn't say her name, I just said "her", and you smiled. You were in a good mood that day. Your eyes shone, you raised your right hand to sketch a question mark, and you said, "There. Among the rocks," and fell silent. It became my job to collect your asides and mutterings and turn them into a story to tell you.

Now you can't stop me talking. I can say whatever I want, and I'm telling you that this is your story. My goal isn't to make one up; I'm only a half-doctor awaiting death at the hands of the family of Shams, who want their revenge.

I promised I'd start with the ending, and the ending will be your getting up from this coffin-like bed. You'll get up and you'll be tall and broad-shouldered, carry a stick and return to your country. There you will go first to the cave of Bab El Shams. You won't go to Naheeleh's grave, as everyone expects you to. You'll go to Bab El Shams, enter your village of caves and disappear.

This is the only ending that goes with your story, which you'll never betray.

I know what you'll say and how you'll roll the word *betray* around in your mouth before announcing that you had no choice. Your life was a series of betrayals. You'll say that in order for us not to be traitors, we have to change – that is, to be traitors.

You'll tell me how the youth you were during the Holy Struggle alongside Abd El Qadir, God rest his soul, was related to the young man you became in the Arab Commando Brigades, and then in the Arab Nationalists Movement.

You'll say that the man you became in the Lebanon Regional Command of the Fatah Movement was the continuation of that same young man but different from him in every way. You'll speak to me of the older man you became, the one dreaming of a new betrayal, because one has to begin somewhere.

Where were we?

Did you know that all this sitting in your room has made me incapable of concentrating? I jump from story to story and lose track of things, and I forget where I began.

I was telling you about Amna. No, Amna wasn't the point. I was telling you how they brought you to the hospital half dead. We carried you into your room and put you on the bed. Your eyes were closed, and you were shaking with fever. They gave you a drip-feed in your right hand, first tying your hand to the edge of the bed so the needle wouldn't rip the artery, you were shaking and twitching so much.

I stood there not knowing what to do. I was alone in the room, listening to the nurses' voices in the corridor and smelling the smell. That was the first time I smelled the smell of Galilee Hospital. I thought, Why don't they clean the place? And why hadn't I noticed the smell before? I come to the hospital every day – it's true that I don't really work, because I refused the demotion from doctor to nurse – but I'd never smelled that horrible smell before. Tomorrow, I thought, I'll clean every-thing.

But the next day I didn't clean everything, and another day passed, and after it another without my doing anything. It seems I've got used to it. The smell is not a problem. Smells work their way into us, and we absorb them, which is why they only exist at the beginning.

Let's return to the beginning.

I left your room in search of Dr Amjad and found him sitting in his clinic, smoking, drinking coffee and reading the newspaper.

He invited me to sit down, but I remained standing.

"Sit down, man, what's the matter with you?"

Hesitantly I asked him about you.

"Blood clot on the brain," he said.

"Treatment?"

"'Strokes have no cure,'" he quoted at me.

"I can't believe it."

"It's in God's hands," he said. "Leave it, Dr Khaleel. It's over. I don't give him more than seventy-two hours."

"What about a blood thinner? Didn't you give him a blood thinner?"

"There's no point. We did a scan and found that the haemorrhage has spread over half the brain, which means it's over."

"And the fever?" I asked.

I asked as though I didn't know even though I did. It's amazing how one can turn ignorant. Standing in front of Dr Amjad, I forgot all my medical training and found myself behaving like an imbecile, as though I knew nothing.

I stood in front of Dr Amjad asking and asking, and the doctor answered me tersely, impatient with my questions, as though I was keeping him from something important.

He explained that you'd die within three days and asked me to contact your relatives about the funeral, but instead of trying to get hold of Amna I returned to your room and began my work.

You've brought me back to the medicine I hated and had forgotten, and I want to tell you not to be afraid of the fever. My opinion is that the clot occurred somewhere near the area of the fever in the brain, and the pressure is interfering with your body temperature, which means that the fever will disappear once the blood is drawn off.

Don't be afraid.

I disagreed with Dr Amjad when he said that the shaking was your death tremor. You were shaking with fever, and the fever would go. As you see, I was right. But do you remember what Nurse Zeinab did? She bent over and started massaging your chest. When I asked what she was doing, she said she was helping your soul escape from your body.

"Don't you see how his soul is shaking?" she asked.

"That's fever, you idiot," I shouted and I chased her out of the room, locked the door and sat down, not knowing what to do.

During those first days I despaired. For three days I didn't leave your room. I changed your drip-feed and put antibiotics in it; Dr Amjad made fun of me, telling me that the fever had nothing to do with any inflammation.

But I wanted you not to die – not because I'm a non-believer, as Nurse Zeinab said, but because I don't want you to die in bed.

Do you remember what you told me when I visited you to offer my condolences after Naheeleh died? You received me calmly and handed me an unsweetened coffee. I asked you, as people offering condolences usually do, about the circumstances of her illness and her death, but you didn't give me the details. You said she'd died in the hospital in Nazareth. Then you started murmuring some verses by Al Mutanabbi.

You recited the poetry as though you'd composed it yourself, and you said you'd never die here. You said you'd go and die over there.

"And if I die here, try to bury me over there," you said.

"As you wish, Abu Salim," I said.

But you looked at me strangely and said it was impossible, because you knew the end would be a grave in the camp that would be made into a soccer pitch a few years later. You were referring to the mass grave containing victims of the 1982 Shatila massacre, where children play soccer and there's rubbish all over the place. Then you returned to Al Mutanabbi's verses:

We make ready our swords and our spears
And the Fates destroy us without a fight.
We bury each other, and the heads of those who came first
Are trampled by the feet of those who came late.

That day – do you remember? – that day I suggested that you go to Deir El Asad immediately, and you said the time hadn't come and that you'd make your Return when you were good and ready.

For three days I did the impossible to save you from death in your room. You'd open your blood-shot eyes and I'd close them for you, because leaving them open endangers the corneas. The eye isn't one mirror, it's a network of mirrors that must not be exposed to the air for too long or they're ruined. I focused my attention on your eyes so you wouldn't lose your sight. Because in those early days, I was certain that you'd awake from that sleep.

The strange thing is that, on the fourth day, when your temperature came down and you were lying quietly, I felt very afraid, because I was certain the drop in your temperature would begin your return to consciousness. But stabilisation led to lethargy. Now you never open your eyes. I've taken to opening them myself and passing my finger in front of them, but the pupils are unmoving. Leucoma has begun. The redness has gone, and this bluish whiteness has come.

"He's entered a state of lethargy," said Dr Amjad.

"What does 'state of lethargy' mean?" I asked.

"It means I don't know," he said. "He'll stay like that till he dies."

"And when will he die?"

"I can't specify the time, but he will die."

Dr Amjad decided to substitute a feeding tube for the drip-feed. At first I objected, but then I realised that he was right, as the tube will put life back into your guts.

And I started to prepare your food myself. Dropping the ready-made hospital food, I mixed bananas with milk. Bananas, milk and honey: for the last three months, you've been eating like a baby.

Is it true that new-born babies are as happy as they look, or are they like you, opening their eyes in pain, refusing to take part in the life we're forcing on them? You've changed my thinking about being a baby. All the same, and despite the pain, I dream of having one, because a baby gives you the sense that you'll live on through other people.

"That's not true," you'll say.

I agree, but I told Shams, when I fell in love with her, that I wanted to have a child with her that would be brown-skinned like her. No, it's not true that I was involved in her murder. I swear I had nothing to do with it. The problem wasn't with me but with Samih Abu Diyab. They killed her to revenge Samih. I swear I did nothing to hurt her. I loved her the way one does, but she went and died. She killed him and then died, and that was that. I don't want to talk about her any more.

I'm worried about you. You've settled into death. As though you've turned your temporary unconsciousness into a permanent one.

Would you like to know what happened to me after you'd settled into this state of withdrawal?

To begin with, I was overwhelmed by a criminal idea: the only solution was that I should place a pillow over your face and press down till you died of asphyxiation – that I should just kill you, cold-bloodedly and calmly. I felt real hatred for you. I pretended I hated the world for what it had done to you, but that wasn't true. I didn't hate the world, or Fate, or God. I hated you, Yunis, or Abu Salim, or Izz El Din or whatever name – I don't know what it might be – suits you here in this bed.

No, it's got nothing to do with wanting to murder my father, as the psychologists would claim. You're not my father. I was the one who killed my father, and his picture, after they killed him in front of our house all that time ago. And I lived with my grandmother, who slept on her amazing pillow. I promised I'd bring you the pillow, but I forgot. I'll bring it tomorrow. Anyway, my grandmother's pillow doesn't look like a pillow any more. It's turned into a heap of thorns. The flowers inside have faded and dried and turned to thorns. My grandmother used to stuff her pillow with flowers, saying that when she rested her head on it she felt as though she'd returned to the village, and she'd make me rest my head on it. I'd lay my head on her pillow and smell decay. I joined the fedayeen when I was nine years old to escape the flowers of El Ghabsiyyeh that my grandmother would pick at the camp's rubbish dump. I hated the perfume of decay and ended up connecting the smell of Palestine with the smell of the pillow. I was convinced then, and I still am, that my grandmother was afflicted with floral dementia – a widespread condition among Palestinian peasants who were driven from their villages.

The day she began her long final illness, she summoned me to her side. My uncle came to me in the village of Kafar Shouba in southern Lebanon, where the fedayeen set up their first camp, and asked me to go to Beirut. In her house in the camp, the woman was dying on her pillow. When she saw me, her face lit up with a pale smile, and she gestured to the others to leave us alone. When everyone had gone, she asked me to sit down next to her on the bed. She whispered that she didn't own anything she could leave me but this – and she pointed to her pillow – and this – and she pointed to her watch – and this – and she pointed to her Koran.

She pulled on my hand as though she didn't want to die and said she missed my father. Then she closed her eyes, and her breathing became irregular. I tried to pull my hand away, but I couldn't, so I yelled and the women came and started weeping. She didn't die, however. I stayed for three days waiting for her to die, then returned to Kafar Shouba and, two weeks later, had to go back to Beirut again, for her funeral.

I don't know where I put the watch, the women in the camp decided to bury the Koran with her, and I still have the pillow. I thought of my grandmother's pillow because I was going to kill you with a pillow. Tomorrow I'll bring it to you before I throw it away; I must get rid of that pillow full of flowers that stink of decay. The strange thing is that no-one who comes to my house notices the smell. Even Shams didn't smell it. I'm the only one who can smell that secret smell that makes me feel faint.

I wanted to kill you with the pillow because I hated your incredible insistence on clinging to life, but I hesitated and became afraid, and that was the end of it.

Tomorrow I'll bring you my grandmother's pillow and open it up so I can see what's inside. My grandmother used to change the flowers at the beginning of each season, and I think she expected me to continue this tradition. I want to open up the pillow to see what happened to the flowers. Why does a person turn to dust when he dies, when things turn into other things? Strange. Didn't God create us all from dust?

Tomorrow I'll open up the pillow and tell you.

I said I'd wanted to suffocate you and then the desire faded. It was a strange, passing feeling and never recurred, but I did feel it. How can I describe it? It was as though there was another person inside me who leapt out and made me capable of destroying everything. Whenever I became aware of that other person, I'd run out of your room and roam around the hospital. This would calm me down. Now I'm calm. Feeling that things around you and me are moving slowly, I've decided to kill time by talking. Have you heard that fearful expression "to kill time"? It's time that kills us, but we pretend it's the other way round!

So as to kill time and stop it from killing me, I've decided to examine you again.

At the beginning – that is, after you'd settled into your lethargy – you smelled odd. I can't explain what I mean, because smells are the hardest things to describe. I'll just say it was the smell of an older man. It seems there are hormones that set different ages apart from one another. The smell of older men differs fundamentally from the smell of men in their prime, and especially from that of thirteen-year-old boys, who start to give off a smell of maleness and sex. The smell of older men is different, quiet and pale. Like my grandmother's pillow, it's a disturbing scent. No, I wouldn't say it disgusted me – God forbid. But I was disturbed, and I decided I ought to bathe you twice a day – but the smell was stronger than the soap. Then the smell started to go away, and a new smell took its place. No, I don't say this because I've become accustomed to your smell. It's a medical matter and clearly has to do with hormones. And I believe that – I don't know how – you've started a new life phase which I can't define but which I can discern through your smell.

And because "one thing reminds one of another", as the Arabs say, I want to tell you you're wrong, your theories about age and youth are a hundred per-cent erroneous. I remember I met you one rainy February morning when you were out jogging. I stopped you and told you that jogging after sixty was bad for the heart and lungs, and that you should practise a form of light exercise such as walking to get rid of fat and keep your arteries open. I told you older men should do older men's sports.

That day you invited me to have a coffee at your house and subjected me to a long lecture on aging. "Listen, son. My father was an old man – I knew him only as an old man. Do you know why? Because he was blind. A person will grow old at forty, not at sixty, if he loses the two things that can't be replaced: his sight and his teeth. Being old means having your sight go and your teeth fall out. At forty, white hairs invade your head, your teeth rot, and your vision becomes dim, so you look like an old man. But inside you're still young; your age consists of how other people see you, it comes from your children. Yes, it's true: in addition to eyes and teeth, there are children. We peasants marry early. I got married when I was fourteen, so just think how old my children and grandchildren were when I was forty. There's no such thing as being old these days, for two reasons. The first is the invention of spectacles, so weak eyesight is no longer an issue, and the second is dentistry, so people don't have to have all their teeth out by the time they're seventy or eighty. Here I am today, with all my own teeth and glasses that let me read, so how can you call me an old man? Old age is an illusion. People get old from the inside, not the outside. So long as there's passion in your heart, it means you're not an old man."

On that occasion I meant to ask when you'd last seen her, but I felt shy. I stood up and started looking at the pictures on the wall. Seven sons, three daughters and fifteen grandchildren, and in the middle, the picture of Ibraheem who'd died as a baby. Twenty-five people, the first fruits of the adventure you forged.

You told me about Ghassan Kanafani.

You told me he came to you with a letter of introduction from Dr George Habash, asking you to tell him your story and he'd write it down. It was you who trained Habash and Wadi' Haddad and Hani El Hindi and everyone else in the first cadre. Why didn't you tell me what that first experiment was like? And also why you joined Fatah and the Asifa Forces. Was it because of Abu Ali Iyad, as you told me, or because you were opposed to plane hijackings? Or because you enjoyed change?

Ghassan Kanafani came, you told him your story, he took notes, and then he didn't do anything. He didn't write your story.

Why didn't he write it? Did you really tell him your story? You never used to tell anyone your story because everyone knew it, so why bother?

Writers are strange. They don't know that people don't tell real stories because they're already known. Kanafani was different though. You told me you liked him and tried to tell him everything. But he didn't write anything. Do you know why?

It was the mid-'50s when he came to see you, and your story hadn't become a story yet. There were hundreds of people slipping across from Lebanon to Galilee. Some of them came back and some of them were killed by the Border Guards' bullets. That, maybe, is why Kanafani didn't follow up on the story – because he was looking for mythic stories, and yours was just the story of a man in love. Where was the mythology in that? How did you expect he'd believe the story of your love for your wife? Is a man's love for his wife something to write about?

However, you became a legend without realising it, and I want to assure you that if Kanafani hadn't been killed by the Israelis in 1971, when they blew his car up in Beirut and ripped his body to shreds, he'd be sitting with you now in this room, trying to piece your story together.

Times have changed.

Then, you'd have to have died in this cold bed to have been a story. I know you're laughing at me, and I agree — the important thing is not the story but the life. But what are we supposed to do when life tries to force us out? The important thing is life, and that's what I'm trying to get at with you. Why can't you understand? Why don't you get up now, and shake the death off your body and leave the hospital?

You don't love the moon, and you don't love the blind singer, and you can't get up.

But moonlight is true light. What is this sun culture that's killing us? Only moonlight deserves to be called light. You told me about moon-stroke. You said that in your village people feared it more than sunstroke, and that was why you'd seek cover in the shade from the moon, not the sun.

The fact is, master, your theories on aging are erroneous: it's not teeth and eyes, it's the smell. Aging is that implacable death that paralyses body and soul, and it always comes as a surprise. Of course, I agree that in your case the psychological factor was decisive: you became old at one go when Naheeleh died — though in fact her death doesn't explain everything because other women still love you. Despite which you got away.

Don't put your finger to your lips. I can and will say whatever I like. You don't want me to talk about Mme Nada Fayyad? Very well, I won't say a word — but she came yesterday and stood at the door to your room and wept. A woman of around sixty, she came and stood at your door and refused to enter. This is the fourth time she's come in three months. Yesterday I ran after her and invited her in. I stopped her in the corridor, lit a cigarette and offered it to her. She was weeping convulsively, mascara running into her eyes.

She said she didn't go into your room because she didn't want to see you like that. "Unbelievable!" she said. "How can it be? Screw the world!"

Her tone took me aback.

She told me she was from El Ashrafiyyeh, in Beirut, her name was Nada Fayyad, she'd known you for a long time and used to work with you in the Fatah media office on El Hamra.

Did you work in media? What did you have to do with media and journalists and intellectuals? You always used to say you were a peasant and didn't understand all that nonsense! Or is Mme Nada lying?

She asked me if I was your son and said I looked a lot like you. Then she kissed me on the cheek and left. You must have seen her when she came in, but you didn't want to talk to her. Why don't you talk to her? Does she know about you and Naheeleh? Or did you hide that story from her and give her a different account of your wife and children and your journeys to your country?

Tell the truth, confess you had a relationship with this woman, maybe loved her. Tell me you loved her so I can believe the story of your other love. How do you expect me to believe you were faithful to one woman your whole life? Even Adam, peace be upon him, wasn't faithful to his only wife.

You used to hide your truth with a smile and, when I asked you about other women, say, "No"; a big "no" would emerge from your lips. Now, master, you've been exposed: Amna and Nada and I don't know who else. One after the other they'll come, as though your illness has turned into a scandal trap. I'll sit with you and count your scandals.

Please don't get upset – I'm only describing the facts. Shams taught me to do this. She said she'd never lie to me. She'd lied to her husband and there was no reason to lie to me. She said she'd learned to lie after the long torment she'd lived through with him, and she'd relished it because it had been her sole means of survival. Then she started to get sick of it. She said that when she lied successfully she felt she was disappearing. In the end she decided to run away so the lying and disappearing would stop. She said she wanted an innocent relationship with me. Then I discovered that she was lying.

When I fell in love with her, she said she hated sex because her husband had raped her, and I believed her and tried to build an innocent relationship with her. But of course I was lying to her: I used the phrase "an innocent relationship" so I could sleep with her. Then I discovered she was raping me.

I say she was raping me, but I'm lying. We lie because we can't find the words; words don't indicate specific things, which is why everyone understands them as they wish to. I meant to say she enjoyed sex, as I did, which doesn't mean she raped me. On the contrary, it means we loved sex, revelling in it, laughing and frolicking. She'd yell at the top of her voice – she said her husband had forbidden her to yell, and she loved me because of the yelling. She'd yell and I'd yell. I've no right to call that rape, so I withdraw what I said and apologise.

I'm certain Naheeleh was different. You don't want me to talk about Naheeleh? Very well, I'll shut up. With Shams it wasn't a question of sex; I lost myself in that woman. I was lost all those years, and then I discovered I'd been deceived. I don't concur with Shams's theory of love, that every love is a deception. She dominated me completely, and she knew it. Once, after disappearing for two months, she turned up as though she'd never been away, and instead of quarrelling with her, I dissolved into her body. That was when I told her I was done for, and she knew it. She'd disappear for days and weeks at a time, and then appear and tell me unbelievable stories which I believed. Now I've found out what a fool I was. Love makes a person naïve and drives him to believe the unbelievable.

The woman was amazing. After we'd made love and screamed and moaned, she'd light a cigarette and sit on the end of the bed and tell me about her adventures and her journeys. Sometimes she'd tell me she'd been in Amman, or Algiers, or Tunis. She'd tell me she thought of me every day and heard my voice calling to her every morning. And she'd ask me to say her name over and over again and never get tired of listening to it. I'd say it once, twice, three times, a dozen times, then I'd stop, and I'd see her face crumple like a child's, so I'd start saying her name again and we'd start making love again.

Then I discovered she was lying.

No — at that moment, when I was repeating her name, I knew, but I used to relish the lie. That's love — enjoying a lie, then waking up to the truth.

After the killing of Samih Abu Diyab, I looked everywhere for her. My first feeling was fear. I was afraid she'd kill me as she'd killed him. I told myself she was a madwoman who murdered her lovers. Instead of feeling jealousy or sorrow, I discovered fear. Instead of looking back over my relationship with this woman, I took to shivering in my sleep.

Then she died.

No. Before she died, I went and looked for her so I could warn her of her fate.

Do you believe me now? I know that the day her death became known you looked at me suspiciously and said, "Shame on you! That's not how a woman should be killed. A woman in love must never die."

I told you she was a killer. She killed the man she loved and then claimed she'd done it to revenge her honour because he'd deceived her. He'd promised to divorce his wife and marry her but didn't do it.

I told you, "Shams is lying. I know her better than any of you."

"And why should she lie?" you asked.

"Because she loved me."

You told me then that I was naïve, because the heart is a storehouse of secrets, and the point of her relationship with me might have been to rid herself of the ghost of her love for Samih. You explained to me that a lover takes refuge in other relationships in order to escape the incandescence of his passion. You despised me because I was "the other man", and you didn't believe I'd had nothing to do with the killing. It's true I appeared before the investigating committee in Ein El Hilweh camp, but I didn't participate in the massacre.

I call Shams's killing a massacre now rather than an execution, as I always used to. And it was a terrible massacre. They tricked her, asking her to go to El Miyyeh wi-Miyyeh camp to be reconciled and to pay blood money, and they were waiting for her. A man with a machine gun came from each family, they hid behind the mounds lining the highway, and when she arrived . . . You know what happened. There's no need to describe the shreds of woman stuck to the metal of the burned-out car.

Why am I talking about Shams, when we're supposed to be talking about Mme Nada Fayyad? Was Nada your way of escaping the incandescence of Naheeleh?

You don't want me to talk about Nada? Okay, suggest another subject.

I know you don't like talking about these things, and I never meant to end up here. I wanted to tell you the story you don't know, and I don't know how the subject got changed. I must concentrate because one subject leads to another.

I was describing your health situation to you. After they pulled out the drip-feed needle, they put the feeding tube into your nose. Yesterday I decided to add a drug called L-Dopa that's used for epileptics and has proven effective for those suffering from brain death. This is something I should have done earlier. How come I never thought of this medicine before? Never mind. We shall have to wait a few days before its positive effects become apparent.

I know you feel pain, and I can sense your rigidity in the white air. This is you – a man in white air, surrounded by dust and noise and incomprehensible murmurs.

As for this catheter that bothers you, it has to be there or you'd be poisoned by your urine, because you don't urinate on your own any more, and instead of wetting yourself, as Nurse Zeinab expected, you retain everything, and there's no need for the oil cloth they put under your sheet so you wouldn't wet the mattress.

I know your back hurts a lot. I removed the oil cloth and I promise you you'll feel better. I rub your back with cream to improve your circulation. I won't allow poor circulation to give you ulcers. There's no way around pressure sores; we just need to deal with them quickly. Whatever we do, however much we massage you, we'll never be able to prevent the sores that come from lying motionless in bed.

We've created a permanent catheter, which will most likely lead to inflammation of the urethra. That's why we take your temperature every day. I know you hate it, but I have to do it. Please let me use the suppositories three times a week, so the milk is converted into faeces. God, how horrible we discover our bodies to be – a feeding tube at the top, a tube for waste below, us in between.

Please don't hate yourself. If only you knew how happy I was when I discovered it wasn't over, that cells were renewing themselves even in the midst of this death.

I cut your hair, clip your nails and shave your beard, but the most important thing is your new smell, a smell of milk and powder like a baby's.

I'll describe how I spend my day with you, so you can relax and stop muttering.

I enter your room at 7.00 a.m., pour the urine into the lavatory and clean your nails. Then I mop your room. After that I give you a flannel bath with soap and water, for which I use an expensive soap I bought myself, because here at the hospital they refuse to buy "Baby Johnson" on the excuse that it costs a lot and is supposed to be for babies. Then I change the white shift in which we wrap your body and call Nurse

Zeinab to come and help me lift you and sit you in the chair; she holds you up and I change the sheets. I don't want to give you more to worry about, but the sheets were a problem. What kind of hospital is this? They said they weren't responsible for sheets, so I was forced to buy three and asked Zeinab to wash them for a small sum, which I pay. That way I don't have to worry any more. Next I put you back in bed, get the mucus extractor (because you can't cough now), extract the mucus from your windpipe, clean the extractor and rest a little.

At 8.30 a.m. I get your breakfast ready and feed it to you gently through your nose. At 12.30 I get your lunch ready and, before feeding you, tip you a little on your side and wipe your face with a moistened towel.

At 5.00 p.m. I make your afternoon snack, which is a bit different because I mix honey into the milk, farm honey from the village of El Sharqiyyeh in the south.

At 9.00 p.m. I rub your body with white spirit, then sprinkle powder on it. When I find the beginnings of an ulcer I stop rubbing and bathe you again. The evening bath isn't mandatory every day.

At 9.30 p.m. you eat dinner.

After dinner, I stay with you for a while and tell you stories. Sometimes I fall asleep in my chair and wake up with a start at midnight. Or I leave you quietly and go to my room in the hospital, where I sleep.

The problem is my room.

They all think I sleep there because I'm scared and on the run. Truth to tell, I am scared. Ameen El Sa'eed came to see me three months ago. You know him: he was a comrade of mine in Fatah's Sons of Galilee brigade and now lives in El Rasheediyyeh camp near Tyre. He told me they'd decided to take special security measures because Shams's family had sent a bunch of their young men from Jordan to Lebanon to avenge their daughter, and he asked me to be careful. I told him I didn't care because I had a clear conscience. But, as you see, I'm stuck in this hospital and unable to leave.

The surprising thing, master, is how much you've changed. I won't tell you how much thinner you've got, since I'm sure you're aware of that. And your little paunch, which you used to hate and run five kilometres every day to get rid of, isn't there any longer. I think you've lost more than half your weight.

Nurse Zeinab thinks your new smell is the result of the soap, powder and creams I use to massage you, but that's not true. You smell like a baby now because you eat what babies eat. Your smell resembles milk — a white smell on a white body.

Maybe tomorrow, I don't know, I'll bring a tape measure. I suspect you've started to shrink a little. Don't be frightened, it's just your bones contracting because of the lack of movement or the cells not renewing themselves due to your age. Your bones get shorter and you get shorter, but so what? Don't get upset: soon, when you get up, I'll organise a special diet full of vitamins for you, and everything will be as it was, and better.

Do you hear me?

Why don't you say anything?

Didn't you like the story?

I know what you want now. You want me to leave you alone to sleep, and you want the radio. The bastards stole the radio. Last night I left the radio on all night. I thought it would keep you company while you were on your own, but they stole it.

I know who they are. They haven't forgotten the status and money they had during the Revolution. Don't they know I'm the poorest person here? True, I'm a nurse and a doctor, but I'm a beggar. Those days are over, but they haven't yet taken it in that we're back where we started – poor.

And you, have you forgotten those days?

Have you forgotten how Abu Jihad El Wazeer, God rest his soul, would take a tattered piece of paper and use it to disburse unimaginable sums to people in need of budgets? Disgusted, I mentioned it to you, but you didn't agree with me. I told you to make the point that money had corrupted and would destroy us, but you explained everything to me then and asked me not to say anything about Abu Jihad that I'd regret later. "Two men, son, represent all that's best among the martyrs – Abu Ali Iyad and Abu Jihad El Wazeer." Could you have been prophesying his assassination in Tunis? Did you know about it then, or did you just see it coming? You said Abu Jihad used a tattered bit of paper to disburse money to show his contempt for it, because money is nothing.

I'll buy you a new radio tomorrow.

What?

You don't want one?

You don't like listening to the news any more?

I'll buy you a tape recorder and some tapes. You love Fayrouz, and I'll buy you every Fayrouz song, especially the one that goes, "I'll see you coming with the cloudless sky, disappearing through the cloudless sky among the almond leaves." Tomorrow I'll bring you the cloudless sky and the almond leaves and Fayrouz, and all the old songs of Mohammed Abd El Wahhab. I'll bring you "The wasted lover is spurned by his bed" – how I love Ahmad Shawqi, the Prince of Poets! Tomorrow I'll tell you the story of his relationship with the young singer Mohammed Abd El Wahhab.

He was my lord, my soul was in his hands.
He squandered it – God bless those hands!

How I love love, Abu Salim! Tomorrow we'll sing and relive our loves. You'll love and I'll love – you and I, alone in the only hospital in a corner of the only camp in the city of Beirut.

Say with me, "Say, 'I seek refuge in the Lord of men, the King of men, the God of men, from the evil of the slinking prompter who whispers in the hearts of men of jinn and men.'"

Say it. The Koran comforts the heart.

I'm going now. Good night.

W hy don't you answer?

Why don't you ask, "Where shall we find the 'good'?"

Why do you believe me?

Last night I told you "good night", but I didn't go to sleep. Every night I tell you the same thing and don't go. I told you "good night" because I was sick of everything. I sit with you and get upset. I sit and get fed up. I'm sick and tired of waiting. And I still can't sleep. I yawn, I feel the exhaustion in my body, as if all I need to do to drop off is to put my head on the pillow, but I can't sleep.

Sleep is the most beautiful thing.

I lie down on the bed and close my eyes. The numbness that comes before sleep steals into my head – and then my body convulses and I wake up. I light a cigarette, gaze at the glowing end in the dark, and my eyelids start to droop. I put out the cigarette, close my eyes and let the phantoms take over. I think about Kafar Shouba; for ages now Kafar Shouba's been my sleeping companion. I lie down on the bed, and I go there and see the flares.

I was seventeen when I saw flares for the first time. At the time, I was a fedayeen fighter, one of the first cadre, which came via Irneh in Syria to southern Lebanon to build the first fedayeen base.

I heard of Kafar Shouba as I was on my way there, and the name stuck in my mind. In fact our base wasn't in Kafar Shouba but in an olive grove belonging to a neighbouring village called El Khreibeh. All the same, when in my drowsiness I travel back to those days, I go to Kafar Shouba.

I was the youngest. I'm not certain about that, but I was certainly young for the job of Political Commissar that Abu Ali Iyad gave me.

I was scared.

A Political Commissar having no right to be scared, I covered up my fright with a lot of talk, and the military commander of the base, a blond lieutenant aged twenty-eight called Abu El Fida, used to call me the Talk-a-lot-ical Commissar.

I talked a lot because I wanted the fedayeen to acquire political consciousness: we wanted to liberate the individual, not just the land.

During those days – July 1969 – the Americans made it to the moon and Armstrong walked on its white face.

I remember that that was when Abu El Fida got very angry and punished me. Is that any way to deal with people – punishing a Political Commissar in front of his men for expressing an opinion?

The thing is that, as was the fashion in those days, I made no secret of my lack of faith. If humankind could go to the moon, that meant there was no God. May God the Exalted, the Almighty, forgive me for such thoughts, but when I expressed them I only meant the idea. Atheism was just an idea, and I didn't express it because I believed in it but because it was logical, even though, like the rest of the boys, I fasted during Ramadan and repeated Koranic verses to myself. How can you not repeat Koranic verses when you confront death every day? What else can you say to death than "Count not those who were slain in God's way as dead!"

Abu El Fida got angry with me and ordered me to hand over my weapon and crawl on the ground in front of the platoon. And I crawled. I won't lie to you and say I refused to carry out his order. I crawled, got filthy and felt like an insect. I decided to hand in my resignation and join the fedayeen in El Safi Valley. Things heated up soon afterwards, the Israeli planes started shelling our positions, and we were too busy dealing with the large numbers of martyrs to remember Armstrong and the moon and my declarations and my atheism.

It was there that I discovered the incandescent flares that set fire to the olive trees and, as we shot at the lights, saw Palestine for the first time. The flares spread themselves over the shiny green olive leaves. I can see them now, and I see you making your way alone, carrying your rifle through the hills and looking for a drop of water among the shattered rocks so as to get to Bab El Shams, where Naheeleh was waiting for you.

I see you making your way beneath the flares, feeling no fear.

Dear God, how selective our memories are! Now I remember the light dropping in flares, but then, after the flares had burned the camp, after the flies had devoured me on the main street of Shatila, and after I'd returned to this hospital with its pervasive smell of death, all I retained was the memory of fear.

That's the difference.

You remind me of the light, even though you're half-dead, while the corpses of the Shatila massacre make me think of fear, even though they were piled on top of one another in twisted heaps, like living people frozen in place.

That's how I start my journey towards sleep, watching the firing at the light grenades and the face of Abu El Fida shining under the Doshka machine gun aimed at the sky. I run through the olive grove, take cover behind a rock and fire. Then I find myself in El Hama taking part in general staff meetings and discussing military plans. Then I fall asleep. The memories come like swarms of ants to take over my head, and with their spiralling motion I sleep.

I lie on my bed and try to summon up the image of the ants, but it doesn't come. I think of Shams, I see her cut into pieces, and sleep doesn't come. I think about love. Why didn't I go to Denmark with Siham? I see her walking in the streets of Copenhagen and turning around as though she's heard my footsteps. That was how our story, which isn't even really a story, began. She came to the hospital complaining of stomach pains. When she lay down and uncovered her belly, I trembled. I saw a bit of sun that seemed to have been polished with olive oil. I prescribed a painkiller and explained that the pains were just symptoms of nervous tension. From that day on, whenever I saw her on what was left of the roads of this devastated camp, she'd turn and smile, because she'd heard my footsteps and knew I was hurrying to catch up with her. Our relationship developed through walking, turning and smiling. Then she went abroad. Should I go to her? Or stay? Indeed, why should I stay? But what work would I find in Denmark?

Siham doesn't care because she doesn't understand that I'm almost forty and that it's difficult for someone of that age to begin again, starting from zero.

"But you're at zero now," she'd say.

She's right. I have to acknowledge that zero to be able to begin my life. But what does it mean to "begin my life"? When I say "begin" does it mean that everything I did before was nothing?

I think of Siham, try to sleep, and go with her to Denmark and become a prince like Hamlet. Hamlet lived in the Rotten State, and I live in the Rotten State. Hamlet's father died, and my father died. True, my uncle didn't kill my father and marry my mother like Hamlet's, but what happened to my mother was perhaps more horrible. Hamlet went mad because he was incapable of taking revenge, and I'm on the verge of going mad because someone wants to take revenge on me. Hamlet was a prince and saw something that was rotten, and I see something rotten too. Hamlet went mad, and so did I.

When you told me about Ibraheem, your eldest son, with his curly hair, black eyes and long eyelashes, I thought of Hamlet. You say Ibraheem, and I see Hamlet.

The image of Hamlet started to form when you told me of your son's death. At the time it amazed me that people could remember such painful things. Why wouldn't they forget? And a terrible thought came into my mind – that people are only the phantoms of their memories. The story of Ibraheem came up when you were telling me about the beneficial qualities of olive oil and how your mother never used medicine.

"Medicines never entered our house," you told me. "My mother treated herself and us with olive oil. If she felt a pain in her belly, she'd dip a piece of cotton wool in the oil jar and swallow it, and if my father came back from the fields with his feet covered in cuts, she'd dab oil on them, and if her son was in pain and crying, she'd run to the demijohn of oil for the perfect cure."

When Naheeleh told you that three-year-old Ibraheem only liked to eat bread dipped in oil, you told her the boy was like his grandmother. He'd dip his bread in oil and eat it with onions, only onions, never any thyme or *labneh*. Only onions – except he liked honey too.

You didn't know your son.

His mother brought him to the cave several times, and you saw him in his swaddling bands by candlelight, but you didn't really see him. All that stuck in your memory was a white face and half-closed eyes. You loved him, of course – could any man not love his first-born son? You'd hold him in your arms and kiss him and then, when his mother came close, forget him. When he got a little older, Naheeleh no longer brought him to the cave.

She'd describe him to you and imitate his walk, his movements and his words, but she adamantly refused to bring him to the cave. She said he could understand now and talk, and that the poor child shouldn't be exposed to danger, what with the village being full of informers. You'd agree with her, ask her to imitate the way he talked, and then forget the boy in your feverish efforts to hold on to time as it drained out of the cave. You'd bury your head in her hair and tell her you wanted to sleep with your head resting there, but you wouldn't sleep.

One day, when Naheeleh was telling him about her son, Yunis left the cave. He left his wife with her talk and went off. Naheeleh knew he'd go to the house, but she didn't go after him. When he returned, she'd tell him she'd been rooted to the spot with fear.

Yunis reached the house, pushed open the old wooden door, went into his wife's room, turned on the electric light and saw. The boy was sleeping on his left side, his head resting on his hand, which was curled under the pillow, and his curly black hair covered his face.

Years after that visit, he'd tell his wife that when he stood in front of the bed he forgot where he was and was overwhelmed by beauty. He'd tell her that beauty was the curly hair flowing over the face sleeping on its side on the pillow.

Yunis doesn't remember the time, but he remembers his mother's footsteps. The old woman had been awakened by the light, gotten out of bed and gone towards the room, asking if he was Naheeleh.

"When I heard her, I turned off the light," he told his wife, "and tiptoed out of the house."

Naheeleh would tell him that his mother never stopped interrogating her.

"Your mother hates me," she said. "You know she's hated me since day one because she thought I was to blame for the mess-up that forced her to cut my finger to bloody the bedsheet, and for the rest of her life she'd say she never felt such shame as on that night. But the night you visited, everything changed. I came back, and she was in my room waiting for me. I saw something like tenderness in her eyes. I opened the door – it was 4.00 in the morning – and I heard her voice. She was walking back and forth and talking to herself. I came in as the last shadows slipped off the house before dawn.

"'Was it him?' she asked. 'He was here, and you were with him?'

"I asked her to keep her voice down because I was afraid she'd wake Ibraheem. She lowered it, but it still sounded loud. She shook with excitement as she talked, her words tumbling over one another. She didn't ask me anything, and I don't remember what she said. Then she calmed down. She went to the kitchen and returned with two cups of tea and sat down on the floor. I was sleepy and felt as if my body was slipping away. I drank the tea quickly and went to my bed. Looking at me affectionately, she told me not to worry, she'd take care of Ibraheem when he woke up.

"'Get some sleep,' she said.

"I felt her eyes boring into my belly and from that night on whenever she looked at me she'd start with my belly. I lay down on my bed. She came and sat on the end of it and asked me to take her there with me. She didn't ask me where I went, or how, or where 'there' was.

"'Tell Yunis: Your mother wants to see you before she dies. I know he doesn't have much time, daughter, but tell him.'"

Naheeleh told Yunis, but he warned her, "Don't bring that woman here. I'll go and see her."

He didn't go, though, except when his father died, and after he'd been, his mother said it was like she hadn't seen him.

You didn't go, you told me, because after Ibraheem's accident you were no longer capable of going. "How could you expect me to enter that house after Ibraheem died? His mother," you said. "His poor mother. I saw how Naheeleh died and came to life again. I somehow knew he'd died; nobody told me, I swear. I heard his voice calling for help, and I went and found that he was dead. After my only visit to the house, when I saw him sleeping, a special bond grew up between us. You could say I started to love him, and I started to find a place in my pack for small presents I'd buy him. Naheeleh didn't understand at first why I insisted she dress him in the pyjamas I'd stuffed into the pack. She said they were too big for him, so I asked her to shorten them, and when I explained the reason to her, she laughed. She said I was crazy, wanting my son to wear the same pyjamas as me. Then she took things one step further. She took to giving us the same clothes. I told her I wouldn't wear Israeli clothes, and she said they weren't Israeli, she sewed them herself. She said, 'This shirt's just like Ibraheem's,' and that when I wore it I looked amazingly like my son. She'd make us the same clothes and say that when Ibraheem grew up we'd be like twins. I started wearing my clothes and imagining my son wearing his clothes and me talking to him as though he was a man. We became like one man divided in two, one half in the cave and one at home."

That was your game.

Naheeleh would say that when she missed her husband, she'd dress Ibraheem in his pyjamas and that would take care of it. And Yunis used to tell her that when he didn't change his shirt it meant he was longing for her and her son. "See, the shirt's torn and I haven't changed it. That means I was really homesick. Plus it means you have to make us new clothes."

Clothes became the subject of the meetings of husband and wife in that cave suspended above the village of Deir El Asad. The husband would bring cloth from Lebanon and the wife would sew it, saying she didn't want to turn into a tailor and had to take care of the unborn child growing in her belly.

"I started holding conversations with my son without realising what I was doing. He became part of me. Even after Naheeleh delivered our second son, Salim, and in spite of all the problems associated with the birth, we never forgot the game of the clothes."

Yunis said that somehow he knew.

"I was in Lebanon, hiding in Nizar El Saffouri's house, God bless him, when I had that dream. I dreamt I saw Naheeleh weeping for me. I dreamt I was thrown into the rubbish pit and Naheeleh was standing at the edge of the pit trying to get me out and weeping, and I was telling her to go back to the house. I don't know how I spoke, as I was dead, or how I looked into the pit and saw my pyjamas.

"It was 5.00 a.m. and raining heavily. I got dressed and decided to go to Deir El Asad. The dream had frightened me a lot because I had had it more than once. I awoke in a panic, put on my clothes and set off. At Nizar's house, I remembered seeing the dream for the third time, each time repeated detail for detail. The two times before, I'd seen it in prison and thought it was a nightmare caused by the torture, because in prison you become incapable of distinguishing between sleeping and waking. That morning I got up in a panic and heard the sloosh of the rain, and I decided to go. I thought it was my father, that the old man had died and I had to go. I don't know; when I thought of my father's death, I felt relief, even though I'd grown to love the blind sheikh in his last days. But a father's death comes quietly.

"Nizar El Saffouri had also awoken in a panic, and tried to stop me leaving. He said they'd kill me this time, that I'd never be able to stand the torture. I was worn out after three months in prison. I don't know where they held me – I was in an underground vault, in darkness, damp and cold. I only saw the interrogator's face once. The cold got into my body, and the pain, the pain of cold bones, crushed you from the inside. When cold gets into your bones, it turns you into solidified bits of agony. It was as though my skeleton had turned into bits of ice inside my body.

"You know, I used to hope I'd be beaten because it was my only way of getting a little warmth. I'd look forward to the beating party and rush to it. They must have noticed how I enjoyed the warmth while they were punching and kicking me, so they decided to do something different.

"I was laid out in the centre of the beating circle, with three men above me kicking every part of my body, while I rolled among their feet, unseeing. Just the boots; the boots above my cheeks and eyes. The interrogator came in, and the boots withdrew from my face. They stood me up, I couldn't do it on my own, and one of them propped me up against the wall with his arm around my neck while the other started hitting me on my mouth with a chain wrapped around his fist, and the floodgates of pain opened. I remember the interrogator's voice as he told me to swallow. I spat and gagged, and the man held my mouth shut with his hand to force me to swallow my shattered teeth.

"The Lebanese interrogator spoke to me in a fake Palestinian accent as though he was making fun of me, and he threatened me. Then he said they were going to let me go, and they knew everything, and woe betide me if I tried to cross the Lebanon–Israel border again because they'd make me swallow all my teeth.

"I listened and didn't answer. No, not because I was afraid of him really. I couldn't talk without my front teeth.

"Nizar took me to a dentist, a friend of ours, and he put in a temporary bridge and told me to rest for a month before he put in a permanent one.

"Nizar didn't ask me why I was wearing a torn shirt; his only concern was to stop me from going out. I told him I wouldn't be long but I had to go, and I set off. That day I was wearing the torn blue shirt I'd been wearing in the rubbish-pit dream. I found the shirt at the bottom of my pack – I'm the only man in the world who lives out of his bag: I put all my possessions in my bag, and it goes wherever I go.

"I won't describe how I got there, because you'd never believe me. It's true the distance between southern Lebanon and the village of Tarshiha in Galilee is short and you can do it, walking, in four or five hours, but in those days it took about twenty hours because we had to avoid the Israeli patrols. I don't remember how, but I flew. Now, as I tell you the story, I see myself as though I wasn't walking – no, I swear I was moving over the ground as though I was skating, and I arrived at noon.

"I went to my cave at Bab El Shams thinking I'd wait till evening and then go to the house, and I found her there, waiting for me."

"'You're late,' she said."

Yunis didn't hear and didn't see. Naheeleh stood with her back to the entrance of the cave. The cave was dark, and the sunlight splintered against his eyes so he saw nothing. He saw a wavering shadow and what looked like bowed shoulders.

She said she'd spent the whole night waiting for him.

She said she wanted to die.

She said she had died.

And her words mixed with her moans.

"She wasn't weeping," said Yunis. "I didn't hear sobbing or screaming. I heard moaning like that of a wounded animal. I went to her. She shook me off and fell to the ground. Then I understood, and I started to rip up my shirt.

"She said, 'Ibraheem'. Silence and the madness of sorrow struck me, and I heard a low moaning coming from every pore of her body.

"I tried to question her, but she didn't reply. I sat down on the ground and reached out to her shaking body, but she moved away. She opened her mouth to say something, and a grating, gasping sound emerged, as though she was in her death throes.

"Poor Naheeleh, she stayed that way for more than a year. For a year her eyes were swollen with repressed tears. Her milk dried up, and Salim, our second son, almost died.

"To tell the truth, I didn't understand her behaviour. Can a mother lose her instincts, or refuse to let her second son live, as though she wanted him to join the first?

"Her milk dried up, but she went on feeding Salim as though nothing was wrong, and my mother didn't notice. The child wept night and day. She would give him her breast, and he would fall silent for a while. Then he would start crying again. My mother discovered the truth when he wouldn't stop crying even when he was feeding.

"Do you know what my mother did?

"She stole the child. She snatched him away and took him to Umm Sab', Nabeel El Khateeb's wife, and asked her to suckle him and keep him with her. My mother was afraid the old story would happen all over again, and my children would die just as hers had.

"Poor Naheeleh. Mothers, friend, are really something."

I didn't ask you then what you did, and how you bore the death of that son of yours that you looked like. "You look like him," Naheeleh used to say, when she found you sad in the cave because she hadn't cooked you *mihammara* and *kibbeh nayyeh*. She said it wasn't just your features and your clothes but the way you moved. This would make you laugh, and you'd accept the dish of leftover food she'd brought from home.

I didn't ask you because on that occasion you seemed like someone who was just telling the story. You told me how you'd spent two months in the wild out of fear for your wife. You tried to calm her down and told her that Salim had to stay with Umm Sab' so he'd survive. She'd speak disjointedly and say your mother was a liar and that her milk hadn't dried up and she was going to die. You spent two months moving about in the fields and going to see her three times a week and taking her to Bab El Shams.

After staying with her for two months, you went back to Lebanon because the temporary bridge the dentist had given you was starting to crumble, and in Lebanon you forgot about everything and went for more than a year before visiting Galilee. You told me you were delayed by your many preoccupations and that you were getting things ready for the first groups of fedayeen, but I didn't believe you. I think you fled because you had no solution. Your wife was on the verge of madness, and nothing would console her, so what were you to do? As men always do, you fled. Manliness, or what we call manliness, consists of flight because, inside all the bluster and bullying and big words, there's a refusal to face up to life.

You went back to her after more than a year. You were embarrassed and timid, but you went back, knocked on the window and raced off to your cave.

She came.

She was like a new woman. Her hair was long and tied back; she smelled of a mixture of coffee beans and thyme, and her face looked like his. You only knew Ibraheem from photos; you only saw him sleeping, hair covering his pillow.

You said the woman had come to resemble her dead son and that when you smelled the coffee beans and the thyme rising from her hair, you fell into that feeling that never left you. You said that when you returned to Lebanon after that visit, you were like a lost man, talking without thinking, moving like a sleepwalker, unaware of your own existence except when you were on your way to Bab El Shams.

"That's real love, Abu Salim."

You refused to acknowledge this blazing truth and said that something inside you, something that had come out into the open after being secret, made you incapable of putting up with other people, and that you were like a wolf that prefers to live in the open.

During that time, you lived in the forest for sixteen continous months. You didn't tell Naheeleh you were living nearby. You'd visit her twice a week, amazing her with your ability to traverse such distances and dangers. You didn't tell her you had no distances to traverse, only time

– the time that became your cross during the days and nights of waiting.

You told Dr Mu'een El Tarshahani, who was in charge of the training camp you'd set up at Meisaloun near Damascus, that you were going on a long surveillance trip. "I'll be away for a few months, maybe a year. Don't ask about me, and don't issue any statements. I won't die, and I will come back."

At the time, Dr Mu'een thought you'd been hit by "Return fever", that disease that spread among the Palestinians at the beginning of the '50s and led hundreds of them to their deaths as they tried to cross the Lebanese border on the way back to their villages. He tried to dissuade you, saying that the Return would come after the Liberation.

"But I'm not going back," you told him. "I'm going to scout out the land, and I'll come back so that we can return together."

Dr Mu'een explained that those who succeeded in reaching their objective couldn't live decent lives because they were treated as "resident absentees" and permitted neither to work nor to move about.

"I don't want a communiqué or a death notice. I'm coming back."

And you left.

There you were, pretending that you wanted to explore Galilee inch by inch, but you were lying. You didn't explore Galilee. On the contrary, you just kept hovering around Deir El Asad and making a circuit of Sha'ab, El Kabri and El Ghabsiyyeh. You lived among the ruins of the villages and would go into the abandoned houses and eat their stocks of food. You'd pounce on what people had left behind in their houses and savour the vintage olive oil. You said oil's like wind – the longer it matures in its jars the smoother it gets. And you gave me your views on bread. You made me taste the bread you ate when you were on your own during those long months, kneading the dough and cutting it and frying the little pieces in olive oil. You said you'd got used to that kind of bread, and you made it now in the camp whenever you had a yen for it.

"But it's bad for you and raises your cholesterol," I said as I experienced its burning taste.

"We don't get cholesterol. Peasants are cholesterol-proof."

A year of living in the open around Deir El Asad.

A year of loneliness and waiting.

You didn't tell anyone, and no-one was willing to listen to you. In those days people played games with death every day.

Who remembers that woman?

You told me you prayed that God would bless you with forgetfulness and that you didn't want to remember her, but she kept coming into your thoughts, like a phantom.

She was alone – a woman on her own wandering among the destroyed graves of El Kabri. And they weren't even graves: the Israeli Army didn't leave one stone on top of another in El Kabri after they occupied it.

The woman was picking things up and putting them in a bag on her back. Yunis approached her. At first she looked like an animal walking on all fours. Her long hair covered her face, and she was muttering. Yunis moved towards her carefully, ready to fire his rifle. Then she turned and looked him in the eye.

"My hands shook and I nearly dropped the rifle," he told his wife. "She seems to have thought I was an Israeli soldier, and when I got close to her she slung her bag over her shoulder and started running through the rough. I stayed where I was and looked around but saw nothing on the ground. I found dried bones, which I thought belonged to dead animals. I thought to catch up with her to ask her what she was doing, but she ran as fast as an animal. When Naheeleh told me who she was, I went back to the place, gathered the remaining bones and buried them in a deep hole."

The woman's story terrified the whole of Galilee.

In those days, Galilee quaked with fear – houses demolished, people lost, villages abandoned and everything topsy turvy.

In those days, the woman's voice was like a wind whistling at the windows. People became afraid and called her the Madwoman of El Kabri; she crept along the ground and leapt from field to field, carrying her bag of bones on her back.

It was said that she gathered the bones of the dead and dug them graves on the hilltops. When she died, the bones from her bag were scattered in the square at Deir El Asad, and people came running and gathered them up and made a common grave for them. The Madwoman of El Kabri was buried next to the bones she'd been carrying.

Who was that woman?

No-one knows, but people learned her story from her bag.

Yunis said he met the madwoman of the bones and spoke to her, and that she wasn't mad as people said. "She gave me wild chicory to eat. She was looking for wild chicory, not bones. What happened was that she stayed behind in El Kabri after the Jews demolished it to avenge the victims of Khirbet Jiddeen. The woman didn't run away with the others because they left her behind."

"In those days we forgot our own children," said Umm Hassan when I asked her about the Madwoman of El Kabri.

"In those days, son, we left everything. We left the dead unburied and fled."

In those days the people lived with fear, military rule and the death of border crossers. People no longer knew who they were or who their family was or where their villages were. And there was her voice. She would go around at night and wail, like a whistling wind colliding with the tottering houses.

All that the people saw in the square at Deir El Asad was a dead woman. She was dead and spread-eagled, her arms outstretched like a cross, her black peasant dress torn over her corpse, her empty bag at her side, bones everywhere.

Sheikh Ahmad El Shatti, the sheikh of the mosque at Deir El Asad, stood next to the corpse and ordered the women to leave. Then he wrapped it in a black cloth and asked the children to gather the bones and placed them on top of the corpse. "The children of Deir El Asad will never forget it," Rabee' told me at our military base in Kafar Shouba. Rabee' was a strange young man who laughed all the time. Even when Abu Na'il El Tirawi was killed by a bullet from his own machine gun, Rabee' laughed instead of crying like the rest of us. Abu Na'il was the first dead person I'd ever seen. I'd only seen my dead father through my mother's description. I saw Abu Na'il dying and the blood spurting from his stomach while we stood round him not knowing what to do. We carried him to the car, and on the way to the hospital he screamed that he didn't want to die. He was dying and screaming that he didn't want to. Then he suddenly went stiff, his body slumped, and his face disappeared behind the mask of death.

I don't know how Rabee' escaped from Israel, but I do remember his terror-stricken eyes as he said he hadn't forgotten the bones. "Sheikh Ahmad El Shatti was sure they were human bones, but we children thought they were animal bones. That's why we played with them till the sheikh made us put them on top of the corpse. There was a single human skull in the madwoman's bag, and this the sheikh wouldn't let us touch. He took it and put it in a bag of its own, and the rumour went round among the children that he'd taken the skull to his house to use in magic séances."

Rabee' left Kafar Shouba and joined one of the Hebrew–Arabic translation bureaux belonging to the Resistance. He died during the Israeli bombardment of Beirut's El Fakahani district in 1981.

Yunis was sure that the madwoman collected people's bones and put them in her bag, and that she'd been killed by mistake; the Israelis had killed her during the sweeps ordered by Prime Minister David Ben Gurion in 1951.

In those days the villages of Galilee were haunted by border crossers at night, and there were clear orders to shoot anything that moved.

The madwoman used to move around at night, alone, like the ghost of the dead she carried in her bag. People were afraid of her. Nobody saw her and everybody saw her, wearing her long black dress and walking among the patches of darkness.

When you told me the story of those long months spent among the abandoned houses, the night ghosts and the sound of the Israeli guns harvesting people, you told me everything except the word I was waiting to hear.

Are you scared of the word *love*?

I am, I swear; that's why I can't sleep: frightened people can't sleep. I lie on my bed, and I ask the memories to come like swarms of ants, and I follow their spiralling motion. I think of Shams, and I get scared.

What if I couldn't open my eyes again? What if I slept and didn't get up? What if they came and killed me? I'm scared.

No, not of them, nor of the rumours, which I don't believe. I'm scared of sleep, of the distance it erases between my dreams and my reality. I can't tell the difference any more, I swear I can't tell the difference. I talk about things that happened to me and then discover they were dreams.

And you, do you have dreams?

Scientists say the brain never stops producing thoughts and pictures. What do you imagine? Do you see your story the way I tell it to you?

Anyway, I'm scared. There are rumours all over the camp. They say Shams's gang will take revenge on everyone who took part in her murder. I'm ready to explain that I had nothing to do with it, but where are they?

Is it true they killed Abu Ali Zayid in Ein El Hilweh camp? Why did they kill him? Because he whistled? Can a man be killed because he whistled? They say he was standing at the entrance to El Miyyeh wi-Miyyeh camp and that when he saw Shams's car he put two fingers under his tongue and whistled. And the bullets rained down.

They'll kill me too.

I didn't do anything. They took me to court, I gave my testimony, and that's it.

I'm sure they're just rumours. Dr Amjad and the crippled nurse think I'm hiding in your room because I'm afraid of them, and two days ago I heard Nurse Zeinab telling Dr Amjad she wouldn't try to stop them if they came. I gathered she was talking about me.

You know I don't live here out of fear of Shams's ghost or her gang. I'm here so you're not on your own and I'm not either. What kind of person would leave a hero like you to rot in his bed? And I hate being on my own with no-one to talk to. What kind of days are these, swaddled in silence? No-one knows anyone else or talks to anyone else. Even death doesn't unite us. Even death has changed and become just death.

I lie on my bed, open my eyes and stare into the darkness. I look at the ceiling, and it seems to get closer, as though it's about to fall and bury me beneath the rubble. But the darkness isn't black, and now I'm discovering the colours of darkness and seeing them. I extinguish the candle and see the colours of the dark, for there's no such thing as darkness: it's a mixture of sleeping colours that we discover, slowly. Now I'm discovering them, slowly.

I won't describe the darkness to you because I hate describing things. Ever since I was in school I've hated describing things. The teacher would give us an essay to write: "Describe a rainy day." And I wouldn't know how, because I hate comparing things. Things can only be described in their own terms, and when we compare them, we forget them. A girl's face is like a girl's face and not like the moon. The whiteness and the roundness and everything else are different. When we say that a girl's face is like the moon, we forget the girl. We make the description so that we can forget, and I don't like to forget. Rain is like rain, isn't that enough? Isn't it enough that it should rain for us to smell the smell of winter?

I don't know how to describe things even though I've memorised a lot of ancient poetry. I'm not intimidated by Imru' Al Qays – king, poet, lover, drunkard, debauchee and semi-prophet. What wonderful poetry! "Her breast polished like a looking-glass" describes a woman's breast as being like a mirror. I listen to poetry and say, "Amazing!" and love it, but I've a problem with the descriptions. How, I mean, can a woman's breast be like a mirror? It won't do. Isn't he saying in effect that he's not seeing her, he's just seeing himself? And that he's not making love to her but to himself? Which would lead us to a terrible conclusion about our ancient poets. Of course Imru' Al Qays wasn't a sodomite, nor was Al Mutanabbi; it's the description that's at fault.

All the same, I love ancient poetry, and I love Al Mutanabbi. I love the melody that makes the words revolve inside their rhymes and rhythms. I love the rhythm and the way things resonate with one another and the reverberation of the words. When I recite that poetry, I feel an intoxication equalled only by the intoxication I feel when I listen to Umm Kalthoum. It's what we call *tarab*. We're a people of *tarab*, and *tarab* doesn't go with description, so how can I describe things to you when I don't know how?

I don't sleep, and I don't describe, and I don't feel *tarab*, and I don't recite poetry. Because I'm afraid, and fear doesn't sleep.

Tell me about fear.

I know you don't use that word. You'll say that you "withdrew" because you use words to play tricks with the truth. That's the game you play with your memories – you play tricks and say what you want without naming it.

I know you want me to leave after this night of drowsy sleeplessness and darkness. I'll go; just tell me how Ibraheem died.

Naheeleh told the story two ways, and you believed both.

The first time around, she lied because she was afraid you'd do something stupid. Then she told the truth because she could tell from your eyes that you were going to do something stupid anyway, so she preferred you to do something meaningfully stupid.

Yunis went into the cave, the sun burning his sweat- and fatigue-rimmed eyes, and he saw her. She was a motionless shadow at the back of the cave, her back turned to the entrance. She heard his footsteps and smelt the smell of travel, but she didn't turn around. Yunis went towards her and saw she was staggering, as though she'd waited for him to come before falling to the ground.

He saw her shoulders, outlined by shadows, shaking as if she was weeping. He went to her, gasping for breath as though all the distances he'd traversed and that had been imprisoned in his lungs were about to explode. When he tried to grasp her shoulders, she started moaning and said a name.

Yunis tried to make her explain, but she wouldn't stop repeating "Ibraheem", which had become part of her moaning. He tried to ask about his father, but she didn't answer and burst into a long fit of weeping that grew louder before being choked off.

She said the boy had died because she'd been unable to take him to the hospital at Acre.

"His head fell forward while was eating. He said his head was ringing with pain."

She tied a cloth around his head and rubbed oil on his neck, but the pain didn't stop. He held his temples as though hugging himself and writhed in pain. So she decided to take him to the hospital at Acre.

Naheeleh went to the headquarters of the military governor to ask for a pass and was subjected to a long interrogation.

"They threw me into a darkened room," she said, "and left me there for more than three hours. Then they took me to the office of a short man who spoke with an Iraqi accent. I said my son was sick and he asked me about you. I wept and he threatened me. I said the boy was dying, and he asked me to co-operate with them and questioned me about the border crossers. Then he said he couldn't give me a permit if I didn't bring him a medical certificate to prove my son was sick."

"There's no doctor in the village," I told him.

"Those are my orders," he said. "If you don't co-operate with us, we won't co-operate with you."

When she returned to her house without a permit, she found her son dying, with the blind sheikh whispering the last rites.

When Naheeleh finished her story, she saw how calm your face was. Your panting had stopped, and you looked at her suspiciously, as though you were accusing her. Naheeleh saw how calmly you took the news as you sat down, lit a cigarette, asked about Salim and told her you'd be away for a long time.

She understood that you'd never come back.

You asked about the new Israeli settlement being built near Deir El Asad, and then you stood up, said you'd have your revenge and walked out. She grabbed you by the hand, brought you back into the cave and told the story over again.

She said Ibraheem had been playing with the other children.

She said the new settlement had sprung up like a weed, and they'd fenced off the land they'd confiscated with barbed wire while everyone looked on, seeing their land shrinking and disappearing, unable to do anything.

She said, "They took the land and we watched like someone watching his own death in a mirror."

She said of the children – "You know how children are – they were playing close to the barbed wire and talking to the Yemeni immigrants in Hebrew – the children speak Hebrew – and the immigrants were answering them in an odd Arabic – our children know their language and they don't know ours. Ibraheem had been playing with them, and they brought him to me. God, he was shaking to death. They said a huge stone had fallen on him. I don't know how to describe it; his head was crushed, and blood was dripping from it. I left him in the house and ran to ask for a permit to take him to the hospital in Acre, and at the military governor's headquarters they made me wait for more than three hours in a darkened room, the Iraqi threatening to beat me when he interrogated me. He said they knew you came, that their men could do what you came for better than you could, and that they'd kill you and leave you in the square at Deir El Asad to make an example of you. And he asked for information about you while I pleaded for the permit.

"And when I got back to the house, Ibraheem was dead, and your father was saying the last rites."

You sat down, lit a cigarette and put a thousand and one questions to her. You wanted to know whether they'd killed him or he'd died accidentally; had they thrown the stone at him, or had he just got in the way of it.

Naheeleh didn't know.

You stood up and said that you'd kill their children as they'd killed your son: "Tomorrow you'll ululate for joy, because we'll have our revenge."

For three nights you circled the barbed-wire fence. You had your rifle and ten hand grenades, and you decided to tie the grenades together, throw them into the Jewish settlement's workshop, and, when they exploded, fire at the settlers.

It was night.

The spotlight revolved, tracking the barbed-wire fence, and you hid in the olive grove close by. You started moving closer, crawling on your stomach. You got the chain of grenades ready and tied them to a detonator, deciding to throw them into the big unfinished hall where the Yemeni Jewish families slept practically on top of one another. You wanted to kill, just to kill. When you described the event to Dr Mu'een, you said that during your third pass you imagined the dead bodies piled on top of one another and felt pleased.

"I was thirsty; revenge is like thirst. I would drink, and my thirst would increase, so that when the time came and I began to crawl, a refreshing coolness filled my heart. When everything was about to happen, the thirst disappeared, and I set out not with revenge in my mind but because it was my duty, because I'd promised Naheeleh."

Yunis never told the story of what really happened.

He said later that it was impossible to carry out the operation due to the huge losses the villages would incur as a result of the predictable Israeli response.

He crawled towards the fence, and after the spotlight had passed over him a number of times, heard the sound of firing and dogs barking. He flattened himself to the ground. Then he decided to "withdraw", running, paying no attention to the spotlight. When he ran, the bullets flying around him, he disappeared into the olive grove, and instead of hiding there until the morning, kept going till he reached the Lebanese border.

He said later that he decided not to go through with the operation because it was an individual act of revenge and because the Israelis would take it out on the Arab villages. But he never spoke of the fear that made him freeze or of why he fled all the way to Lebanon.

Now, master, I have a right to be afraid.

But not Yunis; Yunis wasn't afraid, his heart never wavered. Yunis "withdrew" because he was a hero. I, on the other hand, am hiding in his room because I'm a coward. Have you noticed how things have changed? Those days were heroic days, these days are not. Yunis got scared, so he became a hero; I'm scared, so I've become a coward.

When Yunis returned to Bab El Shams, he didn't tell Naheeleh about the revenge that never happened. But me — the crippled nurse looks at me with contempt because she's waiting for me to justify my staying in the hospital. Shams was killed and I'm expected to pay the price for a crime I didn't commit.

I don't sleep.

And you — did you sleep after you postponed your revenge?

You want a story!

I know you want to change the way the conversation's been going as you don't agree with my way of telling the story of your son's death and your revenge. You'll ask me to tell it a different way, to say, for example, that when you got up to the barbed wire, you understood that individual revenge had no value and decided to go back to Lebanon to organise the fedayeen so we could start the war.

"I swear that was no war. I swear it was like a dream. Don't believe, son, that the Jews won the '48 war. In '48, we didn't fight, we didn't know what we were doing. They won because we didn't fight, and they didn't fight either, they just won. It was like a dream."

You'll say you chose war instead of revenge, and I have to believe you. Everyone will believe you, and they'll say you were right, and I'm trying to cover my fear up with yours.

You weren't afraid that night in March 1951.

And I'm not afraid now!

When Yunis told how his son Ibraheem died in 1951, he spoke a lot about Naheeleh's suffering. He didn't speak about his own suffering, saying only that he felt the thirst for revenge and then falling silent.

"Didn't you feel pain?" I asked him. "Didn't you want to die? Didn't you die?"

"I don't understand, because I'm only afraid of one thing," I said to Shams as I was flying above her.

"I'm afraid of children."

When we made love, she'd scream that it was like the sea. In bed, she was next to me and over me and under me, swimming. She said she was swimming in the sea, the waves cascading inside her. She'd rise and bend and stretch and circle, saying it was the waves. And I'd fly above Shams or under her or in the midst of her, flying above her undulating blue sea.

"You're all the men in the world," she said. "I sleep with you as if I'm with all the men I've known and not known." I'd fly above her listening to her words, trying to put off the moment of union. I'd tell her to go a little more slowly because I wanted to smell the sky, but she'd pull me into her sea and submerge me and push me to the limits of sorrow.

"You're my man and all men."

I didn't understand the expanses of her passion and her desire to control her body. She'd massage her body and grasp her breasts and faint. I'd see her faint and it was as though she wasn't with me, or as though she was in a distant dream, a sort of island encircled by waves.

I didn't dare ask her to marry me because I believed her. She said she was a free woman and would never marry again. I believed her and understood her and agreed with her, despite feeling that burning sensation that could only be extinguished by making her my possession.

I agreed with her because I was powerless and didn't dare force her to choose between marrying me and leaving me, for the idea of not seeing her was more difficult than death.

Then I found out she'd killed Samih because he'd refused to marry her. They said she'd stood over his body and said loudly, so everybody heard, "I give myself to you in marriage" and left.

That's what they said at the interrogation, when they arrested me. I said nothing. I was incapable of speech because I felt tricked and frightened. It was there, in the eyes of the committee members, that I discovered she'd been sentenced to die. The head of the committee was in a hurry, as though he wanted to use me as new proof to justify the decision to kill her.

The committee eyed me, the duped lover, with contempt, though I wasn't duped. But what could I say to them? I used to smell the other men on her body, but it never occurred to me that she loved another man the way I loved her. There – with him – she'd have said nothing and been on the verge of tears as she listened to him saying that with her he was sleeping with all other women.

I understand her, I swear I do: love's only solution is murder. I never came close to committing the crime, but I did long for her death, because death ends everything, as it did that day.

Shams is a hero because she put an end to her own problem. But me, I'm just a man who grew horns, as the head of the committee said, thinking he was making a joke that everyone could appreciate.

I refused to answer their questions. All I said was that I was convinced she was "not a normal woman". I know I was hard on her, but what could I say? I had to say something, and that expression popped out of my mouth. As for all the other things I'm supposed to have said, they're not true. Liars! I never said anything about orgies. My God – how could we have held orgies in my house when it was surrounded by all those other wrecked houses? They put words into my mouth so as to come up with additional justifications for killing Shams. All I said was that she was my friend and that she was a woman of many moods. I heard their laughter, and the joke about my horns.

The head of the committee ordered me to be released because I was pathetic. "A pathetic sort, no harm to anyone," he said.

"Pathetic" means stupid, and I wasn't stupid. I wanted to tell them that love isn't stupidity, but I didn't say anything. I left and went looking for Shams, and I was arrested again before being released and returning to Beirut.

This isn't what I wanted to say. I wanted to tell you that when I was caught up in that wave, I'd dream of having children and get scared. I told Shams that the most horrible thing that could happen to a person was to lose their son or daughter. Even though I live in the midst of this desolate people that has grown accustomed to losing its children, I can't imagine myself in that situation.

Shams laughed and told me about her daughter Dalal, in Jordan, and about how missing her was like having her guts ripped open.

And when I asked Yunis about the death of his son, he told me about Naheeleh.

The woman almost went mad. All the people of Deir El Asad said the woman had lost her mind. She took to walking outside the village as though chasing her own death – going to areas the military governor had decreed were out of bounds (and almost everywhere was out of bounds) and walking and walking. Then she'd return home exhausted and sleep. She never asked about her second son, Salim, whom his grandmother had smuggled out of the house because she was frightened of his mother's madness.

It took Naheeleh a year to return to her senses, after she got pregnant with her daughter Nour – "Light". The girl's name wasn't originally Nour: her grandmother named her Fatimah, but Yunis said her name was Nour because he'd seen Ibraheem in a dream reciting verses from the chapter of the Koran called "Nour".

"Listen, woman, to what he was saying." Naheeleh looked and she saw a halo round Yunis's head as he said,

God is the Light of the heavens and the earth;
the likeness of His Light is as a niche wherein is a lamp
(the lamp in a glass, the glass as it were a glittering star)
kindled from a Blessed Tree,
an olive that is neither of the East nor of the West
whose oil wellnigh would shine, even if no fire touched it;
Light upon Light;
(God guides to His Light whom He will).

Yunis said he'd been able to bear his son's death because he hadn't believed it. "When you don't see, you don't believe. I used to tell Naheeleh that Ibraheem would come back once he'd tired of playing with death. I swear, son, as far as I'm concerned Ibraheem is still alive. I'm waiting for him."

She came into your room today as I was laughing. The crippled nurse had made me laugh by telling me how she'd hit Dr Amjad. I'd thought that Amjad Hussein was a respectable man. I don't know where they got him from to play the doctor here. Some say Mme Widad, the Director of the Red Crescent, got him the job because he's a relative of hers. But he's not one of us, because he didn't fight with us and the Israelis didn't hold him at Ansar detention camp. So where does he come from? Don't ask me now why I didn't go to the Biqa' when our battalion withdrew from El Nabatiyyeh during the Israeli incursion — that's just the way it happened. I withdrew with the battalion and went to Ein El Hilweh, and that's where I was arrested. A month later, they released me, and I found myself going to Beirut. On the other hand, I've no idea where you disappeared to. You told me that when you heard the Israelis had entered Beirut, you fled to the village of Batshay and hid there with the priest.

"The priest's an old friend of mine, and he thinks I'm a Christian," you told me.

Me, on the other hand, they tied up in that net that looks like a cage, blindfolded me, wound what felt like ropes around me, and took me to the Israeli prison before I was moved to Ansar.

I won't tell you now what I told everyone about our life in the detention camp. In Ansar, I lost twenty kilos and became thin and sick. Everyone was at the camp except Dr Amjad. Even Abu Mohammed El Rahhal, President of the Workers' Federation, left sick and died two months later. I haven't told you this dream he used to tell us every day. I don't know what happened to Abu Mohammed in the detention camp. There were thousands of us in the middle of a bare field surrounded by barbed wire, "treating our cares with our cares", as we used to say — all of us except Abu Mohammed, who visited a new tent each day and told the occupants the same dream.

"Yesterday," he'd say, "I had a dream," and he'd start telling the same dream, till it became a joke.

"Yesterday I had a dream that I was – I don't know how – standing on the pavement with my manhood (he used this curious term for his member) sticking out, and it was, I don't know, sorry to mention it, *sooo* long, longer than the street from side to side, and an Israeli tank came along and drove over it."

"Did the tank cut it off, Abu Mohammed?"

"Did it hurt a lot?"

Abu Mohammed would say he was afraid he was going to die, because "when a man sees his manhood cut off in a dream, it means he's going to die".

"Where did you get that from, Abu Mohammed?"

"I read it in Ibn Sirin's *Dreams*," he answered.

"And who's this Ibn Sirin? An interpreter of dreams about reproductive organs?"

"God forbid! Ibn Sirin was a great Sufi and a great scholar, and his interpretations of dreams are never wrong."

Anyway, master, Ibn Sirin was right, because Abu Mohammed died. This Dr Amjad, though, wasn't with us at Ansar, and no Israeli tank cut off his manhood, but he's here; a respectable man who likes everything to be clean. I've never seen a man who bothered so much about being clean as he does. He lives in the middle of this shit and reeks of cologne. He washes his hands with soap, then scents them with cologne and turns his nose up at everything. I don't know what to make of the man. You haven't seen him, so I'll have to describe him to you (even though I don't like descriptions): bald, short, thin, with an oval face, high cheek bones, small eyes. He wears glasses with gold frames that don't suit his brown complexion, and his pipe never leaves his mouth. He has narrow shoulders, as though he has no width, and he speaks fast, looking off into the distance to make what he says seem important.

He wasn't with us in the war or the detention camp, and I don't understand why he's working in the hospital here. He says he's half Palestinian because his mother's Syrian, from the region around Aleppo, and he doesn't speak Palestinian but a funny mixture of classical Arabic and Lebanese.

Nurse Zeinab told me today about a pious Muslim woman wearing a headscarf who struck him because he tried to molest her.

"I heard the woman's scream, then the sound of slapping. The woman came out, threatening to come back with her husband, and the doctor started pleading with her in an embarrassed voice. Later the woman emerged with her husband, who was carrying a bag of medicines, and the doctor thanked the husband, practically falling over himself he was bowing so low."

Today I'm happy. Dr Amjad was humiliated, and I want to enjoy the thought of him bowing in front of the husband and cringing like a dog. I want to have a quiet cigarette and think about life. What do you want from me today? I've bathed you and fed you. We sucked out the mucus and everything else. Today I'm happy.

I swear I don't know any stories. Where am I supposed to get stories when I'm a prisoner in this hospital? Okay, I'll tell you the story of the cotton swab. You're the one who told it to me, I'm certain of that. You know, when I heard the story, I was very aroused, even though I pretended to be disgusted and presented a long defence of women's rights, saying that our bad treatment of women was the reason we'd failed and been defeated. But when I fell asleep, I was possessed by the demon of sex, and I won't say any more because it wouldn't be decent.

In those days, says the story, in a small village in Galilee called Ein El Zeitoun, Sheikh Ibraheem Ibn Sileiman El Asadi decided his only son should marry. The boy had reached adulthood, his beard sprouting when he was fourteen years old. The blind sheikh urged his wife to find a bride for her son quickly, for the sheikh had one foot in the grave, and the grave cries out for grandchildren.

The wife was of the same mind, for she too wanted her son to marry so he would settle down and become mature and find himself work and end his long absences and his life in the mountains with the Holy Warriors.

The story is that the young man, who was called Yunis, had no objection to the idea, and when his mother told him she was going to ask for the hand of Naheeleh the daughter of Mohammed El Shawwah he agreed, even though he'd never met the girl. He said yes because he liked her name and in his head drew himself a picture of a fair-skinned girl with long black hair, wide eyes, broad cheeks, full calves and round breasts.

He fantasised about a woman sleeping next to him and letting him make love to her.

But Yunis got a surprise. The woman wasn't a woman, she was a twelve-year-old child. The girl wasn't fair-skinned; her complexion was the colour of wheat, and her hair wasn't long but like tufts of black cloth stuck to her head, and her calves weren't . . .

Ten years later, when he was about to make love to her at Bab El Shams, he discovered he was wrong. The girl was a woman, and fair-skinned, and her eyes were large, her hair long and black, and she was overflowing with secrets and treasures.

On which occasion he said she'd changed.

On the same occasion she laughed at him because he hadn't seen what was in front of him. "Now, after I've had children and got fat and flabby, you come to me and say I'm pretty . . . ? Now, after all the hard times, you think . . . You men! Men are blind, even when they can see."

But Yunis insisted, and embraced the roundness of her calves and saw the white sky in her broad, high brow and ate Turkish delight from her long, slim, smooth fingers.

He told her he could smell Turkish delight on her neck. He'd open his pack after he'd taken her and get out a tin of Turkish delight while she made tea. Then he'd sit hunched up inside the curve of her body as she lay on the rug, and she'd feed him Turkish delight, the fine white sugar falling onto his chest. He told her he loved eating Turkish delight from her fingers because they were white, the same as the sweet, which was the best thing the Turks had left behind when they'd abandoned our country, and because her smell was musky, like the white pieces when they melted in his mouth.

At that time, says the story, the world was pregnant with war, and when there's a war, things take on a different shape. The air was different, the smells were different, and the people were different, as if war was a ghost that wore clothes like people and walked among them.

Ein El Zeitoun, in those days, was a small village that slept on the pillow of war. Everything in it rippled. The people collided with the electrified air and tasted the taste of war. Nobody called anything by its proper name, for in those days war wasn't like its name. Everyone thought it would be like the war tales of their ancestors, in which mighty armies were defeated, locusts devoured the fields, and there were famine and pestilence in the land. They didn't know that this time it was the war that had no name.

The blind sheikh told his wife that he could see, even though his eyes were closed, but he couldn't explain why he'd come to fear the water.

Weeping, the woman told her son that the man had become senile. She said she felt ashamed and begged her son to come back from the mountains and the Sacred Struggle to look after his father.

The sheikh told his wife he couldn't bear to live any longer now that they'd appointed a new sheikh to be imam of the village mosque. He said an imam couldn't be deposed and that he'd never abandon his Sufi companions in the village of Sha'ab. And he said that Ein El Zeitoun would be destroyed because it had rejected the blessings of its Lord.

The sheikh explained everything to his wife, but he couldn't explain why he'd come to fear the water. He said that the water was dirty and that when he touched it it felt sticky, as though he was plunging his hand into dead, putrifying bodies, and that ablutions could be performed with dust, and that dust . . .

He took to using dust to wash with.

The woman would look at him, and her heart would be torn to pieces. The sheikh would go out into his garden carrying a container, squat as though he was preparing to pray, fill the container with dust and go into the bedroom. He'd remove his clothes and bathe with the dust, which stuck to his body as he moved and sighed.

The sheikh said he was afraid of the colour of the water.

"Water doesn't have a colour," said his wife.

"You don't know, nobody knows, but the water has its own colour, like gluey blood that slides over the body and sticks to it."

At the time, Ein El Zeitoun was preoccupied with the story of its blind sheikh who bathed with dust. It had no idea that after a little while the dust bath would move to a neighbouring village, called Deir El Asad, and that the sheikh would die in his new village.

Ein El Zeitoun was built on the shoulder of a hill, as though it wasn't a real village. Its square was long and sloping, as though it wasn't square. Its houses were built of mud and rose up above one another in piles atop neighbouring terraces. To the left lay the Honey Spring, which the village drank from and which the villagers said was sweeter than honey.

Ein El Zeitoun was suspended between the land and the sky, and Sheikh Ibraheem, son of Salim, had been the imam of its mosque since he was nineteen years old.

Everyone looked like everyone else in Ein El Zeitoun, and they all belonged to the Asadi clan, the Asadis being poor peasants who'd come from the marshes of the Euphrates in southern Iraq during the seventeenth century. No-one knows how or why they came. The blind sheikh said they weren't Asadis and didn't come from Iraq, but the Asadi name got attached to them because they worked as hired labourers for a feudal landlord of the Asadi clan who was said to have come from there. It was said that the landlord's descendents had sold the land to the Lebanese family of Sursuq towards the end of the nineteenth century. The question of land sales in Palestine has "no end and no beginning", as they say. As to how the Asadi came to possess the lands of Ein El Zeitoun, no-one has any idea. Did he buy these wide and extensive holdings, or was he a brave warrior in the army of Ahmad El Jazzar – the governor of Acre who defeated Bonaparte – to whom the governor granted lands in Marj Ibn Amir, along with a group of villages including Ein El Zeitoun, Deir El Asad and Sha'ab? Or did he flee Acre with a band of horsemen following the governor's death, and was it them who occupied the land? The blind sheikh didn't know, but he preferred the story with the band of horsemen, so he could say that the natives of Ein El Zeitoun were originally cavalrymen with the Asadi sheikh in Acre and came with him to the village and established it and came to be known by that name, which was nothing to do with them because they were originally from the districts surrounding Acre – "though we're all sons of Adam, and Adam was created from dust".

As for the Sursuq family, it's even more complicated.

Did the Sursuqs buy the land, or was it given them as a fiefdom because they were friends of the Turkish governor of Beirut?

The inhabitants of Ein El Zeitoun never saw anyone from the Sursuq family. It was Kazim El Beiruti, a man dressed in Western clothes and wearing a fez, who used to come after each harvest, count the sacks of wheat and take half. The peasants parted with half their crop of wheat and maize to the agent without protest. The olives, however, were a different story; Kazim El Beiruti didn't dare demand the owner's share of olives or oil. "The oil belongs to him who sows it," the blind sheikh told Ahmad Ibn Mahmoud to his face when he came demanding his share.

When the disturbances in Palestine spread during 1936, the inhabitants of Ein El Zeitoun refused to give Kazim El Beiruti anything. Ahmad Ibn Mahmoud chased him away after humiliating him in front of everyone by knocking his fez off with his stick, trampling it underfoot and announcing that the land had returned to its rightful owners. And Ahmad Ibn Mahmoud El Asadi declared himself as head of the clan, sole legal heir of the original El Asadi, taking the fertile lands belonging to the village and giving the peasants of his family the liberty to exploit the land they worked without paying the owner's share. However, he tried to take some of the olives and the oil, and this was what caused the problem between him and Sheikh Ibraheem.

Ahmad Ibn Mahmoud was one of the local bosses of the Revolution of '36. It's said that he met Izz El Din El Qassam and was injured in the Revolution, and that he declared that anyone who sold land to the Jews was a traitor who had to be killed.

Yunis doesn't know why Ahmad was killed, because he's convinced that he didn't sell land to the Jews, and that anyway he didn't have any land to sell since he'd taken the land he controlled by force, and the deeds were in the Sursuq family's possession.

When Ahmad was killed by the revolutionaries' bullets in 1946, Yunis, who was then seventeen years old, became severely confused, because, despite the rumours, he wasn't the one who'd killed his cousin, and he was sure that Ahmad, who'd become the village headman, hadn't sold land to the Jews. True, he was domineering, arrogant and rude; and true, he hated Yunis and would say that the youth had abandoned his father and mother and wife to beggary while he worked as a bandit in the name of the Revolution; and true, he beat his two wives terribly and treated everyone with contempt, but why had he been killed? Yunis was convinced that Ahmad hadn't been a traitor.

Everyone hated him, even his children. The strange thing was that at his funeral, his wives yelled as though they were being beaten. The two women wept, their children around them, just as though they were being beaten. They screamed at him to raise his hand, they pleaded with him to get up, they swore they'd never leave the house again. Everyone was dumbfounded. No-one mourned The Thief (as his relatives called him in secret), but everyone was amazed at his wives' behaviour and how unconvinced they seemed that the man had died. They seemed to be afraid that he might get up and, seeing they weren't weeping enough, shower them with blows.

Ahmad died without anyone knowing who killed him, but the way he was killed seemed to suggest that he'd been a collaborator or had sold land. The killer came to his house at night, knocked on the door, and, when the man opened it, shot him and left. Then, when the killer got to the Honey Spring, he fired two shots into the air. The firing of the two shots gave the impression that Ahmad had been executed rather than murdered for some personal or family reason. The reason suspicion hung over Yunis was the quarrel between Ahmad and Sheikh Ibraheem, which had ended with the sheikh being expelled from his position at the mosque.

It was Ahmad who engineered the substitution of a new sheikh for Sheikh Ibraheem and presented reasons that convinced everybody, saying that the sheikh was blind and unable to teach his pupils reading and writing, and also had started to forget names, and verses of the Koran, and couldn't conduct prayers properly. Once shamefully dismissed from his responsibilities, Sheikh Ibraheem became a beggar, at a loss as to how to provide for his needs and those of his family.

Into the house of Sheikh Ibraheem came Naheeleh, the twelve-year-old daughter of Mohammed El Shawwah. They had asked for her for Yunis because her family was the poorest in the village. Her father, who'd died when she was six, had only had daughters, and her mother had inherited nothing from her husband. She took up work in the fields, and Ahmad didn't let her keep the land her husband had worked because women, in his words, "should never be entrusted with land". Thus the woman ended up working on Ahmad's land and as a servant in his house and got beaten the same as his wives. When Yunis's mother decided to arrange a marriage for her son, she consulted one of Ahmad's wives, who advised her to go to Naheeleh's mother, saying, "Go and take your pick – five poor, fatherless girls who need someone to give them a respectable home." She went to choose, but Naheeleh's mother wouldn't let her.

"If you want a bride for your son, take this one," she said, pointing, and wouldn't have any discussion.

"This one" was Naheeleh.

Yunis would never forget the wedding and the wedding night.

How could he forget when he hated himself till he died and could smell the blood for days and days?

How could he forget the girl's face as she shook with fear?

How could he forget his mother closing the door behind them and waiting?

How could he forget that he fell asleep with the girl next to him in the bed, and didn't take off his clothes?

How could he forget the ululations of joy outside and the mother waving a white handkerchief with a spot of blood on it to announce the girl's virginity?

How could he forget that room, filled with the smell of bird-lime?

The mother took the girl and didn't argue. She wanted a wife for her son. Marriage would steady the boy and force him to come home.

The sheikh took the girl and didn't argue, because he'd despaired of his son and wanted a grandson. He'd wanted his son to be a sheikh, a scholar and a Sufi, but all the boy had memorised of the Koran was the first chapter. He sent him to the elementary school in Sha'ab, but instead of studying he'd made off with the others into the mountains. He'd picked up a rifle and started moving about among the villages, taking part in attacks on British patrols.

Yunis could see that his father and mother were sunk in poverty, but he had no concept of what that meant. He must have wanted to escape from the company of that old man who cursed Fate and sat all day in front of his house, and who'd go every Friday morning to the mosque of Salah El Din in the village square, where there would be problems that would end with his being thrown out while Sheikh Kamil El Asadi led the worshippers. This Kamil was neither a sheikh nor a scholar. He hadn't memorised the Koran, he hadn't studied in a religious school, and he didn't take part in the devotions of the Sufis who'd built themselves a small mosque in Sha'ab dedicated to the Yashrati master of whom Sheikh Ibraheem was one of the first disciples.

They said, "Let's get him married," so they got him married.

And Yunis agreed. He heard the name "Naheeleh" and said, "I agree," and he gave his mother ten Palestinian lira – God knows where he got them – for the wedding, the dowry and the rest.

And the wedding occurred.

The boy sat at the centre of the men's circle, and things almost ended up in a mess: Sheikh Ibraheem threw Sheikh Kamil out and performed the rites himself, after which there were ululations of joy. Naheeleh put candles on her ten fingers and entered the house – there were ululations and the young man was receiving congratulations when the door opened and the girl entered, holding her fingers out in front of her with a lit candle on each one. She was covered from head to toe by a robe behind whose colours her face was lost.

Yunis didn't see her.

He saw a girl on the point of collapse, swaying as though dancing, who approached the chair on which her husband was seated and then knelt. The candles shone in Yunis's face, the flames dazzled his eyes, and he didn't see.

Yunis doesn't remember how long she knelt, for time seemed endless that day, his eyes burned with something like tears, his shadow swayed on the walls, and the ululations pounded in his ears.

He would never say he was afraid. He would say instead that when his shadow leapt up in front of him that night he didn't recognise it, as though it was the shadow of some other young man, lengthening and breaking off and barging about against the ceiling and among the guests and against the walls. And he'd also say that when he bent over to put out the candles, his mother stopped him and made him sit upright again and asked him to smile. Then his mother knelt next to the girl, took hold of her right arm and raised her up, and the two of them walked among the guests as the showers of rice started to fall on them. Sheikh Sa'eed Ma'lawi stood up, struck his tambourine and shouted, "God is Living," and the cry was taken up by five bearded men who'd come from Sha'ab at the behest of the grand sheikh of the Yashrati Shadhili order, to bless Sheikh Ibraheem's son's marriage and recite the prayers that would help him follow in the path of righteousness like his father before him.

The woman and the girl disappeared into the bedroom. After what seemed like a long while, they returned carrying olives and grapes. The girl tossed the olives one by one among the guests while the woman bent over and laid a large cluster of white grapes before the girl's feet and asked her to walk over them. The girl took off her slippers, raised her right foot with care and stepped on the grapes; then she placed both her feet on them and walked.

Yunis, telling me of his love of white grapes as we drank a "tear" of arak once at his house, said that the women sitting in the reception room stood up and started laying clusters of white grapes before the bride, and that the bride walked on them, the tears from the grapes soaking the ground.

He said he saw the tears. "Wine is the tears of grapes. That's why we say 'a tear of arak' – not because we want to drink it in small quantities, and not because we put the arak in the small flask we call a *batha* and which is tear-shaped, but because when the grapes are pressed, the juice oozes out like tears, drop by drop."

Years later, when Yunis and Naheeleh were in the cave at Bab El Shams and night fell, Naheeleh lit a candle she'd hidden behind a rock she called "the pantry". Yunis leapt up and brought ten bunches of grapes he'd cut from the vines scattered around Deir El Asad, and he spread them on the ground and asked her to walk over them.

"Take off your shoes and walk. Today I'll marry you by the laws of God and the Prophet."

She said that that day the man was mad with love. She bent over, removed her headscarf, placed the grapes on it, wrapped them up and shoved the bundle to one side. She told Yunis that at the wedding, she'd only stepped on one bunch, that she hated walking on grapes, that she'd slipped and almost died because the grape juice had clung to her heels, and that when she came to marry her daughters, she'd never make them walk on grapes – what a shameful idea!

Naheeleh walked over the grapes, which exploded beneath her small, naked feet, then went into the bedroom and did not come out again.

"You know the rest," Yunis said. "My mother by the door and me inside.

What are these ugly customs? You have to fuck for their sakes, strip off your clothes and get it over with in a hurry so they don't get bored waiting outside."

But I don't know "the rest", father, and you're lying when you say the rest was the way it usually is.

It wasn't the way you told it me, and I know so because Abu Ma'rouf filled me in.

Abu Ma'rouf was a pleasant man I met in 1969 at the Nahr El Barid camp in northern Lebanon, after the commander of the base at Kafar Shouba had thrown me out for being an atheist. I'd gone to Nahr El Barid to take up the position of Political Commissar for the camp militia, when clashes broke out between us and the Lebanese Army. The November cold was intense and made the bones ache. They put me and Abu Ma'rouf on the forward road block, which was supposed to be a lookout position. We were opposite a hill occupied by the Army, and it was our job to engage the enemy briefly if the camp was attacked and then to withdraw, in other words to delay their advance as much as possible so the other groups could block the roads leading to the camp.

A naïve plan, you'll say.

It wasn't even a plan, I'll answer, but I'm not interested at the moment in a critique of our military situation, which I don't understand much about. I'm interested in informing you that the rest was not "the way it usually is".

Abu Ma'rouf was a grown man.

In those days, when we hadn't yet reached the age of twenty, we wondered at the way these men would come and fight with us. We thought they must be brave, if only because they were what we thought men should be like. Abu Ma'rouf was in his forties. A thick black moustache covered his upper lip and curled into his mouth. He would grab the Degtyaref machine gun, wrap the ammunition belt around his neck and waist, and sit in silence. I gathered that he was from the village of Saffouri, that his wife and children lived in Ein El Hilweh camp, that he'd fought in 1948, and that he didn't believe that Palestine would ever exist again.

I never asked him why, in that case, he was fighting. In those days I believed that the "people's war" (which, inspired by the Chinese experience, is what we called ours) would liberate Palestine. These days, the issue's become more complicated, even though I do believe that Palestine will return, in some form.

Abu Ma'rouf, that silent man from whose lips I used to have to wrest words as if by force, told me a story similar to yours.

You'll be surprised, since you never met Abu Ma'rouf El Abid, and Ein El Zeitoun isn't close to Saffouri. All the same, this man made me understand your generation's stories about women, which can be summed up in the one about the cotton swab. Yes, the cotton swab. Don't tell me I'm making up a story to put you down. I swear I'm not making up a word of it. But I understood.

It was 4.00 in the morning. We'd gone more than two days without sleep, dumped in the trench under the light November rain, with the cold stealing into our bones.

He said he was going to warm himself by talking about women, as nothing warmed a man's bones like a woman's body. He told the story of his first night with his wife from Saffouri. At the time, I didn't ask him any questions; it may be that he spoke because I didn't say or ask anything. He said, "Let's warm ourselves with women," so what was I to say? Then I got scared. I thought maybe he was "one of those" and wanted to string me along till he could stick it in me. The man wanted me to keep quiet so he could talk, so I listened, but I didn't believe him. Now I know that I should have believed him, because the story of Abu Ma'rouf and his first wife, who died in Saffouri, could well be your story too.

Abu Ma'rouf said his first wife died during the bombing of Saffouri by Israeli planes on 15 July 1948 and that it was the fault of Abu Mahmoud, the village's commander in the Holy Struggle: "After the fall of Shafa Amr and the displacement of more than three thousand of its inhabitants to our village, he should have realised that the battle was over, but he insisted on staying put. We gathered in the square in front of the mosque, and he said we could hang on for a week and then the Arab Liberation Army, which was based at Nazareth, would come. But we didn't hang on. In fact, I swear I can't remember if we even fought. The planes came, three of them circled above the village, dropped barrels filled with fire and gunpowder, and the houses started to collapse."

He said he saw how the houses would blast open, doors and windows flying out, and then the flames would rise. He said his wife and three children died in their house: "I was at the roadblock at the entrance to the village, and when I heard the bombs I ran towards the house. They said I got scared, but no, I wasn't scared for myself, I was afraid for her and the children. I ran to the village carrying my English rifle, and when I got to the house, there were flames everywhere. I swear I didn't even have time to bury my wife and children. I was driven, with everyone else who fled, from Saffouri to El Ramah and from El Ramah to El Bqei'ah and from El Bqei'ah to Sahmata, then to Deir El Qasi and finally to Bint Jbeil in Lebanon.

"We spent three days in the fields of El Ramah, where we had nothing and almost died of hunger. My mother asked me to go back to her house in the village to get a little flour and cracked wheat. I found the village empty and didn't see any Jews. I met three men and a woman who was bent over as if her back had been folded in half. They said they'd given up because they didn't know where to go. One of them was a relative of mine, Ahmad El Abid. I was surprised that his son hadn't taken him with him and asked if he wanted to come with me. He raised his head to say no, and then I realised he'd stayed behind because he was sick; he was spitting and coughing, and his eyes were running. I went to my mother's house. The door was open and the food in its place, untouched. I got a bag of flour and left. On the way back, they fired at me, and I left the bag in the field. Later we found out that they'd killed Ahmad El Abid and the two men and the woman. We were in the fields at El Ramah when we heard the news. It seems Ahmad's son went back to look for him and found the four bodies lying in the road.

"We never fought. Now we say we fought and that Palestine was lost because the Arab countries betrayed us. That's not true. Palestine was lost because we didn't fight. We were like idiots; we would take our rifles and wait for them in our villages, and when they came with their motorised units and their heavy machine guns and their airplanes, we were beaten without a fight."

He said he'd married again in Lebanon and had had seven boys and girls and had given the first three new children the names of the children who'd died, but the taste of his first wife was still in his bones: "She was like fire. She set me alight whenever she came near me."

He related how he'd married her when she was fourteen and he was fifteen.

"Impossible! At that age!"

He started laughing, the tears pouring from his eyes it was so cold. Then he told me about the cotton swab.

How to tell you the story, father? Abu Ma'rouf said incredible things, but I believed them – perhaps because we were alone in the trench, perhaps because of the dawn and the changing colours of first light, perhaps because my bones were cold. I don't know.

Abu Ma'rouf said, "After the wedding party was over – and as you know, a wedding, my friend, is no joke – we went inside. You know, I swear I had no idea. Well, no, of course I used to indulge in the 'secret habit' and play around with my mates and everything, but getting married is different. As soon as I went into the room, I saw her. She was young. She was sitting on the end of the bed all wrapped up in her clothes and crying. I sat down beside her, my body feeling icy all over. She told me she liked sewing and embroidery and that she'd made all her wedding clothes. Then she started to yawn. She lay back on the bed, and I stretched out beside her. She didn't take her clothes off, and I didn't take mine off either. I went to sleep. Or no, before I dropped off I got on top of her, and as soon as I was on top of her it happened. I came and got it all over my trousers. Then I got off and lay down next to her. I think we must have dropped off quickly because I woke up to hear a loud knocking on the door. I opened it and found my mother asking for the sheet. Then she rushed into the room, pulled out the sheet from under the girl and ran out. We heard the joyous ululation. My mother told me later she'd wiped the sheet with chicken blood and wished the earth could have opened up and swallowed her."

Abu Ma'rouf said that two days later he went into his bedroom and found the girl naked, and everything went fine.

"Do you know what my mother had done? She'd taken the poor girl into the bathroom, stripped off her clothes and started inspecting her body minutely, touching her everywhere. The girl didn't know what to do – laugh at the touching or scream at the pain of my mother's pinches. Then my mother scrubbed her with scented soap, poured water over her and dried her off. She brought a cotton swab and asked her to open the thing between her thighs; then she placed the swab there and told her, 'Tonight take off your clothes and wait for him in bed. Take hold of his member and insert it here where the cotton is. Put a pillow under your behind and lift up your legs."

"When I got into bed and lifted the coverlet so I could lie down, I found her naked. She gestured to me to take off my robe, so I took it off, the sweat dripping off my face and eyes, and I stretched out beside her and did nothing. She reached out her hand, took hold of my thing and pulled me towards her, and I found myself on top of her, with her holding onto it with both hands as though she was pulling on it. I moved up, and the sweat — I bathed her in sweat and fear. She reached towards the place where the swab was and put it there, and I found myself getting bigger and bigger and bigger. Then I was inside her, and I got bigger inside her and learned the secret of life. She put her hands on my shoulders and screamed. That was the night I really came for the first time. Before that it wasn't the same. That night my whole being was there, inside her.

"When I rolled off her, the blood had stained the sheet, and I saw she was searching for something like a madwoman. She went through the whole bed because she was afraid the swab had gone inside. I looked with her for a bit, then dropped off, so exhausted I didn't hear her questions. The next morning she said she'd found the swab, but I don't think she had. I think my mother had just reassured her that it wouldn't do her any harm."

Abu Ma'rouf said he'd never forgotten the taste of her.

"And your second wife?" I asked him.

"At first I didn't want to get married again; Umm Ma'rouf had been part of my flesh. But my mother, God rest her soul, knew better. She knew a man shouldn't stay a bachelor or he'd mate with the Devil, so she convinced me to marry the second Umm Ma'rouf, like us a refugee girl, from Sha'ab. I married her in Ein El Hilweh, and she bore me seven children."

"And what happened?" I asked.

"Shame on you, man — you can't ask things like that. With the second one I knew what to do, and everything went fine from the first night."

"Did you tell her about the cotton swab?"

"Of course not. You don't understand women. You mustn't tell a woman about the others. If a woman doesn't think she's the centre of your life, she'll become miserable and make your life a misery too."

Abu Ma'rouf's story amazed me. I thought he was lying, thought, "It's not possible" and then forgot all about it.

But now I see it could be true. I see you before me, and I see Naheeleh, and I see everything. I see you, a child, going into the room and playing about with the girl. Then the child lies down next to her. I won't say you were innocent, but you didn't know what to do. Your mother comes. She takes the girl to the bathroom. She soaps her and pours water over her, then puts the cotton swab inside her – and you discover the secret of life.

I know you'll never like this story, and you'll think it's a slur on your manhood. You prefer to talk about the grapes and the "tear" of arak and the dance of the girl with the candles before her groom, and you don't want to admit that you didn't know how to do it.

It's as though you were denying the whole thing.

Fine. I'll agree with you. I won't say you lay down beside her in your clothes like Abu Ma'rouf did. Maybe you took your clothes off and made the poor girl take hers off too, and you didn't know how to do it, and your mother had to make do with a drop of blood from her finger on the sheet. Then she waited seven nights for you two and in the end was forced to put the cotton swab inside the girl to guide you to the place.

"It's not true!" you'll say.

Okay. So where is the truth? Tell me, since I'm still confused about the dates. Did Ibraheem die in 1951 aged three, meaning he was born in 1948? And what was going on between 1943, when you got married, and 1948, the year your first child was born?

Didn't your wife get pregnant?

Would you people put up with a wife who wouldn't get pregnant? Why didn't you divorce her? Your mother used to say she was still a child and would get pregnant when she grew up. So didn't Naheeleh grow up until 1948?

Did you love her?

No, you didn't. You yourself said you only learned to love a long time after you married her, when your visits to her came to be your whole life.

So when?

You'll tell me it was the war, and you paid no attention. I swear you're confusing me — I don't understand anything any more. Even your own story seems muddled and mysterious. Even my presence in this hospital seems like a dream, but one I'm not dreaming, because I'm not asleep.

Say something, father. I'm sick of it all. Say something, just one word, then die if you want, or do whatever you want, or say that you want something.

Okay, okay, fine! You didn't have the cotton swab when you got married, and it never crossed your mind to divorce your wife because she hadn't borne children, and you felt no fear at the outskirts of the Jewish settlement, and you didn't kill Ahmad Ibn Mahmoud, and you didn't cry when your teeth hurt etc., etc.

Happy now?

Content and sleeping? I swear you're a lucky man. What have you got to worry about? You sleep on the surface of death, and death doesn't come near you.

Death is afraid of you, you'll say, or you used to say.

But me, right now I'm not in the mood to listen to heroics. Do as you like — die or don't die, dream or don't dream, it's up to you.

How did we get here?

Honestly I don't understand how what was could have been. What happened and what didn't. How I stayed here or how I didn't go with you or how you . . .

Who says I had to stay?

I'm not talking about the hospital now: the hospital means you, and I couldn't abandon you even if I weren't afraid or a fugitive or hadn't fallen into Shams's trap.

I'm talking about Beirut, because I didn't have to stay on in Beirut as I said I did to Shams. I told her I felt I had to stay and that it just wasn't possible for us to turn our backs on the people here and go.

But I was lying.

Well no, I wasn't lying. At that moment, with Shams, I believed what I said, but now I don't know any more. I was with her in my house here in the camp. I closed the windows tightly so no-one would see us. The cold was intense, but I didn't feel it. My body was shivering with heat.

I wanted to prostrate myself in front of her. She was naked and beautiful, wrapped in a white sheet, her long hair adorned with drops of water. I wanted to kneel down and place my head on her belly. Everything inside me was quivering. It was the thirst that can never be quenched.

I wanted to kneel, rub my head all over her feet and pour myself out in front of her. And instead of kneeling, those stupid words came from my lips.

She asked me why I didn't go with them, and I answered with my little sentence and waited. I heard her laugh. She turned around in the white sheet, sat down on the bed and laughed. She didn't say my words had bewitched her, the way words are supposed to in moments of passion.

She laughed and said she was hungry.

I suggested that we make some food and asked if she wanted her usual pasta.

She yawned and said, "Whatever you want."

She stretched her hand behind her back and the sheet fell away from her brown breasts, still wet from the bath. I leapt towards her, but she raised her hand and said, "No. I'm hungry." I ran to the kitchen and started frying cauliflower and making *taratur* sauce.

"You're the champion at *taratur*," she used to say, licking the last of the white sauce – made from sesame paste, limes and garlic – from her fingers.

She said she didn't like fried cauliflower, but the *taratur* was fantastic.

I didn't say . . . well yes, in fact I did repeat what I'd said. I said I felt that I had to stay because we couldn't turn our backs on the people here. She laughed again and said she'd eaten enough and wanted to sleep. She pushed the tray to one side, put her head on the cushion and slept.

At that moment I told her I wanted to stay because I wanted to impress her. But now, no. I feel there's no reason for me to stay. I stayed so as not to go. I don't know where you were in those days. The truth is, I didn't ask about you. I was like someone who'd been hypnotised. I picked up my bag, took my Kalashnikov, barrel pointed at the ground, and made my way to the municipal stadium in Beirut to leave with the rest. And there, in the midst of the crowd and the long, white faces, I made up my mind to go back to the camp.

You'll remember how the fedayeen left Beirut during the siege.

You said you were against leaving. "Better death!" you told me. "Live guarded by Americans and Israelis? Never!" But you were the first to leave. You went to that Christian village and hid yourself there and made up a story about the priest who thought you were a Christian so he hid you in his house. I believed you at the time. At the time I too claimed to have refused to leave – "Shame on you, man! Like the Turkish Army? Never! We can never leave Beirut!" But at the same time I was convinced that we had to leave. We were defeated, and we had to withdraw as defeated armies do. On my way to the stadium, I imagined myself part of a Greek epic setting out on a new, Palestinian, Odyssey. I'm not sure if I imagined that Odyssey then or I'm just saying it now because Mahmoud Darwish wrote a long poem about such an Odyssey, even though he didn't get on the Greek boats that would carry the Palestinians to their new wilderness either.

I put on my uniform, picked up my small pack, took my rifle and went. I glanced back and saw the camp looking like a block of stone and felt I was extruding the place through my skin. Suddenly the camp became a block of ruins, a place unfit for habitation, and I decided to leave it for ever. What would I do in the camp after the fedayeen had pulled out? Would I end my life there, meaninglessly, the same way I'd lived all those years doctoring the sick when I wasn't a doctor, and love a woman I didn't love? At that time I was on the verge of marrying plump, white-skinned Noha, who worked with us at the Red Crescent. The only thing Noha wanted was to get married. She'd take me to her parents' house at the camp entrance near the open space that later became the common grave, and there we'd eat and I'd see a spectre called "marriage" in her mother's eyes. I don't know how I came to find myself half married without realising it. Then came the Israeli invasion and the decision to move us out of Beirut.

I looked back and I saw the heap of stones called Shatila camp, and I started running in the direction of the stadium. I was afraid that Noha would come, persuade me to stay and take me to her parents' house. I reached the stadium convinced she'd be there. I kept my head down and mixed with the crowd so she wouldn't see me. I didn't want her, and I didn't want to stay or to get married. I'd look up from time to time so

I could see her before she saw me and run away. But I didn't see her. Instead of relaxing and looking for my friends, however, I was seized with anxiety, as though her not coming had frightened me. I didn't want her to come, and she didn't, and I found myself searching for her.

You remember those days – women and tears and rice and shots fired into the air. I never saw anything like it in my life – a defeated army withdrawing like victors! That burning Beirut summer was cooled with tears; August scorched the earth and the people and the tears with its savage sun and I searched for Noha. I thought: It's impossible – Noha's given up her best bet after all that? She was bound to come and ask me to promise to marry her, and I'd promise and then forget her. But where was she? I walked through the crowds like a stranger, because if your mother doesn't come to say goodbye, it's not a real goodbye. Mothers filled the place, and young men were eating and weeping. Food and tears, that was the farewell. Mothers opening food wrapped in cloths and young men eating, and ululations and bullets.

At that moment, master, I thought of my mother. At that moment I loved her and forgave her and said I wished she was there. But I didn't know where she was. At that moment I didn't know she was in Ramallah. At the stadium, I was sure my mother would come, that she'd suddenly appear at Noha's side and open a cloth full of food in front of me, and I'd eat and weep like everyone else.

I stood there alone, and nobody came.

Then I don't know what happened to me – I looked at the people and they were like the ghosts of the dead.

I told you about the siege and the hospital and death, how we lived with death and couldn't take it in. I stayed in the hospital for a month treating the dead, eating aubergine and watching the Israeli planes making bombing raids as if they were competing in fireworks displays. I lived with death, but I couldn't absorb it, and everybody died. They came, and as soon as we put them in beds, they died. They were strange days. Do you remember how we used to tell tales about the walking dead? Did I tell you about Ahmad Jasim? The man was hit at the Museum crossroads, in the neck, but he walked. He fell to the ground, then got up like a chicken with its throat slit and, to the astonishment of his comrades, set off in the direction of the Israeli positions. After about ten metres, he fell down dead, motionless. They picked him up and brought him to the hospital. I checked him over and ordered them to throw his body into the morgue. "The morgue?" shrieked one of his comrades. "Why the morgue?"

"Because he's dead," I said.

"Dead? That's impossible!" the man cried.

I ordered Abu Ahmad to take him to the morgue.

Then the yelling started. They seized the body, picked it up and left. I tried to explain that he was dead and that walking after being hit didn't mean anything because it was just an involuntary reflex, but they called me names, wrapped him in a woollen blanket and went off with him.

We lived with death for three months and didn't believe it. But in the middle of the stadium I believed it. They were all like dead men, eating and firing into the air and weeping.

Just as I came to the stadium running, so I left it running.

I won't tell you how I looked for Noha like a madman. God, why didn't she come? For some reason I couldn't cry. I hated this farewell of theirs – why were they eating and weeping and shooting? There shouldn't have been a farewell. At that instant, master, I was ready to buy a farewell for myself at any cost. I wanted to weep as they wept and shoot as they were shooting.

Why didn't she come?

What had happened to Noha? Had she understood that I didn't want her any more? Had love ended along with the siege?

"Why the tears?" I ask, and you close your eyes that swim in their blue whiteness. Yesterday I brought you eye drops and opened your eyes and put the drops in. Do you know what the drops are called? They're called Artificial Tears. They call drops for washing out the eyes "tears". They go to the chemist's and actually buy tears while we can barely hold ours back.

"Tears are our medicine," my mother used to say.

My mother used to cry beneath the beating rain that crackled on the zinc sheets we'd made into a roof for our tottering house in the camp. She'd cry and say that tears were medicine for the eyes. She'd cry and get scared. Then she fled to Jordan and left me with my grandmother and the flower pillow. I told you about my grandmother's pillow, so why am I telling the story again now? I just wanted to say that I bought this eye dropper made in Great Britain so I could put tears in your eyes, which are dry as kindling. Brother, cry at least once. Cry for yourself and for me, I beg you, for you don't know the importance of tears. The best thing for the eyes are tears, tears are indispensable. They are the water that washes the eye, the protein that nourishes it, and the lubrication that allows the eyelid to slide over it.

You've made me weep, and you refuse to weep yourself.

I administer the drops, wait for your tears and feel the tears in my own eyes. I'm not weeping for you; I'm weeping for Umm Hassan, not because she died but because she left me the videocassette.

Sana', the wife of the *kunafa*-seller, came. She came and stood by the open door of your room and knocked. I was sitting here reading Jabra Ibraheem Jabra's novel *In Search of Waleed Mas'oud*. I was absorbed in Waleed Mas'oud, the Palestinian who disappeared leaving a mysterious tape in his car, to unravel the riddle of which Jabra had to write a long and beautiful novel. I love Jabra because he writes like an aristocrat — his sentences are élitist and beautiful. It's true he was poor when he was a child, but he wrote like real writers, meaning he formed expressive, literary sentences. You have to read them the way you read literature, not the way I'm talking to you now.

Sana' knocked but didn't enter. I put my book aside, stood up and asked her to come in, but she stood by the door and handed me the cassette.

"This is what Umm Hassan left you," she said. "Umm Hassan entrusted me with this tape to give you."

I took the videotape and offered her a cigarette, which she smoked greedily. I used to think that women who wore headscarves didn't smoke, but Sana' talked and stammered, swallowing the smoke between words.

I didn't understand about the cassette, because Umm Hassan had visited Galilee three years before, and when she'd returned she'd brought me a branch of oranges and told me of her visit to El Ghabsiyyeh, where she'd lit a candle under the lotus tree and prayed in the mosque.

Sana' said Umm Hassan had visited El Kweikat again, six months earlier, and had seen her house and made up her mind to die. Every day she'd watch this cassette and tell stories while others joined her in her lament, her sorrow and her memories.

"She stopped sleeping," said Sana'. "She came to me and said she'd heard the angel of death because she couldn't sleep. Her death was marked by weeping, and she told me to give you this tape. I don't know what you'll see on it. It's falling apart it's been used so often, but she left it for you."

I thanked Sana', nodded goodbye, but she didn't move; it was as if she was stuck to the door. Then she spoke. She blew smoke in my face, and her eyes filled with tears.

Sana' told me about that journey. At first I couldn't understand a thing. Then the words started forming themselves into pictures. She spoke abut Fawzi, Umm Hassan's brother, and about the village of Abu Sinan, stammering and repeating herself as though she had no control over her lips. Then she got to the point.

"I won't tell you to take good care of it," said Sana'. "That cassette – I mean, you know."

"God rest her soul," I said.

"God rest all our souls," said the pious woman and started to go. After taking two hesitant steps, she came back and said, "Please, doctor, watch the cassette carefully."

Is it true?

Can it be that a woman died because she saw another woman?

Umm Hassan's story shook me to the core, not just because she died, but because she thought of me and bequeathed me this tape.

What can have happened in El Kweikat for the woman to die?

You know Umm Hassan better than me and you know her courage. She left El Kweikat when she was twenty-five carrying her son Hassan on her back and holding on to her daughters Saleema and Hanan. They walked from El Kweikat to Yarka. In the olive orchards of Yarka, the wife of Qasim Ahmad Sa'eed discovered that what she was carrying in her arms was a pillow and not her baby son, and started wailing. Her husband sat on the ground like an imbecile while she implored him, "Go and get the boy!" But the man was incapable of getting up. The mother moaned like a wounded animal and the husband sat unmoving, but Umm Hassan – do you know what she did? Umm Hassan went back on her own. She left her children with Sameerah, the wife of Qasim Ahmad Sa'eed, went back to the village and snatched the child from the hands of the Jews. She didn't tell anyone what she'd seen and what the Palmach men were doing to El Kweikat. She returned exhausted, breathing in great gasps as though all the air in the world wouldn't fill her lungs, set the child down in front of its mother, took her own children and went to El Zeitouneh, where her husband and brothers were. Sameerah ran to kiss her hand, but Umm Hassan looked at her with contempt and pushed her away.

Umm Hassan didn't think she'd done anything extraordinary. She'd gone and got the child, and that was all there was to it. No-one considered her a heroine. In those days, surprise had disappeared from people's faces; only sorrow wrapped itself around them, like a cloak full of holes.

El Kweikat fell to the Jews without our knowing it. On the night of 9–10 June 1948, everyone came out of their houses in their night clothes. The shelling was heavy, and the artillery thundered into the night of the unsleeping village. People took their children and fled through the fields to the neighbouring villages of Yarka and Deir El Qasi and from Deir El Qasi to Abu Sinan and Ya'thur, and on from there. Abu Hassan drove four head of sheep and three of goats along the road, but the flock died at Ya'thur, and Umm Hassan wept for the animals as a mother weeps for her children.

"God, I wept, son! How I mourned those animals! How could they have gone as though they'd never been? Wiped off the face of the earth, dead. How were we supposed to live?"

But Umm Hassan lived long enough to bury her sons one after the other.

Sana' said Umm Hassan never stopped weeping. She'd put on the cassette and weep and tell everyone the story of the two visits she'd made over there. "Dear God, people. What we've lived through and seen! Would that we'd neither lived it nor seen it!"

Sana' said the woman died of grief over her house.

"She knew?" I asked.

"I've no idea," she answered. "Maybe it was because she saw it for herself. Hearing's not like seeing."

And you, father – did you know these things? Why didn't you tell Umm Hassan what had happened to El Kweikat? Didn't you spend your days and nights in those demolished villages? Why didn't you tell the woman that the Jews had occupied her house?

"Why the fuss?" you'll say. "Umm Hassan didn't die because she saw the house. She died because she'd got to the end of her life."

That's what you'd say if I told you about Umm Hassan's house.

Umm Hassan said she'd gone there. It was her second visit to her brother Fawzi's house in Abu Sinan.

"My family fled from El Kweikat to Abu Sinan and stayed there. I wish my husband had done what my father said, but he wanted to stay with his own family; his brothers had decided to go to Lebanon, so he went with them. My father disagreed. He hid with his wife and children and grandchildren in the olive groves for more than a year. Then he appeared in Abu Sinan and stayed there. I don't know how they managed. My father used to grow watermelons. After the Israelis moved in, the watermelons belonged to Israel. They worked as builders' labourers and got by. Then my father bought a piece of land and built a house. It was to my father's house in Abu Sinan that I went, and there I found my brother, sick. He had pneumonia, and we feared for his life. That's why we didn't go to El Kweikat. Was I supposed to go on my own? I went to Deir El Asad and Sha'ab and visited our relatives there, but El Kweikat had been demolished, and my brother was sick. All the same, once when we were coming back from Sha'ab and my nephew was driving me in his little car, I begged him to go by El Kweikat. "No, auntie," he said. "It's all Jews," and kept going. I begged him, but he wouldn't agree. We went on the road parallel to the village, but I couldn't see a thing.

"The second time was different.

"My brother was in excellent health, and he took me to El Kweikat. I asked him to do it, and at first he said the same as his son, then later he said yes. We went and he took his son Rami, who had a videocamera. He's the one who shot the film, God love him. We went into El Kweikat, and I didn't recognise it till we got to the house."

How can I tell you about Umm Hassan?

Should I mention the tears, or the memories, or say nothing?

The woman sat in the back seat of the little blue Volkswagen looking through the back window and seeing nothing.

"We're here," said Fawzi.

Her brother got out of the car and held out his hand to help her do the same. Umm Hassan reached her hand out, and then moved her stout body, but she couldn't raise her head. It was as though she was unable to do so, or as though her breasts were pulling her down towards the floor. She was bent over double and rooted to the spot.

"Come on, sister."

Fawzi pulled her by her hand and helped her get out of the car. She remained doubled over. Then she put her hand to her waist and stood upright.

He pointed to the house, and she could see nothing.

Her tears flowed without her weeping. She wiped them away with her sleeve and listened to her brother's explanations while his son played around with the camera.

"They demolished every single house, sister, and built the settlement of Beyt ha-Emek – all except for what had been new houses on the hill."

Umm Hassan's house had been new and on the hill.

"All the houses were demolished," said the brother.

"And my house?" mumbled Umm Hassan.

"This is the house," he said.

They were about twenty metres from the house, and the branches of the china-bark tree were swaying. But Umm Hassan could see nothing. He took hold of her arm and they walked. Then suddenly she saw everything "as though no time had passed, son".

What happened to that time the woman was talking about, father? Can we discover it in the videotapes that have become our only entertainment? Shatila camp has turned into Camp Video. The cassettes circulate among the houses, and people sit around their television sets and remember and tell stories. They tell stories about what they see and out of the pictures of the villages they build villages. Don't they ever get sick of repeating the same stories? Umm Hassan didn't sleep. She kept telling stories till she died amid her tears.

She said that suddenly everything came back to her. She went up to the door but didn't knock. She stood back a little. She walked around the house, then squatted on the ground with her back to the china-bark tree as she'd used to when she'd moved into the house. She'd been afraid of the tree, so she'd turn her back to it, and her husband would make fun of her for ignoring the view and looking at the stones and the walls. Her brother took her by the hand and helped her up. For the second time, she had difficulty standing, as though she'd become stuck to the ground. Her brother dragged her to the door and knocked. No-one opened, so he knocked a second time. The ringing sound started to grow louder in Umm Hassan's ears; everything seemed to be pounding in her ears, her body was trembling, and her pulse was racing. The brother stood waiting.

And the door opened.

In the opening a woman appeared, aged about fifty, with a dark complexion, black hair streaked with grey and large eyes.

Fawzi said something in Hebrew.

"Why are you speaking to me in Hebrew? Speak to me in Arabic," said the woman with a strong Lebanese accent.

"Sorry, madam. Is your husband here?" asked Fawzi.

"No, he's not here. Is everything all right? Please come in."

She opened the door wider.

"You know Arabic," Umm Hassan whispered as she entered. "You're an Arab, sister — am I right?"

"No, I'm not an Arab," said the woman.

"You've studied Arabic," said Umm Hassan.

"No, I studied Hebrew, but I haven't forgotten Arabic. Come in, come in."

They entered. Umm Hassan said, like everyone else who's visited their former home, "Everything was in its place. Everything was the way it used to be, even the water jug.

"God of all the worlds," sighed Umm Hassan, "what would Umm Eesa have said if she'd visited her house in Jerusalem? Poor Umm Eesa. In her last days she spoke about just one thing — the saucepan of courgettes. Umm Eesa left her house in Katamon in Jerusalem without turning off the flame under the saucepan of courgettes."

"I can smell burning. The saucepan's burnt. I must go and turn off the flame," she'd say to Umm Hassan, who nursed her during her last illness.

And Umm Hassan, who'd felt pity for the dying woman, stood in her own house in front of the water jug that was still where it had been, smelled the courgettes in Umm Eesa's saucepan and said that everything was in its place "as though those people had come in and sat themselves down right where we'd been sitting".

The Israeli woman left her in front of the water jug and returned with a pot of Turkish coffee. She poured three cups and sat calmly watching these strangers whose hands shook as they held their coffees. Before Umm Hassan could open her mouth, the Israeli woman asked, "It's your house, isn't it?"

"How did you know?" asked Umm Hassan.

"I've been waiting for you for a long time. Welcome."

Umm Hassan took a sip from her cup, the aroma of the coffee overwhelmed her, and she burst into tears.

The Israeli woman lit a cigarette and blew the smoke into the air, gazing into space.

Fawzi went out into the garden where his son Rami was playing with the videocamera and filming everything.

The two women remained in the sitting room, one weeping, the other smoking in silence.

The Israeli turned and wanted to say something but didn't. Umm Hassan wiped away her tears and approached the water jug, which stood on a sidetable in the sitting room.

"The jug," said Umm Hassan.

"I found it here, and I don't use it. Take it if you want."

"Thank you, no."

Umm Hassan went to the jug and picked it up. Then she balanced it on her arm, went over to the Israeli woman and gave it to her.

"Thank you," said the Palestinian woman, "I don't want it. I'm giving it to you. Take it."

"Thank you," said the Israeli woman, who took the jug and returned it to its place.

The silence was broken as the two women burst out laughing. Umm Hassan started looking around her house. She stood at the bedroom door but didn't go in. Next she went to the kitchen. She stood at the sink and saw the piles of dirty dishes. Umm Hassan turned on the tap and the water gushed out, and the Israeli woman ran in saying, "I'm so sorry. It's a mess." Umm Hassan turned off the tap and said, laughing, "I didn't leave the dishes. That was you."

The two women went out into the garden.

The Israeli woman gave Umm Hassan her arm and told her about the place. She told her about the orange grove where Iraqi Jews worked and about the new irrigation projects the government had started and about how difficult life was and about their fear of the Katyusha rockets. Umm Hassan listened and looked and said one word: "Paradise. Paradise. Palestine's a Paradise." When the Israeli woman asked her what she was saying, she answered, "Nothing. I was just saying that we call it an 'orchard,' not a 'grove'. This is an orange orchard. How wonderful, how wonderful."

"Yes, an orchard," said the Israeli.

Then the roles were reversed, and Umm Hassan started telling the Israeli woman about the place.

"Where's the spring?" asked Umm Hassan.

"What spring?" answered the other woman.

Umm Hassan told her the story of her spring and how she'd discovered water in the field next to the house. When her husband had built the house, close to the china-bark tree, there'd been no water. It was Umm Hassan who'd discovered it. Seeing the water welling up from the ground, she'd said, "We must dig here," and they dug and the water came gushing out, so they surrounded the spring with stones and put up a fence, and it became known as Umm Hassan's spring.

"Where's the spring?" she asked.

The Israeli woman couldn't answer. "There was a spring here," she said, "but they dug an artesian well around it and laid pipes. Would that be it?"

"No, the spring's a natural one," said Umm Hassan, and told how they would have planted apple trees after they discovered the water, but for the war.

Umm Hassan guided the woman to where her spring had been.

Instead of finding a spring, she found a well fenced with pipes and iron with a small tap on each side. Umm Hassan bent over and opened the tap, and when the water gushed out, washed her face and neck, sprinkled the water on her hair and clothes, and drank.

"Drink," she said. "Water sweeter than honey."

The Israeli woman bent over and washed her hands, and then turned off the tap without drinking.

"This is the most delicious water in the world."

The Israeli woman turned on the tap again, drank a little and smiled.

Later Umm Hassan would say that the Israelis don't drink water, just fizzy drinks: "They only drink out of bottles, even though Palestine has the best water in the world."

In vain we tried to explain to her that they drink mineral water, not fizzy drinks, and that the people of Beirut have started to drink water out of plastic bottles too, but she stuck to her opinion and said, "They don't drink water. I saw them with my own eyes. You want me to disbelieve what I saw with my own eyes?"

After they'd had a drink, the two women walked round the house. Umm Hassan told the woman about the china-bark tree and the olive grove and pointed out the stone that looks like the head of an ox and took her round behind the house and showed her the cave behind the hill.

Umm Hassan talked and the other woman discovered, and showed her surprise, because she'd never noticed that the stone looked like the head of an ox or gone into the cave. Then Umm Hassan told her how she'd learned her profession as a licensed midwife from her grandmother on her father's side, Hajjeh Maryam, and that she had an official certificate from the British Government. She recounted how she'd got married at fifteen "to chase away the chickens from the front of the house", as her mother-in-law had said when she'd asked for her hand.

Umm Hassan told her stories and walked from place to place, and the Jewish woman followed along behind and listened and shook her head and said nothing.

Umm Hassan would tell her visitors that she saw her life falling away in front of her: "What's life? Like a grain of salt in water, it just melts away." She'd tell them that over there she'd gone back to the way she'd been, as though no time had passed, and she'd seen the young woman who'd gone to live in her new house when she'd been twenty years old. She'd told her husband that she wanted a house – "I was no good for chasing chickens any more and I wasn't a child." They got the land and built the house with their own hands, and she discovered the spring and the cave and the ox's head, and became the midwife for the entire Acre district.

The women went back inside the house and sat in silence.

Umm Hassan stood up and went into the bedroom. She looked at the bed that occupied the centre of the room. It was the first bed she'd slept on in her life. At home with her family and then at her husband's house she'd slept on bedding on the floor and got up every morning and folded it up and put it at the far end of the room. But in this house the bed couldn't be folded up.

"A room just for sleeping in," her husband had said.

"The other woman sleeps here every night," thought Umm Hassan, "with her husband, in the same bed, in the same room, in the same house, in the same . . ." But no, not in the same village: the village didn't exist any more. Umm Hassan could no longer see the close-packed houses of the village – the houses had gone. Nothing was left of El Kweikat.

When she finished her tour, Umm Hassan wept. She sat in the sitting room and wept. Her brother came in to hurry her up so they could return to the house in Abu Sinan and found her weeping. He wept too, and the son with the camera wept.

"Do you know what she said to me?"

Umm Hassan would relate the same conversation every day, adding a word here, deleting one there, as though gulping back her tears.

"She asked me, 'Where are you from, sister?'

"I said, 'From El Kweikat. This is my house and this is my jug and this is my sofa, and the olive trees and the cactus and the land and the spring and everything.'

"'No, no. Where are you living now?'

"'In Shatila.'

"'Where's Shatila?'

"'It's a camp.'

"'Where's the camp?'

"'In Lebanon.'

"'Where in Lebanon?'

"'In Beirut, near Sports City.'"

When the Jewish woman heard the word *Beirut*, she jumped up and changed completely.

"You're from Beirut?" she cried, the words tumbling out of her mouth and her eyes filling with tears.

"Listen, sister," the Jewish woman said. "I'm from Beirut too, from Wadi Abu Jmeel. You know Wadi Abu Jmeel, the Jewish district in the centre? They brought me from there when I was twelve years old. I left Beirut and came to this dreary, bleak land. Do you know the Ecole de l'Alliance Israélite? To the right of the school there's a three-storey building that used to be owned by a Polish Jew called Elie Baron. I'm from there."

"You're from Beirut?" Umm Hassan asked in amazement.

"Yes, from Beirut."

"How did that happen?"

"What do you mean, how did that happen? I've no idea. You're living in Beirut and you've come here to cry? I'm the one who should be crying. Get up and go. Get up, sister, and go. Send me to Beirut and take this wretched land back."

Umm Hassan said she talked with the Jewish woman for a long time.

The Jewish woman's name was Ella Dweik, and hers was Nabeelah, daughter of El Khateeb from the family of El Habit – "The Fallen" – wife of Mahmoud El Qasimi. "El Habit isn't the family's real name, but my grandfather used to spend all day sitting down so they called him that. Our real ancestor was Iskandar, and before Iskandar there was El Khateeb."

Ella Dweik spoke of Beirut.

And Nabeelah El Habit talked about El Kweikat.

Ella said she'd married an agricultural engineer who worked here, and they'd given them the house and she hadn't had any children. Her husband was Iraqi, from the suburbs of Baghdad; she'd like to visit Baghdad. She had a brother who worked in Tel Aviv, but she didn't see him.

Umm Hassan told her about Beirut. About the sea and the Manara corniche, the shops in Hamra Street, the affluence and the beauty and the cars. She said the war hadn't been able to destroy Beirut. It had destroyed a lot, but Beirut was still as it had always been.

Umm Hassan said that over there, in El Kweikat, she'd seen the Beirut she didn't really know. "All I know is Umm Eesa's house in America Street near the Clémenceau cinema.

"In El Kweikat I saw Beirut," said Umm Hassan, "but I don't live *in* Beirut, I live in the camp, and the camp's like a lot of villages piled up on top of one another."

The Jewish woman stood up.

When someone stands up, it means it's time for the guests to leave. Umm Hassan didn't grasp the meaning of the signal, however; when her brother said they had to go, she looked at him in amazement and didn't respond.

"And now, what can I do for you?" said Ella.

"Nothing, nothing," said Umm Hassan as she began to get up ponderously.

The Jewish woman took the water jug and gave it to Umm Hassan without saying anything. Umm Hassan took it without looking at it and went back with her brother to his house in Abu Sinan.

"The jug is still in its place," said Sana'.

Umm Hassan said nobody should move it and that she was sorry she'd brought it with her, it should have stayed in its own house.

"Then what?" I asked Sana'.

"'Then what?'" she said. "Then she died in the camp, and the Jewish woman is living in her house."

Can you imagine, father, that Umm Hassan would die weeping for the jug she brought with her from her house? That she'd die because a woman said to her, "Damn El Kweikat! Take it!" Why didn't she just take it? Why didn't she tell the woman she was welcome to the whole camp, the whole of Wadi Abu Jmeel, the whole world?

Umm Hassan said she wept over what had happened to her. "The Jewish woman bought my silence with the jug and her stories about her mute childhood, and I came back to the misery and poverty of the camp. She's taken the house and I'm here. What's the point?"

So the story was turned into a videotape that now belongs to me. Rami didn't film the conversation between Umm Hassan and Ella Dweik; he made the camera roam over the house and around the land and the olive orchard. But it's a beautiful tape, made up of lots of snapshots joined together. I'd rather he'd done a panorama, but never mind, we can imagine the scene as we watch. We've become a video nation. Should I be watching the tape every night and weeping and dying, or should I be filming you and turning you into a video that can go the rounds of the houses? What should I film, though? Should I ask someone to play you as a young man? What do you say to my doing that? That lady asked me if I was your son – I'll say I'm your son and play the role, but I'm not an actor and acting is a difficult profession. I wish I did know how to act, I'd have enacted Shams's crime, and the interrogators wouldn't have laughed at me and humiliated me with their pity.

"Pity is the ugliest thing," you used to say. "We shouldn't pity ourselves. When a man pities himself, he's done for."

But I'm very sorry to have to tell you now that I pity you. I swear you stir more pity than Umm Hassan's jug or that mute Jewish woman.

The Jewish woman told Umm Hassan she hadn't forgotten her Arabic and said she'd been struck dumb when she'd come to Israel.

"I was on my own, the only child from Lebanon; they all spoke Hebrew. I went for five months without saying a word in class. I didn't dare talk to anyone, I didn't answer the teachers' questions, and I refused to read aloud. Then I began to speak. It was as though I'd tried, in my silence, to become part of these people I didn't know. French was my first language because at the Alliance school in Beirut we were taught Arabic, like all other school children in Lebanon, but our language in school and at home was French. I knew a little Hebrew because we also studied it at school, though we didn't like it. I also learned Hebrew at the Maabarot, but in the classroom, in the midst of all the children, I was struck dumb before I could speak."

She told Umm Hassan how she'd lived in the Maabarot, where they'd sprayed the Eastern Jews with insecticide as though they were animals before admitting them to the stone barracks. She'd cried when they'd forced her to remove her clothes; the usual blonde woman had sprayed every part of her body mercilessly with a long, cylindrical sprayer. Her father, a man in his fifties, had started howling when they'd ordered him to remove his red fez, and the men had started playing football with it. He ran around after it while the soldiers played and laughed. When he saw that his fez had been destroyed, he started howling and repeating "There is no god but God," so they assumed he was a Muslim and subjected him to a prolonged interrogation before making him remove his clothes and be sprayed, and become accustomed to standing naked, without a fez, for ever.

Ella Dweik told Umm Hassan El Habit her story. And Umm Hassan told everyone that she'd wept.

"Damn, how I cried! 'Take this bleak, dreary land,' she told me, 'and send me back to Wadi Abu Jmeel and the Elie Baron building!'"

"And what did you reply, Umm Hassan?"

"I didn't. I said nothing and wept."

Did you know, father, that the medical profession is anti-pity? You can't be a doctor and feel pity for your patients. That's why I'm a failure as a doctor. In fact, I'm not a doctor. I came to the profession by accident; it never occurred to me to be a doctor until the Chinese lady doctor decided for me. She assigned me to be a doctor, ordered my military training stopped and put me into medical school. I don't like medicine. I found myself in China and had to acquiesce. The way people regarded my new profession won me over. They call you a *hakeem* – a "wise man" – and think you're a magician. I think that magic aura was what made Shams love me. Don't say Shams didn't love me – she loved me in her own fashion, but she loved me. I'm convinced her death contains a riddle that needs to be solved. The riddle will only be solved after the emotional shock has passed along with my voluntary imprisonment in this accursed hospital. There's dirt everywhere. The walls of the room are no longer white, the paint is peeling and yellowed, and something is smeared on them. I cleaned them with soap, but it made no difference.

What do you say to Denmark?

You know Dr No'man El Natour? I don't know him, but he wrote an article that made me weep. I didn't weep for Old Acre, which has nearly collapsed, but I wept for the key.

Shall I tell you what happened to No'man?

He went to Acre – he can visit Israel because he has a Danish passport. He boarded a plane at Copenhagen airport and got off at Lod. He disembarked like any ordinary passenger, presented his passport to the security man and waited. The man took the passport, looked at it closely and asked Dr No'man to wait. He waited for about quarter of an hour, and then a young woman in military uniform arrived. She returned the passport to him and apologised, smiling. He took his passport and went out to the baggage hall, got his suitcase, which he later discovered had been opened and carefully searched, and left the airport.

These formalities had no impact on him because he was in a dreadful state, with everything tumbling around inside him. He thought he'd have a heart attack the moment he left the airplane but was surprised to find himself behaving like an ordinary traveller, as though this wasn't his own country.

He left the airport and got a taxi, which took him to Jerusalem. He spent the night in a hotel in the Arab city and in the morning, instead of touring Old Jerusalem as the tourists do, he took a taxi to Acre, where he alighted in the square close to the Jazzar mosque. He walked and walked and walked, lost and alone in his own city. He said he wanted to find his house without help. He was like me – born outside Palestine and with no memories of his country except what his mother had told him. No'man walked, got lost in the alleys, stood and scrutinised the houses and walked some more. In the end he got to the house. He said he knew it as soon as he saw it. He knocked on the door and was greeted, as Umm Hassan had been, in Arabic, but they weren't Jews, they were Palestinians.

He went into the house, said hello to everyone and sat down.

When the woman went to make coffee, he got up and started to look around, refusing the company of the man of the house. As he went through the rooms, No'man recalled his mother's words, which became his guide. He came to the kitchen, and there he saw his mother standing in front of the big saucepan of cracked wheat. No'man said that in Yarmouk camp near Damascus, where he'd been born, they ate nothing but cracked wheat. His mother would stand in their small kitchen in front of the saucepan of cracked wheat, and No'man would hold onto the hem of her dress and cry.

But in the spacious kitchen in Acre, it wasn't his mother he saw. He was a child alone, and in front of him stood the Palestinian's wife making coffee. The woman tiptoed out when she saw No'man wiping away his tears.

They drank coffee, and the Palestinian man explained to No'man that he'd been waiting for him for a long time, that he'd rented the house from the official in charge of absentee property after they'd thrown him out of his own house, and that he was ready to leave whenever No'man's family wanted them to.

No'man listened and said nothing, as though he'd forgotten how to speak.

The Palestinian tried to explain their circumstances and the difficulties of their life and to reassure No'man that he didn't want the house and had been forced to rent it because his own house had been demolished.

No'man stood up and excused himself.

"Stay for lunch – the house is yours," said the man.

"No. Thank you," said No'man and left.

No'man didn't look back. He wrote that he didn't. Before, he'd needed to preserve the image of the house in his head, but now that image had evaporated, and nothing was left but the words of his mother that had engraved it in his memory.

No'man said he walked and walked, and then he heard the Palestinian man shouting, so he turned and saw the man running after him, waving something in his hand.

"The key. I forgot to give you the key to the house. Take it, it's yours."

"There's no need," said No'man. "We still have the old key in Damascus."

Dr No'man returned to Denmark, the key is still in Damascus, Umm Eesa died muttering about the saucepan of courgettes, and her son Eesa is in Meknes looking for the keys.

Umm Eesa used to talk about her son as though he belonged to a different world, as though he was dead, which is what Umm Hassan thought when she heard Umm Eesa talking about her son almost as though she was mourning his death. Then she found out that Dr Eesa Safiyyeh wasn't dead – he was living in a faraway city in Morocco called Meknes, where he taught Arabic literature at the university.

He'd been seduced by a woman from Meknes, said Umm Eesa. "He met her in New York, where he was teaching, and began a relationship with her. I saw her once when they visited me in Beirut. Damn her, how beautiful she was! Huge eyes and long, smooth black hair, with something strange about her. She put a spell on him for sure. I know women, and I know that that one had shown him the fish that talks."

Umm Hassan agreed, even though she didn't believe in the existence of a magic fish in a woman's private parts. Also, she didn't give a damn about "Dr" Eesa, who did his doctoring in literature instead of learning medicine and becoming a proper doctor and helping people. But then, "maybe our Christian brothers from Jerusalem have a fish we don't know about."

"The woman from Meknes took Eesa to her country, and they left me alone in Beirut. Why don't they come and live with me here? Eesa writes to me, but the letters don't arrive when there's a war, and in the last one he said he was collecting keys. Dear God, now we're collecting the keys of the Andalusians! He said the descendants of the people of Andalusia who were chased out of their country and who migrated to Meknes still preserve the keys to their houses in Andalusia, and he was going to make an exhibition and write a book about them. Read the letter, Umm Hassan."

Umm Hassan's sight was failing, and she could no longer read, the words looking to her like little jumbled-up insects. Umm Eesa asked if she had read it, and Umm Hassan nodded as though she had.

"What do you make of that? He said he wants to collect the keys and write a book! He says we have to collect the keys of our houses in Jerusalem. What do you make of it? He says we're to collect our keys, when the doors are already broken!"

Umm Hassan told me the story of Dr Eesa Safiyyeh's keys when I asked her where I could find Dr No'man, since she knows everybody. I told her I didn't want to collect keys, I wanted to ask him about emigrating to Denmark, but she didn't believe me. She thought that I too had been struck by key fever and told me that our house in El Ghabsiyyeh didn't have a door and wasn't a house any more because the weeds had devoured it.

I'm not interested in keys. These emotions don't concern me. I was only thinking about emigrating, and I said Denmark because lots of the young men from the camp have gone there. And I thought of Dr No'man because he was a doctor like me. I thought he'd be able to get me a job in one of the hospitals over there. But I forgot about it and stayed here.

Umm Hassan said, "Stay in your house here, and forget about keys."

Can we call these wretched huts in the camp houses?

Everything here is falling down, wouldn't you agree, my dear Mr Abu Salim?

Do you know where you are, master?

You think you're in the hospital, but you're wrong. This isn't a hospital, it's a mock hospital. Everything here isn't itself but a simulacrum of itself. We say "house" but we don't live in a house, we live in a place like a house. We say "Beirut" but we aren't in Beirut, we're in a place like Beirut. I say "doctor" but I'm not a doctor, I'm simply like a doctor. Even the camp – we say we're in Shatila camp, but after the War of the Camps and the destruction of eighty per cent of Shatila's houses, it's no longer a camp, it's just something like a camp – and so on and so forth to the end of all these boring "likes".

You don't care for what I'm saying?

Look around you, and you'll see the truth in what I say and be convinced.

Let me walk you round the place.

This is a hospital. You are in Galilee Hospital. But it's – what can I say? It's better I don't say. Come, let's start with this room.

A small room, four metres by three, with an iron bed next to which is a bedside table on which are a pack of paper hankies and a mucus extractor (a round glass instrument connected to a tube). To the left, opposite the bed, is a white metal cupboard. You think everything is white in this room, but in fact nothing is white. Things were white, but now they've taken on other colours – yellowish white, flaking walls, a cupboard discoloured with rust, a ceiling covered in spots where the paint has blistered and burst because of damp, neglect and the shelling.

A white patched with yellow and grey, a yellow patched with grey, a grey patched with white or . . . etc.

You don't care, but I'm repelled by the sight. You'll say I worked here for years and never gave any sign that it bothered me, so what's so bad now? What's changed?

Nothing has changed, master, except that I've become like a patient myself, and a patient can't tolerate such things. As you can see, when a doctor starts to feel like a patient, it's the end for medicine. And medicine has come to an end, my dear Mr Yunis, or Izz El Din, or Abu Salim, or I don't know what I should call you. In the past you were content with all the names people called you by, as though you didn't care. And when I asked you your real name, you gestured broadly and said, "Forget all that, call me whatever you like." And when I insisted, you replied that your name was Adam: "We're all children of Adam, so why should we be called by any other name?"

I found out the truth without your telling me. I found it out by accident. You were telling the story when I came to visit and your relatives from Ein El Hilweh were there. When I saw them I tried to leave, but you told me to sit down, saying that Dr Khaleel was family, and went on with your story.

You said your father had first wanted to call you Asad — "Lion" — so you would have been Asad El Asadi, "Lion of the Lions," and everybody would have been terrified of you. He did name you Asad but changed his mind after a couple of days because he was scared of his cousin Asad El Asadi, a village notable who'd indicated displeasure at his name being given to the poorest of the poor in the family. So he named you Yunis — Jonah. He chose Yunis to protect you from death in the belly of the whale, but your mother didn't like the name, so she chose Izz El Din and your father agreed. Or so the woman thought, and she started calling you Izz El Din while your father was still calling you Yunis. Then he decided to put an end to the matter and said that the name Abd El Wahid was better. He started calling you Abd El Wahid, and you and everybody else got confused. In the end, the teacher at the primary school didn't know what to do, so he went to the blind sheikh to get some clarification, on which occasion the sheikh expounded his theory about names and about Our Master Adam, peace be upon him. He said, "All names are borrowed from other things. Thus the only true name is Adam. God, Mighty and Glorious, applied this name to man because the name and the thing named were one. He was called Adam because he was taken from the adeem — 'the skin' — of the earth, and the earth is one just as man is one. Even after his fall from Paradise, Our Master Adam, peace be upon him, gave no thought to the matter of names. He called his first son Adam and his second Adam and so forth. So it was up until the disaster occurred;

for when the first crime was committed and Cain killed his brother, Abel, Adam was obliged to use borrowed names to distinguish between the murderer and the murdered. So Gabriel inspired him with the names he gave to every Adam he sired so things wouldn't get mixed up and the names get lost.

"All our names are borrowed," the sheikh told the school teacher. "They have no value, and you may therefore call my son whatever you like. But his name and your name and the names of everyone are one. Call him Adam if you like, or Yunis or Izz El Din or Abd El Wahid or Wolf . . . Why don't we call him Wolf? That, I swear, is a name I never thought of before!"

You told your relatives you only discovered the wisdom of your father's words during the Revolution. You were the only Holy Warrior, and then the only fedayeen fighter, who wasn't obliged to take an assumed name. You used all your names, and they were all real and all assumed at the same time.

I came close then to discovering the essence of your secret, master, and understood that truth isn't real, it's just a matter of convention; names are conventions, truth's a convention, and so is everything else.

When your relatives left your house, I asked you about truth and you said you'd been telling the truth. Listening to you, I'd thought you'd been making the story up as you went along, perhaps to make yourself even more mysterious, but you assured me you'd told them the truth and that to this day you still didn't know your real name. Then you told me the men were your relatives from Ein El Zeitoun and lived in Ein El Hilweh camp and had come to invite you to be the head of an Asadi clan association they'd decided to form, and that the business of the names was the only thing you could think of to make them drop the idea. "Names and families and sects have no meaning. Go back to Adam," you told them as they left. So they left with gloomy faces. They'd wanted you to be head of the association because you were the family's only hero, but as you were pouring the tea and stirring in the sugar, you said, "I seek refuge with God, I seek refuge with God! There are no heroes. We're all from Adam, and Adam is from dust."

Come with me then, Mr Adam, to your hospital room. There's only one small window, which is covered with a metal grille like the window in a prison cell. The yellow – or sometime yellow – door opens onto the corridor, from which comes the smell of ammonia. Why the smell? Nurse Zeinab says it's to kill germs, but I'm convinced there are germs nesting in every cranny here. That's why I bought cleaning supplies just for us and clean your room every day. I wash it down with soap and water, taking care that the smell of the soap gets into every corner. All the same, whatever we do, the smell of ammonia seeps back in and threatens to choke us. I thought of washing down the corridor during the night but gave up on the idea as it would be impossible for me to clean the whole hospital on my own, and the other people here seem to have got used to the smell.

We leave your room now for the corridor, where we find rooms that exactly resemble your own on either side. You, however, are the only patient with a private room. Why this special treatment? That's something I won't go into. You think you're here because they respect your history, and that's what I tell myself too so I can put up with the situation. The truth, however, is different.

When they brought you here, Dr Amjad put up his hands and said, "There is no power and no strength but with God." Everyone dealt with you as though you were dead, so they didn't allocate you a room. Nurse Zeinab understood that you were to be left in the emergency room till you died – they left you lying there untreated and went away. When I saw you in that state, with the flies hovering round you as though you were a corpse, I rushed to the doctors' room, put on a white gown and ordered Nurse Zeinab to follow me, but she didn't come. Nurse Zeinab, who throughout the war used to tremble when I ordered her around, looked at me with contempt when I told her to prepare a room for you.

"No, Khaleel. Dr Amjad said to leave him."

"I'm the doctor and I tell you . . ."

Bitch! She left my sentence hanging in the air, turned and went off, and I stayed with you on my own.

You were ready for death – lying on the ground on a yellow foam pad and shivering. And the flies. I started shooing the flies away and yelling. I left you and went in search of Nurse Zeinab, ordered her to follow me and went back to you. Even Ameen, the young guy in charge of the emergency room, had disappeared. I became obsessed with finding

Ameen. Where was Ameen? I started yelling for him, and then a hand came from behind and covered my mouth.

"Shush, shush. Snap out of it, Khaleel."

Dr Amjad covered my mouth with his hand and dragged me to his clinic on the first floor, where he explained that Ameen had disappeared and started telling me a strange story about the killing of Kayid, the Fatah official in Beirut, and the Kurdish woman and the car, going into an exhaustive analysis of the political assassinations that had taken place recently in Beirut.

You remember Kayid.

He was quiet and gentle and brave – you don't know that he's dead. No, you should know – Kayid died two weeks before your stroke, he was the last to die. Is it true he married a Kurdish woman before he died? And if he did marry her, why did he make an appointment to meet her at Tellet El Khayyat near the television building? Who makes an appointment with his wife to meet her on the road? And where did the new Japanese car disappear to?

"They buy luxury cars instead of spending money on equipping the hospitals," said Dr Amjad. "The Kurdish woman stole the car. She was a spy and inveigled him into meeting her and they assassinated him. And it seems Ameen had something to do with the affair."

Amjad speaks and I tremble.

Amjad tells his stories and you're left lying there.

Amjad analyses Kayid's killing, and when I'm trying to say something his hand comes and covers my mouth.

When we're puzzled, we always say, "*Cherchez la femme!*" and we solve the problem. I'm convinced the Kurdish woman doesn't exist and is an invention of the young Iraqi who calls himself Kazim.

Do you know Kazim? He was Kayid's personal bodyguard. He came here twice to see you, claiming he wanted to set his mind at ease regarding your health. But he didn't know you. He came to clear his conscience because I'm sure he was involved in the assassination. And why did he come to visit me? I have nothing to do with the matter; Kayid was my friend, but I wasn't his only friend, so why did he choose me to tell the story of the Kurdish girl to? Did he want to get me involved? Or maybe he was part of the plot to take my life. Does he know Shams's family?

Did he come to check the place out? I don't want my imagination to get out of hand because it's nothing to do with me and Kazim has immigrated to Sweden. He said he was waiting to get refugee status, but I didn't sympathise and I made sure he understood that. Then he stopped coming to see me, and we were rid of him.

I know, but I haven't told anyone. The girl whom Kayid loved wasn't Kurdish; she was a Jordanian from Krak, an engineering student at the American University in Beirut. Kayid did love her. I met her with him a number of times. She was tall and fair and had enchanting eyes. They weren't large like the eyes we usually describe as beautiful, but they were enchanting. And her name was Afeefa.

I smiled when she introduced herself to me: "An old name that isn't used much now." She said that her father, who'd been living in Beirut for twenty years, had named her Afeefa after her mother, who was living alone in Ma'daba, and that she'd discovered that her uncle on her mother's side was a priest called Nasri who lived in Deir El Seidnaya near Damascus and painted beautiful icons. Her eyes watered – no, they didn't water, but they had something of that watery blue in them. Kayid loved her and said she bossed him around: "People from Krak are always bossy."

There was no Kurdish woman or anything of the sort. Kayid loved a girl from Krak, and all his friends knew about it, but that's not a sufficient reason for his death. It's true that after falling for Afeefa he abandoned many of the security precautions Fatah officials in Beirut had had to take, once it had been decided to liquidate the Palestinian political presence in the city, but his death had nothing to do with his being in love. It was connected with something else, and I don't think the Israelis had anything to do with it.

Dr Amjad put me off my stroke. Where did he get all this information? Is it true the so-called Kurdish woman stole the car, suggested they meet in front of the television building and, when he arrived, asked him to get out of the car so she could tell him something and they killed him? A man fired five bullets at him from a silenced revolver, and the Kurdish woman disappeared with the car.

Was the whole thing just a car theft?

But why did he get out?

Didn't he know his life was in danger?

If we're to believe Dr Amjad's version, Kayid was supposed to drive past the television building, and the Kurdish woman was meant to get into the car next to him.

How could that be? He stops his car, gets out and dies? Where was his Iraqi bodyguard, Kazim, and what did Ameen have to do with it?

Kazim says he didn't go to the appointment: "You know, meetings of that sort require privacy" – and he winked at me.

Privacy! What privacy is there in the street at 11.00 in the morning? They're all lying, and Kazim has disappeared. He came to say goodbye because he was travelling and to "set his mind at rest over the health of 'Uncle Yunis'".

I never heard anyone else use this term "Uncle". You're "Brother" Abu Salim or Yunis or Izz El Din – you're only "Uncle" to people who don't know you. The easiest way to get close to a man we don't know is to call him Uncle. Uncle and Hajj are titles we give to men of over fifty when we don't know what we're supposed to call them. It's laziness; our language, master, is a very lazy language. We don't look for the names of things; we name them by happenstance, and it's up to the listener to understand. The other person has to know what it is you mean to say in order to be able to understand you, or we get into misunderstandings.

That's the word I was looking for: what happened between me and Dr Amjad was a misunderstanding.

Dr Amjad was talking about the disappearance of Ameen after Kayid's killing and presented an exhaustive analysis to prove that Ameen had a relationship with the Kurdish woman, as though I cared.

"She used to come here to visit him and I think . . . I think she came the last time in the Japanese car, so Ameen killed him and not Kazim. He killed him for the woman and the car. It's an expensive car as you know – Mazda, fully automatic. I'm certain it was the car, but I don't know."

Dr Amjad doesn't know, but he wants me to know. I didn't say anything, gave no support to his hypotheses and didn't tell him about the girl from Krak who's studying at the American University. I wish I could contact her; she's really fantastically beautiful, or not beautiful but striking (observe with me the precision of the word *striking*, meaning more than "pretty" and implying presence and authority).

God rest your soul, Kayid, but on the occasions when I met her I never saw her as being bossy. She had a certain indescribable delicacy. Her neck was long and smooth, and round it she'd wear a silver necklace with the Throne Verse, or so I thought till Kayid explained to me that it was a picture of the Virgin Mary. He said the girl from Krak loved the Virgin and would tell him not to be afraid because she'd made a vow on his behalf to the Mother of Light. I didn't ask who this "Mother of Light" was, guessing it must be one of the innumerable names of the Holy Virgin.

I said I want to meet her, but not to clear things up, since they're beyond being cleared up now. No, I want to contemplate her beauty. Shameless, really. Instead of mourning my friend Kayid and bemoaning his horrible death, I desire his girlfriend. They left him on the pavement in Tellet El Khayyat for more than five hours before taking him to the hospital. A man, and a pool of blood, and people looking and not wanting to see. For five hours under the Beirut sun, Kayid was in agony from his wounds. Well, there you are. But I still don't know why I desire his girlfriend. My desire isn't sexual; I just desire to see her. Men are traitors from the beginning, from the moment they discover their names. To know your name is to be a traitor. Wasn't that your blind father's theory about names?

Where were we? It seems I've become like Dr Amjad. All doctors are that way: I've left you lying there to amuse myself with the story of Kayid.

That day I swear I could have committed murder, but I was paralysed by lassitude. I was half paralysed and half speechless. I was asking for Ameen when the hand covered my mouth; then Dr Amjad got deep into the analysis of Kayid's assassination and started chewing over the possible explanations and insisting that Israeli intelligence had been involved. But that wasn't enough. If he'd stopped there, that sound would never have come, involuntarily, from deep inside me. Nurse Zeinab told me that I bawled, and that Dr Amjad fled the hospital because he was afraid of me. It was when he started on the disgusting stuff about women that I yelled. You know how men are. Amjad was talking about Kayid and the Kurdish woman when he suddenly switched to his sexual experiences with Kurdish women. Can you credit such obscenity? He said a Kurdish woman used to call him every day on the telephone, sigh down the receiver and tell him the colour of her knickers.

That was when I exploded.

I didn't explode for your sake but for the sake of that woman he'd invented.

He said she used to sigh down the telephone, but he didn't say what he was doing – how he'd sigh and masturbate and jump like an ape from sentence to sentence.

Plus, how dare he talk about Kurdish women that way? Even if we suppose that one Kurdish woman did that, is it reasonable to suppose that all Kurdish women are like her? I hate this stupid machismo. I think it's a cover-up for men's deep-seated impotence.

I exploded, yelling and screaming and bellowing like a wounded bull. Dr Amjad fled, and Nurse Zeinab came running. Nurse Zeinab's stupid, and I didn't need this further proof of her stupidity. She's not really a nurse or anything of the kind: all she can do is take blood pressure and give injections, and yet she's still called a nurse. The stupid woman, instead of realising I was yelling because of you, thought I was the one needing attention, so she ran and got me a glass of water and started to calm me down. I threw the glass on the ground, grabbed her hand and ran to you, and she got a woollen blanket and I covered you with it.

"What shall we do with him?" she asked, looking at me like an imbecile.

"Hurry, hurry! We'll carry him to a room."

It was then that Nurse Zeinab opened her mouth to say that Dr Amjad had said you were to be left there because there was no hope.

I told her to shut up and help me.

We tried to carry you, but it was impossible because the yellow foam mat on which they'd thrown you down wasn't rigid. I ordered Nurse Zeinab to bring a stretcher and off she ran.

From the moment I yelled at her, Nurse Zeinab changed completely. She started running blindly every time she heard me order her to do something. I'd give an order and she'd set off running like an idiot. I could hear her clattering around everywhere – on the stairs, in the room, in the corridors. I could hear, but I couldn't see anything. All she brought was a woollen blanket with a mouldy smell. So I picked you up – I couldn't wait any longer. I picked you up, committing an unforgivable medical sin. I doubled you over and threw you across my shoulder, your head on one side, your feet on the other, your stomach on my shoulder. You were heavy and shaking. God, how heavy people are when they're dead or close to dying, as though, as Umm Hassan explained it to me, the soul was a means of combating gravity, and half your soul had left your body. I took you out of the emergency room and climbed up to the first floor, where I found Nurse Zeinab saying there weren't any empty rooms. I climbed up to the second and final floor and took you into Room 208, which you now occupy. I put you into bed and ordered Nurse Zeinab to take the second bed out of the room.

The room you're in is now tip-top. It's clean and attractive and tidy. Forget that stuff about the colours – it's impossible to maintain the colours of the walls and doors in a place that's eaten away by damp. There's no solution to the humidity in Beirut, which is between eighty-five and ninety per cent most of the time. However, it's not a matter of humidity, as you know, but of the water pipes and the sewage mains, since the hospital was exposed to shelling ten times, and on each occasion they repaired it from the outside, that's to say patched the holes in the walls and sealed off the water that was spurting from the pipes at the joints. However, it seems the whole system's in need of a radical rethink, which is impossible at the moment. The pipes leak, the damp creates patches on the walls, and the smell – a mixture of Nurse Zeinab's ammonia and standing water – spreads everywhere.

All's well.

I say "all's well" because I know you're in a place that's relatively safe from all those smells, because the soap, the insecticides, the cologne and the powder fill your room with the scent of Paradise.

Of course, everything's relative. It's a relative scent in a relative paradise in a relative hospital in a relative camp in a relative city. And so on.

Everything is relative. Even the Arabic calligraphy that I've hung on the wall above you is relative, since it isn't a picture in the precise meaning of the term, though it is beautiful. I brought it from my house because Shams refused to take it – a beautiful picture with the name of the Almighty written in Kufic script. I like that script. I see its angular forms as re-drawing the boundaries of the world, and I see it curving and rounding everything off. It's true it's not a curved script, but everything's round in the end. *Allah* in Kufic lettering is above your head because Shams didn't realise the picture's artistic value when I offered it to her at my house. She looked at it with something approaching revulsion, said, "You want to make me into one of those women who cover their hair?" and laughed treacherously.

When Shams laughed, she laughed treacherously. I'd smell the smell of another man on her breath and "avert my gaze", as they say. I'd feel I was with her and not with her. I'd see them all hovering around me and her, and I'd try to push them away so I could see her. Then I'd forget them, and forget the betrayal, when I penetrated her undulating body.

Shams laughed treacherously.

We were in my house. I told her I'd bought her a present and went to the bedroom, got the picture, which was rolled up in white paper, and ripped off the paper while she watched me curiously. The picture with the Kufic lettering shone.

"Lovely. A lovely picture," I said. "Don't you love Arabic calligraphy?"

She looked closely at the picture, read it carefully, then pulled back.

"You want to make me into one of those women who cover their hair?"

Shams thought I was asking her to place her faith in God and gave me a lecture on her particular view of God and existence. I'll spare you her theories about the oneness of existence and how God is present in everything and so on.

She didn't take the picture because she imagined I wanted her to adopt the headscarf in preparation for marriage. She spoke of her faith in women's liberation.

I had no such thoughts; I bought the picture because I love Arabic calligraphy, and that's all, and I wanted to give her a lovely present.

This picture, Mr Abu Salim, cost more than fifty dollars, and it was the most beautiful thing in my house. Shams didn't take it, and I didn't hang it up because it wasn't for me. I said to myself, I'll hang it in the living room when Shams comes and lives with me. But she died, so I decided I deserved the present and ought to hang it on the wall above my bed. Then things got mixed up, and there was talk of a list of people to be killed and of Shams's relatives seeking revenge, and of my name being at the head of the list, so I forgot about the picture and everything else.

But then, after I put you into bed and cleaned everything, I went to my house to get a few things and remembered the picture and decided its place was here. *Allah* in Kufic letters wraps you in its aura and protects you.

I didn't bring the map of Palestine or the posters of martyrs or anything since those no longer have a meaning. Do you remember how we used to tremble in front of the martyrs' posters and feel they were about to burst through the coloured paper and jump out at us? Those posters were an essential part of our life, and we filled the walls of the camp and the city with them, dreaming that one day our own pictures would appear on similar ones. All of us dreamed of seeing our pictures outlined in bright red and with the martyr's halo. There was a contradiction to which we paid no attention: we wanted to have our pictures on the posters and also to see them, meaning we wanted to achieve martyrdom without dying!

Tell me, how have we managed to separate the pictures of dead people from their deaths? How did we attain this absolute faith in life?

I know one thing, which is that after the massacre I hated the posters of martyrs. I won't tell you what happened and about the swarms of flies that almost devoured me because the time isn't right for those memories. They need the right time. We can't just toss off memories like that. We don't have the right to remember any old how.

I brought you the picture and said the name of *Allah* in Kufic lettering would remain however circumstances and conditions changed. The pictures and posters were temporary, but the name of the Almighty can never be dislodged from its place and will hang before our eyes for ever.

You don't like the words *for ever*. You used to say, "What small minds the Jews have! What is this silly slogan of theirs – 'Jerusalem, Eternal Capital of the Jewish State'? Anyone who talks of eternity exits history, for eternity is history's opposite; something that's eternal has no existence. We Arabs even used to eat the gods: in our Age of Ignorance we made gods out of dates and ate them, because hunger is more important than eternity – and now they come and tell us that Jerusalem is an eternal capital? What kind of shit is that? It's fatuous – which means they've started to become like us, meaning defeatable."

You said we'd never defeat them: on the contrary, it was up to us to help them defeat themselves. No-one is defeated from outside; every defeat is internal. Once they'd raised the banner of eternity, they'd fallen into the whirlpool of defeat, and it was up to us to help them.

You didn't tell me how we were supposed to help them. So far, the only people we've helped to defeat have been ourselves – carpeting our land with our blood for the Israelis so they could walk over it like victors.

Things have changed, master.

If you'd become sick, God forbid, ten years ago, I wouldn't have brought you this picture. I would have hung a map of Galilee above your head, to show how proud I was of you. You are the pride of us all. You made our country that we'd never visited come to life within us and traced our dream with your footsteps.

Now it's not the dream I put up but the reality.

Allah in Kufic lettering is the one absolute reality we can depend on.

No, I won't let you speak.

You're in a mysterious place now and approaching the moment when nothing but faith can help you. Please don't blaspheme. You're a believer, your father was a Sufi sheikh.

You'd like to say – though I won't let you – you'd like to say that someone who's lived your life will submit to nothing and that even the gods change; our forefathers used to worship other gods.

Be quiet, please – I don't want to listen to your theory of temporariness. It's time for the temporary to become permanent. It's time for you to relax. You shocked me to the core with your theories, you seemed not to care, but you were lying, because you too have become sick of the temporary and can't take it any more. Do you want proof? Shall I remind you about Adnan Abu Odeh?

I know you don't like this particular biography because it scares you. Have you forgotten the day you returned from visiting him, trembling with terror, and came to ask me for sleeping pills?

You came to me doubled over as though you were looking for death. Why don't you face the truth? Why don't you say you became frightened for yourself and not for Adnan? And why, after I'd given you the sleeping pills, did you go back to making fun of everything?

Heroes aren't supposed to be like that.

A hero has to remain a hero. It's a crying shame – you all left Adnan and abandoned him, and all you remember now is his legend. As for the man himself, he went to his fate without anyone batting an eyelid.

You're acting all macho now because you forget. Have you forgotten Adnan?

Adnan Abu Odeh came back to Burj El Barajneh camp after twenty years in Israeli prisons. He came back a hero, and you went to welcome him because he was a comrade and your friend and life-long acquaintance. You always used to speak of him as The Hero, with the definite article.

What happened to The Hero?

It was 1965, and you were five fighters on one of your first operations inside Galilee. Adnan was taken prisoner, three others died, and you survived. What were the names of the three martyrs? Even you've forgotten their names – you were telling me about that fedayeen operation and you hesitated and said, "Khalid El Shatti. No, Khaldoun. No, Jamal . . ." Even you couldn't remember any more. You survived and they died. Death isn't a good enough reason to forget, but you did.

You survived, you told me, because you "withdrew" forward after you'd fallen into the Israeli ambush, while your comrades "withdrew" backward, as soldiers normally do. They came under fire from two sides and died, while you continued your journey to Bab El Shams. Adnan didn't die even though he received appalling wounds in his stomach. The Israelis took him prisoner and treated him in hospital before putting him on trial.

You'd tell the story tirelessly, as though it was your own. Then you suddenly stopped going to see him after he came back and no longer talked about him.

Adnan stood up in court and said what he was supposed to say.

He said he didn't recognise the court's authority as he was a fedayeen fighter and not a saboteur.

"This is my land and the land of my fathers and my grandfathers," he said, refusing to answer any questions. They asked him about you, and he said nothing.

During the interrogation he spoke of the three who'd died in front of

him, but he didn't say one word about you. Although the Israeli interrogator informed him of your death, he didn't believe it. The interrogator
showed him the news as reported by the Lebanese newspapers; the Fatah
leadership had issued a statement announcing the death of four martyrs.
But Adnan didn't believe it because he'd seen you move forward and
disappear (which doesn't change the fact that that statement in the papers
was a terrible error that cost you dear, because it exposed you and led
to Naheeleh being arrested).

You realised Naheeleh had been arrested when she stopped visiting
you in your cave. You stayed in your hideout for more than a month,
only going out at night to pick wild herbs to eat and to fill your flask
with dirty water from the irrigation ditch.

You lived for five months at Bab El Shams, which turned into a prison,
and you almost went mad. You sat all day long without moving, daring
neither to sleep nor to go out. You became like a vegetable. Have you
forgotten how a man can become a vegetable? How his thoughts can be
wiped out, his words disappear, and his head become an empty pot full
of ringing noises and incomprehensible sounds?

When Dr Amjad informed me you'd entered a vegetative state and
there was no hope, I couldn't understand why he'd despaired: you'd
already been through the vegetative state once and come out on the other
side.

Naheeleh woke to their violent knocking, and when they failed to find
you they took her in for a week-long interrogation. When she left the
prison, she found the village surrounded and realised they'd let her out
as bait to lure you with. She acted out her celebrated play and buried
you, praying for your absent corpse and receiving condolences while she
wept and wailed and smeared ashes on her face. Naheeleh's excessive
carrying-on drove your mother crazy – the old woman couldn't see why
she was behaving that way. She understood the play had to be staged to
save you, but Naheeleh turned the play-acting into something serious.
She wept as women weep. She lamented and wailed and fainted. She let
down her hair, and tore her clothes in front of everybody.

"This isn't how we mourn martyrs," everyone told her. "Shame on
you, Umm Salim! Shame on you! Yunis is a martyr."

But Naheeleh paid no attention to the sanctity of martyrs. She wept for you till she could weep no more, and her sorrow was mighty unto death. And death came: your mother believed Naheeleh caused your father to die. After his only son's death – i.e. after your death – the man went into a coma that lasted three years, then slept in his bed for more than a month, and then, when he got up, started using dust to perform his ablutions prior to chewing up the words of the prayers. Then he died.

"Naheeleh killed him," your mother told everyone.

Your mother tried to explain to him that what Naheeleh was doing was just play-acting, but he couldn't understand. She'd speak to him and he wouldn't reply. She'd look at his face and all she could see would be his closed eyes. She'd tell him you were alive, and he'd shake his head and moan.

In the past his wife had been able to understand him from the way he moved his eyebrows. After your death, however, his eyebrows stopped moving, and the woman felt she was talking to herself as he sat there in front of her like a cipher.

Why did Naheeleh do it?

Was she afraid for you, or did she hate you, or what?

Did she reach into herself "where the tears are", as the Sufi sheikh would say to his disciples? "In our depths is nothing but water. We go back to the water to weep. We are born of the water, and we go to the water. And when the water dries up, we die," he would say, and he'd repeat words attributed to one of the Sufi imams: "The sea is the bed of the Earth, and tears are the bed of man." Having finished their chanting and whirling, the dervishes would fall to the ground and weep – that's what the Sha'ab Sufi chapter did following the Catastrophe. Sheikh Ibraheem, son of Sileiman El Asadi, would go every Thursday evening from Deir El Asad to Sha'ab to lead the séance and return home borne along by his closed eyes, red as two specks of fire.

But Naheeleh?

Why did Naheeleh do it even though she knew you were still alive?

I know: Naheeleh wept for herself and for the oppression under which she lived.

You'd say, if you could speak, "She wept for love."

No, master, Naheeleh went to the lake of her tears in order to find herself. The woman lived her life alone among the blind, the refugees and the dead. Then you'd turn up at the cave of Bab El Shams, place grapes beneath her feet and go away, leaving her sad, abandoned and pregnant.

What did you expect her to do?

Yearn for you?

Wait for you?

You want to believe she did nothing but wait for you, a woman who filled her days with bearing children and waiting for her husband who didn't come, and when he did come did so secretly and stealthily, once a month, or every three months, or whenever he could.

Naheeleh got fed up with her life with an old blind man, his wife obsessed with cleanliness, and the children crawling around on the ground and never getting enough of anything.

On top of that, you wanted her to be happy to see you and lie down on the floor of your sun hidden inside the cave?

Naheeleh left the prison barefoot and when she got to the garden of her house fell to the ground and started wailing and weeping. People thought the blind sheikh had died, so they raced over, only to find her weeping for you. Everyone in Deir El Asad had learned of your death because Israeli radio had broadcast the military communiqué announcing it. However, the villagers hadn't dared to think of holding a big funeral. They mourned you in silence and told one another that Naheeleh had been relieved of all the torment, the child-bearing, the oppression, prison and the interrogations.

People ran and found Naheeleh kneeling at the door of her house lamenting and rolling her head from side to side in the dust. When they gathered around her, she stood up and said, "The funeral is tomorrow. Tomorrow we will pray for his soul in the mosque," and she went into the house.

Naheeleh held a wake the likes of which had never been seen. Her weeping obliged everyone else to weep. "As though he was Imam Hussein," people said. "As though we were performing the rites of Ashura." Food was served, coffee was made, the turbaned sheikhs came, and the chanting circles formed. Naheeleh went unveiled to where the men had gathered and recounted the news of your death. "They killed him and left him gasping with thirst. They hit him with three bullets to the chest. He fell to the ground, and they fell on him. He said 'I want water,' and the officer kicked him in the face." Then she wept and the men's tears fell, while the blind sheikh sat in the place of honour and red streaks like tears furrowed his creased, aged cheeks.

The village turned into a place of lamentation, and your mother said, "Enough!"

But Naheeleh wouldn't be silent. Three days of tears and lamentation. Even the Israeli officer who came to monitor the wake stood there dumbfounded. Did he believe Naheeleh's tears, call himself a liar and disbelieve what he knew to be the facts? Can weeping deceive the eyes?

You think she did all that to protect you from them. As though the Jews didn't know you'd escaped and were probably hiding somewhere in Galilee.

But no, that's not how it was. It was about weeping.

The woman wept because she needed to weep. Naheeleh needed a false death in order to weep because a real death doesn't make us weep, it demolishes us. Have you forgotten how the death of her son Ibraheem annihilated her? Have you forgotten how she was incapable of weeping and overwhelmed by moaning?

You, master, were merely the pretext for all that weeping, which brought up from her depths the water imprisoned there for a thousand years.

No, she didn't weep for you.

During the false funeral, and after it, you were besieged in your distant cave. You and the night – a long night, thick and viscous, a night without colour or eyes.

When Naheeleh finally came to the cave of Bab El Shams, she was afraid of you because she found you looking like a corpse. She came in carrying food, water and clean clothes, found you lying on your belly and smelled the smell. Your foul smell, like that of a dead animal, filled the cave. She tried to wake you. She bent over you and listened to your rasping breath. She tried to wake you again, taking hold of your shoulders and attempting to make you sit up, but you fell over backward. She took your head in her hands and spoke to you. Your head kept falling forward, and she'd pull it back up. When you opened your eyes, you didn't see her. She said she'd brought you food, and you moaned. Then you turned and started trying to sit up. You raised yourself on your hands and knees, then sat up and looked around as though you were frightened.

"It's me," said Naheeleh. "Me, Naheeleh."

You started peering around in terror while she tried to persuade you to wash and change your clothes.

Naheeleh told you that you stayed that way for more than two hours before you came to your senses. After she'd succeeded in stripping off your clothes, she bathed you in cold water while you were semi-comatose, and that was the only chaste bath that took place in Bab El Shams.

She covered you with soap and her long black dress was soaked, her body sticking in patches to the dress, outlining its rounded shapes, and instead of leaping out of the water like a fish, you submitted beneath the mantle of soap as though you were weeping.

Naheeleh didn't say you wept, but she felt you were on the verge of weeping. She said it wasn't you. It was as though you were another man, as though the fear had paralysed you and made you surrender.

You, however, when you returned to yourself, would deny all that and claim that you hadn't slept for four weeks and that when you heard the sound of her footsteps, you felt safe and surrendered yourself to sleep.

I don't know who to believe.

Should I believe the sleep or the fear?

Should I believe Naheeleh, who saw her husband disintegrating, or the husband who claims he was sleeping peacefully to the sound of his wife's footsteps?

I've thought about the story of the cave a lot since you went into a coma, and about your destiny and that of Adnan. I've thought about those long weeks in the cave and your sleeping while your wife tried to wake you. I wish I could ask Naheeleh about it. Naheeleh knows the secret, but you, you're locked up tight, like all men. You've turned your life into a closed story, like a circle.

How am I to bear the death of Shams and my fear, if not by telling stories?

But you, whom were you afraid of?

Why did you always tell the story of your life as though it was only the story of your journey over there?

You'll say I talk about Bab El Shams because I'm in love: "You're the one who's in love. You want to use my story to fill the holes in your own and paper over your wash-out with the woman who betrayed you."

Please don't speak of betrayal – I don't believe there was a betrayal, and if they hadn't treated me like shit while they stared at me and searched for the cuckold's horns in my hair, I wouldn't have cared.

No, master, I'm not using your story to serve my own. I lost my life right at the beginning, when my mother left me and escaped to Jordan. But you, you won everything.

The way you are now is like how you were in the cave, the difference being that that woman won't come and save you from death, so I have to find a woman for you. What do you say to Mme Fayyad?

"Mme Fayyad only exists in your imagination," you'll say.

But I saw her with my own eyes. She came to the hospital and kissed me. I know you don't want me to pursue this line of exploration, but before I shut up I want to ask you why you didn't tell me what went on in the cave during those weeks.

When I asked you, you replied that you'd sat and waited, and that nothing happened.

Is waiting nothing? You're mocking me: waiting is everything. We spend our whole lives waiting, and then you say "nothing" as though you want to dismiss the whole meaning of our life.

Get up now and tell the rest of the story.

The story isn't you, it's Adnan. Get up and tell me the story of your friend Adnan. You tell it better than I do.

Adnan heard the sentence of thirty years in prison and burst out laughing. So the judge added another ten years for contempt.

Before the sentence, Adnan stood in the dock and put his hands on the bars like a caged animal. He struck the bars and shouted and cursed, so the judge ordered his hands to be tied behind his back, at which he decided to remain silent. The judge asked questions, and Adnan said nothing. Then the blonde Israeli woman lawyer, the only Israeli lawyer who dared defend Adnan, explained the reason for Adnan's silence, so they untied him, and he spoke once before being sentenced.

"This is the land of my fathers and my forefathers. I am neither a sabo-teur nor an infiltrator. I have returned to my land."

When the judge announced the sentence, Adnan burst out laughing and slapped his hands together as though he'd just heard a good joke. The judge asked him what he thought he was doing.

"Nothing. But do you really think your state is going to last another thirty years?"

The judge listened to the translation of the defendant's words, and, as they were leaving, Adnan began yelling, "Thirty years! Your state won't last, and I'll put you all on trial as war criminals."

The judge came back to the dais and added ten years for contempt of court, while Adnan kept up his clapping and fooling around, as if he was dancing in the Israeli dock.

That's how you told me the story. You weren't at the trial, naturally, and the details of the trial weren't published in the Arab papers, but you knew all that from your private sources, whose source is known to none!

Tell me, now, why did you return in such a state from visiting Adnan when he came out of prison after the celebrated prisoner exchange in 1983?

Were you afraid? If so, what were you afraid of?

Were you afraid of Adnan's sickness?

I told you he had a neurological disease and that neurological diseases could be treated, but you continued to feign ignorance.

Adnan was mentally disturbed, which doesn't mean he'd gone mad. He returned as a semi-imbecile; that's the correct term to describe his condition. He spoke calmly and with self-possession. He recognised everybody and knew the names of all the members of his family, even the grandchildren who'd been born during his long absence. He knew them and embraced them as grandfathers do their grandchildren.

He spoke slowly and calmly, and that's all.

After a few days, however, he started to lose his temper at unexpected moments, speaking to people as though he was talking to the Israeli gaoler and jabbering in Hebrew. Then, as time passed, he started yelling and going out of the house naked.

You returned from your last visit to him in Burj El Barajneh camp despairing and defeated and asking me for sleeping pills, and you decided to stop going to see him. His son Jameel wanted to send him to the mental hospital. You objected and wept. Everyone saw you weep. You wept and said, "Impossible! Adnan is a hero, and heroes don't go to the lunatic asylum." It's said you pulled out your revolver and tried to kill him. Everyone said, "Shame on you!" and you said, "The shame is that he doesn't die. The shame is that he should live like this, you bastards."

Why didn't you tell me you pulled out your revolver? And why you didn't kill him? And why did you let them take him to the Dar Al Ajazah home for the infirm? Do you imagine Dar Al Ajazah is a hospital? I swear it wouldn't do as an animal pen. The mental patients there are crammed together like animals and live a living death.

This time I'll change the story.

With your permission I won't let Adnan end like that. I'll tell what happened a different way.

Yunis, Abu Salim El Asadi, went to visit his friend Adnan Abu Odeh in the Burj El Barajneh camp. This wasn't his first visit to Adnan since the latter's release from the Israeli prison where he'd spent eighteen years. When Adnan had been freed, Yunis had been at the head of those who'd welcomed him home. He'd fired his rifle into the air, slaughtered animals and danced with the others. He'd embraced Adnan and told everyone, "Hug him and smell the smell of Palestine!"

Everybody sat in the Abu Odeh clan's guest hall eating lamb and rice and drinking coffee, and Adnan said nothing except for a few words that were lost among the sounds of men and women whooping for joy. That day the men ululated like women, and everybody drowned in a sea of colours – the women wore their coloured peasant dresses and came out onto the unpaved streets of the camp as though they were the streets of their villages.

When the party was over and everyone had departed, Adnan went back with his family to his house and sat down in the midst of his sons and daughters and grandsons and granddaughters. He embraced them all and said, "Praise be to God!" Everyone laughed when Yunis related the events of the trial.

"Stand up, Adnan, and tell us the story!" said Yunis.

Adnan didn't stand up, or tell them the story, or laugh, or strike one hand on the other as he asked the judge: "Do you really think your state is going to last another thirty years?"

So Yunis told the story instead and everyone laughed while Adnan remained immersed in his deep silence.

"See, Adnan? Twenty years have passed, and there's still plenty of time!"

At that moment Adnan began to manifest strange symptoms. He yelled once, then fell silent. He uttered an incomplete sentence and said some Hebrew words.

Yunis thought he was tired. "Let the man rest," he said. "He's tired."

He said goodbye to Adnan and promised he'd visit him in the next few days.

A week later, the news of Adnan's madness arrived, but Yunis refused to believe it and went to his friend's house and saw and wept and returned distraught.

But things didn't end there.

One morning, Adnan's son Jameel came to Yunis, informed him of the family's decision to move Adnan to the lunatic asylum and asked him to get a report from a doctor at the Palestine Red Crescent.

This is where Dr Khaleel – that's me – comes in. He went to Burj El Barajneh camp, examined Adnan and said he was suffering from depression and in need of long-term neurological treatment, but there was no need to put him into hospital. However, Adnan's condition worsened and things got to the point where he'd leave the house naked. People started saying that he should be admitted to hospital, and Jameel came to me asking for help. I explained my diagnosis and the man started screaming in my face that he couldn't take it any longer and that he'd made his decision and it didn't matter whether I wrote the report or not.

Yunis decided to intervene.

He went to Burj El Barajneh camp and knocked on Adnan's door. Jameel welcomed him, then started complaining and telling him stories. Yunis told him to be quiet.

Yunis went into the living room where Adnan was sitting in his pyjamas listening to Umm Kalsoum's song "I'm waiting for you" on the radio and swaying to the music. Yunis greeted his old friend, but Adnan remained absorbed in Umm Kalsoum, as though unaware of him.

Yunis pulled out his revolver, fired one shot at Adnan's head and yelled, "I declare you a martyr."

Then he bent over his blood-covered friend and embraced him, weeping and saying, "It wasn't me that killed you, it was Israel."

Adnan died a martyr. They printed his picture on big red posters, and he had a huge funeral the like of which had never been seen before.

Don't you agree this ending's better than yours?

You should have killed him as the horseman does his wounded stallion instead of letting him be taken there.

Instead, you came to me asking for sleeping pills and left your friend to his savage death in the hospital.

I saw him in the hospital and I know he spent his final days screaming and in a coma and having shock treatments, but I never told you because you were busy and only wanted to hear what made you feel good.

As far as you were concerned, Adnan ended in the courtroom with his "This is the land of my fathers and my forefathers." You'd clap your hands and laugh, saying, "Thirty years! God bless you, Adnan. There's still plenty of time, Adnan. The years have passed, and we're still in the camp."

"It was time that drove Adnan mad," you told me. "Don't count the years. We need to forget. The years pass, that doesn't matter. Twenty, thirty, forty, fifty, a hundred years, what's the difference?"

You let Adnan die like a dog in the hospital, and his son didn't dare to announce his death. The Abu Odeh family didn't take part in his funeral. They buried him secretly, as though there'd been a scandal. Even you, his life-long friend, didn't go to his funeral.

Now do you understand my confusion?

Temporariness perplexes me because I fear it.

"Everything's temporary," you told me when we met after the disaster in 1982. And during the long siege at Shatila in 1985 you said it was temporary. "Listen, we have no choice. However bad things are, we have to keep on living or we'll become extinct."

I know your views, your eloquence and your ability to make the impossible sound reasonable.

But what would happen if we were to remain in this temporary world for ever?

Do you believe, for example, that your present situation is temporary?

Do you believe that I'll stay here in your temporary world trying to wake you when you won't wake up, telling you stories I don't know, and visiting countries with you that I've never visited?

What kind of a game is this? You're dying in front of me, so I take you to an imaginary country!

I hear you saying, "Don't say 'imaginary'! It's more real than reality."

Very well, master. I take you to a real country. Then what? I can't bear more illusions. I want something other than these stories filled with heroic deeds. I can't live within the walls of a story for ever.

Shall I tell you about myself?

There's nothing there, master. I have nothing to say except that I'm a prisoner. I'm a prisoner of this hospital. Like all prisoners, I live on memories. Prison is a storytelling school: here we can go wherever we want, play with our memory however we please. Right now, I'm playing with your memory and mine. I forget the danger my life is in and amuse myself with yours, and I try to wake you up. The fact is, I no longer care whether you wake up; your return to life no longer has any meaning. But I don't want you to die, because if you die, what will become of me? Will I go back to being a nurse or wait for death at home?

As you see, you're right.

You were always right: the temporary is preferable to the permanent, or the temporary is the permanent. When temporariness comes to an end, so does everything else. I'm in your temporary world now: I visit your country, live your life and make imaginary journeys. I'm your temporary doctor who isn't really a doctor. Do you believe I became a doctor? Do you believe three months' study in China can make someone a doctor?

Would you like me to tell you about China?

I'll give you your bath first, then order a dish of beans from Abu Jabir's restaurant, eat it and tell you afterwards, because I'm hungry and the hospital food is uneatable. Believe me, you eat better than I do. You can't taste anything now because you eat through your nose, but the taste of bananas with milk is delicious. Our food on the other hand is disgusting, and I'm obliged to eat it. What else can I eat? Do you think I'm going to pay for a dish of beans every day? I had to fight a huge battle to get

Dr Amjad to take me back onto the hospital payroll as a mere nurse, at half pay. He said I wasn't working and you didn't need a full-time nurse and all I did was take care of you.

That bastard of a doctor only agreed to pay me half salary after Nurse Zeinab intervened and told him his conduct was unbecoming "because Dr Khaleel was a founder of this hospital, and he has a right to return to it". She used the word *doctor* after hesitating and eyeing me like an idiot, as though she'd done me a huge service.

Do you know how much I make?

I make, master, two hundred thousand Lebanese liras a month, or the equivalent of a mere one hundred and twenty American dollars. A doctor for a hundred dollars, what a bargain! A hundred dollars isn't enough to cover the cost of cigarettes, tea and arak. And I only rarely drink arak because it's got expensive.

What sort of era is this?

"We were willing to take the shit, but the shit thought it was too good for us," as they say. Between you and me, Amjad's right. He found out I wasn't a doctor, so he offered me a job as a nurse and I refused it. And then when I agreed, he made me half a nurse!

Do you believe I'm a doctor?

You encouraged me when I came back from China to work as a doctor, telling me revolutionary medicine was better than regular medicine.

But how sad it is when revolutions come to an end! The end of a revolution's the ugliest thing there is. A revolution is like a person: it gets senile and rambles and wets itself.

What matters, master, is that revolutionary medicine no longer exists. The Revolution's over, medicine's gone back to being medicine, and I was only a temporary doctor.

And now I'm returning to being my real self.

But what is my real self?

I swear I don't know. I know I became a doctor by accident, because I fractured my spine. I don't remember how the accident happened – we were in the Burjawi district, whose main street forms a tongue of land descending from El Ashrafiyyeh in East Beirut to Ras El Nab' in the west, a perfectly formed salient we were able to occupy to announce that we were liberating Beirut.

It was Lebanon's civil war.

When the war began, I thought of Amman and how we were thrown out without having lost; in 1970 we were defeated without a war and left for the forests of Jerash and Ajloun, and that was the end of it. Amman – today it seems like a white dream; Black April was my white dream. We called that April "Black" to convey its significance, but Amman was white, and there I discovered the whiteness of death. Death, master, is white, white as these sheets you're wrapped in in your iron bed.

I was a young lad at the time. I fought in the El Weibdeh district near the Fatah office. To tell the truth, I'd been enthusiastic about going to Amman so I could look for my mother, but that's a long story I'll tell you later.

The war in Beirut was different and went on for a long time. When it started, I thought it would be Amman all over again, and the fighting wouldn't go on for more than a few weeks and then we'd "withdraw" somewhere. But I was wrong because Lebanon blew up in our faces. Whole towns turned to splinters, and we found ourselves running about among the shattered fragments of districts, cities, villages, sects.

I won't present an analysis of the Lebanese war right now, but it terrified me. It terrified me that the belly of a city could burst open and its guts spill out and its streets be transformed into borders for dismembered communities. Everything came apart during the years of the civil war; even I was split into innumerable persons. We changed political discourse and alliances from one day to the next, from support for the Left to support for the Muslims, from the Muslims to the Christians, and from the Shatila massacre, carried out by Israelis and Phalangists in '82, to the siege-massacre of '85, carried out by Amal with support from Syria.

How can this war be believed?

I see it pass in front of me like a mysterious dream, like a cloud that envelops me from head to toe. I was able to swallow an amazing number of contradictory slogans: words were cheap at the time, as was blood, which is why we didn't notice the abyss we were sliding into. None of us noticed, not even you. I know you hated that war and said it wasn't a war, but, with all due respect, I disagree because I don't think you can apply the concept of blame to history. History is neutral, I tell you –

only to hear you answer, "No! Either we apportion blame where blame is due or we become mere victims." I don't want to get caught up in that argument since, as you can see, nowadays I tend to agree with you, but you have to explain one thing to me. Some day soon, when you wake from your long sleep, you must give me your explanation for the way clouds can so fill someone's head that he goes to his death without noticing.

In the war, the Khaleel who's sitting in front of you now was the hero of Burjawi. No, I've started to lie. I wasn't a hero. I was with the boys when we occupied that salient that climbs towards El Ashrafiyyeh, and that's where I fell: the world turned upside down, I couldn't hear a sound, and I understood that death has no meaning and that we can die without realising it.

Like all fedayeen, I expected to die and didn't care. I thought that when I died, I'd die like a hero, meaning I'd look death in the eye before I closed mine. But when the world turned upside down in Burjawi and I fell, I didn't look at death. Death occupied me without my realising. It was only in hospital that I found out that four of my comrades had been killed, and then I was stricken with the crazy fear that I'd die without knowing I was dead.

If you were alive, my dear Mr Yunis, you'd laugh and tell me that no-one knows he's dying when he's dying. But it's not true, I've seen them dying and knowing. A doctor sees a lot, and I've seen them frightened and trembling in terror of death, and then dying.

It's not true that the dead don't know; if they didn't, death would lose its meaning and become like a dream. When death loses its meaning, life loses its meaning, and we enter a labyrinth from which there's no exit.

You tell me: when you were struck dumb and fell, did you know you were dying?

Of course not. I'm sure you didn't. In medical terms, the moment you lost the power of speech, you were afflicted by intense confusion. Because Amna couldn't understand what you were saying, you thought she'd gone deaf, so you raised your voice and repeated what you'd said, explaining your thoughts with your hands and tongue. Then, with the second stroke, you lost all comprehension. It follows that now you're just lying here and know nothing.

I, too, when the world turned upside down, didn't recover consciousness for three days and was afraid. The doctor at the American University in Beirut hospital said I had to remain motionless for a week. The spine – the L6 vertebra – was crushed to powder, and the only cure was to lie without moving, waiting to be saved from semi-paralysis.

If I told you the pain was unbearable, I'd be lying. The pain was appalling, as pain always is, but it could be borne. It was like a savage hand grabbing my chest and neck. I was paralysed, my chest was constricted, my breathing was shallow, and the pain was in every part of my body. But I knew I wasn't going to die and that if I did die, I'd die with my comrades who'd been killed by the heat from the B7's. The B7 was our secret weapon – a small rocket-propelled grenade carried on the shoulder, capable of piercing tank armour because it gave off two thousand degrees of heat.

We were in our hiding place in an old house in El Burjawi when the grenade fell on us and we ignited. Later they told us our bodies had turned black, that I was as black as charcoal. They'd thought I was dead and took me to the hospital morgue, but a nurse noticed I was breathing so they moved me to the emergency room, where they worked for hours to remove the black coating that clung to my skin and whose traces are still visible on my upper back.

The doctor said my life wasn't in danger; the only danger was that I'd be paralysed, but I'd probably "got away with it", and he made a gesture with his fingers like popping an almond from its skin. I wasn't afraid of paraly-sis. I was sure it wouldn't happen to me. But I was frightened of the idea that I'd die without knowing. That would be terrible. Everyone else knowing and not me. Everyone weeping and not the dead man. A farce. That's what they mean by the "farce of death".

I got better, of course. After a week I got out of bed and was as I'd been before; I even forgot the pain. Pain is the only thing we forget. We're capable of remembering and being exercised by many things but not pain. We either have pain or we don't – there's no halfway house. Pain is when it's there, and when it's not, it isn't, and the only feeling it leaves is of lightness, the ability to fly.

Why am I telling you about my back?

Could it be because I've been in constant pain since Shams died?

Shams has nothing to do with it. God knows, when I was with her I didn't notice my back. I was like a god. With her I loved in the way you described it: you said God had made a mistake with men — he'd created them with all the necessary parts except one, which there was no doing without and whose importance we only discover when we need it and can't find it.

Why am I telling you about the missing part now, when I'm supposed to be telling you about China?

Could it be because that was where I became aware of how ponderous my body was and discovered I was unfit for war? Do you know what it means to be unfit for war during a war?

I won't take any more of your time with this. I sense you're fed up with my stories and would prefer to have me take you back to Bab El Shams, to that day when you wept for love and told Naheeleh you felt impotent.

"Women have it," you told me. "I discovered there that women have it — because it's their entire bodies — and that I was lacking, lacking and impotent."

Naheeleh looked at you in amazement because usually you couldn't get enough. She couldn't believe you felt impotent; she thought you were talking about sexual impotence and burst out laughing. After that journey of the body through the realms of pleasure, you stop and tell her you're impotent! After she felt she'd been purified inside and out and was shining and her eyes were two mirrors reflecting the world!

You tried to explain, but she didn't understand. You explained that you needed another part because the sexual organ was not an instrument of love. It was its doorway, but when the chasm opened you needed another part, for which you were searching in vain.

Naheeleh thought you were saying that as a way to return to making love and she had no objection; she was always ready, always ardent, always waiting. So she said, "Come to me." But you didn't want to. You'd just been trying to tell her about your amazing discovery. Of course, you went to her; and there, amid the waves of her body, you discovered that women surpass men because the woman's body itself is the part the man doesn't have, and because she's a wave without end.

I won't tell you now the details of that night at Bab El Shams. I want

China. Come with me on a short journey to China, then we'll go back to the cave.

In China I discovered I was unfit for war and was transformed from an officer into a doctor. I studied medicine in spite of myself, because I had no other option.

In classical Arabic mixed with colloquial Egyptian, the woman told me I was unfit for war and should go back to my country or join the doctors' course. I accepted even though it had never occurred to me to study medicine. Like all my generation, I'd had no serious schooling. From elementary school we joined the cadet camps of the various military forces. We set off to change the world and found ourselves soldiers. We were like the soldiers in any ordinary army, the only difference being that we talked about politics, especially me. I started my active military life as an officer, a Political Commissar with the commandos, because I loved literature. I used to read novels and memorise long passages from them. I read Jirji Zeidan and Naguib Mahfouz, but my special favourite was Ghassan Kanafani. I learned *Men Under the Sun* by heart, like a poem. Then I broadened my horizons and memorised bits from Russians novels, especially Dostoevsky and *The Idiot*. How I felt for Prince Mishkin! How sweet he was, caught between his two lovers! How wonderful his naïvety, like that of Christ! I'd read *The Idiot* and never tire of it. How I wished I could be like him!

No. When I stood before the investigating committee, I didn't feel like an idiot; I felt humiliated. Being an idiot is not the same as being humiliated. It's a position one takes. But there I stood before them, humiliated, and I lost my ability to defend myself.

I memorised literature because it was my refuge. In the days of Kafar Shouba, when we were naked beneath the aerial bombardment and the only things covering me were the branches of the olive tree those books were my shelter. I'd imitate their heroes and speak their language so as not to die.

I became a Political Commissar because I love literature, I became a fighter because I was like everyone else, and I became a doctor because I had no choice.

I became a doctor because of my back: after a week I was completely recovered and rejoined my battalion, which had been transferred to fight at the Jebel Sanneen crossroads. There among the snows of Lebanon I grew to hate the war and to love that white mountain. I lived in the mire of blood-spattered snow.

Blood spattered the snow on both sides of the front, which stretched to the horizon. There I understood why my mother had fled the camp, for in the camp we don't see, we remember. We remember things we never experienced because we assume the memories of others. We pile ourselves on top of one another and smell the olive groves and the orange orchards.

At Sanneen I realised that those far horizons were an extension of man and that if God hadn't made those curves, we'd die and our bodies would turn into coffins.

I was in Sanneen when Colonel Yahya from the Mobilisation and Organisation Office came and informed me that I'd been chosen to join a training course for battalion commanders in China.

And I went.

From Sanneen to China in one go: "Seek knowledge, though it be from China," as the Prophet said. I descended from the highest mountain in Lebanon to the lowest point in the world, and there my final destiny was decided. "No soul knows in what land it shall die."

It never occurred to me that I'd switch from military to medical college. Such are destiny and fate. My destiny was not to be a soldier, and my fate took me where it willed. I understood that that fall on the Burjawi steps had determined my future, and once I accepted my future as a doctor in the armed forces, things began to change. Now I'm no longer a doctor, and it's up to me to decide whether I remain a nurse. I'd prefer something else but don't know what it would be. You'd say it was my own fault – I should have left with the others in '82 – and blame me because I returned from the stadium to my house.

When I recall my moments at the stadium, where the fedayeen gathered amid rice and ululations, I don't know what happened to me. I had no justification for staying in Beirut. I had no family, only Noha, whom I didn't want.

"You should have gone with them," Nurse Zeinab said when she learned they'd decided I wasn't a doctor and had to work as a trainee nurse.

Do you see the significance of the insult, father? A trainee nurse!

After all those years of being treated as a doctor, I become a mere wretched servant in the hospital whose founding physician I was. But even if we suppose I'd gone with the fedayeen, where would I find myself today?

I'd probably be in Gaza, and my status would be ambiguous. Do you think they'd have accepted me as a doctor there? Our leaders, as we understand it, are setting up an Authority, and an Authority needs educated people, crooks, merchants, contractors, businessmen and security services. Our role has ended; they don't need fedayeen any longer. If I'd gone with them, it would have meant choosing between working as a nurse and joining one of the intelligence services, and I'd have felt my destiny was in a state of suspended animation.

We've ended up in a state of suspended animation, master. Our lives have become a burden to us.

The decision to return to Shatila from the stadium wasn't a mistake, as you think. It's true it wasn't a conscious decision, but like all critical decisions, we take them, or they take us, and that's the end of the matter.

In China the only thing I had to worry about was my role as a doctor, which I became convinced of despite myself. After two weeks of intensive non-stop military training, the doctor discovered I was unfit for war. She didn't take me to the X-ray room or subject me to medical tests; she looked at me and understood everything.

I went to see her bare-chested just as my comrades had done. She looked at me, walked round me, asked me to bend over, put her finger on the place where it hurt and pressed. I screamed in pain.

"When did your spinal cord get broken?" she asked.

"What? Two months ago."

She asked me to bend over again, brought her face close to the place where it hurt, and I don't know what she did, but I could feel her hot breath scorching my bones. Then she went back behind the desk and asked me to get dressed and wait.

I put my clothes back on in the waiting room and waited. After everyone had left, she came and sat down beside me. She was wearing khaki trousers, a khaki shirt and a khaki cap. All I could see of her was a small face and Mongol eyes. I couldn't work out her age; I thought she was in her thirties, but someone told me she was in her fifties. I've no idea.

She sat down and said that the way my broken spine had knitted didn't permit me to continue training, or any military work, as it might cause pain at any moment. She said this meant I had to get ready to return to my country.

I tried to explain that she was putting an end to my life and that I had to continue the military course at any cost.

She patted my hand to reassure me — the only time my hand touched a Chinese woman's — and advised me to go back to Palestine to work with the peasants, and that her best memories were of when she'd worked in the countryside.

"But I can't go back," I said.

"Of course you can," she said.

"If I go back, I won't work with the peasants because we're not living in our own country and because there aren't any peasants . . ."

She seemed amazed that there weren't any peasants and that we didn't live in Palestine, so I explained that we were refugees and she became even more surprised. I said we were making our revolution from the outside, surrounding our land because we were unable to enter it.

"You are surrounding the cities," she said, looking relieved, "as we did on the Long March."

"No," I said. "We're surrounding the countryside because we're outside our country."

Numerous questions flitted across her face, but she didn't say anything; she didn't understand how you could surround the countryside or how there could be no peasants. She asked me to prepare myself to go back to the place I'd come from, so I left the clinic and went back to the camp as though nothing had happened.

The next morning I went out to join the line-up as usual, but the trainer, who was accompanied by a social worker who spoke classical Arabic, ordered me to leave. I went to my room to wait to go home, but instead of sending me back to Beirut, they took me to another camp, where I spent the training period in a field hospital belonging to the Chinese People's Army. It seems that what I'd said had had some effect on the doctor. Medical training wasn't very different from military training. We drank the same water, ate the same food, ran in morning line-ups and trained on medical instruments as though they were weapons. The only difference was the language.

In the camp we did our training in Arabic. In the field hospital, however, it was in English. It's true that I don't know the language very well, but I understood everything. The truth is I learned English in China! Imagine the paradox; imagine that I learned the importance of drinking water warm in English! In China they always drink their water tepid, which is why no-one gets fat there. You open your eyes in the morning, and you're desperate for a drink of cold water. But you get warm water, so you drink and you drink and you're still thirsty. For the first few days there, I was thirsty all the time. I would drink and get thirsty. Then I became accustomed to their water, discovered the secret and grew to like it. Warm water enters you as if through your pores: you drink as though you aren't drinking, as though the water is already inside you. To this day I yearn for warm water, but I don't drink it any more the way I used to during the first days after I returned to Beirut. Perhaps the climate is the reason. The climate is what makes our men fat.

After the first days in China we were overcome by the feeling that we were outsiders. This happened when we visited the tunnels of Beijing – Tunnel City – which had tunnels everywhere, tunnels full of rice and wheat depots, tunnels amazingly camouflaged. Once we went into a small shop to buy clothes. The salesman stood up and pushed aside piles of khaki garments, and we found ourselves descending into a tunnel more than thirty metres deep, equipped for people to live in for months.

Tunnels are what it's about: a whole world under the ground, a world of war and a world of history. In China we learned how people can live in history. How can I describe history to you?

Once, some middle-school children came and took part in our military training. We competed with them at target practice with Simonov rifles. It's a useless rifle, or that's what we think here, but there they respect the Simonov enormously, because it's the rifle that played such an important role in bringing American planes down in Vietnam.

The point is that Chinese children, not more than fifteen years old, beat professional officers at target practice! That was our first lesson – respect your weapon. Of course, you'll say, we forgot everything the moment we returned to Beirut, but it's not true. I didn't forget everything, but I couldn't apply it on my own. How can you apply these things on your own? How can you convince people here to drink water warm? How can you teach them to respect an ordinary rifle when Kalashnikovs are cheap as dirt, along with Belgian and American and all the other rifles?

This isn't what I was going to tell you about.

I wanted to draw your attention to the sight of the people doing their morning exercises. I know this is difficult to believe, but I saw it. At 7.00 a.m., in the streets, sports music comes out of loudspeakers dotted around everywhere, and the people do their exercises. The whole Chinese people doing morning exercises!

Can you imagine how these scenes affected us?

First the warm water, then the Simonov children, then the morning exercises, then the soy bean that swells up in water and turns a milky colour and which we ate, and then the long, thin bag of rice that every Chinese soldier wraps around his neck and waist.

It took us into history.

That's the way history's supposed to be.

Today I'd say it's an uncivilised feeling, but at the time we were intoxicated by the wine of revolution. Imagine with me a billion Chinese men, women and children coming out every morning for their street exercises. Imagine the tunnels and the grain and the thoughts of Chairman Mao Tse Tung.

I was convinced and bewitched.

No, I can't say I was convinced one hundred per cent, but I started repeating phrases to myself as though they were prayers; "Chairman Mao Tse Tung, a thousand years more". Of course Mao died, and stayed good and dead, and the Cultural Revolution ended, the crimes were revealed, and these things no longer stir up any emotions in us.

But then.

Then, master, we felt we were making history and that we were like books. We behaved and talked as though we were heroes in novels without authors, novels we all knew and which we narrated every day. We ended up not speaking when we spoke but repeating sentences we'd learned by heart. We would ask and we knew the answer and our memories would speak through us. It was as though we were mimicking ourselves; yes, mimicking ourselves.

That's the way history's supposed to be.

It takes you to two contradictory places: where you're everything and where you're nothing. That way you can be both monster and angel, kill as though you're dying, pursue gratification and fear it, and become your own god.

History is us becoming gods and monsters.

I say that now because I've seen it. No, it's not about China, it's about us. I don't want to desecrate anyone's memory, but do you know Ali Rabih? The martyr Ali Rabih whom we mourned so bitterly?

Ali Rabih was the hero of Maroun El Ras, in 1978: he didn't run from the Israelis who swept over our positions in their first incursion into Lebanon. Ali Rabih, along with a small group of fighters, stuck it out and fought and became a hero. We thought he'd died because in those days we used to assume that anyone who didn't "withdraw" was a dead man, and we used to call running away "withdrawing". Ali Rabih came back alive, told his story and became a hero.

I saw an unrecognisable monster emerge from inside Ali Rabih. We were fighting in the Burjawi district – this was before my fall and before China and before I became a doctor. Abu George was there. This Abu George wasn't important enough to be mentioned in the history books. He was just an ordinary citizen living on the ground floor of a three-storey building located at the crossroads that divides El Burjawi in half – a safe half and a half exposed to gunfire from the Phalangists who'd occupied the tall buildings of El Ashrafiyeh.

Abu George lived alone, cooking for himself, listening to the radio and looking at us with sleepy eyes. He was short and fat with a broad brow and a round white face full of wrinkles. He didn't talk to us about politics; he told us about his son, who'd emigrated to Canada, and his daughter Mary, who lived in Paris. He said he couldn't abandon the house because it was bound up with memories of his wife, who'd died there as a young woman, and that he also hated the idea of emigrating to Europe: "Better the tares of your village than the Crusaders' wheat," he'd say. Then he'd watch us rushing up to the roof in our khakis and with our weapons and he'd say, "My my, what fine tares!"

Abu George didn't object when we occupied the third storey of the building he lived in, where Ali assembled a Doshka cannon. He limited himself to directing a long look at our weapons when he invited us for a coffee and to saying "My my, what fine tares!"

I'm confident that the man didn't like us or, if "like" isn't the right word, didn't think too much of us, and that was his right, not to mention the fact that we hardly induced admiration; now, in fact, I'd say we invited pity – the way we'd talk, set up ambushes, build bunkers, shoot and drop dead.

In El Burjawi, our wounded dropped by the dozen. It wasn't logical to turn the street into a second front: anyone who occupies El Burjawi has to get all the way to El Nasirah in the centre of El Ashrafiyyeh or "withdraw". However, we stayed on so we could die. It wasn't our decision, as you know; we were just troops, potential martyrs.

One day, after Ali had finished his morning coffee with Abu George, he thanked him and was already climbing the stairs to the third floor when he heard Abu George say, as he had dozens of times before, "My my, what fine tares!"

"So we're tares, you son of a bitch?" Ali yelled.

Without preliminaries, he started beating Abu George savagely. Ali was exhausted that day – I think he was frightened – but I saw the fire in his eyes. He was beating the man, fire in his eyes, while Abu George doubled over, shielding his head with his hands and moaning as Ali hit and kicked him, demanding an answer to his question.

"Spy, agent, where's your communications set-up?" Ali yelled, panting and hitting.

This had nothing to do with Abu George, because the man was innocent and no spy. It's true that he wasn't enthusiastic about our cause or our war, and it's true that his eyes showed contempt for those times in which we were allowed to boss him around, but he was neutral.

Ali, on the other hand . . .

Ali was a monster. The cause of his fury was unclear; it was as though there was a monster inside him, as though the war had become a spirit that possessed him. We were afraid he'd kill the man. It wasn't just a beating, it was murder. Ali was killing Abu George with his hands, his feet, his brown, full face and his crinkly hair, as though Abu George was his prey.

We feared for Abu George. All of us said we feared for him.

"And what did you do?" you'll ask.

Nothing. I'm telling you, we froze in place and watched and didn't say a word. We waited for Ali to finish, we saw that Abu George had come out of it alive, and then we started talking!

We didn't freeze because we were afraid of Ali. No, we stood and watched as though we too had become like Ali, as though we were watching a wrestling match.

All the others said they'd been afraid for Abu George, but I was afraid for Ali. I saw he'd turned into another man, a man I didn't know, a monster.

History, my dear Mr Abu Salim, extracts from our inner selves people we don't know, people whose presence we don't dare to acknowledge. In China I found myself in history and felt capable of doing anything, and I wasn't afraid of myself or for myself because I couldn't see. When you're surrounded by mirrors on every side, you lose your ability to see, and the monster of history makes you its prey.

In China, master, we opened the book of history and learned the art of war and the art of exploiting advantage. Our Chinese trainer told us that the central idea in a people's war is to exploit advantage. We withdraw when we're unable to achieve victory, then attack in large numbers, concentrate our forces and wipe out the enemy. In the battles we choose to enter, we have to be greater in number and better armed than our enemy and then we win.

By exploiting advantage, we can delude our enemy into thinking we're capable of permanent victory.

He'd use the word *victory*, and we'd hear it and feel victorious, as though words were magic spells – for words are either magic or they're to be thrown into the bin. That's revolution – a word with magic properties that resemble . . . magic.

We started saying things we'd learned by heart, fighting as though we'd fought before and dying as though we were mimicking our deaths.

God, what times!

I say "what times" as though they were over, but really they're both over and not over. We're "caught", as Major Mamdouh used to say. We're caught and have no alternatives. We get out of one tight place only to get into another. "All that's wrought is caught," as the proverb has it. That's how history is: when you have no alternatives, you get caught and twist in the breeze in spite of yourself.

I sit before you, Major Mamdouh's words boring into my ears. I'm stuck here, and so are you, and Dr Amjad, and everybody. Even Mamdouh – he thought he'd got out of the tight place because he managed to get a visa for Paris. Even Mamdouh, what did he do? Did he become a millionaire and live "safe as a tiger's arse", as they say? Of course not. Mamdouh got to France, married for the sake of getting married (as he said in the only letter he sent his mother) and died of a heart attack. "No soul knows in what land it shall die."

I was talking to you about history, and I don't want to upset you with Major Mamdouh's tragic end – even though it wasn't a tragedy, for tragedy calls for tears while Mamdouh's death made me laugh. Imagine, a man who spent all his time saying he was searching for a way to get out of the trap and then, when he gets out, dies! Mamdouh died in 1981, so one year before the Israeli incursion into Lebanon, so a year before his appointment with death. If Mamdouh had remained stuck with us in Beirut, he would've died in '82 as thousands did, but he moved his death date forward.

I revert to China to tell you that history bewitched me during those two weeks of intensive military training. I discovered how it was possible for me to open a book of history and enter into it and be the reader and the read at the same time. This is the illusion that revolution creates for us. It makes us believe we're both the individual and the mirror, and it leads to monstrosity.

I'd fallen under the spell of all of that when the doctor said I was unfit to continue training and told me to get ready to go back to my country. But instead of taking me back to Beirut, they took me to another camp and announced that I was a doctor.

I won't bother you with stories of Chinese medicine, which I never learned – I remember almost nothing of it, especially not the names of herbs, which our teacher knew only in Chinese. But I discovered the human body. I discovered the existence of an interconnecting natural logic with a precise regime that controls our bodies. Through the body I discovered the soul of things, the links between our bodies and nature, and the limitlessness of man.

You'll say these philosophical theories I'm repeating are an attempt to cover up my ignorance of medicine, but it's not so. I'm convinced of these things, and that's why I'm treating you according to my own methods. Of course, you're not the issue; Dr Amjad was right when he pronounced you a vegetable. But I'm convinced the soul has its own laws and the body is a vessel for the soul, so I try to awaken you with my stories out of a conviction that the soul can, if it wants, wake a sleeping body.

In China, in spite of everything, and in spite of the madness of history raging in my head, I learned the most valuable thing in my life. I learned that each individual's body incorporates the history of the whole human race; your body is your history. I'm the proof. Look at me. Can't you see the pain tearing at me? The Chinese doctor was right. The break in my spinal column, dormant for many years, has suddenly come to life. The pain is everywhere, and painkillers don't work.

The body is our history, master. Observe your history in your wasting body and tell me, wouldn't it be better if you got up and shook off death?

I learned medicine in China and returned to Lebanon as a doctor who knew English but who understood nothing of medicine beyond its general principles.

After I transferred out of the training course, I was taken to a field hospital belonging to the Chinese People's Army, and there a tall man – the Chinese are not all short, as we think – asked me if I knew English. He asked me in English, so I answered, "Yes." I answered in English because I used to think I knew English, which we studied in the UNWRA schools. So they put me with a group of trainees, most of them Africans. The doctor who taught us would give his lessons in English and I'd understand nothing. Or I'd understand a bit, so I decided to pretend that I understood; thus I learned to imitate parrot-fashion everything that was said in front of me and ended up understanding. I discovered that I was no worse than the others, English being a language you don't have to know to be able to speak; this is the source of its power. With amazing speed I learned to memorise what the doctor said and came back from China gabbling English and throwing in a few medical terms to convince people that I was a real doctor, so everything was fine.

What I can't forget is that, when I spoke English in China, I felt I wasn't me. Sometimes I'd be my Chinese professor or my African colleague, or I'd imitate the Pakistani. I forgot to tell you that our group was composed of ten students, eight from Nigeria, plus me and a Pakistani. The Pakistani knew more than we did; he said he'd been a student at the Faculty of Medicine in Karachi, had been thrown out because of his political activism and had come to China to study the science of revolution. He didn't want to study medicine, but they'd forced him to join this course before training him for guerrilla warfare.

I'd imitate him and feel myself becoming another person inside the English language. I'd react as they did and especially like the Pakistani, who'd change totally when he got excited, stretching his mouth so that he looked like the heroes in American films when they scream, "Fuck!"

I told you I worked out the most important thing in my life. I worked out that when I speak, I imitate someone. Every word I spoke in English had to pass through the image of another person, as though the person speaking wasn't me. And when I returned to Beirut and started speaking Arabic again, I returned to myself, as though I'd come back to the Khaleel I'd left behind.

In China I discovered that when I speak the language of others I become like those others, which is a mistaken point of view, of course. But what if? What if even in Arabic I was imitating someone else? What if the difference was that here I forgot who it was I was imitating? We learn our mother tongues from our mothers, but we forget that, and when we forget we become ourselves, which is why we think we're speaking when we speak.

Now I've started to understand your feelings about your father's voice. You told me that sometimes you felt that the voice emerging from your throat was that of the blind sheikh: "It's amazing, but I came to look like him, and when I spoke I came to feel it was he who was using my tongue."

No, I don't agree with that theory. It's true we imitate, but we manufacture our own special language in sync with our manufacturing of our lives. I didn't know my father. All I remember is a phantom, and I can't say now – not after twenty years – that it's that phantom's voice that emerges from my throat.

Of course we imitate, but we forget, and forgetting is a blessing. Without forgetting we would've died of fright and maltreatment. Memory, master, is the process of organising what to forget, and what we're doing now, you and I, is organising our forgetting. We talk about things and forget other things. We remember in order to forget, this is the essence of the game. But don't you dare die now! You have to finish organising your forgetting first, so that I can remember afterwards.

Even now, when I say the word *fuck*, I see the Pakistani with his distended mouth, white teeth and fine oblong jaw like the beak of a bird, and I feel his voice in my throat and smell the smell of China.

I studied medicine for three months and then returned to Beirut carrying with me my new education in the English language, in drinking warm water and in the performance of simple field operations such as removing bullets, bandaging wounds, treating fractures, giving injections and so on.

I wasn't a doctor, but they believed me. I worked in a field hospital in Tyre, stretched my mouth while repeating words I'd memorised from the Pakistani and became a doctor. Time's wheel has turned, as they say, and now here I am, a temporary doctor, in a temporary hospital, in a temporary country. Everything is waiting for something, and these waitings breed and are eliminated and accumulate and interact.

I look at my life and see images. I see a man who looks like me, and I see men who don't look like me, but I don't see myself. It's strange how we deal with life. We go to one place and find ourselves in another. We search for one thing and find something else. Alternatives pile up on top of us. In place of Noha came Siham. In place of Siham came Shams, and in place of Shams I don't know. But now I have to wise up and marry. I'm forty years old, and at forty you either get married or life becomes hell. When a man says he "has to" get married, it means he's reached rock bottom. Marriage is supposed to happen without that "has to".

No. With Shams, no. Marriage never occurred to me because I was living like someone under a spell. Now when I remember that magic, I see another man. The Khaleel sitting in front of you isn't Shams's Khaleel. Shams's Khaleel was different. He didn't eat, because love suppresses the appetite, and he didn't speak, because love has no language, and he didn't get bored, and he didn't mind waiting. When she was there, he was fully there. When she was absent, he invested himself totally in waiting.

Then the love went.

The only thing that destroys love is death. Death is the only cure for love. It ought to have been me. It ought to have been me that killed her. I'm the one who . . . But I didn't.

Now I'm looking for an alternative. I'm not looking for a woman like Shams but for any woman. How good it is to find a woman in your bed! Aaah! But my bed's empty, and I couldn't possibly ask anyone to help me find a woman. A woman is something you have to find for yourself.

A dupe and a cuckold and he's looking for a woman?

So what? All men are betrayed by their wives, and all of them are dupes. I know. I discovered this here in the camp, in the house of the Green Sheikh, and I mourned and wept for Shams.

I was passing through the moment of my great weakness. Shams had died, and rumours of a death list were everywhere. "I'll go to them," I said. Abd El Latif with his one closed eye took me to the house of Sheikh Hashim, who used to be called the Green Sheikh. I removed my shoes and stood in their ritual circle and swayed and twisted with the chanting, shouting the name of God and timing my breathing to the hand of the sheikh that clapped and guided us to the final ecstasy, where we touched the universal presence. I swayed with them, experienced the intoxication, and my tears flowed involuntarily. After the people had dispersed, the sheikh asked me to stay behind and said he was pleased with me and it was time to repent, and he accepted me as a disciple in his chapter, which the people of Sha'ab had brought with them from their village. He gave me a book by the great Yashrati sheikh and told me to come and see him whenever I wished.

On my second visit, when I went to ask him about the story of Reem at Sha'ab, which I'd heard from everyone, I saw his wife knock on the door of their house and the sheikh refuse to open. "She's mad," said the sheikh.

Then I found out the truth.

She was sixty-three years old, sitting on the bench outside her sister's house and telling everyone the story – how she'd gone in and found the sheikh panting with the wife of one of his disciples in his arms.

"I saw him," the woman was saying, "and her cuckold ass of a husband believed him and wouldn't believe me. He said I was mad and took his wife home in the car."

The sheikh's wife said that when she saw them she started screaming.

People, including the woman's husband, rushed over, and the hullabaloo commenced. Then the Green Sheikh raised his hand, everyone fell silent, and he declared, "I divorce you." "And he ordered me out of the house," his wife went on. "I tried to tell them the truth, but no-one believed me. A man in his seventies, the old bastard: I saw him hugging the woman to his belly and the woman between his legs while he panted like a dog. They said I was mad, and the husband took his wife and spat on me. He should have spat on himself and on his wife, but he spat on me."

In the house of the Green Sheikh I understood that Shams hadn't betrayed me: she'd been under the man's spell, or I don't know what . . . I left the Sufi circle and never went back.

I understood Shams, but I was very angry with her. I should've known. If she'd told me about her relationship with that other man, I'd have advised her not to kill him. But she was right; only death can put an end to love, and she was the more daring because she killed her love. Not me; I waited for my love to die. And with death came death, for at death love evaporates and turns into nothing.

I don't care about people. They pity me because they don't under-stand anything. They pity me because I loved her and she betrayed me, and because I fear her ghost and because . . . I don't know. For my part, I don't care. I'm in China. The hospital sent me back to China, where I recovered my English. I can't be a doctor just in Arabic, and without warm water. There, master, I was reborn. There, when everything seemed to end, when they said I couldn't continue my military work, everything began. Khaleel the officer was swept away, and in came Khaleel the doctor. Instead of going to war, I went to the hospital. And today Khaleel the doctor has been swept away, and in has come Khaleel the nurse.

Do you know what Dr Amjad said?

He invited me into his office and started talking incoherently. He sat behind the desk and spoke as though he was the director of a hospital. Of course, he is the director of a hospital, but what a hospital! A hospital lacking the bare necessities – no hygiene, no medicines, nothing, like a prison. And this lightweight stammers in front of me, saying I'd better work full time. He stretches his words out, hesitates and leaves half of them suspended in mid-air before snatching them back and continuing. He trips over the letter "r" and says, "You're a 'nu'se' and you have to work as a 'nu'se.' This won't do. It can't continue this way." I tried to explain the conditions under which I was working and how you take up all my time.

"All your time!" he said mockingly. "The fact is, we've started to worry for your sanity, doctor, talking to yourself all the time. You think we don't know what you do in that room? You think talking's a cure? If talking were a cure, we'd have liberated Palestine long ago. No, it won't do."

I told him I took half a salary and was content with that, and he told me that what I called a half salary was a full salary now that the Red Crescent's funding had been cut off.

"The money evaporated with Kuwait's oil, Dr Khaleel. There is no money. There's war and America, but the oil has gone, and the Arabs are bankrupt, and the Revolution's bankrupt, and your salary isn't half a salary, so you have to choose between working with us as director of nursing on a full-time basis and leaving the hospital."

He said the hospital wasn't a place of asylum, and he only wanted what was best for me, and he respected me and my history. "But you must work. And don't be afraid; you're under our protection."

I didn't answer. He was trying to manipulate me by using my fear against me and trying to let me know that he was aware of the Shams issue. All the same, I was on the verge of refusing his offer when he threatened me with you.

"We'll take care of Yunis," he said. "Anyway, he no longer needs attention, and the question of whether he should stay in the hospital is still on the table. I'm in the process of getting his papers ready for transfer to Dar Al Ajazah. People like him are put there, not in a hospital. His condition's hopeless, and clinically he's dead."

Do you see what the son of a bitch doctor wants? He wants to throw you into a home. Yunis – Abu Salim, Izz El Din, Adam – is to end up in Dar Al Ajazah? Woe betide him! Do you know what that means? Listen to me, please. I didn't promise Amjad that I'd consider the proposal seriously out of concern for myself. After all, what can they do to me? It's God who decides when you die. I said I'd consider the proposal because the idea of the home struck terror into my heart. Do you know what moving you there means? It means you'll rot alive – yes, you'll rot, and the worms and the ulcers will devour you. I didn't tell you about Adnan because I didn't want to upset you, but I'm the only one who visited him, because they sent for me, and while I was there Dr Kareem Jabir showed me something horrifying.

"I'm not a relative of the patient," I told him.

"Precisely," he answered. "We reviewed his medical file and found the report you wrote, and we'd like to discuss his condition with you."

When I said I knew nothing about neurological diseases, he eyed me with distaste and corrected me: Mr Adnan's illness was not neurological but psychiatric, as he was suffering from schizophrenia and receiving electric-shock therapy.

I won't bother you with a discussion of the doctor's diagnosis as I'm certain he understood nothing. He invited me to meet Adnan, and we walked through the place, to which I'd give any name but "hospital."

Heaps of lunatics, the smells of lunatics, the sounds of lunatics.

Moaning from every corner.

Moans rising like smoke.

At the entrance to the conjoined clumps of tin shacks in what in the past had been called Sabra camp, there's a dingy yellow building walled in on all sides called Dar Al Ajazah.

In this building, which isn't part of our world, I walked and walked until I got to a room that looked nothing like other rooms and saw an old man tied up with chains who they said was Adnan.

We walked through the first floor, which has the large wards. "Here," said Dr Kareem, "is where we put the mental patients who aren't dangerous."

We walked among them. They clung to our clothes as though they wanted something they couldn't articulate. The smell of food and the sight of the patients in their dirty white garments gave the impression that the rooms hadn't been aired for years.

I told Dr Kareem that I felt suffocated because of the lack of ventilation, and he patted me on the shoulder, saying that the hospital had been built to the proper standards and was equivalent to the best in Europe.

"And the smell?" I asked.

"The smell's nothing," he said. "Just the smell of an agglomeration of people. Any agglomeration, whether of humans or of animals, has a strong and penetrating smell, that's all."

We continued down the corridor, which opened onto the patients' rooms, and I noticed that they weren't wearing day clothes but pyjamas. I wanted to ask why they weren't wearing clothes, but I didn't.

We went up to the second floor, and there I saw!

On the first floor the conditions were more or less humane. The patients' rooms opened onto a relatively large corridor, and they could choose to stay with their companions in the corridors or sit in their rooms, in each of which there were four beds.

Upstairs was unbelievable.

We came first to a large ward full of cots with metal sides. "These are the incapacitated," he said. Then we turned right and entered the hall of horrors. I saw thirty children tied to their beds and immobilised. "These are the mentally retarded," he said, smiling.

"But this is torture," I said.

"It's better this way, for them and for us," he replied.

He led me down the long corridor and said we were coming to the "dangerous" ward.

And I saw Adnan.

It wasn't a ward, or a corridor, or rooms. It was a group of small, dark cells, and Adnan was tied with a metal chain to a bed fenced with metal bars, snoring.

The doctor tried to wake him. "Adnan! Adnan!" he said.

The reply was a staccato and fidgety snoring.

The doctor put his hand on the black metal siding surrounding Adnan's bed and talked about his case. He said they'd made a mistake with Adnan. "It seems the doctor on duty didn't read his medical file carefully and had him tied down, and you can imagine. The man had spent twenty years in solitary confinement under restraint, and when he saw the restraints here he was stricken with nervous paralysis, and the doctor had to take him to shock therapy. Then he had him tied to his bed, and his condition began to deteriorate. He wouldn't stop screaming and trying to attack the nurses, and he's very lucky they didn't kill him. These errors occur, but as soon as I got back I took things in hand. As you can see, there's not much hope and his situation's getting worse."

"But he's still tied up!" I said.

"Of course, of course," answered the doctor. "I was away, as I told you, and I had no choice but to tie him up so he didn't endanger himself and the nurses."

"You ordered this?"

"Yes, sir, I did. As you can see, the physician can be forced to take harsh measures. What would you have me do? I undid his restraints and he started beating one of the nurses and fractured his hand. So I ordered him to be taken back to shock therapy and tied up."

"But he's half-dead now!"

"Precisely. That's why I called you in," said Dr Kareem. "I don't think he'll get up again after the last shock treatment, and I want you to get in touch with his family and explain the situation to them so they can come and visit him before he dies. Maybe if he sees one of his children he'll improve a little. Can you get in touch with them?"

That's where Dr Amjad wants to send you – to the place where they tied Adnan up and tortured and killed him; to the place where Adnan hovered on the verge of death for six months between the shock-therapy room and his cell before dying.

"Impossible," I said to Amjad.

I said I'd think about the situation, gave him the impression I'd agreed and then implored him to leave you here. I said it was a scandal. I said, "By all you hold dear!" I said, "It's out of the question."

I talked and talked and talked, saying I don't know what. I implored him not to transfer you to the home, and he promised to reconsider, so I was happy. I left his office in good spirits, but now I'm sad.

I stand in front of you confused, scared, despairing.

But in Dr Amjad's office I was happy because he's going to reconsider, which means I shall remain here, and if I stay you stay, and vice versa.

When he does reconsider, he'll find he can't expel you from the hospital because that would be shameful. True, the hospital is like a prison, and true, we're both prisoners here, but it's better than dying.

But all the same.

I shouldn't have agreed to his conditions. I should have threatened him, don't you think?

In your room I saw the scene with new eyes, and I imagined what I should have said and said it, or as good as.

It was 9.00 a.m. and I'd finished giving you your morning bath and was standing at the window drinking tea and smoking an American cigarette when I found Nurse Zeinab in the room.

She said Dr Amjad was expecting me.

I threw my cigarette out of the window, put the tea cup on the table and followed her. I knocked on the door of Amjad's office and entered. The doctor was reading the newspaper. He moved it a little to one side, said, "Please sit down" and went on with his reading. I accepted his kind invitation, sat down and waited. But he didn't interrupt his reading, muttering in disapproval as he read. Finally he threw the paper onto the desk, said, "Welcome" and fell silent.

"Nice to see you," I said.

"Can I do anything for you?" he said.

"Thanks. Zeinab told me you wanted to see me."

"Ah yes," he said. "How's the old chap?"

"Better," I said.

I told him about the drops and your reaction when I prick your hand with a needle and the clear signs of improvement.

He took off his dark glasses – I forgot to tell you, he wears dark glasses when he reads. Strange. I'm sure this doctor doesn't understand a thing about either medicine or politics, but what can we do? "God's the boss," as they say. He took off his dark glasses, blew pipe smoke in my face and informed me that I was being transferred to full-time work as director of nursing.

I didn't agree.

I explained the importance of my work with you and was getting up to go when he informed me of the decision to transfer you to the home.

I tried to say something but couldn't. My tongue was as heavy in my mouth as a piece of wood. Then the words burst out. I said that transferring you meant throwing you onto the rubbish dump and leaving you to die, and that I knew the place was neither a "home" nor a hospital but a hodgepodge of the living and the dead.

Amjad, however, insisted on having his way.

"Do you know what you're doing?" I asked.

"Of course I know, and I'm doing my duty. The hospital can't take a case like Yunis. People like him die in their own homes."

"There's nobody at his home," I said.

"I know. That's why we'll be transferring him to Dar Al Ajazah," he said.

"Impossible," I yelled. "You don't know what you're saying."

"On the contrary, I know more than you do."

"You know nothing."

"I'm doing my duty. There's no room for pity in our profession."

"Pity! You're an imbecile. You don't know what Yunis means."

"Yunis! What does Yunis mean?"

"He's a symbol."

"And how are we supposed to treat symbols?" he asked. "There's no place for symbols in a hospital. The place for symbols is in books."

"But he's a hero. It's impossible! A hero doesn't end up in a cemetery for the living."

"But he's finished."

When I heard the word *finished*, everything changed. I told him I don't know what – that you were the best there was, that you were Adam, that nobody was going to touch you or I'd kill them.

The doctor tried to calm me down, but I got more and more excited.

He said he was the one who made the decisions here.

I said, "No. No-one decides."

I took his newspaper and started ripping it into little bits and chewing them. I chewed and spat and yelled, and the little bits of paper dropped onto the table and the ground. I kept on ripping away, and the doctor shrank back behind his desk. As I spat, he started to disappear till all that was left of him was his head above the desk, and then the head disappeared and his body grew smaller and smaller in the chair till it disappeared as though the desk had swallowed it up.

I left him under the desk and stormed out of his office. That's how I like to think of my exit from his office – "stormy".

And I came to you.

I'm sure now that you'll stay here even though I didn't say what I meant to in Amjad's office.

Tell me, how is it possible? How could Amjad dare to speak of you in that way? Doesn't he know? Everyone knows your story. Doesn't the story mean anything to him or what? Has he lost his memory? Are we a people without a memory? He said what he did as though he didn't know, but I'm sure he does. What's come over him? What's come over all of us? In the end is there nothing left but the end – you and me in a world that's hurling us into oblivion?

You're fortunate, Mr Yunis.

Can you imagine yourself without me?

If you were in my place – and only if you were in my place – you'd understand that the worst is yet to come. I know you want me to tell you about the political situation, but I hate politics because I no longer understand what's going on. I just want to live. I flee from my death to your death and from my self to your corpse. What can a corpse do?

You can't save me and I can't cure you, so what are we doing here? I'm in hospital and you're in prison – no, I'm in prison and you're in hospital – and memories come. Do you expect me to make myself a life out of memories?

I know you'll say you don't like memories. You don't remember because you're alive. You've spent your whole life playing cat and mouse with death, and you're not convinced that the end has come, the time for you to sit on the sidelines and remember. "We only remember the dead," you said to me once, but no, I differ entirely with you about that. Through you I remember so that I can live. I want to know. At least to know.

I heard the stories that all the children in the camp heard, but I didn't understand. Do you imagine it's enough to tell us we weren't defeated in 1948 because we never fought to make us content with the dogs' life we've lived since we were born? Do you imagine I believed my grandmother? Why did my mother run away to Jordan? Why did my grandmother tell me my mother had gone to see her family and would come back? She didn't come back. I went to Jordan to look for her and couldn't find a trace of her, as though she'd vanished into thin air. That's how we are: nothing begins but it disappears, as in a dream.

Now, in this long dream in the hospital, I want you to tell me the story. I'll tell the story, and you can explain and make comments. I'll tell you the story, and you can give me information, but before that I want to tell you an enormous secret on the condition that you don't get angry. I watched the video Umm Hassan brought, and I saw El Ghabsiyyeh. I saw the mosque and the lotus tree and the roads smothered in weeds, and I felt nothing. I felt no more than I felt when I went to the centre of Beirut devastated by the civil war and saw the vegetation wrapped around the soaring buildings and the ruined walls. No, that's not true. In the middle of Beirut I almost wept, and I did weep, but watching Umm Hassan's film I felt a breath of hot air strike me. Why do you want me to weep for what history has ruined? Tell me, how did you leave them there and come here? How did you manage that? How did you live in two places and inside two histories and two loves? I won't take your sincerity at face value nor your enigmatic talk about women. All I want is to understand why Naheeleh didn't come with you to Lebanon. How could you have left her? How could you have lived your story and let it grow and grow until it killed you?

My question, master, is, "Why?"

Why are we here? Why this prison? Why do I have no-one left but you, and you no-one but me? Why am I so alone?

I know you're not able to answer, not because you're sick or because you're suspended between life and death, but because you don't know the answer.

Tell me, for God's sake tell me, why didn't you make your wife come with you to Lebanon, and why did Naheeleh refuse to come?

She said she'd stay with the blind sheikh and you didn't believe her, but you left her and went. You left her and you left your first son, who died. You left her because the blind man told you, "Go, son, and leave her. We're not up to moving."

The blind man who'd moved from village to village and from olive grove to olive grove till fortune brought him to Deir El Asad to die told you he couldn't move, and you believed him?

Why did you believe him?

Why didn't you tell them?

Why did you turn your back on them and go?

I know you were one man lost among the villages along with the other lost people, that you were clumps of humanity in despair. But what did you do after the fall of Tarshiha? Why didn't you go to Lebanon with the fighters? You went to the hills of El Kabri and fought with the Yemenis, then went back to Sha'ab and found the village empty. You looked for them everywhere, and it took you a month to find them. You went to Deir El Asad, where you found them living in half a house, and instead of looking after them you left them and went away.

Tell me, what came over you?

Inform me.

Whenever I ask you what happened, you start mixing events up chaotically, jumping from month to month and from place to place, as though time had melted away among the stones of the demolished villages. My grandmother used to tell me her version as though she was ripping the stories up into little pieces; instead of gathering them together, she ripped them apart and I understood nothing. I didn't understand why our village fell or how.

I can understand my grandmother and forgive her her pillow full of the smell of decay. But you, you who fought in 1936, who took part in all the wars, why don't you know?

Do you want me to believe my grandmother and lay my head on the pillow of dried flowers and say, "This is El Ghabsiyyeh"? Do you want me to be like her and sleep and not see? Her only son came back, and she didn't see him. She was standing under the olive tree, undoing her hair and dancing in sorrow, when her son, my father, came back carrying the sack of vegetables, and she didn't see him. The boy coming back from the whining of bullets grabbed his mother's dress, and the two of them started weeping together, she because she'd lost him and he because she was weeping.

I won't tell you about my father who died in a heap at the threshold of his house. They killed him and threw him down there. I didn't see him. My mother and his mother were there, and when I see him now it's with my mother's and my grandmother's eyes. I see him dying in a pool of his own blood like a slaughtered sheep, and I see white.

But no.

The story that's told is that the sky fell. My grandmother, describing the terrible dispersal into the fields, said the sky fell to earth, the stars turned to stones, and everything went black.

Tell me about that blackness. I don't want the usual narration about the betrayal by the Arab armies in the '48 war, because I'm sick of armies. I want to know what you did yourself. And why you're here and they're there. And why fate led me to you at this late date.

I won't go back as far as Ein El Zeitoun because our story begins as the story of Ein El Zeitoun is ending.

That was on the night of 1 May 1948. You'll never forget this date because you scratched it with a piece of hot iron onto your left wrist. On that day Ein El Zeitoun was wiped out of existence. The Israelis entered the village and demolished it house by house till it was as though it had never been, and in place of the village they planted a pine forest.

Where were you on 1 May?

I know you were organising the defence of Sha'ab. You'd been summoned by Abu Is'af, and you'd gone because you weren't expecting an attack. The Holy Struggle battalions were re-organising themselves after the volunteer Arab Liberation Army led by the Lebanese Fawzi El Qawuqji decided to go into Galilee.

Suddenly the village was overrun and destroyed and wasn't there.

When you returned to your village carrying your English rifle, you saw Palmach men everywhere and you didn't do a thing; you didn't fire a single shot. You took a bit of iron, heated it in the fire and scratched the date on your left wrist. Then you ran off to the fields, heard how the village had fallen and swore vengeance.

Ein El Zeitoun marked the major turning point in the war for Galilee. On the night of 1 May 1948, a Palmach unit with mules carrying ammunition advanced on Ein El Zeitoun via the hill of El Dweirat, which overlooks the village from the north, and from the hill the Palmach men rolled barrels of explosives down onto the village.

Umm Sileiman said, weeping, that they'd killed your father.

You reached the olive grove and saw their forlorn wandering ghosts moving about aimlessly. You grabbed Umm Sileiman by the shoulder, but she didn't stop. She kept walking and you kept trying to catch up with her.

"Umm Sileiman, I'm Yunis," you yelled.

Then she turned and saw you, but she didn't stop. She walked on and said, "They killed your father. Go look for your mother and your wife up ahead."

You ran and then you saw your mother and Naheeleh in the crowd. Salty sweat mixed with your tears as you searched for your small son. You got close to them and saw that your mother was leading the blind sheikh and Naheeleh was walking next to them carrying her child.

You walked beside them and said nothing. You didn't ask about your father's death because you saw he was alive. You'll tell me you were done for, mistaking the living for the dead and the dead for the living. Everything got confused for you people, and you spent years after this first great disaster trying to draw a line between the dead and the living.

Your father didn't die and Umm Sileiman was wrong and you didn't ask about it. But when you reached Sha'ab and the Khateeb family house, you started searching and asking. You saw Umm Sileiman sitting at the threshold of the mosque with her hands clasped like a little girl at school. You told her the sheikh hadn't died, and she looked at you as though she didn't know you. People started gathering in the courtyard of the mosque and Hamid Ali Hassan arrived.

Hamid Ali Hassan's clothes were dripping with blood when he reached the courtyard of the mosque of Sha'ab. Hamid was in his early twenties with green eyes like those of his dark-skinned Bedouin mother, and he'd only left the village when he'd found himself alone with bombs exploding around him.

Hamid Ali stopped in the courtyard of the mosque and said that Rasheed Khaleel Hassan had been killed.

"We went back," said Hamid. "We were six young men from the Hassan family. We wanted to get the money buried in the courtyard of our house. Rasheed Khaleel was the first to enter the village, and he washit by a bullet in the neck. Bullets rained down on us from all sides, and we were driven off. We have to go back and find a grave for Rasheed."

He sat down. Your mother ran over and gave him some water to drink. He drank and sighed, but no-one moved. No-one got up and said, "Come on. Let's go and fetch the body."

They were in the courtyard of the mosque of Sha'ab, wrapped in their stupefaction like ghosts in long black mantles.

It was there that you found out what had happened.

On the morning of 2 May, the armed men withdrew from the village and the people were penned up inside their houses, pinned down by gunfire. When the Palmach soldiers arrived, they ordered the people to gather in the courtyard of Mahmoud Hamid's house.

Umm Sileiman had hidden in the stable close to her house, then decided to go out. She carried a white flag and joined the people in the court-yard.

"What can I say, son? We were standing there, and they were firing over our heads. We started to crouch down, some of us kneeling, some squatting, some lying flat on the ground. Then Yusif Ibraheem El Hajjar stood up. His wife was next to him and she tried to pull him down, but he stood up. He raised his hands as though surrendering, but the firing didn't stop. Yusif Ibraheem El Hajjar went towards the soldiers, bearing the seventy-five years of his life on the shoulders of his huge body.

"'I want to say something. Listen to me.

"'We surrender. Our village has fallen, and our men are defeated, and we surrender and expect to be treated humanely. Pay attention now. We are captives, and you have to treat us the way captured civilians are treated in wartime. We're not begging for your sympathy. We're requesting it and will repay it. If you treat us well, we'll repay your good deed with even better ones. Tomorrow, as you know, Arab armies will enter Palestine, and we'll defeat you, and then we'll treat you as you treat us today. It would be better for you that we come to an under-standing. I declare that I have said what I must, as God is my witness.'

"A young officer went up to Yusif and slapped his face. Then he pulled out his revolver and fired at Yusif's head, and the man's brains scattered over the ground. None of us moved. Even his wife remained kneeling. Then the soldiers chose about forty young men and drove them ahead of them, and after they disappeared from sight we heard firing. They killed the young men and then drove us like sheep towards the valley of El Karrar, where we gathered before setting off towards Sha'ab."

As they walked you looked for Hanna Kameel Mousa. Hanna was the leader of the village militia and closer to you than a brother. You'd met Abd El Qadir El Husseini with him in Saffouri and you were inseparable.

"Where's Hanna?" you yelled.

Ahmad Hamid said he'd seen him.

"I saw him, son. I was hiding in my house and then I decided to give myself up. I went out and walked along the street in front of the houses of the Hamid clan, making my way to the square. Before I got to Abu Sultan Hamid's house, they stopped me and started dragging me along: I'd put up my hands in surrender, but they dragged me along as though they'd captured me. It was behind the square that I saw him. He was on the oak tree. I don't know if he was alive. I couldn't get close to him because they were dragging me along as if they'd tied a rope round my neck; one of them had his hand on my neck and I couldn't resist. I didn't want to resist. I tried to stop in front of the oak tree, but they wouldn't let me. Then they took me to the square where they killed Yusuf Ibraheem El Hajjar and where they dragged the sheikh your father — didn't your mother tell you? Where is the blind man? Did they take him away?

"Hanna Kameel Mousa is still crucified on the tree. Go and get him down, son. I wish I could go with you. I don't know where his family are. They've probably come to Sha'ab. Perhaps they went to Amqa, lots of people went towards Amqa. Go to Amqa, maybe you'll find his mother or father there. Tell them Ahmad Hamid saw him crucified and we have to get him down from the oak tree."

You went to the Khateeb house and confirmed, for the thousandth time, that your father was alive. You found the sheikh sitting in the court-yard drinking coffee and talking about the terrible events of the First World War!

You were gone for three weeks. Everyone believed you'd gone to Ein El Zeitoun to get Hanna down from his cross, and when you came back you didn't tell anyone about what you'd seen.

Tell me, is it true they crucified him? And what does it mean that they crucified him? Did they drive nails through his hands? Did they tie him to the tree with a rope and then kill him? Or did they tie him and leave him there to die, the way the Romans did with their slaves?

You don't know, because when you slunk into the village and went to the oak tree, you found no-one.

Was Ahmad Hamid hallucinating?

Or were you no longer able to see?

You didn't see your father walking beside your wife and your mother in the exodus from the village.

"It was as if I could only see darkness," you told me.

Is it true that the area around the spring was piled with the bodies of the forty young men who were killed there in cold blood?

Is it true too that they didn't bury the dead but brought a bulldozer which pushed them all together into a pit, which didn't get covered over properly so that people's remains stuck out, mixed up with the earth?

Is it true that their demolition of the village was meant as revenge for Khirbet Jiddeen?

Salih Ahmad El Jashi claimed that you didn't take part in the battle at Khirbet Jiddeen. I know he's lying, and in any case no-one in the camp believes anything he says after the strange scene he made in 1972 following the Munich operation. People saw something they'd never seen before – a father jealous of his dead son!

Everyone raced to his house to offer their condolences after his son Husam was killed at Munich airport, but instead of talking about Husam, he couldn't stop talking about himself and his own acts of heroism, about how he'd killed seventy Israelis in the battle at Khirbet Jiddeen.

Of course you remember the Black September operation and the kidnapping of Israel's Olympic athletes in Munich. I know what you think about that kind of operation, and I know you were one of the few who dared take a stand against the hijacking of airplanes and operations abroad and the killing of civilians. People said your position sprang from your fears for your wife and children in Galilee, but you said no, and you were right. I'm completely convinced of your position now, even though at the time I said what everyone else said about your being afraid for your family. As you used to say, "If you want to win a war, you don't go in for acrobatics, and if you don't respect the lives of others, you don't have the right to defend your own."

Salih Ahmad El Jashi claimed you didn't take part in the battle of Khirbet Jiddeen. We didn't believe him, though. That elderly stooped man with his large nose sat in his house receiving condolences, or congratulations, on his son Husam's martyrdom, and made use of the occasion to recount the tales of his own glories and those of the bands that came from El Kweikat and Sha'ab and Ein El Zeitoun to support the fighters of El Kabri. And when someone asked about you, he raised his finger and said, no, he didn't remember you being with them. Puffing out his chest, he told the story of the ambush: "The people of El Kabri won't forget the victory they tasted at Khirbet Jiddeen! If we'd fought throughout Palestine the way El Kabri fought, we wouldn't have lost the country!"

"But we're fighting now," someone said. He was a youth, one of the martyr Husam's comrades.

"We'll see, son. We'll see what you can do," Salih Ahmad El Jashi said and started telling us about the Israeli convoy that fell into the ambush.

I want to ask you: Was the fall of Ein El Zeitoun, El Kabri and El Bruwweh revenge for Khirbet Jiddeen?

Umm Hassan said she went past there on her way to El Kweikat and amid the ruins saw a burned-out bus and the remains of an armoured car; the Israelis had set up a monument to their dead.

"And us, what will we put up there?" I asked her.

"What will we put up?" she asked in surprise.

"After the liberation, I mean."

She looked at me with half-closed eyes as though she didn't understand what I was getting at. Then she laughed.

Umm Hassan's right. We'll never put up anything – not even a decent burial ground, let alone a monument – for the fifteen hundred people who fell at Sabra and Shatila. We built nothing. The mass grave has turned into a football ground where children play, and there are those who say, I don't know if it's true, that the whole of Shatila is going to be bull-dozed soon.

Monuments aren't important. What matters is the living. But why did Salih El Jashi claim you didn't take part in the battle, and why, instead of weeping for his son, did he sit like a puffed-up cockerel boasting of his own heroic deeds?

You tell me what went on.

I don't want to listen to that cripple boasting that a hand grenade went off in his pocket and didn't kill him. I didn't believe the story, but you confirmed it, laughing and saying, "The poor man was frightened for his manhood. Blood was spurting out of him, and he put his hand between his thighs, and when he was sure the injury was somewhere else he started jumping for joy before fainting from the pain. We were a band of fighters on our way to El Bruwweh, and Salih El Jashi was hanging out of the window of the bus when the grenade went off in his pocket and he fell. We took him back to El Kabri and continued to El Bruwweh. Then he met up with us again at the Sha'ab garrison after he'd become a cripple."

That was in March 1948.

El Kabri had been in turmoil for two months. At the beginning of

February, a band of Israelis attacked the village and tried to blow up the house of Faris Sirhan, a member of the Arab Higher Committee. The attack failed, and the band that got to Sirhan's house would've been wiped out if they hadn't withdrawn under a hail of bullets.

On the same day, the commander of the El Kabri militia saw a Jewish armoured car leave Jiddeen at the head of a convoy of cars and lorries in the direction of the main road that leads to Safad via Nahariyyeh. He rushed to Alloush, commander of the Arab Liberation Army in the area, to ask him for help, but Alloush refused because he hadn't been given any orders.

Ibraheem gathered the fighters and divided them in two, the first group in the area of El Rayyis, two kilometres south-west of El Kabri, and a group at the cemetery.

The first group blocked the road with rocks and stones while the second set up an ambush in the cemetery under the command of Salih El Jashi.

The Israeli convoy stopped where the road was blocked but didn't retreat. The armoured car pulled back and the bulldozer moved forward, with three armoured cars, two lorries and a bus following.

Then all hell broke loose.

The battle began at noon. After the bulldozer succeeded in clearing a way, Salih threw a hand grenade, but it didn't explode. He threw another and it made a terrible noise and a lot of dust, but the convoy continued its progress. Suddenly one of the armoured cars turned and burst into flame. How did it catch fire? No-one knows. Did a third grenade hit it, or did it collide with the pile of rocks at the crossroads?

Salih doesn't know.

But he does know that after the Israeli car caught fire, the convoy halted in its tracks and the firing started. It was a blood bath. The firing went on till dawn.

Sitting among the mourners in his house, Salih described what happened:

"They started getting out of the armoured cars and tried to spread out among the olive trees while we fired at them. We had one Sten gun, English rifles and hand grenades, and not one of them got away. They couldn't fight, and they didn't wave a white flag. We fired and received occasional fire from the windows of the bus or from the area of the ambush. The firing didn't stop till we'd killed every last one of them.

"In the morning the British came. I stayed the whole night in the cemetery, and I had with me a band of young men from El Bruwweh and Sha'ab who'd come to support us. The rest seized the Israelis' weapons and went home to sleep. The British removed the bodies, and General Ismail Safwat, chief of staff of the ALA, came, was photographed in front of the destroyed Israeli vehicles, and then set about confiscating all the weapons we'd taken, from which he made us a donation of eleven rifles and seven boxes of ammunition.

"What kind of army was that? And what kind of liberation?"

Didn't anyone ask him what they did after the battle?

Didn't they expect a counter-attack? Did they prepare for one?

But tell me, my dear Mr Abu Salim, what did Khaleel Kallas, commander of the group of thirty ALA men stationed around Faris Sirhan's house inside El Kabri, do?

"'Withdrew',," you'll say.

"When?" I'll ask.

"Three days before the village fell."

"Why?"

"Because he knew."

"And you? You people didn't know?"

Salih said they were taken by surprise by the attack on El Kabri.

However, Fawziyyeh, widow of Mohammed Ahmad Hassan and wife of Ali Kamil, knew, because she left the village the day the ALA men left.

Fawziyyeh, whose husband died in the battle of Jiddeen, didn't remarry for twenty years, and Ali Kamil, her second husband, discovered that she was a virgin!

Her first husband died in the battle of Jiddeen without taking part in it. He was a cameleer, transporting goods among the villages. On that day in March 1948, he was returning from Kafar Yaseef to El Kabri when he passed the Israelis who were pinned down by gunfire from the village militia in the ambush. He was hit and died. The man fell, but the camel continued on its way to the village, ambling along in its own blood, till it reached its owner's house, where it collapsed.

Fawziyyeh said the camel was hit in the hump and belly, and the militia men ate it to celebrate their victory. "No-one paid any attention to my tragedy. I was seventeen years old and hadn't been married more than a month. My husband died, and they slaughtered the camel and ate it, and invited me to eat. I won't deny that I ate, but I could taste death and from that day I haven't eaten meat, not even on feast days or holidays. When I see meat, I see the body of Mohammed Hassan Ahmad and feel faint. I only ate meat with my second husband, Ali Kamil. Poor thing, he couldn't believe his eyes when he saw that I was a virgin. I married him after twenty years; he was a widower, like me, and when he took me and the blood came out he went crazy. He kissed me and laughed and danced. I was frightened, I swear I was frightened. I mean, how could it be? As if I'd never married and blood had never spotted the sheets in El Kabri. He wanted to say things about Mohammed Hassan Ahmad, but no, I swear, Mohammed was a real man, it was just that I'd turned back into a virgin. My virginity came back when I saw them eating the camel and wiping the grease off their hands.

"Ali Kamil, poor chap, couldn't make sense of it. He went to a doctor and came back reassured. The doctor told him it meant I hadn't had sex since the death of my first husband, but how could I have done? Poor me, I lived in a hut with my father in Shatila and he watched me like a hawk. He even stopped me from working in the embroidery workshop – he said he'd rather die of hunger than see his daughter go out to work. Then this widower with no teeth comes along and goes around saying he's taken my maidenhood! But it wasn't so; Mohammed Hassan was the one. The other was like glue – he'd stick to my body and lick me like I was a piece of chocolate. Umm Hassan laughed at him. He told her he wanted a child, and she explained that I wasn't a virgin, but he didn't understand. So she explained that his seed was weak – a man over sixty, a woman in her forties, and he wants children!"

Fawziyyeh sits alone at the wake and El Kabri rises up before everyone's eyes. Salih El Jashi tells of his feats of heroism and the village dissolves like an old picture.

"But we left the dead behind, and that was shameful," said an elderly man, getting up and leaving.

Umm Sa'd Radi wasn't at the wake to tell her story.

Ameena Mohammed Mousa – Umm Sa'd Radi – died a month before Husam was martyred. If she'd been there she'd have told you, and she'd have stopped the flood of nostalgia and memories in which you're drowning.

If Umm Sa'd Radi had been there she'd have said: "My husband and I left El Kabri the day before it fell. We were on the Kabri–Tarshiha road and they slaughtered us. I wasn't able to dig a grave for my husband. I see him in my dreams, stretched out on the ground. He sits up and tries to speak, but he has no voice, I don't know why.

"We were on the road when darkness fell. My husband decided we should spend the night in the fields, and we slept under an olive tree. At dawn, as my husband was getting ready to say his prayers, our friend Raja passed and urged us to flee. He said the Jews were getting close. My husband finished his prayers and we kept going to Tarshiha, where we ran into them. They were coming from the north and the south towards El Kabri. They stopped us, searched us and took us in an armoured car to our village.

"They left us in the square, where I saw the troops dancing and singing and eating. A Jewish officer came over to us, chewing on bread wrapped in brown paper and started asking us questions. He pointed his rifle at my husband's neck and asked in good Arabic, 'You're from El Kabri?'

"'No,' I answered. 'We're from El Sheikh Dawoud.'

"'I'm not asking you, I'm asking him,' he said.

"'We're from El Sheikh Dawoud,' said my husband, his voice shaking.

"At that instant a man with a bag over his head came over. I recognised him. It was Ali Abd El Azeez wearing a sackcloth bag with three holes, two holes for his eyes, and one lower down for his mouth. The man with the bag nodded. He was breathing through his mouth, the bag was stuck to his nose, and he was puffing as though he was about to choke. I knew him from his nose, and from the way the bag stuck to his face.

"The bastard nodded his head, and I recognised him.

"'You're from El Kabri,' said the officer after the man with the bag had confirmed it for him.

"They took my husband, along with Ibraheem Dabaja, Hussein El Khubeizeh, Osman As'ad and Khaleel El Timlawi, and left the women in the square. We stood without moving while they danced and sang and ate around us. Then the officer came over and said he would have liked to bring my husband back to me except that he'd been killed. He said not to cry and showed me a picture of Faris Sirhan and asked if I knew him.

"'Tell Faris we'll occupy all of Palestine and catch up with him in Lebanon.'

"I started crying, but it wasn't real crying. I discovered real crying on the second day when I saw my husband's body and tried to carry it to the cemetery and couldn't. That's when I cried, the tears coming out of my mouth.

"The officer raised his rifle and ordered us to leave the square. We slept in the fields, and in the morning Umm Hassan and I returned to El Kabri and saw the chickens in the streets. I don't know who'd let the chickens out. Their feathers were ruffled and they were making strange noises. Umm Hassan tried to round them up. I don't know what we were thinking of, but we started rounding up the chickens. Then I got scared. Scared of the chickens. They seemed wild and were making strange noises. I fled to the spring. I was thirsty, so I left Umm Hassan rounding up the chickens and fled. On the way I found Umm Mustafa. She hugged me and started weeping: 'Go and gather up your husband, he's dead.' She took me by the hand and we ran to the square.

"I found him there.

"He was lying on his stomach and had been shot in the back of his head. And the sun. The sun burned everything. What, dear God, was I to do? I carried him into the shade. No, I dragged him into the shade. I didn't dare turn him over. I left him like that, took hold of his feet, pulled him into the shade and looked around. Umm Mustafa had disappeared, and Umm Hassan was still over there with the chickens. I went looking for her and I found her in the street, bleeding, the chickens jumping around her. I pushed her ahead of me to where my husband was. When Umm Hassan saw my husband's body, she calmed down a bit and went off and came back with a wooden board. We turned the man over onto his back and carried him to the cemetery. We weren't able to dig a grave for him. We pushed the earth aside a bit and buried him above his mother. To this day I pray I buried him properly. We didn't wash him because he's a martyr, and martyrs are washed by their own blood. And anyway, dear God, how were we to wash him in such conditions?

"But the chickens!

"I don't know what got into the chickens.

"I went back to my house on my own and stayed in El Kabri five days, not daring to go out as we could hear scattered shots. On the sixth day when I went out of the house, I found blood everywhere and couldn't see the chickens. I'm sure they'd shot them all and eaten them. I didn't see a single chicken. I went to Umm Hussein's house. Where was her husband? Her husband had been with mine and had to be buried too. The door of her house was off its hinges, and I didn't find anyone inside. I looked around for her and came across Abu Saleem. Abu Saleem was looking for his son – a seventy-five-year-old man saying he'd lost his son and asking me for help. I came to my senses again.

"Suddenly, I saw things straight. During those five days I spent in my house after burying my husband, it was as if I was someone else. I remember nothing, or I remember that I fried some dough and ate it. I was like a lost person, as though the soul of some other woman had entered my body. Five days like one day, or one hour. Ah me.

"When I ran into Abu Saleem and walked through the deserted streets with him in search of his lost son, I returned to myself.

"I took the old man's hand, took him with me to Tarshiha and told him he was the one who was lost, not his son. He went with me and didn't say a thing. He bowed his head and went like a little child. Upon entering Tarshiha I saw my sister. I rushed over to her. Then I couldn't find the old man again. His son said he looked for him everywhere but never found him. I swear I don't know. Maybe he went back to El Kabri and died there."

Umm Sa'd Radi died before the families of the Northern District assembled at Salih El Jashi's house to congratulate him on the death of his son.

If she'd been there she'd have told everyone her story, and told Salih to stop boasting of his non-existent heroic deeds.

I visited her a few days before her death. She wasn't sick; it was as though her life force was draining away. I prescribed some vitamins even though they wouldn't do any good. But I did my duty; a doctor has to do his duty to the end – to him falls the task of protecting the spark of life. I'm the guardian of the life force, Mr Abu Salim; that's why I won't leave you: it's my duty to defend the life in you against all odds.

With Umm Sa'd Radi I did my duty. Radi was there, a man aged about sixty, his children and grandchildren with him, hovering around his mother's bed, afraid of death.

Umm Sa'd Radi spoke in a low voice, almost inaudibly. "His grave," she said, almost as if she could see him shaking the earth off his bones, raising his head a little, then sitting up with his pale, cracked face and looking at her as though in reproach. "His grave," the woman repeated. "Go to his grave."

Umm Sa'd Radi died in fear. She lived her whole life in fear, going to the fedayeen, waiting at the entrance of the camp for the fighters coming back, or going to southern Lebanon and imploring them, one by one: "I beg you, go to the cemetery at El Kabri."

And the young men would nod their heads and run off as though to escape her words.

"The grave is the fourth on the right, near the oak tree. You'll recognise it, son. Just dig a little. I couldn't dig. Dig a little and you'll find him. Make sure his head's facing Mecca, and if it isn't, I beg you, move him into the correct position. God will reward you."

Everyone promised her and no-one went. Who'd be so stupid as to go to the cemetery at El Kabri? And supposing anyone went, who'd go scratching around in a grave?

Even you, father, promised her and lied to her, telling her you hadn't been able to travel that far. Even you didn't dare tell the truth – that El Kabri no longer existed – the cemetery had been erased, the oak tree cut down, the olive groves uprooted, and palms and pines planted in their place.

Abu Salim never told her he hadn't looked for the grave, and he never told her the story of the madwoman of El Kabri and the bag of bones thrown down in the square at Deir El Asad. He listened to her like all the others, and like all the others he nodded his head hurriedly and went on.

Umm Sa'd Radi said she wanted nothing. "They took Palestine? Let them have it. I just want to visit the grave to make sure I buried him correctly. I don't care about El Kabri or anywhere else, they're all going to disappear. They took them? Let them have them. But they should give me the grave at least."

Abu Salim agrees but says nothing.

And we say nothing.

All of us were afraid, and we didn't dare visit her and give her a proper answer.

A good question – why?

Why didn't we lie to the woman and let her die with her mind at peace?

Why didn't anyone dare release her from the ghost of the man sitting in his grave looking at her through his eye sockets, moving his head as though he wanted to say something and not saying anything?

Why didn't we lie to her?

We're not even capable of lying. Incapable of war, incapable of lying, incapable of truth.

Umm Sa'd Radi wasn't there, and she didn't tell her story.

As for you, master, you were sitting in the midst of them, calm and silent. Everybody knew you'd taken to criticising everything, and no-one took you seriously any more. You were depressed, they said. Even I thought so. You'd got fed up and dismissive; we thought you'd become depressed because the way over there had been blocked. After the fedayeen were thrown out of Jordan in 1970 we only had the Lebanese front, and it was swarming with fighters. They told us we had to climb Mount Hermon to protect Palestine from vanishing, so we climbed it and set the ice on fire with our fighting and dying. This made your route to Bab El Shams difficult, albeit not impossible, since I know you managed to find your way through and slipped into your village many times, which is another story, which I'll tell you tomorrow.

On that day, however . . .

On that day, you stood up and explained things to us. The house of Salih El Jashi was sailing along on memories and the stories were flying from people's mouths. Everyone told some story or other and believed the story he wanted to remember.

And the curses rained down on Kallas and Alloush, and how could the ALA have withdrawn, and how they betrayed us, and how this and how that.

Then your quiet voice came from a corner of the room, cutting through all the others. You were holding a thin stick like a long pen, and you drew imaginary lines and circles on the dark red carpet and said that Galilee had collapsed.

"The whole of Galilee collapsed between operations Dekel and Hiram, and we had no idea.

"The Dekel plan began with the occupation of Kaswan on 9 June 1948. Then El Mukur, El Jdeideh, Abu Sinan, Kafar Yaseef and El Kweikat were occupied. On 13 June they occupied Nazareth, and then Ma'loul, linking Kafar ha-Horesh with the rest of the settlements south of Nazareth. On 15 June an Israeli unit moved from Shafa Amar and occupied Saffouri, and a thorough mopping-up operation followed that led to the occupation of El Bruwweh.

"What did we do after the fall of El Bruwweh? We were besieged in Sha'ab. Sha'ab didn't fall; every village and city in Galilee fell in the war except Sha'ab. We stayed up to the end of Operation Hiram, on the night of 28 September, which concluded with the fall of the whole of Galilee in sixty hours.

"We never . . ."

You stood up *like a man* I didn't recognise, said half a sentence and sat down again without finishing it. You put your head in your hands and closed your eyes.

You were *like a man*, which is to say like somebody I didn't recognise. When we call someone we know "a man", it means we don't recognise him any more, or he's taken us by surprise. That's why a wife addresses her husband as "Man" – because she doesn't know him.

And Naheeleh, what did she call you?

You didn't tell me your names as they came from your wife's lips, but I don't think she addressed you as "Man" despite the fact that she was the most ignorant woman in the world about her husband.

This man, you, his head crowned with white, stood up and tried to respond to one of the women, and all the woman said was what we say every day and what we'll always say because it's easiest.

"So they sold out," said the woman.

But instead of letting the words slide past, as words usually do on such occasions, you stood up and said, "We never . . ." and fell silent. And everyone else fell silent.

You used classical Arabic on that occasion, as though you felt yourself to be an orator or wanted to say the final and unanswerable word. So you said, "We never . . ." in classical Arabic and sat down.

I want to ask you: Why did you stop? You waited for the teardrop to be suspended in Noha's eye before speaking. You stood up twice and started to tell the story of what happened to you in Sha'ab, which was your last war. You said that all the villages fell except for Sha'ab: "Sha'ab didn't fall. We evacuated it because defending it was impossible after the rest of Galilee had fallen. Sha'ab isn't a country, it's just a village."

You said you understood the meaning of the word *country* after the fall of Sha'ab. A country isn't oranges or olives, or the mosque of El Jazzar in Acre. A country is falling into the abyss, feeling that you are part of the whole, and dying because it has died. In those villages running down to the sea from northern Galilee to the west, no-one thought of what it would mean for everything to fall. The villages fell, and we ran from one to another as though we were on the sea jumping from one boat to another, the boats sinking, and us with them. No-one was able to conceive of what the fall would mean, and people fell because everything fell.

You talked and talked; you were at boiling point, almost exploding, and we couldn't grasp what you were trying to get at, and why you said that Palestine no longer existed.

"Palestine was the cities – Haifa, Jaffa, Jerusalem and Acre. In them we could feel something called Palestine. The villages were like all villages. It was the cities that fell quickly, and we discovered that we didn't know where we were. The truth is that those who occupied Palestine made us discover the country as we lost it. No, it wasn't just the fault of the Arab armies and the ALA; we were all at fault because we didn't know. And by the time we knew, everything was over. We found out at the end.

"Listen. All of them sold out and we want to buy it back. We tried to buy it back, but we were defeated, utterly defeated.

"Listen. They were less traitors than miserable wretches because they were ignorant; they didn't know what was really happening. Would you believe me if I said that none of us – not I, not Abu Is'af – knew their plans or understood the logic of their war? We didn't know the difference between the Palmach and the Stern Gang.

"Why call it a war when you aren't really fighting?

"We thought we were fighting to defend our homes. But not them; they didn't have any villages to defend. They were an army that advanced and retreated freely, as armies do.

"We didn't put up a defence. At Sha'ab we discovered we were incapable of defending our houses. My house in Ein El Zeitoun disappeared into thin air; all the village houses were blown up the moment they entered. I fought at Sha'ab, but it wasn't my village.

"We fought and fought. Don't believe all that lying history. We have to go back there to fight, and I'm there, and that's enough."

Do you remember how Salih got up, all macho, and said that he got angry when he heard that kind of talk. "The army they called the Arab Liberation Army never fought. The Arab armies just entered Palestine to protect the borders that had been drawn for them, and left us on our own."

You tried to explain that we fought but we didn't know. When you fight and don't know, it's as though you aren't fighting. But no-one wanted to listen. Only Noha. Do you remember Noha? Noha was there. She came and sat close to you and stared at the imaginary map you'd drawn on the dark red carpet. Then she took the stick from your hand, re-drew the map of Galilee and asked you about El Bruwweh.

That was the day I fell in love with Noha and a one-sided love story began that only turned to real love six years later, when she came to the hospital to ask for my help in looking after her dying grandmother.

After Noha finished drawing her map, she turned to you and asked, "Why?"

I think I saw a tear suspended in the corner of her eye, and that tear was the start of my love, a love that began with a teardrop that didn't fall and ended in the municipal stadium under the downpour of tears that covered eyes and faces.

But Noha, when she fell in love with me years later, denied the story of the tear. She said she hadn't cried, she'd felt pity for all of you because you were living on memories and could come up with nothing better than the past to base your lives on.

Her voice halting and punctuated by white spaces, as though emotion was spotting her words with silence, she asked you a question.

"Why did you believe Mahdi?" asked Noha, looking at the map.

The room exploded in silence.

Is it true, father, that El Bruwweh fell because you believed Mahdi and Jasim and the ALA band stationed at Tell El Layyat?

Answer my question. I don't want anecdotes but a clear-cut answer.

I know you don't know the answers. I can see you with the eyes of those days. You were a young man who didn't think ahead – that's how everyone who knew you describes you. Despite that, or because of it, you succeeded, you and the band from Sha'ab, in breaking through to El Bruwweh and taking it back.

But, to be accurate, before the breakthrough and the recovery, El Bruwweh had fallen without a fight.

Sun-dust enveloped the fields, the wheat shining with the special yellow light that precedes the harvest. And the village was afraid. After the fall of Acre, the villages of El Mukur, El Jdeideh, Julis, Kafar Yaseef and Abu Sinan surrendered, leaving El Bruwweh swinging in the wind.

And they attacked.

No-one was ready. Our ambushes were laughable. Now we've worked out how to do things and we have these amazing numbers, glory be, of fedayeen. But then we were forty men and Father Jibran. The priest of El Bruwweh didn't negotiate a surrender with the Jews, that's a lie. He negotiated for our return, and that's an issue that's sparked great debate.

Noha's grandmother, who came to be known as Umm El Hajar, would tell the story and say, "If only . . . !

"If only we'd believed Father Jibran! We were nothing, daughter – just forty men and up above, at Tell El Layyat, more than a hundred soldiers of the ALA under their leader Mahdi, who used to come down like a monkey asking for chickens. We named him Lieutenant Chicken Mahdi and would give them to him. What are a few chickens? Let them eat and good health to them! The important thing was for the village to survive – better a village without chickens than chickens without a village.

"But the chickens did no good, daughter, because when the Jews attacked, Chicken Mahdi didn't fight."

They were forty men. They'd sent their wives and children into the surrounding fields and sat in their ambushes waiting. The Jews chose to attack from the west at sunset, so the sun would be in the peasants' eyes. Three armoured vehicles advanced under a heavy cannon bombardment but were brought to a halt. Then the Jews retreated and dug themselves in, renewing the attack at dawn.

"We ran," said Noha's father. "Yes, we ran. We had no means of defence and the army up above us didn't fire a single shot. I said to Mahdi, 'Aren't you even going to defend your chickens?' He replied, 'No orders.' The village fell and we left everything behind. The ALA didn't ever try to save the chickens."

Noha said her father lived with sorrow in his heart: he said his dearest wish was not to kill the Jews but to kill Chicken Mahdi.

It would be lawful to kill Mahdi, isn't that right, father? It would be lawful to kill him not because he didn't fight with you, but because after you took the village back he asked you to "withdraw" and join your women and children and said the ALA would protect the village. And you believed him.

Why did you believe Mahdi?

Yunis said he didn't believe Mahdi, "but what could we do?

"Listen, daughter. They occupied the village, so the fedayeen withdrew and joined their women in the fields nearby. They slept and lived under the olive trees, waiting for an end to their sufferings. When they got hungry, they decided to take back their village. The Jews occupied the village on 10 June 1948, and we waited in the fields for two weeks. Then we came together, people from El Bruwweh, Sha'ab, El Ba'neh and Deir El Asad, and we decided to liberate the village. The wheat and maize were there waiting to be harvested, and people couldn't even find a dry crust to eat.

"The fighters gathered at Tell El Layyat, and there the Iraqi officer Jasim stood up and made a speech. He said the ALA didn't have orders to help, but they were with the villagers and would be praying for their success.

"We mounted our attack. We attacked the village from three directions – Jebel El Taweel on the north, Sha'ab in the south-east and Tell El Layyat in the east – and we won.

"We won because they were taken by surprise and didn't fight. They did just as we'd done: instead of resisting, they ran away to Abu Laban. So we entered the village. They fired at us before leaving, but it seems their numbers were very small so they withdrew.

"In El Bruwweh we found everything in its place and Father Jibran there to greet us.

"He said, 'You should have agreed with me and given me time to finish negotiating with them, but this is better. God has granted us victory.'

"The priest suggested we harvest the wheat before they came back, and we agreed. We started inspecting the village and the houses. Then we heard ululations coming from the house of Ahmad Isma'eel Sa'd. When we got there, we found everyone's clothes stuffed into bags in the centre of the house. People started sorting out their clothes, which were all mixed up together. I swear no-one knows what he took and what he left behind: the clothes were all mixed up, and no-one could tell his clothes from those of his neighbours. The priest asked us to leave the clothes and go out to the fields. Saniyyeh, the wife of Ahmad Isma'eel Sa'd, ululated and we all laughed; it was a rag wedding – we discovered our clothes were only rags. Why would the Jews take rags? And we too, why were our clothes rags? We celebrated. I can hardly describe it, daughter – the clothes were flying around, and everyone was trying things on and taking them off. Everyone wore everyone else's clothes, and we mixed ourselves together and made a wedding. That was our victory celebration, but we couldn't enjoy it because we heard gunfire from the direction of the threshing ground, so we thought the counter-attack must have begun. Leaving our rags, we ran to get our rifles, and we found Darwish's son, Mahmoud (not the poet Mahmoud Darwish, who was only six years old then and hardly knew how to talk – he was his cousin, I think) standing in the middle of the field, firing his gun in the air and pointing to the threshing floor. There we discovered the sacks: a large part of the wheat harvest had been placed in sacks in the centre of the threshing floor. We started taking the sacks while Saleem As'ad stood by in the uniform of the British police, which he'd never left, next to seven harvesters the Jews had abandoned when they ran.

"We climbed on top of the harvesters, but then the shooting started, and the dying.

"We left the harvesters, picked up the sacks of wheat and rushed towards the village; the women began to leave.

"Bullets, women leaving carrying sacks of wheat on their heads, men spreading out to their positions – the men decided to stay in the village after they'd been joined by eleven fighters from the village of Aqraba who announced they were withdrawing from the ALA."

"We were like drunkards," said Noha's father.

He said he got drunk on the smell of the wheat and the sun-dust.

"Can you get drunk on dust?" she asked Yunis.

Yunis said that Mahdi committed suicide in Tarshiha. "It wasn't his fault, son. Mahdi was just carrying out orders. In Lebanon we found out that Mahdi had died in Tarshiha. When he heard the final order to withdraw, he said, 'I spit on the Arabs,' pulled out his revolver, shot himself in the head and died.

"At some point, Mahdi came and said, 'Okay. Go away and rest up with your women.' And Mahdi was right – the big push was over. We rushed to El Bruwweh and liberated it, and then we returned to our villages, leaving thirty-five men there who were too exhausted to move.

"When we talk about the war, you think of us as regular soldiers, but that wasn't the case at all. Listen.

"After we liberated El Bruwweh, three United Nations officers arrived carrying white flags and asked to negotiate with our commanding officer.

"'But there isn't a commanding officer,' said Saleem As'ad.

"'We're just peasants,' said Nabeel Hourani. 'We don't have a commander, we're just peasants who want to harvest our crop and go back to our houses. Would you rather we died of hunger?'

"'But you broke the truce,' said the Swedish officer.

"'What truce, sir? We've got nothing to do with the war. We wanted to go back to our village, so back we went.'

"The Swedish officer asked permission to search the village and go to Tell El Layyat to meet with the commanding officer of the ALA, but we refused. We were afraid of spies working for the Jews, so we ordered the officers to leave the village.

"We weren't an army. We were just ordinary people. More than half the fighters knew nothing about fighting, I swear. For them, war was shooting at the enemy. We'd stand in a row and fire; we knew nothing about the art of war. That's why, when Mahdi came and asked the fighters to withdraw and leave the village in the hands of the ALA, we agreed without thinking. The peasants did what they set out to do, took part of their crop and handed the village over to the regular army.

"Forty aging men and women who refused to leave their houses were all that were left in El Bruwweh, plus a young man called Tanyious El Khouri, the priest's nephew, who said he'd rather stay with his uncle and later was killed when the Jews reoccupied the village.

"The shelling started and no-one knew what was happening, because they found the Israelis in the square but there was no sign of the ALA. The Jews started blowing up houses and then asked everyone to assemble in the square. When they did so, the Israelis discovered that there were only old people, the priest and his nephew left in the village. Tanyious helped his uncle in the church and was preparing to take holy orders, and when the village fell the priest dressed him in a black cassock like the one he himself was wearing, and they went to the square and stood there with the others.

"An Israeli officer came forward and took the youth by his hand, dragged him out of the crowd and ordered him to take off his cassock. The youth hesitated, then took it off under the officer's steely gaze and stood trembling in his underwear. The July sun hit the people's faces, and dust spread over the village as Tanyious trembled with cold and the priest tried to say something and the shots buzzed over their heads.

"The officer ordered Tanyious to walk ahead of him. The youth walked till they reached the sycamore-fig tree at the edge of the square. There the officer fired a single shot from his revolver. Returning to the little clump of people he ordered them to get into a lorry. Everyone rushed towards the lorry, including Father Jibran, who didn't look back at his dead nephew. But before the priest reached the lorry, he fell, striking his head on a stone. He started bleeding, and the blood seemed to wake him from his stupor. He stood, or tried to stand, staggering as though he was about to fall, then regaining his balance. Instead of continuing his dash for the lorry, he turned and walked back to the tree, where he knelt and started to pray.

"The lorry took off, and no-one knows what happened to Father Jibran, as he wasn't seen again. He didn't catch up with everyone at El Jdeideh, and no-one saw him at Kafar Yaseef. Maybe he fell near his nephew. Maybe they killed him. Maybe we just don't know. Some say he went to Mi'ilyah, to the Shufani family, to whom he was distantly related, and changed his name there and took off his priest's clothes.

"The old people were dumped at Kafar Yaseef and the priest disappeared.

"When the Israelis entered El Bruwweh, they blew it up house by house. They didn't take our clothes and rags. They were like madmen. They blew up the houses and set about bulldozing them, and they trampled the wheat and felled the olives with dynamite. I don't know why they hate olives."

Indeed, why do they hate olives?

You told me about Ein Houd and the peasants they chased out of their village, which was renamed En Hod. The peasants wandered the hills of Jabal Karmal, where they built a new village which they called by the name of their old village.

You were telling me about them because you wanted to explain your theory about the secret nation that stayed behind over there.

"I wasn't the only one," you said. "We were a whole people living in secret villages."

You told me how the Israelis transformed the original village into an artists' colony and how the peasants live in their new, officially unrecognised village with no paved streets, no water, no electricity, no anything. You said there were dozens of secret villages.

And you asked yourself why the Israelis hate olive trees. You mentioned how they planted cypress trees in the middle of the olive groves at Ein Houd, and how the olive trees were ruined and died under the onslaught of the cypresses, which swallowed them up.

You asked yourself, "How do they eat without oil? We live on the oil, we're oil people, but them, they cut down the olive trees and plant palms. Why do they love palms so much?"

"Poor little Tanyious," Noha's father went on. "They killed him before our eyes, and God, what a sight he was. He arrived in the square all puffed up in his uncle's cassock, which looked as though the air had got into it and filled it out. The uncle was short and fat, but Tanyious was tall and slender. Tanyious put on the cassock and went out with the priest, in his short, puffed-up cassock that ballooned like a ghost; we could see his calves, covered with thick, curly black hair. He took off the cassock and shivered as he walked, then we heard the fatal shot, and everything went dark. Sweat covered our eyes and we could hardly see – when people are scared, their bodies sweat amazingly. The sweat was dripping into our eyes, and Father Jibran wiped the blood from his forehead and knelt in front of his nephew's body making the sign of the cross over the thin young man, then stretched his arms out under the tree as though he'd become a tree himself or as though he was crucifying himself on the air, while the village collapsed."

Tell me, Yunis, how, why, did you believe Mahdi? Did you have to believe him?

You'll tell me we shouldn't have believed him, but we did. "We believed him because we had no choice at the time. Only the priest suggested reconciliation with the Jews, but who could guarantee that it wouldn't turn out with us as it did at El Kabri? The priest said he'd be the guarantor, but he couldn't save his nephew's life."

Noha, who told me the story of El Bruwweh, wouldn't accept this. Noha was different from Shams. She allowed me a small peck on the corner of her mouth, whose taste I'd steal as I listened to the endless story of El Bruwweh.

Sometimes she'd say she'd seen the rags in a dream.

Sometimes she'd say that Father Jibran had put the cassock on Ahmad Yasseen the grain measurer, who hadn't "withdrawn" with the others because he wanted to steal one of the harvesters the Jews had left behind on the threshing floor, and that the officer recognised Ahmad and ordered him to take off his priest's clothes and killed him. And that the priest didn't go back to the body under the tree but that an Israeli soldier pushed him and he fell and his head was cut open, so they dragged him away and killed him as well as Ahmad. And that her grandmother, who witnessed the scene, swears that Father Jibran didn't have a nephew called Tanyious and that the young man disguised in the cassock was the son of the grain measurer.

"El Bruwweh, it's gone," said Noha. "All I see are the shadows of the houses drawn in my grandmother's unsleeping eyes." This grandmother was the cause of all the trouble. "She turned my father into a stone. She turned him from a man into a stone and killed him, killed everything inside him, like mothers kill their sons and claim they love them. I lived with him. He lay there in our house like a stone."

Noha said her grandmother walked and walked until her feet swelled because when the lorry dumped them in El Jdeideh she refused to enter the village and started to search for her children. She got down from the lorry and walked. She went to El Damoun and from there to Sikhnin and from Sikhnin to El Ramah and then on to Ya'thur. In Ya'thur she found her son and his family, and they crossed over into Lebanon, where she found her four other children.

The grandmother walked alone, entering the villages and sleeping in the open. She entered the villages a stranger and left them a stranger, and all she ate was bread moistened with water. She ate so she could walk, and she walked so she could look, and she looked but she didn't find.

Noha said she was frightened by the pain etched on her grandmother's face – a woman etched with pain and stories. "She didn't love us; she loved only my father, whom she treated as though she couldn't believe he hadn't died. Every day – every day, I swear – she'd touch him all over to make sure he was still alive. She didn't want him to work; when they settled in the camp near Beirut and he found work in a chocolate factory, she said no. 'You stay in the house and we'll work,' she said. 'You're the pillar of the house, and the house will fall down without you.' My mother couldn't understand her mother-in-law – a woman stopping her son from working, not wanting him to leave the tin shack, so that no harm might come to him, while we were dying of shame and hunger? He'd sit next to his mother and they'd listen to the radio and analyse the news and whisper to one another. She'd make plans and he'd agree with her. Then they decided to go back to El Bruwweh, and so we returned."

The story as Noha related it to me was as distorted as her grandmother's memory. Noha was a child and her grandmother an old woman. The child couldn't remember, and the old woman couldn't speak. The grandmother would raise her hand and point upwards as though invoking the help of mysterious powers and all Noha would see was dust.

"I was two years old," she said, "so I remember nothing. I remember vague images, an old woman speechless in the house, my father looking at her with hatred. My father became like a stone. He would enter the house in silence and leave it in silence, so my brothers and sisters and I called him The Stone, and he was like a stone. My father spoke in 1967, after his son died in Ghour El Safi in Jordan during the battle for El Karameh, but his speech was shrouded in silence. He speaks like one who never speaks and he never raises his voice, as though he's afraid of something. My father tried many times to work. He tried at the soft-drink factory. Then he became a taxi driver, so they put him in gaol because he didn't have a work permit. He tried unsuccessfully to get that impossible permit, because as you know a Palestinian can only work in secret in Lebanon, and my father wanted to be a driver and a driver can't work in secret. He loved to drive. Since he was a child he'd loved cars, but it was difficult for him to buy one, so he decided he'd work as a driver. He wasted his life running around in pursuit of a work permit that never came. We only survived because it was easier than dying.

"My mother worked as a seamstress. She wasn't a good seamstress, but she managed to make a living with the women in the camp. She sewed a little and earned a little and we survived. The Stone would leave the house every morning and not come back till evening. He wouldn't speak to us, and he'd even refuse to eat the food we'd prepared. My mother had a relief card so she'd go at the beginning of each month to get flour, milk and cooking oil from the Agency. But he wouldn't touch it. I don't know how he got by. He wouldn't ask my mother for money, and he didn't steal as most of the men in the camp did. He'd get up at dawn, drink his coffee before we woke up and leave, and he wouldn't come back again till evening. My mother would beg him to taste a mouthful of the food she'd prepared and he'd refuse. He'd turn away, open his newspaper and read. My father wasn't illiterate – he was semi-literate and could spell out the words – but he'd learned to read from the newspapers. He'd sit and read in silence. We'd see his lips moving, but we couldn't hear a sound. He'd read without a sound and speak without a sound and come and go without a sound.

"I heard the story just from my grandmother. I thought she was rambling on like all old people, but she told me the truth.

"'We went back, daughter, but it was hopeless,'" she told me. She said they'd demolished El Bruwweh and she couldn't stand to live in any other village, so she decided to move to Lebanon again. Her son left them in the fields outside the village and went to Kafar Yaseef, then came back to tell them that they should all go there.

"'But I couldn't agree to live in Kafar Yaseef, daughter; I wanted El Bruwweh. I said we should go back and live with the El Bruwweh people that were left, go back and sow our land. What were we supposed to do for work in Kafar Yaseef? Your father said he'd met Sa'd's son who worked in the building trade, and he'd promised him a job. I said no, and I picked you up and started walking. Your mother caught up with me with your brother Amir, leaving your father standing there. He screamed at us; he wanted us to stay with him, but we left. We found him again here in the camp. I thought he'd stayed behind. I said, "Let him stay, God damn him, but I can't," and your mother caught up with me and he screamed at us, but we couldn't hear his voice, as though there was no sound coming out of his mouth. I think he caught up with us, and when we got to the camp he went into the lavatory, and then he left the house and became like a stone. Our feet were sore, and all we wanted to do was sleep, but he went out. I was right. I mean, how could we go back to El Bruwweh when we couldn't find El Bruwweh? What were we to do? Go to another village and become refugees in our own country? No, daughter.'"

Noha said she'd pieced the story of their return together from scraps of stories. She could see the scene as though she was remembering it. "Going back", her mother told her, was difficult, but people did return. "All the members of a family would suddenly disappear, and we'd know they'd gone back. Your father was like a madman, hunting for scraps of news and abusing his mother. One morning in April 1951, he told us, 'Come on, we're going back.' We didn't take anything with us. We returned as we'd left, with nothing but our clothes, two flasks of water, a bundle of bread, two kilos of boiled potatoes and ten eggs. We got a taxi to Tyre and from there another to Rimeish. From Rimeish we started our march to El Bruwweh. Going back was easy. We went around the villages and walked in the rough, The Stone walking as though on the palm of his hand – he'd stretch his hand out in front of him and read from his palm; he said he had everything written on his palm. We walked behind him in silence, your grandmother carrying you, me carrying your brother, and The Stone walking ahead of us. Finally we arrived. We'd walked the whole night, and we arrived at dawn. At the outskirts of the village, he ordered us to wait under an olive tree.

"There, The Stone started walking differently. He bent over as though he was getting ready for a fight and started leaping until he disappeared from view.

"Your grandmother was like a zombie. She wanted to go after him, but he waved her off, placing his finger on his lips to ask us to be quiet. Then he disappeared.

"As for us, what were we to do? How could I wait when I had this half-paralysed old woman with me? Suddenly your grandmother had become half paralysed. All the way there, she'd been like a horse, but at the outskirts of the village her knees gave out and she sat down pouring with sweat. She was carrying you in her arms and the sweat dripped onto you. You started crying, and I took you from her and gave you my breast. No, you weren't still breast feeding, you were two years old and I'd weaned you more than a year before, but I don't know why, I took you from her arms, dried the old woman's sweat off you and gave you my breast, and you stopped crying and fell into a deep sleep.

"The Stone came back.

"The sun was starting to set and your grandmother was sitting on her own under an isolated olive tree. She saw her son and started to stand up so she could come over to us, but she couldn't so she crawled. We helped her to sit up; her eyes were fixed on her son's lips.

"We sat around him. He drank some water, ate a boiled egg and said, 'Wait for me.' Then he disappeared into the olive grove.

"He came back the next morning and said he was going to Kafar Yaseef.

"We understood.

"The old woman bowed her head and started sobbing. I tried to question him. I asked him about my father's house – I thought, never mind; if our house has been demolished, we can go and live in my father's house. 'Listen, woman,' he said, 'I'm going to Kafar Yaseef.' And we understood. I said to him, 'They demolished all the houses, right?' And he said, 'Yes.'

"When I heard the word *yes* I fell to the ground. I couldn't see; everything had gone black. The Stone tried to bring me round.

"He explained everything to me.

"'El Bruwweh is dead,' he said. 'You wait here and I'll go.'

"He didn't wait for nightfall. He said he'd go, and he went. His head must have been hurting him because he kept putting his hands to his temples and pressing. He ordered us not to move from where we were.

"We waited for three days and nights. It was the cold time in April, and we had only brought two woollen blankets. The four of us slept underneath them, the old woman shivering and talking in her sleep. No, we weren't hungry. I had bread with me, and your grandmother gathered thyme and plants from the land and we ate.

'On the third night the old woman disappeared.

"I woke up and didn't find her with us under the blankets. I searched for her, but she'd disappeared.

"When The Stone came back, I told him his mother had disappeared. He'd come to tell us that we had to go to Kafar Yaseef in the night: El Bruwweh had been destroyed, and they'd built the Jewish settlement of Achihud on top of it. Kafar Yaseef was the solution.

"He asked about his mother, so I told him I'd looked for her in the fields, where she'd gone to gather thyme, and couldn't find her.

"'She's there,' he said. 'I know her. I'll go and get her, and don't you move from here.'

"I wanted to tell him not to go, but I didn't dare. Can you tell someone to abandon his mother? I begged him to wait for night to fall, but he didn't answer. He left and didn't come back until sunset. He said he'd seen her and she'd refused to come back with him. She was sitting alone on top of the ruins.

"A ruined village, and a woman sitting on top of the remains of her house, and a man trying to persuade her to go with him, and her not answering. He talked to her and she remained silent. He asked her and she paid no attention.

"He said he'd told her about Kafar Yaseef, that he'd found a house and that everything would be all right, but she said no.

"He slept with us that night, got up at dawn and brought her. He brought her like a prisoner and said, 'Now let's go to Kafar Yaseef.' I started getting ready. I folded the blankets and was checking around the huge olive tree among whose roots we'd been sleeping when I heard the old woman say, 'No' and saw her pick you up and start walking in the direction of Lebanon."

Noha said her grandmother had told her about three young men who'd approached her and how they'd pelted her with stones. She'd told them she was so-and-so, the daughter of so-and-so and that this was her house, so they'd pelted her with stones.

"'I told them I was staying.

"'I told them this was my house, why did you destroy my house?

"I told them they were stupid because they'd cut down so many olive trees.

"I told them these were Roman olive trees and how could anyone dare to cut down Christ's olive trees? These were Father Jibran's olive trees.

"'I told them lots of things.'

"She said she told them she didn't care – 'You took the land – take it. You took the fields and the olives and everything else – take them. But I want to live here. I'll put up a tent and live here. It's better than the camp. The air is clean here. Take everything and leave me the air.'

"The three young men backed away and started throwing stones at her.

"'They were afraid,' she said.

"The stones started raining down on her and piled up around her and she became a mass of wounds.

"She said they spoke Arabic to her. They spoke like the Yemeni headman she'd met in 1947 when she went into the Jewish settlement near Tiberias by mistake: 'To begin with, they came over to me and seemed nice. They weren't aggressive. But when I told them I was so-and-so, daughter of so-and-so, they began moving away. One step back for every word I said. Then suddenly they all bent over as if they'd received some kind of signal, and the stones started raining down.'

"The old woman sat under the olive tree and my mother went to get a rag and a flask of water so she could clean the old woman's wounds. At the same time The Stone was telling them about Kafar Yaseef and the house Sa'd's son had found and the job in his workshop. He said, 'We're here now and we can't go back to Lebanon.' He said, 'We'll live in Kafar Yaseef, then we'll see.' He talked and talked and talked; the old woman sat on the ground looking into the distance. She didn't tell them what had happened to her. She didn't say she'd tried to talk to the Yemenis. She didn't say she'd talked about a tent she was going to put up in the ruins of El Bruwweh. She was like a tree with its branches broken. Suddenly she got up, picked me up and set off in the direction of Lebanon."

Noha's mother said she'd caught up with her mother-in-law. "I took your brother by the hand and we started running after her. The Stone stood like a stone. And we found ourselves in the camp."

What do you make of Noha's story, master?

Naturally, Noha didn't describe her grandmother as looking like a tree with its branches broken. I added that detail to convey how the old woman looked, her psychological state and her bleeding wounds. Noha wasn't that interested in the story; she just told it to me when she was explaining her own situation. She doesn't believe in the possibility of our returning to Palestine. "If we go back, we won't find Palestine, we'll find another country. Why are we fighting and dying? Should we be fighting for something only to find ourselves somewhere else? It would be better to marry and emigrate."

Noha cried a lot when her grandmother died. She told me how her father started to speak after his son was martyred in the battle of El Karameh. She said that even though he didn't talk, he didn't stop fathering children.

"Wouldn't you agree the man was a bit strange – not talking to his wife but sleeping with her every night?" I tried to ask Noha about her grandmother's story, but she said she didn't know and didn't care. She loved Egyptian soap operas and said she had to get out of this cesspit; she called the camp a cesspit. Her father, whom I met numerous times at their house, was very nice to me. He was a strange man, eyes hanging vacantly in his face, always clicking his prayer beads and talking about everything. He knew a lot about agriculture, medicine, politics and Palestinian history. He talked to me a lot about my father, about how his was the first calamity in the camp.

In fact I wanted to marry Noha, but then I don't know what happened. I started to feel stifled when I was with her. We couldn't find anything to talk about. She'd tell me about her soap operas and their heroes and I'd feel immensely bored. Even my desire for those little pecks on her lips began to fade.

I never told you the story of Noha and her grandmother before because I thought it wouldn't interest you. You didn't talk about the past except incidentally; the past would come up in the form of illustrative examples, not as lived reality. Then you were transformed into the unique symbol in the stories of the camp people, the symbol of those who kept slipping back there. You know you weren't the only man who'd go over there and come back. Thousands went, and maybe some of them are still going over now. I know at least three cases of married men whose stories are like yours. They go over, leave their women pregnant and come back to the camp. The story that intrigued me was Hamad's. I won't tell it to you now because I'm tired, and the woman of El Bruwweh has wrung out my heart.

The first time I heard the story from Noha, it made no impact on me. I was absorbed by the story of The Stone and paid no attention to the grandmother. Now it occurs to me, master, that that woman (who was called Khadijeh) was remarkable. I wish I'd known her better: I only saw her once, when she was sick. A woman I saw only once but who I think was more beautiful than her granddaughter who tried to seduce me into marriage.

I forget to mention that Noha was white, whiter than any woman I've ever seen. Her skin was so white that the whiteness almost seemed to be bursting out from inside her. She thought she was beautiful just because she was so white. She was a bit short and plump, but her whiteness made up for everything.

I was taken by her whiteness, I won't deny it, but I never discovered beauty till I met Shams. It was then that I found out the meaning of "wheat-coloured". That brown shading into yellow is *the* colour because it undulates infinitely. Noha's whiteness, on the other hand, blocked my spirit – no, I'm talking through my hat, saying anything that comes into my head. Please don't believe that stuff about whiteness – I'm not against white, but I did suddenly stop loving her. All my feelings evaporated, and when I looked at her I could no longer see her. I only felt anything for her at the stadium, when I stood there with hundreds of fedayeen waiting for the Greek ships that were to take them from Beirut into their new exile. I searched for her there but couldn't find her. Do you know what that feeling is like – to leave when there's no-one to bid you farewell?

I searched for her and didn't leave. I went back to my house, not because she didn't come and not because I wanted her; I went back because I felt everything was meaningless. Everything had lost its meaning, so I couldn't bring myself to go away with everyone else; a journey has to be more than just a journey, and I noticed, after the siege and all the waste, that I wasn't capable of such things. So I returned to my house and never saw Noha again and forgot her. I forgot what that girl I'd loved looked like. Now, when I try to recall her, I see her as a trembling image, a shapeless woman. I see her white face, and I see her lips quivering on the verge of tears, and I see her grandmother Khadijeh.

I think, master, that I fell in love with Noha in the shape of her grandmother.

Imagine the woman of El Bruwweh with me.

A woman walking alone through the rubble of her village looking for the stones that were her house. A woman alone, her head covered with a black scarf, hunched over on herself in that emptiness that stretches all the way to God, among the hills and valleys of Galilee, within the circle of a red sun that crawls over the ground, passing slowly and carrying with it the shadows of all things.

All the woman saw was shadows. She sat down alone, and they came and she spoke to them. It may be that she didn't say the exact words her granddaughter recounted to me. Maybe she said something else, and maybe they didn't understand her language.

Noha said they were Yemenis, and Yemenis understand the Palestinian dialect, or a lot of its words anyway. But probably they didn't understand anything. When she spoke they were terrified, because they thought she was a spirit who'd come out of the tree, and they started to throw stones at her. They were just adolescents, so they didn't call the Border Guard from the kibbutz that had been built on top of El Bruwweh.

Maybe. I don't know.

Anything's possible.

But why wouldn't she agree to go to Kafar Yaseef?

Was it because . . . ?

She probably regretted it afterwards, so she didn't tell her story to anyone, unlike Umm Hassan, who never stopped telling people the story of the woman of Wadi Abu Jameel.

The woman of El Bruwwch said nothing.

And I'm telling you now to prove that you weren't the only hero, or only living martyr.

Don't worry, you'll die in peace. But I want you to know before you die that this protracted death of yours has turned our life upside down. Did you have to fall into this death for your memory, and mine, and everyone else's, to explode? You've been stricken with a brain storm, and I'm stricken with a storm of memories.

You're dying, and I'm dying.

God, it's not about Shams, or Dr Amjad, or this Beirut that no longer looks like Beirut. It's to do with me staying here and starting work in the hospital tomorrow. Don't be scared. I won't leave you. I'll continue to work with you as usual and tell you stories and the news.

Think about me a bit, and you'll see I can't take it any more.

True, nobody cares any more. Nobody believes anyone any more. Those who'd got used to me as a doctor will get used to me as a nurse. But me – how can I adjust to this new me I'm being forced to accept?

We'll find out tomorrow.

But before tomorrow comes, and before the hospital, I want you to tell me who the woman of Sha'ab was.

I want the story from you. I've heard it dozens of times from different people, but I'm not convinced. In Ein El Hilweh camp I got to know Mohammed El Khateeb, who claimed that the woman of Sha'ab was his mother, Fatimah. Then I met a man from the Fa'our clan who said his mother, who was called Salma, was the woman of Sha'ab. And then of course there's that legend about the woman called Reem, to whom the story became attached.

Let's go back to the beginning.

You went back to Ein El Zeitoun only to find the village demolished. At that point you were with Abu Is'af on a mission to carry weapons to Galilee from Syria. I don't want to hear now about the humiliations you suffered trying to find weapons and about how Colonel Safwat treated you like shit, saying you weren't a regular army and that he wasn't about to throw away the few weapons he had on peasants, who were known for their cowardice and slyness.

That was how the "general of the defeat", as he'd become known to the fighters who withdrew to Lebanon to the beat of the Arab leaders' mendacious war drums, talked to you.

You returned, you and Abu Is'af, bringing nothing with you. You left Abu Is'af in Sha'ab and continued to Ein El Zeitoun, discovering that the village had fallen without a shot being fired, and that your friend and twin Hanna Kameel Mousa had died crucified on an oak tree.

You all ended up in Sha'ab, and you only left after the whole of Galilee had fallen.

Now tell me about the woman. I know that the story of the Palestine of your generation is a difficult one and that we can find a thousand ways to tell it, but Sha'ab, and that woman, and the men of Zubouba – I want to hear about them from you.

You left Ein El Zeitoun and went running to Sha'ab. You told me you ran there even though you went by car. What matters is that you got hold of a house in Sha'ab because the headman, Mohammed Ali El Khateeb, gave it to you, telling you he'd built it for his son Ali, and that Ali and Yunis were one.

Sha'ab became your new village, and it was there that you saw the miracle.

I don't want to hear the history of the village, because I'm not interested in the brawl that broke out between the Fa'our and Khateeb clans in 1935 and how it grew during the Revolution of '36, when the Khateeb clan took revenge for the murder of Shakir El Khateeb by killing Rasheed El Fa'our, headman of the eastern quarter, and how all of you – you were still a young man – took action. You came with the fighters of the Revolution and imposed a settlement, which was concluded on the threshing floor, where they slaughtered more than four head of sheep and people came from all the villages in the area to eat and offer their congratulations.

I don't want to get into the labyrinth of families and sub-clans about which I understand nothing. I know you always cited the example of the Sha'ab settlement when you were conducting training courses for fighters. Instead of theorising about the Sha'ab war, as we did, you'd tell stories and cite examples. And instead of asserting that family and tribalism had to be transcended, you'd explain to the fighters how you succeeded during the '36 Revolution in fusing families together, and you'd cite the example of Sha'ab.

You'd tell them about the moon.

Your moon wasn't my mother's full moon; your moon never became full. I think I read the fable of the moon in a Chinese book translated into Arabic, but it sounded more beautiful coming from your mouth than from any book: "The moon is full only one day a month. On all the other days it's either getting bigger or smaller. Life's the same. Stability is the exception, change the rule." You'd ask the boys to follow the movement of the moon on training nights so they could get some practical political culture instead of book culture, which goes in at the eye and out at the ear.

Now tell me about Sha'ab.

Was it Abu Is'af who made the arrangements with the headman for you to have a house, the leader of the Sha'ab garrison thus guaranteeing that you'd stay with him?

You found yourself in the Sha'ab garrison after you'd failed — yes, failed — to form the mobile military unit you'd dreamed of. The war was speeding up, and the Arab armies that entered Palestine in 1948 were being defeated by the larger, better-armed Israeli Army in record time. God, who'd have believed it? Six hundred thousand Israelis assembled an army larger than all seven Arab armies put together!

You started military patrols, you begged weapons, you took part in the battles of El Bruwweh and El Zeeb, but the rapid fall of the villages and hamlets of Galilee made it impossible for you to move and turned you into a garrison of not more than two hundred fighters centred on the little village called Sha'ab. Later, the garrison would end up in prison in Syria, and its heroic deeds would disappear among the flood of displaced people who invaded the fields and groves.

All the stories of the displacement have collected in your eyes — shut over the tear drops I put in them — and in place of heroism I see sorrow and hear the voice of my grandmother telling about the woman who sewed up the loaf. I'm listening to the story of the woman in the fields of Beit Jann and I see my grandmother, like a mime, screwing up her eyes so she can put the imaginary thread into the eye of the imaginary needle, then take the imaginary loaf in her hand, divide it in two and start to sew it up.

"The woman sewed the loaf, and the boy was crying. She gave him the whole loaf and asked him to be quiet, but he tore it into two halves and went on crying. At which point the mother killed her son!"

I see the displacements in your eyes and I hear my grandmother's voice, which has changed to a low mutter full of ghosts.

"We reached Beit Jann, but we didn't go into the Druze village because we were afraid."

She tells me about fear and the Druze, and I swallow the pitta bread stuffed with fried potatoes and feel the potatoes sticking to the roof of my mouth, as though I'm going to suffocate.

No, I'm not complaining about the potatoes – they were my favourite food. I loved fried potatoes and still do. They were incomparably better than the boiled plants my grandmother cooked. She'd leave the camp I don't know where for and come back loaded down with all kinds of greens, wash them, cook them, and we'd eat. The taste was – how can I describe it? – a green taste, and the stew would make a lump in my mouth. My grandmother would say this was healthy food: "We're peasants, and this is peasant food." I'd beg her to fry me some potatoes; the smell of potatoes gives you an appetite, but those cooked weeds had no smell and gave you no appetite; it felt as if you were chewing something that had already been chewed.

You don't like fried potatoes, I know. You prefer them grilled and seasoned with olive oil. Now I've come to like olive oil, but when my grandmother, who cooked everything in olive oil, was around it felt sticky to me and I didn't like it, but I couldn't say so in front of her. How can you say what you think to a woman when she doesn't see it? She used to live here as though she was over there. Can you believe it? She refused to use electricity because she hadn't had it in her village and didn't want to get used to things that didn't exist there because she was going to go back! If only she'd known what Galilee had become! But she died before she knew anything.

You won't believe the story of the loaf, and you didn't believe the story of Umm Hassan and Naji, whom she picked up and put in the basin. You believe, as I'd like to, that we don't kill our children and toss them under trees. You like things clear and simple. The murderer is a known quantity, likewise the person killed, and it's up to us to see that justice is done. Unfortunately, master, it wasn't as simple as "them" and "us". It was something different that's hard to define.

I'm not here to define things. I have a mission. As usual I'll fail, and as usual I won't believe I've failed, and I'll claim I succeeded or put the blame on others. How stupid habit is; if only we could kill it! If only I could be rid of this past that hovers like a blue ghost in your room! Come to think of it, why do I see things as blue? Why do I see Shams looking at me with a blue face as though she was about to kill me?

If I could, I'd go to Shams's family and tell them the truth and let them do what they want. I'm innocent of her murder, and of her love, and of everything, because I'm an imbecile. If I hadn't been made a fool of . . . everything would have changed.

Tell me, who in the Shams story wasn't made a fool of?

The whore killed him. She told him, "I give myself to you in marriage," and then she killed him.

She loved him and he loved her, but like me he felt the woman would slip out of his hands. Is it possible for a man to marry a woman who leaves someone else's bed to go to him?

Why did she kill him?

Was the fact that he'd lied to her enough to make her kill him?

We all lie, so it really was unreasonable. Just imagine – if the penalty for lying was death, there'd be no-one left alive on the surface of the Earth.

Now I've started to doubt everything. I no longer believe it was a matter of honour. Shams is the first woman in the history of the Arab nation to kill a man because he was unfaithful to her.

But slow down . . .

Did she kill him?

They said she killed him in front of everybody. Everyone saw her, but does that mean anything? What if everyone's lying? What if everyone just believed what other people, passing on what they'd heard from others, told them?

No, that's impossible. If that were believable, my whole life would turn into an unbearable lie. But she was a liar anyway. Shams lied to me, and everyone lies to me now and passes death threats on to me. And I'm afraid of a lie. When you're afraid of a lie, it means your life is a lie, wouldn't you agree?

I'm scared and I hide in the hospital, and the memories pour down on me and I have no idea what to do with them. What do you say to a novel-writing project? I know you'll tell me I don't know how to write novels. I agree, and I'd add that no-one knows how to write because anything you say comes apart when you write it down and turns into symbols and signs, cold and lifeless. Writing, master, is confusion; tell me, who can write the confusions of life? It's a state between life and death that no-one dares enter. I would never dare enter that state unless it were to say that, like all doctors and failures, I'd become a writer. Do you know why Chekhov wrote? Because he was a failed doctor. I imagine that by becoming a writer he was able to find a solution to his crisis. I'm not like him; I'm a successful doctor, and everyone will see how I was able to rescue you from the Valley of Death.

I'm certain she killed him, because I know her and I know how death shone in her eyes. I used to think it was love that changed her eyes from grey to green, then back to grey, but it was death. Grey-green is the colour of death. Shams used to talk about death because she knew it. But not my grandmother.

Shaheeneh didn't dare say the child had died. She said they went by Beit Jann and were afraid. The airplanes were hovering above their heads, and when night fell their journey to Lebanon began.

My grandmother said she found herself in a group of about thirty people wandering the hills looking for the Lebanese border. She didn't say how she came to find herself among women, old men and children from the village of El Safsaf. "Me, my daughter and my son walked with them. I don't know how we ended up in that terrified group. We were afraid, but we weren't like them. When they spoke they whispered. When we got to Beit Jann, they refused to go into the place. Their leader said they'd rob us and ordered us to continue marching. I told him not to be afraid, and he told me to shut up and we left. When we got to Lebanon, we'd lost our voices because the old man had made us whisper so much."

It seems that my grandmother's voice became husky on that journey. I forgot to tell you that my grandmother had this husky voice, as if it was coming out of a well deep inside her, which made it seem broad and full of holes.

"The child began crying from hunger; a child of three or four years of age crying to say it was hungry, while everybody looked askance at its mother and asked her to make it shut up, and the woman didn't know what to do. She picked it up and started shushing it, but it went on crying. And the old man . . . I can't forget that old man."

My grandmother always used the old man of El Safsaf to scare me. When I refused to eat her greens, she'd tell me she'd ask the old man of El Safsaf to come at night and strangle me, and I'd be scared and chew my pre-chewed food.

She said she realised why they were so terrified when they reached Tarshiha. There their fear disappeared and they ate and wept, and the old man told the story of the white sheets.

"We received them with white sheets. We went out carrying the sheets as a sign of surrender, but they started firing over our heads. Then they ordered us to gather in the square. They chose sixty men of different ages, tied their hands with rope and stood them in a row. Sixty men of different ages standing like a wall threaded together by a rope that linked their hands, which were tied behind their backs. Then they started firing. The sound of the machine guns deafened us, and the men dropped, and the people gathered in the square fled into the fields. Death enveloped us."

"After we reached Tarshiha, he became a different man," said my grandmother, "but on the road, during those silent nights, he was a monster. A tall, thin man with a hunchback. His moustache looked as if it had been drawn with a pen. His hair was grey, his moustache black, and he ordered us about furiously. We could see the sinews of his small, veiny hands as he motioned to us to be silent."

My grandmother said she gave the mother the one loaf she had hidden underneath her dress. She said she was afraid of the old man because he was determined to kill the child if he went on crying. The woman tried to make her son shut up – holding his hand, lifting him up, carrying him, putting him back down on the ground, letting him walk between her legs – but the child went on crying. The woman took the round loaf from my grandmother and divided it into two halves. She gave her son half and gave the other half back to my grandmother. But the boy refused; he wanted a whole loaf and started crying again. The old man came over and took hold of his clothes and started shaking him. My grandmother rushed to give her half of the loaf to the mother, who gave it to her son. But the boy wanted a whole loaf, not two halves. The woman put the two halves together, extracted a needle and thread from the front of her dress, inserted the thread in the eye of the needle and started sewing up the loaf.

My grandmother said she saw things as though they were enveloped in shadows. The meagre crescent moon that would slip out from among the branches of the trees turned people into colliding shadows. And I listen to the story and am scared of my grandmother's husky voice which swallows up the scene and makes it a story of genies and afreets.

The woman sewed up the loaf and gave it to the boy, and he stopped crying. He took his loaf happily until he discovered that it wasn't a loaf. For the woman had sewn it quickly in the dark and not made the stitches tight. The boy took his loaf and the stitches started to pull apart, the gap between the two halves widening. And he started to cry again. He held the loaf up to give back to his mother and cried.

The old man came over, took the loaf, put it in his mouth and started gobbling it down. He swallowed more than half the loaf along with the thread and went up to the woman.

"Kill it," he hissed.

"Throw it down the well," said a woman's voice from within the dark, shadowed crowd.

"Give it to me. I'll take care of it," said the old man.

He went towards the child, whose screams grew louder and louder. The woman took a wool blanket, wrapped her son in it and picked him up. She put his head on her shoulder and kept pushing him down onto it as she walked, stifling the child's cries with the blanket. The old man walked behind them; my grandmother said the old man walked behind the woman and kept pushing the child's head down onto its mother's shoulder.

In Tarshiha the mother put her son down on the ground. She pulled back the blanket and started weeping. The child was all blue.

The old man changed when they reached the last Palestinian village and started looking for his daughter, eagerly asking people about a short, fat woman with five children.

My grandmother said the people of Tarshiha brought them food, but the man refused to eat. He became a different person. The veins disappeared from his face and his hands, his body slumped, and he started weeping and asking to die.

"And the child?" I asked.

"What child?"

"The child with the loaf."

"I don't know."

She said she didn't know, though she knew the boy had died.

Its mother killed it – do you hear, father? – its mother killed it because she was afraid of the old man, who was afraid of the Jews. The mother didn't carry her child on her breast, and she didn't support his head on her shoulder the way my grandmother told me. She wrapped him in the blanket and sat on him till he died.

That's the way our relative Umm Fawzi told me the story. Umm Fawzi said they walked for five days without a sound so the Jews wouldn't hear them, and when the boy cried its mother killed it because the old man threatened to kill them both.

"Umm Fawzi's raving," said my grandmother.

You'll say I'm raving too because you don't like hearing the story about the boy, or the story about the people of Saliheh, who were executed wrapped in their bed sheets. The Jews wrapped more than seventy men in the white sheets they'd been carrying as a sign of surrender and fired on them, and the sheets spurted blood.

You don't want to hear about anything except heroism, and you think you're the "heroes' hero". Listen then to the story of another hero, a mixture of you and your father, a hero who didn't fight. A man from a village called Mee'ar. It's close to your new village. His name was Rakan Abboud.

When Mee'ar fell, the man refused to leave his village and stayed on, with his wife, after the rest of his family had gone. This is what Nadia told me. Do you know Nadia? Didn't you meet her? She was in charge of the People's Committee in the camp. Nadia said the Jews drove her grandfather out along with two other men from the village three months after they'd occupied it. The two men died on the road, near Jenin, but Nadia's grandfather, who was in his eighties, went to Aleppo and stayed with someone he knew there. Then he joined Nadia's father in Baalbek camp.

"My grandfather was an unbearable man," said Nadia. "He hated Baalbek. He hated its snow and its cold weather. He used to scream that he didn't want to die there, so my father decided to move to the camp at Burj El Shamali near Tyre. We lived in a shack there, like everyone else. His condition got frighteningly worse. He'd go out at night and only come back at dawn. Then he informed my father that he'd decided to go back to Mee'ar to look for his wife. That was in 1950, and we were waiting. All my father did was listen to the radio and set dates for the Return. Each month he'd say our time would come next month. My father tried to stop him and begged him to wait one more month, but the man had made up his mind. He went off secretly and hired a guide and a donkey and left.

"He made it to his house – imagine! – knocked on the door, and a woman opened it. The poor man thought she must be a spirit and ran off, tripping over himself, and left Mee'ar, never to return. He spent what remained of his life in the fields. My grandmother, who lived in Majd El Kuroum, found out and began her long search for him. She looked for him for more than a year before she found him. When she found him, the poor man had completely lost his sight, so she took him to Majd El Kuroum, where he died."

Nadia went on at great length about how her grandfather died. She told how he lived his last days like a thief, a blind, infirm thief. Despite this, his wife had to hide him from the police so he wouldn't be expelled like others who'd got back in. He'd gone to see his village and his wife, but he saw nothing. He lived in secret, and his presence was made public only when he died.

Blind and infirm, living in secret – but when he died, people wept openly. All those people who'd now become the people of Majd El Kuroum wept. You know the villages aren't the old villages any more: they've become full of abandoned houses and houses lived in by refugees from other villages, and the people are all mixed together. The people in Majd El Kuroum didn't know the blind old man. They knew that

Fathiyyeh Abboud was hiding "Lebanon" in her house. They called him Lebanon because he'd slipped in from there. When the secret got out, the whole village wept for the blind man. He hadn't died in his own house surrounded by children and grandchildren; he hadn't died, as everyone dies, wrapped in trivial memories. He went back and died in the secrecy of that town that lived under the secrecy of military rule, and curfew, and the footprints of those who slipped back in.

"That was a blind old man, nothing like me," you'll say. "I didn't go back to end my life wrapped in memories. I went back to start again, to remember the way, so I could love my wife."

Nice words, master, and everything you say is correct. And I'm not going to talk to you about the beginnings of the fedayeen, which coincided with your journeys to Deir El Asad and your repeated fathering of children.

Tell me, how did Sha'ab fall?

Very well, tell me how Sha'ab didn't fall.

Without heroics, please. I've put the question to you to find out who the woman of Sha'ab was.

Naheeleh, or who?

Who was that woman who stood up six days after the village fell and said she was going to go back? The men tried to stop her, but she left and you had to catch up with her.

Did people get confused and mix up the woman who carried a jerry can of arak on her head with the woman who led them in liberating their village?

And why didn't you tell me about the smuggling of arak? Because it was shameful? What's shameful about smuggling arak from Lebanon to Palestine? Is it because you don't want to acknowledge that the Lebanese arak they make in Zahleh is the best in the world? Or are you embarrassed because the smugglers made use of the Revolution of '36 and became revolutionaries in their own way?

Reem belonged to the Sa'd family, which was famous for smuggling. It was the smugglers' sheikh, Hassan Sa'd, who came up with the brilliant idea of smuggling arak on women's heads. He'd put jerry cans of arak on the heads of the women, who looked just as though they were carrying water.

The column set off, crossed the Lebanese border and came to the outskirts of Tarshiha. The column was composed of eight women in long peasant dresses and, for protection, three armed men, Hassan Sa'd at their head.

A column of eight women, moving rhythmically as though they were coming from the well, armed men at the rear, and Hassan Sa'd about three hundred metres ahead, to scout out the unpaved road joining Tarshiha to El Kabri.

Hassan came back suddenly, having spotted a British patrol. He ordered the women to scatter in the fields, and the women began to run. All of them ran except Reem. It appears she was paralysed with fear. Hassan yelled, but Reem stayed frozen to the spot. Hassan pulled out his revolver and fired at the jerry can. Reem started running, the arak pouring down over her face and clothes. Then she fell. Apparently she'd drunk a large quantity of the arak, or perhaps it was just the fumes. The girl staggered and fell. Hassan tried to hold her up, but he couldn't, so he left her and hid in the field by the road. Having heard the shot, the patrol approached and found the girl awash in arak. They tried to question her and searched at the sides of the road but didn't find anyone. One of the soldiers went over to her, held out his hand to help her up . . . and shots rang out. Hassan had seen the soldier going up to Reem so he fired, and battle was joined.

This is where accounts differ.

Some people say Hassan killed three members of the patrol and took Reem and fled with her to Sha'ab, others that Hassan fired into the air so no-one was hit, and all that happened was that the soldiers retreated, thinking they'd fallen into an ambush set by the revolutionaries. This is what allowed Reem to escape and reach Hassan, even though she tripped over her long, wet dress.

Hassan became a hero. When he arrived at the village, he was treated like a revolutionary.

Even Reem believed in his heroism and fell in love with him. Their love persisted for more than five years, Reem's father refusing to marry his daughter to her smuggler cousin and Reem refusing marriage to any other groom. Things reached an unexpected conclusion when Reem broke all the traditions and declared in front of everybody in the reception room of the headman of the Western Quarter, Shakir El Khateeb, that she loved Hassan and would never belong to anyone else. The old story of blood feuding would have been repeated if Abu Is'af hadn't intervened by claiming that Hassan had become a Holy Warrior and that he would stand guarantor for his becoming a reformed character.

And Reem married her hero Hassan.

Reem of the jerry can full of arak became Reem the heroine. Incredible as it may seem, most people attribute the decision to return to Sha'ab to her.

The truth, on the other hand . . .

Please tell me, wasn't Naheeleh the woman of Sha'ab?

Naheeleh stood up. She was like someone whose patience has run out – a woman faced at every turn by a blind man and his wife – and took her unweaned son in her arms. Her first village had been demolished, and her second had been occupied.

Naheeleh stood up, and Reem joined her.

But why did people say it was Reem?

Was it because that woman who'd carried the jerry can of arak and staggered under the shot fired by the man she loved lost everything the moment they entered the village?

Her husband, Hassan, was the first to join her, and he was the first martyr.

Reem was at the front beside Naheeleh, and Hassan was behind them. He was the first to attack and the first to die. On that day in July 1948, Reem came to the end. After the village was liberated and her husband died, she took her three children and went to Deir El Asad. From there she fled to Syria, and nothing more was heard of her. She lived in Yarmouk camp outside Damascus and ceased to be of interest to all of you.

The question that puzzles me is: Why did everybody forget all the other stories but remember Reem at the instant the decision to enter the village was made?

They forgot Hassan the smuggler-martyr, they forgot Naheeleh, who led the march, and they forgot you too. There's no mention of you at the battle of Sha'ab. Nobody ever told me anything about you. They all said you were there, but you weren't what people were interested in. What they were interested in was your father, the blind sheikh, who refused to leave again after the village had been liberated. He said he couldn't leave because he had responsibilities at the mosque. You begged him to leave, and he refused. You begged him and you begged your mother and you begged Naheeleh. The decision you'd taken was clear: no-one but militiamen were to stay behind in Sha'ab; the residents were to take their belongings and leave, because it was no longer possible to live in the village, which was under constant fire from the Jews concentrated at Mee'ar.

But your father refused, and then he refused again when you decided to withdraw to Lebanon.

Let's get back to Sha'ab.

I'll try to put together the fragments I've heard from you and from others. When I make a mistake, correct me. I won't start at the beginning because I'm not like you. I can't say "in the beginning".

I'll start after the fall of El Bruwweh, and with the story of Mustafa El Tayyar.

After you'd mobilised your men and matériel, you liberated El Bruwweh, seizing weapons, ammunition and harvesters. Then Mahdi, the commanding officer of the ALA detachment, surrounded you and yelled, "Everything on the ground!" He wanted to confiscate the weapons and claim he was the hero of the liberation.

You were dumbstruck. The battle of El Bruwweh was your first offensive. You'd tried to co-ordinate your fire and organise the assault; you'd put great effort into mobilisation and you were exhausted from the victory, your first; and along comes this officer whose soldiers hadn't fired a single bullet and yells, "Everything on the ground"!

Up jumped Mustafa El Tayyar, a fighter from El Bruwweh who'd die in the last battle, between the Yemeni volunteers and the Israeli Army, which took place on the hills of El Kabri.

El Tayyar jumped up and yelled, "We're the Arabs and you're the Jews," and threw himself to the ground holding the machine gun Ali Hassan El Jammal had pulled out of the Jewish redoubt during the battle.

The Iraqi sergeant Dandan intervened and said, "This won't do. Arabs don't fight Arabs." He prevented a massacre. Things were worked out, and they took half the weapons.

Mahdi came back afterwards and convinced you to leave El Bruwweh

and hand it over to the ALA. And you were persuaded! You abandoned
El Bruwweh only for it to be surrendered to the Jews twenty-four hours
later without a fight. And Dandan stands up and says, "Arabs don't fight
Arabs"! Poor people! Say you agreed with Mahdi because you were
incapable of staying, because you were exhausted and the village was
surrounded on all sides, so you abandoned it before the ALA did the
same.

After El Bruwweh fell, you only had Sha'ab.

And Sha'ab didn't survive either.

On 21 July 1948, the shelling of Sha'ab began, from the direction of
El Bruwweh. Then an infantry unit advanced from Mee'ar and swept
through the village. The first shelling was intermittent but accurate. Ten
minutes after the first shell fell on the threshing floors, the second one
fell on the houses of Ali Mousa and Rasheed El Hajj Hassan and destroyed
them. The villagers started fleeing in all directions. In the chaos, everyone
found themselves outside the village except for a small group of fighters
concentrated in El Abbasiyyeh on the eastern side.

On 21 July Sha'ab fell for the first time, without a fight!

The ALA, concentrated in Tell El Layyat, Majd El Kuroum and El
Ramah, didn't intervene. It seems the Israeli attack took everyone by
surprise. War was everywhere, and it took you by surprise!

The village collapsed before its defenders fired a single shot, and the
Jews got in.

You said you lived those six days in the fields and could see Sha'ab
from a distance. It was as though it had fallen into the valley – Sha'ab is
hemmed in by hills on all sides – and had become a Valley of Death.
After the fall of El Bruwweh and Mee'ar, Sha'ab was under fire and the
only way to protect it was by concerted military action. Abu Is'af tried
to organise the fighters. He divided them into four detachments and
assigned each one the task of protecting one of the village borders, but
he didn't leave a central emergency force.

Practically speaking, there was no battle.

The shelling and screaming caused terrible confusion among the peasants and the fighters, and the battle ended before it had begun.

In the fields, the Sha'ab fighters discovered they were impotent.
Attempts at surveillance and infiltration were useless. "We can't attack,"

said Abu Is'af, "without preparatory shelling, and we don't have any artillery." He assigned the task of contacting the ALA to assure artillery support to you.

Yunis went to Tell El Layyat and entered into impossible negotiations with Mahdi and Jasim. Every plan he proposed was rejected on the grounds that it would cause huge losses to both peasants and fighters.

"I suggested an attack from Tell El Layyat, and they said the artillery at Mee'ar would wipe us out. I suggested an attack from the fields to the east, and they said they'd discover us and wipe us out before we arrived. I suggested that the ALA unit move to give the impression that the attack would come from their positions while we attacked from the east, and they said they had no order to move. All my plans were refused, and their suggestion was to reflect and wait. I told them, 'You're the army. You propose something and we'll do it.' They said, 'Of course, but we're waiting for orders.' I said we couldn't stand about waiting. They said, 'In war, you have to obey orders.'

"I said, they said . . . My mission ended in failure. I went back to the field where everyone was waiting for me. Everybody thought I'd come back carrying the order to liberate Sha'ab in my pocket. When I told them, their faces darkened and they made no comment, as though I was telling them about some other village."

The table for breaking the fast was set out at sunset – hungry, poor and fasting.

When I ask you about the meal they provided, you'll tell me you were tired and not hungry. You'll tell me you never used to feel real hunger unless you were with her, after you'd made love to her in the cave of Bab El Shams, but on ordinary days you didn't feel hungry, you ate just to fill your stomach. On that day, however, you did try to eat from that empty table. There was almost nothing – greens and weeds. There wasn't even any bread.

Perhaps that was the reason.

Why didn't you tell me the Jews attacked Sha'ab precisely at sunset in the month of Ramadan, as the villagers were around their tables, breaking their fast? The shelling started, your defences collapsed, and you were defeated. Hungry, you fled to the fields in that terrible chaos; then, as you were leaving, you saw the flames springing up in the middle of the village. You thought they were burning the village, and this added to your panic and drove you out into the neighbouring fields.

When Yunis got back, he found everyone eating. He was hungry, but he didn't eat. He put his hand out, and before the food reached his mouth, he threw it down and said, "We'll attack on our own." There followed a long, noisy, involved discussion about military plans, but there wasn't a plan. Only Yunis's blind father said, "There's no hope. Everything's lost." People saw the tears falling from his closed eyes while the gathering broke up without a decision. That night everyone slept like the dead, even those who'd taken it upon themselves to act as guards; in the face of the despair, the fear and the hunger, only the door of sleep remained open.

In the morning, the two women were struck by something resembling madness.

They were discussing ways of getting water from the spring, when suddenly a cry went up and everyone saw Naheeleh and Reem leaving.

Naheeleh said she couldn't take it any longer.

Reem said death would be more honourable.

The other women set off behind them. Abu Is'af and Khaleel Sileiman Abd El Mu'ti tried to stop them, but they were like a torrent that sweeps everything before it.

"At the outskirts of the village, the firing started. We attacked without a plan. We were running and firing at random. It wasn't a battle, it was like a Bedouin brawl, and we found ourselves in the village with the Jews gone. A few of our people were dead, first among them Reem's Hassan. If you want me to describe the battle, I can't because it wasn't a battle, it was a charge. We got back into the village in less than an hour. Afterwards we found out that Dandan's group of Yemeni and Iraqi volunteers had mutinied when we started our attack and opened fire from their positions at Tell El Layyat, deluding the Jews into thinking there was a co-ordinated attack and withdrawing. Then Dandan and his men came and said they'd been thrown out of the army, so they joined us."

Yunis said that when he met Abu Is'af more than twenty years later, he was astonished to hear the Sha'ab garrison leader's version of the story.

"Abu Is'af is more than a brother to me, as you know. Being comrades in arms is something time can't erase; after you haven't seen him for twenty years, your comrade in arms turns up and you discover he still has his place in your heart. Abu Is'af came and we sat and drank tea, and the conversation took us back to '48.

"Abu Is'af said the Israelis threw white powder into the square at Sha'ab as they withdrew and set fire to it to frighten us. He said that when he saw the fire, he felt he couldn't take one more retreat, threw himself into it and discovered that it was just flames.

"I remember things differently – the fire started when they occupied the village, not when they withdrew. But that's not important.

"Abu Is'af knew very well that I was the military official in charge of the whole South Lebanon sector, but he still treated me as though I was a junior officer, raising his hand and expecting me to stop speaking, like in '48.

"I stopped speaking so as not to upset him. After all, Abu Is'af is one of those who are truly dedicated to the struggle, and I respect him immensely, and when we disagreed over the flame powder and he started to get upset, I lied and said he was right. I recounted how I too had followed him and thrown myself into the flames, and let him tell whatever stories he liked in front of his sister and grandchildren – how he caught on fire himself and how all the other fighters followed him and this scared the Jews."

"We were like demons," said Abu Is'af, "like demons that spring from the heart of a fire, and they fled, leaving their weapons on the battlefield."

I asked you about the woman of Sha'ab and you told me about the flames. So be it. Now I want a clear explanation of why you said that Sha'ab didn't fall.

What did happen?

"The truth is . . . ," said Yunis, "the truth is that after we'd liberated the village, we buried the four martyrs and met on the threshing floor and decided that the women, children and old men should leave and only the militiamen should stay. Everyone agreed. They took their supplies and left in the morning. All the women and old men and children left, except for my father, my mother and Naheeleh.

"My father said he'd never go, that he was going to stay so he could conduct the prayers. And my mother said she'd never leave him. And Naheeleh stayed with the two of them. Then we discovered that a lot of the older men had stayed behind or come back in secret.

"That's how Sha'ab became a place of fighters and an old people's home – about two hundred fighters and more than a hundred old men and women.

"We waited for three months, the women coming into the village at night to get supplies and other things, and us acting as guards. We waited for their attack, but they didn't make a serious assault; they launched limited attacks. The first was on 27 July, the day after the liberation of the village. The attacks continued through August and September, but there were no incursions. They'd open fire without attempting to advance. We provoked them into fighting on many occasions, even though our ammunition was low. Then we withdrew."

You withdrew, just like that, for no reason?

"No, we withdrew because it became impossible to stay any longer. On 29 November 1948, the Jews bombed Tarshiha from the air. Then the bombardment expanded to include El Jish and El Bqei'a, and the ALA began its withdrawal to Lebanon. Jasim came to Sha'ab and said, 'Friends, they've betrayed us all. The Sha'ab garrison should withdraw before they close the Lebanese border.' We realised that everything had collapsed.

"That day, Abu Is'af took the decision and said, 'We'll withdraw. If everyone else withdraws and we're left on our own, it won't work.' He said, 'We'll go, then come back.'

"I told him, 'If we go, we'll never come back.'

"'What do you suggest?' he asked.

"'Nothing,' I said.

"He said, 'We'll withdraw, then come back.'

"So we withdrew. All the fighters withdrew with their weapons.

"But the old people refused to withdraw.

"Hussein El Fa'our, who was to die later in the mud of Zubouba, said, 'Take your weapons and go. We're going to stay in our village. They can't do anything to us. We're old people; they have nothing to gain from killing us."

"But they killed them.

"Naheeleh told me about the massacre of the old people in the village and how the Israeli officer called Avraham came in and ordered them all to gather near the pond. He stood among them like an officer inspecting his troops, as though they were a military line-up. He even ordered El Hajj Mousa Darweesh, who was disabled, to be brought from his house. It was his wife's fault. She told the Israeli officer she'd left her husband in the house because he was disabled. She told him about her husband because she was afraid they were going to blow up the houses, as they'd done in El Bruwweh. The officer ordered her to get him. She said she couldn't carry him on her own and a man volunteered to help her, but the officer waved his rifle in his face and said no. She went on her own and came back dragging her husband along the ground. She was weeping and dragging him. The woman was dragging her husband and the officer was smiling, pleased with himself. We saw his white teeth. There was something strange about the whiteness of his teeth. When the woman had brought her husband to the officer, El Hajj Mousa Darweesh gave a loud snort, black liquid gushed from his mouth, and he died.

"The officer saw nothing; he appeared to see nothing of the man's death. Instead he started pointing at men. Anyone his finger pointed to had to move to the other side. He chose about twenty old men. Then he pointed at my blind father. My father didn't see the finger, so the officer pulled out his revolver. My mother screamed 'No!', went over to her husband, led him to where the others were and then went back to her place. A lorry came and the officer ordered them to get in. My mother ran up and took hold of my father's hand and said that he was blind.

"'Get back, woman,' the officer yelled.

"Naheeleh ran over, carrying her son on her arm, and took told of the blind sheikh's hand. 'Get back, all of you,' screamed the officer.

"They didn't go back. They took my father and went back to the pond where most of the people were, and the lorry set off. The Israelis started firing over the heads of the people, who scattered into the fields looking for new villages or the Lebanese border.

"The story of Zubouba, my son, is the real embodiment of our tragedy," said Yunis.

No more was heard of the twenty men whom the officer's finger had put onto the lorry till Marwan El Fa'our appeared in Lebanon. Marwan El Fa'our was the only one to survive what we would later come to call the Massacre of the Mud.

Marwan El Fa'our told of the rain.

"The rain was heavy and the lorry drove through it. We reached Zubouba, close to Jenin and on the Jordanian lines. They made us get down from the lorry, ordered us to cross to the Arab side and started firing over our heads."

It was a march of rain, death and mud.

The mud covered the ground, and the rain was like ropes. Cold, darkness and fear. Twenty men walking, sliding, grabbing at the ropes of rain hung down from the sky and falling. They'd try to rise, and they'd get stuck in the mud.

Twenty men hanging onto ropes of rain, sobbing and coughing, trying to walk and sliding and sticking in the mud.

The mud was like glue.

They stuck to the ground. They fell and the mud-glue swallowed them.

The threads of water falling from the sky began to turn to mud.

And the dying started.

That's how the men of Sha'ab died in the Massacre of the Mud, which took place on a day in December 1948.

The Sha'ab garrison congregated and withdrew in orderly fashion in the direction of the Lebanese border.

The detachment commanded by Dandan, however, left them and joined the Yemenis concentrated in the El Kabri hills, where the final battle took place and all the Yemenis and Iraqis died. That was where Dandan, and Abdallah, and El Mosulli died.

The Sha'ab garrison congregated at Beit Yahoun and Ein Ibil and started making forays from Jisr El Mansourah.

An army unit surrounded them, disarmed them and ordered them to join the Ajnadayn Brigade near Damascus. There they were put in prison.

You came to the Ein El Hilweh camp from the prison, stood up and screamed among the tents, "We're not refugees!" The rest you know, master.

Shall I tell you the rest? Why should I tell you when you already know everything?

On the other hand, you don't know what happened to Abd El Mu'ti.

Abd El Mu'ti died yesterday, here in the hospital. He breathed his last after suffering an angina attack. We tried to treat him, but he died.

What can we do for a man of seventy who's decided to die? Let him go – it's better for him and for us. We tried to save him, but "There is no power and no strength but in Almighty God."

When they brought him in, he was breathing with difficulty, opening his mouth as though there wasn't enough air, or as though his spirit was trying to depart his body but couldn't.

"Another leech" I thought, because Sha'ab men refuse to die. Then I remembered you're not from Sha'ab, which meant that the man wasn't like you and wouldn't do what you did over again, just as he wasn't your relative as I first thought, based on the resemblance between you. Later I discovered that he didn't look like you; you old men end up like small children – you all look like one another at first glance, and we have to look hard to discover that the resemblance is only in our heads.

Abd El Mu'ti died and took his story with him.

Did you know he destroyed us with his great achievement during the long siege of Shatila camp? And you were the reason, because you . . . I don't know why you took such pleasure in that story of the nuclear bomb that you made up with the Lebanese woman journalist to break the siege of the camp.

I wasn't in the camp for the entire siege because I'd been given the mission of going out for antibiotics, which we needed desperately, and when I came back I found that the ways into the camp had been closed off once and for all. That was the day I met Shams, in our office in Mar Elias camp, and she took over the mission. She said she could get things in via her private network, and she took the medicines and disappeared. Then I learned that she'd entered the camp and stayed there for about two months, leaving again after a dispute with its military commander,

Ali Abu Toq. It was after she left the camp that our love began. She'd come to Mar Elias camp, sit with us in her uniform, draw maps and talk about her impossible plans for breaking the siege of Shatila. That was when my passion began. I didn't tell her or make the first move. I just waited and she would come, and that burning passion that erupts from deep inside your chest would hit me and cut off my breathing. It seems she noticed, because she behaved like she'd noticed. At the time I thought she was trying to convey her lack of interest, but I found out later that that kind of sideways way of showing interest was her way. She'd glance at me obliquely as though desire had made its abode in the corners of her eyes.

My love for Shams started with the antibiotics, in Mar Elias camp. I didn't run away during the siege, as was said; I was on a mission. And anyway, when I came back, no-one looked on me as a traitor. The camp had been wiped out, and none of the siege fighters were left. Even Shams refused to stay in Shatila and joined the fighters of Ein El Hilweh, using a village east of Sidon as her base.

I didn't return to the camp because I was afraid to take part in the fighting in Maghdousheh but because I'd lost any desire for war. War is an urge, as you used to say. You said that war burned inside you and you couldn't wait for the Arabs to complete their military arrangements so you joined Fatah and fought the way you wanted to.

In those days I didn't like fighting any more. What was I supposed to do east of Sidon? Plus why continue with the Lebanon war when it wasn't a war any more? I will never say, as you do, that it wasn't ever a war, that it was a trap we set with our own hands and fell into. I disagree. We got into the civil war in Lebanon because all roads were closed to us and because it was our duty to bring the world down on the heads of its masters. That's what I believed in 1975. But after the fall of Shatila in 1987 and our conversion into bands fighting around Sidon, I was no longer convinced.

Abd El Mu'ti was different.

His war urge never died.

During the siege, when the camp was surrounded by Amal men, Abd El Mu'ti took his Czech rifle and hunkered down in one of the forward positions. The young fighters felt sorry for him being so old, but he was like an ape, as though the years had left no trace on his well-muscled body, white moustache and bald head. The firing from his rifle used to reassure us because it signified that we were still capable of resistance.

Abd El Mu'ti said he fought so they wouldn't give him another "sunbath".

Before talking about "sunbathing", do you remember what Abd El Mu'ti did during the siege?

You were all cut off and half-starved and your morale was pitiful. So Abd El Mu'ti decided to let off his secret weapon. He telephoned the Agence France Presse office in Beirut and talked to a woman, asking her to repeat her name several times before he gave her the news. He said he wanted to be sure of her identity. She said her name was Jameela Ibraheem and that she was Lebanese, from Zahleh.

You listened to him in amazement. He made up a story about a meeting to be held by the fighters in the camp to discuss the situation. He said that the fighters had decided to ask a religious authority for a ruling permitting the eating of human flesh. "We're dying of starvation. We've eaten the cats and the dogs, and there's nothing left to eat, and the militias surrounding us have no mercy, so what are we to do? We've decided to eat the flesh of our fallen comrades, and we're asking for a ruling to allow this."

He said they couldn't call from the camp and asked the journalist to contact a religious authority, promising to call her back after an hour.

An hour later, the news that shook the world was out. Abd El Mu'ti called Jameela, and she told him of the good news that Sheikh Kamil El Sammour had ruled that it was permissible to eat human flesh in situations of urgent necessity. Agence France Presse sent the news out over its international network and television and radio stations, and the world press went into an uproar.

The people of Shatila didn't eat human flesh, and the Syrian army that was surrounding the area ordered the Amal militias to make a partial lifting of the siege.

I entered the camp after Abd El Mu'ti's bombshell. I went in with medicines and rations, and there I met Jameela Ibraheem.

The journalist came to the camp looking for Abd El Mu'ti. She came carrying a cooking pot full of delicious food – God, how good her food was! A pot of cracked wheat, cooked cracked wheat with mutton and onions and chickpeas piled on top, plus a big container of milk.

Jameela said she'd cooked it for Abd El Mu'ti, and everyone ate. When she saw the number of people hovering around the pot, she said she was ashamed, and if she'd known Abd El Mu'ti was going to invite the whole camp she'd have made more. Abd El Mu'ti told her, his mouth full of cracked wheat, that he'd repeated the miracle of the fishes. "Didn't your prophet make five fishes go round a thousand people?"

We ate and laughed, and Jameela's round face was flooded with happiness. I never saw a woman so happy. She didn't touch the food herself, and Abd El Mu'ti sat next to her and tried to make her eat from his hand, as though they were two old friends, and she called him "my partner" because he'd written the news item that led to the raising of the siege with her, and he called her "my partner" because she'd cooked for him.

Where is Jameela now?

I ought to contact her to tell her of Abd El Mu'ti's death, but what if she doesn't remember him? What if she talks to me as though the pot of cracked wheat never existed?

I won't get in touch with her, but how I wish she'd bring another pot of cracked wheat. The man is dead, and death calls for food; nothing stimulates hunger like death.

Abd El Mu'ti is dead and with him has died the story of El Ba'neh and its square and his stubborn refusal to stay inside his house in the camp.

"I'll fight and I'll die, but I'll never let that happen again."

Abd El Mu'ti said, "After Sha'ab, we fled to the forests of El Ba'neh and lived there. We turned our blankets into tents. We'd throw the blanket over the branch of a tree, tie it to the ground, and that would be half a tent. We lived in those half-tents for more than a month. Then El Ba'neh and Deir El Asad fell. We knew they'd fallen when the Jews surrounded us and took us to the square at El Ba'neh. El Ba'neh doesn't really have a square; I don't know another village in the world like it – the square of El Ba'neh is shared with Deir El Asad, as though they were one village. They collected us in the square and left us crucified under the sun. That was the first time I heard the term 'sunbath'. A man next to me said, 'They're going to give us a sunbath before they kill us.' I found out the full horror of what it meant later in Ansar detention camp. In that vast camp, which the Israelis built after the occupation of '82, 'sunbathing' was a basic means of torture. They tie your arms and legs and throw you down in the sun, so you twist and turn and roll, trying to get a moment's relief from the burning. That would be from sunrise to sunset. Then the officer comes and gives the order for your arms and legs to be untied and asks you to stand up, and you discover you can't do anything. The sun has set under your skin, and fire has made its home inside you. Sunset is tribulation and death. When the sun disappears on the horizon, the burning inside begins, as though the sun had gone to its rest in your bones instead of in the sea.

"We were in the square of El Ba'neh and there was the sun, and the man said, 'They'll give us a sunbath before they kill us,' and I didn't understand what he meant till they killed us.

"We were a vast mass of humanity twisting under the sun and waiting for death. Later we discovered that we were to spend the rest of our lives in the 'sunbath'. What do you call the refugee camp? Now you see houses, but in the beginning the camp consisted of a group of tents. Then later, after we'd built huts, they allowed us to roof them. It was said that if we put proper roofs on our houses, we'd forget Palestine, so we put up zinc sheets. Do you know what zinc sheets do to you under the Beirut sun? Do you know what it means to be under zinc at night, after it's absorbed the sun all day?

"In the square of El Ba'neh-Deir El Asad they left us to bathe in the sun all day long after they'd separated out the women. They ordered the women to go to Lebanon and left us to burn.

"Two men I didn't know asked permission to fetch water, and the officer told them to follow him. They left the square and walked towards the spring. We heard the sound of two bullets. The officer returned and the men didn't, and after that no-one dared say he was thirsty.

"After more than an hour an old man stood up and asked for water. The officer looked at him with contempt, pulled out his revolver, brought the barrel close to the man's forehead, placed it between his eyes and didn't fire. The old man started to shake. I was sure he was going to kill him, but he didn't. The officer put his revolver in his belt, and the man went on shaking for a long, long time.

"Then they searched us and stole everything — money, watches and rings. When the search was over, the soldiers pulled back and we saw the officer's hand going up and down and the soldiers dragging away the men tapped by the officer's hand. The hand fell on more than two hundred men, who were loaded onto lorries that took them in the direction of El Ramah. To this day we don't know what happened to them. Then they ordered us to go to Lebanon. The shooting started. We found ourselves in the fields with our wives and our children, and we walked for endless hours. We walked till we got to the village of Sajour, where we slept in the fields; we continued our journey in the morning to Beit Jann. There the Druze gave us food. We walked for more than two days before we got to Lebanon.

"My son Hamid was ten and had been hit in his right knee. I tied up his knee and carried him, but I became exhausted and put him down and he walked. By the time we reached Lebanon, he was crippled.

"Sahirah, the daughter of Ibraheem El Hajj Hassan, gave birth to a girl in the fields of Sajour. We didn't know what was wrong with her; she pulled out a girl from under her and started dancing.

"Ibraheem El Hajj Hassan tried to calm his daughter, but the woman didn't care. She danced like she was at a wedding party and said she could hear drums beating in her ears. She said she wouldn't stop dancing till her husband came back. Poor husband! How was he going to come back after they'd taken him to El Ramah?

"Sahirah kept dancing till we reached Lebanon, where they said she'd gone crazy, though only God knows.

"Do you understand, son, why I don't want to stay at home? I'm an old man who fights because I prefer death to a sunbath. They gave me a sunbath in El Ba'neh in '48, and they gave me a sunbath in Ansar in '82, and now I've had enough — I'd rather die than face another."

"You are dying, Abd El Mu'ti."

The rigid body slackens. Your features return to you; your face clears, the wrinkles are wiped from your broad brow, and the cloud over your eyes parts.

I stand up.

What am I to say to this man I call my father but who isn't my father? I open his eyes, put "tears" in them, and he doesn't weep.

*

Abd El Mu'ti dies, and you don't weep. You're dying and you don't weep.

I bring you news and tell you stories and you don't hear. Tell me, Abd El Mu'ti, what to do. Take me with you on your journey to that place, for I yearn to see all of you. I live among you and I yearn for you and you leave.

Weep a little, father. Just one sob and everything will be over. One sob and you'll live. But you don't want to, or you no longer want to, or you've lost your will. And I'm with you and not with you. I'm busy, I have to check on the other patients; that's what Dr Amjad has decided. Don't be scared, I won't leave you for long. I'll just slip over, check on them and come back to your side.

And then what?

What indeed?

For three months I've been telling you stories, some of which I know and some of which I don't. And you're incapable of correcting my information, so I make mistakes. Freedom, father, is being able to make mistakes. Now I feel free because with you I can make as many mistakes as I like and retract my mistakes whenever I like, and tell story after story.

My throat's dry from so much talking. I've dried out, become desiccated.

I feel water coming out with my words and spotting the ground around me. I feel I'm drowning in my own water. Do you want me to drown? Reach out your hand, I beg you, reach out your hand and pluck me from the pool of storytelling in whose waters I'm drowning. I'm a prisoner who owns nothing but the stories he makes up about his freedom. I'm a prisoner of the hospital and a prisoner of the story. I'm drowning in the water, the water that's around me. I swallow the water and swallow the words and I tell the story.

What do you want from me?

I've told you all your stories, about the past and about the present, and you don't care.

Now you know the whole story, but I don't. Can you believe that? I've told you a story I don't know. I understand nothing; things are collapsing inside my head. I've almost forgotten your names, and I mix them all together.

You know, but I don't.

I don't know, but I have to know so I can tell. But I don't know the story, and I'll have to go back to the beginning to look for it. What do you think?

Do you want the beginning? This time, though, I'll tell it the way I like it; I won't subject it to your distorted memory or to the phantoms that hover about your closed eyes. I'll tell you everything. But not now. I have to go now. I'll turn on the radio so you can listen to Fayrouz. Her voice calms the nerves and spreads its lilac shade over the eyes. I'll leave you with the lilac shade and go.

Part Two

NΛHEELEH'S DEATH

I want to apologise.

I know that nothing can excuse my leaving you on your own for more than two weeks. Forgive me, please, and try to understand. I don't want you to think for a moment that I'm like them – certainly not, master. I despise positions, and my new one is of no importance. I don't know what came over me. I left you that night and went to my room to sleep. And when I was in bed, I began to suffocate as though there was no oxygen left in the air. I lay down on my bed, and without realising what I was doing I started searching for the oxygen bottle I'd put in your room in case of an emergency. I set up the oxygen equipment in your room and went off to sleep. While I was sleeping, everything became constricted. I woke up. My heart was beating rapidly, I was bathed in sweat, and the air . . . the air wasn't enough any more. I started breathing loudly, gasping for air, but there was no air. I felt a tingling sensation in my head and left hand and belly and back. I tried to get up. I raised my head, sat up sluggishly and pushed the electric bell, but there was no electricity. I put my hand to my head and there was the dark; a thick darkness was drawing closer. I raised my hand to push back the dark, but my hand was paralysed. Everything was murky, and there was no oxygen. I thought, "I'm going to die." But instead of lying on my back and waiting for the angel of death, I jumped out of bed like a madman, ran to the window, put my head out and started breathing as though I was eating. I ate all the air in the world, but the world's air wasn't enough. I dressed quickly and left my room. I walked down the corridor and down the stairs to the ground floor and then climbed back up. It was what one might call the Night of the Stairs. I jogged up them and down them, panting and running, as though I wanted to prove to myself that I was still alive. Imagine the scene: a man on his own in the darkness running and panting and breathing, running up and down the stairs dozens of times so he won't die. At that moment, I took my decision, went back to my room and lay down on the bed.

So, finally, Khaleel Ayoub, whom you see before you, has become head nurse at Galilee Hospital. I accepted Dr Amjad's proposition and went to tell him the next morning.

Forgive me.

Strangely the two weeks passed quickly. I swear I couldn't find the time to scratch my head. I asked Nurse Zeinab to look after you, but I don't know, master, why I couldn't do it myself. I'd get to the door of your room and instead of going in I'd back away, as though a barrier had gone up in front of me.

It has nothing to do with my new position: I'm not like that, as you know. But I felt, I just felt I was living suspended in space, and I thought that maybe, just maybe, my fear would come to an end and I'd go home. I miss my house and my grandmother's cushion and the smell of decayed flowers. I told myself I could go back, but I didn't. I swear it was only when the French delegation came that I dared go out into the streets of the camp. I found Saleem then, and I'll tell you more about him, but my uselessness and my fear drove me back to the hospital.

Have you forgiven me?

I came back to you, organised everything and convinced myself that leaving the hospital wasn't worth it. We're back the way we were, and I bathe you and perfume you and take care of you, and I'll tell you the story from the beginning, just as I promised I would two weeks ago. That was when I left you, hoping I'd see you in the morning, and the oxygen night happened and I went in the morning to Dr Amjad's office, knocked on the door, went in and stood there. As usual he had his feet up on the desk and was reading a newspaper, and as usual he pretended he hadn't noticed me.

I stood there like an idiot and coughed in the smoke from his pipe which rose from behind the newspaper that obscured his face.

"I accept, doctor," I said. "Dr Amjad . . . Dr Amjad . . . I . . ."

He moved the paper aside.

"Hello, hello! Please do sit down. I didn't see you."

"I accept the job," I said.

He removed his feet from the desk, sat up straight in his chair, put the paper aside, lifted his finger, raised his voice and said, "You assume your duties immediately." Then he rang the bell on his desk and Nurse Zeinab came into the office.

"He's responsible for everything from now on," he said.

Dr Amjad hid behind the newspaper again and Nurse Zeinab stood there with no idea what to do.

"But, doctor . . ." she said.

"You're still here?" he asked from behind the newspaper.

I asked him to explain a little about my new job.

"Later, later," he said. "Go with Nurse Zeinab and take over."

So I took over.

You think, master, that I took over the administration of a hospital! It's true that I am, practically speaking, the hospital's director, now that Dr Amjad has found that by appointing me he has an excuse to absent himself from work on a permanent basis. I'm back to being a doctor, the way I used to be, but . . . This "but" tells the whole story. I'm a doctor, but Dr Amjad's the real doctor! I examine and decide and prescribe medicine and everything, but the patients say they're waiting for the doctor's opinion.

When the doctor comes, he doesn't have an opinion. He agrees with my diagnosis and my prescription, but the patients wait for him just the same, as though the only thing they have faith in is his degree certificate. I swear he knows nothing, but never mind, it's better this way: I make the decisions and don't have to take the responsibility.

I took over the administration of the hospital and became head of the nurses – Nurse Zeinab, whom you know because she was the person who received you here at the hospital; Kameel, who stole the radio but who's a nice lad – he has a lovely voice and knows all the songs of Abd El Haleem Hafiz by heart – and who's waiting for a visa so he can leave the country; and the Egyptian, Hamdi, who's not a nurse, but we call him one so the hospital won't seem empty (can you imagine a great big hospital with more than forty beds and only two nurses!?). Also Hamdi's started helping us move patients and take care of them, even though basically he's a doorkeeper. And there's Kamilya the cook, who's told me she's decided to leave the hospital at the end of the month. We added Kamilya to the nurses' list too, and I started teaching her the basics.

So things were moving along.

I'd managed to set things to rights in a minimal way, and that was my mistake, because when things are set to rights we discover what's wrong – and here everything is wrong. There are no medicines, no serums, nothing. It's as though we aren't in a hospital, and in fact we aren't. We're in an off-white building suspended in the air, and I'm its director and head of nursing. I try to organise things and I turn up the impossible and the temporary. When I accepted my new job, I thought I'd find a solution to my problem, but now my problem has become part of the hospital's.

Hamdi the Egyptian was replaced by Dr Amjad. He threw Hamdi out without warning and replaced him with a Syrian youth called Umar. Poor Hamdi was crying as he got his things together.

"What are you crying for?" I asked him. "Go and look for work. You barely earn enough to eat here." He said he'd go back to Egypt, that they'd thrown him out because he didn't have a work permit.

"I don't have a work permit either," I said.

He said he'd been here for three years and that he'd come to Beirut through a smuggler in Damascus because Egyptians don't need a visa to get into Syria. He'd paid seven hundred dollars to the Syrian smuggler who got him to Beirut. He'd wanted Beirut as a stop on the way to migrating to Germany. He said he didn't want to leave because he needed two thousand dollars to fix a visa for a European country from which he'd slip into Germany. Now he'd be deported to Egypt and go back to his village penniless, so how would he get married?

The Syrian called Umar talks to no-one. He's supposed to work as a guard and a servant, but he doesn't guard and he doesn't clean. He has a small car he runs about in all day, and at night he comes back to sleep in the hospital.

Dr Amjad asked me to do nothing to get in his way.

"Leave him alone, my friend. He's free to do what he wants. I'm sure you'll understand without my telling you that we don't dare let ourselves think about these things. We have to accept them and that's it. They made me throw out the Egyptian and got me this person to keep an eye on the hospital, so you'll just have to keep quiet and take it as read."

"It", master, means that we live in a place filled with security services, each of which is keeping an eye on the others, and we're supposed to deal with them as though we don't know. I don't have any dealings with Umar, and practically speaking it's Kamilya who guards the hospital at night. She stands at the entrance, lets people in, writes down their names and that's all.

We don't need a lot of staff. True, we have fifteen patients, but their families take care of everything. They change the sheets, fetch food and clean the rooms. I don't understand why they bring their sick to this hospital; they'd be better off at home. But they feel safe here, or they use it as an excuse to get out of the house. All we offer is free medicine; any cure is in God's hands.

I won't go into the details of this strange world in which I find myself with you because you're tired and need your rest.

I've come back to you now, and everything's going to be as it was. Your condition isn't too good because of the ulcers. Nurse Zeinab looked after you while I was away, but she didn't do the things I used to do. She gave you a bath every two days, which is why the ulcers on your back have got so bad. Don't worry, they will go away in less than a week and you'll be my spoiled child again, and I'll bathe you twice a day and put on ointment and everything.

Have you forgiven me?

I swear you're better company than any of those others. I see them walking and talking as if they're dead. We, though, aren't dead, because we seek the aroma of life and are waiting.

I know you're waiting for the end, but I assure you, as I have in the past, that the end can only be a man disappearing into the cave of Bab El Shams.

I'm optimistic! Saleem As'ad has promised to find a waterbed for you. When you sleep on water, you'll find that your body will return to you.

I forgot to tell you about Saleem As'ad.

The lad's driving me insane. I came across him by chance, and now he comes to my office every day asking for work. He's a good-looking youth, and strange, always seemingly on the verge of flying away. When he stands up to say goodbye, I feel that he's not going to walk away but to fly off. He stands in front of me holding out his hand; I hold mine out, shake his quickly and then withdraw.

"Any work, doctor?"

"I'm not a doctor, and I don't have any work."

He smiles, stands up, shakes my hand again, gets ready to fly off and leaves.

The lad enchants me, and I'm prepared to do anything to find him a job. What do you say I appoint him to look after the records? We need someone to put the hospital's files in order. I know Amjad will never agree, but I'll make him agree in spite of himself.

Why am I telling you about Saleem As'ad?

Because he astonished me by convincing me that anything's possible.

Saleem As'ad taught me that deception is life.

Listen. I was in my office (I now have my own office and a telephone) when Nurse Zeinab came and said there was a group of foreigners asking for the doctor. Amjad, as usual, wasn't there. I told her to bring them in. Why not? Foreigners wanting a doctor and I'm a doctor.

There were three of them, two men and a woman. They spoke to me in French, so I answered them in Chinese English, so they switched to French English and we understood one another.

The bald, tall man who seemed to be their leader said they were French actors who'd come to Beirut to visit Shatila. They said they'd met Abu Akram, the Popular Front official in the camp, who'd advised them to visit the hospital. They said they wanted to learn about the camp.

Nurse Zeinab offered them tea, they lit cigarettes, and I was caressed by the smell of toasted French tobacco.

Their leader said they were members of a theatre troupe and were getting ready to put on a play by a French writer called Jean Genet entitled *Quatre heures à Chatila*. Before starting rehearsals they'd decided to come to Beirut to acquaint themselves with the conditions in Shatila camp. He introduced me to the French woman, who was going to be the only person acting in the show.

"It's a monodrama," he told me.

The woman smiled and said her name was Catherine. She was white and her short black hair could hardly keep still on her head. Everything about her seemed to be on the verge of coming apart, as though her limbs were joined together artificially, and she looked at me, and around her, with dancing eyes.

"The actress," said the tall, bald man.

"It's a play with just one performer, her," he said and pointed at Catherine. "She tells the story alone on the stage."

"A play without actors?" I asked.

"There's just one. We wanted to preserve the spirit of the text; we wouldn't want to do violence to Jean Genet's work. You know of him, I'm sure."

I said I knew of him, though it was the first time I'd heard the name.

"He's the French writer who lived with the fedayeen in Jordan and wrote a beautiful book about them called *Un Captif amoureux*. Did you ever meet him?"

"No, I never met him, but I've heard a lot about him."

"Have you read his books?"

"No, I haven't, but I know the sort of thing he wrote."

"He's a great writer," said the tall, bald man. "He wrote a most beautiful text about the Shatila massacre."

"I know."

"And he was a supporter of yours."

"I know."

"So that's why we're asking for your help."

"For *my* help?"

"Mr Abu Akram suggested we begin our tour with the hospital. He said that talking to Dr . . ." He pulled a piece of paper out of his pocket and read the name: "Dr Amjad. You're Dr Amjad?"

"No, I'm Dr Khaleel."

"And you're in charge?"

"More or less."

"And Dr Amjad, will we meet him? Mr Abu Akram said he was a knowledgable man."

"Tomorrow, if you come by at the same time, he'll be here."

I said "tomorrow" even though I knew he wouldn't come either today or tomorrow because he'd managed to get himself a job at the Dr Arbeed Hospital in Beirut, where he was paid a proper salary, not like here – but what was I to say? We don't wash our dirty laundry in front of foreigners!

The tall, bald director said he wanted to ask a few questions, but she stood up – the actress stood up – and said something to him in commanding French.

The director apologised and asked me, if it were possible, to accompany them on their tour. "Catherine would rather we see things for ourselves before asking questions."

"But I can't leave the hospital."

"Please," he said.

He said "Please" knowing that I'd agree. These foreigners think that just visiting us is such a big sacrifice that we'll agree to anything they ask. I don't belong to that school, but it occurred to me that it would be an opportunity to get out of this accursed hospital. I've been a prisoner here for three months, and it's about time I got out to try my chances. It would be a kind of protection to be part of a group of three French people: no-one would dare to kill me in front of them. So I came over all courageous, master, and agreed. I asked them to wait so I could take care of a few things and rang the bell. Nurse Zeinab came and I ordered three cups of coffee and left them. I went to my room and took a shower. I was like a small child who's going on an outing. I took a shower, put on clean clothes and went back to them. The girl smiled at me; it seemed she'd noticed the change in my appearance and smelled the smell of soap that came off my white hair.

"Let's go," I said. "But what do you want to see?"

"Everything," said the girl.

The director said he'd like to speak to families of the victims if it was possible. I understood him to mean the victims of the massacre of '82, not those of the massacres that came later.

"The cemetery," said the second man, whose name I found out, when we lost him in the alleys of the camp, was Daniel. He was the set designer and spoke a little Arabic.

"The cemetery," said Daniel.

I explained that the victims' mass grave no longer existed because it had ended up outside the boundaries when the camp was made smaller during the War of the Camps. I also explained that the grave of the martyrs who were killed after the massacre was now inside the mosque. I asked them which one we should start with.

"You decide and we'll follow you," said their leader.

We left the hospital. I'd made up my mind to walk in the midst of them; Daniel was in front while the short, curvaceous girl kept moving about, walking around us and raising a pen she was holding to her lips as though she wanted to say something but then not saying anything. When we got to the main street, I said, "This is the street. The bodies were piled up here and in the surrounding alleys." The girl came up close to me, raised her pen to her lips and repeated, "This is the street." Then she leaned against me, put her head on my shoulder and held the pose. I tried to move away a little, for that kind of thing isn't looked kindly upon in the camp, but she wouldn't change her pose. I thought she must be weeping because I could feel her shaking against my shoulder. I twisted towards her; her head fell onto my chest. I took hold of her shoulders, pushed her back and said, "Let's go."

Daniel asked me about the "vertical" bodies: he said that Jean Genet had described the bodies as being "vertical".

"Of course, of course," I answered. "Everything happened here." I didn't tell them about the flies; I felt I couldn't. I don't know why I kept silent, even though I'd been determined to tell them the story. While I was taking my shower, I'd told myself that the story of the flies would be the high point of the visit. I'd tell them how I left the hospital and how the flares fired by the Israeli army had lit up the night, turning it into a day of blood and fear.

I told the armed men who broke into the hospital that I was Turkish. I spoke English to them and told them I was a Turkish doctor and couldn't permit them to violate the sanctity of the hospital. And they believed me! You know what they did to the Palestinian nurses, but me they believed, or forgot. So I fled the hospital. I know I should have stayed, but I left and wandered like someone lost in the midst of that night illuminated with fire. Dear God, all I remember of that night is the shadows. I ran, and the houses would emerge from the darkness into the light and then submerge themselves again in the darkness. I ran to Umm Hassan's house, shaking with fear. I'm telling you now, and I'm ashamed of myself – as though a man can become, in an instant, what he truly is, and then forget. I've forgotten that crying that turned me into drops of water at Umm Hassan's house. Umm Hassan cried too, but she never reminded me even once of my weeping and my fear. Even – do you remember? – even when we finally succeeded in building a wall round the mass grave and the women congregated and wailed, Umm Hassan upbraided them and said, "No weeping! Praise God we were able to bring them together in death as fate brought them together in life!"

She said it couldn't be allowed, and everyone stopped weeping.

Then Umm Ahmad El Sa'di sang a song of celebration and yelled, "We won, everybody. We won, and we have a grave." Umm Ahmad El Sa'di, who was ululating and leaping about, had lost her seven children, her husband and her mother in the massacre; all she had left was her daughter, Dunya. She sang and leapt and the tears started. Everybody left the grave and gathered around the woman.

Umm Ahmad El Sa'di held more sorrow than the grave. She said that her belly was a grave. She said she could smell death in her guts, could smell blood.

The people gathered round Umm Ahmad, whose daughter was standing there with her crutches. I saw Dunya again today. She was just a pair of eyes suspended in an oval, wan face, eyes that looked as though they'd fallen from some distant place and got stuck in that sandy face. Her face was sandy, yellow or brown. She was standing with her wide-open eyes, putting her crutches under her arms. She turned, thinking someone was talking to her. I asked her how she was. She said she was looking for work and I suggested the hospital, but she said she'd spent two years in hospitals and detested them. She said she wanted to go to Tunis and asked if I could do anything.

At that point I didn't know her story. Her story then, as far as I was concerned, was that of a lump of bloody flesh thrown down in the emergency room. I tried to treat her, then proposed that she be moved to the American University hospital because we didn't have the means to treat her. She was a wreck. Fractures in the chest and pelvis. Blood and holes everywhere. They moved her to the American University hospital, where she stayed for about two years, and it never occurred to me to visit her; like everyone else, I was astonished at her mother's loss. Umm Ahmad was the story, and the strange thing is that the woman never mentioned her daughter, as though Dunya had died along with the others.

Dunya was standing near the wall. I asked how she was, and she asked about the possibility of going to Tunis to work in one of the Palestine Liberation Organisation's offices.

When I left, she walked with me.

She said, "I'll walk with you to the hospital."

"I'll walk with you to your house," I responded.

She smiled and said she was strong now. I asked about her injuries, and she said she didn't remember anything, or rather she remembered running in the street and didn't come round until she was in hospital.

She told me how the men from the Lebanese Red Cross had discovered she wasn't dead. They were at the edge of the mass grave, sprinkling quick lime on the bodies, when a fat man discovered her and picked her up and came running with her to the hospital. He stood in front of me sobbing like a child.

"Doctor, doctor, not dead. Still alive, doctor."

They threw you down in the emergency room and that fat young Lebanese man, his white gown almost bursting at the seams, begged me to go with him, saying we had to dig around at the grave site: "We may have buried people who're still alive. Please, doctor, come with me." He grabbed my hand and I went with him, and there was the smell and the flies. All I remember is the flies. I didn't see the bodies. They were sprinkling quick lime over the piled-up, puffed-up corpses, and the flies were buzzing and making insane sounds. The man in white led me by the hand and I crouched down for fear of the flies. They were like a cloud or a woollen cover of black and yellow buzzing. I was bent over and he led me on, jumping over the corpses. I jumped too. I let go of his hand and fell down and rolled over in that white stuff and got up again supporting myself on the ground and the lime and ran towards the hospital. I ran turning and looking back for fear that he was following me. I ran with the quick lime dripping off me. I wiped my eyes so I could see and the flies were creeping into my hair and taking up residence in my insides. I wiped my hair and my face and I ran. When Nurse Zeinab saw me enter the hospital, she fled. In those days, master, we used to fear the dead. We didn't fear those who killed them; we feared the people who'd been killed. We feared the quick lime. We were afraid they'd rise up and come towards us, covered with quick lime, shaded by their clouds of flies.

That's how the camp lived and its people died. They covered them with quick lime to kill the germs and wiped away their faces before throwing them into the hole, which became a soccer pitch.

I didn't tell these stories to Catherine and her group, and I didn't tell them about Dunya. I walked with them through the streets of the camp and took them to the mass grave, which is outside the camp borders now, and there they saw three children playing soccer. Catherine went up to the fence and laid her head on it. I thought she was going to cry, but she didn't.

"Is that really the grave?" she asked me.

I nodded, but her dancing eyes and short black hair seemed not to believe me. The tall man, whose name I've forgotten, asked me about the numbers.

"Fifteen hundred," I said.

I told them about the wall and said we'd built one round the grave, but that that proper wall had been destroyed during the War of the Camps and replaced with this fence.

The tall man said he wanted to talk to people.

"Of course, of course," I said.

We went back to the main street and took the first turning on the right. We found children running through the alleys and women sitting in front of their houses washing vegetables and talking. We stopped in front of one of the houses.

"Come in, come in," said the woman.

"Thank you," I said. "I have a delegation of French actors with me, and they'd like to talk to you a little."

"Welcome, Dr Khaleel. It's been ages! How are you? I hope your mind's at peace."

Now the trouble starts, I thought, and what I was afraid of is happening. Now she'll ask me about Shams and I'll have to lie. But she didn't, thank God; I ignored her words and said the French visitors wanted her to tell them about the massacre.

When the woman heard the word *massacre*, her face fell.

"No, son. We're not a cinema. No."

The woman went into her house and closed the door in our faces.

I was embarrassed because I'd told the French group that the people here loved guests and talked naturally, and that we only had to knock on the door and go in.

After the first door was closed in our faces, all the others were too, and no-one spoke to us.

The fourth and last woman whose door we knocked on was very kind, but she said she wouldn't talk.

"My story? No, Dr Khaleel. I don't want to talk about my children. Come and talk to me about something else. Not my children." Then she came up close to me and whispered, "Don't tell them what I'm going to tell you now; it's a secret. Can you keep a secret? Every time I talk about them, or say something to them, they come to me at night. I hear their voices speaking like the wind. I can't make out what they're saying, but I know them from their voices. I know they don't want me to talk about them. Maybe whenever I talk about them they remember the massacre. The dead remember, and their memories hurt like knives."

"You're right, sister. Do whatever you like," I told her and made a sign to the visitors to leave.

"No, please. Have some tea!"

We drank tea in a living room whose walls were covered from top to bottom with photographs banded with black ribbons. Catherine got up and bent over the sofa to examine one of the photos close up. It showed a girl of about ten standing with her short skirt riding up a little on her left thigh. She was wearing sandals and playing with her plait. Catherine bent even closer till her face was almost touching the picture, but the woman pulled her back and said, "Sit down." Catherine almost fell over, but she sat down silently. When we left, however, the tall man asked me what the woman had said to Catherine. I told him she'd asked her to sit down and keep away from the picture.

"Why?" he asked me.

"I don't know," I said.

"We're bothering them, and I can understand," he said.

"We oughtn't to have come," said Catherine.

Then Daniel disappeared. We left the house, walked on a little, and Daniel was no longer with us.

"Where's Daniel?" I asked.

The tall director said Daniel was like that: he had to explore places by himself.

"Do you want to wait for him?" I asked.

"No need," said the tall director. "He'll work out how to get back to the hospital on his own."

"Is that all?" asked Catherine.

"There's the mosque that was turned into a cemetery," I said, and explained that during the long siege we'd turned the mosque into a cemetery because the original cemetery had been occupied and destroyed.

"I don't want to go. *Nous sommes des voyeurs*," Catherine said to the tall director, who tried to translate what she'd said, to the effect that it was the tragedy of intellectuals and artists that they had to go and look and react, and then they forgot. When he read Jean Genet's text on the massacre, he said, he felt as though he'd been struck by lightning; he said he hadn't read the words, he'd seen them – the words emerged from the pages and moved around his room. That was why he'd decided to come here: "I had to see the people so the words would go back into the book and become just words again."

I didn't get into a discussion with him because I couldn't understand what lay behind all that finickiness of his. I understood what *voyeurs* meant and said one didn't have to be an intellectual to be a *voyeur*; we're all *voyeurs*. Voyeurism is one of the human race's greatest pleasures; uncovering what others want to hide justifies our own mistakes and makes life more bearable.

Catherine said the people were right. "Why should they talk to us? Why should they give us information? Who are we to them? It's not right."

I didn't tell them what the fourth woman had said to me; I felt I had no right to reveal her secret. I also felt a certain pride, believe me, for when we suppress pain it shows we know its meaning. Nothing equals pain but the suppression of it.

On our way back to the hospital, we met Abu Akram, and he invited us to the Popular Front office, where I was introduced to Saleem As'ad.

You agree that people took a noble stand when they refused to talk, right? They were right not to talk. How could they, after all? We don't tell these tales to one another, so why should we tell them to foreigners? Plus, what's the point? And those voices – is it true that the voices of the dead flow through the alleys of the camp?

And Dunya? Why do I keep seeing Dunya, with her wide eyes, standing in front of the tall French director and speaking?

I don't know Dunya. I just encountered her eyes, suspended in her face, near the cemetery wall, promised I'd try to work something out for her in Tunis and forgot the matter. Then I discovered that Dunya *was* the matter, the reason being Dr Muna Abd El Kareem, professor of psychiatry at the Lebanese University. Dr Muna works with the Association for the Disabled in the camp, and Dunya was a regular visitor there. We thought Dunya had found a job for herself, but Dunya wasn't working, she was talking. Foreign journalists would come and Dr Muna would take them to the office, where Dunya would tell her story with Dr Muna translating. Dunya had become a new kind of storyteller, one who tells her stories only to foreigners, and she became a story herself. I don't have any objections – everyone's free to do as they please – but a month after the Carlton Hotel Women's Conference they brought her here to the hospital and Dr Amjad refused to receive her. He said she was a chronic case and untreatable, but Saleem As'ad and I got her in by force. She's living in a room on the second floor now, close to yours. Her situation is precarious because her pelvis has been shattered again. I think there must be some problem with her bones because they're disintegrating. Today Dunya looks like a corpse and needs a private nurse. Her mother visits her every day, but instead of helping us she weeps. And Dunya says nothing. Her eyes, suspended in her thin, pale face, look without seeing, and she doesn't open her mouth.

Dunya talked too much – it was Dr Muna's fault. We all thought she was working at the Association for the Disabled, but she wasn't working, she was talking. Dr Muna had made her into a tool for "fund raising." Let's contemplate this expression that has entered our language from the American dictionary. In order to collect money we need pity, and Dunya could summon forth tears. Dr Muna Abd El Kareem would make her tell her story, and the "fund raising" went ahead. I don't know what's come over us since the Israeli invasion of '82: every intellectual and activist has started talking about nothing but the international organisations that give out money. The activists have turned into thieves, master, with all this "fund raising" going into their own pockets. Maybe they're doing the right thing! I swear I don't know any longer.

But no.

This has nothing to do with Dr Muna. The psychiatrist was just doing her job, and maybe she believed that Dunya, having told her story so often, had ended up merely acting. Acting isn't confession, and has no impact on the actor's life. It seems, however, that Dunya wasn't acting; she was telling her own story.

I saw her. I was watching the Women's Conference on television when they announced a "Palestinian testimony", and I saw Dunya come forward, borne on two sticks. Her feet struck the ground hard, her pelvis swivelled, she walked slowly and calmly. She was neither hurried nor embarrassed, as though she'd learned her role well. She reached the podium, supported her weight on it and let the crutches fall with a clatter. Dunya paid no attention either to the noise or to the man who hurried to pick the crutches up. She looked straight ahead and started speaking. And she amazed me. This woman was telling a completely different story. I'd no idea she'd been . . . had no idea how she could have hidden all these things from us and could now be saying them in front of these foreigners. She spoke in English, sometimes slipping into Arabic, which Dr Muna would hasten to translate.

"I ran," she said. "Then they raped me." She said "raped me" in English and then stopped, to let the hall fill with the stains of silence.

"They came into the house and started firing. We were wearing our night clothes and sitting in the living room. Our house has two rooms, one for sleeping and the other for the television. When we heard the explosions, we all went into the television room. The electricity was cut, but we found ourselves going there without thinking, to listen to the news."

She said that all the members of the family were round the television when armed men entered carrying torches. "The light from the torches was terrifying. We had sat round the silent television and lit a single candle. Then the ropes of light started, and the firing. I fled. Without looking behind me, I went to the door, which the armed men had ripped off. I walked away calmly, I didn't run. I saw the flares, like little suns. I walked and I walked, then I felt something hot in my right thigh. I started running, or I felt I was running, but I wasn't. I was moving very slowly in fact. I ran and heard the bullets, and they sounded as though they were exploding in my ear."

Dunya said she was running on the spot when he brought her down. "I thought I'd fallen, but it was that man. I didn't see his face. The flares seemed not to provide light, as though they were surrounding the darkened faces with light but not lighting up their features. He fell on top of me. They all fell on top of me. I'd reached the corner of the main street. From our house to the main street was about ten metres. I was in front of Abu Sa'du's shop when I fell and the faces fell on top of me. *They raped me* and I felt nothing. I thought that the hotness that exploded from my right thigh was blood. Everything was hot, everything was black, everything was . . . I can't tell you how long it went on. I was like someone in a coma. I saw without seeing, felt without feeling."

Dunya's face filled the small screen, a black cloud seeming to me to hover around her eyes. She spoke and spoke, in a flat white voice without any trace of excitement, as though she was telling some other woman's story. As though it had nothing to do with her.

Later I learned from Dr Muna that all Dunya did was relate what had happened to her, and yet her listeners would be taken by surprise each time by some new thing she hadn't mentioned on previous occasions. The journalists and representatives of international humanitarian organisations would come, and Dunya would sit in the office of the Association for the Disabled in the camp and speak, and Dr Muna would translate what Dunya didn't know how to say in English.

Dunya became a story telling its own story.

When Dr Muna came to the hospital to visit her, she said she understood now. "Dunya collapsed because she stopped speaking after the Carlton conference. That was the first and last time she spoke about the gang rape. The story went round the camp, her mother got very angry, and everyone . . . well, you know the people here better than me, doctor."

Dr Muna said she'd had a disappointment. "A German journalist said he wanted to do a piece about the camp and the 'trauma' of the massacre.

I told him about Dunya, and he asked to meet her. She came, but she didn't say a word. She told me the pain in her pelvis had come back and was so terrible that she couldn't talk through it. I begged her because I'd told the German journalist about her and he was very interested. He wanted to hear a story from a victim, but the victim wouldn't talk. I tried to persuade her, but she shook her head, tears flooding from her eyes, so I left her alone and apologised to the journalist, who was very sad because he wouldn't be able to use Dunya's story in his article. Then her mother came and told me that Dunya couldn't get out of bed and asked me to get her into the American University hospital. We don't have a *budget*, doctor, for such cases, so I advised her to put her in Galilee Hospital. You know the rest."

Dunya lies on her bed sleeping with her eyes open, or so Saleem As'ad informed me before he disappeared. He said he went into her room to check because he thought he heard a moan, and he saw her swathed in the woollen blanket up to her neck and her eyes . . . her eyes were open in the darkness, and a white light was coming out of them.

Saleem said he'd gone over to her because he'd thought she was awake. "I went close," he said, "but she didn't move. I bent down and whispered her name and she didn't answer. I put my ear close to her nose, and her deep, slow breathing brushed my ear. She was asleep with both eyes open. Is that possible, doctor?"

Saleem said he'd been frightened and asked me my opinion, which is, of course, that it's impossible; no-one can sleep with their eyes open. But I don't know any longer; anything's possible these days. Isn't your own death a clinical reality, father – despite which you don't die? Everything's become strange. Tell me, is it true the voices of the dead roam the streets at night? I don't believe such superstitious nonsense, but we weren't able even to collect the names of the dead properly. The community committee met and decided to make a list of the names. We collected lots of names but still couldn't arrive at a final record. Differences arose among the different political organisations and the project folded. We don't have the names of our dead, we only have figures. We put figures next to figures, subtract them, add them, multiply them – that's our life. Even the Lebanese journalist Georges Baroudi, when he came to the camp and asked for a list of the names of the victims

and we said we didn't have a complete list, said that made things complicated. He suggested that a memorial be erected to the martyrs. You know
how those intellectuals think: they imagine they can solve the problems
of their consciences with statues, or poems, or novels. I told him that
memorials were impossible here because we didn't know what would
happen to us tomorrow – whether the camp would remain where it is
or not. But he insisted on his idea. He came back a few days later with
a Lebanese sculptor sporting a straw hat. He was wearing shorts and
they went round the camp together, then walked to the grave. The women
rushed over – in those days we were still capable of defending our dead
– the women ran and started yelling and hurling abuse and a brawl started
that only ended when you intervened. You came and dispersed the
women, invited Baroudi and the sculptor for a coffee, and explained that
no-one was allowed to walk over graves. They apologised profusely and
told you the details of their project, and you asked them to co-ordinate
with me.

More than three weeks later, Baroudi came back and told me that a
committee of Lebanese artists and intellectuals had been formed to
prepare plans for a Martyrs' Garden.

"We're going to call it the Martyrs' Garden – what do you think?" he
asked.

I said the name was satisfactory and asked for details of the project.
He said the committee hadn't finalised the plans yet and promised to
discuss them with me and the community committee before work started.
Then he told me he was writing a book about the Shatila massacre. He
said there were only two books about the massacre, both by Israelis. One
was by a journalist called Amnon Kapeliouk, the other the report of
Israel's Kahane Commission. "Don't you think it's shameful – shameful
that we don't write our own history?" he asked. Baroudi told me he'd
translated the Kahane Report into Arabic, but he felt that we should
write a book that would bring eyewitness accounts together.

He invited me to lunch at Rayyis's restaurant in El Jimmeizeh, so I
said, "Why not." We drank arak and ate a good, cheap Lebanese stew.
My attention was drawn to the Lebanese man they call Shoukri. Shoukri
was sitting at a table in the midst of the customers, peeling enormous
quantities of garlic. Baroudi told me that Rayyis's was the best popular

restaurant in Beirut, that he always went there to meet a group of young men who'd been fighters with the Lebanese Forces militias, and that he'd heard the story from Boss Josèph – one of those who'd taken part in the massacre – himself. What he'd had in mind in inviting me to the restaurant was to arrange a meeting between myself and Boss Josèph. "A Dialogue between the Executioner and the Victim" would be the first chapter of the book.

He asked me what I thought.

I said I didn't know because I didn't know about that kind of book, but it might be a good idea.

We sat and waited, but Boss Josèph never appeared. Baroudi ordered food and arak, and then he took me on a tour of El Ashrafiyyeh and told me about the massacre as it had been described to him by Boss Josèph.

Do you want to hear? Or are you in some other place, and would you prefer me to tell you about Saleem? I think you liked the story about Saleem because he was a pleasant young man, bright and a real son of a bitch.

Where was I?

Abu Akram came and invited us to drink tea at the Popular Front office. The tall director hesitated and said he was waiting for Daniel.

"Where's Daniel?" asked Abu Akram.

"I don't know. We lost him in the camp," said the director.

"I'll send someone to look for him. Please come with me."

So we went with him.

In the office I was the translator.

Abu Akram delivered a short speech in his awkward English about the sufferings of the Palestinian people. He was followed by a man I hadn't met before; his stomach hung down over his leather belt, the smoke from his cigarette trailed through his thick moustache, and he held forth. The director and Catherine found their attention wandering and I translated a bit. I skipped the slogans because they bored me, also because they sounded ridiculous in English. China taught me a valuable and unforgettable lesson. There I was required to translate whatever I said in Arabic into English, and I discovered that I could dispense with half the expressions we use. Even my way of talking changed: I started to avoid the long introductions we usually put in front of what we have to say and started coming straight to the point instead.

The fat man's speech resisted translation. How was I to translate the words for suffering, torment, oppression and persecution that he used one after the other? He'd use strings of adjectives without indicating what he was describing, so I summarised his long Arabic sentences in brief English ones.

He interrupted me to say, "I said more than that."

"It doesn't matter," I told him. "English is a short language."

"But you cut out half my speech. How do you expect them to understand our sufferings when you cut them out?"

He looked at the tall director and asked if he understood what he was trying to say.

"Translate, son, translate. Ask him if he understood what I was trying to say."

"I understood," said the director in response to my translation, adding that the aim of their visit was to acquire knowledge. He didn't say one word to indicate solidarity, as Abu Akram and the fat man expected he would. He said he'd come to learn so as to be able to transfer an accurate picture to the stage.

Saleem was sitting behind the room's only metal table, while we, Abu Akram and the fat orator sat on low sofas against the walls. Saleem said nothing during the speeches; his looks moved between the French woman and me. But when we'd subsided into silence and were sipping our coffee, he asked me, without any preliminaries, why I didn't dye my hair!

"Why should I dye it?"

"To make you young again," he said.

"I am young. I don't need to prove it."

You'll remember, master, that my hair started to go white when I was twenty-one. My grandmother, God rest her soul, told me the family was like that and that my father's hair had been white before he was twenty-five.

My grandmother said my father had loved his white hair because it made him look old and young at the same time. She also told me she'd insisted on washing his hair before he was buried. She'd got a bowl of water and washed his hair, which had been dyed with his blood, till it was white as snow, and wept. My grandmother said she didn't weep till the hair was shining white once more. At that moment she'd understood that her son was dead and plunged into a bout of weeping that only ended when she died. I wasn't in the house when she died. They sent for me and told me the end was coming, and I came up from the south, and she gave me the cushion and the watch and the Koran, but she didn't die. Her last days dragged on, so I went back to the south, and she died when I wasn't there.

Saleem asked me why I didn't use a shampoo to dye my hair. He said he had a wonderful French shampoo. "Would you like to try it?"

"No, thank you."

"I use it; look at my hair."

"You?"

"Certainly. I've been using it for eighteen years."

"You!"

He said the shampoo had removed all traces of white from his hair and told me his story.

Now that's a story, I said to myself. No-one had agreed to describe his experience of the massacre to the French people, so I asked if he'd let me translate it into English.

Saleem said he could speak English if he wanted to and didn't need me to translate, and he didn't want to tell them his story.

When Saleem said his hair had turned white, Abu Akram shrugged his shoulders as though he already knew and looked at me in amazement, as though I ought to have known too.

I asked him apologetically how his hair had come to be white, and he smoothed it with his right palm and said it had turned white during the massacre.

"How old were you?" I asked.

"Five," he said. He said his mother had picked him up; they'd both been bleeding, and his mother had run through the fire.

"There wasn't a fire," I said.

"Oh yes there was," he said. "The fire was everywhere, and we jumped over it."

"It was the flares," said Abu Akram.

"No," said Saleem.

"Of course," said the fat man. "What's the problem? Everyone tells the story his own way. There wasn't any fire, son, it was the flares, but you were young, how would you know."

"I know all right," said Saleem and pointed at his head.

He said his mother ran with him, picked him up and ran, and they were shooting in all directions. He'd clung to her neck, then everything went sticky and bloody, and he'd come to in the hospital with his hair as white as snow. The nurses had been afraid of him.

"In America I shaved my head."

He said he'd gone to America with his mother after all the members of his family had been killed. "My mother emigrated to join her sister in Detroit and took me with her. That was in '84, but they refused to give me a resident's visa. I stayed with her for two years in secret, then I came back. She told me, 'You go back to Lebanon and I'll send for you when they give me a Green Card.'"

"And did she send for you?"

"No, I swear. I waited and waited, but it was no use. Abu Akram is my father's first cousin. He took me in and is letting me live in this office till my mother sends for me. I wrote her letters, but I didn't receive any answers. It seems the Americans don't like white hair, or she's forgotten about me. God knows where she is now. I asked to meet the American ambassador in Beirut. I phoned the embassy several times, but they never gave me an appointment, I don't know why, even though I spoke Classical English to them."

"There's no such thing as Classical English," I said.

"What are you talking about, man? All languages are the same. There's colloquial Arabic and classical Arabic, and there's colloquial English and Classical English, am I right or am I not?"

"No," I said, "but it doesn't matter."

"Do you want some shampoo?"

He got up and fetched a black leather case, opened it and took out a number of bottles.

"I sell shampoo to keep myself busy."

He went over to the French actress and indicated that she should buy some. Catherine took a bottle and seemed embarrassed, not knowing what she was supposed to do.

I snatched the bottle from her and gave it back to Saleem.

"Forget it. Try it on someone else."

"Let them make up their own minds, brother. Maybe they would've bought some."

"Leave it alone, son. Forget it," I scolded him loudly.

"Why don't you buy some, doctor, and dye your hair?" asked Saleem.

"What's he saying?" asked the director.

"He's selling hair dye," I answered and quickly told him the story of Saleem's white hair.

"Don't tell him," said Saleem. "If you want, I'll tell him myself. But did you believe my story? I only tell it to sell shampoo."

I looked at Abu Akram and saw his lips curling in a kind of smile, and his small white teeth, as white as those of a little child, appeared.

"What? What?" asked Catherine.

"Buy the shampoo and I'll tell you," said Saleem.

The girl took the bottle of shampoo and asked how much it was.

"It doesn't matter," said Saleem. "Pay whatever you want."

Catherine took a hundred-franc note out of her little purse and gave it to Saleem. Saleem took the note, looked at it for a while, then handed it back to Catherine and turned to me and said, "No, brother. I was just joking."

"Which was the joke," I asked him, "the shampoo or the white hair?"

"You guess."

Saleem took the bottle from Catherine, put it back in his leather case, said goodbye and went off.

Abu Akram said Saleem joked around all the time, treating his tragedy as comedy because he had no-one and needed work.

"What did he study?" I asked him.

"Nothing, my friend," he said. "We're all children of the Revolution, and what can you study in the Revolution?"

"Tell him to come and see me at the hospital. Maybe I can find him some work. But is his story true?"

"Of course, of course," said Abu Akram. "He's the only one of his family to have survived the massacre."

"What about his mother?" I asked.

"His mother died, but he insists on saying she picked him up and escaped with him. She didn't pick him up. They found him under the bodies; they pushed the bodies away and took him to the hospital, and there they discovered that every hair on his head had turned white."

"And America?"

"What America, brother? His aunt lives in Detroit, that's all. Do you think someone like Saleem or like us can get a visa for America? Out of the question! He just loves the cinema. He goes to see Al Pacino's films ten times and learns the dialogue by heart. He puts the films on the video machine and says the words along with the actors. That's how he learned English – monkey see, monkey do."

"And the shampoo?" I asked.

"That's a different story," he said. "The shampoo came after the 'Ekza'. Do you know what he was doing for a living last year? He'd go out to Fakahani with a bunch of small bottles, stand in the middle of the road and shout, 'Ekza for pain! Ekza for rheumatism! Ekza for impotence!' He'd invented a medicine he called Ekza and he'd package it in empty bottles and sell the bottles for three thousand lira each.

"'Ekza!' he'd shout, opening a bottle and drinking the contents in front of everyone. 'Drink and get well! Rub it on where it hurts and the pain goes away!' And people bought. Then they arrested him.

"They took him to the police station on the new highway, where he confessed that Ekza was a mixture of water and soya oil, and that it was harmless. The officer smiled and told Saleem that he'd overlook it this time on condition that Saleem didn't do it again. But instead of leaving, Saleem took out a bottle and offered it to the officer saying he'd give him a good price and sell him the bottle for two thousand, now he'd become his friend, and that Ekza cured everything, especially constipation.

"The officer lost his temper and ordered him to be beaten and put in gaol. They practically beat him to death and left him to rot for more than a month.

"When he returned to the camp, he said they'd released him because they were scared of him. They were scared of him because of his hair, which he told them had turned white overnight.

"After his experience with gaol, Saleem decided not to leave the camp. He stopped making and selling Ekza and started selling shampoo. Yesterday, if you'd seen him, you'd have understood how he works."

"And is it real shampoo?" I asked.

"I don't know," said Abu Akram, "but he lets his hair go white, then stands in front of the mosque, washes his hair and people buy."

"What's he saying?" asked the director.

As I told him the story of the shampoo and was looking at Catherine, expecting a reaction, we heard a racket outside the door. The bodyguard Abu Akram had gone to look for Daniel had returned with him. Daniel came in with three children larking about while he handed out chewing gum and chocolates and they argued over them.

"Get the children out of here!" shouted Abu Akram.

"Where were you?" I asked.

"Looking around," he said. "And, as you can see, I like children."

The director stood up and Catherine got ready to go; it seemed they'd lost interest. They didn't ask for more information about Saleem.

Abu Akram asked if I'd taken them to the mosque-cemetery.

I said no.

"I'll take them," he said. "Thank you, doctor."

I was on the verge of leaving when Catherine asked me what Abu Akram wanted.

"He'll take you to the cemetery," I said.

"But we've already seen the cemetery," said the director.

"The one at the mosque," I said, and explained how we'd turned the mosque into a cemetery during the siege.

"Another cemetery!" exclaimed Catherine, and her lower lip started to tremble. "I don't want to, I don't want to. I want to go back to the hotel."

I told Abu Akram that our friends were tired and it would be better to take them back to the hotel, but Abu Akram insisted and asked me to translate what he said. He started talking about death, and about how we as a people regarded the dead as holy, and said that if Shatila hadn't stood fast during the siege, the Gaza and West Bank *intifada* would never have happened.

I interrupted and said I wasn't going to translate. "Can't you see, my friend, the woman's crying and the man's trying to calm her down, with his pale face and his bald spot shining with sweat? Drop it and let them go."

I heard the girl whisper to the director that she wouldn't do the part:

"I'm scared. I won't do the part, and I want to go back to the hotel."

I translated this to Abu Akram, and the fat man said he understood and went over to pat her on the shoulder. The moment his hand touched her, she trembled and pulled back as though she'd had an electric shock, and I saw a sort of fear mixed with disgust in her eyes.

I left them with Abu Akram and the fat man and walked out without saying goodbye.

What blindness!

Is this what things have come to? They're afraid of the victim! Instead of treating the patient, they fear him, and when they see, they close their eyes. They read books and write them. It's the books that are the lies.

But why does the image of Catherine stick in my mind? Perhaps because she's short and young and loose-limbed, or perhaps because of her hair, cropped like a boy's. It seems I fancied her, especially when her lower lip started trembling. It started when I translated bits of the anecdote about Saleem, especially the bit about how he used to stand in front of everybody and dye his hair in order to sell the shampoo. Catherine, instead of laughing like me and Abu Akram and the director, hid her face as though she'd seen us playing out our own deaths. I think she thought we were beasts. How could we do that and not implode?

In fact, father, wouldn't it be better if nobody saw us? And what's to be done if they do? Why are they going to build a wall around the camp? The Lebanese journalist I told you about spoke to me about the wall. He said the government would soon complete the rebuilding of Sports City, which was demolished by the Israeli planes, and that Beirut was going to host the next Arab Games, and it would be better for the Arab athletes if they didn't see.

They solve the problem by covering their eyes. And maybe they're right! We, in this place, we're a kind of dirty secret. A permanent dirty secret you can only cover over by forgetting it.

"I'd like to forget too," I said when he invited me to Rayyis's restaurant.

I'd prefer to forget. And my encounter with Boss Josèph, as Baroudi called him, changed nothing because I'm not seeking revenge.

Can you believe it? The man invites me to meet with one of the butchers of Shatila, and I tell him there's no point because I don't hate them.

"There is a point," said the journalist. "I want you to come because I'm going to write about reconciliation and forgiveness."

"But I haven't forgiven him or the others," I answered.

"Never mind, never mind. What matters is how you feel."

"And what about how he feels?" I asked.

"About what who feels?" he asked me.

"This Josèph I don't know."

I went out of curiosity, since I don't know East Beirut and I'd never met someone we'd fought and who'd fought us. The civil war had become a long dream, as though it had never happened. I can feel it under my skin, but I don't believe it. All that remains are the pictures. Even our massacre here in the camp and the flies that hunted me down I see as though they were pictures, as though I wasn't remembering but watching. I don't get upset; I feel astonishment. Strange, isn't it? Strange that a war should pass like a dream.

What do you think?

If you could speak, you'd say that the whole of life seems like a dream. Maybe, in your long sleep, you're floating over the surface of things, as eyes do over pictures.

We went to Rayyis's restaurant and waited, but he didn't come.

We sat at a table for four. The journalist ordered two glasses of arak and a bowl each of *hommous* and *tabouleh*, and we waited. Then a group of young men came in, their hair cut like that of fighters in the Lebanese Forces.

"Nasri!" yelled Baroudi, jumping up from his seat and embracing this Nasri.

"What are you doing here?" asked Nasri.

"What am I doing? I'm getting drunk," answered Baroudi.

"Come and get drunk with us," said Nasri.

"I can't. I have a guest. And we're waiting for Boss Josèph."

Soon I found myself at their table. There were six young men and a dark-skinned girl in a very short skirt and a shirt open all the way down. It seemed to me she must have been Nasri's girlfriend because whenever she got the chance she'd put her hand in his.

They laughed and drank and ate and told jokes. I tried to match their mood, but I couldn't; it was as though my mouth was blocked with a stone, or I was ashamed of my Palestinian accent.

Baroudi broke the ice and told them who I really was: "I forgot to tell you that Dr Khaleel works for the Palestine Red Crescent in Shatila camp."

"Welcome, welcome," said Nasri. "You're Palestinian?"

"Yes, yes."

"From Shatila?"

"Yes, yes. I live in Shatila, but I'm originally from Galilee."

"I know Galilee well," he said, and he started to tell me, to the delight of his companions, about a training course for parachutists that he'd taken part in in Galilee.

"Have you visited Palestine?" he asked me.

"No," I answered.

"I know it well. You have a beautiful country, I swear, a lot like Lebanon, but the Jews have fixed it up and it's in good shape. The way it's organised is astonishing – gardens and water and swimming pools. You'd think you were in Europe."

He said they'd done their training in a Palestinian village. The village was just as it had been, but weeds had sprouted up everywhere.

"What was the name of the village?" I asked.

"I don't know. They didn't say, and we didn't ask."

"It's a small village," said another youth, called Maro, "and in the middle there's a big rock."

Nasri said he'd fired at a tree, to amuse himself, and the Israeli trainer had scolded him and told him that he was lucky he'd missed because in Israel they loved trees and forbade anyone to cut them down or do them any harm.

"They're taking care of our trees," I said.

"When you see it, the whole area is planted with pine trees. God, how lovely the pines are! You'd think you were in Lebanon."

"Pine trees! But it's an area for olives."

"The Jews don't like olives. It's either pines or palms."

"They killed the trees," I said.

"No. They uprooted them and replanted."

Nasri used the odd Hebrew word I didn't understand to prove that what he was saying was right, and said he'd been a fool because he'd believed in the war. War was meaningless. Soon he was going to go to America to continue his studies in computer engineering.

The strange thing, master, was that I listened to this young man, who'd jumped with his parachute over Galilee, without feeling any hatred. I'd imagined that if I ever met one of those people I wouldn't be able to hold myself back, but there I was drinking arak and laughing at their jokes and watching the girl as she tried to hold Nasri's hand and he pulled it out of hers, while Baroudi observed me and looked at his watch and tut-tutted because Josèph was late.

"That Josèph of yours is full of bullshit," one of them said, and he started telling tales of Josèph's cowardice, especially at the battle of the Holiday Inn, when he threw himself from the fourth storey to escape and ran on a broken leg.

"A dope-head and an arsehole," said another.

"Look how he's ended up – calling himself a boss just when there aren't any bosses left," said Nasri.

I felt a desire to defend Boss Josèph. I thought it wasn't fair to talk about him behind his back and that if he were there, he'd show them what being a boss meant. And as to his being a coward, I didn't believe it, especially after what Baroudi had told me about how particularly savage he'd been during the Shatila massacre. However, I preferred to remain silent. I was in a strange position. How can I describe it? I really can't say there were no crimes. We too killed and destroyed, but at that moment I felt just how banal evil is. Evil has no meaning, and we were just its tools. We're nothing. We make war and kill and die, and we're nothing – just fuel for a huge machine whose name is War. I said to myself, it's impossible. Especially with this Nasri, I felt as though I was standing in front of a mirror, as though he resembled me! If I'd been able to talk, I'd have talked more than he did, but a big stone stopped up my mouth. Then the stone started crumbling to the rhythm of the girl's hand that reached out for Nasri's hand and then pulled back. He was drinking arak in a special way: he'd suck the glass, leaving a little of the white liquid on its lip and then licking it off with his tongue. He was a white-skinned youth with broad shoulders. I think he must've been a body builder because his chest rippled under his blue shirt and he kept coming back to the story of the parachute training and how he'd felt as though he was flying through Israel.

He'd say "Israel" and look at me apologetically: "Sorry, sorry –

'Palestine', to make you happy." He said he'd flown over Palestine, and looked at me with eyes full of irony and complicity.

After my third glass I asked about the war. "What do you feel now?"

"We don't feel anything," said Nasri. "And you?" he asked me.

"I feel sad," I said.

Nasri said he didn't feel regret or sorrow for his friends who'd died in the war. "That's life," he said, shrugging his shoulders with indifference.

"But you were defeated," I said.

"And you were defeated," he said.

"Not exactly," I said.

"Tell me about your life in the camps, and then talk to me about victory and defeat."

"I'll tell you about my death," I said. "You killed me."

"We killed you, and you killed us. That's what I was trying to explain to you," said Nasri. "We were defeated, and you were defeated."

"All of us were defeated," Maro said and raised his glass. "Knock it back, boys – a toast to defeat."

The young men raised their glasses and drained them.

"We have to go. It was good to meet you, doctor. Don't be upset, we'll talk some more," said Nasri, who asked for the bill and paid it. Then they all left.

I wanted to – but didn't – mention the *intifada* and say, "It's true we were defeated, but the game's not over." That stone stopped up my mouth.

Nasri paid and left, and I was embarrassed because my friend the writer didn't even take out his wallet.

I felt nauseous among the piles of empty dishes, but I wasn't drunk. I'd only drunk three glasses of arak, but I'd had a psychological reaction. I looked at my watch and said Joseph wasn't coming.

"How about a coffee?" said Georges.

I said, "Great," and put up my hand to order, but Baroudi pulled it down.

"Not here," he said. "Let's go to a café."

I sat next to him in his red Renault and he took me through streets I didn't know. That's how I finally became acquainted with El Ashrafiyyeh, East Beirut's Christian quarter which they also call "Little Mountain".

He switched the car's tape player to the Fayrouz song 'Old Jerusalem'.

"We're enemies," I said to Baroudi.

"Don't worry about it," he answered me. "It's all bullshit."

Then we entered a beautiful street. It was how I imagined the streets of Haifa. My grandmother told me tales of the city by the sea, where the streets were shaded by trees and jasmine and there was the scent of frangipani. "We're in the Circassian quarter," Baroudi said. "This is where the rich people live. They were just translators for the foreign consuls in the days of the Ottomans, and look at their palaces!"

He said he dreamt of having a house here.

He said that during the illness of his aged father, who was now dead, he'd come with him every day to this street and they'd walk.

He said his father loved to walk here. "I want to die and take these colours with me to the grave," he'd say. Then Baroudi told me a strange story about a woman his father had been in love with before he'd married his mother. He spoke of an old hunch-backed woman who lived close to the cemetery: "She was ten years older than my father, worked as a seamstress and spent her money on him. She had no family, her only brother had died when he was young. My father didn't marry her. His family forced him to marry his cousin, who became my mother. The strange thing was that the woman encouraged him to get married. He went on loving her even when she grew old and her back was bent, but he took to sending me to her because he couldn't bear to see her in her wretched old age – a woman with a hunched back who wore black clothes and walked as though she was crawling, as though she'd turned into a tortoise. I was afraid of her. I'd put a bag of food at the entrance to her house, knock on the door and flee. She'd yell at me to come in, but I was scared of the tortoise's shell that had sprouted on her back."

He stopped the car, turned to me and asked, "And you?"

"And me what?"

"What about your father?"

"My father died long ago, and I don't remember him."

Before we got to the café, he pointed out the cemetery of Mar Mitir. I saw what looked like marble palaces with angels, statues and doves that could almost fly above them.

"These are their tombs," he said.

"Whose tombs?"

"The tombs of the owners of the palaces we saw in the street."

"Those are tombs!"

"Indeed, my dear sir. They live in palaces, and they're buried in palaces. It's the way of the world."

We sat in Joachim's Café close to Saseen Square in El Ashrafiyyeh, whose name has since been changed to Phalange Martyrs' Square. In the middle of the square is a memorial to the victims of the blowing-up of Phalange House on the Feast of the Cross, 14 September 1982, when President-elect Basheer Jmayil met his end. The base of the monument bears a large picture of Basheer shaded with grey lines. His assassination a few days before he was to assume the post of President of the Lebanese Republic was the reason given for the Shatila massacre. It was said that his men committed the massacre, in co-ordination with the Israeli Army, because they were so blinded by sorrow for their leader.

Pointing to the monument, Baroudi said that the massacre had been an instinctive act of revenge, and he just wished Boss Josèph had come so I could hear his version of events.

I said I knew what had happened and I didn't need Josèph to tell me because I'd been there.

"You know nothing," he said, and told me what Josèph had been going to tell me. As I listened, the cold crept into my bones, as though the words were bits of ice dropping onto my spine.

What did he hope to achieve with his story?

I'd believed that he sympathised with us and wanted to build a memorial to the victims. Then he brings me to this café and talks to me as though he was Josèph.

When I think of him now, master, I can only see him in the form of Josèph. After that trip to El Ashrafiyyeh, the man disappeared. He gave me a lift to the camp entrance and promised he'd come back with the plan for the memorial garden, but he didn't. The war started up again, and there was the long siege that destroyed the camp and the cemetery and memories of the massacre. As with all disasters, the only thing that can make one forget a massacre is an even bigger massacre, and we're a people whose fate it is to be forgotten as a result of its accumulated calamities. Massacre erases massacre, and all that remains in the memory is the smell of blood.

Baroudi disappeared and never contacted me again. I phoned the newspaper where he worked a number of times but didn't find him. The switchboard operator said he wasn't in even though I was sure he was there. I didn't want anything from him, I just wanted him to publish our news, for in those days, master, I was living in two deserts: my little desert was the camp, and my big desert was Shams.

I left the camp to get some antibiotics, got held up in Mar Elias and couldn't go back to Shatila. In Mar Elias I met Shams and was smitten, and then she disappeared. When I think of that day, master, I feel ashamed, but I wasn't interested in the fate of the camp, I was running after that woman's shadow. Something inside me was stronger than I was. Something made me forget everything and nailed me to the cross of her eyes. I was like a madman. You understand; you must have gone through a similar experience with Naheeleh because you're like me, you weren't married. Or at least let's say that your marriage wasn't like a marriage. You didn't possess the woman you loved in such a way that you could quench your thirst, and you stayed suspended between places just as I was during the siege. I used to feel a savage loneliness, which is why I phoned Georges Baroudi, but he avoided me because he didn't want to get involved.

That day at Joachim's Café, however, Baroudi forgot himself and assumed the character of Josèph. At first I thought he was talking the way he was because he was drunk, but then again maybe he was with them in the camp! How, though? He was an intellectual and a writer and a journalist, and they don't go to war or get involved; they observe death and write, thinking they've experienced death.

On that rainy day, however, he was different.

I forgot to say that it was raining, and in Beirut, as in Haifa, the rain comes down like ropes, then suddenly stops. I almost said the man was raining! I can see him in front of me through the café window, the ropes of rain around his thick lips, the smoke from his cigarette, abandoned in the ashtray, ascending; and his words hurt my ears, and the sloosh of the rain drowns the road that descends from Saseen Square to the Church of Our Lady of the Entry.

Why did he tell me the story?

I'm certain he wasn't watching for my reactions – a drunk doesn't observe a drunk. So why? Because he was one of them? Did he want to confess? Christians confess to a priest. Their confessions are like the self-criticism sessions I learned in China and tried to apply here, and which made me a laughingstock: I'd call a self-criticism session and start with myself to encourage the others, and the meeting would end in jokes. No-one was capable of confessing to his own mistakes, and they'd all find justifications for their actions. To put an end to the joking around and the obnoxiousness, I'd be forced to agree with them that we hadn't made any mistakes at all, even in the case of the village of El Eishiyyeh in South Lebanon, which we entered in the summer of 1975 after a gruelling battle with the Phalangists. Our commanding officer ordered the armed fighters who'd surrendered to stand against a wall and executed them all with machine guns. The execution of captives is forbidden, as you know, by the laws of the Fatah Movement, but we discovered justifications for our mistake-crime. We said we were taking revenge for the massacres that had been committed against us, that civil wars always involved massacres etc. Rasim, the militia commander, God rest his soul, cited Sholokhov's novel *And Quiet Flows the Don* and said that during the civil war in Russia the Bolsheviks would ask their captives to take off their clothes before they executed them so they wouldn't get torn by the bullets. The captives would stand naked in the snow, shivering; then they'd shoot them so they'd fall into the graves they'd dug with their own hands.

"We're more merciful than the Bolsheviks," said Rasim. "We don't force them to dig their own graves or take off their clothes."

That was when I became convinced that self-criticism was useless, since everything will be found to have its justifications, its reasons, its special circumstances and so on.

Sitting in the café, Georges Baroudi exploited the rhythm of the rain with its long ropes to confess. He said he'd recorded more than three hours of confessions by Boss Josèph and wanted to publish them in a book to be called *The Banality of Man*. He said he'd brought a tape recorder with him to record our conversation and that he'd make that the intro-duction to his book. But Josèph didn't come, so he asked me to tell him my version of what happened so he could put the two versions into the book. "A page for you and a page for him – what do you think? The killer and the killed in conversation."

"But I wasn't killed," I said.

"You can represent the dead," he said.

"The dead don't talk and they don't have representatives," I said.

"Aren't you a Palestinian like them? Look at Israel; it represents the victims of the Holocaust."

"That's the difference," I said. "I don't believe victims have representatives, that they . . . that they . . ."

"You understand nothing," he said.

I told him his project was meaningless, you couldn't sit the victim down next to the perpetrator. I told him, "Your book will be as banal as its title" and burst out laughing.

At that instant, the man before me was transformed. Even his white face became tinged with green. He said, as though it was Josèph speaking, "They took us to the airport – I was leading a detachment of twenty boys. We were wasted. Basheer died and Abu Mash'al gave me a load of cocaine and asked me to distribute it to the boys. We were sniffing cocaine like it was snacks, like we were eating nuts. Then we went down to the camp and began. There were flares. We didn't take prisoners or fight with anyone. We went into the houses, sprayed them with bullets, stabbed and killed. It was like a party, like we were at scout camp dancing round the campfire. The fire came from above, from the flares the Israelis were sending up, and we were down below having a party."

"A party", he said!

He said Boss Josèph had come across three children and asked one of his colleagues to help him grab them. He said he asked his colleague to push them together on a table. "I took out my revolver. I wanted to find out how far a shot from a revolver could go." One of the children slipped off onto the floor. The light was burning our eyes, and I asked my colleague to turn his face away. He didn't understand what I wanted, so he let go of the two children and went out of the house. I went up to them. I wanted to tie them up and then get some distance, but I couldn't find a rope, so I jammed them together, put the muzzle of the revolver close to the head of the first one and fired. My bullet went through both heads, so they died right off. I didn't see the blood because inside that weird Israeli light I couldn't see blood. When I left the house, I came across the third child, the one who'd fallen. I stepped back and fired at this small moving thing, and it came to a sudden stop where it was."

At this point Monsieur Georges got into a complicated analysis of Boss Josèph's state of mind, saying Boss Josèph wasn't aware of what he was doing and thus couldn't be considered responsible for his crime, and he got into a complex thesis about death. Then he asked me if I'd ever killed anyone.

"Listen, Monsieur Georges, I'm a fighter; your friend's a butcher. Can't you tell the difference between a criminal and a soldier?"

"You're right, you're right. But I want to know."

"What do you want to know?"

"I'm asking you, have you ever killed anyone? What did you feel afterwards?"

In the middle of this maelstrom, he asks me if I've ever killed anyone! Where does this man live?

"Of course," I said. I said it simply, even though I'd never asked myself that question before. I hadn't killed anyone, in the sense of getting close to an unarmed man and firing at him and seeing him die. But I said with a simplicity that astonished Monsieur Georges that I'd killed.

He asked me about my feelings.

"What feelings, man? There are no feelings."

He doesn't understand a thing. Imagine, master. Imagine that Monsieur Georges comes to you and asks you the same question. How would you answer? For sure you'd throw him out of your house and tell him to go to hell. What kind of questions are these? Doesn't this genius know that death means nothing, all his talk of blood instinct means nothing, it's just literary talk? In war, we kill like we breathe. Killing means not thinking about killing, just shooting.

Can you credit it that someone would come along in the middle of the whirlpool of this war and ask me about my feelings when I kill?

First, I haven't killed.

Second, even if I've killed, there are no feelings.

Third, I'm a fighter. Either I die or I live, so what am I supposed to do?

Monsieur Georges asked about my first time. He said he was starting to understand my answers because anything could become a habit, and habitual behaviour loses its impact.

"Tell me about the first time," he said.

"There wasn't a first time," I said.

"No, no, try to remember."

"The first time I saw a man die, he was screaming that he wanted to die."

That was my first time.

Do you remember your first time, master?

I think that kind of question leads nowhere.

I can only remember myself when I was a cadet. When Monsieur Georges asked me about my first time, in my mind I saw myself running with the shaven-headed boys and the cry going up: "We'll die, we'll die, but we'll never submit!"

The trainer was running in front of us shouting, "We'll die," and we were running behind him, our mouths filled with the fruit of death. That was my first time – putting death in my mouth like a bit of gum, chewing on it, running with it to the end of the world and then spitting it out. But Monsieur Baroudi wanted to know my feelings when I killed a man – so I asked him about his feelings. He said he'd never fought in his life. I don't understand how a man can be an intellectual and a writer and let war go on right next to him and not try to find out what it's like.

He said his first time was when he truly saw, and he told me the story of the barrels in Jisr El Basha camp.

He told me he went with the militia to provide press coverage for them and saw how they forced their captives to get into barrels. He said the fall of Tell El Za'tar and Jisr El Basha camps had been barbaric.

I told him I didn't want to hear about it – not about the barrels that seeped blood, or the captives rolling around inside the barrels, or the rape, the killing and the eating of human flesh.

I've got enough to deal with as it is.

I told him I hated myself now. I hated myself for the way I'd stood spellbound in front of that yellow poster designed by an Italian artist – I've forgotten his name – as a salute to the martyrs of Tell El Za'tar. I hate those three thousand vertical lines the artist put on his poster. I hate how we used to celebrate death. The number of our dead was our distinguishing feature – the more our deaths increased, the more we increased in significance.

I said I no longer liked our game with death.

He said death was a symbolic number and numbers had been the sole stable element since the dawn of history. "Numbers are magic," he said. "Only numbers can bewitch men. That's why death expressed in statistics turns into a magic charm."

We left the café. He gave me a lift to the camp entrance and went away. I don't know what he wrote in his newspaper about the meeting with Boss Josèph that never took place; I ceased to be interested the moment I got to the camp. Even the idea of reconciliation ceased to make any sense: the reconciliation has happened without happening, as should be clear from my telling you about the incident without being upset.

The reconciliation happened when Dunya became the victim of her own story; when her story was transformed into a dirty secret, when the woman fell from grace, and when all that was left were her two eyes suspended in the emptiness of her sandy face.

I believe she became separated from her own story when she agreed to participate in Dr Muna's game. I saw her on TV; I saw how she bent over the microphone after the horrible clatter made by her crutches falling. And she was lying, I swear she was lying. How can you rape a girl with a shattered pelvis? She said she'd been hit in her right thigh, that's to say in her pelvis, and that she then fell and they threw themselves on top of her – which is impossible. But that was the story the public wanted to hear. Rape is a symbol. I'm not talking just about Arabs but about everyone on earth. Man connects war with rape. Victory signifies the victor raping the defeated enemy's women; it's only complete when the women are subjected to rape. This isn't something that happens in reality, of course; it's a fantasy. No! God forbid – Dunya didn't say she was raped because she wanted to be. I don't accept the superficial, trivial opinion that most men hold about women wanting to be raped; rape is one of the most savage and painful things there is. Dunya said she was raped to please the psychologists, the sociologists and the journalists, who were expecting to hear that word from her. She said it, and they relaxed.

That's the problem with the Lebanese war. It entered the world's imagination pre-packaged as insanity. When we say that its insanity was normal, the same insanity as in any war, our listeners feel thwarted and think we're lying. Even Boss Josèph's story – I wouldn't say it didn't happen; it probably did, and there may have been worse outrages. The issue isn't what happened but how we report and remember it.

I'm convinced that if Boss Josèph had come to the restaurant and told me the story, he would've been compelled to introduce fundamental modifications. He was used to telling it in front of people who believe that what happened in the camps was heroic. With me, however, he wouldn't have been able to talk about heroism. He'd have had to have described what he did in a cold and neutral, maybe even apologetic, fashion. And that would've changed everything; even the significance of that bullet penetrating the heads of two children thrown down on a table in a house somewhere in the camp would've changed.

I haven't forgotten how the flies hovered over and pursued me. I haven't forgotten the blue flies that buzzed over those bodies acting as reservoirs for all the death in the world. I haven't forgotten how we stepped over the distended vertical bodies, holding our noses.

I told Monsieur Georges there was no such thing as "the first time", no such thing as "the first", except in stories.

You used to say, "Back to the beginning" and talk, and we'd listen. It was enough for us to hear your footsteps for "the beginning" to return, for things to start.

Not now.

Now there's no-one, and no beginning.

The issue is war, and war has no beginning.

I was prepared to meet Boss Josèph even though I felt no curiosity about him. I was prepared to meet him because I'd learned the secret of war. The secret of war is called "the mirror". I know no-one will agree with me, and they'll say I talk like this because I'm afraid, but it's not true. If you're afraid, you don't say your enemy is your mirror, you run away from him.

I agreed to meet Boss Josèph despite the fact that I didn't expect to hear anything I didn't already know. The man would start – as indeed he did start – with cocaine. He'd say he took huge amounts of cocaine before going to the camp, so he'd be exonerated from responsibility for his acts. He'd say the Israelis lit the place up and that his boss, who was sitting with the Israeli officers on the roof of the Kuwaiti Embassy overlooking the camp, expected something extra-special from him. He'd say that when he entered the darkened camp and had trouble with his torches, the famous flares blinded him, which made him fire randomly and without thinking, and that when he entered that particular house and opened fire and saw people falling over on the sofas where they were sitting, he felt a strange intoxication, and that he never meant to kill the two children but was just joking around with his companion about the effectiveness of the gun, and then he killed them, just like that, without thinking.

This is something about us that you won't understand, father.

You didn't get caught up in your war the way we did in ours. You went to war, but we didn't. Our situation was more like yours when you were in Sha'ab, except that we couldn't withdraw. Do you remember Sha'ab after you got it back from the Jews? Did you hesitate even once? Of course not. The only time you hesitated was when the ALA informed you of the decision to withdraw before the Lebanese borders closed. Then you hesitated, but you withdrew with the rest. When you met Naheeleh, you told her you'd made a mistake and asked her to stay because you thought it would be possible to correct that mistake, and quickly.

Do you remember those long months after Ibraheem died?

Do you remember how many decisions you made and how often you swore you'd stay? You lived in caves. The earth, the rocks, the trees and the wild animals were your companions, and you said you'd never leave. And when you recovered from the shock of your son's death, you went back to Lebanon and started designing your story as a permanent journey between the two Galilees. You'd go from Lebanese Galilee in the south to Palestinian Galilee in the north and would invent yourself as a story.

But we, master, we moved from war to war as though we weren't fighting. We didn't fight a war, father, we lived war, and to us it was just numbers added to numbers.

When the Lebanese war ended, I didn't feel it had ended. The war ended but didn't end, which is why I didn't pay any attention to the question of what and how our life would be afterwards.

My trip to that restaurant in El Ashrafiyyeh permitted me to meet my enemies, but unfortunately I didn't feel they were my enemies. At Rayyis's restaurant it was as if I was in front of a mirror, as though I was seeing my own image. No, I'm not defending them. If the war began again, I'd fight them again. Despite that, I want to say that real war begins when your enemy becomes your mirror so that you kill him in order to kill yourself. That's what history is. Can you see the sordidness and inanity of history? History is inane because it dislikes victors and defeats everybody.

Take yourself. When you told the tale of your journeys and your wars, when you saw that woman kneeling near the Roman olive tree in the middle of the sun's red circle, you were designing your mirror. You saw your own image in their mirrors. No, I'm not equating executioner and victim. But I do see a mirror broken into two halves which can only be mended by joining the parts together. Dear God, this is the tragedy: to see two halves that come together only in war and ruination.

I say these things to you, and you can do nothing from your bed, which has become your ship on the sea of death. I hear you saying no and telling me the story of Naheeleh and the Israeli interrogator.

"I'm a prostitute. Write that I'm a prostitute, what more do you want from me?"

Please tell me that story again, I like it so much. The first time you told it to me you didn't say the word *prostitute*. You said she said, "I'm a pro . . ." And when I asked what that meant, you burst out laughing and said "prostitute": "You've always been stubborn and you don't understand anything."

I asked you, "What did she say? Did she say 'pro . . .' or 'prostitute'?"

"She said 'prostitute'. She said the word the way it is. Quite a mouthful, huh?"

Naheeleh was pregnant with her fourth child. Ibraheem had died, Sameer was two, Nour was nine months old, and Naheeleh was pregnant.

Nour saved her. After the birth of her daughter, Naheeleh recovered from her sorrow, and the chronicle of her never-ending pregnancy began: her beauty would round out, her long black hair would hang down her back, and she would sway as she walked, as though, when pregnant, she was filled with an inner light that radiated from her face and eyes.

You told me that your lust for her would explode whenever you saw her belly growing round. Naheeleh would get as round as a ripe apple and give off a smell of thyme mixed with sour apples. She would ripen. When she came to you pregnant at the cave of Bab El Shams, she'd be overflowing with love and drowsiness.

The incident with the Israeli interrogator occurred nine months after Nour was born. Your mother went to register the girl and get an Israeli identity card for her, and they refused to register her.

The Israeli registrar asked for the father's name, and the old woman said it was registered on the headman's document and it was Yunis Ibraheem El Asadi.

The registrar said he wouldn't register the child till he'd seen her father. This happened even though your mother had brought an official document from the headman of Deir El Asad and had thought that registering Nour would be a mere formality. But the Israeli official insisted on the father coming, so the old woman took the document and went back to her house.

Naheeleh told the headman and all the men of the village that she wouldn't register the girl. "Forget it," she said. "I'm the one responsible for my children." From that moment, Naheeleh ceased to be an ordinary woman in the eyes of the villagers: she began to mix with the men and sit in their councils.

Soon after, soldiers came and escorted her to an interrogation. They entered the house, turned it upside down, and found nothing except the blind sheikh, his wife and two small children. They took Naheeleh and put her in a dark solitary-confinement cell for three days before starting to ask her questions.

At the time, the Israelis didn't employ the art of torture with chairs; they invented that after invading Lebanon. This consists of tying the detainee to a chair and leaving him sitting there for a week with a black bag over his head. The detainee remains tied to the chair inside the darkness of the bag. Soldiers lift the bag once a day and give the prisoner a crust of bread and a mouthful of water, and they take him, with his head still covered, to the bathroom once a day. In the end the prisoner forgets who he is, his joints stiffen up, and he's crushed by the darkness. By the time he's taken to the interrogation, he's lost all sensation in his body, and his back feels like a sack of stones he's carrying on his spine. He stands before the interrogator staggering, on the verge of collapse.

In those days the Israelis didn't have a particular way of dealing with women. The first charge against Naheeleh was that she'd had two children, and the second charge was that she was pregnant. They kept her for three days in a solitary-confinement cell and then summoned her for interrogation.

There were three interrogators in the room. The first sat at a small metal desk and the other two on chairs on either side of him. Handcuffed, Naheeleh stood.

He asked her her name.

"My name is Naheeleh, wife of Yunis Ibraheem."

Then she said, "Yay! It's so nice!"

"What's so nice?" the interrogator asked.

"The light," she said. "The light, sir. Glory be to God, three days in the darkness and then the light came. Praise God, praise God!"

The interrogator began questioning her in classical Arabic, and Naheeleh stared out the window and didn't respond.

"Can't you hear?" yelled the interrogator.

"Yes, I can hear. I just can't understand."

"You've been charged, and the charges are serious."

"What are the charges?"

"You're pregnant, right?"

Naheeleh burst out laughing and the two assistant interrogators looked at her with fury in their eyes. One of them got up, slapped her and started questioning her in Moroccan dialect. Naheeleh couldn't understand a word; the Moroccan words spewed from the interrogator's mouth, fell on her ears and wouldn't go in.

The man sat down again and Naheeleh was left standing, the slap ringing in her left ear. After a short silence, the Classically tongued interrogator, who was sitting at his desk, said he'd been patient long enough.

"I'm at your service, sir," said Naheeleh.

"You're pregnant, right?"

"Yes, sir."

"So?" asked the interrogator.

"So I'm pregnant, you're right. Is there a law against pregnancy in your state? Do we need a permit from the Military Governor to get pregnant? If so, we'll ask next time. I didn't know there was a law like that."

"No! No!" yelled the interrogator.

"Okay, what do you want? I confess that I'm pregnant. Happy? Can I go home?"

"We're asking about him," said the interrogator.

"Who?"

"Your husband, Yunis. Is Yunis your husband?"

"What's Yunis got to do with it?"

"We're asking you, where is Yunis?"

"I don't know anything about him."

"How?"

"How what?"

"How did you get pregnant?"

"I got pregnant the same way every other woman in the world gets pregnant."

"Meaning him."

"Who?"

"Your husband."

. . .

"He's your husband isn't he?"

. . .

"Why don't you answer?"

. . .

"Answer and have done with it."

"I'm embarrassed."

"Embarassed? Forget modesty and answer me."

"Okay."

"So Yunis is the father of your child."

"I don't think so."

"You'll confess under duress. We have methods you can't imagine, and we'll force you to tell us everything."

He looked at his assistants and said, "Take her."

"No, no!" she screamed. "I'll confess."

"Excellent," said the interrogator. "I'm listening. Please go ahead."

"I've been pregnant for four months."

"Fine. Continue."

"That's all, sir. You ask, and I'll answer."

"Where's your husband?"

"I don't know."

"Is he the father of the child in your belly?"

"No. No, I don't think so."

"It's not him? Then who is it?"

"No, it's not Yunis."

"Who?"

"I don't know."

"You don't know?"

"Right. I don't know. Or at least I'm not sure."

"You're not sure! What does that mean? You mean you're a . . . ?"

"Yes, I am. I can do as I like. What's it to you, brother? I'm a prostitute. What, there aren't any prostitutes in your respected country? Think of me as one and let me go."

The interrogator spoke with his companions in Hebrew, expressions of alarm appearing on their faces.

"I confess I'm a prostitute; I don't know who the father is."

"You don't know the child's father?"

"No."

"Who do you think it might be?"

"Everybody. Nobody. What kind of a question is that, sir? Can a woman like me be asked who she thinks it might be? Shame on such questions!"

"So it's not Yunis?"

"No."

"And how can your uncle the respected sheikh accept a fallen woman under his roof?"

"Go ask him."

Naheeleh sat down on the ground, the cuffs on her hands, the laughter fluttering over her face, in the midst of that bizarre interrogation, which took place in three languages. She sat and told them they'd smashed everything to pieces and now they were defending honour and morals!

"You destroyed the sheikh's house twice, sir: once in Ein El Zeitoun and again in Sha'ab. This isn't his house. You commandeered his house.

This is my house, and I support him and his wife, and I can do what I like."

"Stand up, prostitute!" screamed the interrogator.

Naheeleh rose slowly in the silence.

"Are there any more questions? I'm tired, and the children are alone in the house with the old people."

"You won't say where Yunis is?"

"I don't know anything about him."

"And you acknowledge that you work as a whore?"

"I'm free to do as I like. You can think what you like, but I don't work and I don't take money for prostituting myself."

"Disgraceful!"

"Disgraceful! You stole our country and drove out its people, and now you come and give us lessons in morals? My dear sir, we're free to do as we like. No-one has the right to ask me about my sex life."

The interrogator wasn't convinced but didn't go on with the interrogation. What could he do with a peasant woman who stood in front of him and told him she was a prostitute? He spat on the floor and ordered her released.

When Naheeleh got back to the house, she ululated for joy, and everyone gathered round her. That day, she told them, she'd become Yunis's bride: "Before I was arrested, I didn't deserve to be his wife. Now, though, I'm his wife and the mother of his children." She told them what she'd said to the interrogator, and the villagers laughed till they cried. They laughed and wept while Yunis's mother passed among them with glasses of sugared rosewater, ululating for joy.

You told the story, but you didn't finish it.

The story, father, doesn't end with a woman standing alone before an interrogator and protecting you in such an inventive way – a woman taking disgrace on herself to protect your life and wrapping you in her love.

You used to tell bits of the story and look at me to see my astonishment and admiration, and I was astonished and admiring – all our stories are like that: they make you laugh and cry and squeeze joy from sorrow.

But come. Let's take a look at that woman.

I don't want to rewrite our history, but tell me. You say you didn't understand, and that in 1948 all of you slipped helter-skelter from your villages into the darkness. And Umm Hassan says she carried the basin on her head and went from village to village, from olive grove to olive grove, without knowing where she was going.

That day – no, before that day – when you were a young man in the Revolution of '36 and afterwards: tell me, did you know anything about them?

You were peasants and didn't know anything, you'll reply.

Where was Palestine? You'll agree that Galilee wasn't the issue. Galilee has its magic because it's "Galilee of the Nations", as they call it in books. Today we've become "the Nations of Galilee" – we others, or *goyim*, as the Jews call us.

But tell me, what did the nationalist movement centred in the cities do apart from demonstrate against Jewish immigration?

I'm not saying you weren't right. But in those days, when the Nazi beast was exterminating the Jews of Europe, what did you know about the world?

I'm not saying – no, don't worry. I believe, like you, that this country must belong to its people, and there is no moral, political, humanitarian or religious justification that would permit the expulsion of an entire people from its country and the transformation of what remained of them into second-class citizens; so, no – don't worry. This Palestine, no matter how many names they give it, will always be Palestinian. But tell me, in the faces of those people being driven to slaughter, didn't you see something resembling your own?

Don't tell me you didn't know. Don't say, "It wasn't my fault."

You and I and every human being on the face of the planet should have known and not stood by in silence, should have prevented that beast from destroying its victims in that barbaric, unprecedented manner. Not because the victims were Jews but because their death meant the death of the humanity within us.

I'm not saying we should have done something. Maybe what we should have done was understand, but we – you – were outside history, so you became its second victim.

I don't mean to preach – even though I am preaching – because the settlers who set up the early "companies", and who are still setting them up today in Jerusalem, the West Bank and Gaza, don't resemble those who died. The settlers were soldiers who possessed the means to kill us – as indeed they did, and as they'll kill themselves as well.

But the ones who died, they're like Naheeleh and Umm Hassan.

I see Umm Hassan in the midst of the thousands of homeless in the fields. I see her and I hear the whistle of the train. I know there weren't any trains in Galilee; they came later, in Lebanon and Syria, when the refugees were rounded up and distributed round the suburbs of the cities, which then turned into camps.

The whistle rings in my ears. I see the people being led towards the final trains. I see the trains, and I shudder. Then I see myself loaded into a basin and carried on a woman's head.

I confess I'm scared.

I'm scared of a history that has only one version. History has dozens of versions, and for it to ossify into one leads only to death.

We mustn't see ourselves only in their mirror, for they're prisoners of one story, as though the story had abbreviated and ossified them.

Please, father – we mustn't become just one story. Even you, even Naheeleh – please let me liberate you from your love story, for I see you as a man who betrays and repents and loves and fears and dies. Believe me, this is the only way if we're not to become ossified and die.

You haven't ossified into one story. You're dying, but you're free. Free of everything, and free of your story.

Saleem As'ad taught me the meaning of freedom.

I was pre-occupied with the French visitors when he pointed to his head, described the child he'd been and led me to the story of the shampoo. Saleem would stand in front of the mosque that had been turned into a cemetery, expose his white hair and wash it in front of everyone, invoking a miracle.

"The old man made young again!" he'd shout.

People would form a shoving crowd around him. There was nothing magical or exotic – everyone knew the white hair would turn black and the old man in front of them become young again. His back was hunched, his legs shook, and his voice croaked as he invited everyone to the show, which he put on at 5.00 on the first Thursday of every month. He'd stand

there and ask one of the onlookers to help him to pour the water over
his head. The onlooker would pour the water, the old man would groan,
he'd apply the shampoo, rub it in well, pour on more water, and all of
a sudden there he was, leaping about, a young man again. The tremor in
his legs was gone, his voice was loud and clear, and his head was covered
in black hair. "The old man's return to his youth! A shampoo for every
part of the body! I'm the old man who returned to his youth – wash
your limbs with it and they'll be young again, every part of you will be
young again. Try it, you'll never regret it." And he'd start handing out
the little bottles and taking the on-lookers' money. Women, old men,
children, they'd gather in the forecourt of the mosque to watch the
miracle of the old man returned to his youth.

As you can see, there's nothing to it as a story. It's just a trite re-
enactment of the massacre.

Then I saw him for myself.

I went to the mosque out of curiosity, no more. I overcame my fear
and isolation, and I went. The youth bewitched me. He acted his part
amazingly well.

He comes forward, his back hunched, walking in circles and groaning.
Then he draws an imaginary circle around himself and walks round and
round inside it. He goes round in circles without getting tired until the
number of on-lookers is sufficient. Then the show begins.

A voice like a death rattle, a back hunched and broken, and a face –
the face is the real genius: he turns and swallows his face, sucking in his
lips and swallowing them so that it becomes a mask, as though he's put
on the mask of old age. His eyes sink into the skull, his mouth widens,
his gums become toothless. He goes around in circles, groaning, his legs
shaking, staggering, almost falling but not falling, and then says in a low
voice, "My children, my children. Your old father is about to die. Come,
my children." He puts out his hand like someone begging and asks for
help. One of the younger on-lookers comes forward, and the old man
shows him the bucket of water. The young man picks up the bucket, the
old man bends over till his head is almost touching the ground, and the
young man pours the water over the old man's head as he totters under
its force. Then he puts his hand into his pocket, pulls out a little bottle,
puts a small amount of the green liquid on his hand and shows it to the

people. He raises it to his head and rubs and groans and shakes. He asks for more water. His voice disappears. He opens and closes his mouth as though he wants to speak but can't, as though he's pleading for help. A woman goes up to him and gives him water to drink from a bottle she's holding. He drinks a little, then is taken with a fit of coughing like an outburst of sobs. He raises both hands, and the young man comes forward and starts pouring water on his head again. The water gushes and the old man drowns. The pool of water around him becomes wider. He goes down on all fours and splashes about in the water. He goes round and round, the water dripping off his head. Then suddenly he jumps up — he's young again, and he shouts, "The old man's return to his youth! A shampoo for every part of the body! And especially . . . especially . . ." — and he puts his hand to his crotch. "Welcome, welcome to Eternal Youth!" he cries. Then he starts handing his little bottles out to the on-lookers, while everybody laughs and claps and shoves and pays.

The French actors should have come to see this play *The Old Man's Return to His Youth*. "This is the play of the massacre," I'd have told Catherine if she'd been standing at my side watching Saleem's transformation from youth to old age and from old age to youth, as though he was purchasing his life by acting it.

I went up to him, bought a bottle and laughed. When the crowd had dispersed and he'd paid the young man with the bucket and the woman with the bottle their share, he saw that I was still standing there.

"See, doctor. You liked us."

I took his hand and asked him to come to the hospital the following day to start work.

"You can work," I said, "but without these antics."

"Whatever you say, doctor," he said, selling me another bottle. "I have to sell all the bottles before moving to my new job."

He took five thousand lira and said he would come the next day. And he came. He worked here for about a month and turned the place upside down. He filled the hospital with craziness: he stole medicines and sold them, he flirted with Nurse Zeinab, he told anecdotes, and he went into the patients' rooms and sold them medicines he'd made himself from herbs and which he claimed were more effective than the ones we used.

I knew all about it but was incapable of reining him in. He had amazing powers of persuasion and claimed that what he was doing was in the patients' interest.

"There's no such thing as illness, doctor," he'd say. "Half of all illness is psychological, and the other half is poverty. I'm treating them psychologically. Leave me alone and you'll see the results."

I left him alone because I didn't know what else to do about him.

"What do the patients want? I make them laugh, so they die laughing. What's the problem?"

He even tried to joke around with you, so I explained to him that such things stopped here, at the door to your room, and to Dunya's. But he wouldn't understand, or rather, he understood as far as you were concerned, and he stayed away from your room, but it was different with Dunya. He'd go into her room and do his act and sell her mother weird and wonderful things. And the mother was happy. She said Dunya smiled at him.

"It's the first time she's smiled, doctor. Please don't stop him from coming to her room." She said Dunya responded to the medicine Dr Saleem prescribed for her.

"Dr Who?" I asked.

"Dr Saleem. Really, he's better than all the other doctors!" said the mother.

When I asked him about the amazing medicine he'd made for Dunya, he looked at me from behind the mask of the old man I'd seen in front of the mosque.

"Get away from me, man. You don't understand."

And I didn't.

If I'd understood, I wouldn't have been taken by surprise when he disappeared. He stayed for about a month, then disappeared, and I never came across him again. I don't think he went back to doing his play in front of the mosque.

Nurse Zeinab said he'd said he wanted to go to Ein El Hilweh camp, where he was going to marry his cousin.

"What will he do for a living there?" I asked.

"Nothing," she said.

"I know," I said. "He'll act the old man there. He'll find a new audience."

"No," she said. "He'll live in his father-in-law's house. He told me her father works in Saudi Arabia and sends them dollars, and he was going to live like a king there."

Have you accepted my apology?

Saleem As'ad bewitched me with his stories and his play and his white hair. He bewitched me and made me forget you. You will, no doubt, appreciate what a difficult battle I got into with Dr Amjad over creating a job for him. Amjad refused, saying the budget wouldn't cover it and that Saleem As'ad would turn the hospital into a circus, but I insisted and won.

I won, meaning I lost, because he doesn't want to work. He worked for a month and then left without saying goodbye. What did I do to him? Nothing, I swear. I let him do as he pleased, just forbade him to go near your room. That was all. But he's a bastard – really a bastard – who doesn't want to work. He's got used to being unemployed and acting and bullying people into giving him money. What more could I have done for him than I did?

"This isn't a hospital." Every time I commented on his behaviour, he'd look at me in astonishment, shrug his shoulders and say, "This isn't a hospital."

Once he came into my office.

"What, Saleem?" I asked.

"I have some bottles, doctor. Haven't you made up your mind yet about changing the colour of your hair?"

"Get out of here. Leave me alone so I can work."

"Work!"

"Of course. Please leave me alone."

"Work, doctor? You think you're working, but you're a fool (sorry, doctor, I say whatever pops into my head). You're a fool, and you're cheating everybody by making them believe they're in a real hospital. You sell them things you don't have. I'm better than you, I sell them the real thing, the white-haired man who gets rid of his white hairs and feels as if he's become young again. But you give them nothing, just a continuation of the lie. Stop lying, please; stop lying and let people get on with their lives."

Is it true, father, that I cheat people?

Have I been cheating you?

You too would prefer things to be solved by Saleem As'ad's methods, with a little bottle containing a liquid made of soap and herbs. But where am I going to find a liquid that will restore consciousness to your paralysed brain?

No, don't believe Saleem.

Saleem is just a game, just a play, just a show. The real thing is hiding here, in these two rooms. You're here, and Dunya's there. Dunya's dying, and you're dying. She can no longer tell her story, and you, since Naheeleh's death, can no longer stand your story.

And I'm a play actor.

I'm the real actor, not Saleem. I'm acting your story, and Dunya's story, and Saleem's story, and all your stories.

If Saleem had understood what goes on in this room, he wouldn't have gone away. I'm sure the story about him marrying his cousin isn't true, and he'll come back the first Thursday of every month to act out his play in front of the mosque so he can purchase an imaginary old age with his youth to help him face these times.

Saleem left, and I didn't look for him.

I'm here, and I've a lot of work to see to. I've returned to you, as you see, and I'll come three times a day and spend most of my time in your room. I'll supervise the distribution of morning tasks and then come back to you. We'll go back to the way we were – me telling your story and you telling mine – and we'll wait.

B ack to the beginning, I tell you.

We're at the beginning.

At the beginning, I see my father. I see him and I don't see him, for Yasseen Ayoub died before I could set eyes on him. I see him as a photograph hung on the wall, a big photograph with a brown frame within which he stands, next to the wall, looking into the distance, his tie with its vague intertwined patterns hanging down like a long tongue. Above it are his stern face, his sculpted chin and his tired eyes. I'd like to ask him about his death. My mother went away and never told me, and my grandmother died before I could find out.

Why did they kill him in 1959? Why did they throw him down in a heap in front of the house, after his white hair had become stained with blood?

That was when everything ended: the civil war that had broken out in Lebanon in 1958 had collapsed, peace was concluded between the Christians and the Muslims, the US Marines withdrew, and the commander of the Lebanese army, Fouad Shehab, was elected President of the republic. Everything went back to the way it had been before except for us. Everyone was celebrating peace and life, and my grandmother celebrated the death of her son!

You're the only one who knows his story, so why don't you tell it to me?

Before you — that is, before this endless illness and coma of yours — I wasn't interested in him and I didn't love him. I'd look at his picture without seeing it, and if my grandmother hadn't been so obstinate, the picture would've died.

Shaheeneh, Yasseen's mother, had a theory about pictures. She thought pictures died if we didn't water them. She'd wipe the dust from the glass over my father's picture with a damp rag and place a container full of flowers and sweet-smelling herbs beneath it, saying that the picture lived off the water and the good smell. She'd pick basil and damask roses and put them in vases underneath the picture, bending over it with a damp rag and talking with her son. My grandmother would talk to the man hung on the wall and hear his voice, and I'd laugh at her and fear her.

"You'll understand when you grow up," she'd say.

I grew up and didn't understand.

Maybe the picture died because I didn't water it. Maybe it died the day my grandmother died. Maybe it ought to have been buried with her. I was young and didn't care; even her death happened without my being aware of it. I didn't shed a single tear for her. I came, and they'd buried her, so I returned to my military base in southern Lebanon, and it was there that the pain struck me. Can you imagine, I waited a month to feel the sorrow? On the day itself, I didn't feel any sorrow – it was as though I'd been hypnotised. I remember sitting. I remember that I took the pillow and the watch. I remember that I put the watch on my wrist and discovered it was broken. I tried to wind it but the spring wouldn't move. So I took the watch off and threw it in a drawer and forgot about it.

Can it be that my grandmother wore a broken watch all those years – as though she'd killed the time on her wrist? Did she sometimes look at her watch?

I don't know because I didn't see her during her last days. I came and stayed for part of her last illness, then came again after she was dead and threw her watch into a drawer before returning to my base.

It was there, at the base, that fierce sorrow struck me, and I didn't dare tell anyone why I was sad. How could I? You're living in the midst of young men who fall in battle every day and you mourn an old woman who waters her son's picture, tells delirious tales and sleeps on a pillow of flowers?

The sorrow struck me fiercely. Her voice came and went among dreams filled with horror and empty picture frames. At the time I didn't confess to myself that my sorrow was for her.

Today, faced with your eternal sleep, I understand my sorrow.

There, master, at the base we built in the olive grove at El Khreibeh, death came and spoke to me. My sorrow was indescribable, as though I'd lost the meaning of life, as though my life had been dependent on this woman who'd departed, on her tall tales and memories.

On that day I was possessed by an intimation of death, and I became convinced I was going to die because the woman had died. However, it was my duty to come back to life – that's what I told myself then, and that's what I told myself after the massacre of the camp in 1982. I didn't go to Tunis with the others because I was afraid of the death I saw on the faces of those who were saying goodbye. I stayed here and lived death. Then along came your sickness to bring me back to the beginning. When I'm with you, master, I feel as though everything is still at its beginning, my life hasn't started yet, your story is still before me to try to unravel, and my father has come back to me, as though he'd stepped down from the picture on the wall and is speaking to me.

Do you know what I did yesterday?

I left you to sleep and went home. I lit a candle in the sitting room, took a wet rag, and wiped the picture and told it I'd come back tomorrow with flowers and basil. I didn't go back, however. It was an insane thing to do, don't you think? There, beneath the picture, I understood why my grandmother said I was like him, because in fact I really do look like him. I don't know why I used to hate myself when my grandmother told me I was like him. Perhaps because I was afraid of dying like he had.

Where is my mother now?

Even her pictures have disappeared from the house. My grandmother said she'd run away and taken her pictures with her. Maybe my mother was afraid of what my grandmother might do to her pictures. Maybe she was afraid the old woman would find a way of talking to the pictures, so as to compel her – Najwah, wife of Yasseen – to come home. Or no, maybe my grandmother tore the pictures up so all that would be left to me would be his picture, which talked to her. My grandmother would say she heard him order this or that to be done, and I believed her. She'd attribute all her orders to him. Which is why I hated the picture and hated her and hated my father.

I told you I looked like him, and I hated myself because of that. No longer. But in those days, when the white was starting to invade my hair, I felt a terrible hatred for that man, and for myself, but I didn't dye my hair. I don't have Saleem's degree of irony. Maybe if my life had started like his, with the Shatila massacre, I'd have become an actor like him. But let's slow down – I also started my life with a massacre; what else would you call my father's murder? True, I was young and can hardly remember anything, but I can still imagine the scene. What my grandmother told me about his death turned into pictures that haunt me.

I sit and talk to you and hear that man's voice coming from my heart. What does one call that? The onset of old age? Maybe. I stand at the crossroads of my forties, and at this crossroads the picture of that man who left me so he could die comes back to me.

Shouldn't he have given some thought to his son's fate, which was to be decided by two women – one who'd run away and another who'd collapse under the weight of her memories? Shouldn't you all have given this some thought?

Before going on about my father, before getting to the beginning, I want to tell you that your high temperature isn't a cause for concern. Don't be afraid and don't fidget about on the feather pillow I put under your head. And – the miracle finally has occurred: I've managed to buy you a waterbed. I bought it with my own money, with Saleem As'ad acting as the intermediary. It was the last job he did at the hospital before he left to go who knows where. He went and bought the waterbed, brought it to the hospital and gave me back twenty thousand lira.

"From you, doctor, I'd never take a commission," he said.

He took a hundred dollars from me and gave me back twenty thousand lira, and everything was settled.

This bed will solve the problem. Your ulcers will get better because waterbeds don't stick to people's bodies like ordinary beds do. In the beginning, I substituted a cotton mattress for the hospital mattress, which is made out of foam. Cotton is more comfortable, but it's soft. As soon as you start sleeping on cotton, the mattress fills with lumps. I thought of cotton because I was afraid of the heat of the wool we normally stuff our mattresses with.

And look at the result.

I left you for three weeks only to come back and find you covered in sores. That's why I thought of the waterbed, and Saleem As'ad solved the problem. He said he could rustle one up, and he did. Nothing to worry about from now on. The cause of your high temperature this time is the ulcers, not the catheter as it usually is. All the same, I've decided to give you a rest from the catheter once in a while – I can't do more than that. I left you for four hours without one so you'd feel your freedom again. But more than that means blood poisoning, so I put it back even though you objected. I expect your temperature to decrease gradually with the ointments and the antibiotics I've mixed into your food. Don't be afraid. We can go back to the beginning. I'll bathe you twice a day, apply the ointments, put powder on your ulcers and perfume you. Rest easy, father, and don't be afraid. I say "father" and think of how you used to call me "nephew". When you came to visit us at home or dropped in on the cadets' camp, you'd hug me and say, "This one's a champ, a champ like his father." Now you've worked out that I'm not a champion like my father. I'm just a semi-unemployed nurse in a hospital suspended in a void. Also, I don't resemble him in anything but my prematurely white hair, my stooped shoulders and the business of my short stature, which came suddenly to an end. My mother used to say I was to be pitied: "Poor boy, he'll grow up short. He'll be no taller than a waterpipe." My grandmother would rebuke her and shout, "No. He's like Yasseen. Yasseen was that way, then suddenly he shot up and became as tall as a spear." She'd talk of the Calamity: "The Calamity shortened our lives and made us grow up short too, all except Yasseen. Suddenly the short boy became like a spear. We got to Lebanon after all that torment and there I suddenly noticed, God knows how I'd failed to see it – I opened my eyes and there he was, tall and beautiful. Amazing how he grew up like that all of a sudden, without my noticing. This boy's like his father, and you don't know anything about our family."

My mother knew nothing and would curse the luck that had brought her here and say she hated Beirut, and hated this camp, and hated El Ghabsiyyeh and its people, and didn't know why she'd married that man who was destined to die.

Would you like me to tell you how my father married her?

Or maybe these things don't interest you since you only like stories of heroes and heroic deeds, and you'd rather hear the story of how the man died on the threshold of his house.

But I don't know that story.

Listen. I'm going to tell you a story I don't know. My story isn't beautiful like yours, but I'll tell it so we don't get bored.

I know you're fed up with me. This way we can save some time and kill it before it kills us. I'm certain you can hear, and are laughing to yourself, and want to say lots and lots of things. Never mind, father, say what you like, or say nothing at all; what matters is that you arise from this sleep. I'm certain you'll wake up one day and discover that I bathed you in words, and washed your wounds with memories.

Fine words, you'll say, but I don't like them.

You like words when they're like a knife's edge. You used to make fun of people's speech, if instead of stating their opinions directly they took refuge in ambiguities and metaphors: "Words must wound," you'll say. But where do you want me to find you words that wound? All our words are circular. From the beginning, which is to say since Adam, our language has been circular. No matter how hard we try to break its circles, we find ourselves falling into new ones. So bear with me and play the game. Come, let's circle with our words. Let's circle around the sun, let's circle around the camp, let's circle around Galilee, let's circle around Naheeleh and Shams and around all the names. Let's circle with names, let's circle without names. Let's circle and come back to the beginning. Come with me to the beginning so we can get to the starting of the story.

I see the starting as a long dress. I don't know if it's my mother's dress or my grandmother's. Two tall women covered from head to toe by long, full, black dresses. Two women waiting, sitting on the doorstep of the house with me between them not knowing which is my mother and which my grandmother.

When I was little – you know how mysterious childhood is – I had two names and two mothers. My first mother called "Khaleel!" and my second mother called "Yasseen!" The first told me stories about the death of the man, the second about the loss of the child after the village fell. Both stories belong to me, and I play with them, becoming both child and man. You'll understand what I'm saying because you yourself are living the moment that everyone yearns for: you're in your second childhood – helpless as a child, speechless as a child, resigned as a child. Ah, how good you smell! Didn't I tell you we'd go back to the beginning?

Your childhood smell has returned to you, your childhood has returned to you. Even your shape has started to change. I'm convinced you've started to get shorter, that you've lost a lot of weight, and that you've returned to that mysterious moment that confuses our memory when we try to recapture our childhood.

Put out your hand so I can prove it to you.

I open your hand and place my finger in its palm; your hand closes over my finger. Do you know what that means?

It's the first test we give a child at the moment of its birth. It's an involuntary reflex. So now you're at that stage: you've become a child again, and instead of being my father you've become my son. I open your hand for you again, we repeat the action, and I'm as proud of you as any father of his child. I play with you and hug you, and you surrender to my game and play and squirm. I hug you and sniff you, and your smell fills my nose. It isn't the smell of soap and ointment and powder; there's something that comes from deep inside you, a new smell that takes you to the beginnings of childhood, to the life that has barely started to live, where we find the beginnings of speech.

I can go there too and see those mysterious days that I lived between two mothers. Najwah went away to her family and left me with Shaheeneh, daughter of Rabbah El Awad – the leader of the El Ghabsiyyeh militia – and wife of Khaleel Ayoub, who was killed in 1936, when he was a bodyguard for his wife's father in the Revolution. I see the two as one woman. They looked as alike as two sisters, the same dark complexion, small eyes, high forehead and long hair rippling with blackness. When Shaheeneh died, I felt that Najwah had died too. I won't talk to you about Najwah now because I know nothing about her. I just know that I looked for her once. I went to Jordan and looked for the wife of Ayoub and daughter of Fayyad in El Wahdat but could find no trace of her. Then I got that mysterious letter from Samih's wife in Ramallah, and after that heard no more of her.

I asked you why my father died, and you didn't answer me.

I asked my grandmother, and she said they killed him because he was going to die like his father.

"God! How could the dream come twice," she asked, "and both times the man dies? The first time was in '36, when I saw, as a dreamer sees, the light that goes out, and the second time was in '59, when the light went out again. How can I describe what I saw to you, son? A light like no other light, a light white and brilliant, a light that was above me as I sat on the ground. The light came in through the window and drew closer and closer to me. I got up and went towards it, and when I got there I saw the face of your grandfather Khaleel. 'What's the matter, man?' I asked, and his face started to crack into bits like glass. He came to me and hugged me, and suddenly he went out. People, like lights, go out. The light that came from the faces of your father and grandfather went out before my eyes, and I said, 'The man's dead.'"

Both times, my grandmother saw a light that went out. She never tired of retelling her dream, as though the dream was the issue.

"El Ghabsiyyeh was like a light, and it went out," said my grandmother as she listened to her son-in-law telling of his visit to the village.

"El Ghabsiyyeh went out," said Shaheeneh. "I was alone that day. My late husband and my father were commanding the militia, and I had Yasseen and his brothers with me. Suddenly they attacked. The Jews broke into the village from the north and south-east. They occupied the house of Osman As'ad Abdallah in the southern part of the village and seized him and his son. Then the shelling started, and we fled."

My grandmother told the story of the man who fell from the minaret of the mosque. She said she saw him falling like a bird. She said his name was Dawoud Ibraheem and that he climbed to the highest point of the mosque during the shelling carrying a white rag, so as to hang it on the minaret to announce the village's surrender. She said she saw him there at the top waving his hands. Then he hung the rag, but it fell. He picked it up, looking into the distance, towards the source of the shelling, as though he wanted them to stop firing for a while. He tried to hang up the rag again, was struck by a bullet in his chest and fell like a bird. He hugged his arms to his chest and plummeted. My grandmother said that when she saw him she understood how birds die, that Dawoud was like a bird. She gathered her children to her and ran with the others, scared of the tall trees — she ran looking upwards, scared that people would fall from the trees.

She kept running until she reached the fields of Amqa, where she lived with her children beneath the olive trees.

My grandmother said she lost all her relatives and her father disappeared.

I'm sure, master, that you must know my grandfather because he joined up with you following the fall of El Ghabsiyyeh on 21 May 1948. He went to Sha'ab and stayed there with its garrison until that ceased to exist and you were all arrested. He died in prison in Syria, and you got out of prison and went to Ein El Hilweh camp, there to proclaim your unforgettable madness by occupying the police post, seizing rifles and disappearing.

The story I want to tell you is the story of my father in Amqa.

Listen to me. I swear it's as though I was the one who lived the story, as though it was my story. My grandmother told it to me hundreds of times, and every time she'd say to me, "You did such and such," and then catch herself and say, "Drat, I was starting to get you and your father mixed up." I'd enter the story and correct the details because she'd forget names or mix them up. Telling me the story of my father and the donkey she'd even forget the name of Azeez Ayoub, my father's uncle, which no-one from El Ghabsiyyeh could ever forget.

They were in Amqa.

My grandmother had her four children with her – three daughters and Yasseen – and they were living like everyone else under the olive trees.

Let's suppose now that I'm her son, by whose name she used to call me. I'm her son and I'll tell you the story.

I was twelve years old, short and round, and no-one could believe that that was my real age. They thought I was just a child, and they only believed my age when I came back to them carrying the vegetables.

We were in Amqa, and the hunger began. Do you know what we ate during that long month? Nothing – bread and thyme and weeds. Then the bread ran out. Can you imagine a whole people living without bread? We'd sleep under the trees, we'd gather greens and weeds, and we'd eat them and not be full. We slept under awnings made of woollen blankets spread over the branches of the olive trees, and we waited. My mother wasn't afraid. The olive trees weren't so tall that she had to be afraid of dead men falling out of them, and her father let her know he'd joined the Sha'ab garrison and asked her to stay put with her children because he'd come and take them to Sha'ab. But he didn't come, and the woman couldn't take it any longer. She told her children that hunger had made her long for her village and she'd decided to go back to gather some vegetables from her field and get supplies of flour and oil. She told her children to stay together and to be careful while she was away.

So I volunteered.

"Yasseen volunteered," said my grandmother, "and insisted on coming with me. I refused and asked him to stay with his sisters. 'You stay and I'll go,' he said and, to cut a long story short, Yasseen came with me."

We walked with the others who were going to the village, each one carrying sacks and intending to gather food. My mother had a donkey she'd got from a relative in Amqa. We kept walking till we reached El Sheikh Dawoud. There the firing started from the rampart that dominates the village. The Jews were hiding behind the barrier, and the firing began, and people got scared and returned in defeat to El Kweikat and Amqa. I lost my mother and didn't know how to find her. She'd gone off with the donkey towards Amqa and I kept going towards El Kweikat, running and shouting, and then suddenly there was a man standing in the middle of the road with a donkey holding its head directly in line with the firing while the man stood at the donkey's tail. "Help, Uncle Azeez!" I say, and he says, "Get behind me" as if the donkey was a barricade. I got behind him, and after a little the firing stopped and I left Azeez and his donkey and went down towards the valley. He told me he was going to El Ghabsiyyeh to stay. "I'm the guardian of the mosque," he said, "and I won't leave it. Come with me." "I want my mother," I told him, and I left him and went down the valley. I heard firing and thought, "Uncle Azeez is dead" and started crying, and when I saw my mother I told them Uncle Azeez had died behind his donkey and they all believed me.

But Uncle Azeez, as you know, father, didn't die. He remained dead in the memory of the people of El Ghabsiyyeh until 1972, when my sister's husband returned from his visit and told the amazing stories of Uncle

Azeez. Then people found out that my father had lied and he hadn't seen Uncle Azeez dead. Yasseen died before the visit his son-in-law made to the village, so he won't be able to tell you about it, so I'll tell you but not now.

Where were we?

We left Yasseen in the valley of El Kweikat, crying with fear. Then the bullets became fewer.

"I pulled myself together and climbed in the direction of Amqa. As I was going along, I found a bundle of okra and vegetables. Someone must have thrown his bundle down and fled for his life when he heard the shots. I picked the bundle up with difficulty; in fact, I couldn't really lift it, so I dragged it and the vegetables started spilling out onto the ground. Then I slung the bundle on my back and set off."

Shaheeneh reached the olive groves of Amqa and said she'd lost her son at El Sheikh Dawoud and she'd fled along with everyone else. She said she'd led the donkey through the valleys looking for her son, and that she was afraid of losing the donkey because it wasn't hers. She'd held on to the donkey's halter and shouted her son's name, and on the outskirts of Amqa she realised that she'd lost him. She returned the donkey to its owners and stood in front of her blanket-tent, waiting and weeping.

She said she was weeping, and she didn't see him.

Yasseen returned carrying the bundle of vegetables he'd stumbled across in the valley of El Kweikat. He was small and bent over, and the bundle hid him completely.

"I was tired, my back was bent, and the vegetables were on top of me – I was all sweat and okra pods. I got to the entrance to the olive grove at Amqa with the okra spilling from on top and beneath me. I was tired and couldn't believe I'd made it. Instead of throwing the bundle down and running towards my mother, I stood where I was. I stood with my back nearly breaking, and then I started to go to my mother. She was tall and thin and kept waving her hands about and crying while everyone looked on and wept with her. Everyone was standing where they were while I drew closer, the bundle of vegetables on top of me, till I reached her. Then I threw the bundle on the ground and stood up. Everyone said, 'Yasseen's here! Yasseen's here!' They all saw me except her. She kept crying and waving her arms around, and I didn't know what I was supposed to do. I grabbed hold of her long black dress and started tugging on it. She bent down and saw me and fell to the ground, and it was as if she'd fainted, and everyone went and got water and sprinkled it on her."

My grandmother said that when she saw her son she lost her voice and couldn't remember anything after that.

Everyone saw him except her, and when she recovered from her faint, there were Yasseen and his three sisters. He opened the bundle on the ground and told her he'd gathered all these things: "I went and harvested the land, and I wasn't afraid of the Jews." The mother slowly got up, asked her daughters to start the fire underneath the stew pot, and the bustle of cooking began.

My grandmother said they attacked the village at dawn.

The village was half empty because after the fall of El Kabri and what happened to its inhabitants we'd understood that everything was over. "But my father, God bless his dust in its foreign grave, didn't leave," said my grandmother. "He stayed with the militiamen, so we stayed. Do you know, son, I don't know where they buried my father. They said he was killed in the military camp. They said he was trying to escape from prison."

My grandmother said she went to El Neirab camp in Aleppo and looked there and visited her uncle and his children, who lived in a strange barracks the French army had built. They were squashed on top of one another like flies, in long, oblong rooms. Her husband's brother said he wasn't sure, but he thought they'd buried him in Yarmouk camp and suggested she forget the matter.

"The man's dead," Azmi, as he was called, said, "so he can be counted as having died in Palestine."

But Shaheeneh wasn't convinced.

"Forget it, Shaheeneh, and look after your children."

But Shaheeneh didn't forget.

She went to Yarmouk camp and visited Abu Is'af, the commander of the Sha'ab garrison, who was living in the camp alone under a sort of house arrest.

In his small house, which consisted of one room without a bathroom, Abu Is'af told her he'd heard shots, but he wasn't sure if the man had died. He said the camp they'd been in resembled a prison.

"They took our weapons and said the war was over. We said, 'Okay, let us go to our wives and children.' They said no, you will stay as our guests. You know what Arab hospitality is like: we were prisoners without a prison, we were like people abandoned in the desert. In fact, we were in the desert. Then your father disappeared and we heard shots, but we didn't know then that it was him. He did disappear, though. God rest your soul, Rabbah El Awad, you were the reason for our being released, because after he disappeared, we went on a hunger strike. Yunis — you know him — he was the one who proclaimed the hunger strike and yelled in the officer's face, 'A strike to the death!' Then they let us go. Everyone went to his family except for me. They said that in view of my military experience, it had been decided to put me 'at the disposal of the Leadership'. Imagine my situation! I'm now at the disposal of the Leadership, and I don't have a latrine to use in my old age nor can I visit my children in Ein El Hilweh. Go, daughter, and take care of your son: Rabbah is a martyr and buried God knows where. Forget the grave and see to the living. Go, God keep you, and if you pass by Ein El Hilweh, ask for my son Is'af and tell him his father wants to see him before he dies."

My grandmother said she was convinced.

"Listen well, daughter," said Abu Is'af. "Death is destiny. Someone who was destined to die in Palestine and didn't is going to die somewhere else."

He said he'd wanted to die there himself because "Palestine is closer to Paradise."

My grandmother said she stayed in El Ghabsiyyeh and didn't move out with the others three days before the battle because her father was fighting there, but he disappeared. "I waited for him at the house during the shelling, but he didn't come. So I got myself and the children ready and left. They were shelling as we fled, the houses were collapsing, and they died – Mohammed Abd El Hameed and his wife Fathiyyeh, Ahmad El Dawoud, Fayyad El Dawoud, I saw them lying in the street, as though someone had come along and thrown them down outside their houses." She said the houses weren't pulled down: "The houses were left standing, but their roofs flew off."

I didn't believe my grandmother: the story of that bird-man who fell from the minaret with his hands stuck to his chest seemed like an image that had broken loose from memory and alighted in the woman's consciousness.

"That's history," you'll tell me.

However, I'm not concerned with history any more. My story, master, isn't an attempt to recapture history. I want to understand why we're here, prisoners in this hospital. I want to understand why I can't free myself from you and from my memory. I'm chief nurse now, and I've returned to the position I deserve, as the hospital's effective director.

Is that because the hospital isn't a hospital any longer, in fact has been turned into something less than a clinic?

Or because I saw an image of my own death in you and rushed towards death to talk with it?

Or because, deep down, I'm afraid of Shams (whose story I'll tell you later, when you'll understand why I'm afraid)? I'm not afraid of death but of her; yes, of her, and of her voice, of her voice when it shakes with hoarseness, with anger, with intoxication, and of her body, with its tattoos of sex, men and death.

I don't believe my grandmother, and I don't believe history, but that day I found myself wearing the name my grandmother had used for me. She'd dressed me in the name of her dead son, ruffling my hair and weeping for her husband who'd died in the Revolution of '36 at the village of El Nahar, which neighbours our village, and whom they brought back to her in his shroud, so that she was unable to see him.

My grandmother said she smelled the same smell when Yasseen died.

"He was jerking about in his blood, and the smell of it escaped from the cracks of his disintegrating body till the whole house was filled with the smell, there in El Ghabsiyyeh and here in the camp."

"Like that smell, grandmother," I said sarcastically, pointing to the pillow.

"His smell was like our smell. It's the smell of the El Awad family, the smell of blood mixed with the scents of flowers and herbs."

She ran to her pillow.

"Smell it," she said.

I clasped the pillow to my chest, smelled it and started to laugh.

"It's the smell of henna, grandma. It's the smell of your head. Did my grandfather dye his hair with henna?"

She took the pillow away from me angrily. "You don't understand anything," she said. "When you grow up, you'll understand what I'm saying – the same dream and the same smell. They brought my husband and his smell came off him and filled me up. They took him into the house for a few minutes and stopped me from going to the grave. They carried him once around the house and asked me to ululate for joy, but I didn't, not because I don't believe in God, as they said, but because I couldn't. The smell had taken me over, and I could feel it creeping into my bones and inhabiting them. You have to ululate for martyrs, and I've ululated for many. In fact, our lives take place between one ululation and the next. Every camp ululates, for we're all martyrs, son. But when they brought him to the house, I couldn't; the smell was in everything."

She recounted my father's death.

When she recounted his death, she'd stand and act out the crime. The truth of the matter is that the story changed after my mother disappeared. When my mother was here, she was the one who'd tell the story. My mother would speak and my grandmother would sigh. My mother would say the man fell like a sack, motionless, as though he'd died before they shot him.

My mother said she opened the door, with Yasseen behind her, and saw three men. Yasseen said, "Is everything okay? Please come in." One of them pulled out his revolver and fired three bullets. She said she was standing in front of him, saw the gun and heard the shots. She said that everything happened very fast – they fired the bullets at him and left.

"I turned and saw him on the ground, motionless. I bent over him. His mother came and pushed me away. Then everyone came."

My mother said my sister died two weeks after my father. "He took my daughter and went away," she said, "so what am I doing staying here?"

I don't remember my younger sister Fatmah. My grandmother said she was pink and blonde and white, like the middle of the day, and that the Jew Aslan Durziyyeh, when he visited us, couldn't believe she was my father's daughter, she was so beautiful and white. The old woman yawns and raises her hands to her head as though she's going to throw the days behind her. "God bless him, Aslan Durziyyeh. I don't know what's become of him."

My grandmother doesn't remember my sister well. I ask her and she says she doesn't know. "I told Najwah, 'You take care of Fatmah, and Khaleel's mine,'" so the work was divided between the two women from Fatmah's birth. But Fatmah died; she was struck by intestinal inflammation and became dehydrated. The doctor said she was dehydrated – her temperature went up and she dehydrated.

"We got up in the morning, and she was like a piece of cold wood. Your mother picked her up and ran with her to the doctor. He told her that she'd dehydrated."

I lived alone. My mother stayed up at night, waiting for the moon of El Ghabsiyyeh that she never saw, and my grandmother wept and called me Yasseen. Between the two women I listened to stories I thought were my stories and got confused. I would tell stories about my father as though I was telling them about myself. I'd imagine him through my mother's eyes and see him fall like a sack. Then I'd see him in my grandmother's words, see the blood staining his white hair as he convulsed between life and death on the threshold of our house.

So, right, why did they kill him?

The papers wrote that he'd been killed because he'd resisted the police patrol that came to arrest him. My mother said he was behind her when he went to the door and didn't possess any weapons. And my grandmother says the weapons were there, but they didn't find them. "They came the next day and turned the house upside down. I'm the daughter of Rabbah El Awad and you think they're going to find the rifle? The rifle's there, son, and when you grow up you'll have it. But they were liars. He didn't resist. If he'd resisted, he'd have killed them all. He greeted them because he didn't know they were coming to kill him, so they killed him, the sons of bitches."

My grandmother doesn't know why they killed him.

You, father, on the other hand, know everything.

My grandmother said you showed up at the funeral when no-one was expecting you, appearing among the mourners and raising your hand in the victory salute. You'd covered your face with your *kufiyyeh*. In those days, the *kufiyyeh* wasn't our emblem; we didn't have an emblem. You came with the *kufiyyeh* covering your face and head and you shouted "God is Most Great!" and everyone shouted the same thing. Then you disappeared.

Tell me about those days. Tell me how you held on to the courage of the beginning after all that had happened.

You'll tell me that in those days you weren't aware of the beginning. You continued your journeys over there as though things hadn't been interrupted, as though what had been etched on our bodies hadn't been etched on yours. You moved among the forests and hills of Galilee, continuing your life and returning to the camp. You appeared only to disappear.

I know you know things weren't that simple.

I know you were a wolf and like all wolves didn't like to settle down in one place. In the early years, you felt a strange wildness and a killing loneliness.

But my father.

Why did he die that way?

Why didn't he go with you?

Why did he leave me?

Dr Amjad is wrong. Do you know what he told Nurse Zeinab? He said, Khaleel is going through a psychological crisis, driven by the need to find his father; leave him with that corpse till he gets tired.

He spoke of you as a corpse, of me as an idiot and of our story as nonsense. The son of a bitch, I wish I could peel away that shell he hides behind, and those thick glasses of his, thinking he's discovered a meaning for his life in the pursuit of money. I know he steals. He steals here and he works at another hospital, where he dons the skin of the all-knowing, all-understanding doctor — but he doesn't know a thing. No-one who hasn't crossed a desert like the desert of Shams has meaning to his life.

Excuse me, father, if I say that love is not as you describe it. Love is feeling yourself to be lost and unanchored. Love is dying because you can't hold on to the woman you love. Shams would slip through my hands, and she was a liar: she'd say she wanted me, then go to some other man. That's love, master — an emptiness suddenly filled, or a fullness that empties and melts into thin air. With her I learned to see myself and love my body. Before, I knew nothing. I thought that love was Noha plus her mother's stew and her father's throat-clearing, and the desire that awakes and then dies away. But Shams taught me how to be a man, how to die in her arms and cease to exist. Please don't laugh. I don't remember if I became aroused with her the way men do, the way I would when I took hold of my member and discharged it with my hand. With her I didn't have a member. Naturally, I'd become aroused but — how can I put it? — it was more like melting and coming out of the water. We'd bathe in the water of desire and dissolve — but the desire never died. Her water . . . her water, master, would burst out like a spring emerging from the depths of the earth, and I'd drown.

That's what Amjad doesn't know, since, if he had done, his life would've been squandered as mine has been.

How can you expect me to fix my life now that she's dead?

Shall I tell you a secret? The secret is, father, that now, when I'm scared of her ghost, I feel the same desire that used to take me into her limitless world, and I tremble with lust, and I'm afraid.

But why?

I used to think that Samih's death would be swept under the carpet the way we've swept so many hundreds of deaths under the carpet. Why did they sentence her to death?

Was it because . . . ?

Or because she . . . ?

But I knew she would die, because death lurked in her eyes. You told me about the death that blazes from people's eyes. Do you remember that girl, what was her name? Dalal? Yes, Dalal El Maghribi. Do you remember the suicide operation she carried out in Tel Aviv, convulsing the camp as though it had been struck by an earthquake? We were unable to believe that Dalal, that melancholy, meek girl who worked in the sewing studio, had been capable of taking command of a boat that would set her down in Haifa and of kidnapping an Israeli bus full of passengers and dying that way.

That day you told me you'd seen death in her eyes and explained that you could tell the fighter who was going to die from his eyes, since death covers the eyes like an invisible film and the fighter is bewitched by his death before he dies, and so goes obediently. That day I thought of the Lebanese youth Mohammed Shbaru, whom we called Talal. You don't know him because you weren't with us during the Lebanese war. That was our war, master. I say that in all sorrow because whenever I talk about memories of the Lebanese war, I feel as though my face is falling to the ground and shattering. I could see the death in the eyes of that youth, whom we called the Engineer because he was a student at the Jesuit University in Beirut. He'd put on his thick glasses, wrap the patterned *kufiyyeh* round his neck and go out looking for death. He died in Sanneen because he'd decided to die. He didn't have to die, but he was chasing after his eyes. The image of the Engineer floated before me as you told me about the connection between my father's death and his eyes. You'll say that my father carried his death in his eyes and that it wasn't your fault, or Adnan's, God rest his soul. In those days you were all in a hurry to carry out armed operations, and the central authority that emerged out of the Lebanese civil war of '58 had decided to teach you a lesson. My father was the lesson. They came and killed him to deter you. You weren't deterred, though. My father died and my mother paid the price.

Did my father understand the danger he'd put himself in? Why didn't he hide? Why didn't he flee the house? Why didn't he get his weapon and fire before he died?

He fell like a sack, as my mother said, or he flailed around in his blood like a rooster with its throat cut, as my grandmother said, or he was a hero, as all of you said.

But shouldn't he have been worried about us?

I know you didn't worry about your children, but why didn't he?

Tell me, what was this life you led? You left your children with a woman living on her own over there, and you were between here and there, living your heroism the way heroes do.

Tell me, is that what heroism's about? You abandon your children to fear and despair and go off and die?

I told you I hated my father and lived alone with my grandmother.

Do you know what it means for a person to live in a vacuum? Do you know why my mother left me, and where she went?

You want the beginning!

That's the beginning. The beginning, master, is death. In the beginning my father died and in the beginning my mother disappeared. My grandmother knows the reason for her disappearance, and I'm certain she encouraged her to flee; she may even have given her a push. After the death of my little sister Fatmah, my mother spent five years with us, weeping. Then she disappeared. I don't remember the day because I didn't notice her absence. Then it became as though it'd always been that way. My grandmother said my mother had gone to visit relatives in Jordan, and the visit had turned into a long one. The woman disappeared as though she'd never been, and when I became aware of her absence, it was too late. I used to long for her at night. Just at night, I used to feel as if something was gnawing at my chest. I'd get up from the mattress and go to hers, and not find her. I'd sleep next to her when she wasn't there. Then my grandmother decided to change the way the house was arranged. She bought two beds, one for her and one for me, and my mother didn't have a place any more, and I could no longer go to her mattress at night to sleep next to her or smell the smell of her hair. No, no. It didn't happen the way it was supposed to happen, such as me coming back to the house, for example, and not finding her and then crying, and everyone coming and starting to search for her; my grandmother sitting among the women and weeping, and the women paying particular attention to me and one of them saying, "Poor boy, no father and no mother!" Nothing like that. I told you, I don't remember the day she disappeared because I didn't notice, and then I got used to it. My grandmother didn't tell me what had happened, but I understood my mother wasn't going to come back.

"She's gone to her family," the old woman said.

"Aren't we her family?" I'd ask in amazement.

I don't remember if she answered, and I don't remember that we discussed the matter. My mother's phantom would hover over me in the night, and the pain would gnaw at me. Then the light would come and she'd disappear.

Yes, master, I lived an ordinary life. I thought that everyone was like everyone else and all houses were like all other houses. I was sure that those distant memories of the village that had been erased were memory itself, and that my grandmother and my aunts were all the women there were.

So, right, why were my aunts like that? Why did they refer to me as "Najwah's son"? Was it because I was dark-skinned like her or because they wanted to erase my father's image from their lives?

My grandmother said that Lebanon was the beginning of a change for the better, in spite of everything. She said her daughters married in Lebanon within two years: "We came to Lebanon, my daughters got married, each one went her own way, and I'm still waiting to find my own path."

"And what's your path, grandma?"

"My path is the one that will take us back."

"Where will we go back to, grandma?"

"We'll go back to El Ghabsiyyeh."

"When are we going to go?"

"How should I know? But my heart tells me I'm not going to die here. I'm going to go back and put my head next to that man's and close my eyes and rest.

"We get no rest. Since that day, we've been going from place to place like gypsies." She said she picked up her children and ran. She said she saw the man fall from the minaret like a bird. She said she heard the screams of the dying, but she didn't look back and found herself in the midst of throngs of people on the outskirts of Amqa, and there, among the olive trees, she set up her tent made of two woollen blankets and lived for three months. Then she found herself among those going from Amqa to Yanouh, and from Yanouh to Tarshiha, and from Tarshiha to Deir El Qasi, and from Deir El Qasi to Beit Leef, and from Beit Leef to El Mansourah, and from El Mansourah to El Rasheediyyeh, and from El Rasheediyyeh to Burj El Barajneh, and from Burj El Barajneh to Shatila.

My grandmother said it was a long journey and that she'd thought that all the moving from one village to the next would bring her back to El Ghabsiyyeh in the end, but she discovered that she'd ended up in Lebanon. And in Lebanon fate took her three daughters by storm and they married, and she was left on her own with her husband-son until she married him to Najwah.

I saw my grandmother's sisters only rarely. My grandmother used to visit them three times a week at Ein El Hilweh camp, but she didn't take me with her and they didn't come to us. Though, in those last days, when I was summoned from the south as she succumbed to her last illness, I went to see her and they were seated around her. She gestured to them to leave the room. They went out, indignation written all over their faces, and I was left alone with her. That was the day she gave me her bequest. She tried to say something, but she couldn't, the words emerging in fragments from between her lips like unconnected letters. The words broke up into letters and the letters rang in my ears as I bent over her trying to understand, but all I could understand was that these things were for me: the watch that didn't work, the pillow of flowers and the Koran. I nodded to show I accepted them, she put her hand on my head to bless me, and I heard her say, "Yasseen." I pulled away. At the moment of truth, the woman revealed the secret of her relationship with me: she didn't know that I wasn't Yasseen, that I didn't love Yasseen and that I didn't want to be him. I'm a different man, and I don't look like the picture. I'm not a picture hung on the wall. At that moment, master, I hated everything, and I decided to leave the base in the south and go abroad. I don't want to die the way my father died, and I don't want to become the captive of this mysterious village I've never seen, and I don't want to become the captive of El Ghabsiyyeh's moon when it's full or of the man who killed himself by hanging himself from the lotus tree.

I left her room after putting the watch in my pocket and let my paternal aunt Munira take the Koran from my hand and sat in the sitting room listening to my aunt's husband.

"What's this?"

He questioned me about my grandmother Umm Yasseen's bequest, and, taking me by the hand and seating me next to him, started telling his story. A man of about forty-five with a white bald patch that shone as though he'd rubbed it with olive oil, and a face full of pimples and pock marks, and a hand that trembled, holding a lit cigarette.

"Come and listen," he said. "This is a story you must hear."

Ahmad Ali El Jashi began his story. I forgot my grandmother dying in

and his voice disappeared. I was afraid. I thought, 'I'm on my own, and if the Jews come now, what am I going to say?' I threw the pomegranates away, keeping just one, which I put in the pocket of my coat, and I shouted to him, 'Let's meet at the mosque.'"

Ahmad Ali El Jashi told me how he'd gone around the whole village before reaching the mosque, and how he'd been afraid the weeds would eat him, and how he'd heard something panting and it scared him, and how he'd decided never to go back to El Ghabsiyyeh again.

"Then I found the gap in the wall," he said.

He said he'd walked a lot but kept looking back, for the pomegranate tree was his only landmark in the middle of that obliterated landscape. He returned to the tree, walked three steps backwards and found himself in front of the opening. He jumped through it and was in their orchard. From there he returned to the mosque to find his uncle waiting for him.

Ahmad Ali El Jashi said El Ghabsiyyeh was the way it had always been.

He said it had been waiting for him.

He said most of the olive and carob trees had been cut down, but we'd plant new ones.

He said it wouldn't take much work. We'd pick ourselves up and go. What could they do to us? We'd pitch our tents there just as we'd pitched them here and wait till we'd rebuilt the houses that had been knocked down.

He said they hadn't really been knocked down, it was just the earthen roofs that had collapsed, and we could rebuild them in days.

He said and he said and he said, his bald patch shining like oil, and I listened to him with half an ear. I thought, "People like that never tire of repeating the same thing, and they live in the past. Why don't we pay attention to our present? Why must we remain prisoners of the past that overshadows us?"

Then he asked me about the base in South Lebanon and said that, if I wished, he could come there so we could go to El Ghabsiyyeh together. "It won't be a military operation," he said. "Fighting isn't the point. I'll take you there so you can see your village. Wouldn't you like to see your village?"

When he said the words *your village*, we heard a wail from my grandmother's room and realised the woman was dead. None of the men moved, but their tears flowed copiously, as though they'd been waiting for a signal and the signal had come from my grandmother's room. No-one said anything and no-one went into the room. They were sure the end they'd been waiting for had come, and the crying began.

My aunt's husband wiped the tears away with his hand and whispered suspiciously: "What are you going to do with the house?"

"What house?" I asked, thinking he was continuing the conversation about our houses in the village.

"This house," he said.

"Nothing," I said.

"You don't want to sell it?" he asked.

"Why would I want to sell it?"

"Because you live at the base, and my son is coming next year to study at the university in Beirut, so I'll buy it."

"I'm not selling," I said. "I'll never sell my house."

He said he was ready to give me whatever sum I named right now.

I said I wasn't in need of money and I'd never sell my house.

The man stood up, joined the men's circle and resumed his weeping. Then my aunt came out of the room, silenced everyone with a wave of her hand and announced that the woman wasn't dead. The crying came to a sudden halt, and the men returned to their conversations. My aunt's husband resumed his story, but I decided to go back to the base. It seemed the woman was never going to die, and I had to get back.

My grandmother died when I wasn't there, just as my father had.

Why does the memory of my father come back when I want to root it out?

The fact is, I did root it out long ago and had forgotten about it, and the only reason it's come back is you, because you want the story to go "back to the beginning". I don't know the beginning of the story. It's not me; I didn't move from village to village, or go back to the field in Amqa carrying a bundle of vegetables on my back, or hide among the maize stalks, and I don't know Aslan Durziyyeh and his son Simon or the story of the crime in Wadi Abu Jmeel.

All the same, he comes back and haunts me.

It's as though that woman who raised me on the smell of decaying flowers had superimposed me onto another man and given me another name. It's as though I'd become the Other that I'd never been.

My grandmother said the days passed. "I was like everyone else. I worked the land my late husband had left me. I worked the land before he died and after he died, and he, God bless him, was a fighter, meaning that he'd leave me and go off. If I hadn't cultivated and looked after the land, well, we'd have died of hunger. God rest his soul, he was full of talk, a peasant who didn't know how to work the land and whose head was stuffed with gunpowder and weapons. We peasants don't fight. I told them we don't know how to fight. Tomorrow the Arab armies will come and make war. But he didn't take any notice and left me and went off. He took to coming back every now and then, and then he died and that was the end of him. It was my father's fault. He was their commander and he married me to Khaleel without consulting me. He came and said they'd read the first Sura of the Koran and the wedding was to be the next day. The wedding took place and I had a God-awful time. I lived with him for five years and bore him three girls and a boy, and then my husband went off. The girls worked with me in the fields, and the boy we sent to the school in Acre."

When Yasseen finished memorising the Koran in the village, his mother sent him to Acre, where he joined the fourth-year class of the elementary school. In Acre, he stayed at the house of Yusif Effendi Tobil. This Yusif Tobil owned the oil press in the village and a small shop in Acre, and only came to the village in October and November, when he'd press his olives and those of the peasants and then return to Acre.

"Your father, God rest his soul, worked in the press, helping with the oil pressing; then he'd go back to Acre. He only studied in Acre for two years. He'd come to the village every Friday. He'd pass by the mosque and say his prayers before coming to the house, where he'd open his books and read, and I wouldn't see him. I'd ask him about his life in Acre, and he'd read in a loud voice to make me stop talking. I tried to read his books, but I couldn't. We knew how to read the Koran: we could open the Koran and read easily, but the books your father brought were impossible. My daughters and I tried to read them, but we couldn't, even though they were written in Arabic. In those days, God help me, I used to think there was an Arabic language for men and an Arabic language for women. Our language was the verses and chapters of the Koran, and God knows where they got theirs from. Yusif Effendi, God bless him, persuaded me to send my son to school. He said, 'Your son's a beacon of intelligence, Shaheeneh, and he has to go with me to Acre.' I told him, 'The boy'll be scared there because he's never seen the sea in his life.' Yusif Effendi laughed and said the sea was the most beautiful thing in the world, and he'd teach him to swim in the sea. 'The sea of life is harder than the sea of Acre,' he said and took the boy. Yasseen lived with them as though he was a member of the family, eating with them and sleeping in their house. He'd go to school in the morning and help Mr Yusif in his shop in the afternoon. I thought the boy would do as well in his life as he did in school, but, poor boy, he only studied in Acre for two years. Then the disasters started, the war came to Galilee, and we started running from village to village till we reached Lebanon."

My father, Mr Yunis, didn't understand what was going on. He was young and short and round. He carried the vegetables on his back and stood watching his mother cry, and then resumed the journey of displacement with her till they reached Tarshiha, and in Tarshiha he died. No, he didn't die, but he saw death with his own eyes when the house collapsed on his head as the Israeli planes shelled the town.

"In Tarshiha we lived in the house of Ali Hammoud, who'd fought with my father," said my grandmother. "Yasseen stopped going to school, and I worked with Ali Hammoud's women on the olives, and we waited for the ALA, of which there was news everywhere, and we said, 'Things are fine.' Fine how, son? We lived like dogs. True, Ali Hammoud offered us a house, and true, we worked on the olives, but God, we were so hungry. I never slept a night in Tarshiha with a full stomach. You know, son, from the day we left the village I've never slept with a full stomach. I eat and I don't feel full, like there's something open at the bottom of my stomach. I have no appetite, and my stomach hurts I'm so hungry."

My grandmother's appetite was never satisfied. She'd say she wasn't hungry, put the plate in front of me and sit watching me. Then, all of a sudden, she'd reach towards my plate, wolf everything down at one go and say she'd eaten nothing. The woman was a strange case. She'd only eat from my plate, and she'd wolf everything down, put her hand on her stomach and complain of pain, then start eating again. I used to think she'd taken to eating that way as a compensation mechanism following my father's murder. Then I found out that her pains preceded his death and she treated his food the same way she did mine. I remember the story of the string stew only vaguely, but my paternal aunts, on their rare visits, used to talk about little else, starting with laughter and ending in a sort of quarrel.

"You loved Yasseen more than you did us," one of the aunts would say.

"God forgive you," Shaheeneh would say. "It wasn't like that at all. I used to make string stew because the boy was short and we were poor, not like now."

You hear what she says? As though we weren't poor now. We say we used to be poor so that we don't have to talk of our present reality. But the important thing is, master, that she had this strange way of cooking. She'd make a hotpot the way everyone else did. She'd fry bits of meat with onions before adding the vegetables on top. But she'd take the bits of raw meat and thread them on a string and tie the ends together before frying them. When the family sat down at the table, she'd pull the meat string out of the pot and say, "This is for Yasseen." I don't know what happened next. Did my father eat the bits of meat while his sisters looked on, their eyes wide with desire? Or did he distribute the bits of meat among them? Or did he leave the string untouched, to be wolfed down by his mother?

My grandmother only stopped cooking string stew when my mother left. I vaguely remember those days. I remember how I hated the string on my plate. I remember that I wouldn't touch it, and that my grand-mother would try to force me to eat it and I'd refuse. Maybe I ate it once or twice, or a dozen times, I don't know, but the taste of string stuck in my teeth or on my tongue has never left me.

My grandmother stopped threading the meat after my mother left, and I didn't think of it again till one of the fighters with us at Kafar Shouba told us about his mother's string stew, which was like my grand-mother's. In the fedayeen camps we ate lots of meat, and Abu Ahmad used to take my share, saying that I didn't understand anything about food because I hadn't tried string stew, and I'd say that I hated the taste of meat precisely because of string stew. Abu Ahmad would eat the meat in a strange way – but was his name Abu Ahmad? The name's not impor-tant because in those days our names were all made up. I, for example, wasn't called Khaleel. My name was Abu Khalid, even though I'd wanted to call myself Guevara. The fact is, I love Guevara, and whenever I see his picture, I see the light in his eyes as something holy. I think that he, like Mohammed or the Talal you told me about, had his death lurking in his eyes, which is why they were beautiful and radiant. I wanted to call myself Guevara but discovered someone else had beaten me to it. Amir El Faisal said, "We'll call you Abu Khalid." Then the Abu Khalids multiplied. Gamal Abd El Nasir was the first Abu Khalid because he called his oldest son Khalid, and when he died in 1970 the young men all wanted to name themselves after him, so you ended up finding it everywhere. I was the first Abu Khalid in South Lebanon, but following the September massacres in Jordan the fighters fleeing from there poured in and we couldn't distinguish among all the Abu Khalids any more. My name thus became Abu Khalid Khaleel, and gradually the Abu Khalid part faded away in favour of Khaleel. To this day, however, I still turn when I hear the name Abu Khalid, even though I know people have forgotten that's what I used to be called.

Meat was Abu Ahmad's only joy. He'd leap on the supply lorry, pick up the meat platter, put it under a tree, pull out the knives and start cutting it up, singing. He sang to the meat because meat was *the* food, he said, and I despised him. Not exactly despised him but felt disgust when he ate bits of raw meat and invited me to join him.

"That's disgusting, man," I'd tell him.

"What's disgusting is your not eating it. Don't you know what Imru' Al Qays said were the three most beautiful things in the world – 'Eating flesh, riding flesh and putting flesh into flesh'?" – he'd say, his tongue, extended to lick his lips, mixing with the red meat he was chewing.

"All our lives, brother, the only meat we ate was the string. We used to fight over the string and the little bits of half-melted meat scattered along it. All we ate was the string. Now we eat properly. Long live the Revolution – the best thing about this revolution is the meat. It's the Meat Revolution."

He'd chew raw meat and start preparing *maqloubeh*. We ate *maqloubeh* once a month, when the supplies arrived, and Abu Ahmad would put huge quantities of meat on top of the rice cooked with aubergine or cauliflower; everyone at the base dived into the "meat of the Revolution". Our great problem was that the Revolution was rich while our people are poor. The problem's over now – the Revolution's moved on, leaving nothing here in the camp but this poverty that's destroying us. I don't know if people have gone back to their old habit of cooking meat on a string because I live on my own, and so do you, and I don't like meat. I like lentils and cracked wheat and broad beans, and you like olives.

I know the story. You don't have to tell me what your mother did with black olives, how she sliced them over bread cooked in the peasants' clay oven and said they were "chicken breasts" and that olives were tastier than chicken. I know the story, and I don't want to repeat the virtues of olives again, or talk about the Roman olive tree that provided you with shelter during the winter and inside whose huge hollow trunk you'd spend the day before continuing your journey to Bab El Shams.

As a doctor, I acknowledge the beneficial properties of olive oil, but I can't agree with your mother's theory about dentistry. I remain unconvinced by her belief that ground olive pits make a good painkiller for toothache. A handful of cloves will act as a painkiller, and arak acts as a painkiller, but olive pits – impossible! It seems your mother found a solution to her poverty by transforming olives into something similar to Saleem As'ad's little Ekza bottle (before he discovered the virtues of shampoo and became an actor). No, master, olive pits are no use as a medicine, and olive leaves are no use for fumigating houses. Were we – were you – that poor in Palestine? Were we too poor to buy a handful of incense? Was it poverty that made your blind father take dry olive leaves and use them as incense when he led the Sufi devotions every Thursday night? They'd use dry olive leaves for incense: the men would gather around the blind sheikh, who stood in the middle of the circle clapping his hands and saying, "There is no god but God," and the circle would start to turn. Then you'd come, carrying a vessel full of dry olive leaves with three lit coals placed on top of them. You'd give the vessel to your father and withdraw while he tried to make you join the others – you'd run away and stand at the far end of the room, near the door, where the women were gathered, and you'd watch a little before leaving quietly. The sheikh would blow on the coals, the coals would ignite the olive leaves, and the incense would rise. The circle would begin revolving fast, and the men would fall down until the tambourine player himself fell to the ground, shouting "Succour! Succour!"

The smoke blinded you, father. Your incense wasn't incense, it was smoke, which blinded you and made you fall down, but your poverty caused you to transform olives into an entire way of life. You transformed them into meat, chicken, incense and medicine. Explain to me now, why all this nostalgia for those days of poverty? Why did my grandmother hug her pillow and take such care to change the flower heads she stuffed it with, saying it was the smell of El Ghabsiyyeh? Have you forgotten how poor you were there? Or do you feel sentimental about it? Or is memory a sickness – a strange sickness that afflicts a whole people? A sickness that has made you imagine things and build your entire lives on the illusions of memory? I still remember the song we chanted at our bases in South Lebanon. Listen to these words and think with me about the meaning of imagination:

> Abd El Qadir pitched a tent
> Above the tent were olive plantations
> I'm a fighter and so's my dad
> We go out together on operations

Imagine with me how Abd El Qadir imagined his life: he'd become a refugee, so he put his olives on top of his tent and sat underneath and sang songs. That's how we express our nostalgia. We believe the olives are on top of the tent and that the homeland is a plantation. We feel sentimental about our poverty and our demolished villages. And we forget ourselves and die.

But not me.

Never! You know my commitment to and faith in our right to our country. I just talk that way. We're not in a meeting or at a lecture. We're conversing, so let the stories take us where they will.

Where were we?

I was trying to pull scattered anecdotes together about my father. They were in Tarshiha, and that's where Yasseen died. Not really died but fell beneath death's wing and survived. It was after Qal'at Jiddeen fell into the hands of the Jews. "We took refuge at Tarshiha while waiting to return to our villages," said my grandmother. "But instead of us getting closer to our villages, the Jews got closer to us. Jiddeen fell and Tarshiha started to be exposed to intermittent shelling."

One day – the day Yasseen came to call the day of his death – the planes started shelling Tarshiha: "I was in the market and suddenly found myself running with everybody. I holed up in Ahmad Shirayh's shop, and suddenly the shop started shaking and the walls toppling, and there was smoke. A shell fell into the shop, and everything was demolished and everyone died. I was standing in the only corner that wasn't demolished, and I found myself with rubble above me, below me and around me, that and the dead. I started groaning. I don't know if I was in pain, but the groaning emerged from deep inside me. Then I felt a hand pulling me. Everything was on top of everything else. They picked me up, shouting 'God is Great!' and I found I hadn't died."

Yasseen said that when he discovered he was still alive, he freed himself from the men's grasp and started running in the direction of the house they'd been staying in. The mother had got everything ready and was standing with her three daughters, and they'd lifted the woollen blankets and pots and pans onto their heads waiting for Yasseen. The second they saw him, their new march began.

"My mother didn't ask me where I'd been or why I was covered with dust. She was in a hurry. She set off, my sisters set off behind her, and I was behind everybody, till we got to Deir El Qasi. There we couldn't find a house so my mother set up her tent beneath the olive trees and made up her mind yet again that this life was intolerable and that she'd go to her village to get supplies.

"My sister Muneerah said, 'No. I'll go.'

"My mother yelled, but the matter was settled, and my sister Muneerah and I and a girl whose name I can't remember who was a friend of my sister's and lived in a woollen-blanket tent close to ours set off. We went down to the Acre plain and hid in the maize fields. The stalks were tall, more than a metre and a half, and we started picking okra, cucumbers and tomatoes. Suddenly, a man carrying a rifle came towards us. My sister and her friend were in front, and I saw the man go up to them and take the stuff away from them. This man with the rifle was the guard. They called him the *mikhaddir* because he guarded the *khudar*, or vegetables. He was a Jew called Melikha, and we knew him and he knew my sister – so why did he get out his weapon and threaten us and confiscate the vegetables we'd taken from our land? I saw my sister giving him everything and raising her hands. Then she looked back to warn me and went off. This made the man notice my presence. I'd been standing stock still and was about to put my hands up so Mr Melikha wouldn't kill me, but I found myself throwing my sack to the ground and running as I heard the sound of shots. I ran and ran, and when I reached my sister and her friend I felt something hot trickling down my left thigh, which at that moment I didn't know was blood. But my sister tore my shirt and tied up the wound and ran in front of me, crying. It wasn't a wound in the proper sense of the word; it was gunpowder from the double-barrelled shotgun the guard had fired. It had burned my trousers, and several grains of buckshot had lodged in my left thigh, and there was blood everywhere. My sister tied up my wound, and we ran back to our tent and weren't able to pick anything. That was my second heroic deed. The first time I was the only person who managed to get vegetables from El Ghabsiyyeh, and the second time I returned wounded like the martyrs. I can't describe what my mother did when she saw the blood covering my trousers."

"What can I tell you about him, son?" my grandmother would ask.

"Your father was a hero. I saw him and I saw the blood, and I ran to him, my tears flying ahead of me – my only son dying for the sake of a handful of okra – and started screaming that the Jews had killed him, that I'd killed him. 'I've killed my son. Come, everyone, and see!' I didn't stop when I discovered the injury was trivial. I made him a wedding, as they do for martyrs. I ululated and wailed and waved his blood-stained trousers. I made a commotion and said, 'Praise God!' and did what the mothers of martyrs do. I waved the trousers over my head, and our neighbour, Umm Kamil, came and censed me and censed the trousers and censed you. I thought, 'This is my bit of martyrdom.' I did what the mothers of martyrs do so I could pass that cup from me. I thought, 'My son has died. That means he'll never die again after today.' But he betrayed me and betrayed his wife and betrayed you. He left us and died on the doorstep of this house that I built with my tears. God help me, in Deir El Qasi I thought death had ended and I could escape from it with my children, but it caught up with me here and snatched my son away and left me on my own with this boy who's the spitting image of Yasseen. My son was scared of the vegetable guard. He didn't surrender because he was afraid of death – they were killing all the young men – he didn't put his hands up so he wouldn't die. At the door he tried to put his hands up. He saw the revolver pointing at him, but he didn't have enough time to put his hands up, and they didn't let him surrender, and they killed him."

Why did they kill him?

My grandmother asked you the question, and I'm asking you too.

Wouldn't it have been better if he'd died among the maize fields? Was it necessary for him to go through that long agony from Deir El Qasi to Beit Leef and from Beit Leef to El Mansourah and from El Mansourah to El Rasheediyyeh and from El Rasheediyyeh to Shatila, and to death?

My grandmother hates bananas.

No-one in the world hates bananas, but Shaheeneh hates them.

You don't know the story of this woman and bananas because you don't know how she used to use banana leaves to cover the floor of her tent in the El Rasheediyyeh camp. Banana leaves were the only thing they could find to protect them from the rain that was drowning them. You weren't there to see how the banana leaves covered them, and you weren't there to see how Naheeleh stole her food and food for her children from her appropriated land.

You were in Nowhere. You'd entered your secret world that made you think that things were the way they'd always been, while Shaheeneh was spreading the floor of her tent with banana leaves and eating dust, and Naheeleh was stealing olives from her appropriated land, before your father the sheikh returned to his post and started receiving his livelihood from the Deir El Asad Mosque Endowment. You may or may not know that there was no such endowment or anyone to make one – the Israelis had confiscated all the land. The sheikh convinced himself of the endowment's existence so he wouldn't have to acknowledge that he'd become a beggar, a beggar living off the donations of people who were poorer than himself but were embarrassed to look into his sightless eyes and by the belly of his daughter-in-law, always swollen with children.

My grandmother hated bananas, and Naheeleh hated the endowment and went to work in the *moshav* the Yemeni Jews had built along the edges of the rubble of the village of El Bruwweh. You don't know these things.

You'll ask why she didn't let you know. Do you have to be told in order to know? I'd like to believe you and forgive you now, because you didn't know how we and they lived, but tell me, what did you do for them and for us? Why did you let us go through such hell?

I hear your laughter breaking through the veil of your death. You're laughing and dragging on your cigarette till it burns down to nothing, and you raise your hand nonchalantly. Your voice shouts, "Hell? You, Khaleel, are talking to me about hell? What do you know about hell?"

And I hear, coming from the depths of your voice, the voice of Yasseen, bringing with it the stories of the banana leaves that covered the ground and the roof of the tent so that those inside wouldn't drown.

My grandmother said she entered Lebanon on a donkey. "We hired a donkey and travelled on it as far as the Lebanese border. We left every-thing behind in its own country and took nothing with us."

But in fact, my grandmother brought her gold jewellery, which allowed her to live reasonably during the first few years in Lebanon. She said she'd been in Deir El Qasi. All the people were asleep in their tents, but she couldn't get to sleep. She said she felt as though everything was lost. It was night and the stars were like red spots in the sky, and the sounds of distant howling mixed with those of scattered gunfire and silence. The armed young men who guarded Deir El Qasi's tents stuck close to the olive trees as though fear had frozen them in place.

A woman on her own, sitting in front of her shelter of olive branches, seeing nothing but darkness. A dead husband, four small children, a father whose whereabouts were known only to God, an unsure future and a village that had died. My grandmother said that during those moments, when night was concealed in her eyes, she realised that El Ghabsiyyeh was dead and that she had to do something to save her own life and the lives of her children, and she remembered that she'd left her gold jewellery and twenty Palestinian lira – her entire dowry – at the bottom of a chest.

The woman sat in front of her tent, the howling around her, the night covering her, the tears flowing from her eyes. Then she found herself in front of her eldest daughter, Muneerah. Muneerah was sixteen years old and greatly resembled her mother. Shaheeneh went up to her sleeping daughter and shook her gently. The girl woke with a start.

"Get up! Get up!" said her mother.

The mother took her daughter's hand and led her out of the tent. Outside the girl listened to her mother and understood nothing.

"I don't understand a thing," said Muneerah.

The mother explained her plan to her daughter. She hadn't had a plan when she'd awoken her, hadn't known what she was going to say to her; she just wanted to banish her own loneliness and talk to someone so she could mourn the loss of her dowry. But instead of complaining, she found herself explaining the plan to her daughter. She said she was going to go there at dawn to get her money and her jewellery, and that something might happen to her, and that if anything bad should happen, God forbid, Muneerah was to go with her brother and sisters where everyone else went. She said people might go to Lebanon: "Go with them and ask about your grandfather Rabbah El Awad. You grandfather's still alive, he's fighting now with the others, I don't know where. Look for him, and he'll take care of you." Muneerah proposed that she go instead of her mother, but her mother refused. "No, daughter. I'll go on my own. You're still young, and your life's ahead of you. Just don't forget to ask for your grandfather, his name's Rabbah, Rabbah El Awad, and he's with the Sha'ab garrison now, and everyone knows him. Wait for me till tomorrow night. I'll come back tonight, but something may hold me up. Wait two nights for me. If I'm not back, something will have happened. Forget me, go with the others, and put your trust in God."

Muneerah said she understood and went into the tent and fell into a deep sleep. Shaheeneh couldn't believe her eyes. How could the girl sleep after what her mother had just told her? Shaheeneh went into the tent again and bent over Muneerah, who was breathing quietly.

Shaheeneh put a crust of bread inside the front of her dress and set off. It was dark. Shaheeneh doesn't know what time it was, but the veil of night was breaking to reveal dim coloured lights. She walked and walked, and no-one appeared to stop her – not the camp guards, who kept close to the olive trees, nor the Jews, who'd invaded the villages and spread out over the hills. The woman walked alone on paths she knew. She bent over and stumbled and almost fell and righted herself. She walked for about two hours. Distances in Galilee aren't great – as you once told me, Galilee is like the palm of a hand. She walked till she reached the Bubbler. She bent over the water, washed her hands and her face, drank and entered the village.

The spring called the Bubbler isn't more than two kilometres from El Ghabsiyyeh, but it was the longest leg of her journey. She walked and walked and never arrived. Shaheeneh knew the road and could have done it with her eyes closed as she'd fetched water for the house from the Bubbler every day, but what did every day have to do with that day? Her head felt heavy, as though she was carrying three water jars on it. She walked weighed down by her head, and her fear welled up out of her mouth as laboured breathing.

Long years after this journey she'd tell me that it taught her to see.

"You know, son, it was there that I saw. Before I hadn't seen, and after I left the village I didn't see again."

"And what did you see, grandma?"

"I saw everything there. It's difficult to explain, son. With one look I saw all the houses and all the trees, as though my eyes had pierced the walls and seen everything."

On her journey to El Ghabsiyyeh, Shaheeneh walked bent over. She bent over to avoid the branches of the olive trees, she bent over because of the night, she bent over out of fear, she bent over for the water from the Bubbler, and she bent over for the lotus tree. When she passed the mosque, however, she suddenly straightened up. She held her head high and walked calmly into the village as though she'd never left it. Her frightened panting subsided and she saw everything. She saw the houses and the trees and the orchards, and she heard the voices of the people and the cries of the children. The woman walked calmly towards her house. The door was open. She ran into the room, opened the chest and reached in. There she found her money and her jewellery – her gold signet ring, her twisted bracelets and her pearl necklace. She put every-thing inside the front of her dress and decided to go back. No. She felt intensely hungry. She took the crust of bread out of the front of her dress and started to gnaw on it. Then she hurried into the kitchen, found the bread in its place, looked round for the molasses, mixed it with *tahini* and stood in the kitchen eating. She ate three pieces of bread with molasses, then got the tea kettle ready. She sat and drank and began to feel sleepy. Having stood up sluggishly, she found herself lying down on the bed and slipping into unconsciousness. She slept like one who doesn't know she's asleep – that's how she'd describe it later. She didn't shut the door and she didn't take off her clothes. She lay down as she was, her hands sticky with molasses, and drowsiness overcame her. When she awoke, darkness had started to steal into the house. She opened her eyes and was lost.

"I was lost, son, and didn't know where I was."

For a moment, she didn't dare move. She opened her eyes and went rigid.

"I slept on the only bed we owned. My husband, God rest his soul, bought a brass bed unlike any in the whole village. I didn't sleep on it after he died, because a bed's for men. He'd sleep on the bed and I'd sleep on a mattress on the floor beneath. Then he started making me sleep in the bed next to him. He said it was because he loved me. In our day, son, no-one used that word. A husband loved his wife, but he wouldn't tell her. But your grandfather Khaleel, he made me sleep on top, and that's all there was to it."

That day Shaheeneh slept on the brass bed. "I hadn't slept in the bed since his death. It was his bed. I used to make it every day and wash the sheets once a week, but I never slept in it. That day, though, when my eyes grew heavy with sleep, I threw myself down on it and slept. You can imagine what it was like when I woke up and saw darkness everywhere. For an instant I didn't know where I was; it was as though my husband had never died, the village hadn't fallen, and the children weren't waiting in a field in Deir El Qasi. I forgot everything and found myself at home. When I remembered where I was and where I'd come from, I became frightened and started shivering. I jumped off the bed, patted my chest, found the jewellery in its place and thought I'd better go back."

Shaheeneh said she regretted one thing. "I'm sorry I didn't make the bed. In my fear and haste, it was like I didn't care. I know my husband was angry with me: I dreamed of him, son. We were here in the camp and he came to me in a dream and said, 'Even so, Shaheeneh, is that any way to leave my bed? Where am I going to rest now?' I went to the Green Sheikh, God set him straight, and told him about my dream, and he reassured me and said the dead don't return to their houses, and your husband was a martyr, and the martyrs are in Heaven, and he asked me to come and visit him from time to time. I didn't visit him, though. I'd seen that look in his eye; praise God, I never visited him even once. He looked me up and down and licked his lips, saying, 'The martyrs are in Heaven, where there's ease, and houris. Your husband, Shaheeneh, is enjoying his fill of the houris now.' As he said 'houris', he licked his lips as though he were, God forbid . . . ! Is that how they treat martyrs' widows? I mean, who did that old man think he was? No, dear God, I spit on his beard and the beards of all like him. He picks up the Book of God and looks with that lustful look?"

Shaheeneh said she came to her senses and started to shiver.

"I got up, drank some water and left."

She said the village was empty – no-one. Not a sound, not anything. Only the wind whispering to the branches of the trees and the sound of her footsteps.

In front of the mosque, she heard someone quietly clearing his throat. She threw herself on the ground and saw the man coming.

"Who's there?" whispered the man.

Shaheeneh couldn't find her voice to reply. She tried to make herself as small as she could when she saw the White Sheikh coming towards her, carrying what looked like a rifle in his hand.

Shaheeneh said she closed her eyes and started reciting the Throne Verse in her heart. Then the stick tapped her and she heard her name.

"Get up, Shaheeneh my daughter. What are you doing here?"

She opened her eyes and screamed, "I seek refuge with God from Lapidated Satan – I beg you, please not me! Don't take me, Azeez! Please, I have children."

He held out his stick as though he wanted her to take hold of it to raise herself.

"What's the matter, daughter? I'm Uncle Azeez Ayoub."

"You're dead, uncle. Leave me alone. I have children."

"Me, dead! Have you gone crazy? Did you ever hear of a dead man talking? Here I am in front of you. Get up."

"I beheld my uncle, Sheikh Azeez Ayoub, and discovered Yasseen had lied to me. Azeez Ayoub hadn't died; there he was, taking me inside the mosque, lighting a fire, giving me tea and asking after my children. But you know, son, not one person believed me. They said I'd seen a ghost.

Even his daughter Safiyyeh laughed at me and said that he was dead and gone, but I'm sure. I saw him, and he gave me tea and said he couldn't leave the village because he had to guard the mosque and the tree."

Nobody believed her, father. Even I didn't believe her, and in the end she started to doubt herself. Poor grandmother. She died before Umm Hassan returned from her journey over there and told us the man wasn't a ghost, and that he died in a strange way.

Azeez Ayoub told Shaheeneh they'd been guarding the tree for five generations and they couldn't abandon it. "I asked my wife to stay on here, but she refused because she was afraid of the Jews. 'What can the Jews do?' I asked her. 'The worst has already happened.' And she said, 'I'm afraid of Deir Yasseen.'"

Sheikh Azeez said he wasn't afraid. "I'm the fifth generation, and I won't leave the lotus tree. Who will look after the holy saints? Who will pray in the mosque? Who will wash the graves?"

Shaheeneh listened to what the man said as though she was in a dream, and in dreams words have no meaning. "He asked me to tell his wife that he was still alive. I didn't ask him anything. It was very strange – whenever I was about to ask him something, I'd hear the answer before I could ask. In the Name of God the Merciful, the Compassionate, it was as though he could read my heart. He said the Jews came from time to time. A patrol of three armed soldiers would come, roam around the village, then go into the houses and loot the gold. 'You found your gold things by God's will, but the gold's flown away, daughter. They think I'm mad. When they see me, they run away, so I climb the minaret and recite the call to prayer; the call frightens them and protects me. Off with you now, daughter. Go to your children.'"

My grandmother said the journey back to the fields of Deir El Qasi was as quick as a flash. "I ran the whole way. I ran, and I didn't look back. I felt there was someone running behind me. I couldn't hear a thing, as though my ears had been blocked by the wind. I ran and the wind carried me till I arrived. I arrived at our camp and saw my four children sitting there, waiting for me. I arrived and threw myself among them. I took them into the tent and told them to sleep. They pressed up close to one another in silence. It was then that I smelled myself. It was sweat; it had stained my clothes, and the smell of it spread inside the tent. I was embarrassed and asked Muneerah to get up and help me to wash. That day I divided the wealth between me and her. I put ten liras into the front of my dress and ten into the front of hers. I took the signet ring and the necklace and gave her the twisted bracelets. With this money we were able to live for a whole year in Cana before my girls had to go and work in the stone quarries."

You don't know Azeez Ayoub, or you didn't tell me anything about him or about the life he lived alone in our village. Didn't you visit El Ghabsiyyeh? Didn't you hear the story of the holy saint who was killed? If it hadn't been for Umm Hassan, I'd have known nothing. You ought to have heard her telling me. How wonderful Umm Hassan was – I wish she'd been my mother! At least I'd sleep comfortably. Did you know I'm afraid of sleeping? I told you, I'm scared of sleeping and waking up to find myself in a strange land whose language I can't speak. I'm scared I won't wake up. I'm scared I won't find my house or I won't find you or I won't find the hospital or I don't know what.

With Umm Hassan I would've slept. My grandmother used to scare me at night. I'd hear the sound of her footsteps in the house as though she couldn't sleep and couldn't let me sleep. She'd walk and walk, then come to my bed and ask me if I was asleep. I'd jump up in a fright to find her at my side saying she'd remembered something, and she'd start to tell me her boring story about Yasseen, his life and death, and so on.

With Umm Hassan sleep comes to you. With her you feel the world is steady, not about to be dislodged. Where are you now, Umm Hassan? And where's the nursing certificate you kept from the days of the British Mandate? Umm Hassan told me about my grandfather's uncle, Azeez Ayoub. She said he'd become a saint and that people made oaths in his name and that he could cure illnesses. She said that during her visit to her brother in El Jdeideh, she'd remembered her promise to my grandmother to visit El Ghabsiyyeh and light a candle under the lotus tree.

Have you seen the lotus tree, father?

Have you tasted its fruit?

Umm Hassan said its fruit were called *doum* and were like medlars, or even better than medlars.

Umm Hassan told the people in El Jdeideh that she had to go El Ghabsiyyeh to fulfil her vow before the lotus tree, and she went on her own because her brother was afraid to go with her. He told her that since the Ayoub incident and the building of his tomb there, the Israelis had started to clamp down and stop people from visiting the village. El Ghabsiyyeh was a military area, and if anyone was seen there they were taken to prison and made to pay a huge fine.

Her brother took her to the village of El Nahar and showed her the way. She said that when she reached the tree, she made a prostration. She saw melted candles and ribbons hung over the fine small leaves, which covered the branches in profusion. She said she made a prostration and then entered the mosque, where she knelt in a corner and prayed.

When she returned, she told me about Ayoub.

She said the people in El Jdeideh talked about him. They told her about a white man with a white beard and white clothes who guarded a tree and talked to its branches. People would come from the surrounding villages to fulfil their vows to the tree and see the man. Umm Hassan told them it was Azeez. "It's Azeez," she'd say. "No. His name's Ayoub," they'd say.

Umm Hassan said Azeez cleaned the mosque every day. The Israeli settlement that had been built on the edge of El Ghabsiyyeh used the mosque as a cow pen. Ayoub would get up every day and set about cleaning the mosque, picking up the dung with his hands and throwing it into the fields. Then he'd sprinkle water and pray.

Umm Hassan said that at first the people thought he was Jewish, for he resembled the Iraqi Jews who were common in the area and had set up the settlement of Netiv ha-Shayyara. They thought he was the guard for the cow pen. Then they discovered the truth because whenever more than three women gathered round the lotus tree, he'd climb the minaret and recite the call to prayer. Many, both men and women, had attempted to talk to him, but he wouldn't speak. He seemed to be from another world, as though he was a ghost, with his eyes sunken in his oval face and his shoulders that drooped as though his body was no longer capable of holding them up.

"That's Azeez Ayoub," said Umm Hassan, and she told them his wife and children lived in El Burj El Shamali camp near Tyre, and that she'd seen his son, who'd grown into a fine man and worked as a broker for the lemon growers in Tyre.

The people of El Jdeideh couldn't believe that their Ayoub was that Azeez Ayoub.

Their Ayoub was a phantom; our Azeez was a man.

Their Ayoub was a saint; our Azeez died when the young Yasseen left him and fled into the valley.

Ayoub, or Azeez Ayoub, lived his life a lonely phantom in a village inhabited by ghosts. He lived alone close to the tree and the mosque, eating the plants that grew on the land and the remains of supplies that had been left behind in the abandoned houses, and sleeping in the mosque with the cows. They'd see him walking through the fields or sitting under the lotus tree or praying in the mosque or giving the call to prayer. His clothes were shining white, as though all the muck that surrounded him left no mark.

People called him White Ayoub.

After lighting their candles under the tree, they'd approach him hoping for a blessing and he'd run away. No-one was able to touch him. Umm Hassan didn't know how they knew his name. "He doesn't speak and he doesn't answer, so how did they find out his name? I swear, son, I don't know. They said he was as clean as the angels and that he'd clean out the mosque and become even whiter."

Umm Hassan said she thought half the stories about Ayoub were just fantasies. The mosque wasn't used permanently as a cow pen. She said she'd gone into the mosque and seen traces of cows and gathered that the Jews used it to pen their cattle in winter, and she didn't think they'd leave their cows with Ayoub.

"Ayoub went mad," said Umm Hassan. "How could anybody live alone among those ruins and not lose his reason? If he hadn't lost his mind, he'd have left El Ghabsiyyeh and gone to another village and lived there."

"This isn't the point of the story, son," said Umm Hassan. "The point of the story is Azeez Ayoub's becoming a saint after he died."

One day a woman came to the lotus tree to fulfil a vow, and she saw him. She threw down her candles and ran to El Jdeideh, and everyone came. Ayoub was dead beneath the holy tree, his neck tied to a rope, the rope on the ground, as though the man had fallen from a branch of the tree. At one end of the rope was Ayoub's neck, which had turned thin and black, and at the other end was a branch of the lotus tree that had been torn from its mother and fallen to the ground.

"No-one touch him," said someone. "The man committed suicide, and suicide defiles."

The people backed away from the body of White Ayoub, whispering in strangled voices. One woman left the throng, went over to the corpse, took off her headscarf and covered the face of the dead man. Then she knelt bare-headed and started to weep.

"They killed him," said the kneeling women. "They killed the guardian of the lotus tree, and it's a sign."

Sheikh Abd El Ahad, sheikh of the Jdeideh mosque, said that Ayoub hadn't committed suicide. "Ayoub is a martyr, friends."

The sheikh gave orders to take the body into the mosque, where it was washed and wrapped in a shroud. The burial took place next to the lotus tree, where they built Ayoub a tomb.

"Now, son, when you go to El Ghabsiyyeh, you'll see prickly pears everywhere. Only the prickly pears bear witness to our endurance. And there next to the tree, you'll see the tomb of Ayoub. The tree is lush and beautiful and green. Ah, how beautiful lotus trees are! Have you ever seen a lotus tree in your life? Of course you haven't. Your generation hasn't seen anything. There, son, sleeps Azeez Ayoub, or Saint Ayoub. People visit his tomb and leave him gifts and votive offerings, and he answers their prayers. I saw the tomb. A small tomb with a window. I stuck my head inside and shouted, 'Azeez. Can you hear me? I swear you merit your name of "Precious"! You were better than a whole people. You ended your life on the tree you guarded. Azeez! Saint! Beloved of God!' That's how they call to him, son. They come from all the villages and stick their heads through the window and shout, 'Ayoub!'"

Umm Hassan said she thought Azeez Ayoub had committed suicide. "A man all alone, afflicted by madness, what was he to do? But he was transformed into a sheikh and they swear by his name and await his blessing. Poor humans!"

Even though Umm Hassan didn't believe that Azeez Ayoub had become a saint, in her last days she'd swear by his name and ask me to tell her the story of how I'd stood with my father behind the donkey, and how Azeez had grabbed the donkey's tail and told him to stand behind him. I'd describe the scene to her and she'd laugh: "What was he thinking of? Did he think the donkey would act as a barrier and protect them from the bullets?"

As you see, master, things have become mixed up in my mind just as they have in yours. I've got nothing to do with it: it was Yasseen, my father, who stood behind him. But, as you also see, I've caught Umm Hassan's infection and started talking about these people as though I knew them, which I didn't. But Ayoub did become a saint. What do saints do to become saints? Nothing, because people invent them. People invent wonders and believe in them because they need them. True as that is, it changes nothing. Ayoub's a saint, whether we wish it or not.

Azeez was guardian of the mosque and guardian of the lotus tree and guardian of the cemetery. He'd inherited his profession from his father, who'd inherited it from his father, who'd inherited it from his father, who . . . till you run out of fathers. Every day he filled his water jar, washed the graves, cleaned the mosque, walked around the lotus tree and slept.

"A man who sleeps in a cemetery." That was how Umm Hassan described him.

And the man who slept in a cemetery started curing the sick, helping women get pregnant, bringing back those who'd gone away and finding husbands for girls.

Ayoub became another name for the tree, which became known as the Tree of Ayoub.

Now I understand why you get things mixed up, father. I asked you about the lotus tree, and you answered that there was no such thing as a lotus tree in El Ghabsiyyeh, and that the people of Deir El Asad used to talk of a tree called an *ayoubi* and you didn't know what kind of tree that was.

The tree, father, is the lotus, and its guardian is Ayoub – a man who hanged himself from the branches of his tree, so the tree proclaimed him a saint.

"Listen, Khaleel," said Umm Hassan. "It could be that he hung himself, or it could be that the man tied the rope around his neck and climbed onto a branch of the tree to put an end to his misery and loneliness, but the tree took pity on him and broke so as not to allow him to commit the defilement of suicide. The tree, which is ruled by a saint, proclaimed him a saint, so now it has two saints, the first one, whose name we don't know, and Ayoub, of our village, whose name was Azeez. The sheikh of

El Jdeideh has a different opinion. He believes the Israelis strangled him, then tied a rope round his neck to make people think he'd committed suicide. 'Why should he commit suicide?' the sheikh asked when I met him. 'The man chose to live alone in the service of God, so they killed him. They killed him because they wanted to uproot the tree, but we'll never let them do that. I'll appoint a new guard for the tree and the tomb.'"

The sheikh of El Jdeideh didn't appoint a guard as he'd promised Umm Hassan, and the tomb remained alone, but no-one raised a hand against the holy tree.

Would you like me to make a vow to Ayoub for your recovery?

I'm certain you know Azeez Ayoub. You may not have liked him because he wasn't a fighter. You told me you despised anybody who didn't carry a gun: "The country was slipping away before our eyes, and they sat there doing nothing." Azeez Ayoub didn't carry a gun and he didn't fight, but look what he became and what we've become. He's now a saint to whom people make vows and we're alone.

Leave Azeez Ayoub in his tomb and come with me to look for Shaheeneh. We left her in front of her tent in Deir El Qasi. She went into the tent and lay down next to her children after her long journey to El Ghabsiyyeh. And before she fell asleep, she smelled her own sweat, left the tent and asked Muneerah to help her to bathe. She washed herself, divided her wealth into two halves and lived off it for more than a year.

From Deir El Qasi to Beit Leef, from Beit Leef to El Mansourah, from El Mansourah to Cana. Shaheeneh told how the people were like locusts: "The Israeli planes hovered overhead while we scurried through the emptiness looking for a refuge, until we reached El Mansourah. There we crossed the border, the noise stopped, and the terror was extinguished. We found ourselves in Cana, and there we rented a house from the Atiyyeh family. Yasseen went to the school, and the girls and I sat in the house, and I spent all my money. Cana was beautiful and quiet, like our village in Palestine."

My grandmother didn't tell me much about Cana because she believed that her journey into exile only really began when they gathered everyone together in the camps around Tyre.

"In Cana, we weren't in exile, or refugees. We were waiting."

Do you know what waiting, and the hope of return, meant to these people, master? Of course you don't. However, the story of the buffaloes of El Khalsah astonished me. When my grandmother told me the story, I thought she was telling me something like the stories grown-ups tell children that they don't expect them to believe. The story concerns a man called Abu Arif, one of the Bedouins of El Khalsah, who belong to the Heib tribe. He came to Cana along with everyone else and stayed with his wife and five daughters. And he brought his buffaloes. Seven buffalo cows, God protect them. "We all drank their milk, for the man used to give it away free to everybody. He refused to sell it, saying the buffaloes were an offering to El Khalsah – 'When we go back, we can buy and sell.' He was generous and stubborn, like all Bedouin. When spring, which is when buffaloes become fertile, arrived, people saw the man leading his herd south. His wife said he was mad because he believed the buffaloes could only conceive in El Khalsah, and he'd agreed with a cousin of his to hand the buffaloes over to him at the Lebanese–Palestinian border on condition that he return them two weeks later. The man set off for the border, and his wife stood in the square at Cana and bade him farewell, mourning him and mourning the buffaloes, but the man would have nothing to do with her. Then the buffaloes disappeared from view and everyone forgot about the story.

My grandmother said Abu Arif returned alone, cowering, his spirit broken. He wouldn't speak to us. "He was bathed in tears and we didn't dare ask him anything. He returned alone, without the buffaloes."

"We've lost everything," said Umm Arif.

Abu Arif drove his buffaloes to El Khalsah because he was convinced the buffaloes could only conceive in the land where they were raised, and at the border post the firing started. The buffaloes sank to the ground, their blood blotting the sky, and Abu Arif stood there in the midst of the massacre.

He told his wife he was standing at the border waving for his cousin when the firing started.

He said he ran from buffalo to buffalo. He said there was blood everywhere. He said he raised his hands and screamed, but they were dying.

He said his dog of a cousin never turned up. He said he'd taken off his white *kufiyyeh* and raised it aloft as a sign of surrender, then started running with it from buffalo to buffalo, trying to staunch their wounds, the *kufiyyeh* becoming drenched in blood. He said he raised the stained *kufiyyeh* and shouted and begged, but they didn't stop. "The ground was covered in blood, the buffaloes were dying, and I was weeping. Why didn't they kill me too? I wiped my face with the blood-soaked *kufiyyeh* and sat down among the buffaloes."

The man returned to his wife, cowering, frightened. He returned without his buffaloes, carrying the blood-stained *kufiyyeh* and the marks of despair.

That was Cana, master.

My father went to the school and my grandmother got out her Palestinian liras and spent them one by one, then sold her gold bracelets and her necklace; however, she didn't sell the signet ring, which remained on her finger till her death. I think my Aunt Muneerah took it. I don't know. My grandmother sold everything and then started working with her daughters crushing stone in the village. Waiting was no longer viable. The borders were closed; people had entered a labyrinth. The Lebanese police came and said they had orders to gather the Palestinians into the camp at El Rasheediyyeh. This was when the agony began. They drove Abu Arif, tied up with rope, with whips while he screamed that he couldn't bear to be taken away from his buffaloes.

They assembled everyone in the square, put them on to lorries and trains, and moved them away from the borders of their country.

My grandmother said the agony started in the camp. "They dumped us at the seashore in winter. The wind blew hard from all directions, and we were left in the dark."

She said she couldn't remember daylight. "During those days, everything was black. Even the rain was black, son. We drowned in the mud. Your poor father, God rest his soul, was only knee-high, and I was afraid for him and told the girls to watch out for Yasseen because he'd drown in the mud. I'd yell and hear nothing; my voice flew away in the wind. God, what terrible days those were!"

How can I tell you of those days, father, when I didn't experience them myself and my father didn't tell me? My father died before he and I reached the age when fathers tell their sons their stories.

They were known as "the banana days."

The only shelter people could find was under big, dry banana leaves. They'd buy ten leaves for five Lebanese piastres and make roofs for their tents and spread the leaves on the ground.

"They were the banana days," said Shaheeneh.

When Shaheeneh told about those days, it was as though she wasn't describing the past. It was as though time had stopped. She told of the crowded buses, of the wooden pattens they wore as protection from the hot sand, of the tents in which the wind was a permanent occupant, of the rain that pierced the bone.

She told of moving from Cana and of how the Lebanese officer came surrounded by his men and ordered the Palestinians to congregate in the square, of how he beat Abu Arif with his whip till he was soaked in blood.

"It was all banana leaves," she said.

"We spread the leaves on the ground and covered the roofs and the sides of the tents with them, and lived with the rottenness. The leaves rotted, and we rotted beneath them and on top of them."

It was then that Shaheeneh decided that Yasseen's schooling was over and it was time for him to work.

"No, that's not true," she said. "I begged him not to leave school. I said we'd live off the rations we got with the relief card." But he refused. He found work in the sheet-metal factory at Meena El Hisin, which landed him in prison, though that's another story.

Shaheeneh told of three months in the camp before we were moved to Beirut and stayed in the house of the Hammoud family. She and her children stayed about two months in that ancient Beirut house, which belonged to a family of fighters from '36, before moving to Shatila camp.

Shaheeneh met Ahmad Hammoud in El Rasheediyyeh camp. He was one of a group of young men who came from Beirut to distribute relief supplies to the refugees, and when he found out that she was the daughter of the '36 fighter Rabbah El Awad, he bowed and kissed her hand. Two days later he returned with his father and asked Shaheeneh to come to Beirut.

"We went to Beirut," said my grandmother, "and lived for about two months in their beautiful house, but people get on each other's nerves."

My grandmother didn't tell me about her life in that house or why people got on each other's nerves. She said she'd taken her children and gone to Shatila, set up her tent there and lived. From the tent, to the concrete room roofed with canvas, to the corrugated-iron roof, to the "Revolution roof" – she had to wait twenty years, until 1968, to get a concrete roof. The concrete roof came with the Revolution and the fedayeen. Only then was she able to get any sleep. She said that before she got the concrete roof, she hadn't been able to sleep at night because she felt she was sleeping in the open.

My mother told me nothing.

She moved within her silence, which she wore like a cocoon. When I remember her now, I see her as an evanescent phantom.

She was there and not there, as though she wasn't my mother, as though she was a stranger living with us. She disappeared and left the story to my grandmother.

I wasn't interested in the story. You think that to gather the stories of El Ghabsiyyeh I had to search and ask around, but it's not true, master. The stories came to me without my having to chase them. My grand-mother used to drown me in stories, as though she had nothing to do but talk. When I was with her, I'd yawn and sleep and the stories would cover me. Now I feel that I have to push the stories aside in order to see, for all I see is spots, as though that woman's stories were like coloured spots drifting around me. I don't know a whole story; even the story of Abu Arif's buffaloes I don't know in full – why did the Israelis open fire on the buffaloes, and why didn't they kill the man, why did they leave him unharmed in the midst of the massacre?

My grandmother said his wife didn't believe him. "He disappeared for a month and then returned saying they'd killed his buffaloes! Abu Arif lied to us because he didn't dare to tell the shameful truth of his disgrace. He said he wanted to have his buffaloes conceive in El Khalsah and his cousin would meet him at the border and take them from him, then return them after a week. Fine. But he didn't come back after a week, or after the massacre. He was away for a month. Then he came back carrying his *kufiyyeh* and saying the Israelis had killed them."

"I'm certain the Jews didn't kill them," said his wife. "Why would they kill them? They'd take them. And how could they have killed the buffaloes and not killed him as well? It would've been good riddance! No, the

Jews didn't kill the buffaloes. I'm certain his cousin stole them. Took them and disappeared. The man waited a month at the border, then despaired and had no choice but to make up the story of the buffalo massacre. Everything stupid we do we blame on the Jews. No, the Jews didn't kill them. And all of it for what? We could have sold them and lived off the money."

My grandmother said Umm Arif grieved for her buffaloes as much as if her husband had died. She'd insult him and grieve, weep and get up and sit down again, while the man behaved like an imbecile, carrying his *kufiyyeh* around and showing it to people in Cana. Everyone believed him and cursed the times. Everyone believed him except his wife, who knew him better than anyone else.

"So what do you think, son?" asked my grandmother.

I said I didn't know because I'd only seen buffaloes in Egyptian films and didn't know we raised them in Palestine.

"Did we raise buffaloes?" I asked her.

"Us, no. We raised sheep and goats, cows and chickens. The people of El Khalsah are Bedouin, and the Bedouin raise buffaloes, not us."

She started telling me the story of Abu Arif again.

"You told me that story, grandma."

"So what? I told it to you, and I'll tell it again. Talk's just flapping the lips. If we don't talk, what are we to do?" The man was a pain in the arse and a fool. Wouldn't it have been better to slaughter them and eat them? In those days we were dying for a bit of meat. All we had to eat was *midardara* – lentils, rice and fried onions."

"But I like *midardara*, grandma."

What did they eat, there in their village in Palestine? I'm convinced *midardara* was the only thing they ate. But my grandmother always had an answer "under her arm," as they say. She'd say that things over there had a different taste. "Real oil – olive oil – was enough. You could thrive on olive oil and nothing else, and there were lots of things you could use it for."

Have I told you what Shaheeneh did to my father on their wedding night? She made him drink a coffee cup full of olive oil before going in to my mother. "I made him drink oil. Oil's good for sex. One day soon, son, God willing, one day soon, at your wedding, I'll give you oil to drink the way I did your father, and later you'll say 'Shaheeneh knew, God rest her soul!'"

Father, I don't know Shaheeneh's story well enough to be able to tell it to you. The stories are like drops of oil floating on the surface of memory. I try to link them up, but they don't want to be linked. I don't know a lot about my paternal aunts. All I can tell you about is the husband of one of them, who had a bald patch that looked like it was polished with olive oil. I've told you about him, so there's no point in repeating it. I hate things that repeat, but things do repeat, infinitely.

Would you like to hear the story of my father and the Jew?

I'll tell it to you, but don't ask for the details. I'll ask my grandmother one day – meaning when we meet one another, after a long life, God willing, there in the real world. I'll ask her because she knows more than I do, and she'll tell you the story of the rabbi properly. All I know are the broad outlines, which I'll try to tell you.

I apologise.

I return to you with apologies. I'll give you your bath now and feed you. Then I'll tell you the story of the rabbi. Tell me you're comfortable – your temperature's gone down, and everything's back to normal; all that's left is this small sore on the sole of your left foot.

Tell me, what you do think of the waterbed?

If Saleem As'ad, God send him good fortune, did nothing else in his life but come up with this mattress for us, his heavenly reward will still be great.

I told you I was apologising because I had to attend to other matters. I witnessed a sad scene, but instead of crying I laughed uproariously. Something was flowing inside me like tears, but I laughed and I could only settle the matter the way Abd El Wahid El Khateeb wanted it settled.

Do you know Abd El Wahid?

I doubt it. I didn't meet him till his son brought him to the hospital a month ago. He arrived in a bad state, with pain throughout his body. I examined him along with Dr Amjad and suggested having him transferred to El Hamshari Hospital in Ein El Hilweh so he could have X-rays, as we don't have any equipment here – even the blood-testing lab has closed. We're more of a hotel. The patients come, they sleep, and we provide them with the minimum of care. Despite which, we call this building suspended in a vacuum a hospital.

Abd El Wahid came, and I examined him. My diagnosis was liver cancer; his liver was enlarged and cirrhotic. But Dr Amjad disagreed, as usual. He said the man was suffering from the onset of amyloidosis of the liver and prescribed medicines for him. I advised his son to take his father to El Hamshari Hospital to be sure. Father and son left with Amjad's prescription and my advice, and it seems that after a few days of Amjad's medicines, they decided to go to El Hamshari Hospital. There the man underwent examinations that showed he was suffering from liver cancer. They came back to me carrying the report. The father sat down, his son at his side. They'd undoubtedly read the report and discovered that the case was hopeless, since it ends with the recommendation that the patient be taken home to rest with powerful painkillers.

I read the report while the two men sat in my office, their eyes trained on my lips. People are strange! They think doctors are magicians. What was I supposed to do for them?

"You must take the medicines regularly," I told the sick man.

I told the son he could phone me if there were any developments.

The son made a move to go, but Abd El Wahid didn't budge and asked me, with trembling lips, "Aren't you going to put me in the hospital, doctor?"

"No," I said. "Your condition doesn't warrant it."

As he spoke, he bit his lower lip; he was wracked with pain, and his eyes were tearing. I don't know what the eyes have to do with the liver, but I could see death like a bleariness covering his eyes. The man, with his red face, his little pot belly and his sixty years, didn't want to leave the hospital.

"I don't want to. No. I'll die," he said.

"How long we live is for God to decide," I said. I didn't hide from him the fact that his case was serious because I believe the patient has a right to know.

"How much time do I have?"

"I don't know," I said. "Probably not much."

"Why won't you treat me here?"

I explained that we didn't have the means to treat him and that anyway his case didn't require a hospital.

He said he didn't want to go home: "You're a hospital, and it's your duty to treat me." He looked at his son for support, but the son sat in silence and looked at me with complicit eyes, as though . . . I don't want to say he was glad his father's end was near, but he was indifferent.

I stood up to show that the visit was over, and then, without any preamble, the son began abusing me. He said he wouldn't take his father because it was the hospital's duty to care for difficult cases, and he threatened me, saying he'd hold me responsible for any harm that might come to his father.

I had to explain our situation again and tell him how, since the Israeli incursion of '82 and the massacres, the siege and the destruction that had come with it, we no longer had the necessary equipment.

"Why do you call it a hospital?" screamed the son.

"You're right." I told him. "But do you want to change the name of the place now? Go and take care of your father."

The son took his father and left, and I forgot about the incident. I didn't even tell you about it.

Yesterday there was a surprise. I was in your room when I heard Nurse Zeinab scream. I went out and found Abd El Wahid there. He had come to the hospital barefoot and wearing his pyjamas. I saw the man standing there and Nurse Zeinab on the ground, pulling her skirt over her thighs while he mumbled incomprehensibly.

Nurse Zeinab said he'd pushed her and tried to go up to the rooms.

Where he got the strength when he was already in the jaws of the angel of death I don't know. I know he ran into the hospital and started climbing the stairs to the rooms. Nurse Zeinab, running after him, tried to ask him what he wanted, and he answered her with incomprehensible words as though he was howling, and when she tried to stop him he shoved her to the ground.

When he saw me, he ran towards me shouting, "I beg you, doctor, put me back in hospital." He grabbed my hand and tried to kiss it, saying he didn't want to die.

"Don't treat me if you don't want to," he said, "but I don't want to die. People don't die in hospitals. I implore you, doctor, by all that you hold dear, don't send me to die at home."

It was then, master, that I burst into tears inside but started to laugh.

I was laughing, Nurse Zeinab got up, and the man was trembling. When I asked Nurse Zeinab to prepare him a room, he seemed to fly with joy. I saw him climbing the stairs behind Nurse Zeinab, in his dirty white pyjamas, his feet hardly touching the stairs, as though I'd saved his life or promised him a place in Paradise.

Believe me, master, when I tell you I never saw such joy in all my life. Naturally, nothing changed. His joy disappeared when he lay down on the bed and the pain renewed its onslaught. His son's wife came to be with him. I think he heard her ask me when he would die and then start grumbling when she heard me say she had to take care of him and give him his painkillers regularly.

"Regularly!" she said with the surprise of one who hadn't expected to hear this answer. "You mean I have to stay here full-time?" she asked, gesturing in my face.

"Of course," I said. "Everyone knows that here families have to look after the patients."

"We'll take him home," she said. "Home's better."

When the man heard "home" he started to cry.

I said, "No. Abd El Wahid has to stay in the hospital."

Hearing my reply, he relaxed on the bed and eased himself into his pain, as though he'd found comfort.

Abd El Wahid, father, will die in flight from his death. He'll die without knowing it. He fled from having to stare death in the face and came to the hospital so he could close his eyes before dying.

No, master, I beg of you.

Please don't misunderstand. I just wanted to apologise because I neglected you for a while, and I don't mean to compare you with him or with my father. I don't know if my father saw his death in the muzzle of the gun or whether he shut his eyes before he died. I told you, I don't know much about the man. My mother said one thing and my grandmother said something else, and I'm not that interested in the subject. I just want to know why my mother ran away.

You don't know anything about my mother, so listen to what I tell you. My mother ran away because she'd made a bad marriage, and the reason was "the Jew." This is how my grandmother told it – my grandmother whose circumstances improved after my mother ran away, as though she'd found peace. From then on, my father's horrendous death no longer constituted the mainspring of her life. From then on, her muscles relaxed, her face rounded out with tenderness, and she never stopped abusing "the Jew" who was the cause of the marriage. I was only little and incapable of making sense of things so I didn't understand that when she abused "the Jew" she was talking about a specific person. Later I discovered that "the Jew" was the reason for my father's marriage to my mother, Najwah.

My grandmother said my father had to go to work young. His sisters were married and the UNWRA assistance wasn't enough, not to mention that the boy hadn't done well at school. So he started work at Shukri's chemist's shop in Bab Idrees. Then he found work in a sheet-metal work-shop at Meena El Hisin that belonged to two Jews called Aslan Durziyyeh and Sa'eed Lawi. That was where the scandal occurred.

My grandmother said they arrested my father and threw him into prison for more than a fortnight. "Poor dear, he was just a child. True, he was tall and mature, but he was only sixteen. He liked reading a lot but behaved badly at school, so he left his studies to work. At the chemist's, his wages were a joke: seven liras a week, and he worked from dawn to the afternoon. I asked him to put up with it so he could learn something useful."

The young man who was my father was spellbound by Beirut, espe-cially by Abu Afeef's restaurant on El Burj Square, close to the chemist's where he worked. He'd leave the camp at 6.00 in the morning, walk from Shatila to El Burj Square in half an hour and arrive at work at 6.30. Then he cleaned the shop before opening for customers at 7.00.

Before going to the chemist's, he'd pass in front of Abu Afeef's, which was at a crossing, and smell the beans, onions, oil and mint, and feel hungry. He'd sit on the edge of the pavement opposite, spread the food he'd brought with him on the ground and wolf it down. The food his mother had made was divided into two, half for breakfast and half for lunch, and consisted of squares of bread baked and sprinkled with thyme or pounded spices, three boiled eggs, two loaves of flat bread and a tomato. But the youth seated on the pavement in front of the restaurant would smell the food and see the men sitting at the small tables inside devouring their meals, and he'd eat all the food he'd brought with him at one go. He'd eat breakfast and lunch together as though he couldn't get enough. And when he went back to the house, at 7.00 in the evening, he'd be overcome by hunger again, so he'd eat his dinner quickly and go out into the alleys of the camp.

My grandmother didn't know that my father longed for a dish of beans, but when she found out, she made it for him as a surprise. She woke him at 5.00 one morning, after setting out a special table with beans and mint and onions and tomatoes and a pitcher of tea. The youth got up and looked at his mother's table with neither hunger nor appetite. He ate to please her and told her the smell was different. Then he took his picnic and left. When he came back in the evening, my grandmother discovered that he hadn't touched his food and wasn't hungry. He confessed that he'd eaten beans at the restaurant. He said he hadn't been able to resist. He'd gone into Abu Afeef's at 10.00 in the morning and eaten two plates of beans and paid a whole lira. He said his stomach hurt and he felt guilty, but the restaurant beans were tastier than the beans she made at home. "Then he started eating beans at Abu Afeef's every Friday morning, and he remained faithful to his dish of beans till the day he died, God rest his soul."

It wasn't the dish of beans that enchanted my father, it was the city. He beheld a new world, without names, and wanted to know everything. I don't know, master, about how well educated he was, except that I found his library in a box in my room and saw novels by Jirji Zeidan on the history of the Arabs, and the books of Taha Hussein, as well as a collection of yellowing Egyptian magazines. My grandmother said that if my father had finished his education, he'd have been a great scholar. All mothers say the same, right? I'm the only one who has none of that self-confidence mothers can give.

I won't talk to you about my mother now but about why my father married her. What happened was that after about a year of working at Shukri's chemist's shop, my father transferred to a job in the sheet-metal workshop at Meena El Hisin.

After Mr Emile Shukri threw him out for being rude to the customers, the young man hung around the Beirut streets. My grandmother said my father denied the accusation and said he'd never pestered customers for tips, and she believed him because he never came back at the end of the week with anything but the six and a half liras which were his entire wages minus the cost of the weekly dish of beans.

"But he smoked," I told her. "Where did he get the money to buy cigarettes?"

"How should I know?" she asked.

My father was thrown out of his job over the tips because Mr Emile said it wouldn't do: "You can't force something on a customer. If he gives you a quarter of a lira, how can you tell him it's not enough? The customer's free to give you what he wants." It seems, though, that my father insisted on what he felt was his due and insulted one of the customers, so he was thrown out of his job.

The young man without a job loitered on the city's streets, left El Burj Square going in the direction of the sea, kept on till he reached Bahri restaurant, and from there walked in the direction of El Zeitouneh. In the Meena El Hisin district he went into a petrol station to ask if they needed help, and there he saw a small notice advertising for workers for the sheet-metal workshop.

My father said, "I went into the workshop through the old arch at the entrance and saw a man wearing a fez and a long, open-fronted gown. I asked if they needed workers. He looked me up and down and asked where I was from. When I said Palestine, he took me inside and said, 'Get started.'"

It was because of the workshop that my father went to prison.

The sheet-metal workshop owned by the Jews Aslan Durziyyeh and Sa'eed Lawi was small and employed about twenty young men, most of whom were Lebanese Christians. The two owners differed in every respect. Aslan Durziyyeh loved the workers and mixed with them. He even invited my father to his house in Wadi Abu Jmeel once Yasseen got to know his son Simon and they'd started going to the cinema together. Sa'eed Lawi, who wore Western dress, was tough on the workers and docked their wages if they were even a few minutes late.

I won't tell you about the work because I don't know what it was like. What I know is that my father told my mother he'd visit the Durziyyeh family at their home in Wadi Abu Jmeel and that they'd feed him mutton-sausage sandwiches and that Simon suggested he work with him in a dairy

Simon managed close to the fish market. But everything came to an end when the Lebanese police surrounded the workshop and arrested all the young men who worked there.

That was 1953, the year Rabbi Ya'qoub Elfiyyeh was stabbed to death in his home in Wadi Abu Jmeel. It seems the police suspected that the gang responsible for the crime consisted of workers at the sheet-metal workshop owned by Durziyyeh and Lawi, so they raided the place and took all the young men for interrogation.

"Your father went straight from the prison to his wedding," said my grandmother.

The story spread through the camp. At the beginning, the newspapers hinted that the presence of three Palestinians among those arrested pointed to it being a revenge killing. You know how they make a big thing out of any crime committed by a Palestinian in Lebanon, so how much more when the victim was a rabbi?

The investigation turned up some amazing facts. The rabbi's wife gave everything away, confessing that her husband had been involved in abnormal relationships with seven young men and had fallen madly in love with the Greek Dimitri Elefteriades and had kept him overnight in his bed despite his wife's objections.

So the investigation turned to Elefteriades, who confessed before the investigating magistrate, Lt Colonel Tanyous El Taweel, that he, along with six of his comrades, had stabbed the rabbi to death. Dimitri said he'd wanted to get rid of the rabbi, who'd forced him to have sex with the youth Saleem Hneineh in front of him, and hadn't paid him the money he'd promised him, and that he'd hated the rabbi but had had sex with him and gone along with his wishes out of avarice.

Elefteriades wept in the courtroom and swore he was innocent and that he'd killed the rabbi unintentionally. The judge, however, accepted the view of the public prosecutor, who asserted that the crime was premeditated and that seven young men had taken part, led by Dimitri.

Naturally, my father was released a long while before the trial. But the details of the sodomy spread through the camp, and my grandmother felt she had to get her son married. She went to visit her daughter in Ein El Hilweh the day before my father was let out of prison. There she met Najwah and her father from El Tirah and the father broached the subject. She didn't mention to him that the groom was in prison for a sex crime, and he didn't ask what the groom did for a living. He just confirmed that he owned land in El Ghabsiyyeh, for in those days people didn't believe the land was lost.

So my father left prison and went straight to his wedding.

It goes without saying that he lost his job, since Aslan Durziyyeh closed his workshop after the scandal and devoted himself to prayer, and my father went on visiting him at his house and eating mutton-sausage sandwiches with him. Aslam Durziyyeh even visited my father in the camp after my sister was born. After the events of 1958, however, he emigrated to Israel.

It was the rabbi's wife who became the story.

She came to the courtroom and spat in Dimitri's face as he stood handcuffed in the dock, and cursed her husband who had besmirched the reputation of the Children of Israel, and said that Beirut would burn like Sodom. She said she didn't know what would become of her: "I'm alone and have no children, and I can't stay in my house, which is filled with the smell of sin." She said she wasn't asking for anything for herself but was ruined: "I'm ruined, Your Honour. I don't have the strength to stay here in Beirut or the courage to emigrate to the Land of Israel. What am I supposed to tell them there? That I'm the widow of the rabbi who was murdered in the bed of fornication and sodomy?"

The judge ordered that she be removed from the courtroom because in those days it was forbidden to pronounce the name of the State of Israel, and here was this woman saying that Beirut was going to turn into Sodom and that she didn't dare emigrate to the land of her fathers and grandfathers, for it would be her fate to be turned into a pillar of salt. "I am the pillar of salt, Your Honour, that proclaims the burning of your city," said the woman before the policemen dragged her out of the courtroom.

The upshot was that my father married the girl from El Tirah.

Najwah Hani Fayyad was fourteen years old when she married Yasseen. Her father handed her over to my grandmother. He took the dowry and left, and the girl entered our house as the wife of Yasseen, who'd found himself work in the sheet-metal workshop owned by the Palestinian Badee' Boulis and called The Light Metals Company, in the Beer El Abid district.

I know nothing about my mother's family. My grandmother said her mother had died and her father agreed to the marriage quickly because he'd got a job in Kuwait and didn't want to take his daughter there with his second wife and her children.

"The wedding was like any other – a party, a procession, ululation, all that. But the girl remained a stranger among us and your father changed after he got married. It was all the fault of the girl from El Tirah. He took to coming home in the evening after work, closing the door of his room and reading. She'd sit with me in the house and do nothing – I swear she did nothing. I'd do all the cooking and wash the clothes and do the washing up and everything. Even you, son: I looked after you, and your father took no interest. He began staying away from home a lot and not coming back till the morning. It seems he left his work at the metals company. I think Adnan Abu Odeh put ideas into his head. Then Najwah had her daughter, and Yasseen died, and his daughter followed him."

Tell me about those days. My grandmother doesn't know. Tell me about the beginning and how you formed the first groups of fedayeen and why my father died and you disappeared and Adnan left the camp.

Tell me why Najwah disappeared.

In Jordan no-one knew her address. It was as though she'd vanished into thin air. My grandmother said she'd gone to her family in Amman, but she didn't have family. Her father was in Kuwait. So where was she? The subject didn't interest me much because when she disappeared I was a child, and when I grew older I harboured a grudge against her and didn't pay much attention to her story. Then I met Sameeh and his wife Samya. You didn't meet Sameeh Barakeh; you hate intellectuals, especially the ones who come and visit the fighters, and theorise and philosophise, and then go back to their comfortable houses.

I first met Sameeh in 1973 when clashes erupted between the army and the camps. He came to the camp with a group of workers from the Palestine Research Centre. They toured the camp and then all went home except for him. Sameeh stayed for more than ten days, lived with us at our guard posts and became our friend. I liked him a lot. There was great suffering in his face, which was broad and brown and etched with pain.

He told me he was waiting for Samya to come from America so they could get married in Beirut. He said he'd fallen in love with her in Ramallah and then gone to prison, and while he was in prison she'd left with her family for Detroit, which has the world's largest concentration of people from Ramallah. I asked why he didn't go to her, complete his education in America and marry her there, and he said he was fully occupied here because he wanted to liberate Palestine. He told me of his long imprisonment in Hebron and of his dream of living with Samya in the stone house he'd inherited from his father in Ramallah. Samya did come and marry him, and now she lives in the stone house in Ramallah while Sameeh sleeps in his grave.

Sameeh said he was imprisoned for the first time in October 1967.

He was distributing pamphlets in the city opposing the Israeli occupation when he was arrested. "In prison," he said, "the Israeli officer taught me the most important lesson of my life. He interrogated me with a copy of the pamphlet in his hand and flung questions at me. At first I said I'd been reading the pamphlet and had nothing to do with distributing it, when in fact I was the one who'd written the pamphlet, which called on the schools to strike in protest against the occupation. He looked me in the eye and said I was a coward. He said that if he were in my place, and if his country were occupied, he wouldn't go about distributing pamphlets, because that would be shameful: you ought to be distributing bombs instead of these bits of paper. I confessed I was the one who'd written the pamphlet, and then he grew even more contemptuous and said we deserved to be beaten. I finished my one year of imprisonment in Ramallah, and when I came out we started the real resistance. We started organising a network for Fatah, but they arrested us before we could undertake any operations. They seized one of the members of the network who'd gone to Jordan and come back in clandestinely, bringing explosives. In the second prison, I learned my lesson well."

Sameeh said he'd been in Hebron prison.

"It was February, and it was as cold as ice. They took me to the interrogator, who ordered me to take off my clothes. Around the interrogator were four men with rippling muscles. 'Take off your clothes,' he said. I took off my shirt. 'Go on,' he said. I took off my vest. 'Your trousers,' he said. I hesitated, but a punch in the face that made my nose bleed persuaded me. I took off my trousers and my shoes and stood naked except for my underpants. With a wave of his hand, the interrogator ordered them to take me away, and we went through the prison door and walked over to a high mound. It was icy. I was certain they were going to kill me and dump me on the ice as food for the birds. At the top of the mound, the beating started. They beat me all over my body. They used their hands and their feet and their leather belts. They threw me down on the ground and kicked me and stamped on my face, my blood turning into icy red spots. At first I screamed with pain, and I heard the interrogator say, 'Coward.' I remembered the first interrogator and the contempt in his eyes as he'd flung the political pamphlet in my face, and I went dumb. They beat me, and I swallowed blood and groans. I rolled naked in the ice, and my skin was torn from me. The beating stopped after what seemed like an infinitely long time, and they took me back to the prison. At the door to the interrogator's room, where they ordered me to go in and get my clothes, I understood everything."

Sameeh said he understood.

The naked, bloodied man stood at the door. He heard the order to enter so he could be given his clothes. The naked man turned to the interrogator, took hold of the sleeve of his thick coat and said to him, "Please, sir, don't go."

The interrogator turned in disgust. He tried to pull his arm away, but Sameeh tightened his grip and said, "Please, sir. I want to tell you something."

"Quickly, quickly," said the interrogator.

Sameeh swallowed his blood and saliva and little bits he later realised were pieces of his teeth and said, "Listen, sir. Listen to me well. I didn't cry out. You beat me and stamped on me, and I didn't cry out even once. Next time, when *you* fall into *my* hands, please don't cry out, because I hate pity."

Sameeh didn't know what happened after he said what he did because he woke up in solitary confinement. When he left that for the common wing, he told the other prisoners only part of his story. He told of the beating on the mound but didn't tell them what happened afterwards at the door to the interrogator's room. He said his words had to remain a secret between him and the interrogator.

"What do you think?" he asked me.

"Do you know the interrogator's name?" I asked him.

"No," he answered.

"So?" I said.

"Any one of them will do," he said.

"And if he cries out?" I asked.

"I'll kill him."

Sameeh died in Tunis, and his wife returned to Ramallah. I learned that he died in his small house in Menzah VI. It's said he died of shock at the Israeli invasion of Lebanon in '82, but I don't believe that was the reason. I mean, after all those who were killed fighting and in massacres, along comes someone who dies of sentiment! It's too much. However, in her letter Samya said that heart disease ran in Sameeh's family and his two brothers died of angina before reaching the age of fifty.

Sameeh said that nothing – not the ice, not the solitary confinement – frightened him so much as the day the prisoners beat him. "In the cell I lost any sense of time. But when the prisoners beat me, I lost my soul."

He said in solitary confinement he had opened his eyes to find himself in darkness.

The cell was very small, and the darkness extended into every corner. He tried to stand, and his head hit the ceiling. He sat and felt as though he was being stifled.

"There wasn't enough air," he said, and he almost went mad worrying about it. He struck the walls of the cell with his fists and discovered that he couldn't find where the door was. The walls seemed to be covered in seamless iron in which the door was lost.

He said he felt as though he was being stifled and started opening his mouth to capture the air.

He said he had a terrible thirst. This was true thirst: true thirst is having no air.

He said it took a while to get used to the lack of air. Then, once he'd regulated his breathing, he relaxed a little and saw the darkness.

"Do you know what darkness means?" he asked. "No-one knows the meaning of the darkness of the grave. Darkness can't be described. Emptiness and stickiness creep over your body and seal your eyes and your pores."

He said he no longer knew who or where he was. Time was lost and with it the man. "To regain my sense of time, I started to count. 'Eureka!' I thought. I spread my ten fingers open and started counting. On the count of sixty, I reached a minute. I'd count sixty minutes and reach an hour. But I began to get confused. Had I reached two hours, or was it more? I'd go back to the beginning and count over again. I'd count and the numbers would get confused, and then I couldn't go on any longer and lapsed into silence."

He said he waited for daybreak, when they brought him water and food.

He said there was no light. "I didn't have a watch or anything. I was on my own in the darkness and with the darkness."

He said he hit his head on the walls. He said he bled and he screamed till he became hoarse. He said he only wanted one thing from them, to tell him what day it was and what time.

As Sameeh told his story, the fear would steal into his words, and he'd shiver and say, "That's the worst torment, being deprived of time. Eternity is true agony."

I asked him what he felt when they took him out of the dark. He was silent for a long time before saying that he felt the beauty of old age. "The prisoner doesn't see himself in the mirror; there are no mirrors in prison. His only mirror is the eyes of other prisoners." He'd felt at ease when he saw his image in the eyes of the other prisoners, who were struck with terror at how he'd aged.

"And the beating?" I asked.

"That was my mistake," he said.

Do you know, master, what Sameeh did when he got out of solitary confinement? He joined the prisoners' Sufi circle. He said he started joining in their prayers and *dhikr*. In fact, he became close to their sheikh, Hameed El Khaleeli, till they found out he wasn't a Muslim.

"When Sheikh Hameed found out I was a Christian, I was terrified," said Sameeh. "On the mound I wasn't afraid. I thought I'd die on the ice, so I surrendered to the ice, and the ice lived in my eyes and took me into the whiteness of death. With the sheikh it was a different matter. I think an informer told the sheikh I was a Christian; he said he'd seen my mother with the other visitors and she was wearing a cross around her neck."

"Is it true?" asked the sheikh.

Sameeh didn't know what to answer. In the end all he could do was confess. They set upon him, but the sheikh raised his hand and they stopped where they were. The sheikh came over to him.

"I said yes. I couldn't find words to justify my position. How could I explain, how could I tell him that after the darkness of solitary confinement, I felt a need to be with them?

"He asked me if I was mocking them.

"I said, 'No, no, I swear.'

"A murmur spread among the devotees as their fury materialised around me. I wished I was dead.

"The sheikh questioned me and I tried to explain, but what I said was the cause of my downfall. I said I was Christian, but also not, because I believed in God, and I loved Christ, but still I was . . .

"'A communist, maybe?' asked the sheikh.

"I said I was a member of Fatah.

"'So you're an atheist,' said the sheikh."

This, master, was where Sameeh made the mistake that almost cost him his life. He said he viewed religion as a social and a literary phenomenon. He said he loved Arabic literature and had memorised the Koran and pre-Islamic poetry, and wanted to join in their experience.

"But that's not what you told us at the beginning," said the sheikh.

The sheikh held his hand up and said, "What do you think, brothers?" The brothers, however, rather than responding, attacked. The sheikh managed to extricate himself, but Sameeh fell beneath their blows and cries.

"On the ice," said Sameeh, "when I saw death, I didn't open my mouth. But there, I screamed and wept and was afraid. The circles revolved around me and by the time I opened my eyes I was in solitary confinement. Then they took me to a new communal cell. There I found Sheikh Hameed, and we became friends.

"I explained to him and he explained to me. He wanted to convert me to Islam, and I wanted to convince him with the mixture of secularism, humanism and Marxism that I believed in. We parted company without him converting me or me convincing him, but he came to understand that I hadn't been mocking them and that I loved religious ritual."

Sameeh was an intellectual. He'd had two books published, plus a number of articles, and he had his own particular analysis of Israel, of which the essence was that Israel would collapse from within and that the moment of liberation was near. He'd mention dates. He was convinced that Israel would collapse at the end of the '80s as a result of its internal contradictions. It was difficult to discuss anything with him as he knew everything. He read Hebrew and English and carried an amazing quantity of numbers in his head, which he'd throw down in front of you so as to convince you of things. Naturally, his predictions didn't come true. The only part that came true was that his remains were transported to Ramallah, where he was buried in his family's grave. Samya was the one who arranged it.

I've told you about Sameeh so I can tell you about Samya. Samya was an ordinary woman, or so she led us to believe in Beirut. All she did was wait for her husband. In two years she bore two children and cooked a lot. When I visited them at home, I'd see her sitting on the edge of the sofa as though ready to get up at any moment. She sat with us as though she wasn't there. I was told she changed a lot after he died. She arranged for herself and the children to return to Ramallah, as she had American citizenship. She'd worked as a librarian and became the official in charge of the Ramallah organisation during the *intifada*. It was as though Sameeh's death had liberated her from waiting and driven her to re-create her life.

The balance of my life was disturbed by Samya's mysterious letter.

I was in Shatila, during the first siege, when a young man called Nadeem El Jamal joined us. He was a friend of the camp commandant, Ali Abu Toq.

Nadeem El Jamal said he had a letter for me from a woman called Samya Barakeh whom he'd met by coincidence in Amman, to which she was returning from a conference in Stockholm. When she found out he was going to see me in Beirut, she asked him to delay till the next morning and brought him a letter for me.

I told you I thought that Samya hadn't been listening to me because she always sat with us as though she wasn't there. Her husband would ask questions and I'd respond, but she wouldn't say anything. Sameeh would always talk about his dream of writing a book without a beginning or an end, "an epic" he called it, an epic of the Palestinian people, which he'd start by recounting the details of the great expulsion of 1948. He said we didn't know our own history and we needed to gather the stories of every village so they'd remain alive in our memories. Sameeh would talk to me about his theories and dreams, and I had nothing to tell him. Or at least, I told him about our village, and my grandmother's stories, and my father's death and my mother's disappearance. With him, or because of his questions, I became acquainted with the stories of my family, put events together and drew a picture of El Ghabsiyyeh, which I hadn't known. I put so much into getting the story ready that I came to know the village house by house. And Samya sat there in silence.

I opened Samya's letter and read it.

To start with, she wrote about her longing for Beirut. Then she informed me of Sameeh's death and about the difficulties of life in Ramallah. I don't have the letter any longer to read to you because we tore up all our papers when we were afraid the camp would fall. I wish I hadn't torn it up, because it was my only evidence that my mother wasn't a ghost or a story made up by my grandmother. My mother is a real woman, not a phantom belonging to the mysterious world of childhood. I followed orders and tore up the letter; Abu Toq called us together during the siege and ordered us to tear up everything. "I don't want any documents falling into their hands," he said. I tore the letter up, but before doing so I wrote down the telephone number Samya had put at the end. I swear I tried that number dozens of times, and every time I got a recorded message saying it was out of service. Did I copy it wrong? Or were the numbers on that little piece of paper I put into the back pocket of my trousers erased or made illegible?

Sanya wrote that she'd met my mother, Najwah, and that Najwah had wept hugely when Samya told her she knew me and had kissed her and held her close, to get the smell of me. Samya wrote that she'd met my mother in the hospital in Ramallah, that she wore a headscarf, and that she worked as a nurse.

Samya had been waiting for her son outside the operating theatre where he was having his appendix taken out when a dark-skinned nurse wearing a white headscarf came over to reassure her.

"Your mother's beautiful, Dr Khaleel," she wrote. I wish I had the letter, but it's gone and I can't get in touch with Samya because the number was either erased or illegible.

My mother's there, a nurse like me! Samya wrote that she knew who she was because she was a nurse. "Nurses look alike, and she resembles you a lot." I'm at a loss. What if I found my mother? I don't want her now, and I don't love her. But why? Why should her ghost come and inhabit this room with me? My grandmother didn't describe her to me, and all I remember is her brown arm. I used to press my lips to her arm and kiss it. All that's left to me of that woman is the image of a face nuzzling her arm, two eyes fixed on it, a mouth caressing the vast, soft brownness.

Samya's letter brought me this new picture of a woman, a woman who covered her hair and worked as a nurse in Ramallah. My mother emerged from the letter looking like any other woman, and when your mother comes to resemble any other woman, she's not your mother any more. What strange kind of a relationship is this that depends on an illusion? But everything's like that. Isn't Shams an illusion? My problem with Shams is that the illusion won't die. When they killed her, they didn't kill her image. I haven't told you what I found out afterwards. When Shams was ambushed, she opened the door of her car and was going to get out. The upper half of her body hung through the open door while the lower half remained inside the car. The number of bullets that poured into her was terrible. More than sixty machine guns firing at one go. Her body was torn apart and scattered. Little bits flew through the air and pelted the trees and houses. After they'd finished, they collected the pieces in two plastic bags and buried them.

As far as I'm concerned, Shams didn't die, for when the body is torn apart there is no death. I wish she'd died, but she didn't. And I'm incapable of loving another woman. No, I'm not saying that I won't ever be unfaithful, because there's nobody who isn't unfaithful, but I can't . . . The problem, master, is not my betrayals but my permanent feeling of being unfaithful. I wish she'd died. No, it's not possible to compare your situation with mine. You died when your wife died, but my wife wasn't my wife, she was another man's wife, and when she died her smell invaded and occupied me. When her image comes to me, I'm overwhelmed by that feeling that my chest is on fire. I get up from my bed and stand in the dark and drink it in. I drink in the dark and rub it into my chest, and the memories possess me.

I was telling you about my mother, and what has Shams to do with that?

I told you I lost my mother, then found her in Samya's letter, then lost her again. All I know is that my father married Najwah after the incident with the Jew, then took a new job in the workshop belonging to the Palestinian Badee' Boulis, then died.

It was a coincidence that my father married Najwah. If he hadn't been employed in the workshop belonging to the Jew in Meena El Hisin, and if the rabbi hadn't been murdered, and if my father hadn't been arrested, and if Najwah's father hadn't been visiting Ein El Hilweh, my father wouldn't have married at such an early age. You know, I feel as though he was my older brother. He was eighteen years older than me. Now do you understand why I hated him, and hated my white hair and my face with its prominent cheekbones and my long jaw? I don't want people to look at me as they did at him. The truth is that that sort of look ceased to exist after the Shatila massacre – as though everyone had died, as though that massacre, with its more than fifteen hundred victims, had wiped out the memory of faces, as though death had wiped out our eyes and our faces, and we'd become featureless.

It was a coincidence, as I said. His coincidences are his story.

Explain to me how that young man could work for a Jew after all that had happened? Please don't talk to me about tolerance; say something else.

Listen! I'll tell you this story, and it's up to you to believe it or not. Do you remember Alya Hammoud, the director of the camp kindergarten? Alya asked me to give a lecture to the kindergarten teachers on preventive health. So I went. When we were having tea after the lecture, one of the teachers started talking about her problems with a child called Khalid Shana'a. She said he was obnoxious and she couldn't put up with his being in her class any longer. He was full of energy and nervous tension, and she asked Alya's permission to expel him from the class. Alya told her to be quiet. The teacher continued with her complaint, at which point Alya said to her in a controlled voice that she couldn't expel him and suggested that the teacher try being lenient and caring with him. When the teacher indicated her dissatisfaction with the director's suggestion, Alya's voice rose.

"Do you know who Khalid is? He's the grandson of that man."

She was speaking of the 1948 occupation of her village, which was located in the district of Safad, and of how they'd taken a group of young men and a bulldozer had come and crushed them; Khalid Shana'a, the child's grandfather, was the only one to survive. She also mentioned how, after the villagers crossed the Lebanese border and took up residence in Yaroun, Khalid was the only one to return to Teitaba. He stole into the village on his own, went to his house, opened the door, and everything exploded. The man opened the door of his house and found himself thrown to the ground, blood pouring out of him. He pulled himself together, returned to Yaroun and spent the rest of his life blind.

"He's a hero," said Alya. "His grandfather's a hero, and I can't expel him."

The teacher couldn't understand where the heroism lay in the story, since she was one of those who'd escaped from Tell El Za'tar camp, where, during the siege which had ended with the massacre of its inhabitants, she'd seen how heroes die and how their heroic acts disappear.

"I don't want to hear such stories," said the teacher and left.

But Alya went on. She said her mother still remembered Saleem Neesan, the Jewish cloth seller who came to Teitaba before it fell and said, "Muslims, stay where you are! We're all in the same boat!" The cloth seller had originally been from Aleppo. He carried his goods on his shoulder and went through the Arab villages selling and not getting paid. He carried a big ledger in which he recorded debts, and people paid what they could – a jerry can of oil, a dozen eggs – and everyone loved him. He'd go into people's houses, eat their food and flirt with the women; his sixty years made him seem an innocuous old man. He'd laugh and tell jokes, and the women would surround him, laughing, and choose their cloth.

Alya was astonished when her mother told her that a number of the women of Teitaba crossed the border to pay him what they owed.

I didn't ask Alya how the women of Teitaba knew where to find Saleem Neesan once the border between Lebanon and Palestine had become a reality.

I listened to the story as one would to a love story, and I didn't ask Alya for the details of the meeting between the women of Teitaba and Saleem Neesan.

"We helped Saleem Neesan out and that teacher won't help Khalid Shana'a out. Is that any way to do things?"

Come, let's return to our story and ask what that young man, which is to say my father, who was one of the first members of the fedayeen groups to start the fight against Israel, wanted by working in Meena El Hisin. Was he attracted to his enemies? Were they his enemies?

Today the Durziyyeh family lives in Israel. I found that out from my aunt's husband, who told me, as he was telling me about El Ghabsiyyeh, that he'd gone to see them in Haifa and had visited Simon at his falafel and *hummus* restaurant, and that Simon had been gracious to him and asked him about the circumstances of my father's death.

What did my aunt's husband have to do with Simon Durziyyeh? Did he also work in the sheet-metal factory with my father, or did he visit him there to see how he was doing, or what? I swear I don't understand anything any more! My aunt's husband said Simon took him on a tour through the whole of Palestine and that he visited Tel Aviv and Nahariyyeh and Safad and was amazed at everything he saw, as though he was in Europe.

Is it true, father, that they've created a European country?

I've tired you out, and I'm tired too.

I've told you story after story, but my mother's secret remains a secret. The only thing I got out of Samya's mysterious letter was that she'd got married and gone to live with her husband in Ramallah, where she discovered that he was already married, and that she works as a nurse.

That's all.

Catherine came half an hour ago. Do you remember her? The French actress I told you about? She said she'd got in a taxi and asked the driver to take her to Galilee Hospital. When he told her there was no such hospital, she explained that she wanted to go to Shatila. The driver was reluctant, but she paid him ten dollars so he brought her to the door of the hospital, muttering complaints.

I ordered a cup of Turkish coffee for her and she drank it down at one go, wrinkling up her face because the coffee burned her tongue. She sat quietly and then asked me why people hated the Palestinians. I didn't know what to say. Should I tell her about the disintegration caused by the civil war? Or say what Naheeleh said to the Israeli officer: "We're the Jews' Jews. Now we'll see what the Jews do to their Jews." I don't agree with these phrases we use so easily. I can understand Naheeleh because she was over there, where the Palestinian finds himself face to face with racism like that faced by the Jews in Europe. But not here. We're in an Arab country and speak the same language.

Catherine said she'd decided not to act in the play, that she'd find it ridiculous if she did. She asked my opinion.

She said she was afraid, and that they had no rights here. Then she burst into tears.

I wanted to invite her to dinner and talk with her, but she said she couldn't act because that much horror couldn't be put into a play.

Why did Catherine come to my office and then leave?

These questions are unimportant, father, but our whole life is composed of unimportant questions which pile on top of one another and stifle us.

I want to rest now.

I've grown tired of talking and of death and of my mother and of you. I want to lay my head on the pillow and travel wherever I wish to.

But please explain the secret of my father's death.

My grandmother told me they were wearing civilian clothes, and my mother said they were soldiers. What do you say?

Do you believe we can manufacture our country out of these ambiguous stories? And why do we have to manufacture it? People inherit their countries as they inherit their languages. Why do we, of all the world's peoples, have to invent our country every day so everything isn't lost and we find we've fallen into eternal sleep?

It's Umm Hassan.

She came to the hospital to visit you three weeks before she died and said you had to be taken back over there.

She came into the room and looked at you out of the corners of her small, sharp eyes. I was sitting in this eternal chair I sit in, and she gestured to me, so I said, "What?" and she put her finger to her lips and made me follow her.

In the corridor she spoke in a low voice as though she was whispering in my ear. When I asked her why she was talking that way, she said, "So he won't hear. They can hear. I know them," she said.

She talked about your other world, which no longer resembled ours. She said you were in torment and mustn't be disturbed. "Talking's no good any more, son," she said. "He has to be taken back over there."

Umm Hassan took me into the corridor and whispered in my ear that it was necessary to take you back to your country.

"Alas!" she said. "He's become like Azeez Ayoub. You can't let the man die alone here, son."

She said you were this way because you refused to die alone. "Shame on you, son, shame. The man spends his life over there and you want him to die here, in this bed? No, I swear, it won't do. Get in touch with his children."

I told her I didn't know how to get in touch with his children in Deir El Asad. She asked about your relative Amna, saying Amna knew, so why didn't I contact her. I told her Amna had disappeared. She said she knew her house in Ein El Hilweh and would go to her and come back with your children's telephone number so we could contact them and organise your return.

"He has to die there. It's shameful. I know him. He'll never die here."

She put her hand on my shoulder and said you were like Azeez Ayoub, who died hanging from the branches of the lotus tree.

I told her Azeez Ayoub had committed suicide and there was no basis for comparison.

She disagreed. "Saints don't commit suicide. They killed him to get rid of him."

"But he wasn't causing any problems, so why should they have killed him?" I asked.

"You don't know anything," she said. "They killed him by hanging him from the tree, and if it hadn't been for God's wisdom and the tree's kindness, people would've thought he'd committed suicide. I didn't see him, son, but people told me: his eyes were open, the rope was round his neck, and he was lying on his back like a piece of wood, like this Yunis. No, son. A man can't die among men. A man needs a woman to die. Women are different, they're stronger and can die on their own if they want to. But a man needs women so he can die. Azeez Ayoub died that way because he was alone. His wife left him and took her children to Lebanon. I don't understand why he did that to himself. He said he was the guardian of the tree and the guardian of the mosque and the guardian of the graves, and he couldn't abandon them. Who's guarding the tree now? God is the guardian. I went there and I saw how the tree guards the whole of Galilee. The tree is the guardian, so why do we guard it? Are we going to put a guardian over the guardian? And this Yunis, Abu Salim, look at him. He's shrinking and becoming like a child. Look at his face and eyes. His face is the size of a child's palm, which means he wants his mother. Why are you keeping him here? Don't you see how he's shrinking? Take him to his mother, son, and let him die in her house. Tomorrow I'll go to Amna and get their telephone number and we'll send him back. I know him better than you. He was a stubborn man, we called him "The Billy Goat". When he came back from over there, his smell was like the smell of a billy goat. When we smelled that smell, we knew Yunis had come back. How that poor woman could abide the smell of his sweat I don't know. A woman is a deep secret."

Umm Hassan placed her hand over her mouth to hide her smile, then drowned in laughter. When I say "drowned", I mean it: she'd fall into her choked-off, silent roar of laughter, and her white headscarf would slide off her hair onto her shoulders. Suddenly she put her scarf back, lowered her hand and wiped away her smile.

I told her Naheeleh would bathe you the moment you arrived at the cave of Bab El Shams.

"And where would that have been, you poor thing?" she asked, turning her face away as though she wanted to close the subject.

I told her about the cave and about the village you built inside the caverns of Deir El Asad. She said she knew those caves, which opened their mouths like ravening animals, and knew that no-one ever went into them. "Those caves are bewitched, son," she said.

And she told me about the goat that got lost in one of the caves of Deir El Asad and re-appeared in Ramallah.

"Yes, indeed, son. They found it in Ramallah, and it was white. Its hair had turned white as though it had seen something terrible." She said people had seen strange things in its eyes, so they shot it dead and no-one dared eat its meat. "And now you come along after all this time and tell me that Yunis lived in those caves and used to bathe there. No, son. I know better. He'd take her into the fields. Who told you about the caves? Yunis would go to his house, tap on the window pane and wait for her. She'd come out and follow him, and he'd take her to the fields, and that was where those things happened. Not in the cave."

I told her that you'd told me, and I tried to explain how Naheeleh had fixed up the cave, how she'd brought mats and the mattress and the wooden chest and the primus stove and so on, but it seems it's impossible to convince Umm Hassan of anything she thinks she already knows.

Then I understood.

This is your secret, father. Your secret is your obscurity. Your secret is your many names and your mysterious lives. You are the Wolf of Galilee, and why should the wolf reveal his secrets? You yourself chose the name Wolf: you told me you wanted to be a wolf so the wolves wouldn't eat you. You were a wolf enveloped in its secret. No-one knew your secret or entered Bab El Shams, which you made into a house, and a village, and a country.

I told Umm Hassan that the Ramallah goat resembled my mother. Najwah seemed to have disappeared via a tunnel from here to there. She disappeared from Beirut only to appear in Ramallah wearing her white clothes in the hospital where she works as a nurse.

"No, son," said Umm Hassan.

"What could your mother do in the face of your grandmother's madness? I swear Shaheeneh destroyed her, and all the people of the camp were witnesses. After the death of your little sister, the life of your mother, Najwah, became hellish. What fault was it of Najwah's that your father died? Your grandmother, God rest her soul, was an excellent woman, but she was the reason. What fault was it of Najwah's? She didn't know anyone there. She was from Tira, near Haifa, and had come on a visit to Lebanon, and your grandmother seized on her and persuaded her father to marry his daughter to her son, who worked in that work-shop that stank of scandal and filth. She wouldn't let her touch anything in the house. She'd do the washing up, and the old woman would come along, sniff the dishes and the pots, and wash them again. She'd mop the floor, and your grandmother would mop it again behind her and curse the filth. Your mother, son, is no Ramallah goat; your mother's an unhappy creature, God help her. Her family must have done terrible things to her to make her agree to marry the Bedouin and live with him in Ramallah."

"The Bedouin! What Bedouin?" I asked.

"Yes, the Bedouin. Abu El Qasim was on a visit to Amman and saw her at Ashrafiyyeh Hospital, where she worked, so he went to her family and asked for her, and they gave her to him without asking her because her stepmother wanted to get rid of her."

Umm Hassan said that in Ramallah Najwah found out that the Bedouin was married to another woman, and lived in misery and humiliation. The Bedouin married her and then regretted it because his first wife, who was also his first cousin, turned the whole clan against him, so that Najwah became a sort of secret wife, which was why she was forced to work in the hospital.

I asked Umm Hassan where she got all this information from.

She said that everybody knew.

"But I didn't know," I said.

"'The husband's the last to know,'" she said.

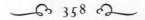

But I'm not her husband, and I don't understand. Why didn't anyone tell me about my mother? When I'd ask my grandmother, she'd shut her face, locking it with the key of silence. I had to wait for that mysterious letter from Ramallah, the one I tore up, in order to know, and I still didn't know. I lost Samya's telephone number, and I lost the name of the Bedouin that had become my mother's name in Ramallah. Even Umm Hassan didn't know the Bedouin's name even though she knew everything. She told me about my Uncle Azeez and about his days and nights in the ruins of El Ghabsiyyeh. "He lived alone for more than twenty years, spending his time between the tree and the mosque and between the mosque and the graves and standing in front of the lotus tree, talking to it and listening to it. He knew everything because the tree would tell him. When people came from the surrounding villages to visit the tree, he'd disappear. He wouldn't talk to them or go near them. They'd see him like a ghost drowning in the shadows of his white mantle. They'd greet him and he'd respond from a distance with a nod. They'd bend over the roots of the tree and light their candles before tying their strips of cloth and ribbons to the branches and going away."

I told her he'd committed suicide and was mad: "Who, aunt, could live alone for twenty years and not go mad?"

Her face lit up, seemingly in agreement, but then she said, "No, no, son. He's a saint, and people invoke his name when praying for their children."

But I, master, have grown tired of saints and heroes and wolves. My father's a hero and you're a wolf, and I'm lost in the middle. I see my father's death in yours and in your new-found childhood I see his. This thing I see is strange: I see you both, but I don't see myself, as though I'm no longer there and everything around me is unreal, as though I've become a shadow of the life of two men I don't know. I swear I don't know you. You I know only through this child-like death of yours, and him I know only through a picture hung on a wall. Even Shams, Shams whom I loved and whose killer I wanted to be, Shams whose vengeful ghost I fear, even Shams seems no more than the ghost of that woman who disappeared and became a white goat in a hospital in Ramallah.

I can't believe Umm Hassan and her righteous saint Azeez Ayoub, or my grandmother and the demon who was the cause of my father's murder.

Instead of telling me about the first fedayeen in whose ranks my father died, Shaheeneh told me about the cave and its guardian.

Shaheeneh would look at the picture of the dead man that she wiped with water to keep fresh and talk about the cave of El Ghabsiyyeh.

She said she'd known that Yasseen would die and that a woman would kill him.

"Damn me," she'd say, "I married him off and thought nothing of it. I was terrified by the rabbi business, so I married him to that girl from Tira and paid no attention to her eyes. Her eyes had something of that fear I saw after the business with the cave."

My grandmother said it was called Eisha's Cave. Eisha's Cave is to the north of the village, on the high ground that separates El Ghabsiyyeh from El Kabri.

My grandmother said that my paternal uncle, Mohammed Abdallah Ayoub, was a religious scholar and a Sufi, and he had power over the genies. "One day he sent his son Mahmoud and a youth called Sa'eed with my son Yasseen to the cave, telling them, 'When you arrive, read this paper and a black dog will appear. Do not fear it, for it is possessed by the genie that rules the cave, and woe betide you if you're afraid!'"

My grandmother said Mohammed Abdallah Ayoub wanted to test the three young men in preparation for their initiation into his Sufi circle.

"At the cave, it happened as he had said, for as soon as Mahmoud had finished reading the paper, the black dog appeared. Mahmoud was afraid and started to run. The dog struck him with its tail, then jumped on him. Sa'eed and Yasseen fled. When the dog struck him with its tail, poor Mahmoud fell to the ground, and the dog pounced on him and stood on his chest. Then we don't know what happened. Mahmoud suffered a fever for three days, and when his temperature went down he left his father's house carrying a stick. He knocked on the first door he came to, and when they opened it he fell on the people with blows. He was like a madman. No, he *was* mad, and went from house to house beating and smashing till the men of the village managed to tie him up and he was sent to the insane asylum in Acre. I don't know what the Jews did with him after Acre fell. During those times, people forgot themselves and their children, so how could they remember the insane? In those times, son, it was as though we were caught up in Judgement

Day. We rushed about in the fields to save our skins, but not one of us was saved; not one, I swear.

"I saw death in the boy's eyes. Yasseen came back from the cave a different boy, and I saw death hovering over him and knew he'd die. And when he married Najwah I saw death in her eyes, but somehow I took no notice, God curse us human beings. I saw death, but I wanted to release him from that thing that hung over him after the incident of the Greek boy and the rabbi. So I decided to marry him off and paid no attention, and he died."

This is how things become linked in the mind of a senile old woman. The whole business of the cave is meaningless. Fantasies, father. Fantasies, son. We invent stories of our misery and then believe them. We believe anything so as not to see. We cover our eyes and set off, and then we bump into one another.

Umm Hassan believed the story of the cave had no basis and that my grandmother was mad, persecuting my mother for no reason and forcing her to run away into God's wide world.

But Umm Hassan knows that God's world is narrow and that "all men meet in the end".

My mother fled from Beirut to Amman and from Amman to Ramallah. She disappeared as completely as if she'd gone into your cave, my dear Mr Yunis. Which reminds me: tell me about the cave. Umm Hassan said the Deir El Asad cave was uninhabitable, so where's the "Bab El Shams" you spoke about? Where is that village that supposedly stretches through interlinked caves, a village that's "bigger, I swear, than Ein El Zeitoun", as you used to say? "I told them, 'Come on, let's look for caves in Galilee and ask the refugees to return to them. A cave is better than a tent, or a house of corrugated iron, or banana-leaf walls. But they didn't agree. Members of the Organisation said it was a fantasy. An entire people can't live in caves. They told me to go look for caves for the fedayeen and I saw the sarcasm in their faces, so I didn't look. I made my cave for myself and by myself and lived in it," you said.

Do you want me to take you back there, as Umm Hassan suggested?

"Go to his house, son, and look. You may find their telephone number. Call them. Call his children, and they'll sort things out through the Red Cross."

I don't think Umm Hassan's suggestion is practical. I'm not selfish, and the reason isn't that I'm afraid. Screw this life. Whenever I think of you, I feel eyes boring into my back and people saying I'm scared. No, I'm not scared. Does Umm Hassan think I haven't tried to contact your children? Do you remember that first day, father, when Amna came to tell me about your fall? That same day I asked her to contact your children, and she did. She said she did.

"What did they say?" I asked.

"Nothing." She said, "Nothing," and I didn't ask what "nothing" meant. "Nothing" means "nothing".

She said "Nothing," and I didn't comment. At the time it never occurred to me that you'd live. Being sure you'd die, I didn't think of sending you over there. What for? Does it make sense? I don't believe they want you any more. This is where things have got to.

Umm Hassan, describing your other world, told me you see God.

"Pay attention, son," she said. "Pay attention to his movements. We may learn something from them. People like him see God."

"How's that, Umm Hassan?"

"I don't know, son, but I'm sure of it."

She told me about an old woman she'd got to know in Acre, before everything happened. Whenever the woman awoke from her coma, she'd tell people of strange things and they'd happen. "It was like she saw God, son. I was there, training as a nurse, and this woman, who was half-way between life and death, would become unconscious for a few days and say these strange things when she awoke. For instance, she'd say that so-and-so's husband was going to die; the man's wife would be nearby and she'd laugh at the old woman's silliness; and when she went home, the prophecy would turn out to be true. They all started to fear her; her children and grandchildren sat around her death bed quaking with fear, and they only relaxed when she died — it was as if a stone had been pushed off their chests. To tell you the truth, Khaleel, I think they killed her. They were scared of her cottony words, her quavering voice and her white hair. I think one of them smothered her with a pillow because she turned blue in death. But I didn't say anything. I returned to the village, dying with fear. And I'm telling you now, this man, Yunis Abu Salim, is in the same place. Take him back to his country and rid us of him once and for all."

*

Can you hear me?

What's happening to you?

You know, I swear you're starting to look like Na'eem, Nour's son. I know you'd rather look like Ibraheem, your first son and your twin, but unfortunately you don't look like him; you look like one of your grand-children. When I went to your house I saw a picture of Na'eem and got a surprise: it was as though I was looking at you, now. I didn't go to your house in order to follow Umm Hassan's suggestion. It's true I searched for the telephone number out of curiosity, and didn't find it, but I went for the pictures. And there I saw you the way you really are. What kind of an arrangement is that, my dear Mr Yunis? A house of two rooms plus a kitchen and a bathroom. The first room is for guests, with an Arab carpet spread on the floor, and there are three sofas, a small table for eating, a radio, a television and video, and one picture on the wall. I went up to the picture and saw a group of children in a circle around an old woman. It's her, I thought. I went closer because I couldn't distinguish the features, which were almost obliterated, as though time had wiped them away – or not time, the photographer. The photographer had taken the picture from a distance in order to get that throng of twenty-five children around the woman into the frame, with the result that all that appeared in his photo was a crowd of indistinguishable chil-dren. I smiled at them. You don't know them; to you they're just numbers and names, these grandchildren of yours whose names you won't tell me. Or at least you told me about Naheeleh No. 2, Nour's daughter; you told me you loved her specially. Where's her picture?

I went into the bedroom, and there I saw them all. It's like a studio. Seven photos frame to frame on the wall and above the bed a large picture of Naheeleh. An amazing number of small photos of children of various ages hung on the other wall. A world of pictures. A strange world. I don't know how you managed to sleep amid all that life.

Tell me, did you sleep?

During the nights of the long Lebanese civil war, when there was no electricity, did you light a candle in your room and see them, trans-formed into shadow puppets flickering on the walls?

Weren't you afraid?

I swear the pictures scared me. I went into your bedroom in the early evening. The clock said 5.00 and it wasn't dark yet, but there wasn't enough light. I tried the switch – no electricity. I seemed to be swimming through the darkness with the pictures. I went up to them one by one and discovered your secret world, a world of pictures hung from the cords of memory. The pictures seemed to move. I heard low voices emanating from the walls and was afraid.

Where did you get those pictures?

When you went, did you go for Naheeleh or for the pictures?

Tell me how you could live with their pictures. How could you restrain yourself from going to their houses and smelling their smells, one by one?

I hear a laugh come out of your eyes, and you tell me you did see them; you entered the house and kissed them one by one, when your father, the blind sheikh, died.

During that bitter winter of '68, the likes of which Galilee hadn't seen for a hundred years, Yunis arrived at his cave in the midst of the pouring rains, exhausted and soaked. The wolf arrived at his cave covered with mud and with every part of him knocking against the other. He lit a candle and searched for dry clothes in the caverns he'd made into his home, and all he could find were a shirt and a woollen pullover. He undressed, put the dry clothes on over his wet body and left the cave. He turned right, behind the hill that hid his cave from the village, and ran into the masses of mud that were sliding down with the rain, forming torrents of mud and water. He fell into the torrent, swallowing a lot of mud before gathering himself up and continuing on his way. He reached his house, gave his three knocks on the window and left. She, however, ran after him and grabbed him by the arm and led him into the house he hadn't entered for twenty years. The blind sheikh was laid out on the ground, dying. He saw his mother sitting by the sleeping man, whose mattress had been placed on the floor. When his mother saw him, a sort of scream emerged from deep inside her. She stood and opened her arms, tried to go towards him, doubled over and sat down again on the floor. Yunis went to her and kissed her on the head. She took him in her arms and squeezed him, and the water started to run off him. The mother wept while the water dripped from the man's clothes, and Naheeleh stood there.

"Now you've come?" asked the mother.

Naheeleh took him to the bedroom, undressed him, dried him with a large white towel, wrapped his naked body, and fetched hot oil and rubbed his back, his belly and all his limbs with it.

"You'll get sick," she said. "Why did you come?"

She rubbed him with the hot oil and left him in order to bring dry clothes, and when she returned she found the water dripping off him. He was naked, shivering from the water, which was coming out of all his limbs — water streaming over the floor, a man enveloped in water as though it dwelt in his bones. She dried him again and told him how the blind sheikh had fallen into a coma three days before and how they'd given him nothing but a few drops of water, and that since the previous evening he'd been shaking with fever.

Yunis left the room, drops of water clinging to his feet, and approached the supine man. He bent over Ibraheem, kissed him and left, saying nothing to his mother, who was reciting verses from the Koran, her eyes drifting in the emptiness.

Yunis returned to his cave and felt hungry but could find nothing to eat. He sat alone smoking. Then she came. She was wrapped in a long woollen blanket that gave off a smell of mould and water. Naheeleh cast the blanket aside and sat down. She said she'd brought him three boiled eggs, two sweet potatoes, two pieces of bread and an onion. He took the food and wolfed it down. He'd tear off a corner of the bread, stuff it with onions, sweet potatoes and eggs, and swallow the whole thing without chewing. By the time she'd made him his glass of tea, he'd polished off the lot. She told him the man had died and that she was tired and was going to go back to help his mother prepare for the funeral.

She stood up, wrapped herself in the woollen blanket and bade him farewell with a wave of her hand. He grabbed her by the waist, threw her to the ground and made love to her. At the time, Naheeleh didn't understand why he behaved that way. She'd come intending to bring him food, inform him of his father's death and go back. Without shedding a tear, he'd listened to her weep for his father, eaten everything, and, when she'd gotten up to go, had thrown her down on the blanket which was sodden with water and mould, and taken her. He was like an animal mounting its mate. He was like he'd been in the beginning, when he was an ignorant, unloving boy. On that stormy night he mounted her. Naheeleh tried to refuse, but he was on top of her. She tried to move so he could penetrate her, but he came. In an instant, the hot fluid spurted and wet her clothes. She tried to get up, but he clung to her neck and broke into loud sobs. She stayed motionless and cradled his head, and his weeping grew louder. "Let me go, darling," she said. "I have to go to your mother. The poor woman's alone with the dead man and the children."

Instead of moving aside and letting her go, he hung on to her. His body covered her entirely, his chest on hers, his belly on her belly, his feet on top of her feet. She had to shove him several times before she succeeded in pushing him off. She got up, straightened her clothes and left, swathed in the damp blanket. Naheeleh couldn't understand how he'd lain with her without her removing any of her clothes. He hadn't penetrated her, she thought on her way back within the black night spotted with drops of rain as large as cherries.

At 11.00 the next morning, the sun wrapped itself around the hills of Deir El Asad and spread itself over Galilee. The procession moved off from the house of Sheikh Ibraheem El Asadi towards the mosque. After the prayer, they carried the bier to the village cemetery. The men walking behind the bier, which was raised up to the height of outstretched arms, bent their heads, covered with their white *kufiyyehs*, as they tried to avoid the mud and the puddles, and kept up a loud buzz of prayers.

Opposite the hill on which the village cemetery lay, Yunis stood alone, holding his rifle and hiding behind a tall palm tree which he'd come to call "Sheikh Ibraheem's palm". There the men turned into ripples of water around the bier as they started to circle it to the sound of Sufi chanting, their voices reaching Yunis: "Succour, succour, Messenger of God, Beloved of God, People of the House, You whom we adore." He ran his hand over his rifle, raised it in the air and placed his finger on the trigger to bid the sheikh farewell with a volley of shots. Instead, however, he lowered it and pointed its muzzle at the ground, bent over where he stood, and started to sing with the others as he had when he was a child, and his father had taken him from Ein El Zeitoun to Sha'ab, and there, in the little mosque, the child Yunis had become submerged in the rhythm of the men as they spun around the blind sheikh, singing, shouting and dancing. Yunis wanted to turn with them and merge with their voices, but he stayed where he was and listened to the voice of the child he'd been.

The funeral came to an end, earth was thrown over the sheikh, everyone dispersed, and Yunis returned to his cave, where he stayed for a week, never leaving it.

Then Naheeleh came and took you to the house. You walked behind her like a sleepwalker and, when you arrived, were a little afraid and said you shouldn't enter, so she dragged you inside. You came to the court-yard, where you saw the children playing, but you didn't go to them. You went in and sat down in the sitting room, and your mother came and sat down beside you, took your hand and said nothing.

You were sitting close to your mother when you heard Naheeleh's voice as she brought the seven children into the house. She'd call to each of them by name, then say, "Shoo!" as though she was herding chickens, not children. They came in and saw you. None of them came over to you, and you didn't open your arms the way a father who sees his chil-dren is supposed to do. They entered and you remained rooted to the spot. They entered and drew back and stood in a row, pressing against the wall as though they were afraid of you. In the silence, you got up, went over to them, knelt and kissed them one after the other. Then you stood up and left. Nour, who was fourteen, cried "Daddy!" as you went away.

That was your only meeting with your children, and when you recalled it, you could only see it as a dream – "as though it never happened" you said when you told me about your father's funeral and how you'd taken part, and how the barbed wire and the electric border fences hadn't stopped you from bidding him farewell.

And now, which is to say yesterday, I stood in your room, beneath the rain of pictures, and saw them. I saw the children and the grandchildren standing against the wall, waiting for you to get up and go to them on your knees and kiss them. I heard Nour's voice and saw your mother's death-haunted eyes. You told me your mother died two months after your father, and that you didn't go to her funeral. That day, when you'd finished kissing them, you'd returned to Lebanon. You came back once more on a short visit, then were absent for more than a year due to your other preoccupations and the tense situation at the border. When you came back, everything had changed. Salim had started work with his brother Mirwan in Mr Haim's garage in Haifa, and Nour was about to announce her engagement to Eesa El Kashif, who'd worked as a builder's labourer before becoming a contractor in the Arab villages, and Naheeleh was exhausted.

"I'm worn out with poverty and the daily grind," she said.

You were together in the olive grove next to your cave, sitting beneath the summer moon that shed its light on the green leaves, colouring them a shimmering blue. You waited for her there because she'd told you, "Under the tree." You tapped on the window and were about to leave when Naheeleh appeared on the other side of the glass and said, "Beneath the Roman tree." You understood that she meant the huge old tree with the hollow trunk that yields small fruit with a special taste.

You love olives.

All of us love olives, especially those little green fruit Naheeleh used to cover with coarse salt in a cloth bag and recommend that you place, the moment you reached your house, in a glass jar filled with water so the salt would dissolve and rise, white and raw, to the top, and into which you were to throw a few bay leaves, leaving the jar for a month before eating the fruit.

You kept those olives for celebrations. You'd celebrate with your olives in Shatila, taking a handful from the jar and steeping them in garlic, lemon and oil, and drinking a glass of arak while you listened to Salih Abd El Hayy singing, "My beloved, he tells me what to do" and taking your "prayer" to the ultimate. You called those moments "the final prayer". You'd . . . but no, I won't tell the truth so that I don't spoil your memories, which you construct to please yourself. But when I listened to you talking about those Roman olive trees, planted before the time of Christ, saying they had an ineradicable hidden bitterness, a bitterness that gave one an appetite for life, and then going on at length about those huge trees with the hollow trunks which they called "Roman" because they're as old as the Romans, I'd imagine you with another woman. Please don't get upset. You know I'm telling the truth, or what do the visits of the two women mean? The first I told you about. She came, then disappeared. The second would come every Thursday at 4.00 in the afternoon. Traces of beauty were discernible on her face, especially in her fine jaw and the two lines that crossed her cheeks. Her name was Claire; she introduced herself as Claire Midawwar. She came into your room and sat down. I was cleaning the mucus extractor. She sat down and didn't acknowledge or address me. She made me feel out of place, so I left the room, and when I came back an hour later she was gone.

She continued to come at her regular time, and I continued to leave her alone with you. Yesterday, however, she was late. Do you know why I haven't spoken of her until today? Because she'd become a part of our life here in the hospital, a routine one paid no attention to till it stopped. Yesterday I became aware of her because she didn't come on time, and I decided to ask about her. I decided to wait for her to ask her who she was. I put on a clean white gown and decided to wear my glasses, which I usually forget in my pocket as I haven't got used to the idea of putting them on. As soon as she entered the room, I went over to her to shake hands.

"I'm Dr Khaleel Ayoub," I said.

"Pleased to meet you, doctor," she answered, sitting down again.

"I haven't had the pleasure of making your acquaintance," I said.

"I'm a friend," she said. "An old friend."

I got into a stop–go conversation with her about conditions in the city, but she didn't seem to want to talk, as though I was stealing the time she'd set aside for you. Despite her deflection of my questions and her brief and irrelevant answers, I decided to be impertinent. I sat on the second chair and leaned forward a little as if to follow what she was saying. As soon as she saw me sit down, she put her hand on her hip as though she was getting ready to stand up. Before the movement of hand to hip could be transformed into the bending of the back that precedes the moment of rising, I got a question in. I asked her, without preamble, what her relationship was to you.

"When did your relationship with him start, Mme . . . ?"

I left my question hanging in the air, and the surprise took the wind out of her sails. Looking at me with startled eyes, she said, "Claire. Claire Midawwar," and stopped.

"Have you known him for a long time?"

"For a very long time," she said and got up.

"Tell me about him," I said.

She picked up her bag and said she was going. "Look after him, and may God make him well."

Perhaps Mme Claire won't ever come again. It's my fault, but I couldn't not ask her. I saw her coming once a week and I imagined her with you, eating Roman olives dripping with lemon juice and oil.

Eating Naheeleh's olives with another woman!

I don't understand any more.

I know you'll ask me about the French actress, but no, I swear it's not true – nothing happened with the French actress. I just felt a strange tenderness.

You'll ask me about my visit to her at the Hotel Napoléon on Hamra Street.

I didn't mean to visit her. I was feeling stifled here, so I went. I'm not going to tell you anything now. I'll behave like Claire Midawwar, who went away without telling me a thing.

Tell me, is Claire the woman you sought shelter with during the Israeli invasion of '82? You pretended you'd fled to a priest's house! Was she the priest? Got you! I've got you now, and it's up to me to interpret what you said. Everything needs interpreting, master. Everything that's said is a riddle and a metaphor which it's up to us to interpret. Now I'm going to interpret you from the beginning. Within your disjointed phrases I'll discover what you're trying to say, and I'll re-compose you so as to get at your truth.

Can I get at your truth?

What does "your truth" mean?

I don't know, but I'll discover things I'd never have thought of.

"And you?" you'll ask.

"Me?"

"Yes, you. What about you?"

"Nothing."

"And the French actress?"

"Nothing."

"And Shams? Where's Shams?"

Please, master, don't say anything about Shams. I promise, I'll forget about Claire and the olives dripping with lemon juice and everything else, but please, not Shams.

Come then. Let's close this chapter and return to the summer moon, and Naheeleh.

That night, the moon was bright in the skies of Galilee. Yunis tapped on the window pane and left, but he heard her whisper. He turned and saw her standing at the window, the moonlight pouring down on to her long black hair. He went closer and she said, "The Roman tree. Go on ahead and meet me at the Roman tree."

He went to the tree, asking himself why she didn't want to go to the cave, surmising that she might have her period, because when she had her period she'd come to him at Bab El Shams and ask him to go out with her into the fields, and he'd stubbornly refuse. The game would end with him sucking every crevice of her body while she screamed at him, "You mustn't, you mustn't! That's wrong!" and he'd give way before this "wrong" and be content with expending himself between her small thighs.

He went to the Roman tree, but instead of waiting for her beneath it, he climbed inside its huge, hollow trunk, which was big enough to take more than three people, and the idea came into his head that he could possess her there. He hid in the trunk, held his breath and heard her circling the tree looking for him. She went around the tree and looked, like a small child lost in the fields. His love caught fire. He waited till she was close to the opening in the trunk, pulled her to him and brought her inside, she in her fright calling on God for protection. He embraced her. She was trembling with fear and reluctance.

"It's me," he said. "Don't be afraid."

She yielded to his hands, and kisses, and his hot breath that burned her every part.

"No, no!" she said.

He pulled her to him, braced himself against the trunk and tried to lift her dress. She pulled back and her head struck the trunk, and she put her hand to her head, moaning. He came close to see, and she pushed him away with both hands and slipped outside. He followed her, reaching out his hands like a blind man searching for something to bump into.

"Listen," she said and sat down. "Sit here," and she pointed.

He asked about her head.

"It's nothing. It's nothing," she said.

She spread out the provisions she'd brought on the ground. "I brought you chicory and *midardara*. No," she said, escaping from his grasp. "Today you must listen."

He listened as he ate, the femininity of the moon creeping inside him and chilling his body. She talked and was born through her words. That day the seventh Naheeleh was born.

The first Naheeleh was his young wife whom he didn't know because he was in the mountains with the fighters.

The second Naheeleh was the beautiful woman who was born in the cave of Bab El Shams as she trod the grapes and married her husband.

The third Naheeleh was the mother of Ibraheem who died.

The fourth Naheeleh was the mother of Nour whom Yunis clung to in the cave and called "Umm Nour" whenever she came to him with the light shining from her eyes.

The fifth Naheeleh was the heroine of the funeral who came out of prison to announce the death of her husband and smeared ashes over herself in front of everybody.

The sixth Naheeleh was the mother of all those children who filled the square at Deir El Asad.

And on that night, the seventh Naheeleh was born.

The seventh Naheeleh was born beneath the olive tree in whose branches the green moon of Galilee was scattered. She was approaching forty, wrinkles had encroached on her long neck, and sorrow extended from her eyes to her cheeks.

The seventh Naheeleh had grown exhausted with all there was to exhaust her. A woman poor and alone.

"You know nothing," she said. "Sit down and listen."

She said she was exhausted. "I'm tired, Yunis; you've no idea. You know nothing. Really, tell me, who are you?"

Did she ask him, "Who are you?" Or did she content herself with telling of her torments, after which he saw himself mirrored in her words?

Yunis sat down and discovered he knew nothing. He'd been concerned only with his Naheelehs, as though he'd married seven women who were different in all things but one, which was the waiting.

Yunis saw his life as scattered fragments – from Palestine to Lebanon, from Lebanon to Syria, from one prison to another.

He lived for his long journeys to Galilee, when he had to get through the barbed wire, past the dangers and the Border Guard and the machine guns that mowed border crossers down.

He'd built up political and military cells composed of the tattered remnants of men who wanted to get back to their land. He'd joined diverse organisations. He'd started as an Arab nationalist with the Heroes of the Return and the Youths of Revenge and moved on to Fatah after meeting Abu Ali Iyad, and there he became an official in the Western Sector.

"I lived in a no-man's-land," he told Naheeleh, "as though I wasn't living, and you were here on your own, and I did nothing for you. Come with me to Lebanon."

She said no. "The children have grown up, and it's over. What do you want me to do in Lebanon? Live in the camp? Become a refugee? No. You come. I know you can't because they'll kill you or put you in prison here. You can't come and I can't either, and you're my husband and I'm your wife. What kind of life is this, Abu Salim?"

The green moon cast its light over Yunis, and the story stole into his eyes and drowned them in a sort of sleepiness. It wasn't tears, things rooted themselves in his eyes and spread out before him, and he became like a blind man who sees. He saw and didn't understand. Thus was Yunis in the presence of the seventh Naheeleh – hearing and seeing and dissolving in the light of the moon that emanated, pure and green, from the woman's eyes.

She spoke of the world she'd divided into two halves, and the life that was like little squares, and her children. She didn't say she'd grown tired of poverty. She didn't say she lived in the squares of fear, and that her children (his children) ground her down with their questions and their eyes filled with fear. She didn't say she'd waited for him to come and say, "Come with me," and that she'd thought he hadn't said it because of his parents, so she'd waited, and when they'd died, leaving was no longer possible. She said only that things weren't easy any more, and that Salim and Mirwan had started working in Mr Haim's garage in Haifa, and that they were happy at the garage. Then a drumbeat of hesitancy crept into her speech, and she started inserting silences between her words.

"You don't know," Naheeleh said. "You don't know anything. You think life is those distances you cross to come to me, carrying the smell of the forest. And you say you're a lone wolf, but no, my dear, it's not a matter of the smell of the wolf or the smell of wild thyme or the Roman olive tree, it's a matter of people who've turned into strangers. Do you know who we are? Do you know what happened to us when we found ourselves following a blind man? Your mother saved him from death, she pulled him out of their midst, and the Israeli soldier looked at her as though he didn't see. She said she asked God to blind them so they wouldn't see her. Then they killed the old men. You know what happened at Sha'ab. We found ourselves with bullets flying over our heads – no, before we fled, they took the men they'd ordered to stand in front of the pond off into the unknown, and then we heard the Israeli officer shouting, 'To Lebanon!' Your mother took your father's hand and led him to where the officer was pointing, but your father walked in the opposite direction so we followed him. A blind man leading two women and a child to we didn't know where. 'Go with the others,' said your mother, but I didn't go. I was afraid to leave them, afraid to meet you in Lebanon, afraid of you and of those crowds racing against one another and treading on one another, and I said, 'No, I'll stay with you.

"So we walked and night came, but the sheikh didn't notice. It was the first time the sheikh failed to distinguish between night and day. Your mother said that was the day the sheikh went blind. You know your father better than me. The sheikh knew the times for prayer by the way the sunlight fell on his closed eyes, but that night he lost the ability to distinguish and became truly blind. Two women walking behind a blind man, in the blackness of the night, and villages shadowed by ruin. We walked for endless hours. Then the sheikh stopped and said, 'We've reached Deir El Asad. Take me to the mosque.' The sheikh had decided that Deir El Asad was his new village, and in the morning your mother went to the headman, who was related to your father; he was called Awwad. But the headman pretended he didn't know them. In those days, no-one knew anyone any more; we'd all become strangers. The village sheikh intervened. He came to the mosque and told your mother there were lots of abandoned houses and that they should go to any house. We went to the first house we found, and it was beautiful, close to the caves that came to be known as Bab El Shams and surrounded by an olive grove. It's the house of Ahmad Kareem El Asadi, who fled to Lebanon with his family at the time of the celebrated incident in the village square when everybody lay down in the road to stop the Israeli bulldozers. Ahmad Kareem El Asadi didn't go to the square. Instead he fled with many others. We went to the house and lived in it, and it became our house, and the village became our village.

"Yes, my dear Mr Yunis, we were strangers, and your father became a beggar. We went to live in the house not knowing what to do and discovered, with the the villagers, that the land had gone. The village wasn't a village any more – the peasants' land wasn't theirs any more, so they were nothing, like you in Lebanon and Syria and I don't know where. No land, no rifles and no horses – and you call those men? There weren't any men left, my dear Mr Yunis. When a woman tried to pick her olives, they detained her and made her throw them away because the land now belonged to the state, and there was nobody left with work except thieves. Yes, we stole from our land and lived like thieves. I don't know how many stayed behind. I stayed because I followed the blind man, and others fled because they ran like blind men."

"There were more than a hundred thousand of you," said Yunis.

"Those who stayed were like strangers to one another. The villages were all mixed up. The Bedouin moved into Sha'ab, we were in Deir El Asad, and El Ba'neh filled up with people from who knows where. People got all mixed up together, and the villages weren't villages any more, and we no longer felt we were in our own country. All you did was savour the taste of the bullets that flew over your heads, of the blood that flowed, and of the young men reaped by death. We, however, could no longer move from place to place. Going from one village to another required a military permit. We weren't even allowed to visit El Ba'neh, which was only a stone's throw away. It was as though they'd built an imaginary wall to divide the villages. And the people turned into thieves, or something like thieves, going to their fields by night and stealing their crops. Strangers stealing from strangers. I would look around me and see nothing but emptiness, as though one had dug a grave for oneself in the air and been buried in it. I hated them all. I hated them for being driven to take jobs working for their enemies, building settlements for the new immigrants with their own hands. We were like idiots, hating one another for no reason. Yes, an idiotic and naïve people. We buried our land with our own hands. Instead of digging the soil to make the plants grow and provide food for our live-stock, we dug the foundations for houses to be built on the ruins of our own. We laboured without daring to look one another in the eye, as though we were embarrassed to do so.

"What could we do? Nothing! We worked so as not to die.

"Then you came.

"You made your way through the blockade of hate that surrounded us and knocked on my window. Did you think you were Qays looking for Layla amongst the ruins? You poor thing, I swear I hated you as much as I did myself. I was afraid you'd take me to Lebanon, and I didn't want you because I didn't know you and was scared of you. All I had in the world was the blind man, who used to go every day to the mosque and try and convince everyone that he was the sheikh of the Shadhliyya order, as a result of which they would take pity on him and throw him a few piasters, which weren't even enough to buy bread with. There was no trace of my mother. It was as though the earth had split and swallowed up my sisters. Do you know anything about my family? Are they in Lebanon? I never asked you about them and you never mentioned them, as though we'd agreed to forget about them. At the beginning I used to see my mother in my dreams. I'd see her sinking into green water and when I got up my neck seemed to be squeezed, as though I was about to choke. Gradually their images started to disappear. I know they're somewhere but I've forgotten them. And I hated my mother. How could she have married me to a man who wasn't even a man, and when I was only a child? How could they have left me to roam from place to place and not asked after me? All I had left was the blind beggar, who succeeded – succeeded, I swear, by a miracle, I don't know how – in turning himself into a real sheikh and finding disciples.

"And you came.

"I'd started to get used to my new life when you returned to us bearing a promise. Why did you promise you'd all come back? Why did you make me believe you, even though you knew otherwise? You knew it was history and that history's a dog. You'd bring me books and go away. And I'd read. I read all the novels and the poetry, and I learned the stories by heart.

Do you know what I used to do? I used to copy the books out. I copied out Ghassan Kanafani's novel *Men in the Sun* innumerable times.

"And what else?

"Your father was fierce as a hawk. He said, 'We'll die before we let our women work for the Jews.' And he didn't let me. My belly would swell up and I'd swell up and my children filled the house. I swelled up so I wouldn't die. I'd get pregnant and I'd feel the life beating in my belly, and I'd fill out."

Naheeleh talked and talked.

She talked of the death of Ibraheem and of her madness.

She talked of Salim, who was stolen by his grandmother so he wouldn't die of hunger for his mother's dry breasts.

She talked of Nour and of the other children who're grown-ups today.

She talked and she talked, and Yunis put his head in his hands, sitting by the Roman olive tree, on the ground that stretched to the horizon of the green summer moon.

She talked of a country that didn't look like itself, and of people who refused to look in mirrors so they wouldn't see their own faces, and of abandoned villages . . . She said she no longer believed this world founded on ruins would last: "We lived in the expectation of something that would come, as though we weren't in a real place.

"That's why I loved you," she said.

"Do you remember the day you came to me and married me all over again? You spread your clothes on the ground, in that cold cave, and asked me to walk over the grapes. There I felt something real. There things were real. But not here. I fell in love with you in that place you called Bab El Shams. I'd come to you as though I'd been sleeping on thorns, for in the house in Deir El Asad, which had become our house, and among the furniture and the pots and pans left by its owners, I felt afraid, and strange, and insecure, drinking out of their cups and cooking in their saucepans. What do the Jews who live in our houses feel? I couldn't, even knowing that I'd return everything to its owners – I swear, I'll give everything back the moment they ask for it. I've lived all my life in the house of El Asadi, who fled to Lebanon, and I felt as though I was no longer me.

"In truth, who am I and who are you?

"Only Ibraheem made me feel I was alive, but he died. They killed him, or it was his destiny to die — I swear I don't know. I don't cry for Ibraheem, I cry for myself.

"One time I made a decision: to work, work at anything, work as a maid — but where? I went to Haifa. I'd never been to Haifa in my life. I got on a bus and went, and I walked the streets aimlessly. In Haifa, I got lost. No, not because of the language. I speak their language, I learned it along with my children; I speak it as well as they do, or even better. I got lost because I felt myself to be a stranger. On the way from here to there I saw the houses that have sprouted up, as though I was in a foreign country. And in Haifa I saw the city. God, Haifa's beautiful: a mountain that runs down into the sea, and a sea that embraces the mountain as though it was rising to meet it. But what good does beauty do? Is it true that Beirut looks like Haifa? You haven't told me about Beirut, but Haifa is beautiful. I wish we could live there with the children.

"I went looking for work and said nothing to the sheikh or his wife. In any case, by that time the sheikh wasn't taking in what was said to him. He used dust to bathe in and lived in his faraway world. I don't know where he was living or who he talked to; he'd talk to strange beings he could see but we couldn't. I went on my own to find a solution to our financial problems, which became serious once the sheikh became confined to the house. But I couldn't find work. And you didn't care and didn't know and didn't come. And when you came, you'd give me the little bit of money you happened to have brought with you. I didn't tell you it wasn't enough so you wouldn't get upset. But the village isn't a village any more. It's become part of a large city that extends from the heights of Galilee to Acre. A city of ghosts, though. The village has died and the city has died, and we try to . . . You know nothing.

"I told the military interrogator — I swear I wasn't afraid — I told him, 'I'm free to do as I please, and it's no business of yours. What's it got to do with you?' I told him, 'You're stronger and richer but you're an impossibility that can't last for ever.' I don't know where I got those words, how I was able to say what I said about the Jews. I told him, 'You were tormented, but your torment doesn't give you the right to torment us.' I told him, 'We have a pain in our guts.' He asked me about my swollen belly and my pregnancy and the children, so I told him, 'Pain generates pain, sir. You don't know the meaning of pain that attacks the guts.' He made fun of me for what I said. He said, 'Go to Lebanon, where your husband is.' I said, 'My husband isn't in Lebanon and I don't know where he is and I'm not going anywhere. You, sir, go to Poland where you came from, or stay here, but leave me alone. You come here and ask me to go? Why?'

"I didn't know how to debate with them. I was – when the interrogator was with me – I'd pretend you were there and say, 'If Yunis were here, he'd know how to make them shut up.' When you talk you convince me of everything. Do you remember the first days in the cave – you'd sleep with me, then light your cigarette and start to talk. You'd talk about politics, and I didn't understand politics; I was waiting for you to take me and cover me with your body and pull the thorns out of it. But all you'd talk about was politics and how you were all ready to liberate the land, and you'd tell me about Gamal Abdel Nasser, who was like Saladin. I believed you. I told the military interrogator about Saladin and he laughed. His large white teeth appeared and he said, 'You Arabs are living in a daydream.' I didn't understand what the term meant, but I told him, 'We're not Arabs.' Why here in Israel, tell me, don't they call the other Arabs Arabs? They call the Egyptians Egyptians, the Syrians Syrians, the Lebanese Lebanese, and they don't call them Arabs. Are we the only Arabs? 'We're Palestinians, sir,' I told him, and he said, 'Just daydreams.' I agree we're Arabs; if we aren't, what are we? But I said we're not Arabs to annoy him, because I didn't understand what 'daydreams' meant.

"Then later I understood.

"My whole life is a daydream.

"You imagine I was waiting for you because I was entranced by your manliness? No, Yunis. I was waiting for you to talk, to escape the daydream that was swallowing my life. But you didn't listen. You'd tell of your adventures, and of the magic nights that bewitched you, but you knew nothing.

"I didn't tell you what the young men here in the village did. I was afraid you'd get upset. On the first of each month, they'd knock on my door and throw down a small cloth bundle. I'd open it and find money, and that was what we lived on. Do you think your blind father supported us – a family of ten? Did you think we were waiting for your visits and the few pennies you brought to get by? No, Abu Salim. We were waiting for the little cloth bundle; I neither knew nor wished to know who left it for us nor how they collected the money.

"Don't say they were your comrades because you know that I know that they had nothing to do with you.

"I waited for you so as to feel that my life was real. Can you believe it – I lived my whole life without being convinced it was life? Maybe everybody was like that, maybe all lives are like my life, I don't know. But I'm exhausted."

The seventh Naheeleh said she was afraid.

"I've started to feel fear. Nour will marry, and Salim and Mirwan go to work every day in the Israeli gentleman's garage, so what's the future?

"I'm afraid for your children. I don't know how they'll live. I don't understand them. They live these things as though they were ordinary things and this reality as though it was the only reality. Do you know what Salim said? He said he was going to open a garage in Deir El Asad. I told him Deir El Asad wasn't our village, and he laughed. He said he dreamed of going to America. And Nour, how lovely she is! She's going to get married, and the younger children are in school and I'm afraid for them. You don't care. You only ask about their health. You don't care about the school and the future. Do you think they'll wait for you, their lives suspended in a vacuum like mine was waiting for your Saladin to put things back the way they were? Things will never go back to the way they were. Don't misunderstand me: I'm not saying . . . I have Israeli citizenship, of course, and I vote the Arab Communist list for the Knesset and I attend the meetings and demonstrations, so as to preserve what's left of the land.

"I told the interrogator they were like an isolated Crusader castle, destined to fade away.

"I told him we'd paid the full price and been destroyed. 'You took us down to the bottom, and after the bottom there's nothing. You'll go down with us and we'll take you to our bottom and you'll taste the fire that burns us.'

"Don't misunderstand me, Yunis, but I want to assure my children's future. I want them to build houses, and find work, and marry and live. I want the illusions to end, I want . . ."

He didn't let her finish the sentence.

Yunis understood that she didn't want him any more, understood that she was tired of him and of his journey across the unknown. He understood, and at that moment he discovered that he'd talked about his journeys over there more than he'd actually gone on them, and that his life too was like a daydream.

He said she was his life.

He said, "You and the children are my life. I don't have any life without you." He said he didn't know what had happened to him, that it was the Revolution.

In 1969 Yunis entered a new phase of his political life. He joined Fatah and became an official in its Western Sector, as well as a member of the Southern Lebanon Sector Command Office.

He told Naheeleh that there was hope once again, that he couldn't abandon everything and come back and live with them.

"No, no. I'm not asking you to come."

He said he'd thought about it, but what would he do here, what job could he find? He said he didn't have a trade and only knew how to live the way he had, but he understood their situation and was there for them.

"I'm here for you," he said.

Naheeleh smiled but didn't say anything.

Silence fell.

Time passed slowly and came between them like something solid and unmoving. Yunis tried to break the silence, but the women's silence spread through the place. He had listened to her and deep down knew it was true and that life had passed him by and never knocked up against him.

"I swear I didn't . . ."

He didn't complete the sentence and felt he needed to sleep. If only sleep would come and take him from here to there. Sleep was everywhere. The village was sleeping, the trees were sleeping, and Yunis sat in silence with Naheeleh.

Naheeleh broke the silence. She said Salim was going to be workshop foreman at Mr Haim's garage and Mirwan was going to work with his brother and learn from him. And that the third boy, Ahmad, was very clever at school and wrote poetry, and that Salma helped around the house and was excellent in English, and that the little ones, Salih and Nizar, were still little.

"Listen, Yunis," said Naheeleh. "I want to open a garage for Salim here. Do you have three thousand American dollars to help us?"

"Three thousand!" he said in a hoarse voice. "Me put together three thousand?"

"Never mind. We'll manage. I just wanted to ask you. Don't worry about it. We'll manage as we've managed before. I shouldn't have asked, I know you're not one of those. But won't you come to Nour's wedding? Of course you won't come, but the groom's insisting on a horse. His family say he's going to arrive on a pure-bred Arabian horse and kidnap Nour from in front of the house. It's their custom, and Nour loves him. I'm sure she loves him. They were at school together, and now he works in Acre and means to move there."

Naheeleh said, "As you see, Yunis, the details of life are stupid and meaningless, but we have to take care of them. Why don't you speak? Cat got your tongue? No, I swear, I don't want anything from you. I just wanted to get it off my chest and talk, and whom do I have to talk to? Before your mother died, God rest her soul, I used to talk to her, but do you think it was possible to talk to her? When I told her I was going to look for work, she went crazy, and when she saw me in the house studying Hebrew with the children, she shook with annoyance. Your mother died and went to live in an unreal world. I had to remind her all the time who we were and what shit we were living in.

"How can I tell you about her?

"A woman to be pitied. She didn't know how to protect your father, or how to make his end easier. She told me he was at the end and that we had to help him to get to the end. Your father was stubborn. He used dust for his ablutions, had no idea where he was and talked with his sister. Why his sister I don't know. He'd say something to her and I'd think he was addressing me, so I'd answer him and he'd avert his face and say, 'You keep quiet!' Your mother told me about his sister who died giving birth to her first son. It was as if his mind had been wiped clean of everything, and all that was left was his sister. He'd even mistake his wife for his sister. She'd order him to do something and he'd obey and your mother would say to me, 'See how it is at the end, daughter. The wife turns into the sister and the son into the father, and everything's all wrong.'

"And you – when will you become my brother? Come on, let's be brother and sister. That way I can tell you everything, and you can tell me everything. A man can't say everything to his wife, and a wife can't say everything to her husband, but a brother and sister can.

"Come on, tell me.

"I know you're upset now. I know I shouldn't have told you those things, but what you don't know is that I'm not upset with you. No, I swear I'm not. When they announced you'd died and become a martyr, I came back from the prison to the house and put on a funeral that had no equal. I wept and smeared my face with ashes and was a model mourner. The Israeli interrogator who summoned me a month later said I could be a cinema actress. What the interrogator didn't know was that I wasn't acting. In my heart I was convinced I'd become a widow and you'd never be my husband.

"The military investigator didn't know I wasn't acting. We've been acting for more than twenty years so we've taken on the role and every day become more like what we're acting. You're acting there and I'm acting here. God, it's funny.

"I'm laughing. Why aren't you?

"You act out your role, and I act out mine, and life is gone.

"Tell me about yourself. Tell me how you live, how you manage your life, how you're able to.

"I've told you my side. I manage mine by acting. I've acted that I'm a widow and it went okay, and I've acted that I'm a hero's wife and I'm getting better and better.

"So what do you act, over there?

"Did I tell you about the case I brought in the Israeli courts when they refused to register your children in your name? Only Salim and Nour got registered, the rest not. I brought a case and appointed an Israeli lawyer called Mme Beida, and we won the case. Before Mme Beida, I commissioned an Arab lawyer from the Shammas family in Fasouta, but he failed; he wasn't able to prove you're alive. The Israeli lawyer turned the whole thing upside down. She asked them to prove you were dead, which they couldn't. The only thing they had to show was the military communiqué in which "saboteurs" announced your martyrdom, which is a valueless document as far as Israeli judicial practice is concerned, because Israel doesn't recognise the legitimacy of "saboteur" organisations, so she forced them to issue a judgement in favour of registering the children. This has been my biggest victory here. We forced them to register the children in the name of a man they are pursuing and whose existence they don't acknowledge. Only on that day did I feel you were my husband, but the feeling faded quickly. How happy I was that day, but you had no idea. How could you know when you only come when it suits you? By the time you came, it was old news. When I told you – did I tell you? – I don't remember that you said anything worthy of this big story, which was my story.

"The story's over now. I'm in my forties, and my life's changing. I'm getting ready to be a grandmother and that's enough. Shouldn't that be enough to make me feel sad? I'll be sitting and I'll feel a desire to weep, and my tears will fall for no reason. My face is going numb, my shoulders hurt, my whole body is falling apart. I feel as though I'm parting from my body, and I'm alone."

Yunis ate a last mouthful, which went down like a knife into his stomach, and put his hands on his knees, which he'd been hugging to his chest. He said he'd come back.

"Where are you going?" she asked.

"To Lebanon," he said.

"No."

She took his hand, left the full plates and the pot of tea, and led him to the cave of Bab El Shams. She took off her clothes and stood in front of him, waiting. Yunis didn't dare look at her naked body in which the desire had ignited. She came over to him and started removing his clothes while he stood there motionless. Then she took him. This time it was she who started it; he felt as though he'd become her plaything and his manhood had been erased. She made him lie on his back and spread her hair and breasts and body over him, and when the water of heaven spurted from her, she began to cry.

She stood up and put on her clothes; the first threads of dawn's light had started stealing into the cave, and she told him to wait.

She returned at mid-day.

She returned with a banquet – *kibbeh nayyeh* with a topping of *hoseh*, cottage cheese, tomatoes and a bottle of arak.

She placed the food to one side, heated some water and bathed him. He was like a small child in her hands, playing around in the water, incapable of issuing his celebrated orders or making remarks about how hot or cold the water was. She took him to the open space inside the cave, which became a bathroom, ordered him to take off his clothes, bathed him with water and bay-laurel soap, dried him and dressed him in new, dry clothes. Then they sat down together at the table.

He poured two glasses of arak, drank from his glass and asked her to do the same.

She said no.

She said she didn't like arak. In the past, she'd only drunk to keep him company, because she didn't like the smell of arak, especially when he slept with her and the scent of aniseed wafted from his mouth.

"I used to drink so I wouldn't smell it."

She said she didn't like arak and wasn't going to drink it again.

Her words took him aback. "What? You don't like arak?"

"I hate it."

"And all these years you drank?"

"I didn't want to upset you."

"All your life you've been drinking something you don't like?"

She nodded.

"I don't understand anything."

She shook her head.

"You don't want to say anything?"

"What am I to say?"

Indeed, what did he want her to say, after she'd said everything under the olive tree? The day before, she'd told him she didn't want him any more, so what more did he want? The day before, a new idea had got hold of him: how had she discovered, or intuited, that henceforth his visits would be difficult, intermittent, few and far between? Southern Lebanon was now full of fedayeen, the country was under constant Israeli bombardment, and the borders were almost impossible to cross. To cross the border now required fighting an entire battle. And then there was his age. The war had stolen years from his life, and now he was too old. He was in his late forties and his body was no longer an instrument that complied with his desires. He wasn't able to walk those long distances any longer. She didn't know what had happened on this visit. He'd arrived at the cave at night and not gone to her straight away, to knock on her window as was his custom. He'd felt a weakness in his joints and decided to rest a little before going. But in fact he'd fallen asleep, woken up at 10.00 the following morning, and spent the day in the cave, waiting for the dark so he could go to her.

How had she found out?

Women just know, thought Yunis as he listened to her. She'd known his visits would be interrupted even before they were, so she'd made her decision. She wouldn't be an abandoned woman; she'd choose her new life deliberately. And now she tells him she doesn't like arak!

Had she forgotten how he'd drunk arak from her mouth? And how after eating she'd washed her hands with arak? Or had she been putting on a show for him, as she had for the military interrogator, and for the village, and her children and everybody else?

She said she'd made this banquet to make up with him and ask him to forget the garage and the dollars and her stupid requests. She was apologising for what she'd said the day before, because he was her husband and the crown of her life, and she knew this was the only way he could live and was proud of him, because people have to live their lives as they find them —

We walked the steps that were written for us,
    And he whose steps are written must walk them.

"You know," she said, "your father, after he forgot everything and started living with his sister's ghost, never forgot two lines of old Arabic poetry, and whenever I wanted him to dig something up that was at the back of his mind, I'd start by saying the first half of the first line, and he'd sit up straight and recite the two lines without a mistake, and I could see the words bubbling up from the well of memory that time had filled in. His voice would return to the way it had been, and he'd say,

Trim your heart as you like to the wind,
    Only the first love's for ever.
Many a dwelling the young man will know,
    But his love for his first home nothing can sever.

You walked your steps and I walked mine. You're my husband and I'm your wife, and please forget what I said yesterday."

Naheeleh said she'd said what she did because she was afraid for Nour because she was young and about to get married – "God protect her and keep her!"

Naheeleh apologised and said the black cloud had lifted from her eyes. And Yunis, what did he say? Did he explain how difficult the situation really is in the south? Did he apologise for all those years? Or did he say that he was trying to live and create a country out of the rubble we call history?

Rather than say anything, he sucked the last drops of arak from his glass, drinking without quenching his thirst, and let the drink take him. Instead of the picture of the lover that had been sketched by his words, the picture of the hero took its place, and one story led to another. He spoke of the prisons and the training camps. He spoke of operations in the Galilee Panhandle and of the young men the bases overflow with and of how they rush headlong into death.

He spoke of the Return. He said he'd return with the others, "for the nation is not a prison. We shall not return as abject prisoners." And he told her of the Revolution he'd been waiting for since the day the Sha'ab garrison had been disbanded and all its members flung into prison. It had arrived, and he couldn't abandon it.

He spoke and spoke and spoke.

And Naheeleh returned to him. She returned to him with every word he spoke, and he could see it. Her face was radiant, her eyes shone, and her hands took the little pieces of bread and transformed them into bite-sized morsels of *kibbeh nayyeh* that she fed to him.

He asked her about Hebrew and if it was difficult.

Of all the things the woman had said, the man picked up only on the language. He knew that Palestinian children in Israel learned Hebrew in school, and he was aware that his own children were just like the others; but he wanted to talk about his children, so he asked about the language.

Naheeleh smiled and said, "*Echad, shtayim, shalosh, arba, chamesh, shesh, sheva, shmone, tesha, eser.*"

"What are you saying?" he asked.

"Guess," said Naheeleh.

"It's Hebrew," he said.

"Correct," she said. "Hebrew's like Arabic. Arabic spoken like a foreign language, if you like, but you have to put in a lot of ch's and sh's. That's how I learned it. The first thing I learned was the numbers, and then I got so I could understand almost all the words. But the children are much better, God bless them. They speak Hebrew better than the Jews."

She said the language was easy. "The easiest thing is learning their language."

He said he was afraid the children would forget their own language.

"That's their problem, not ours," said Naheeleh, meaning it was the Israelis' problem, not the Palestinians'. "They don't want us to forget our language and our religion because they don't want us to become like them."

Yunis didn't understand what she meant, and started talking about the relationship of the children to their history and their heritage, saying that that relationship could only be realised through language. He talked a lot, and mixed up literature and religion and everything else.

She said he hadn't understood her.

"Listen and try to understand. You don't know anything. Try to listen to things the way I tell them and not the way you imagine them in your head. When I said it's their problem, I meant it's the Jews' problem: we can't abandon our language because they don't want us to. They want us to remain Arabs and not to assimilate. Don't worry; they're a closed, sectarian society. Even if we wanted to, they'd never let us."

When you told me, father, about Naheeleh's theory of language, I thought of Eesa who wanted to gather the keys to the houses in Andalusia. I wanted to say that we haven't yet understood the fundamental difference. The Castilians didn't persecute the Muslim Arabs and the Jews simply to throw them out, for no expulsion, no matter on how large a scale and how effective, can drive out everyone. The Castilians imposed their religion and their language on the Andalusians, and that's why their victory was definitive; that's why Al Andalus was assimilated into Spain and that was the end of the matter. Here, on the other hand, our keys aren't the keys of the houses that were stolen; our keys are the Arabic language. Israel doesn't want us to assimilate and become Israelis, and it doesn't impose its religion and language on us. The expulsion took place in '48, but it wasn't total. Our keys are with them, not with us. I didn't say this because I was afraid I'd lose Naheeleh's story through these digressions, the way it was always getting lost.

When I used to ask Yunis about Naheeleh, he wouldn't object or refuse to answer. He'd start to answer, then enter the labyrinth of peripheral stories, and Naheeleh's story would get lost.

On that occasion, I didn't mention my theory about the keys because I was afraid for the other story, but the other story got lost all the same.

He told me about Hebrew and then fell silent.

"And so?" I asked him.

"And so here we are."

"What happened there, in the cave?"

"I returned to Lebanon and we built bases in the south."

"And Naheeleh?"

"Nour got married and Salim opened a garage and . . ."

"Did you visit her after that?"

"Of course, often. You know."

"Often" and "You know" were his only replies.

"And the cave?"

He didn't tell me about the cave even though he talked a lot with Naheeleh that day. He discussed the children's problems and the Revolution, which had started to spread throughout Jordan and Lebanon. He and she talked at length and laughed frequently, him drinking and she filling his glass.

"You're like a bride," he told her.

After he'd finished eating, he was overcome by fatigue. She covered him with the blanket and looked at him with eyes brimming with desire.

"Now?" he asked, and cleared a space for her on the mattress.

"I didn't say anything," she said.

"I'll sleep for half an hour," he said.

"You sleep and I'll tidy up the cave."

"Wake me in half an hour."

She let him sleep and left. But before he went to sleep, she repeated her invitation with her eyes and he repeated his smile as he asked if he could sleep for half an hour. She went into the corner of the cave and washed the dishes, and when she came back found him sleeping deeply, so she left him and went to her house.

When Yunis woke up he didn't find her, and the shadows of evening were spreading over the hills. He found himself filling his water bottle, collecting the contents of his bag and putting into it the two loaves Naheeleh had left, and setting off for Lebanon.

Did he go back to see her after the night of the Roman olive tree?

He said he did, but I have my doubts. Yunis's life changed a great deal at that time. Once the Revolution became an institution resembling a state, Yunis became part of that state. He went abroad as a member of official delegations, phoned his family from various capitals, then became a member of the Fatah Regional Command in Lebanon. His days filled up, especially after the massacres of April 1970 in Jordan and the transformation of Lebanon into the Palestinian Resistance's only refuge following the migration of the leadership from Amman to Beirut.

Yunis became part of that huge machine and ceased to be the homeless fedayeen fighter of old, shifting between Ein El Hilweh camp in the south and Shatila and Burj El Barajneh camps in Beirut. All the same, he remained different. He didn't show the effects of affluence that became apparent among the majority of the Palestinian leaders; he remained a peasant, as he had been and as he wanted to be.

Yunis tried to reconcile his new life with his convictions. It may be that he didn't often succeed, but he preserved his image as Abu Salim, the Wolf of Galilee, who knew the country as no-one else did and who had a story like no other.

Was it during that time that his legend began?

I don't know because I didn't know him then. Well, I knew him, but I was young and I couldn't take things in and grasp their significance. I got to know him well from the beginning of the '70s, by which time he'd become a legend. I got to know him as the man who plants his children in Galilee and fights to liberate them.

All the same, I ask myself as I stand here beneath the rain of images covering the bedroom walls, did the legend begin when the story ended?

Did he start telling people about Naheeleh at the very time he stopped visiting her?

I don't know.

He said he continued his visits over there until '78, in March of which year the Israelis occupied part of southern Lebanon in which they established a dependent mini-state to which they gave the name of The State of Free Lebanon. It was just a narrow strip of Lebanese territory that formed a buffer zone between the fedayeen and the settlements of Galilee, which had been exposed to bombardment by Katyusha rockets.

He said the occupation shut his points of entry in his face, and he took to contacting Naheeleh and his children by telephone. He spoke to me often of his journeys, and of the three little Naheelehs who were born in Deir El Asad: Naheeleh the daughter of Nour, Naheeleh the daughter of Salim, and Naheeleh the daughter of Salih.

He said he'd phone all his Naheelehs and that he received pictures of them via the address of a friend in Cyprus and that he lived with them without seeing them; he lived with the pictures. "The phone doesn't let you do it, son. What can you say on the phone? On the phone you can only say generalities and clichés. Phone talk isn't talk."

Umm Hassan suggested I send you back over there, and then she died and left me alone with you.

Come to think of it, what do you suggest, father? There are me, you and this huge quantity of pictures hung on the walls of your house. The pictures, I swear, have put a spell on me. They're amazing: smiling girls, boys holding themselves stiffly in front of the camera, and a woman gazing into the distance, as if she were looking at you and waiting for you.

Your life is ending with pictures, master. And what about me? What shall I do with them after you die? I mean God forbid, I don't want you to die, but if God decides to reclaim what's His – after a long life – what do you want me to do with the pictures? Should I return them to your children? Should I bury them with you? Or should I leave them as they are for whoever comes to live in your house to throw out with the rubbish?

I don't know.

But I won't be sending you back over there. Even supposing I wanted to send you back, I don't know how, and I don't know if the Israelis would let you return.

And anyway, why all the fuss?

Why don't your children ask about you? Did Amna tell them you're dead, and did they have a funeral for you over there, and was that the end of the matter? Or have they forgotten about you, has the image of the man who knelt and kissed them one by one been wiped from their memories? Or was everything cut off after Naheeleh died?

You didn't tell me about the eighth Naheeleh.

The eighth Naheeleh is *the* woman, father, and I'm prepared to make changes to the numbering because I know you like magic numbers. So, let's throw out Naheeleh number six according to our previous classification and call the Naheeleh of the Roman olive tree Naheeleh number six, and that makes the Naheeleh of the flower basket the seventh and last Naheeleh.

You didn't tell me about that Naheeleh. You only said that Salim told you that all she was interested in was flowers.

"Her senility's expressing itself through flowers," the son said to the father he didn't know.

"What's all this about flowers?" the man asked his wife from his hotel in Prague, where he was visiting the city with an official Palestinian delegation.

"There's nothing to it. I like flowers and your son laughs at me and says I'm senile."

Your son, God protect him, had opened a garage in the village. He left his job in Haifa and opened his own garage. God was good to him, and his two brothers Mirwan and Salih went to work with him. Ahmad had graduated from Hebrew University in Jerusalem with a master's degree in Arabic literature and was preparing his doctoral thesis on the works of Ghassan Kanafani. Nizar was working with Nour's husband as a contractor. Nour was fine, only her husband had kidney stones and suffered great pain, but the doctor said there was no danger to his life. Salma, the pretty one, had refused all suitors because none of them found favour in her green eyes, and she was working as a teacher in El Ramah.

Why didn't you tell me about the Naheeleh you never saw?

About the woman with the head of blazing white hair who'd taken to carrying around a little basket into which she put flowers, as well as little pieces of paper on which she wrote the names of those she loved, mixing up the flowers with the bits of paper and telling her grandsons and granddaughters she'd put a black mark next to the name of anyone who annoyed her.

That was the game she played with her grandchildren. They'd visit her and she'd throw the contents of her basket on the ground and ask them to play the basket game with her, and they'd open the pieces of paper and read out their names and the names of their mothers and fathers, as well as your name, with all its variants.

Naheeleh believed the basket was her family, and when they brought her back from the hospital to the house and she was in the throes of the disease, she gave the basket to Naheeleh the daughter of Nour, and asked her to leave only three Naheelehs in the basket, because Old Naheeleh was going to die. She asked her daughter Nour to change the flowers once a week, and each time she was to change the little pieces of paper with the names written on them.

"Keep the names safe, daughter, and don't you dare not write them and put them in the basket. This basket keeps the names safe from death."

She took the bit of paper with her name on it out of the basket and tore it up, and the next day she died.

Don't tell me now about Naheeleh's death; I'm not here to listen to sad tales. I'm here to tell you I won't send you back over there. I'll bury you in the camp, in the mosque that's been turned into a cemetery, where the young men are buried. Your story will come to an end there, master. I won't tell Little Naheeleh that she has to tear up your names and take them out of the basket. I don't believe that Little Naheeleh has kept up the tradition, for we forget our promises to our dead; we keep them for a few days, and then we forget. I'm sure Little Naheeleh forgot the basket she inherited from her grandmother among her toys, that the basket of flowers ended up like my grandmother's pillow, and that decay will overtake the pieces of paper on which the woman wrote the names of the ones she loved.

Naheeleh was careful to rewrite the names when she changed the flowers in the basket. She'd throw the old flowers under the Roman olive tree, burn the names, and then put fresh flowers and write the names on new little pieces of paper.

Where are the women, master?

Where are the two women who used to come?

Where are the friends and comrades?

Where is everyone?

No-one.

You're dying now, and there's no-one around you. You're dying in silence, and I make you up as I please. I make myself up in you, and see those you saw and I didn't. I speak of a country I never visited, a country I entered a few times with the fedayeen at night but which I didn't see. You told me it was like the Lebanese south, that it was flat and over-looked by low hills, and that it was the epitome of a warm and tender land, which is why it had been fitting for the Messiah. You can't imagine Our Lord Jesus, peace be upon him, without Galilee. This land resembles him and is fitting only for strangers, which is why they call it Galilee of the Nations. The Jews fled to Galilee after the ruin of their kingdom, and we remained in it after the ruin of our history.

You talked to me about its caves and its cactus and its wild animals and its olives that stretch to the horizon. You said Galilee is an island between two seas. In the west there is the Mediterranean, and in the east there is the sea of blue olives. In these two seas, the Messiah learned how to fish and chose his disciples. A land of fish and olives and oil.

You promised you'd take me with you, and you never did. But I saw everything from the olive grove at El Khreibeh, on the Palestinian border. I saw endless olives and young men who never tire of death in that land that has become our graveyard and our promise.

And now we're here. Both of us have ended up in a hospital called Galilee Hospital which isn't a hospital, as I've told you a thousand times. The hospital is coming to an end, and your illness continues.

"We'll have closed the hospital before the man dies."

So said Dr Amjad, laughing. I don't know what brought him here, it's been ages since he visited you. I was sitting with you after giving you that yellow food I introduce with the tube via your nose into your stomach when Dr Amjad came and spoke of the necessity of closing the hospital.

He spoke as if he didn't know what was going on – practically speaking, the hospital is closed already. The first floor has become a congeries of storerooms, and on the second floor there are only five rooms left: a room for you, as a patient, a room for me, as a doctor, and three rooms inhabited by three new patients I haven't yet found the time to examine.

The patients here aren't like patients – two old women and a man of around fifty-five, as though the hospital, or what remains of it, had been transformed into an old people's home. Nurse Zeinab's still here, and the job of looking after the storerooms has been added to her duties. The Syrian guard doesn't guard, the cook doesn't cook, and the operating theatre has been transferred to Haifa Hospital in Burj El Barajneh camp. I heard recently that they may close Haifa Hospital too. As Nurse Zeinab explained it to me, the cost-reduction plan calls for keeping just one hospital in Lebanon, which will be Hamshari Hospital in Ein El Hilweh camp.

You know, things have been turned upside down. The members of the Palestinian leadership who migrated to Tunis and are still alive went back to Gaza, where there's an Authority and police and prisons and all the trimmings. That's why they need every penny and there's no call for all these hospitals in Lebanon.

Why didn't you go with them to Tunis?

I didn't because I couldn't. I felt faint in the stadium and went back to the hospital. But what about you? All the fedayeen went, and they ended up with offices and guards and a Revolution.

Why didn't you go?

Is it true you refused to go and said it was our duty to die in Beirut?

That was a mistake, master. There's no deciding when to die. We die when we die. Deciding when to die is suicide and madness.

Did you feel tired of it all?

Some people said you decided to go back over there after the defeat of '82, but I didn't believe them.

You told me it wasn't possible for us to leave Lebanon like the Turkish Army. Leave our people and go? Impossible! We had to stay with the people.

You stayed. Then what?

They slaughtered us the way everyone knew they'd slaughter us. And nothing changed. Tell me, why did you choose to be a victim?

Rest assured, I'm not going to send you back now, as a corpse. I'll keep you here with us. Staying was what you chose, and I'll respect your choice. But talk to me about your children and your wife. I don't want the story of Naheeleh over again, for I no longer know which bits of it are real and which bits are made up.

Do you remember the day you got furious with me when I refused to join the hospital staff as one of the new conditions they imposed on me after the end of the civil war in Lebanon? I refused because I'm a doctor and not a nurse. On that occasion, you abused me and abused your children. "You're all shit," you said. "Not one of them has turned out like his father. You don't want to work because you're clinging on to your title. Salim is a mechanic, Ahmad's a professor, and Salah's an I don't know what. I didn't beget any real men. Not one of them joined up with us. I was waiting for one of them, just one, to come and be like me and with me, but they're like their mother, peasants stuck to the soil. You too. What does being a doctor matter? The important thing is the work, not the position."

You became furious because your children didn't turn out like you, forgetting that you didn't turn out like your father. Do you understand now how the blind sheikh suffered when you mocked the Sufi gatherings and the prayer circles? Your father swallowed his dudgeon. He never once insulted you the way you did us, even though he wanted you to be a sheikh like him and like his father and grandfather. And here you now are, an officer in a tatterdemalion army in a war that never happened. And when it did happen, you said no, this isn't my war. You didn't want to have anything to do with the civil war, not here and not in Jordan. What were you thinking? That the war would be just the way you like them, simple and clear? Were you surprised by the explosion of this Arab world that lost its soul a thousand years ago and is flopping around today in its own blood, searching and failing to find it?

What did you expect?

The blind sheikh mourned you and took pity on you.

And when you didn't go to Tunis with the leadership, all of us here took pity on you because you'd become a bit of the past, a relic, walking among the ghosts of memory.

You don't know your children, or that country you used to behold through the holes in your cave and its blue night, and now I'm going to be the voice of reality, which you've never heard before, as though fate has sent me to tell you your truth that you hid away in the basket of stories.

"What is reality?" you'll ask.

I won't answer you by philosophising and telling you that the reality of a man is his death because I don't like heavy phrases like that. When I read them in a book, I conclude that the writer has nothing to say.

Reality, master, is what Catherine, the French actress, recounted to me.

Please don't smile. Listen a little. I'm not . . . I don't . . . I didn't . . .

Yes, I visited her. I went to the Hotel Napoléon on Hamra Street because she said she wanted to see me before she left. No, it never occurred to me that I might leave everything and go and work with them in France. First, I don't speak French well and second, I don't like the theatre and third, I hate acting.

I thought I'd visit her to get out of prison. Yes, I feel like a prisoner here. The doors are closed, the light's dim, and there are bars over the windows as though we were surrounded by barbed wire or minefields, or as though the walls were leaning in on top of us and melding into one another and suffocating us. I wanted to get out if only for an hour, and I stayed put all night . . . I don't know. Wait a little and you'll hear the story.

Please hang on a bit, it's not what you think. It's serious. Catherine told me something unbelievable, and I read the book and verified that what she said isn't fantasy.

I went to the Hotel Napoléon and asked for her at the reception desk. They called her on the telephone and I spoke to her and she asked me to wait for her in the lobby.

She came, sat on the edge of her chair and said she was sorry, but she had an appointment with a Lebanese writer who was going to take her to see *Prison of Sand* at the Beirut Theatre.

I said I didn't want anything; I'd just come to say goodbye.

She said she needed to talk to me. "Can you come back later?"

"When?" I asked.

"Tonight," she said. "The play'll be over at 10.00. I won't have dinner with him, I'll come back, and I'm inviting you to dinner."

I said I couldn't stay out that late because getting back to the camp, with all the security barriers surrounding it, was almost impossible at night.

"Please," she said.

"I'm not sure," I said.

As she got up, she said she'd be waiting for me in the lobby at 10.00. We left.

She went over to a man who appeared to be in his mid-forties, wearing glasses and carrying a black leather bag, and I set off with no idea where I was going.

I could've returned to the camp, and that's what I decided to do in fact. But then I thought of the sea and thought: Why don't I go and walk along the Manara corniche a little before going back to the camp.

I got to the corniche and everything opened up. I saw the sea and filled my chest and my heart with the smell of the salt and the wind. God, how good the wind is! Only we, we who've been released from all the prisons of the earth, can take such pleasure in the taste of the wind. I walked and breathed and saw. The sea was every possible shade of blue and I almost wanted to throw myself into the midst of its palette. I ran and walked and danced. I bought some lupin seeds to snack on and sat on a stone bench and watched the people running and striding and strolling. Nobody paid me any attention. I was alone, overhearing snippets of their conversations, which dissipated as they moved away from my seat and which I'd be trying to continue on my own when new stories would steal into my ears.

Time passed without my knowing.

I wasn't waiting because of her. Perhaps I was waiting for her unconsciously, but I didn't sit down and wait deliberately. I sat down to sit down, and then I looked at my watch and it said 10.05, so I started walking towards the hotel. I walked in a leisurely way because I was sure I wouldn't find her there. The writer would invite her to a restaurant, then woo her and sleep with her. That was their world, and I had nothing to do with it. I arrived at about 10.30 to find her sitting on the sofa in the lobby with an empty glass in front of her. She got up, said eagerly, "I was afraid you wouldn't come," and sat me down opposite her.

"What will you drink?" she asked.

"Whatever you're drinking."

"I'm drinking margaritas. Do you like margaritas?"

I'd never drunk one in my life, but I said I liked them.

The waiter brought two glasses, the rims coated with salt.

She said she wanted to ask me some questions.

I said I didn't know anything about the theatre and felt strangled inside an enclosed theatre. I also said the only time I'd watched a play – it was about the history of Palestine – I'd felt stifled by seeing the way the actors seemed to masticate the Classical language they were jabbering in before spitting it out in boring, artificially constructed sentences.

She said she'd decided not to take the part. The massacres of Shatila and Sabra couldn't be acted. She said that when she visited Shatila she felt fear, and that if she accepted the part it would involve her in politics.

"You know, I've visited Israel," she said.

"Really?" I asked coldly.

"Doesn't that surprise you?"

"No," I said.

"You're not upset?"

"Why should I be upset? You visited my country."

"Yes, yes," she said, "I know. But I visited Israel when I was fifteen, and I lived three months on a kibbutz in the north."

"In Galilee," I said.

"Yes. In Galilee."

She said she'd gone there because of the Shoah.

"The what?"

"*Shoah* is a Hebrew word meaning 'holocaust'," she said.

"I understand," I said, and asked if her background was German.

"No," she said, "but all of us (and here she pointed to herself and to me) are responsible for the massacre in which millions of Jews were lost, don't you agree?"

"Agree to what?" I asked.

"It doesn't matter," she said. "I decided not to take the part. I can't. I can't see the victim as someone turned executioner because that would mean history is meaningless."

I finished my drink at one go, and she ordered me a second one.

"Are you hungry?" she asked.

"No. Not very."

She said it would be better if we ate something. "Take me into Beirut and choose a beautiful restaurant."

I said I wasn't hungry and quietly started drinking my second drink, since I don't know any restaurants in Beirut and I didn't have any money on me.

She said she didn't want to act the part because reading wasn't the same as seeing.

"You know, Jean Genet's strange. His language is amazing, and there's that ability of his to move from the most savage to the most poetic expression. But the reality's different. I can't do it."

She looked at me with enigmatic eyes and asked where we were going for dinner.

"I'm not hungry," I said. "I'll finish my drink and go."

She raised her hand, the waiter came, and she asked him about food. He said it was late and the kitchen had closed, but we could order sandwiches if we liked.

She ordered a club sandwich for herself and asked me what I'd like to eat, so I said, "Anything." She ordered me a ham-and-cheese sandwich.

For an instant, I imagined myself in a cops-and-robbers film. The lights in the lobby were dim, and Catherine and I were seated in the bar on our own. At the bar itself were three men in black suits who looked like intelligence agents.

I wolfed the ham sandwich down and she asked if I wanted another.

"Please," I said.

She called the waiter and ordered another ham-and-cheese sandwich. I'd have liked her to have ordered me a club sandwich like hers, but she ordered what she thought I liked, because I'd eaten it quickly.

I ate the second sandwich and felt a little giddy, maybe because of the margaritas or maybe because of the kibbutz story.

I asked her the name of the kibbutz, but she said she couldn't remember.

I asked her if she'd visited the demolished Arab villages in Galilee, and she said she hadn't seen any demolished villages and hadn't known we'd been expelled from our country.

She drank from her glass and said she was sorry but she wanted to ask me an embarrassing question.

"Go ahead," I said.

She said she'd read about "Iron Brain" in a book by an Israeli journalist.

"About what?" I said.

"Iron Brain," she said. "It's the name given to the operation to break into Shatila on the eve of the massacre."

"What's it got to do with me?"

"Nothing," she said and fell silent for a moment.

She said she'd read in the Israeli journalist's book that nine Jewish women married to Palestinians had been killed in Operation Iron Brain.

"How did you know it was called Iron Brain?" I asked.

"The name's given in the book, and the writer's name is Kapeliouk. Have you read Kapeliouk's book?"

"Definitely not," I said.

"Kapeliouk wrote a book about Iron Brain in which she described the death of the nine Jewish women in the massacre."

At this point, master, I felt I'd fallen into a trap. What was this woman saying, and what did Iron Brain mean? No, I swear I'm not paranoid about the intelligence services, and I don't think that everyone who asks questions is in Intelligence, and so far I'd understood Catherine. I'd even felt some sympathy for her: she couldn't take the part because she felt responsible for the Holocaust – that was understandable. But this story of the nine Jewish women had a strange smell to it.

She asked if I'd like another drink.

I said I didn't want the drink that was rimmed with salt.

"How about some white wine?" she asked me.

"Okay," I said. ✦

She ordered a bottle of white wine, and the waiter came carrying the bottle in a container full of ice. He poured a little into my glass and waited. I didn't know what he wanted, but Catherine gestured to me to drink. I drank and nodded my head, so he poured more into my glass and some into hers and left.

"Wait a second," she said. "I'll go up to my room and get the book."

I drank a large mouthful of wine and stood up to go. I didn't want to discuss the Shatila and Sabra massacres over again, and I wasn't going to tell her about Boss Josèph, whom I hadn't met but whose point of view

I'd heard about from the mad Lebanese journalist. I swear they're mad: they invent the news so they can write it. Why did he want to set me up with Josèph? Was it because Josèph was from El Damour? And does one massacre justify another? I don't want to make a comparison. I told him I rejected comparisons: massacres are supposed not to happen, and if they happen they must be condemned and their perpetrators arrested and taken to court. All the same, I'd got involved and had gone with him to the restaurant in El Jimmeizeh, at the bottom of the Ashrafiyyeh district in East Beirut.

Now, however, I was half drunk and didn't want a discussion.

I took another sip from my glass and was getting ready to leave when I saw her coming back, carrying the book.

"Listen," she said.

She opened the book and started reading: "In the count of those lost were nine Jewish women who had married Palestinians during the British Mandate and followed their husbands to Lebanon during the exodus of 1948. The Israeli newspapers published the names of four of them."

She closed the book, drank a mouthful from her glass and asked if I'd been in the camp during the massacre.

"Yes," I said.

"Did you know those women?"

I laughed out loud. "You've come all this way and given me wine to ask that? No, my dear lady, I don't know what you're talking about."

"Listen," she said. "I'm serious. Did you know of the presence of Jewish women in the camp?"

"No."

"I'm trying to discover their names. Can you help me?"

"Why?"

"Because this book saved me."

"Which book."

"Kapeliouk's book. Do you understand the position I'm in?"

"Unfortunately I don't."

"I told you I went to work on a settlement in the north when I was fifteen. I went because I felt guilty. And when I arrived here for the play, I felt guilty again. Then I came across this book, and it saved me. I stumbled across it here in Beirut. I bought it from Antoine's Bookstore on Hamra

Street, and I felt greatly comforted. You know, this book will help me to say to Jews that when they kill Palestinians they're killing themselves too."

"What has it got to do with me?"

"You're Palestinian, and you have to help me."

"Help you do what?"

"Get hold of the names of those women."

"But it says in the book that they were published in the Israeli papers."

"I want the stories," she said.

"Why?"

"To prove my idea."

"Do you know Hebrew?"

"*Ksat*."

"What?"

"A little. *Ksat* means 'a little' in Hebrew. Do you know Hebrew?"

"No."

"Why?"

"Because I'm a doctor and not a linguist. Go, my dear lady, to Israel, or contact the writer and she'll give you the names."

"No. I want the Palestinians to tell me about these women's experiences."

"Are you Jewish?"

"No. Why?"

"No reason," I said. "I understand that you won't act or get involved. Didn't the director say Jean Genet didn't defend the Palestinians, he was just obsessed with death and sex, and that his task as a director was to put on a show that glorified death? You've refused to act in it, and you may be right, because in your view our death doesn't deserve to have a play put on about it. But then you come and ask about nine Jewish women who, you say, or your Israeli writer says, were slaughtered here in the camp. There were more than fifteen hundred killed, and you're searching for nine!"

"You haven't understood me. Please, tell me, do you believe, as a Palestinian, that what the Israeli writer says is true? Tell me about the massacre."

"What do you want to know?"

"Did you witness the massacre yourself?"

*

I told you, master, that I was drinking white wine, the lights were dim, and the noose was round my neck. The wine was going to my head and taking me to places I'd forgotten. It made me think of Jamal the Libyan.

Did you know Jamal the Libyan?

Jamal whose chest was torn open when he was hit by an Israeli bullet near Beirut airport during the siege? I don't know why I told her about Jamal, for I think his story deserves to be made into a book; I wish I'd told it to a writer like Jabra Ibraheem Jabra, to make into an epic. But Jabra's dead now, and I never met him, and all I had in front of me was this French woman half of whose face was hidden behind the bottle of white wine, and I wanted to explain. It didn't matter to me whether she was an actress or a spy. I wanted to make her understand the truth, and all I could think of was Jamal the Libyan. Or no, perhaps I wanted to seduce her. There was the wine, with its whiteness, and there was her head, which looked like a little ball on top of her neck, and it was night, and for the first time in months I felt my loneliness had been breached.

The man who told the story of Jamal the Libyan wasn't me. It was a man who resembled me.

I saw him and observed him and was impressed by his way of talking and how he could convert his fear and doubt into seduction and attraction; how he saw the woman's defences fall before him; and how taken aback he was at feeling himself unfaithful as he approached the female body after his long absence. I saw him shaking off the humiliations his fear had brought upon him. By the way, father, why do fighters, when they feel fear, feel it more than others? If you want to see fear, get a former soldier, or a former fighter, and put him in a frightening situation; then you'll see what real fear is.

I told you I saw Khaleel, which is to say myself, his fear discarded, sitting with this French woman about whom he knew nothing, telling her an amazing story, one that would be suitable for a novel or a film. The truth is that Khaleel Ayoub had given some thought to the matter. Don't think anyone could know a story like this and not get the idea that he might become a writer – though to turn this true story into a novel we'd need at least one military victory so that people would take us seriously and believe that our tragedy deserves to be placed next to the other tragedies mankind has known during this savage century in the gloomy shade of whose final days we're living.

We don't deserve our own story, which is why Jamal never told anyone. He fought in silence and died in silence. But what a story it is.

Why, come to think of it, did he tell me his story?

I remember he came to the hospital among the wounded. They brought him in with another wounded man, both covered in blood. The first one looked dead, his blood clotted on his stiff body. I don't know who examined him. Anyway, he was taken to the mortuary in preparation for burial. Then they discovered he was still alive, so they rushed him to the recovery room, and there we discovered that he was a poet. The papers that came out in Beirut during the siege published long obituaries about him. When the poet awoke from his "death" and read these, he was delighted beyond imagining. His medical situation was desperate: he'd been hit in the spinal cord and his left lung was punctured, but he lived for two days, which were enough for him to read everything that was written about him.

He said he was happy and no longer cared that he was dying because he'd now discovered the meaning of life through the love generated by words. Ali (that was his name) was the only happy corpse I ever saw; it was as though all his pains had been obliterated. He lived for two beautiful days in his bed among the piles of obituaries, and when he died everything had already been written about him, so his second death notice consisted of a few lines and no-one noticed the time of his funeral. We took him in procession from the hospital to the camp cemetery; there were no more of us than there are fingers on one hand.

Jamal the Libyan was wounded along with the poet, fracturing his right shoulder and sustaining scattered wounds to his chest. Jamal suffered acute pain, but that didn't stop him from visiting his dead-alive friend in the recovery room and weeping over his two successive deaths.

Jamal told me his story in the hospital and I told the tale to Catherine, and here I am now, repeating it for your ears so I can unravel, for you and for myself, the meaning of things. I won't lie to you and say that my encounter with this French actress was nothing and ended with the gush of the shower in her hotel room. Something stole into my insides and created a sort of breach, which I wouldn't call passion but which I will say, for the time being, resembled passion.

Jamal the Libyan left the hospital to die, as though it was the fate of this pilot to die on the ground before he could fly. As you know, his real name wasn't Jamal El Leebi; the epithet "The Libyan" got attached to him because he'd studied at the aviation school in Tripoli in Libya in preparation for the formation of the first squadron of the Palestinian Airforce-in-exile. The squadron was never formed, and when the Israeli invasion of Lebanon started, the Palestinian pilots from Libya were summoned to join the defence of Beirut. Jamal died in Beirut, but first he told his story.

"Get to the point," you'll say.

I'll get to the point. I've told you the end of the story before the beginning, but forgive me this time because I'm not telling you Jamal the Libyan's story, I'm telling you my story with Catherine. I didn't tell Catherine the story from the end; I started at the beginning. I didn't, for instance, tell her how Jamal told me his story.

I remember that, when he was speaking about the Israeli Army, he said that his maternal uncles were all in a dither because they couldn't enter Beirut.

"My uncles are very scared of their soldiers dying. They're sick and they need psychiatric treatment."

I didn't say anything when he mentioned his "maternal uncles." At the time I didn't notice because, like tens of thousands of others living in Beirut, I was under continuous Israeli bombardment from air, land and sea and suffering what you might call shell shock.

He said it to give me a chance to stop him at the word *uncles*, and when I failed to notice and got into a political–military debate with him about our likely collapse in the war, he changed the subject and said, "Look, doctor, you don't know them. I know them better than you because I'm a Jew like them."

"A Jew!" I said, and burst out laughing, thinking he was joking.

Jamal wasn't joking, and he wasn't a Jew in the true sense of the word. He said he was Jewish to shock me and push me to ask the question that would let him tell his story.

I didn't tell Catherine the story this way. I told it to her from the beginning. I left things vague and suspended among the various possibilities in order to guarantee her astonishment, and I succeeded in doing so. I didn't make anything up myself – the story's astonishing, and I used it to frame a moment of passion with a beautiful woman in a hotel in Hamra Street in Beirut.

We were drinking the white wine, and Catherine was sitting next to me because when she came back from her room with the book, instead of sitting opposite me, she'd sat down next to me on the wide sofa. She moved close as she read the text so I could see the page she was reading from, but when she finished reading she stayed where she was.

I was surprised.

Really, the text took me by surprise, and I was on the point of expressing doubts about its accuracy and saying, as any of us would, that they'd given us so many massacres they wanted to share them through the nine Jewish women who'd been slaughtered, when I remembered Jamal the Libyan and didn't say what would've seemed stupid with that woman, in that place, and intuitively obvious with you, in this place. It was in China that I learned to distinguish between stupidity and intuition. It takes another culture to show that half the things that seem intuitively obvious are simply stupidities.

I said to her, "Listen. I'm going to tell you a story about a Palestinian family, and afterwards you can draw whatever conclusion you like. But listen carefully."

She said she wanted the answer about the women before the story.

"The story is my answer," I said.

Khaleel started narrating. I see him sitting in the hotel lobby, the words gushing from his lips and eyes. I see him as though he was another person and wish I had a friend like him, because I love people who know how to tell stories.

Khaleel said:

Jamal was born in Gaza City, where his father was a notable member of its affluent class. The man's take on political matters is not known, despite the fact that Gaza suffered a major calamity in 1948, when it was turned into a city of refugees; the city was filled with tens of thousands of those leaving the areas from which the Israeli army had driven them, and it almost seemed as though there were no Gazans left in Gaza – Gaza dissolved in a sea of refugees and became the first place to be collectively Palestinian. It was there that the Palestinians discovered that they weren't groups of people belonging to various districts and villages; the disaster had manufactured a single people. That's why Gaza became the most important hub of political activity in Palestine's contemporary history. The Communist Party was strong there, it was there that the Muslim Brothers arose, and the first Fatah cells took shape in its camps and quarters. The Popular Front would occupy the city by night, under the command of a legendary figure known as Guevara of Gaza, and set up road blocks everywhere. It was there that Hamas and Islamic Jihad were born, and more.

Ahmad Saleem, Jamal's father, lived within this political and ideological whirlwind that battered Gaza. He never participated in politics, but he permitted his sons, when they became young men, to attach themselves to the Arab Nationalists movement, which had caught on among students.

Jamal, his eldest son, finished his secondary education in Gaza and then studied civil engineering at Cairo University, where he was an activist in the Arab Nationalists, which changed their name to the Popular Front for the Liberation of Palestine following the fall of Gaza and the West Bank to Israeli occupation in '67.

Mirwan, the second son, studied agricultural engineering at the American University of Beirut.

Hisham, the third son, was unable to complete his studies as he was finishing his secondary education in Gaza in '67 when everything changed.

Samira, the only girl and the youngest in the family, was one of the first Palestinian women to be arrested on charges of forming cells of "saboteurs," as they're called in Israel.

The four children participated enthusiastically in the demonstrations that swept the streets of Gaza in support of the Egyptian President Gamal Abdel Nasser and his decision to shut the Straits of Tiran to Israeli shipping, which was the reason given for the Six-Day War.

The war came, and Gaza was occupied, followed by curfews, night and fear.

At the beginning of September 1967, as people in Gaza were searching for ways to initiate resistance, a bombshell rocked the house of Ahmad Saleem.

Jamal said that as war became increasingly likely, his mother changed. She didn't share her children's enthusiasm for Gamal Abdel Nasser but remained silent, her face flushed with a blackish redness, saying only, "May the Lord protect us, children!" After the defeat and Gaza's occupation, her silence became heavy and alarming, and her face turned into a black mask.

That evening, when the family were at the dinner table, and the mother's silence had imposed a prickly absence of talk on everyone so that all that was heard was the sound of spoons and knives, the mother broke her silence in a dull wooden voice that seemed to come from far away. What she said she said with a strange rapidity, as though the words had been choking her, leading her to void them at one go before resuming her silence.

The mother said, "Listen. I want to tell you a secret I promised your father I wouldn't tell you because it would create unnecessary problems for you. But things have changed, and you need to know."

The father interrupted her with annoyance to say there was no call for such talk. He pushed his plate to one side, put his head in his hands and bent over, listening.

"I'm not an Arab or a Muslim. I'm Jewish."

Silence reigned.

Jamal said the food stuck in his gullet and he almost choked, but he didn't dare to cough or drink water. Everything became constricted. Even the September air stopped moving.

Jamal looked at his brothers and sister and saw that they were all examining their plates carefully as though they didn't dare to raise their eyes.

Once the mother had let off her bombshell, she seemed relieved, the blackness left her face, she sat up straight, and her voice came back to her.

"Your father isn't from Gaza but from Jerusalem, where he belonged to one of the city's rich and notable families. There, in 1939, he met a German Jewish girl who'd recently immigrated to Palestine with her family. The girl was called Sarah Rimsky. In Jerusalem the girl experienced the difficulties that afflicted German immigrants: German Jews were incapable of acclimatising to the Jewish *yeshuv*, its values and language. She was eighteen years old, a student at Hebrew University in Jerusalem studying German literature. That year she met this man by coincidence and fell in love with him. She went into a shop to buy some clothes, and there was this youth, wearing his red fez and working in his father's shop. The relationship was difficult, if not impossible, at first. She loved him but didn't dare to declare her love, and he behaved as though he was indifferent. He would sit in front of his shop and wait for her, and when she went by, on her way to the university, he'd say good morning to her in English. She'd reply in German and they'd laugh. Things developed from there. He invited her to eat Arab pastries at Zalatimo's; she went with him, saying she loved the smell of orange-blossom water and rosewater. They went walking in the streets of the Old City, discovering it together. He said she taught him to see Jerusalem and that he was seeing the city through her eyes. That was his first declaration of love. After a year of a relationship that came into being around the scent of orange-blossom water and the alleyways of the city, they decided to get married – but getting married was impossible. A Palestinian marry an immigrant German Jewess? Impossible, said everyone. But they decided to get married anyway.

The girl told her friend she was prepared to get married in secret and run away with him, and she suggested Beirut. The young man, however, asked her to be patient and entered into negotiations with his father which lasted two years.

The girl waited and the story got out.

One day, the young man arrived with his father's consent, on condition that they leave Jerusalem and go and live in Gaza, where the father had bought his son land and a house.

The crisis ended with their marriage and move to Gaza, where they lived and worked in the orange business. What's remarkable is that the young woman adapted quickly to her new situation. She started speaking Arabic with a Gaza accent, embraced Islam and lived in Gaza as a Muslim Arab woman with the name Sarah, which was not as widespread among Muslims in those days as it is today, though it was not considered unacceptable.

The mother said she'd told her children the truth so they'd know they had two uncles on her side of the family, the first called Elie, a colonel in the Israeli Army, and the second called Benyamin, an engineer. Both lived in Tel Aviv.

The father removed his hands from his face and said his wife's relatives had tried to kill her in '44 and that a number of armed Jews had attacked the house and sprayed it with rifle fire. The rifle fire had mostly hit the kitchen, where they thought Sarah would be. He said he'd removed the bullet holes from the kitchen walls but had left one "so we wouldn't forget" and proposed that the children get up so he could show it to them. None of them moved.

The mother said she was Palestinian and that that had been her choice, "but you need to know, because the Jews are occupying Gaza now and they won't leave."

"No. We'll throw them out," said Jamal.

"I wish, my son!" said the mother.

"My God!" said Catherine, "Is that possible?"

"I didn't invent the story," I said, "which means it's possible. Didn't you read the book? Did the Israeli journalist make up the story of the nine Jewish women?"

"Of course not," she said.

"There's something mysterious," I said, "but that's not what the story's about."

"They killed her?" asked Catherine.

"No."

"Her brother the colonel came and dragged her to Israel?"

"No."

"Like me, Jamal discovered he was Jewish."

"Like you?"

"No. I mean, I'm not Jewish, just my mother."

"Your mother's Jewish?"

"No, my mother's Catholic, but her mother — her mother's family — were Jews. They converted to Christianity out of fear of persecution, then . . ."

"Then what?" I asked.

"I learned the truth from my mother, so I decided to look for my roots and went to Israel."

"And did you find your roots?"

"I don't know. Not exactly. I discovered that it's not on. No. We don't have the right to persecute another people."

"We don't?"

"Meaning they don't, the Jews don't. That's what I meant."

I told her that Sarah Rimsky's story didn't end with her confession at that family dinner. In fact, that's where it started.

Jamal the Libyan said his mother changed after her confession. The relieved smile that had adorned her lips disappeared, the black spots on her face and neck returned and multiplied, and the family were caught up in the maelstrom of the prison world.

"But I went to see her family," said Jamal.

Jamal said he discovered that he wasn't just Palestinian but could be Israeli or German if he so wished. "I went to their house in the Ramat Aviv district in Tel Aviv's northern suburbs. I knocked on the door and a blonde girl of about seventeen who looked a lot like my mother opened it. I said my name was Jamal Saleem and I was the son of Sarah, her father's sister. I spoke to her in English, but she answered me in Hebrew. I said that I didn't know Hebrew, so she switched to halting English.

"'Come in,' she said.

"I went into the sitting room, where she asked me to sit down and went off to find her father.

"Colonel Elie entered, wearing a brown dressing gown. He came over to me and said something in Hebrew.

"'I'm Jamal, the son of Sarah,' I said in English, after I'd stood up.

"'You!'

"'Yes, me'.

"I didn't expect him to embrace me," said Jamal, "but I did expect he'd be a little curious and ask how his sister was. Instead, he asked what I wanted.

"'Nothing,' I said. 'I want to get to know you.'

"'It's been a pleasure,' he said and turned away as though asking me to leave. I stood at a loss in the middle of the spartan sitting room – no other word fits when you compare their sitting room to the opulent one in our house. I said I wanted to talk with him a bit.

"'You're an Arab, right?'

"'Palestinian,' I said.

"'What do we have to talk about?'

"'Family matters,' I said.

"'What family?'

"'Our family.'

"'We're not family,' said the colonel.

"'But you're my uncle.'

"'We're not family, I tell you. You're a terrorist. I'm sure terrorists sent you here.'

"I burst out laughing and said I brought a proposal for a family meeting.

"'Your mother sent you?'

"'No. My mother doesn't know.'

"'So who sent you?'

"'No-one.'

"'What's your job?'

"'I'm an engineer.'

"'What kind of an engineer?'

"'A civil engineer.'

"'Where did you study?'

"'In Cairo.'

"'They know how to teach engineering there?'

"'So so. It's not bad,' I said. 'The people who built the Pyramids can build a house.'

"'You're name's Jamal?' asked the girl.

"'Yes, Jamal. And you, what's your name?'

"'Leah Rimsky,' she said.

"'A beautiful name,' I said.

"'Do you know Tel Aviv?' she asked.

"'How could I?'

"'Would you like to get to know it? I'm ready to show you around.'

"'Go to your room and leave me to deal with him,' said the colonel.

"But Leah didn't go to her room, and the interview with my uncle the retired colonel was short and brusque. He said he didn't want to see his sister, had no interest in any family meeting, that it was up to us Palestinians to assimilate within the Arab countries ('You're Arabs like the rest of the Arabs') and that he didn't understand our insistence on living in the refugee camps, which had come to resemble Jewish ghettos: 'Go and become Syrians and Lebanese and Jordanians and Egyptians, so that this bloody conflict can come to an end.' I thanked him for his advice and said, 'And you too. Why don't you, my dear European German colonel, become assimilated in Europe? Go and assimilate yourself instead of giving me lessons in assimilation, and then the problem will be over. We'll assimilate with the Arabs, you can assimilate with the Europeans, this land will be empty of people, and we can turn it into resorts for tourists and religious fanatics from all nations. What do you say?'

"'You understand nothing about Jewish history,' he said.

"'And do you understand anything about our history?'

"At this, Leah intervened and said she was ready to show me Tel Aviv. We went out. The colonel said nothing and didn't try to stop his daughter from going with me.

"With Leah I saw Tel Aviv and discovered that strange society, which I can tell you is hard to encapsulate in words. No, I didn't go back and visit the colonel. I phoned Leah several times and went out with her, becoming re-acquainted through her with my mother. It was strange, man. I don't know how it could be. They'd never met but were like one another in every way – laughing, moving their hands – and they liked more or less the same foods. I suggested to Leah that she come with me to Gaza so I could introduce her to her twin, but she asked for time to think about it."

"'And your mother? Have you told your mother?'" she asked me.

"I told my mother I'd visited them, and at first she asked about them eagerly; then the mask reappeared and covered her face.

"'Please, stop visiting them. He's a criminal and he will kill you,' said my mother.

"I told her about our discussion about assimilation and her face lit up for a moment, but then she furrowed her brow and said that history was a savage animal.

"I went out with Leah a number of times, and then she stopped answering the phone and their number changed. I had no other means of getting in touch with her because she said her father wouldn't allow her to meet me. Her father changed the number and she didn't call. Just between us, my uncle the colonel was right: after the bus operations, meetings were no longer possible. Do you remember the bus operations, when the Popular Front planted explosive devices at bus stops in Tel Aviv?"

"Was that you?"

"I wish it had been! I can't claim that honour for myself, but I participated through surveillance. My outings with Leah were a type of surveillance, and I reported on what I'd seen to the Popular Front cell. The cell was uncovered after a sweep in Gaza, and they took me to Damoun Prison, where I was sentenced to twenty years on charges of participating in terrorist activities and belonging to a saboteur organisation."

Jamal said that prison had brought him relief: "The battering torrent stopped roaring in my head. I was twenty-three years old then and I'm twenty-nine now, but all the same, when I remember those days before I was arrested and the feelings that raged inside me when I went out with Leah and took her to Jerusalem . . . ! I swear I took her to Zalatimo's, and when I saw her eating and singing and smelling the scent of orange-blossom water I told her about my mother and how my father had managed to seduce her with Arab pastries and Zalatimo's. When I remember that now, I feel a loss. Prison let me have a rest. Things are clear there – there's them and there's us. We're behind bars and they guard the prison. That way there's no confusion. In prison I read all sorts of books and I learned Hebrew. I thought to myself: When I leave prison, I'll go and visit my uncle and speak to him in his new language.

"My mother came to visit me regularly in prison. My father came with her sometimes, but she'd come every week, bringing cigarettes and food. I learned from her that my brother Mirwan had been arrested too, that Sameerah had been held for several days and then released, and that they were thinking about sending Hisham and Sameerah to Cairo because they were afraid for them. I asked her why she didn't get in touch with my uncle so he could help to get me out, and she asked me never to mention the subject again. I stayed in prison for five years before I was deported to Jordan."

"And your mother? Where's your mother?" I asked.

"I haven't told you that part of the story yet. My mother stopped visiting me a year after I went into prison and my father started coming on his own. He said my mother was sick, suffering from arthritis, and he brought me letters from her. Her letters were short and said only that I was to take care of myself after I came out of prison. You don't know my mother. I swear no-one could've told she was Israeli or Jewish. She was more Palestinian than all the rest of us put together. My father still spoke with his Jerusalem accent, but she became Gazan, loved hot peppers, ate salad without olive oil, and all the rest. Then my father disappeared too. Hisham and Sameerah were in Cairo, Mirwan was in prison like me, and my father didn't visit me.

"Later, a short letter from him reached me via the Red Cross in which he said he'd taken my mother to Europe for treatment.

"When I got out of prison I learned the truth. What a woman she was! I don't say that because she was my mother. All of us love our mothers and think of them as saints, but if you only knew."

"If you only knew," Khaleel said to Catherine.

"You'll never be able to imagine what happened, my dear lady. Sarah didn't go to Europe for treatment. Guess what she did."

"She went to Tel Aviv and returned to her family," said Catherine.

"That possibility did pass through Jamal's mind, but it's not what happened."

"Her brother killed her?"

"Now you're imagining an American film. We can't behave as if we're in American films even if we like watching them."

"What then?" asked Catherine.

Khaleel said that Sarah contracted colon cancer, but they discovered the disease too late, after the cancer had spread through her body.

"You know how women in our country suppress everything. They don't complain and don't say anything and fence themselves in with silence and secrets?"

Sarah treated herself at the beginning, and when the pain got bad she went to the doctor. She was admitted to hospital, had three operations and was sent home after the cancer spread to her bones. She returned home to enter her appalling pain.

One night, when Sarah couldn't sleep because the pain was bad even though she'd had a morphine injection, she went to her husband's bed, woke him and told him she wanted to talk to him about something important.

The man sat up in bed and listened to the strangest request.

Sarah asked her husband to take her to Berlin and bury her in the Jewish cemetery there.

Her husband told her he was prepared to go any place in the world with her for treatment and that he'd call the doctor in the morning to get the addresses of hospitals in Berlin.

"I don't want treatment," she said. "There is no treatment. I want to be buried there."

Khaleel told Catherine that Jamal, as he told the story, was more astonished than he was, as though he was listening, not recounting. He said his father told him, when they met in Amman a few months before his death, that he'd leave this world in peace because he'd succeeded in making Sarah happy.

"She was like a little girl there," the father said. "Every day we'd go out. I don't know where she found the strength. She took me to the places of her childhood, of which not many remained – but she was happy. It was as though the pain had gone or a miracle had occurred. After a week she was no longer able to get out of bed. I tried to take her to hospital, but she refused. Three days later she died, and I buried her there."

Khaleel saw the sorrow engraved on Catherine's face. The French actress who wouldn't act in Jean Genet's play was slumped in her chair almost as though she was unconscious.

"Why don't you drink?" Khaleel asked her.

She looked at her glass and said nothing. Khaleel took Catherine's glass and finished it at one gulp.

Catherine said she was exhausted.

Khaleel looked at his watch. "It's 3.00 a.m.," he said.

Catherine said she wanted to sleep.

"Now you want to sleep! The night is young. I want more wine."

"No. You've had a lot to drink, Jamal," she said.

"I haven't drunk a lot, my name's Khaleel, my mother's name is Najwah, and Jamal died during the Israeli invasion of Beirut."

Catherine stood and Khaleel stood.

"How are you going to get back to the camp?" she asked.

"I don't know, but I'll manage."

"You can spend what's left of the night here, in my room."

"In your room? No . . ."

"I'm tired and want to sleep. Come to my room."

They went up to her room. Catherine undressed quickly and got into bed almost naked. After a little hesitation, Khaleel lay down next to her, fully clothed.

"Take your clothes off," she said. "Don't tell me you're going to sleep in your clothes."

He took off his clothes, Catherine turned off the light, and there, in the darkness of the room, which would continue to cling to Khaleel's skin, they made love.

Khaleel doesn't remember things clearly, but he felt as though he was drowning and caught hold of the woman, who fell on top of him, and they drowned together.

He woke the next morning to find Catherine emerging from the bathroom fully clothed and wearing a lot of lipstick. He dressed quickly, and they went down to the restaurant, where they ate breakfast like strangers.

She told him she was leaving that afternoon and was going to the crafts shop near the hotel to buy some presents. He told her he was late for work at the hospital and would have to get back. They said nothing about the previous day; even the play wasn't mentioned. They finished breakfast and got up from the table. She imprinted a cold kiss on his cheek, and he left.

This was all that took place between me and the French actress.

I told her the story of Jamal, and we slept together. She thought she was sleeping with Jamal the Libyan, who could've been Palestinian or Jewish or German, and I saw in her something of Sarah, who became Palestinian.

Let's suppose now that Catherine had immigrated to Israel, married Jamal, and – after a long life! – the angel of death had come for her. Where would she have asked to be buried? With her Jewish grandmother, with her Catholic mother or with her Muslim children?

I swear our story has no end.

When Jamal told me his story, I couldn't believe it. He told me because he knew he was going to die; now he's resting in his grave in Beirut while his father's in Gaza and his mother's in Germany.

When will the dead be reunited?

Why did Sarah return to the country of her executioners?

"It's the traditional relationship between the executioner and the victim," you'll say.

I'm not so sure. I don't have any strong convictions that would provide me with an answer about the world that drove Sarah to her German grave.

Jamal told me his father had said that Sarah was happy with the language. She gurgled her German the way small children do.

Are we the slaves of language?

Is language our land and our mother and all things?

Catherine went back to her country and didn't take the part she was supposed to in the play about the massacre. She left the play to us so we could go on playing the role of the victim. The role has no end, starting from the fall of the man-bird from the minaret of El Ghabsiyyeh and the men of Sha'ab who climbed the ropes of rain to their deaths.

The French actress left us to play our role and went back to her country with the story of Sarah and Jamal the Libyan. Instead of uncovering the names, she lost them. I asked nothing of her; I found myself in bed with her and she spoke to me in French, which I don't understand, and said "Jamal". And when she got up the next day, she resumed her mask and went back to her country.

She was right, but I still don't understand.

In the morning, beneath her mask of lipstick, she became another woman. She put on her French mask and imprinted a cold kiss on my cheek. She was right: if I'd had a French mask, I wouldn't have taken it off and allowed myself to enter this labyrinth that's called Palestine. I have no choice because I was born in the labyrinth, and nor do you or Jamal the Libyan or his cousin or Sarah or others from an infinite list of names from here, from over there, or even from outside. We have no alternatives and no masks, and even war no longer provides enough of a mask to conceal the whirlpool in which we're drowning. Them and us. As you see, they've become like us and we've become like them. We no longer possess any other memory.

All the stories of the war we entered have evaporated, and all that's left are the massacres. Are we imitating our enemies, or are they imitating their executioners and pushing us to put on that same mask that covered Dunya's face? You remember Dunya? Dunya's dead now. "It doesn't matter," you'll say. I'll say, "It doesn't matter" too – we're all going to die. But Dunya died because she was no longer able to play the role of the victim. That phase is over. The international humanitarian agencies are no longer interested in us. Now what they're interested in is the West Bank and Gaza, and Dunya has lost her audience. That's why she died.

And you.

I know why you're dying, father.

You're dying because the story ended with Naheeleh's death.

Tell me, why don't you open your eyes and speak as Sarah spoke? Why don't you announce your wish to die over there?

Are you afraid of dying?

Or is it that you don't want your story to end, that you want to leave it open-ended so you can force us to keep on playing the role of the victim for as long as God sees fit?

What did you say?

No, my story's different, and I'll tell it to you from beginning to end. Shams's death is no reason for me to die. No, I won't go out on to the street and ask them to kill me. No, what happened last week was an absolute fiasco. I heard shooting in the street near the hospital, which started shaking with the rattle of the Kalashnikovs. I came running to hide in your room. I came and I was shaking with fear. Now I laugh at myself when I remember how scared I was – I was ready to hide under your bed.

In the morning, Nurse Zeinab entered your room with a gloating smile.

"What are you doing here?" she asked me.

I said I'd been afraid for you because your breathing was irregular, so I'd spent the night here.

"Didn't you hear the shooting?"

"No. What happened?"

That was my mistake. When you lie, you discover that you can't correct anything, as though you were naked. I was naked before Nurse Zeinab's smile.

"Everyone heard, and Dr Amjad came from his house to make sure everything was all right and we looked for you. We didn't find you in your room, and Dr Amjad said you'd run away and told me to get everything ready to move Yunis to the home this morning."

"We won't be moving him," I said.

"As you wish. Go and discuss it with Dr Amjad. But why didn't you come out of Yunis's room last night?"

"I didn't hear. I must have been fast asleep."

"Whatever, doctor. I can't understand how you couldn't have heard. Maybe you were in a coma. Fear can cause comas," she said, and she left.

I ran after her. "Nurse Zeinab, come here."

"What do you want?"

I asked her about the day before, fear insinuating itself into my voice.

"It was nothing," she said. "A robbery. Thieves tried to rob the hospital, and when Kamilya noticed them they fired in the air and ran away."

"That's all?"

"That's all. What did you think it was, an assassination attempt? Get a grip, man! No-one's after you. The woman's dead and gone, and if they'd wanted to kill you they'd have killed you. Go back and sleep at home. What kind of person sleeps next to a corpse when they can sleep at home?"

She called you a corpse! Stupid woman.

It's as though she can't see. No-one sees you but me. I said to Amjad – this was the last time we talked about you – I said that I refused to move you to the home and asked him to come to your room to see for himself.

"It's your responsibility," he said. "You want him here, let him stay here. I suggested moving him for your sake." Then he said he refused to examine you personally: "I'm not a forensic physician, to go examining corpses."

I explained, but he didn't understand. He said that what I see as positive signs are really signs of death. God, can't he see how like a little child you've become? You've grown younger, and the signs of aging have been erased from your brow and your neck, and your smell is that of a child. Even your reflexes are those of a new-born. The problem is your closed eyes, and these I still put "tears" into. Your eyes are clear, the whites slightly blue, and your heart's as strong and regular as a young man's.

I told Amjad I could see your improvement in your eyes. I said I could hear your voice, as though you were waiting for something before coming out with the words.

"It's all in your imagination," he said.

"No, doctor, I'm not imagining anything. I speak to him and he understands. I play Fayrouz cassettes for him and see him swimming in his dreams; I play him Umm Kalsoum and see the desire gushing out around him; I play him Abd El Wahhab and Abd El Haleem and see the mist of life curling above his head."

He said he was sure you'd entered the final phase and he expected your heart to collapse – it could happen at any instant and carry you off – and that all my concern for you wouldn't make the slightest difference. You hadn't died already because your constitution was strong and your heart excellent – he'd never seen such a pure heart. He used the word *pure* to mean "regular", but the only true purity, master, is the purity of love, and I'm jealous of you and of your love. I'm jealous of that meeting you had beneath the Roman olive tree when Naheeleh took you to Bab El Shams and poured her rain upon you. When I imagine that scene, I see the woman envelop you like a cloud and then pour her rain upon you. That's the water of heaven, and of life.

How am I to convince them you're not going to die? How can I convince myself?

Your new childhood drives me crazy and crushes me; I never fathered a child and never knew the beauty that you saw when your son Ibraheem's hair covered the pillow.

Now I've started to understand how a man becomes a father.

Will you agree?

You don't have to agree, father, because you're my son now. Let me call you "son", please. Think of it as a game. Don't parents play that way with their children, the father calling his son "daddy" and the son calling his father "son"? I'm the same. I carry the same name as your father: I'm Khaleel, "The Companion", and Ibraheem was "The Companion of God", which is why we've named Ibraheem's city Khaleel, "The City of the Companion". That's why, too, the fiercest battles between the Palestinians and the Jews will take place in that city, and for it.

We won't get into the complications of the relationships between fathers and sons; you know I don't care for religious stories, and the name of the sacrifice that wasn't sacrificed – whether Isaac, as the Jews say, or Ishmael, as we say – doesn't concern me. Neither of them was sacrificed, because Ibraheem, peace be upon him, was able to fetch the ram. The knife passed over both their necks and didn't cut them, so what's the difference?

I don't want to discuss that now. I want you, son, to see life with your new eyes. Start at the beginning, not at the end. Or start wherever you like. I've told you these stories so you can know them and make a new story for yourself.

I can't imagine the world that's waiting for you. You make it. Make it the way you want to. Make it new and beautiful. Tell the mountain to move and it will. Didn't Jesus, peace be upon him, say to the mountains, "Move!" Was he not the Son who took on the outlines of his Father's image when he died on the cross?

Be the Son, and let your bed be your cross.

What do you say?

Don't you like the image of the Son?

Isn't it more beautiful than all the pictures we've drawn during the six months we've spent together here? Come, let's go back to the beginning.

You wanted the beginning, so go to the beginning.

Listen, I don't know any lullabies. Nurse Zeinab does. Nurse Zeinab lost her first-born son in the Israeli air raid on El Fakahani in '82 and she still sings to him. I see her, when she's on her own, cradling her arms as though she were carrying a baby, and I hear her singing:

Sleep now, sleep
I'll slaughter you a dove
Go, dove, fear not
I'm only teasing my son
Come now and sleep

Tomorrow I'll go to Hamra Street and buy you Fayrouz, and that'll be your sixth birthday present. Now I have to go and cook you lunch, and I'll put some orange-blossom water in. There's nothing like orange-blossom water. It's the best flavouring and the best scent. I'll put some orange-blossom water in your food, and your birthday meal will be delicious.

The experiment worked. Didn't I tell you?

After I'd bathed you and scented you and rubbed you with ointment and dressed you in your sky-blue pyjamas, I sat you at the table and I let go of you, and you didn't fall or slump over, which means you've regained your balance, and you can't balance if your brain's damaged.

I stood behind you without touching you. Then I got an idea.

I stood in front of you, placed my hands in your armpits, and the miracle occurred.

It's the first time I've dared to try the experiment. There are three involuntary reflexes made by new-born babies.

The first is the gripping of the finger. We open the baby's hand and put our finger on it, and the baby closes its palm. I've tried that, and it works.

The second is when we put our finger on the baby's cheek close to its mouth. The baby starts to move its mouth towards the finger, grasps it with its lips and sucks on it. I've tried that, and it works.

I hadn't dared to try the third reaction. I was afraid you'd fall and your bones, which have become weak and soft, would break.

I told Nurse Zeinab about the two experiments, and she looked at me blankly and said nothing. As for Dr Amjad, you know better than I that he doesn't give a damn. It's a waste of time – medicine's the least of his concerns now. The only thing that interests him about the hospital is how to steal the medicines we get as donations and sell them.

We all know he steals, but what can we do? He's the Director, so who can we complain to? *Quis custodiet ipsos custodies*, as they say. I'm not going to start belly-aching and complaining. This is the situation we're in, and we have to accept it.

I no longer remember if I told Dr Amjad about those two experiments, but I'm certain his only reaction would be scorn.

The important thing, master, is that I'm happy, and I'm not going to allow anyone to spoil my good mood.

Today I decided to carry out the third experiment, and it was conclusive. I stood in front of you and placed my hands in your armpits and I saw. Before I began, I raised you up a little, the way we do with babies, then I put you back in the chair and placed my right index finger under your left armpit and my left index finger under your right armpit, and I saw you, I swear: you got up and your feet moved as though they were walking. I saw you walking with my own two eyes. Then I got scared. I grabbed you and put you back in the chair, and I saw pain pass over your closed eyes. I picked you up as a mother does her baby – God, how light you've become – I picked you up and put you back on your bed and was overwhelmed with joy.

The third reflex occurred, which means that from the medical perspective you're a child again. You won't progress from sickness to death, as they'd like you to do; instead you've become a baby and begun your life over again.

And that means everything can change.

I have to calculate how old you are now, in your new life. I've decided to calculate from the moment you fell into your coma, which means that as of four days ago you entered your seventh month.

You've been in the womb of death for seven months, and I have to wait for your birth, which will be in two months' time.

Now we're at the beginning, as you asked, and you have to go through all the torments of childhood.

Come on, let's begin.

I spend my time with you, I bathe you, I feed you, and I see you changing in front of my eyes and I'm at peace. I feel my body relaxing, and I feel I can talk to you about what I feel and be free. You're my son, and fathers don't show fear in front of their sons.

Why, come to think of it, was I afraid?

How did fear come to possess me and make me a prisoner, so that I was afraid of everything and always looking over my shoulder, though I didn't see them? I've lived with nothingness for months. Six months I've been with you, paralysed by my fear. Your new childhood has liberated me from it; fathers aren't allowed to show fear in front of their sons.

Now I have no fear.

Do you think I could get you out of here? Why don't we go back to the house? No, we won't go back now; we'll be patient. We'll be patient for two more months, and then it'll be the birth.

*

I was talking to you and I couldn't believe my eyes.

I was bending over you and there was Abu Kamal standing by my side. How did Abu Kamal get in?

"What are you doing here, Abu Kamal? What brought you here?" I said and asked him to sit down, but he remained standing next to you as though he couldn't hear me.

"What were you saying?" he asked me.

I told him I was treating you.

"Treating him with words?"

"I'm treating him. What business is it of yours? Be seated please."

But Sameer Rasheed Sinounou, Abu Kamal, wouldn't oblige. He went over to you, bent over the bed and then drew back. I heard what sounded like a sob and I thought he was weeping, so I put my hand on his shoulder, but then I saw that he was laughing.

"What's that? Incredible! That's Yunis Abu Salim? How are the mighty fallen!"

And he went on laughing.

I tried to take hold of him by the shoulders and push him out of the room and I saw his tears. He was laughing and weeping. His tears were streaming around his gaping lips, and his laugh was a sort of cough.

The bald man of about sixty, known in the camp as "Aubergine" because of his black skin and oblong face, seemed to have lost his ability to balance and hung his head as though he was about to fall to the ground. I calmed him down and made him drink some water.

"How are the mighty fallen," he said. "Is this how a man ends up? This is Abu Salim – God, he's become younger than a suckling child. What kind of sickness turns men into babies?"

I took his hand and led him out into the corridor.

"What's brought you here, Abu Kamal?"

Aubergine hasn't visited you before and I don't believe you were friends; he inhabits a different world and cares only about marriage. He married three times and had ten children, and now he's alone since his third wife died and his two divorced wives refused to come back to him. His children have all emigrated and his life's over, as Umm Hassan said. Umm Hassan felt sorry for him and would visit him and send him food because he was from her village. Abu Kamal is from the Sinounou family, which left El Kweikat when its people were expelled in '48.

"What brought you here?" I asked.

"Poverty," he said.

When I took him out of your room into the corridor, he stood leaning against the wall, but when he uttered the word *poverty*, he collapsed onto the floor and began his complaint. He asked me to find him a job in the hospital. He said Umm Hassan was a relative of his, he knew the esteem in which I'd held her, and he'd come to ask for work.

"I can do any kind of work. Things are unbearable."

"But Abu Kamal, you know the situation better than I do. Things aren't too good."

"I don't know anything," he said. "I don't want to die of hunger."

"And your job? Why don't you go back to your old job?"

"What job, man? Is there anyone left in the camp who reads newspapers?"

"Go to Beirut and get a job."

He said he couldn't work in Beirut any longer. The week before, a policeman had stopped him when he was selling papers on the Mazra'a corniche and asked for his papers and, when he saw he was Palestinian, threatened him and said it was forbidden for Palestinians to work in Lebanon without a permit.

"Now you need a work permit to sell papers, cousin! He confiscated the papers and chased me away. He said if I hadn't been an old man he'd have taken me to gaol."

"In the camp. Work in the camp," I told him.

"You know that nobody here reads newspapers any more. Basically, no-one has the money to buy them, and people have got television and video now. What am I to do?"

He started talking about his problem with video, and about how he couldn't see: everyone else could see, but he couldn't. "They sit around their televisions and run the tapes, and they see things I don't. That isn't Palestine, cousin. Those pictures don't look like our villages, but I don't know what's got into everyone, they're glued to their television sets. There's no electricity, and they still play them, subscribing to Hajj Isma'eel's generator just for the video. They pay twenty dollars a month and go hungry so they can watch the tapes; they sit in their houses and look at those films they say are Palestine. We're a video nation and our country's become a video country."

Abu Kamal said that after the incident with the policeman he tried to go back to his work in the camp. "I opened a news stand, and my only customer was Dr Amjad, but he didn't pay. He'd take the papers, read them and return them, while I sat all day long with nothing to do. Can't you find me a job here?"

I said it was impossible. "Impossible, Abu Kamal. What could you do here?"

"Damn it, man, I want to eat. I can't go on like this. Are you willing to see your Uncle Aubergine become a beggar? It's the bloody limit! Screw life and its ups and downs!"

I tried to help him up, but he refused.

"Get up, uncle. Come along and let's sit in the room."

But he wouldn't get up.

"Get up, man. Shame on you."

He said he didn't want to go into your room because he was afraid.

I told him there was no money and things were tough.

He asked for a cigarette and smoked it greedily, as though he hadn't had one for a long time. I offered him the pack, but he refused it. He took one more cigarette, smoked it and went off.

No. Before he left, he went into your room and said hello to you and I saw a kind of envy in his eyes, as though he begrudged you this sleep of yours. Then he said some words of support and left.

I felt so sorry for Abu Kamal Sinounou. What can I do for him? You don't know him so you won't understand what I'm saying or why I felt so upset about this man. He'd transformed himself from a newspaper seller in Acre into the owner of the largest shop in the camp. Then his shop was destroyed, his life was destroyed, his third wife died, and he ended up poor and alone.

Why are all your stories like that?

How could you stand life?

These days we can stand it because of video; Abu Kamal was right – we've become a video nation. Umm Hassan brought me a tape of El Ghabsiyyeh, and some other woman brought a tape of another village – all people do is swap videotapes in whose images we find the strength to continue. We sit in front of the small screen and see small spots, distorted pictures and close-ups, and from these we invent the country we desire. We invent our life through pictures.

But how did your generation bear what happened to you? How did you go about blocking up the holes in your lives?

I know what your response will be; you'll say it was temporary. You lived in the temporary, the temporary was your way of coming to an understanding with time.

You're temporary and we're video – what do you think?

Abu Kamal used to sell newspapers in Acre and made his life up as he went along. He was about fourteen when he started selling papers. He'd leave El Kweikat on his bicycle each day and reach Acre some forty-five minutes later. He'd get his bundle and sell *The People*. In the afternoons, he carried a big sign around the streets shouting, "Make it an evening at Cinema El Burj!" inviting people to go to the cinema and see *The Thief of Baghdad*, and receiving half a lira for his efforts. Adding this to the lira he'd earned from selling papers, he'd return to his village.

Abu Kamal was known as Aubergine in his own village too; we came here bringing both our made-up and our real names. Aubergine proved he was wilier than all the rest of Kamal Sinounou's children, however. His three brothers worked with their father growing watermelons, but he found himself a job on his own. He went to Acre, saw a paper seller and asked if he could work with him. The vendor took him to the Communist Party's Acre office, where he met a short man and came to an agreement to sell the paper.

Abu Kamal wasn't a Communist; he wanted to leave the village because he didn't like working in the fields. However, it seems that his job selling *The People* had its impact on how he spoke, since for the rest of his life he'd mumble certain phrases he'd picked up from the paper's headlines, about workers' rights, Arab–Jewish brotherhood and so on.

When things started to get complicated, he stopped going to Acre and joined the El Kweikat militia as a bodyguard for Mohammed El Nabulsi, the only man in the militia who owned a Bren gun. When the village fell and Mohammed El Nabulsi died, Aubergine found himself part of the wave of people who moved out. They didn't go to Amqa because of the famous dispute between the two villages that followed the rape of a girl from the Ghadban family at the hands of an Amqa boy.

All the people of El Kweikat went to Abu Sinan, and they all took up residence under the olive trees, where they set up their tents of blanket and sacking. They stayed in the fields of Abu Sinan for about a month. I won't go into what we know now about how people went back to their village by night to steal provisions from their houses, whose doors hung askew, and about how Qataf, an eighteen-year-old girl, died of an Israeli soldier's bullet as she was leaving her house carrying the demijohn of oil, her blood mixing with the oil, and about how, and how . . .

"There was nothing we could do but rob our own houses," said Umm Hassan. "Does anyone steal from himself? But what else could we do, son?"

I didn't ask Umm Hassan why they didn't try to take their villages back the way you did in Sha'ab instead of creeping into their houses and stealing from themselves, because I knew her answer would be, "Go on with you! All that about Sha'ab, and it still fell. Enough nonsense!"

Anyway, Yunis, what was I telling you?

Things have got strangely mixed up in my head. Even the names are mixed up. A name will fly away from its owner and settle on someone else. Even names don't mean anything any longer.

I wanted to say that Abu Kamal tried not to live in the temporary. After Qataf's death and the madness that seized the people of El Kweikat, everyone left Abu Sinan for Jath, and from Jath in Palestine they went to Rimeish in Lebanon and from Rimeish to Rashaf and from Rashaf to Haddatha.

Abu Kamal lived in Haddatha for about two years, working on the construction of the Haddatha–Tibneen road, but he left after a quarrel with his sister-in-law and travelled to Beirut, where he worked as a builder's labourer. He stayed in Beirut for about a month and then went back to Haddatha because of exhaustion and the swelling that had developed in his hip from carrying containers of concrete and following along behind the master plasterer. He returned to discover that the Palestinians had been rounded up and put in Burj El Barajneh camp in Beirut. He went to Burj El Barajneh, but he couldn't find a camp; all he found was a bit of empty land and people sleeping out in the open. A foreign official came, with a Lebanese at his side, and they started distributing tents.

They distributed two or three and then stopped for some reason or other.

Those were the days of waiting.

Abu Kamal went back to Haddatha because working with concrete had tired him out, and he found that the Palestinians had been deported to the suburbs of Beirut. The lorries came, they ordered the Palestinians living in Lebanese villages to gather in their squares, and they were transported to Beirut and the north.

That was how they left Lebanese Galilee following their expulsion from Palestinian Galilee.

Like all of you – like my father, who was led by the feeling that everything was temporary to work for the Jew Aslan Durziyyeh and then to his death – Abu Kamal didn't grasp the reality of what had happened.

You lived in the temporary and died in the temporary; you put up with lives that couldn't be borne and hid yourselves by forgetting what couldn't be forgotten.

What should I have asked Abu Kamal as he sat there clinging to the wall?

Should I have asked him why he'd married three women? Or how his fortune turned and he came to be alone after the death of his last wife, Intisar?

Would I have been able to explain to him why his first wife, Fathiyyeh, and his second, Ikram, refused to go back to him?

And how will Abu Kamal live now?

The children have emigrated. They send a little money to the two women, but he's alone and no-one sends him anything. Should I have told him he was paying the price for the rest of his life? Why should he have to pay? Was the camp destroyed just because he married a third time? His third wife, Intisar, died during the long siege which destroyed our world: our world wasn't destroyed during the great massacre, when we were buried under corpses; our world was destroyed by what they call the War of the Camps between 1985 and 1988, when we were besieged from every side. That was when everything was wrecked.

Later we read all that stuff they threw together in a hurry about how the *intifada* in Gaza and the West Bank was born to the beat of the camp wars. It may be true – I don't mean to ignore history – but tell me, why does history only ever come in the shape of a ravening beast? Why do we only ever see it in mirrors of blood?

Don't talk to me now about the mirrors of Jebel El Sheikh. Wait a little, listen a little.

Before me sits Abu Kamal, who I wish would die.

A man who worked at everything and tried to beat his own path through life. He worked in concrete, then at the Jabir Biscuit Factory. He left concrete with a swelling in his hip and went to work in biscuits, and then decided to sell ice-cream. Then he opened a café, then a shop, which he named the Abu Kamal Minimarket and where he sold smuggled tobacco and everything else. A man who tried to master life by every means possible, and despite it all, all he calls forth in me is pity. I've no solution for his problem. How am I to find him work when I am myself, as you see, only half employed? And then this man comes and tells me his two wives have rejected him and are keeping from him the money his children send?

"If I could just get in touch with Subhi," said Abu Kamal. "Subhi's kind to his father, but I don't know his address. I went to Fathiyyeh and told her. I said I didn't want anything. You don't know, son, what it is to be treated like shit by a woman, a woman who was once . . ."

"Shame on you, Abu Kamal. Don't talk that way about the mother of your children."

"But you don't know anything."

He said that Fathiyyeh had to eat dirt twice. The first time was when he married Ikram, and the second when Intisar forced him to divorce his two other wives as a condition of marrying him.

"It was my fault, son – it was my fault, but I just couldn't resist the Devil. He seduced me and made me accept the woman's conditions, but she died and took everything with her. Now I have nothing. The shop was burned down, the house is half destroyed. Can an old man like me live alone? I said I'd go back, I'd go back to my life the way it was before and to the two women who couldn't do enough to serve me. Do you know what Fathiyyeh did when I went to visit her? She stood at her door and started yelling, and everyone gathered round her. As though I was a beggar. I didn't go to ask for anything, I went because God directed me to. I said, 'I'll get my wife back and I'll be decently taken care of. I'll get my children back. God took Intisar and the shop to punish me.' I went to make amends, and all I got was humiliation and abuse. Now I don't have the price of a loaf of bread."

I put my hand in my pocket but only found ten thousand lira. I gave them to him saying that was all I had.

"No, son, no. I don't beg."

He put out his second cigarette, stood up and left.

I know Fathiyyeh. That woman – I swear every time I think of Naheeleh I see Fathiyyeh's image. A tall, brown woman who covers her head with a white scarf and stands as straight as the letter *alif* – no bending, no shaking and no stumbling, as though the years passed by not inside but beside her.

I don't understand how Fathiyyeh accepted his second marriage. At the beginning the man hid it from her. He bought a house in Burj El Barajneh, where Ikram lived, and divided his time in two. He'd spend the night in his first wife's house in Shatila camp, and he'd spend a portion of the day with his second wife in Burj El Barajneh. Word got out and Fathiyyeh discovered what was going on. When Abu Kamal returned to the house exhausted from work – as he claimed – she asked him about it. A look of uncertainty crossed the man's face, and he thought of denying the rumour because he was afraid of how she'd react, but instead of denying it, he found himself telling the truth.

"Yes, I got married," he said. "And that's my legal right."

He waited for the storm.

But instead of getting angry and breaking dishes, as she was accustomed to do whenever she had a disagreement with her husband over the smallest of things, and instead of killing him, as he believed she might, this woman straight as an *alif* collapsed and broke in two. She bent over her face which she'd rested between her hands and started shaking with tears. Fathiyyeh broke apart at one go and never stood upright again till he divorced her.

That same day she made peace with Ikram, and the two women lived in one house with their ten children. As the family haemorrhaged children through the death and emigration of the boys and the marriage of the girls, the women found themselves alone, breathing the scents of messages sent from far away and chewing over their memories together.

After her divorce, Fathiyyeh became as she'd been before. The slump of her shoulders was erased and they became straight again; the long neck bore its white scarf, and the woman walked the roads of the destroyed camp as though she was flying over the rubble, as though the destruction was a sideshow whose sole purpose was to focus the viewer on the beauty of her commanding height and the splendour of her huge eyes.

When Abu Kamal tried to get his divorced wives back, Fathiyyeh neither yelled not wailed, as Abu Kamal claimed.

She stood at the door, pushed Ikram back and blocked it with her broad shoulders, so Ikram couldn't interfere. She knew Ikram's heart would crumble for the man who'd made her believe that his every footstep shook the earth. She kept Ikram behind her and raised her right hand, straightening her scarf with her left.

"Out!" she said. "Out!"

He tried to speak and she put her hand over her mouth to shut off her hatred and her screams, saying only those two words – "Out! Out!" The man left without daring to speak. He didn't even ask for the address of his son Subhi, who worked in Denmark. He saw the barrier rise in his face and he bowed before turning his back on the door Fathiyyeh had blocked with her body.

And now he comes up with the story that she wailed and made a scandal of him in front of the camp.

Why do people lie like that?

I'm convinced he believed himself. I'm convinced that when he told me the story of how he tried to get his divorced wives back, he heard the yells that never emerged from Fathiyyeh's mouth, covered as it was with her hand.

Tell me – you know better than I do – do we all lie like that? Did you lie to me too?

I told you your story with Naheeleh on the grounds that it was a beautiful story, and I didn't question your version of that last meeting beneath the Roman olive tree. You'll say it wasn't the last and tell stories of your visits that continued up until 1974, but that meeting was the last one as far as I'm concerned and as far as the story's concerned. For after Naheeleh had said what she said, there was no more talk, and when there's no more talk, there's no more anything.

When there's nothing new and fresh to say, when the words go rotten in your mouth and come out lifeless, old and dead, everything dies.

Isn't that what you told me after the fall of Beirut in '82? You said the old talk had died and now we needed a new Revolution. The old language was dead, and we were in danger of dying with it. We weren't fighting not because we didn't have weapons, but because we didn't have words.

On that day the words died, Yunis, and we entered a deep sleep from which we didn't awake until the *intifada* of the people inside. Then the papers published the picture of the child with his catapult and you said to me, "It seems it's begun again." It did indeed begin, but where was it going?

You've never liked this kind of question, even when the self-rule agreement was signed at the White House and we saw Rabin shaking hands with Arafat and we said everything was over.

You were sad, but not me. I seemed to myself to be like someone watching another person's death, and now I'll tell you that deep inside I was happy. Death isn't just a mercy, it's happiness too. That language had to die, and that world manufactured from dead words had to become extinct. I was happy as I watched the end and drew a false expression of sorrow on my face.

Do you remember?

I was at home, we were sitting in front of the television, and you were dragging every last bit of smoke from your cigarette down into your lungs and listening to the American talk. Then you turned to me and said, "No. This isn't the end. There was one end and we got past it, because after what happened in '48 there can't be an end.

"There was an end then, son, but we didn't end. What's happening now is just stages, and anything can change and be upended."

Your words broke up in front of me and scattered in all directions. Then you went out. You left me alone in front of the television tuned to the American talk. I waited for you till the television came to an end, then I turned it off and slept, feeling that psychic confusion that compelled me to mask my joy with simulated sorrow.

And now, tell me: how long are we supposed to wait?

Here am I, waiting for your end – excuse me, your beginning – in spite of everything, in spite of the smell of powder that emanates from your room, and in spite of your face, which spreads over the pillow like the face of a baby that has yet to come into its full roundness. I'm here, waiting for the end. No, I'm not in a hurry, and I don't have the slightest idea what my tasks will be after they close the hospital.

They say they're going to demolish the camp anyway, because the camp is no longer the camp – its borders have shrunk, and its spaces are up for grabs. I don't know who lives here now – Syrians, Egyptians, Sri Lankans, Indians . . . I don't know how they get in or where they find houses. Soon the bulldozers will come. They say the plan is to demolish the camp and turn the land into part of the expressway linking the airport to central Beirut.

Anything's possible here. Maybe we should start our exile again from scratch. I don't know.

I told you I'm waiting for nothing except the end, and then I don't know. Anyway, it's not important. I asked you about speaking the truth so I could understand why Mr Sinounou lied about things that didn't happen and then believed his own lie.

No. Not Shams.

I haven't told you anything about her, not because I don't want to, but because I don't know anything. A man only knows the woman he's loved when the talking ends; then he discovers her all over again and rearranges her in his memory. If she dies before that happens, she remains suspended in the miasma of memory.

Shams remained suspended because she disappeared in the middle of the talking and left me to discover on my own that the meanings of things are infinite. Shams disappeared into the jungle of her words and left me alone. I don't think it was all an illusion and I was just a parenthesis in her life, but I don't understand how anyone could be such a chameleon.

My problem with that woman was that I didn't know. When the love-making was over, she'd turn into a different woman, and it was always up to me to search for the woman who'd been in my bed.

Take it easy, I'll explain everything. Shams would disappear. She'd be with me and there would be her love. Then she'd disappear I don't know where. I'd wait for her and she wouldn't come. Then, when I'd almost given up hope as I didn't have any means of contacting her, I'd find her in my house, and she'd be another woman, and I'd have to start all over again.

I'd get lost in my search for her. I'd walk the roads, my heart thudding whenever I saw a woman who looked like her. And suddenly she'd knock on my door and come in, her long hair cut short like a boy's, her eyes full of wonder as though she was discovering a house she'd never been in before, and overwhelmed by shyness. She'd come to me wrapped in diffidence as though she didn't know me and start talking about politics, saying that she this and she that . . . I'll spare you her speeches on the necessity of re-organising ourselves in Lebanon etc.

When I approached her, she'd draw back and shyness would envelop her. I'd try to take her hand and she'd draw back as though she wasn't that Shams who only a few days earlier had been neighing in my bed. I'd take her slowly and watch her approaching slowly; then, when I had her in my arms, I'd feel the need to be sure she'd truly returned to me, so I'd whisper in her ear and ask her to say that "Ah!" that sharpened my desire, and she'd draw back again.

"I don't want to."

She'd leave me, sit on the sofa and light a cigarette. I'd wait a little, then I'd go back. I'd go back to her, I'd take her hand, and I'd start my journey again and hear that "Ah!" creeping out of her lips and eyes. When I took her in my arms as a man does a woman, she'd twist a little to one side, hide her face in my neck, say "Ah!" and take me to her.

When she was there, I'd forget that she'd disappear in the morning and that I'd have to start my search for her over again.

That's the question, Yunis: where's the truth in this relationship?

Is Shams Shams?

Is this woman that woman? Do I know her? Why did the smell of her body cling to my body and the sound of her voice to my head?

And I forgot to ask you, Yunis; why doesn't the lover feel he's a man like other men? Why to prove our masculinity are we forced to take refuge in lies and false claims and to bulking out our days with idle talk and boasting of our false adventures and then, when we come to the woman we love, to become like women?

Why does something like femininity awake within us?

It's true, the lover becomes like the female.

I confessed, I swear. Yes, I confessed, and I tried to tell her, but she didn't understand, and even if she'd understood . . . what would it have meant? Even if she'd loved me – and she did love me – or she'd betrayed me – and she did betray me – then what?

Come to think of it, why did she want to marry Samih? Why didn't she say she wanted to get married? I was prepared to marry her. I was I don't know what. Yes – why didn't I ask her to marry me? Now I say that I didn't dare, that the story she told about her former husband paralysed my ability to think and that her troubles over her daughter Dalal were the reason I couldn't conceive of marriage.

How do you propose marriage to a woman whose only interest lies in planning an operation to kidnap her daughter? She said she'd have no peace until she'd kidnapped Dalal from Amman and brought her to Beirut, and that she needed a man to help her. And when I said I was at her disposal, I saw a smile of pity.

"You, friend, are a doctor, and no use. I want a *real* man. I want a fedayeen fighter."

Was Samih the man she was looking for?

Didn't she tell me in a satiated moment, "You're my man"? How could I be her man and not be a real man? And how can you ask a woman to marry you when she tells you she's looking for another man? But no, I'm not sure, but I don't think she talked about Dalal with anyone but me. She'd be oblivious to Dalal the whole time, and her daughter would only come alive for her after we'd made love. I'd light my cigarette and take my first sip of cognac, and along would come Dalal and set up an impenetrable barrier between us. The words would die and Shams would be turned into tears – a woman who'd tell stories about her daughter and curse life and fate, and then suddenly jump up and say she was hungry. I don't know how she didn't get fat. She wolfed down huge quantities of food when she was with me.

"Why aren't you eating, Qays?"

She used to call me Qays: "I swear I'm going to treat you the way Layla did Qays and drive you mad."

And Qays, which is to say me, only ate a little. Should I have told her I didn't eat because I was only a lover? Once I said that, and what was her reaction?

"What a crazy idea! 'Seduction requires strength.' Eat, eat! Love needs food."

I was incapable of eating even though I was hungry. I was like someone who couldn't chew food. It was enough for me to keep her company and look at her Satanic eyes stealing glances at me and apologising for her insatiable appetite.

But maybe not. Maybe the reason I didn't ask her to marry me was that I didn't want her because I was afraid of her. Strange. Tell me; don't you think it's strange? Not you – it's impossible to make a comparison with you because Naheeleh was your wife and that explains everything. I don't want to trespass on your life.

But why didn't you do what Hamad did?

Like you Hamad was a fighter in the Sha'ab garrison – don't tell me you didn't know him. Umm Hassan told me his story. She said his sister refused to hold a wake for him after he died in her house in Ein El Hilweh, so the wake was held in Umm Hassan's house in Shatila.

Umm Hassan said they were stupid people: "They say he was Israeli. What do they mean Israeli? When we're treated like shit and go to prison for the sake of our children and our land, does that make us traitors?"

I won't tell you the story of Hamad's return to his village in Galilee because I'm sure you know it. I just wanted to say that perhaps you also were afraid of love.

Take any love story, master. What is a love story? The story we call a love story is usually a story of the impossibility of love. People only write about love as something impossible. Isn't that the story of Qays and Layla, and of Romeo and Juliet? Isn't it the story of Khaleel and Shams? All lovers are like that; they become a story of unconsummated love, as though love can't be consummated, or as though we fear it or don't know how to tell about it, or, and this is the worst, we don't recognise it when we're living it.

What did Qays Ibn Al Mulawwah do? Nothing. They stopped him seeing his sweetheart Layla, so he went mad.

Didn't you make me a promise, heart,
    You'd give up Layla if I did so too?
Behold – I've given up my love for her.
    How then, when her name is said, you swoon?

Nice words and lovely poetry, but the man was crazy and his beloved married another man.

And Romeo, what did he do? He killed himself.

And what about all the other lovers? All of them loved at a distance and lived their love apart, so they became impossible stories.

Don't you agree?

Is it because love is impossible? I swear, every time Shams left me I felt the taste of wood in my mouth.

Was it because I didn't want to be parted from her?

Do you know that beautiful verse from the Koran, "They are a vestment for you, and you are a vestment for them?" How are we to become vestments for one another – I mean, how are we to become one?

That's what love is, which is why we can't talk about it. We talk only about its impossibility or its tragedy or its victims and its fatalities.

The thing we're incapable of describing is when lovers are together. In fact, it may be that no-one lives it and we begin by inventing the reasons that distance us from it.

It's as though love has no language. It's like smells. How can we describe a smell? We describe it in terms of what it doesn't contain, and we don't give it a name. Love's the same. It has a name only when it isn't there.

I don't mean to belittle the importance of your love for Naheeleh. I know that you loved her and that your infatuation was great. I know that she dwelt in your bones. I know that you're dying today because of her.

But why didn't you go back, the way Hamad did?

How was it that Hamad went to prison and succeeded in returning to his house and his wife, and such a possibility never occurred to you?

Don't tell me you sacrificed yourself for the Revolution, because I don't believe you.

Please don't misunderstand. I don't want to denigrate the history of your generation. Your history is my history, and I respect you and honour you and hold you in the highest regard.

But tell me, wasn't there an element of fear of her in your decision? Didn't you prefer – unconsciously perhaps – that Naheeleh would be where she was and you where you were? That way your story would continue and survive across space and time. Every time you went to see her, you put your life in danger. Every time, you purchased your love at the cost of the possibility of your death. Isn't that wonderful? Isn't that a story like no other?

Tell me, when you were walking the roads of the two Galilees, of Palestine and of Lebanon, did you feel that your thorn-lacerated feet bore a love story like no other?

As for me, though, what a let-down!

I know my story doesn't deserve to be put alongside yours. I'm just a duped lover; that's what everyone thinks. But no, Shams isn't so simple that you can sum her up by saying she betrayed me. And "betrayed" isn't accurate. I wasn't her husband, so why did she come to me? If there hadn't been love, she wouldn't have come; if there hadn't been love, her presence wouldn't have bewitched me; if there hadn't been love, I wouldn't have hidden like a dog in this hospital out of fear of revenge. I confess I was afraid and I believed the rumours about the people of El Ammour vowing to take revenge on their daughter's killers. But that time has passed.

If they'd wanted to kill me, they'd have killed me. I live in the hospital because I've got used to it, that's all. I could go back to my house if I wanted to, but my house is near the mosque and I don't like cemeteries.

None of Shams's family put in an appearance except Khadeeja, her mother. She came to Ein El Hilweh camp, took her daughter's things and went back without making contact with anyone here. I heard that nobody visited to pay their respects. She didn't stay in the camp more than twenty-four hours. She went into her daughter's house, closed the doors and windows, remained inside over night and came out in the morning carrying a large suitcase. She spoke to no-one, and at the Lebanese Army barrier at the camp entrance, the one we still call the Armed Struggle barrier, she turned round, spat and left.

There's nothing to fear. The woman came and went, and I'm here not out of fear but out of habit.

Plus, I want to review my life in peace and quiet.

You want the truth, right?

I'll try and tell you the truth, but don't ask me, "Why did you accept?" – I didn't accept. No, I didn't. And no-one consulted me. I found myself in the maelstrom and I almost died, and if Abu Ali Hassan hadn't been there, they would've executed me.

That's right, master. No, not Shams's relatives, the Ein El Hilweh camp militia. They supposed, wrongly of course, that I was the one who put the killers up to it because that way I'd have supplanted Samih and had the woman all to myself. They didn't believe everybody's version that Shams killed her lover herself. They supposed someone else had been involved and arrested me.

I was too embarrassed to tell you about my arrest. The only thing about it that sticks in my memory is their insulting references to "horns" and the way they treated me as a nobody. This was what saved me, and it only happened after Abu Ali's intervention. Can you believe it? He intervened on my behalf to ensure I was mistreated. There was no other way out – mistreatment or execution. Abu Ali saved me by means of that mistreatment; if it hadn't been for him, they'd have killed me as they killed Shams.

I won't tell you about the interrogation. A man came and delivered a letter from the Ein El Hilweh militia inviting me to visit them, and I went. They escorted me directly to Ein El Hilweh prison, where they threw me in a dark underground vault, full of damp and the smell of decay, and left me.

I rotted in the vault for ten days, which were like ten years – time got mixed up in my head, and I lived underground as though I was floating in the night of my entire life.

They took me out to go to the interrogation session. A man came holding the kind of pick we normally use for breaking up blocks of ice and started jabbing it into my chest and asking me to confess.

He'd stab me with the pick and ask, "What did you do to Samih, dog?" and I'd ask him who this Samih was. He'd repeat his question as though he wasn't expecting an answer.

A stupid interrogator, you'll say.

But no, master. He was neither an interrogator nor stupid. He was just a criminal. Crime has spread everywhere in our ranks. We've watered it with blood and stupidities. We've wallowed in error, and error has consumed us.

Can you credit it?

They arrest you and throw you into the darkness and don't ask you a single question? They throw you into an underground vault where you live with your waste and the next thing you see is an ice-pick in your chest, and they ask you about someone you don't know and don't wait for an answer?

Ten days in nowhere, and if it hadn't been for Abu Ali, God knows how long I'd have remained there. Abu Ali Hassan is a comrade of mine from the El Khreibeh base in 1968, and he told me he saved me because he was certain of my innocence. He believed "the whore" had tricked me.

They escorted me to the interrogation and there the contemptuous looks and sarcastic smiles fell upon me and I understood. Instead of feeling furious, however, and trying to defend my honour, I felt afraid for Shams and a single idea possessed me, which was how to rescue her from their hands. I could read the decision to kill her in their eyes, and I didn't want her to die. At the time I didn't know what life taught me later, which is that death is the lover's relief.

Nothing can save you from love but death.

If I'd known that, I'd have killed her myself.

At the interrogation, however, I was possessed by fear for her, and instead of going home and back to work when I was released, I decided to look for her and try to save her. I went to the outskirts of Maghdousheh, east of Tyre, where the fighters had bases. I knew she commanded a military detachment there that they called the Shams Detachment and that she refused to accept orders from the military command in the south because they were directly under the command of Tunis. That's what she told me and I didn't believe her, but when I went to Maghdousheh I found out that this time she hadn't lied. There really was an armed detachment known as "Shams's bunch," but it wasn't at Maghdousheh. I was told that Shams's group had withdrawn towards Majdalyoun.

I went to Majdalyoun and didn't find her.

I was like a blind man, walking the roads of the south, looking for her and not finding her. Everywhere I went I encountered the same strange looks, as though everyone knew the story.

I searched and found nothing. I crossed Majdalyoun, went to the house they told me was the headquarters of Shams's group and found it empty – a five-room house surrounded by a garden with fruit trees. I went inside and found blankets on the floor and plastic bags and cooking pans and a smell of rotten food. It looked as though they'd evacuated the place in a hurry and hadn't had time to organise their departure. I lay down on a blanket and felt like crying. I was like someone besieged by tears, crying without crying, without emotions or feelings – nothing. I existed in the nothing and in tears, and I knew she was lost.

Shams was lost, and I didn't know how I'd manage the empty spaces in my life without her.

I closed my eyes, squeezed them closed as hard as I could, and the darkness filled up with grey holes, and despair overwhelmed me.

My son, Yunis, do you know what it means to feel incapable of living?

Once I told her I couldn't imagine life without her, and she patted my shoulder and picked up Mahmoud Darwish's collected poems and started reading –

Take me to a distant land
Take me to the distant land, sobbed Rita. Never-ending
Is this winter –
And she smashed the porcelain of day on the window's iron,
Placed her small revolver on the draft of the poem
And threw her socks on the chair, breaking the cooing.
Thus she passed into the unknown barefoot, and I was subsumed
in my going.

– naked on the bed reading, the pages gleaming in front of her, her voice twisting, bending and shimmering as I looked at her and failed to understand. I hear the rhythm of her voice mixed with the rhythm of the rhymes, and I see her body shimmering.

She closed the book and asked, "What's wrong? Don't you like poetry?"

"I like it, I like it," I said, "but you're more beautiful than poetry."

"Liar," she said. "My ambition is to become like Rita as Mahmoud Darwish wrote her. Have you heard Marcel Khalifa's song "Between Rita and my eyes there is a rifle"? I'd like to be like Rita, with a poet coming along and putting a rifle between me and him."

She stood up suddenly and said she was hungry and was going to make pasta.

I didn't tell her I wasn't always like that. I like poetry a lot and I memorise it, but when we're in the presence of a wild outpouring of beauty, words are no longer possible.

In those moments when I was alone in the house in Majdalyoun, in the midst of traces of her, I smelled the smell of pasta inside the grey spots dancing in front of my closed eyes and I felt my death. Believe me, without her I'm nothing – alone with the nothing, alone with what was left of her things, alone with her ghost.

I slept deeply among the smells of decay that fumed out of the blankets in that abandoned house.

I fell asleep and floated above mysterious dreams, as though I was no longer me. And I saw her. It was Shaheeneh wearing khaki trousers and a khaki shirt as though she was Shams. I saw her standing in the rain. The ropes of rain tied the ground to the sky, and she stood under a flowering almond tree.

"How can the almond flower in winter?" I asked her.

The branches of the tree shook and the blossoms started to fall. I ran to gather them up and she pointed her rifle at me. "Go back," she yelled. "The Jews are here."

I was a child. No, I became a child. No, I saw myself as a child, and I started jumping to regain my height because I'm not a child and it wasn't Shaheeneh, it was Shams.

"Why are you doing this to me, Shams?" I shouted.

Shaheeneh said she was going.

I went up to her and the earth opened up beneath my feet and I was drowning. I was a child drowning in the rain. The huge drops struck me and I felt pain.

"Mummy!" I cried.

And I saw Shaheeneh who was like Shams turn her back and disappear into the water.

The dreams are all mixed up in my head now, but when I woke there to the sound of their footsteps, I wasn't afraid. I felt feet kicking me and rifles pummelling my head, so I curled up into a ball to avoid as many of the kicks as I could.

They stood me up against the wall and told me to put my hands up. Then they turned me around to face the wall and started searching me for weapons while I remained like a zombie. I didn't resist because I no longer resisted.

Since the stadium, when I'd decided I wasn't going to go with the people who got on the Greek ships, I'd said, "Enough."

But where are we to find this enough?

You say, "Enough," and history drags you by the hair back to war.

I said, "Enough," and was sucked into the massacre. I said, "Enough," and the War of the Camps overwhelmed me. I said, "Enough," and found myself crucified on the wall of an abandoned house in a village of ghosts called Majdalyoun.

And now I say, "Enough," and I find myself with this little child in whom death dances exultantly, as though we were born, and die, in death.

I was standing against the wall, sleepiness spreading through me, and with the image of Shaheeneh in Shams's body as she left me in the rain. Why did she leave me to drown? Who would abandon a child asking for help? To do so would be impermissible and shameful even in a dream. I was standing and the man was searching me as though he was taking my bones apart, piece by piece. Then he ordered me to turn around and I saw four young men, the oldest not more than twenty. They were like children at play. That's war — it should be like a game; when we stop playing, we're afraid, and when we're afraid, we die.

I stood against the wall awaiting my death, but they didn't kill me. Their boss showered me with questions, but I didn't answer. What was I supposed to say? Was I supposed to tell the truth and make myself look stupid?

When the commander despaired of my face, with its sheen of sleep, he ordered them to take me away. One of them came forward, undid the buttons of my shirt and pulled it up to cover my face. They put me into a Land Rover and took me away. In those moments, within the swaying of the furrowed roads and with sleep returning to me, I wanted that woman; I wanted to give her the almond flowers I'd gathered for her.

Sleep, however, wouldn't come, and I found myself in a dark cell like the one I'd been held in before. My guess is that they'd decided to leave me to live out my three days in prison as though in the belly of death. It is I that am Yunis — Jonah — not you. I lived in darkness for three days without food or water. I was sure they'd forgotten me and that I'd die inside that dark vault, and no-one would know what had become of me.

On the third day, however, they took me out of the cell to interrogate me, and the interrogator guffawed in my ear.

"What, Mr Horns!" he said. "What were you doing there?"

I said I'd gone looking for her.

"And why were you searching for her?"

"To understand."

When I said "To understand," the man burst into a long, hysterical laugh and started coughing and trying to say something. Then, in the middle of his coughing and laughing, he gestured for them to throw me out.

Thus it was that I was twice arrested for her sake and twice released.

I returned to my house, leaving Shams to her fate. Don't say I didn't try to save her. I returned to my house and waited for her death, and she died.

What else do you want to know?

I swear I don't know. All I can see now is a question mark. Why did she come from Jordan? And how did she become an officer in Fatah? And how did she put her military group together?

Questions I don't know how to answer. All I know is that I know nothing.

Would you like to hear the story?

I'll tell you as long as you don't tell me it's unbelievable. Believe first, then I'll tell. I'm no longer prepared to go looking for the truth of stories or their lack of it. I mean, none of our stories are believable, but does that mean we should forget them?

I believed it because it resembled your story, but your story, and those of Reem or Naheeleh in Sha'ab, and that of Adnan in the prison or in the mental hospital, are all unbelievable stories, yet they're still true. You know them and I know them and everybody knows them.

My question, then, is . . .

No, there isn't a question.

But let's suppose there was a question. The question would be: Why don't we believe ourselves? Why do I feel that things that happened to me or to others have turned into shadows? You, for instance – aren't you the shadow of the man you were? And that man – was he a hero, or a lie or an illusion?

I know I disturb you when I throw this kind of question at you, and I know you'd rather be on your own now, because now you're . . . God, how beautiful you are! If you could open your eyes just once, you'd see your face in the mirror. An older man opening his eyes and seeing himself as a child, seeing his body liberated from the sack holding his life. You're the one who came up with that theory, remember?

You used to say that the years a man lived were a sack he carried on his back, but we couldn't see it because no-one can see his own life. Our life is like a dream: life trundles us along and time trundles us along and we don't realise. Then suddenly, after we reach forty, we start feeling it, as though time had built up inside a large sack on our backs and was weighing us down.

Do you remember when you came to Naheeleh exhausted and wounded after the Israeli ambush you fell into and which to this day you don't know how you escaped from without dying?

You found yourself lying on the ground in the valley, bleeding. You picked yourself up and went to her. There, in the cave of Bab El Shams, the woman anointed your wounds with oil and brought you back to life. As you made your way heavily towards the cave, you were certain that this time you'd die. And you didn't feel sorrow. You told me that when you tapped on her window and went, you were certain you were going to your death. All the images and memories stopped moving in your eyes, and you saw yourself as a shadow walking towards its shadow.

You came round to find Naheeleh covering your head with her white headscarf, anointing your wounds with oil and rocking you as a mother rocks her child. Naheeleh tried to remove the bullet lodged in your thigh but couldn't, and you got better with the bullet where it was. I feel it under my fingers now when I bathe you. The bullet is getting bigger and you are getting smaller, and there's no need to remove it. We'll let it go with you to wherever you go to.

That day you told Naheeleh that the sack was getting heavy on your back and asked her about her sack, and she smiled and said nothing.

Naheeleh would smile and say nothing, hiding her secret in that broad smile of hers which transformed her eyes into a forest of olives and night.

That day you told her that the years were a man's cross and talked to her about Christ. She listened and loved what you said and said that you spoke like your mother, who hid an icon of the Virgin Mary under her pillow.

You told Naheeleh that Christ was crucified on the cross of the years he didn't live, for life is like the Cross – in the end we'll find ourselves hung upon it.

Naheeleh said you'd started to talk like a philosopher and smiled.

You, however, felt a great load on your back. Your load was heavy and had started to weigh you down. No, your back didn't bend, because you were active to the end, but that accursed sack bent your neck a little, and you started to walk with your eyes to the ground.

Look now and see how beautiful and new you are. You've cast it off your back, and your childhood has commenced. You're an ageless child again. The years that were behind you are now ahead of you.

No-one will believe me.

I tell Dr Amjad or Kamilya or Nurse Zeinab, and they think I'm mad. It's as though they can't see. I say to them, "Look!" and they don't see. Amjad stands at your head and says the danger is now in your heart; at any moment a heart attack might occur and the man might die.

I know more about medicine than he does. I know what the chances are of a heart attack. But nobody wants to see or believe; even you have become like them. I implore you to open your eyes once and look in the mirror, and you'll be surprised. You'll see how a person can cast the sack of years off his back, return to his childhood and find himself at the beginning.

I told you nothing about our story was believable. Shams too is un-believable, but you have to believe me. I know that when I tell Shams's story I'll kill her. This time Shams will be killed by words. All those people who gathered in the hills of El Miyyeh wi-Miyyeh failed to kill her because she's still alive within me, her infidelity radiating from her hot body and her fingers as though I was still holding her hands in mine and watching her long, slender fingers, kissing them one by one, igniting her via her fingers.

Shams still burns, Yunis, but it seems the time has come. I feel I have to shroud her in the little sack of years that she carried on her back. I feel the time for her death has come. So I'll tell you the whole story, from the beginning, and I'll bury Shams with words, as you and I buried Naheeleh.

Now it's my turn.

I can no longer hold on to my woman. I have to bury her as people bury their dead and their stories.

*

Shams's story began in 1960, when she was born in El Wahdat in Amman. Her father was called Ahmad Salih Hussein, her mother Khadeeja Mahmoud Ali. Ahmad had married Khadeeja in their village of El Ammour, in the district of Jerusalem, in 1947. One year later they'd had their first son, Salih, who died in September 1970 in the fighting in Jordan.

Ahmad and Khadeeja found themselves with their baby, Salih, who wasn't yet a year old, among the throngs of inhabitants of El Ammour who were expelled from their village in 1948, following the establishment of the State of Israel. The family took up residence in the caves near Bethlehem, as did all the other villagers, and would slip back to the village to search for provisions. Then everything came to a halt because collective border crossings became more difficult, and because the provisions had run out and all the houses of the villages had been blown up.

In 1950, after a new child, whom they called Ammouri in hopeful memory of the demolished village, had been born, the family moved to Aydeh camp, in the town of Deir Jasir. There Ahmad found himself a job in a pasta factory owned by Abu Sa'eed El Husseini. His wages were a shilling a day, and the shilling was enough because the man used to bring sufficient pasta home from the factory to feed the family.

From then on, the family ate only pasta. Even after the factory closed and they moved to El Wahdat in Amman, Ahmad kept making pasta at home. People even called them "the Italians" because all Ahmad talked about in the camp were the virtues and benefits of pasta and the greatness of the Italian people who'd invented it. Ahmad didn't know that pasta was invented by the Chinese, not the Italians, but how could he have done?

She was known as "the Italian girl" in Jordan, but people forgot the name in Beirut, and Shams, who hated pasta as a child, rediscovered it when I fell in love with her. She said that love had brought her back to her Italian roots, and all we ate was pasta, except on rare occasions when I'd prepare our food, in which case I'd make fried cauliflower with *taratur* sauce.

As you see, there's nothing unusual about Shams's story so far, except for the pasta. We were all expelled from our villages, we all slipped back into them in search of food, we all stopped doing that after the houses and villages were destroyed, and all of us took the jobs that there were.

In 1960, the year Shams was born, Abu Sa'eed El Husseini's factory closed. It's said he went bankrupt when imported Italian pasta flooded the market and the national pasta industry collapsed because there was no tariff barrier.

Abu Sa'eed El Husseini closed his factory in Bethlehem, and Ahmad found himself out of work with a wife and five children (a boy and two girls had been born before Shams). He decided to move from Bethlehem to Amman, to the Ras El Ein district, where he worked on the stone crushers. Then after two years he moved to El Wahdat camp, taking up residence in the development area on the border and building a sheet-metal shack in which he lived with his family. The house resembled a museum of advertisements of every kind and colour. Ahmad Salih got the metal sheets from the cans discarded on rubbish dumps and in the roads and was not alone in doing so, as most of the shacks in the development area were built from sheet metal; people would change the sheets according to the season, since some of them would wear out before others as a result of being exposed to sun, rain and damp.

Shams's house looked very like an oblong billboard.

Shams said she lived a great part of her life in the house of coloured sheeting, a house that turned into an oven in summer and a freezer in winter, and with a father who spoke to his wife only to discuss the need to change this or that wall because it had started to wear out: "I lived all my life in dilapidation: the house was wearing out, my father was wearing out, and everything was drenched in water and sun. My father would go off to his work at the stone crushers and return exhausted and at the end of his tether, and the only thing he could find to amuse himself was to make pasta and yell at my mother because she hadn't made the dough properly."

Shams said that when she remembered those days she did so with a strange tenderness, and she first felt alienation when their house in the camp changed. Concrete arrived and you couldn't change the walls any more. Everything arrived with the Revolution, and Ahmad Salih, whose cousin found him a job in one of the Popular Front offices, left his work on the stone crushers and added two new rooms to his house. That was when Shams said she felt alienated. She was nine when everything in the house changed. The roof stopped leaking, the walls no longer bore the colours of advertisements, and Shams felt some part of her had died.

Her childhood was coterminous with the house being torn down, and her periods started. Her mother told her she was like all the other girls of El Ammour: "We're like that. All our girls grow up at nine." Her mother explained everything to her and told her she had to get ready for marriage. Shams waited for her husband.

She waited for him as a schoolgirl at the UNWRA school.

She waited for him while training at the cadets' camp.

She waited for him as she watched her brother die after being hit by the bullets of the Jordanian Army's Bedouin detachment in 1970.

And she waited for him when she saw how her father was arrested after the closure of the Popular Front office and then found himself a job in a pasta factory belonging to a member of the Alwan family in Amman.

She waited for him as she saw the concrete walls of the house corrode and become like the sheet metal that had enclosed her childhood.

Then came the husband and the nightmares.

How can you expect me to tell you about Fawwaz Mohammed Nassar when I only know him mutilated by Shams's words? When she spoke of him she'd mutilate him: she'd take a small piece of a brown paper bag or a newspaper or a Kleenex or a book and start chewing on it and spitting it out, so I only saw the man drawn on mutilated paper. She would talk and mutilate, and the tears would pour out of her.

Have you ever seen a woman weeping not from her eyes but with everything inside her? Everything in Shams wept as she mutilated Fawwaz Mohammed Nassar and spat out the little bits of paper she was chewing. And then suddenly she'd wipe away her tears as though it was nothing, as though the woman who cried was another woman, and start gobbling the dish of boiled pasta for which she'd made a special sauce of cream and basil leaves. She'd eat and sniff the basil and say the smell intoxicated her. She'd eat as though her appetite had exploded inside her. She'd say she wanted nothing from Fawwaz; she'd just go to Amman, kidnap Dalal and bring her back to Beirut.

"I won't start my life without Dalal. Look."

And she'd take a photo from the pocket of her khaki jacket.

"See how beautiful she is. I swear she's the most beautiful girl in the world."

I'd look and not see the most beautiful girl in the world. I'd see a pretty child with curly hair and a little brown face dominated by large eyes with long lashes.

"Look at her eyelashes! How can I leave her with the Beast?"

When Shams was holding Dalal's picture, she was transformed into another woman. I'd see tenderness and sorrow and weakness gathered on her brow, and I'd try to hug her but she'd push me away as though refusing to share Dalal with me. Then she'd turn to me and say she needed a man to help her kidnap Dalal. If I said that that man was right there in front of her, she'd look at me with pity.

"I need a fedayeen fighter, my dear. Not some doctor like you."

Then I'd tell her I was a fedayeen fighter and talk to her about our first camps in El Khreibeh and Kafar Shouba.

"You? Incredible!"

In fact, I made a mistake. I shouldn't have told her how the officer made me crawl in front of the platoon and how that made me lose my self-respect as a Political Commissar and as a soldier.

That was my unforgivable error, to confess that I wasn't brave enough to prevent the officer from humiliating me.

I wanted to be a blank page with her. I told her I was a blank page and she could write whatever she wanted on it, but she wasn't looking for a blank page. Why, then, did she stay with me? Why was she here, and then with Samih there? I swear I don't know, because I don't understand how the devils that inhabit our bodies think.

Yes, Yunis. I waited for her until she died. I went back from the prison and didn't leave my house until after I heard about her murder, because I thought she might come to hide in my house. How naïve I was. I didn't remain in my house to protest my arrest, as was rumoured in the camp. I remained in my house waiting for her. And I was ready – ah, if only she'd come! Every part of my body hurt; separation causes pain in the joints, the chest, the knees.

I didn't wait to find out what she'd done, because I loved her. It no longer made any difference to me whether she'd been unfaithful or not. It wasn't me that was the point, it was her. But she didn't come. Of course she wasn't aware that I was waiting for her; her crime enveloped her, and the world was blood. I can describe her to you, son, even though I didn't see her. I can see the red halo around her head and the spots of blood. Ever since we sank into our own blood, blood has dogged us and tied us to itself with a long thread looped around our necks.

After she died, I left my house and walked in the streets of the camp as though I'd avenged my honour. I walked like a fatuous revenge-taker even though all the sorrow in the world was pent up inside me. I didn't weep for Shams and I'll never weep for her, for all the tears can never be enough. Like an idiot I walked with my head held high as though I'd had my revenge.

The rumours started and I took refuge in the hospital out of fear. I was afraid because I knew her; she was a woman capable of killing all her men. She did kill us all – me and Samih and I don't know who else. Crime is like love: we kill another person – and we love a man or a woman – because they're a substitute for another man or woman.

I was a substitute for two men I didn't know – Samih, whom I'd never heard of, and Fawwaz, whom I never met. All the same, I was their stand-in. Samih died, Fawwaz took Dalal, and I'm here.

Where were we?

I told you Shams was ready for marriage at nine, and they married her off at fifteen. Fawwaz came, and he was twenty-four. He married her and took her to Lebanon. But it wasn't Fawwaz who came, it was Abu Ahmad Nassar, and he asked for her for his son Fawwaz, who'd finished his engineering studies at Beirut Arab University and was working for the Resistance. Then he took her to Beirut. The girl got to El Wahdat and became acquainted with her husband in a small house in Tell El Za'tar camp, which was situated in the eastern suburbs, and lived a year and a half under the roaring of cannons and the sound of bullets.

She said her husband scared her more than the war.

"He'd only have sex with me when we were being shelled. He was like a devil. I never saw him except in the house. He'd turn up out of nowhere covered in dust, having left his position and he'd come to me with the smell of dust and sweat and take me without taking his clothes off. I never once saw him naked.

"He was an official in the camp militia, but I don't know anything about his duties as he never told me.

"His father took me to Beirut; we had an exhausting journey by car from Amman. When we got to the house in Tell El Za'tar, his father stood at the door and didn't go in. He kissed his son, said, 'I've brought you the bride,' and left. During the six hours we spent together in the taxi from Amman to Beirut, he didn't speak to me. He sat next to me and never spoke to me. He'd look at me from time to time and say, 'Amazing!'

"My father said I was going to get married, my mother nodded in agreement, and I got married. I was like a blind woman. Like a blind woman I covered the distance between Amman and Beirut, and like a blind woman I entered the house of the husband I didn't know. My husband's father delivered me to my new house and left, and I found myself standing in the house, holding my suitcase, as though I was at a railway station.

"'Hello, Shams,' said Fawwaz. 'Come in and have a bath.'

"I went into the kitchen, heated water in a bowl I carried to the bathroom, and washed my body with the bay-laurel soap my mother had put in my case, advising me to wash myself with it before going in to my husband. I bathed and then entered Fawwaz's world to discover that he wasn't an engineer or anything. He'd come to Beirut to study engineering, then taken a job in a tile factory close to Mar Elias camp and forgotten about engineering. With the beginnings of the civil war he'd joined the Resistance and been inducted into the Tell El Za'tar militia.

"I'm not beautiful, but at Tell El Za'tar I discovered that I'm a woman in the eyes of men insatiable for life. There was shelling and war and death, and everything was coming undone.

"Fawwaz would go crazy with jealousy. I won't tell you what he did. At the beginning, he'd bang his head against the wall till the blood ran. He'd sleep with me, and then the scene with the wall would start, and I didn't understand. 'You're a whore and the daughter of a whore,' he'd say.

"I was afraid. I was living through a war that seemed to have no end, and Fawwaz didn't seem to want it to end. I'd ask him when he was going to return to his work, and he'd look at me in amazement and say he wasn't an engineer and didn't want to go back to the tile factory.

"'What's wrong with it?' I'd ask him. 'Those things aren't important. My father was a pasta twister, but we still had our self-respect. What matters are morals.'

"He'd frown. 'Morals, you whore? I got stuck with a whore!'

"I don't know – maybe he wanted me to be a whore, maybe he was afraid of me, but I didn't do anything. I swear I didn't look at another man. Well, I did, but that was after a long time, while we were withdrawing from the camp after it fell.

"Do you know what he did?

"He left his position and rushed to the house. 'Listen,' he said. 'I'm going to withdraw with the other fighters. You surrender with the women. We'll meet in Beirut,' and he gave me the address of someone called Kareem Abd El Fattah, Abu Rami, in El Fakahani.

"'I'll go with you,' I told him.

"'No. This is safer,' he said."

"He looked at me with savage eyes. 'You're afraid of getting raped!' he said, and he left.

"What can I tell you? Of course I was afraid, and I didn't understand why he wouldn't take me with him. Did he want me to die? What had I done to him? I'd lived through the toughest times with him. You know what life's like during a siege. All we could find to eat was lentils. I lived on my own like an alien. I'd go to the public water pipe and wait in the line of death: the water was in their line of fire. We called it 'the blood pipe'. I lived alone with nothing to do but wait for him. He'd come, caked with dust and gravel, sleep with me and leave. He wouldn't eat the lentils I'd cooked because he ate with the boys.

"All I wanted was one thing – to go back to my family in Amman. But how could I leave? The camp was closed by the siege. I wanted him to pay attention to me, but I didn't dare ask for anything: he was a fighter and we were at war. Even his visits and his sex were quick. And every time he slept with me, he'd bang his head against the wall, accuse me of being unfaithful and say I was a prostitute and that my body was a site of evil.

"He came and said he was withdrawing and asked me to surrender with the women.

"I knew what I could expect, so I decided to withdraw with the fighters and went to the eastern edge of the camp. I put on jeans and a green shirt and went to look for Fawwaz but couldn't find him. It seems he was in one of the first groups to withdraw.

"That was when I met Ahmad Kayyali, who gave me a Kalashnikov and said, 'Come with us.'

"We crossed the Monteverde area, which is full of pines. We walked by night and laid up by day. And there, in the midst of scattered bullets and nights of death, I made up my mind to leave Fawwaz. If I lived, I wouldn't go back to him. Ahmad was my first lover. With him I discovered I had a body and that my body deserved the pleasures of life. When Fawwaz had sex with me, he'd say 'Pleasure me,' and I had no idea how to 'pleasure' him. All I was aware of was his panting on top of me and that thing that penetrated me below, as though it was wounding me. With him I'd reach the edge of orgasm but not get there. Ahmad was quite different. I was bedded down with him and invited him to come close. We were lost in the forest. We'd left the camp with about twenty fighters. The first night we walked, then dawn broke and we decided to split up to wait for dark. They started off in different directions, but I didn't know what to do. Ahmad took me with him and we hid on a rocky slope, not daring to breathe. Ahmad asked me – he was a boy of about my age, but he was like the men, he'd use colloquial mixed with classical Arabic to get me to take him seriously – he asked me where I was going to go in Beirut. I said, to the house of Abu Rami, Kareem Abd El Fattah.

"'Do you know him?' he asked.

"'No. They gave me his name,' I said.

"'And your family, where's your family?'

"'In Amman,' I said.

"'My family's in Nablus,' he said.

"'Why did you come to Beirut?' I asked.

"'To join the fedayeen,' he said. 'And you?'

"I felt tears pouring from my eyes. Ahmad put his hand on my head and moved closer to me, so I said, 'Take me,' and he took me. With him I discovered what it means for a woman to sleep with a man. Ahmad disappeared after that; he disappeared at Hammana, when we got to the assembly point. I don't know where he went and I don't know anything about him. We reached Hammana, he disappeared, and I went down with the groups of fighters to Beirut, and I thought of not going to Abu Rami's house. But where was I to go? I thought of going to one of the Fatah offices, but as I wasn't a Fatah member I didn't have a card. Stupid – who'd have asked for a card in those days? So I did go to Abu Rami's house and I didn't find Fawwaz. Umm Rami said he was staying with the boys in the museum district, waiting for me.

"'Go to him now,' said Umm Rami.

"'But I don't know Beirut and I don't know the museum or anything.'

"She asked her son Rami to accompany me. I got into the orange Renault 12 next to him and we left. Suddenly he stopped the car and opened the back windows; it seems I smelled unbearably. He parked the car in a side street, motioned with his hand to a square where people were congregating, and said, 'There.'

"I got out, my rifle in my hand, and walked among the crowds. I was exhausted, and Ahmad's smell went with me everywhere. I looked for Fawwaz for a long time before I found him standing with the weeping women. These were the women who'd arrived in Lebanese Red Cross vehicles and who, the moment they got down from the lorries, started lamenting and wailing – women and children and wailing and pushing and shoving in front of the missing-persons registration office; women telling of people being raped, of executions against walls, of bodies dragged through streets. Fawwaz was standing in the middle of them. I went up to him, but he didn't notice me, maybe because I was wearing trousers and carrying a rifle. I forgot to mention that he'd forbidden me to wear trousers.

"'It's me, Fawwaz.'

"When he saw me, he jumped like a madman. 'I was wrong,' he said. 'I'm crazy. I should have brought you with me.'

"He took me by my arm and took the rifle from me as though to throw it aside.

"'That's my rifle. Leave it alone.'

"I snatched the rifle from his hand and we left. He stopped a car and told the driver, 'To Hamra.' There, near the Cinema Sarola stop, we went into a cheap hotel, where he hired a room on the second floor. As soon as we got inside the room, he attacked me and started tearing at my clothes.

"'Take it easy, man. I want to wash.'

"He slept with me with Ahmad's smell still clinging to me. I don't know if he smelled the other man, but he hit me. In the hotel he hit me; before that, he hadn't. He'd banged his head against the wall and sworn at me. But in the hotel in Hamra Street he hit me after he'd had sex with me twice in succession, and he said he'd fixed up a house in Burj El Barajneh and we'd go there."

Shams lived in Burj El Barajneh until 1982, in other words until the fedayeen left Beirut. She lived that amazing, barely believable life with Fawwaz. True, I'm a doctor, or something like it, and true, doctors, through their long acquaintance with their patients, come to understand people's psychologies, since half of all illnesses at least are psychological in origin, but still I couldn't understand. I asked Shams about Fawwaz's childhood, but what she knew didn't provide me with an explanation.

"Were you unfaithful," I asked, "and he found out?"

She said she never betrayed him except with Ahmad, but Fawwaz made her forget the taste of the love she'd experienced in Monteverde.

She said Fawwaz was always afraid of her and always accusing her and saying he'd got stuck with a prostitute and abusing her because she didn't get pregnant.

"I don't know why I didn't get pregnant in Lebanon and why I did in Jordan, but after the night in Monteverde I wanted to get pregnant so I could have a boy like Ahmad. But I didn't get pregnant and I forgot Ahmad; the only thing I remember about him was the feeling of his lips on my breast – God, how sweet that was! It was the first time a man had sucked on my nipples. Fawwaz would rub my breast and then bite it. But when Ahmad took my nipple between his lips, waves rose within me and I felt my depths moving towards him and taking him. Fawwaz was nothing like that. He was a beast. He'd spread-eagle me half naked and say he could only get aroused when he could hear the bullets, and I was at the end of a gun and afraid. Is that what life is like?" Shams asked me.

She said she'd thought life was like that, and then the Israeli invasion had come and saved her. Fawwaz left with the fedayeen, and Shams went to her family's house in Amman and found herself a job in the sewing workshop owned by Mme Hind Khadir and forgot she was married.

Two weeks later, he came and said he'd decided to settle in Amman – the Revolution was over and he didn't want to go to the camp in Yemen and he'd go back to his original work.

"Meaning you want to be an engineer again?" Shams asked sarcastically.

"Shut your mouth!" her mother yelled at her. "Women don't have the right to make fun of their husbands."

"In El Wahdat, he no longer fired his gun in order to become aroused. He stopped beating me and became kind. He'd go to work in his father's shop and come back in the evening, eat dinner and sleep. He'd tell me he'd dreamt that he'd sired a son. The poor man didn't know I'd had a coil inserted and wouldn't get pregnant if all the semen in the world was stuffed into my guts. Then the mistake happened: I got an infection, so the doctor took out the coil and Dalal arrived."

It's night, and I want to sleep. My eyelids are weighed down with the stories. Now I understand why children go to sleep when we tell them stories: the stories enter their eyes through the lashes and are turned into pictures too numerous for the eyes to process. Stories are for sleep, not for death. Now it's time for us to stop telling stories for a while, for one story begets another, and night covers the words.

All the same, tell me that story about the spirit woman and the man who drowned in the sun's red circles.

This is a story that happened at the beginning, but all the same, it comes at the end.

Naheeleh explained things to you because it was just a misunderstanding. You thought the woman was a spirit, and the woman thought you were a prophet. You ran away, she knelt and Naheeleh laughed.

You told me you named the tree Layla. You used to sleep by day inside the trunk of the Roman olive tree, and when you were with Naheeleh you'd talk to her about Layla and see the jealousy in her eyes.

It was the early '50s and Yunis was making one of his trips to Bab El Shams. That day, Yunis hid during the daytime inside the Roman tree on the outskirts of Tarshiha. When the sun began to set, he came out of his tree and saw the sight he'd never forget.

He said he'd never ever forget that woman.

"She was wearing a long black dress," said Yunis, "and had covered her hair with a black headscarf. Seeing me, she came towards me. I shrank back against the tree. I was wearing my long olive-green coat and carrying my rifle like a stick. The woman came in my direction. She was far away, the sun was in my eyes, and I couldn't see her clearly. I saw a phantom emerging from among the sun's red rays, the black thing inserting itself stealthily like a thread and then disappearing. I leaned against the tree and saw her coming towards me. Then, when she was two hundred metres away, she stopped in her tracks as though she was rooted to the ground, and she knelt, rubbed her brow with dust and raised her face towards me. She put her hands together and said something in an Arabic I'm not familiar with. Then she stood, stumbling over her long dress, and I took advantage of the moment to hide inside the tree trunk. I slipped into the tree with my heart beating like a drum, and stayed inside the trunk until night had covered everything. There was something strange in her eyes. I thought she was a spirit even though I don't believe in spirits; but I was afraid, I swear I was afraid."

Yunis said that when he told Naheeleh how he'd stood close to his tree, wrapped in the red threads of the sun, and how the woman had appeared to him at a distance and how he'd encountered his spirit woman and how she was going to carry his mind off like in the stories, Naheeleh laughed for a long time.

"It wasn't a spirit woman or anything, man. The Yemenis are every-where. That was a Yemeni Jewess."

Naheeleh told Yunis about the weeping that people heard coming from the *moshav* the Yemenis had built over El Bruwweh and spoke of the mysterious rumours of children dying and disappearing. She said the Yemeni Jewesses would go out into the fields and lament like Arab women and that she'd started to fear for her children, for "if the children of the Jews are disappearing, what will happen to ours?"

"That spirit woman was no spirit," said Naheeleh. "She was a poor woman like us who must have lost one of her children. So when she saw you she thought the prophet Elias had appeared to her."

Naheeleh started laughing at Yunis and calling him Elias, and saying that with his beard he'd started to look like a Jewish prophet.

He couldn't forget the scene – a black thread emerging from the midst of the red threads of the sun, a woman kneeling on the ground and crying out in a voice to rend the heavens. To himself he called her "Rachel the spirit", and on his way to see Naheeleh, he'd enter the Roman tree and invoke the Yemeni woman, and then tell Naheeleh that he was Yemeni too: "We were originally from Yemen and we fled. Our tribe migrated from there when the Ma'rib dam collapsed; the dam collapsed and drowned Yemen, and we fled. I'm Yemeni and my sweetheart's Yemeni, and I have to look for her."

Naheeleh would be a little jealous, but then she'd take him into the turning inside the cave that she called "the bathroom", where she'd make him take off his clothes and would bathe him with water and soap. He'd stand there naked and she'd be wearing her long dress, which would get soaked with the water so it stuck to her body, kindling his desire, and he'd grab her with the soap all over him and she'd slip out of his grasp and say, "Go to your Yemeni woman. I don't care."

I told you about the Yemeni woman to wish you sweet dreams.

I too have to sleep so that tomorrow I can try to convince Nurse Zeinab not to leave the hospital. I don't know anything about Nurse Zeinab. I've been living with her here for more than six months and I know nothing. She's been here since the beginning. During these months everything has changed, as you know: Dr Amjad comes only rarely, I've become head nurse and effective director of the hospital, the nurses have disappeared one after the other, the hospital's been converted into a warehouse for medicines, and Nurse Zeinab's still here, as though she was unchangeable. She limps a little, her shoulders droop, her neck is short, and her eyes are small. She moves like a ghost and takes care of everything. The cook left so Nurse Zeinab has become the cook. Nabeel went abroad so Nurse Zeinab took over responsibility for the operating theatre. The Syrian guard disappeared so Nurse Zeinab's become the doorkeeper. Nurse Zeinab, master, is the hospital. I don't care any more. I spend most of my time with you, convinced that it's no use struggling for the hospital's survival. I had many discussions with Dr Amjad and I've tried with Mme Widad El Najjar, the Palestine Red Crescent official in Lebanon, but it's no use.

No-one wants this hospital any more, as though we'd all agreed to announce the death of Shatila camp.

The camp is besieged from the outside and destroyed on the inside, and they won't let us rebuild it. The whole of Lebanon was rebuilt after the war except for here; this witness to butchery must be removed so the memory of us can be wiped out, just as our villages were wiped out and our souls lacerated.

I've lost hope. I said, "If they don't want it, too bad," and I built an imaginary wall around your room and won't let anyone come near you. At first Amjad tried to make me believe that the decision to move you couldn't be revoked, then I forced him to back down. I thought I'd scored a victory, but I discovered he didn't care. No-one cares. They said, "Leave him to get fed up, and if he doesn't get fed up, the old man will die anyway," and no-one expected my treatment method would be so successful. Amjad used to think your death would be a matter of days, and Nurse Zeinab said you wouldn't see the end of your first month, but here we are, past the sixth and into the seventh. We have to hang on to the end of the seventh month. If we get through the seventh, we'll definitely get to the ninth, and the ninth is where salvation lies. But they don't know. They've shut us in here and left us to rot. If only they knew. I'm certain no-one can have the slightest notion of what's going on in this room, here with the world, the women, the words.

I told you Nurse Zeinab's become everything, meaning nothing. When someone becomes everything it means they've lost their specificity. Nurse Zeinab's like that: I wasn't aware of her presence beyond the fact that she was present. I didn't ask her for anything. Then two days ago she came to me and said she'd decided to stop working. It never crossed my mind that Nurse Zeinab could stop working: she exists because she works.

She came to your room and said she wanted to speak to me.

"What, Nurse Zeinab?"

"No, not in front of him," she said.

"Speak up, Nurse Zeinab. There are no strangers here."

"Please, Dr Khaleel. I'm afraid to talk in front of him. Please come with me to the office."

I followed her to Dr Amjad's office, which would have become my office if people took things seriously around here. Nurse Zeinab went out and returned after a few minutes with a pot of coffee. She poured a cup for me and one for herself, and said that the children wanted her to stop working.

"You're married and have children, Nurse Zeinab?"

"Of course, doctor."

"I'm sorry. I thought you weren't married."

"'Cripples don't marry,'" she quoted and smiled.

"I'm sorry, I'm sorry. I didn't mean it like that."

"But I'm not a cripple. I wasn't a cripple when I got married. This is from Tell El Za'tar."

"You're from Tell El Za'tar?"

"I was there and I left with the women. My husband disappeared in Monteverde and I left with the women. We walked towards the armed men with our hands in the air to surrender and they fired on us. I was with my children. They were between my legs and I tried to cover them with my long skirt. Then that man came. The shooting stopped, so we kept going and reached the armed men, and the Red Cross lorries that had been sent to take us to West Beirut were there in front of us. That man came. I don't know why he chose me of all people and yelled to me, 'Over there!' I pretended I hadn't heard and kept going, and the hot red fluid covered my thigh and bathed the head of my daughter Samiyyeh, who was between my legs. I kept going till I reached the lorry. I don't know why he fired only one shot, and why he didn't kill me. These are things I don't understand now, but at the time everything was logical and okay. Our death was so logical that we weren't capable of protesting against it.

"We reached the museum crossing and they decided to transfer me to the hospital. They put me in an ambulance and you can imagine what that did to my children. They started crying. I'd lost half my blood or more and still I jumped from the ambulance and stood with my children. Then the nurse understood and let them come with me. At Makased Hospital, they put me in a room with more than ten beds and the children were with me. Samiyyeh was thirteen and couldn't understand anything, and the youngest was three. Five boys and three girls, God protect them. I stayed in hospital and didn't go with the others to El Damour. It won't do, I thought, when they decided to house the Tell El

Za'tar people in El Damour, which had been cleared of the Christians who'd lived there. I thought, that's what the Jews did to us, and we're going to do the same to the people of El Damour? It's impossible, it's a crime. And I stayed in the hospital. There was a doctor there from the Lutfi family in Tyre, do you know him, he's called Dr Haseeb Lutfi? God bless him, he told me I could work in the hospital and found me a small flat nearby. We lived there, the children and I, until 1982. After the invasion and the massacres, we came to Shatila and I started working in this hospital. I'm not a nurse, but I learned nursing from my work at Makased Hospital. I came here – and there was no-one, so I did everything. But I'm tired, Dr Khaleel. And what are we doing here anyway? You're guarding a corpse and I'm guarding a medicine depot; and also Shadi, God bless him, has told me he's going to send me a visa and a ticket to go to Germany."

"You're going to Germany? What will you do there?"

"Nothing," she answered. "There nothing, here nothing. But I'm tired, and Shadi's wife – I didn't tell you, Shadi married an Iraqi girl who lives in Germany, an Iraqi Kurd and political refugee. She got him asylum and residence – a refugee like us, so, like they say, 'Refugees marry refugees,' and she's expecting and I'll go for the child."

I said I'd feel lonely without her.

She said she knew Shams and knew her husband, Fawwaz, and knew the girl was mistreated: "I swear, doctor, everyone in Tell El Za'tar knows how he treated her. He was mad and heartless. It was like a demon possessed him. Could anyone be that crazy about his wife? He was as crazy about his wife as if she was the wife of another man. He told my late husband Mounir that he used to fire over her head and round her feet to drive the demons out of her. He was mad, and he drove her mad. He wouldn't let her leave the house or receive anyone either. She didn't dare open the door. We'd knock and she'd yell from inside that there was no-one there. And Fawwaz didn't sleep at home. He'd sleep with the fighters and go to her by day, and we'd hear the sound of the bullets and imagine the tears. God knows how she stood it. Then it was said she'd fled with the fighters. Why did she go back to him? I didn't see her after the Tell El Za'tar days, and I didn't ask about her; after what happened there, no-one asked after anyone, as though people no longer want to look at anything but pictures. Instead of looking for the men who disappeared, we've entertained ourselves by looking for their pictures. I swear we're a crazy people, doctor. The only lesson we've learned from our families is that we shouldn't leave our homes without our pictures. Can you believe it, we were in that Red Cross lorry and I was bleeding, nearly dead, and people were piled on top of one another like sardines, and you'd see a woman take a picture out of the front of her dress and compare it with pictures extracted from the front of some other woman's dress. As though if we carried the pictures of the dead around, it would save them from death. Poor pictures! The photo of Abu Shadi, God rest his soul, has lost its colour. I framed it, but photos lose their colours even with frames and glass. He disappeared. We know nothing about what happened to him, and I didn't look for him at first – I was in hospital hovering between life and death, and I had my children with me. Without God's mercy and the generosity of Dr Lutfi, my children would've been lost, as thousands were. A husband may die or disappear and we get upset, of course; but a child – God forbid!

"Once I got better, I went to El Damour and met Riyad Ismat, who was martyred in Tripoli in 1984. Riyad said he didn't know. I went round all the offices in El Damour, but no-one could help me. Everyone did, however, assure me he was dead.

"'If he hasn't come back, it means he's dead. They didn't take prisoners in Monteverde,' said Riyad.

"Last year I went to Monteverde. The war was over, and it'd become possible to go there. Sameer took me in his car – Sameer's my second son, who works as a taxi driver, though God help him if a policeman stops him and finds out he's Palestinian. All Sameer dreams about these days is joining his brother in Germany.

"Sameer took me, and I told him I wanted to take a look at Tell El Za'tar. Poor Tell El Za'tar – it's as though it never existed. I asked people and they couldn't give me directions – just empty ground and nothing else. People have forgotten the war and forgotten the camp, and no-one wants to say its name. I tried to go in – I wanted to look for my house – but they wouldn't let me. There was a kind of guard there who said, 'No entry!' Anyway, even if I'd got in, all I'd have found would've been asphalt: they've spread asphalt on the ground and everything's black as pitch.

"The car managed the narrow hairpin bends in Monteverde. I knew I wouldn't find anything, but I had to do it in honour of Abu Shadi's memory. All we found were Syrian soldiers and tanks. Sameer asked me where to look for his father's grave, and I didn't answer because I wasn't sure that the search was worthwhile; I just wanted to put my conscience at rest. I asked Riyad about the graves – I asked him if they'd buried the boys. He said he didn't know, there was no way to know – the bullets had been whining over their heads and all they'd wanted was to reach Hammana.

"I didn't ask Sameer to stop the car and I didn't feel anything. It was as though those who'd died had been wiped off the face of the earth. War in itself doesn't need graves, because war is a grave. Abu Shadi doesn't have a grave – his grave is war itself. War doesn't call for tombs and headstones, for war is itself a tomb, a tomb in which we live. Even the camp isn't a camp, it's the tomb of Palestine.

"Do you understand? Of course you understand, because you're like me, doctor. You were born in the camp, or in the grave, and the grave will dog you to the end of time."

Nurse Zeinab said she was going to go abroad and leave us.

"When are you leaving?" I asked.

She said she was waiting for her visa, but that she'd come to advise me to abandon the hospital. She said she advised me to leave the hospital and stop watching you.

"Who?" I asked her.

"Yunis, Abu Salim," she replied.

"What's wrong with him?"

"He's dying, can't you see? Leave him be. Let him die. Shame on you! You're forcing him to stay alive."

"But I'm not doing anything," I said.

"You're the one responsible for his condition. Shame on you!"

"No, Nurse Zeinab. Please!"

"Let him die, for shame. Stop this meaningless treatment. Can you change God's will? Leave him with his Lord, brother, and leave the hospital."

Then she returned to the subject of Shams.

"Your fear of Shams is meaningless: no-one's going to take revenge on you. What's it to do with you? She killed her lover and they killed her. 'Warn the killer that he will be killed, though it be after a time': that's God's word as it appears in His Good Book. Samih killed her because he lied to her, and she killed him because she wanted revenge, and they killed her to get justice. That's all there is to it, and you haven't done anything wrong that you should have to bury yourself with this man who's no longer a man. Look at him, it's as if he's gone back to being a baby. In the name of God the Merciful and Compassionate, let him die and release us all."

Nurse Zeinab repeated what Umm Hassan had said: "Where are his family, to take him back to his country?"

Which reminds me, Yunis: why didn't you go back and do what Hamad did?

Don't you know the story of Hamad?

I was told the story by his brother Mansour, who sells fish in the camp. You like fish. "Ah, how I miss the fish of Acre!" you used to say, and you'd refuse to buy Mansour's fish because the Acre fish was better. What is this blind fanaticism? Mansour told you these were fish from Acre that had been smuggled over and become refugees like us. And you'd refuse to buy: "Acre fish is different. We used to fry it and eat it with thyme *fatayir* and *taratur* sauce. It's Christ's fish. That's where he used to fish, peace be upon him."

You said that Christ, peace be upon him, never forbade alcohol because he worked with fishermen and sailors: "How can you convince a sailor not to drink? The sea and fishing are impossible without arak and wine. Fish too – you can't eat them without arak and *fatayir* and *taratur*. The fish of Tiberias are inexhaustible. Fish, Christ and fishermen – that's Galilee. They don't know Galilee. They're trying to create a fishing industry – can you industrialise the water Christ walked on? That's where we'll go back to. Imagine, a whole people walking on water!"

You'd say we'd walk on water, take a sip from your glass and ask me to pour you more.

"Take it easy, Abu Salim."

"Like hell, son. Pour the arak and follow me back to Lake Tiberias!"

It was Mansour the fish seller who told me his brother's story. I'd gone to see him on the morning of the feast at the end of Ramadan because I wanted to mark the occasion by eating fish. I found his stall empty. He said he hadn't gone to Tyre to do his buying because of the feast, and he'd gone to the cemetery at dawn and visited his son and come straight to the shop because he didn't dare to go home and sit there with the pictures of his son the martyr.

"Over here we die, and over there they have children," he said.

Mansour said he was a fool and that his brother Hamad had got away with his life and his children's too.

You know Hamad. With the rest of you, he was a member of the Sha'ab militia, which was the last to leave Galilee, and he was imprisoned along with you. Then he lived in Burj El Barajneh camp. You know him – from Tarshiha, the one who always swore by the *kibbeh nayyeh* his wife Salmeh made: "*Kibbeh nayyeh* with *hoseh* on top. Meat on meat, brother. *Kibbeh* underneath and fried meat with onions and pine nuts on top, and 'Go on, eat, Hamad!'"

He said she was Salmeh, known as Umm Jameel, for her son.

He said he'd left her over there in Tarshiha.

He said he'd found *kibbeh* had no taste after he was parted from Salmeh.

Why didn't you do what he did?

Were you afraid of the Jews?

Of Naheeleh?

Of yourself?

I swear, Yunis my son, the only thing people fear is themselves. You told me the only thing you were afraid of when you crossed the border was your own shadow, which would stretch out on the ground and follow you.

Do you want to listen to Mansour?

Come on, Mansour. Come and tell your story to your Uncle Yunis.

He isn't here, of course, but I'll tell you the story as I heard it from Mansour Ahmad Qabalawi, fish seller, who opened his shop here in Shatila after they closed down his shop in Burj El Barajneh at the entrance to the low-lying area where people from Tarshiha lived because of differences among the various political groups at the time of the Revolution.

Mansour said, "After the fall of Tarshiha, we fled into Lebanon and forgot all about Salmeh and her daughter. It was my fault: the thought of Salmeh never crossed my mind as we were fleeing. It was all shelling and planes and hell let loose, and I wasn't a fighter even though I was in the militia. Between you and me, I was just there to make up the numbers, and when the flight started and the Jews came, I fled with my wife and kids and never thought of Salmeh and her daughter Sawsan. Then my brother turned up. He'd spent a year in prison in Syria. He asked the way to my tent and entered it. Before he could ask, I confessed to him. I didn't tell him she'd died, God forbid. I told him we'd forgotten her and didn't know her whereabouts and that she'd probably stayed in Tarshiha. He called me names and broke the tent pole and left. Later I learned he'd gone there: he went to Tarshiha, stayed with his wife for a few days, and came back and told me. We became like brothers again. I don't have anyone but him, and he doesn't have anyone but me. Every time he went, it'd be an adventure. They'd arrest him and expel him. He didn't stay in Tarshiha in secret: he'd knock on the door of his house and go in for everyone to see. Then they'd arrest him and drag him to the border.

"When they arrested him the last time, the Israeli officer who notified him of the expulsion order told him he was absent when the census was made after the establishment of the State, so he was considered an absentee.

"'Well, here I am, sir. I was absent and now I'm present.'

"'No,' said the officer. 'The absentee is not entitled to be present.'

"'But my wife and children are here.'

"'Take them with you if you like.'

"'But it's my village.'

"They tied him up and threw him out at the Lebanese border and he returned to the camp. He stayed for about a year, then disappeared again, and we discovered they'd thrown him across the border into Gaza, and we tied ourselves into knots getting an air ticket from Cairo to Beirut. Five times he went in and stayed, and five times he was thrown out. The sixth time was the clincher.

"It was 1957, the morning of the Feast of the Sacrifice. My wife was busy cooking, and the smell of *kibbeh nayyeh* filled the house. He looked at my children and his face ran the gamut of the emotions. 'Let's go to Tyre,' he said. I left my wife and my children on the day of the Feast and went with him because I know him, and I knew nothing could stop him.

We went to Tyre, from there to El Rasheediyyeh camp, and from there to the house of Ali Shahada from El Ba'neh. Ali Shahada, who worked as a smuggler, asked for a thousand Lebanese lira to get him to Tarshiha, and a thousand lira in those days was no joke; it was five times the monthly income of a fish-shop owner like me. My brother agreed and said he'd pay over there. Ali, however, asked to see the money before he did anything, and my brother pulled a huge amount of money out of the back pocket of his trousers, showed it to him and gave him a hundred lira, saying, 'This is a Feast present for your kids. Let's eat lunch first and rest. Then let's go.'

"'We'll leave at sunset,' said Ali.

"He slaughtered a rooster for us, and we ate it with rice, drank coffee and chatted. As soon as the sun began to set, my brother Hamad set off with the smuggler Ali and I went back to Beirut.

"My brother reached his house and lived there. Thirty years after all this happened, he got me a permit to visit Tarshiha, and there I found Hamad, living in the midst of his children and his children's children. I told him, 'This isn't Tarshiha: our land doesn't belong to us any more, and our house isn't our house any longer' – Hamad was living in the house of Mahmoud Qabalawi, whose family live in Burj El Barajneh today. He told me our house had been demolished and that all the houses in the lower square had been destroyed and that Salmeh had had no choice but to live in this house. 'I came and stayed here, and I'm ready. Tell Mahmoud Qabalawi I haven't changed anything in their house. When they come back they can take it, and God bless them.'

"'But it's not Tarshiha, Hamad,' I said. 'There are Jews everywhere.'

"Hamad reached his house and stayed a week with his wife before he was seized and deported to the Lebanese border. Before he reached the border check post, he offered the Israeli soldier a bribe, taking off his Swiss watch and giving it to him. The soldier hesitated, then took the bribe and left Hamad on his own.

"My brother returned, was arrested again and sentenced as a saboteur, getting eighteen years. He spent nine of those in prison, then they let him out after a series of remissions for good behaviour and didn't know what to do with him, so they returned him to his house in Tarshiha."

Tell me, Yunis, why didn't you go back for good?

Why didn't you try to go back for good just once?

Were you afraid of dying? If you said you were afraid they'd liquidate you, I'd understand, but then don't talk to me about the Struggle and the Revolution and all that.

Now tell me, what will you do when we've got everything fixed and you're born again? Will you live a new life, or will you repeat the travelling life you lived before?

I hear your voice amid low-pitched moaning. Why are you moaning? Your temperature's normal, everything's tip-top, your heart beats are more regular than those of a young man; I should knock on wood. But tell me, if we could run life backwards, who would you prefer to have been – Yunis or Hamad? Or would you prefer a third option, such as going to Canada for instance? What do you think – go abroad and leave everything behind?

I know you're incapable of answering, and that's why I'm asking. I'm free and not obliged to defer to you in anything. I know what you'd like to say, but you don't, and that's better.

Tell me, what should I advise Nurse Zeinab to do?

Should I advise her to stay here or encourage her to travel to be with her son in Germany? Should I promise her that things will get better for the hospital or promise her Saffouri, which no longer exists?

I'll tell her to do what she wants.

I see Nurse Zeinab now as if for the first time, as if for all those months I didn't. And now, after she's told me how she was wounded by a bullet at Tell El Za'tar, she's no longer "the crippled nurse", as I used to describe her to myself; her name is Zeinab, Zeinab the nurse. Good grief, how long we need to wear our names for them to become ours! Zeinab became Zeinab because she told her story. True, she's leaving soon, and true, she informed me when her work here came to an end, and true, if I'd known earlier, things would have been different, but that's the way it is: a man only discovers his name at the moment of departure or, in other words, when the name becomes his shroud. We shroud him in his name and bury him. Now I understand the wisdom of the pictures that fill our lives: the victims of the massacres have no names and no shrouds. The bodies are covered with lime and pesticide before being thrown into a common pit. People disappear because they have no names and become mere numbers. That's the terrifying thing, son. The terror is the numbers; that's why people carry pictures of the dead and missing, and use them as a substitute for names.

Nurse Zeinab is not convinced.

She says everything I've done for you is for nothing. I wish she knew, but she wasn't willing to listen to the tale from the beginning, plus I no longer have the energy to tell it. If Nurse Zeinab had come and listened to your story, she'd have understood that I wasn't wasting your time and mine but was buying time and history, for me and for you.

Yes, my son and master.

I'm here because I was under the influence of Shams. I thought I'd flee her ghost and her revenge. I wasn't afraid of real revenge or, in other words, that one of her family would come and shoot me. No, I was afraid of everything about her.

Your death came and rescued me. You made me a doctor again, you brought me to live with you here in the hospital, and you allowed me to recover my desire for life. Yes, I was incapable of living. When the air entered my lungs it felt like knives. I'd feel ants burying themselves in my face and I'd become dizzy. In clinical terms it's called "onset of nervous collapse".

When Shams died, everything inside me died. I became a corpse, and things lost their meaning and taste. Life became unbearably heavy. It was as though I was carrying my corpse on my back. Who can carry the sack of life when it's filled with forty years of loneliness? Who would dare to?

Amna came, and she told me about you. By the way, where is Amna? She's gone to ground, like all your women. This means we've entered the dangerous period, for when the women go to ground it means the end is near. Women only run away when life is extinguished.

Amna left and all your women have gone after her and no-one is left in this collapsing place but me. I see cracks everywhere – cracks in the walls and cracks in the ceiling – as though everything was on the verge of collapse.

But I'm not afraid. Things topple and I stand fearless.

We're amazing, wouldn't you agree?

Maybe we haven't been afraid during these long months we've spent together. We've made a house out of words, and a country out of words, and women out of words.

I'm not afraid for you, and I won't comment on what Nurse Zeinab said – don't be angry with her, please: she doesn't understand. She said at the beginning that you'd become young like a baby again, and then she said your shrunken form didn't look human and that I'd created a little monster.

As though she couldn't see.

Never mind; I'm convinced that you're the most beautiful baby, and that's enough, right? And I feel your freedom too. You can die if you want to. I say, "You can" – and I'm not inviting you to do so – because you're free. Choose your death or your life as you wish. Do as you want, want what you want, for now your truth is inside me.

Tell me a little about your daughter Nour. What a lovely name! I don't know her, but I feel as though I do and I long to see her. When you described her to me the first time, I thought you were telling me about Shams. You described her beauty and her dark complexion that made shapes like interconnecting fields of attraction, and you told me about her son Yunis.

You said you'd received a letter from her informing you of the birth of her son Yunis, and that she said your children were calling their boys Yunis. That way you'd live among them and would return to them not as one but as a hundred.

You were carrying the letter and laughing. You read me that passage laughing, then the tears burst from your eyes. You wept and laughed as though your emotions were mixed up and you no longer knew how to express yourself. I promised I'd get you the Fayrouz song that's taken from a poem by the Lebanese poet Bishara El Khouri, known as Little Akhtal, and I recited the line that begins the song, and you took a pen and wrote it on the back of the letter:

He weeps and cries neither in sorrow nor in joy
Like a lover who inscribes a line on love only to rub it out.

You wrote the line and a white mist arose and covered your face and eyes, and I couldn't see you while you were within that mist, repeating the ode, verse flowing around you like water. It was then that I under-stood the meaning of poetry, and the words of Imru' Al Qays – my grand-father and yours, and the grandfather of all Arabs. For Imru' Al Qays didn't see his own image in the mirror of his beloved's breast; he saw the world, he saw the mist that covered it. And, realising that he was living inside that mist, he invented words to assuage his shame and confu-sion. Poetry, my son, is words we use to assuage our shame, our sorrow and our longing. It's a cover. The poet wraps us in words so our souls don't fall to pieces. Poetry is against death – it's both sickness and cure, the soul's covering and its clothes. I'm cold now, so I take refuge in poetry, hiding my head in it and asking it to cover me.

You came with the letter and you described Nour before applying your-self to the reading of it, and when you read you became like a poet. When you read about the hundred Yunises being born over there, you didn't boast and trumpet your triumph. You picked up your triumph and started weeping and laughing, because triumph is not unlike defeat; it is a moment when the soul is exposed from within. You were exposed and wounded, and in ministering to you with Little Akhtal's poem, I poured the voice of Fayrouz on your wounds. The mist of poetry covered you and took you to a distant place.

You're now in the distant realm of poetry, the realm of a hundred Yunises who don't know you're dying or see the footprints you left behind on the roads of Galilee. No-one remembers you now but the forest of oblivion.

I promised I'd tell you about Shams, and I didn't. We got to where she became an officer with the fedayeen. How that came about I don't know. I know she went to Jordan after the '82 invasion of Beirut and her husband, Fawwaz, caught up with her there and worked with his father, who owned a small fabric store in Jebel El Weibdeh.

Fawwaz quietened down in Amman, and the violence that had mani-fested itself in Lebanon in the shape of bullets aimed at his wife's body disappeared.

"Fawwaz didn't scare me any more," said Shams. "Six years in Beirut in which I can only remember myself as naked. I'd stand there spread-eagled, the bullets exploding around me, and then the man would come to me, erect, and bore into my body with a savage shout that emerged from between his thighs. Six years, and I knew I'd never get pregnant because what he did doesn't make pregnancies. He'd ask me before starting my torture party if I was pregnant, and I'd say no and see his snarl and hear the sound of his fury."

Shams said everything changed in Amman.

"It seems the demon left him and he became a different man, stammering in front of his father, addressing his mother respectfully and coming to me peacefully. We lived in one house with his father, mother and unmarried sister. Fawwaz became someone other than Fawwaz, and I became pregnant, and Dalal arrived.

"Three months after Dalal was born, the father died, and died sad because I'd given birth to a girl and not a boy who'd inherit his name. I paid no attention to his harsh looks and his refusal to speak to me after Dalal was born; he took to telling his wife or son anything he wanted to say to me, even when I was sitting right there. He'd say something and not even utter my name. But I didn't care. What mattered was that Dalal looked like me and not like them. The girl was my daughter, not theirs. God, how pretty she was! Soon, when I snatch her and bring her here, you'll see the prettiest girl in the world. I wanted to call her Amal – Hope – because it was with her that hope began, but Fawwaz insisted on Dalal, and later I found out that Dalal was the name of the cousin who'd refused to marry him. I found out that his father had advised his brother not to give Dalal to Fawwaz if she didn't love him; then they stumbled on me for the no-good son who wasn't an engineer or anything else. Fawwaz insisted on the name Dalal and his father didn't interfere, so I submitted to the inevitable and cried because I felt that Amal had died. I named her Amal when she was still in my belly. I'd talk to her and hear her voice, and I knew from the beginning that she'd be a girl, from the first instant that I felt dizziness, nausea and thirst. I spent the first three months of the pregnancy sleeping. I'd drink and sleep and talk to Amal. Then they stole the name. Fawwaz said Dalal, I said Amal. But names aren't important. Dalal fits her and I've got used to it."

Shams told of the great transformation that followed the death of Fawwaz's father and how everything, including her husband, was utterly changed. She said she couldn't believe her eyes.

"The father died of a heart attack and his son inherited everything. Fawwaz changed. He reverted to being the Fawwaz I'd left behind in Beirut. Instead of trembling in front of his father, it was now his mother who trembled in front of him. Instead of stumbling when he walked, it was now his sister who stumbled, and instead of stammering when he talked, we were the ones who stammered. When his father was alive and Fawwaz slept with me, he'd come to me whispering and cover my body, groping in the dark. Only in Amman, and only in the Amman of the whispering times, did I feel something sexual with him. I felt something move and form a hard point inside me. Then the father died, and that page was turned."

Shams said he didn't care any longer: he started making the same noises he'd made in Beirut. "Then he started beating me on my neck, saying he couldn't feel aroused if he didn't hit me. The beating started light but things progressed, and he started hitting me with all his might while I repressed my screams and my pain out of shame before his mother and sister who lived with us. Then I couldn't control myself any more; as soon as he beat me, I'd start screaming. The beating parties followed one after another, and I thought I could hear the two women's footsteps and could imagine them bent over at the keyhole to the door of our room, listening and shaking their heads; then the sister's handkerchief would fall to the ground and she'd pick it up, looking into her mother's face.

"In the morning he'd leave the house and I'd be left on my own with the women, not daring to look at them. They behaved as though they were unaware of what went on in our bedroom.

"Once I said something to his mother, and she looked at me with startled eyes. I didn't really say anything, I just said that Fawwaz pursued me at night and I couldn't take it any more. She looked at me as though she didn't understand what I was saying and mumbled something about life being like that and I should thank the Lord that he was providing me with a home.

"Umm Fawwaz said I should thank the Lord! Imagine! Thank Him for the humiliation and the beatings!

"I don't know whether his mother said something to him or whether things just took their natural course, but after that mistake of mine he became even more savage and went back to acting out the Beirut scenes. In Amman he couldn't fire his gun: there's a state here and we're not in a civil war – but he transformed the bedroom into an arena for civil war. He'd spread-eagle me and point his finger like a gun and make firing noises from his mouth. He'd come close to me and start boring into my body with the muzzle of his imaginary gun. I tried to find a solution. I went to see my mother, but all I got from her was, 'Anything but divorce! Divorce costs a woman her reputation.' So I took my own decision; I decided to run away. But I didn't dare put my decision into action. Every night after he'd gone to sleep, I'd draw up escape plans, and in the morning the plans would evaporate, and I'd find myself just one of three women.

"Where was I to run to?

"The West Bank crossed my mind. God, I even thought of going to the Jews! But I was afraid. I didn't know anyone there and I'd be put in prison. Then I thought of Beirut. I, who couldn't bear to hear the word *Beirut*, decided on Beirut.

"I don't know how I got the words out of my mouth.

"Fawwaz was eating breakfast, sitting alone at the table and eating fried eggs and *labaneh*, while we stood – three women standing in front of him, ready to obey his every demand, while he smacked his lips and drank tea. Suddenly I heard my voice saying: 'Listen. I can't stand it any more. Divorce me.'

"But Fawwaz went on eating as though he hadn't heard, so I screamed, 'Fawwaz, listen to me. I swear I can't go on. Divorce me.'

"He swallowed what was in his mouth and said in a wooden voice, 'You're divorced.'

"I'm certain he didn't take me seriously, but he said it. I ran to my room, put my clothes in a plastic bag, picked up Dalal and left.

"'Leave the girl, you whore,' said his mother.

"My body went slack. I'd thought of everything that might happen except for Dalal. His mother came over to me and snatched the girl from my arms.

"'Go to your family and tell them, "Fawwaz divorced me because I'm a whore,"' said Fawwaz.

"I'm sure he thought I was going to collapse and weep and implore him to forgive me, but I just left the house. I didn't go to my family. Instead, I walked in the direction of the station for taxis to Beirut. I got into a taxi, went to sleep and didn't wake up till we reached the Jordanian–Syrian border. Then I went to sleep again and woke to find myself held up at the Syrian–Lebanese border because I didn't have an entry visa for Lebanon. I stood alone after the taxi left me to continue on its journey. A man came up to me, spoke to me with a Palestinian accent and said he could get me to Tripoli via Homs. At the time Tripoli was a battle zone: the Palestinian fedayeen, or what was left of them in Lebanon, had congregated in the city and it was under siege. I gave him everything I possessed. I was carrying forty Jordanian dinars that I'd stolen one by one from Fawwaz's pocket in preparation for my escape."

Shams said she learned war in Tripoli. She arrived at Fatah's El Zahiriyyeh office and said she'd come from Jordan to join the Revolution. Mundhir, the official in charge, sent her to join the groups at Bab El Tabbaneh, where she met Khaleel Akkawi, the legendary commander who transformed the poor and the young of Tripoli into little revolutionaries and who was to die later in a savage assassination operation that greatly resembled Shams's murder in El Miyyeh wi-Miyyeh.

In Tripoli she also met Abu Faris, an assistant to Abu Jihad (Khaleel El Wazeer), who, before the fedayeen departed the city, appointed her communications officer for Western Sector Command in Tunis, which was responsible for work inside Occupied Palestine.

Shams didn't get on the boats with the fedayeen who left Tripoli in 1984. She said that Tunis was a long way away and she preferred to stay close to Dalal. Abu Faris gave her some money, and she came to Beirut and joined the Palestinian command centre in Mar Elias camp, and from there she slipped into Shatila during the long siege.

Many stories are told about her during that time.

It's said that the Shatila camp commander, Ali Abu Toq, slapped her face in front of the other fighters and told her *he* was the commander in change there.

It's said that she succeeded in forming a network to smuggle weapons and supplies into the besieged camp.

She didn't tell me anything about that. I knew her – we'd run into one another in Mar Elias camp – and I was bewitched by her. Now I don't know, because everything I thought I knew about her evaporated when her murder of Samih revealed that she loved him.

I can say that she was an extraordinary woman. She used to tour Mar Elias camp surrounded by her young men, saying they were members of "Shams's Brigade".

I returned to the camp after it collapsed following the killing of its commander, Ali Abu Toq, while Shams was transferred to the Sidon area. I returned and found it a different camp. I returned and worked for the rebuilding of the hospital. I grew accustomed to the new situation, which you know better than I do and which we don't need to talk about in any detail. When the fedayeen returned, they weren't like fedayeen. I'm not talking here about the corruption and bribes and quarrels we lived through before the '82 invasion. I know there was corruption, and we were ashamed of ourselves. But something made us capable of tolerating the situation; let's say there was an issue that was larger than the bribe-takers and the crooks. After the fall of the camp, however, everything changed.

In the past, death had been everywhere, and it was beautiful. I know we're not supposed to call death beautiful, but there was a certain beauty there that enveloped us in its cloak. In the days following the fall of the camp, however, death was naked.

Believe me, I don't know how Shams got into the camp after it fell. The Fatah dissidents had taken over Fatah's offices in Beirut, and the camps — and only the camps — in the south were left. Everyone knew that Shams was against the split within Fatah and worked with Abu Jihad El Wazeer, and that she was loyal to the leadership and accused the dissidents of many things. All the same, she'd come into Shatila without anyone challenging her. She'd come to my house and we'd spend nights together. I didn't see her often — she was busy all the time and I had no means of contacting her. She'd come when she wanted to and find me waiting for her.

No, master.

No, my son and my beloved, I wasn't afraid of her; I was afraid of myself. Something suddenly died inside me, for when someone we love dies, something dies in us. Such is life — a long chain of death. Others die, and things die inside each of us; those we love die, and our limbs die too. Man doesn't wait for death, he lives it; he lives the death of others inside himself, and when he arrives at his own death, many of his parts have already been chopped off, and only a few remain.

Before Shams, I didn't know. And when she died, I became aware of my amputated limbs and the parts of me that were buried in the ground; I felt that my father and my grandmother, and even my mother whom I'd forgotten, were like parts of my body that had been wrenched off by force.

That's what I was afraid of, and that's why I sought refuge with you.

I wasn't afraid of revenge. Well, maybe I was, but it's not important. I was afraid of my own death. Shams died and I became aware of all the parts of me that had died. I saw death creeping up on what remained of me, and you came. I didn't want you to die, so that the last part of me separating me from my death wouldn't die. Now I laugh at myself: the last part of me has become a child. You've become a child, father, and your smell is like Dalal's, or like that of Ibraheem, your first child, who died. The decision was Naheeleh's. She's the one who decided you shouldn't go on calling yourself Abu Ibraheem. She said, "You're Abu Salim and I'm Umm Salim. We mustn't live with death – the living are better than the dead."

Now I live with your new smell – a fresh smell that invites kisses. The smell of children invites kisses, and you invite me. I hug you and sniff you and kiss you and envelop you in my voice.

You don't believe me?

Shame on you! Shame on you! I swear she loved me, and you've no right to doubt it. I believed all your stories, the believable ones and the unbelievable ones. I even believed the story about the ice worms.

At the time, Yunis was on his way to Bab El Shams. He reached his first hiding place, near Tarshiha, in the morning and lay down beneath the big olive tree he called Layla. He was carrying an English rifle and a bag and wearing a long green coat.

Yunis was beneath the olive tree when the sun began to set and the red covering the hills of Galilee began to spread.

"I'm being unfaithful to you with Layla, my Roman lady," he said to Naheeleh.

"I want to see her," said Naheeleh.

He promised he'd take her, but he didn't.

"Layla's just for me. Layla's my second wife. We're Muslims, woman!"

Naheeleh would laugh at the man's childishness and say she was going to cut the tree down.

With Layla he was Yunis: with the tree inside whose huge hollow trunk he hid and in whose shade he slept – a lone tree, set off a little from the olive groves in the countryside surrounding Tarshiha. There he could rest and sleep, standing or lying down inside the trunk, and there he'd organise his thoughts and his plans, his love and his body.

Then the tree died.

He spoke of the tree as though he was speaking of a woman.

He said it died; he didn't say they cut it down.

Why, in fact, do they cut down the olives and plant pines and palms in their place? Why do the Israelis hate the Tree of Holy Light?

On that day in 1965, after crossing the Tarshiha olive grove, he felt something was missing and couldn't find the tree. The paved road that links Maalot to Carmel had run over Layla.

Yunis said he felt a savage desire for revenge and didn't complete his journey to Naheeleh. He returned to Shatila, shut himself up in his house and didn't receive visitors for more than a week. His face took on a chalky tinge, the tears stood like stones in his eyes, and he announced that he was in mourning for the tree.

He decided to change his route to Deir El Asad.

That was when he discovered the road via El Arqoub, which, three years later – after the '67 defeat, that is – was to become the fedayeen's main route into Palestine. The fedayeen discovered El Arqoub, which came to be called "Fatah Land" and was located on the flanks of Jebel El Sheikh, and learned how to travel its icy roads.

Yunis said Jebel El Sheikh bewitched him.

It was mirrors of ice; a mountain sitting like a crown on the head of three countries – Palestine, Lebanon and Syria. "God's crown," he told me.

Yunis said he discovered the route via Jebel El Sheikh, or Mount Hermon, because Layla was killed.

"Did you know," he asked me, "did you know the ice has worms in it?

I discovered them for myself. I took Naheeleh ten worms wrapped in a piece of cloth. They're little white worms that look like silk worms except that they're white. When you pull them out of the ice, they go hard as pebbles. I told Naheeleh they were ice worms and put a worm in the water jar and asked her to wait. In less than ten minutes, the water was as cold as ice. Naheeleh refused to drink it at first. She said she didn't drink worms. Then she started asking for the worms and giving them away."

Yunis said it was summer. "In summer, the ice of Mount Hermon becomes like mirrors misted with breath. I slept in an old abandoned house. I don't know what came over me that night. There was no problem with the house: it was an old house. The peasants of El Arqoub say a Lebanese émigré returned from Mexico and built it. They say the man, who was from the village of El Kfeir at the foot of the mountain, made a lot of money in America and decided to return to his country following his wife's death, choosing Jebel El Sheikh as his place of retreat. He was an old man, about seventy-five, and it seems that in his dotage he focused on spiritual matters, saying that on the mountain he'd be at the point closest to God. He built the house in the Arab style – a courtyard surrounded by five rooms – and announced his intention to found a monastery there.

"How did he find the courage to live there? You can't imagine the winter on Jebel El Sheikh. Winter there, I tell you, is total whiteness. Scattered ice dust that goes around and around and covers your eyes. Your bones become pieces of ice. You become a piece of ice. I only crossed it in winter twice, and both times, when I got to Deir El Asad, I lit a fire and Naheeleh came and re-arranged my bones. That's what a real woman is, my son – the real woman is the one who can re-arrange your bones. She puts each bone back in its place, and warms you up, and you become yourself again.

"The man, who was called El Khouri, died before the house was finished, and the ice house became known as The House of El Khouri, which is to say, The House of the Priest. I don't know if the house was so called in reference to the man, who belonged to the Khouri family from El Kfeir from which many historic personages hailed – such as Faris Bey El Khouri, a leader of the Nationalist Bloc who became Prime

Minister of Syria – or because the man had decided to become a monk and it was given the name in reference to the unfinished monastery project."

That summer day, Yunis reached the house in a state of exhaustion and decided to spend the night there before continuing to Bab El Shams.

"I was in my room, which is the only one El Khouri finished building before he died. I tried to sleep, but sleep wouldn't come. The August sun burned the ice, and the ice burned my face. I was cold and I burned. I got up, wrapped myself in a wool blanket and sat on the threshold above the dry ice. I could feel the worms moving over me. I must have fallen asleep, and I awoke to find the ice worms, little white worms, emerging from beneath the crust of dry ice and spreading over my feet. I got up in terror and started stepping on them. On that occasion I didn't wait for night to continue my journey to Naheeleh; I travelled by day and God protected me. I don't know how I arrived. Naheeleh didn't believe that the ice had worms.

"A peasant from the village of Kafar Shouba told me that the ice got worms when it got old, and that the ice worms were very beneficial, because they turned water cold.

"I put the worm in the jar and drank, but Naheeleh refused at first. Then she started asking me for worms from Jebel El Sheikh and started distributing them to people in the village – in those days people were poor and no-one owned a refrigerator; to cool the water, they'd put it out in jars over night.

"Naheeleh took to asking me for worms and distributing them, and everyone started calling the ice worms 'fedayeen worms'. The whole village knew that I visited my wife in secret. They knew, but Naheeleh, God protect her, didn't tell even the children about the cave until the end of her life.

"Salim spoke to me by telephone – you know, over there they can talk to us, but we can't phone Israel. He said his mother's health was improving and that she'd told him the secret and asked him to go to Bab El Shams. She told him not to stop going to the cave, to keep it neat and clean. 'Don't let the sheets and the towels and the blankets get mouldy, it's your father's village. Ask him what he wants you to do with it. His house has to be kept neat. And when I die, take everything out and close the door with stones. We mustn't let the Israelis get in ever; it's the only bit of Palestinian territory that's been liberated.'

"After her death, Salim asked me what to do about the things. He said he'd entered Bab El Shams – he called it Bab El Shams on the telephone! No-one knew the name of my village except me and her. There we were on our own, like Adam and Eve, and now along comes Salim and asks!

"He told me about Naheeleh's death and then asked me that. I couldn't breathe.

"He said, 'God compensate you with good health, Dad,' and then asked me what to do with my things at Bab El Shams.

"I said I didn't know.

"He said he'd carry out Naheeleh's wishes.

"I didn't ask him what her wishes were. I found that out forty days after her death. Salim called and said he'd closed the country with stones. He said he'd gone by night with his son Yunis and Yunis, Nour's son, and Yunis, Salih's son, and Yunis, Mirwan's son . . . they'd gone and closed the country. They'd taken out the things and divided them up among them.

"Salim went with the boys and closed the 'country', as they called it.

"Salim told me, and I couldn't speak. I felt my life had ended. Four young men had divided up my clothes and my blankets and my cooking pans and my books among them, and closed the country I'd created for my wife.

"Salim said he'd asked the children to keep the secret of the cave. 'It's Yunis's secret. Leave Yunis in the whale's belly,' he told them, 'and after three days, or three years, or three score years, your grandfather Yunis will emerge from the whale's belly, just like the first Yunis did, and Palestine will return, and we'll call the village we'll rebuild Bab El Shams.'

"'No,' said Yunis to those who came to pay him condolences, 'she didn't die.' But he knew deep within himself that the story was over.

In this last phase he recounted fragments of his stories about Layla the Roman lady and the Yemeni woman.

He said the Yemeni woman was covered by the red of the sun.

He said he saw himself, with his beard and his rifle that he carried like a prophet's staff, within the circle of sun that covered the olive groves that extended from Tarshiha to the sea.

He said he became frightened when he saw her kneeling.

He said he hid himself in the tree and all he heard was the word *Elias*.

He said he emerged from the belly of the olive tree and looked for her.

You are Elias, Yunis. Elias is a new name to add to your others. I told you the story, son, so you don't forget that Elias is one of your names. Elias is the prophet of the fire who never died. He's the only human to have ascended to Heaven without experiencing death.

Death, as you see, isn't required.

Listen to me well.

I know you're tired.

I know you want to die.

But no.

You just have to look at yourself to know that your death would be as harrowing as the death of a child; there's nothing more savage than the death of children.

Do you want to die as Ibraheem did?

I wish she was here. I wish Naheeleh was here, to dress you in Ibraheem's clothes and stop you from dying the way your son died.

But Naheeleh isn't here, and I don't know. Still, please, try to get through this seventh month with me, and afterwards everything will start anew.

But you aren't listening.

I know you never obeyed anyone but the woman called Naheeleh.

Where am I supposed to find Naheeleh?

Salim told you that in her last days she couldn't lie flat or her lungs would fill with water. She'd sit with the basket of flowers and some water next to her, and every day ask Nour's son Yunis to go and pick new flowers. She'd sit him beside her and ask him to write the names. She'd put all your names in her basket and recite from the Chapter of Light:

God is the Light of the heavens and the earth;
the likeness of His Light is as a niche wherein is a lamp
(the lamp in a glass, the glass as it were a glittering star)
kindled from a Blessed Tree,

an olive that is neither of the East nor of the West
whose oil wellnigh would shine, even if no fire touched it;
Light upon Light;
(God guides to His Light whom He will).

"Don't forget, children. Recite the Chapter of Light at my funeral for I always see him surrounded by light. Come, Yunis, and sit beside me, for Ibraheem is waiting for me. We're all descended from Ibraheem, children. Come, Yunis. Come, Ibraheem."

Naheeleh saw her son Ibraheem in the shape of a man called Yunis, and saw her husband Yunis in the shape of a child called Ibraheem.

You're his son, not mine, so why are you tormenting me?

Please. I'll go to your house now and I'll fetch the pictures. I'll hang them on the walls of this room. We'll leave my picture of the Divine Name in Kufic script in the middle and we'll arrange your pictures around it. Your pictures around the Name, and all of you around Yunis.

I'll fetch the pictures and we'll tell the whole story.

The story will be different.

We'll change everything.

I'll hang all the pictures here and we'll live among them.

I'll get a picture down off the wall, and I'll give it to you, and you'll tell a story. Then I'll get another picture and a new story will come, and story will follow story.

That way we can make up our story from the beginning without leaving a single gap for death to enter by.

Now I stand.

I'm alone and it's night.

I stand and speak my last words with you. Talk is no longer possible, master. The speaking's done, the talk's run out, the story's closed.

I stand, neither weeping nor laughing.

As though your death was in the past. As though you died long ago. As though you didn't die.

I stand, without sorrow or tears.

I stand before this grave. I stand before the mosque turned into a grave by the siege. I bear witness that you placed your head in the earth, closed your eyes to the dust and went to a distant place.

What then?

"Tell me"?

Didn't I tell you? Didn't we agree that we had to get through this seventh month? I told you if we succeeded in getting through the seventh month, we'd have outrun death.

Didn't we agree to buy life with those long days and nights we spent at the hospital, as we told stories and remembered and imagined?

I told you they cost seven months, and we entered the seventh month, and your child-features started to take shape. I told you it was the beginning: "We've reached the beginning, father, and now you'll become a son to me."

Why did you do this to me?

I never intended this to happen.

I decided to leave you for an hour to fetch the pictures so we could start the story over again. But I didn't get back till morning. Then I saw Nurse Zeinab waiting for me at the door of the hospital; she ran towards me, rested her head on my shoulder and wept.

I asked her what was wrong, and she shook her head and said, "A heart attack."

Nurse Zeinab wept, but I didn't.

Amjad wiped away his tears as he gave instructions for the burial and I stood by like a stone. As though it wasn't me.

Please don't reproach me – you know what happened to me.

I walked in the funeral procession like a stranger, like any one of the dozens who were there. They put you in the hole, they covered you with earth, and no-one came forward to say a word. They looked at me, and I lowered my gaze. I was incapable of looking, incapable of speaking, incapable of weeping. It was as though a veil had descended over my eyes, as though I saw without seeing.

I had to wait three days before I found within myself the courage to stand at your grave, beneath this rain, the night of the camp covering me and granting me speech.

Now I'm standing, not to apologise but to weep.

I swear the only reason I went to your house was to get the pictures. I thought, I'll go and get the pictures of you and of Naheeleh and of your children and grandchildren and we'll begin the story. I felt my memory had dried out and my soul had gone dead, and I thought that only the pictures could renew our story.

I'd go to the pictures, I'd put them in front of you in the hospital room, and we'd talk.

I thought instead of talking about love, we could talk about the children and grandchildren.

I thought we could tell their stories one by one. That way, with them, we'd get across these two remaining weeks of our seventh month in death's company and make it to the pains of childbirth.

Isn't that life's law?

Didn't we agree we'd try to reach death's deepest point so we could discover life?

No, I won't leave you on this terrible night.

I said I'd go for an hour and come back, and I didn't come back.

Forgive me.

Please forgive me.

I left you with the story of Naheeleh in her last moments, as she talked with you and with Ibraheem, calling you Ibraheem and calling him Yunis, her children and grandchildren around her, weeping.

No. I didn't mean to leave you with death, because it was your duty and that of Ibraheem to guard Naheeleh and accompany her on her last journey.

I wanted a different story.

I wanted to tell you that I believed you when you said you didn't stop going over there after the night of the olive tree, when your wife sat you down and recounted her reality and the reality of her life; when she told you that over there you'd become the Jews' Jews, and over here you were the Arabs' Arabs.

I swear I believe you.

I don't want you defeated and discredited.

I believe you.

After the night of the Roman olive tree you absented yourself for nine months. Then you resumed your old pattern, continuing your journeys over there despite all the difficulties, and you didn't stop going over until after 1982 or, in other words, until after the Israeli invasion of Lebanon, when movement became impossible within Beirut and the trip from Beirut to Sidon an adventure.

That was when you stopped going across Jebel El Sheikh and they started phoning you and you'd talk to them and promise you'd all meet soon, in Cyprus or Cairo. That meeting, however, kept getting postponed, as though neither you nor she wanted it – as though both of you'd agreed, without saying so, to avoid the danger of a meeting outside the place you'd created for such meetings. One time it would be you that put it off, another time it was she who did so. And then Naheeleh fell ill.

I wanted to tell you about your series of visits over there and your trip with Naheeleh to Acre, where you went to the Abu Daoud restaurant in the Old City and ate fish and drank arak. It was there that you said to her, as the alcohol went to your head, "I swear, woman, it's like they weren't here and had never taken our country. Acre's still Acre, the Jazzar mosque is still where it's always been, the sea and the sea bass and the red mullet and the black bream are still the same. I swear, woman, I'll go home with you and stay. What can they do about it? Let what happens happen." When you returned at night, you slipped into Bab El Shams and spent the night there and forgot your talk of all the different kinds of fish and your plans to stay at home. She left you in the morning to return at night and accompany you to the outskirts of Deir El Asad, as she always did.

I swear I was going to tell you stories about Nour and her son Yunis, who excelled in his studies in Acre and went to the University of Haifa to study engineering; and about the second Yunis, Salim's son, who studied business management at Tel Aviv University and is getting ready to marry a Christian girl from Nazareth from the Khleifi family, and how you blessed the marriage. You told Salim that his grandmother used to put an icon of the Blessed Virgin under her pillow and that it was fine, the thing that matters is for us to get married and have children.

I was going to tell you, about the second Yunis, how you told him that God had blessed us by multiplying our descendants: "Here we are, thrown out of our country in 1948, and with only a hundred thousand of us left over there. The hundred thousand have become a million, and the eight hundred thousand who were thrown out have become five million. They bring in immigrants and we have children, and we'll see who wins in the end."

I was going to tell you the story of the pictures, picture by picture, story by story, moment by moment, and so put one over on time and not let it kill us.

My mistake.

Dear God! How did it happen? How did I let it happen? How did I fail to notice? How could I have got drunk?

I left her in the morning and told her I had to go to the hospital because my father was sick. She said, "Go. I know all about it."

Apart from that one sentence she didn't say a thing. And we spent the whole night eating and drinking and making love.

What came over me?

Did her ghost come to liberate me, and to let you die in peace?

I wish she was here. I wish Umm Hassan was here, but she died before you and before me. If Umm Hassan had been here, the funeral would've been different. She would've stood and lamented and made everyone weep.

They picked you up and we walked behind them, and they started dancing. The only ones to walk behind your bier were the men of the Sufi brotherhood in the camp. They remembered your father'd been a sheikh of their order, so they picked up your bier and made a circuit of the camp with it, singing and dancing. Your bier flew on top of their raised hands and they circled the camp, singing their hymns.

And I walked.

I didn't sway or sing or weep.

I walked like a stranger, as though you weren't my father or my son, as though I hadn't been with you on your secret journey to your secret country.

They picked you up and flew with you, singing hymns to the Prophet's family and I stood rigidly by.

I was like one who doesn't see.

The taste of that woman was in my soul, the smell of her on my body, her voice enveloped me.

And now you're dead and departing.

Would you like to know what happened to me? What's the point?

Would you like to hear a new story that its narrator and hero doesn't believe?

We'd decided to stop telling such stories. We'd decided we wanted stories as real as the truth.

That's why I went to your house to get you the pictures and spread them out in front of you in your hospital room or hang them on the walls and show them to you.

But I failed.

I didn't get to your house, and I didn't get the pictures.

I know you want to know, but I feel ashamed: instead of mourning you and opening my house to receive condolences, I spent the last three days looking for her.

I didn't go to the hospital, and I didn't receive condolences along with Nurse Zeinab and Dr Amjad. Instead I walked through the alleys of the camp like a lost soul, and whenever I caught sight of a woman's shadow I'd run after her till I was alongside her and look at her for a moment before resuming my progress, disappointment etched on my face.

I know they thought I'd gone mad.

I know what they're saying.

They're saying Khaleel Ayoub became demented after Yunis died. But no . . . or, well, they may be right. It was dementia; yes, definitely, dementia.

I spent three days searching and didn't sleep for one instant. I was like someone who's lost his mind. How had she disappeared, where had she gone, and what was her name? I don't even know her name. I asked her her name; I did indeed ask. But I don't remember what she said. Did she answer? I don't know.

Maybe she didn't answer. Maybe she smiled and I nodded my head as though I understood.

For three days I forgot that you're my father and my son. I forgot your death and your life and ran after the ghost of a woman whose name I don't know.

And now I've come back to you.

Forgive me. Pardon me.

I know you'll be sympathetic to my situation and accept my apology. After all, you too spent fifty years running after the ghost of a woman.

Do you know how I returned to my senses?

What saved me was this terrible idea that it was her, yes her, and that she'd come back to force me to spend the night away from you and thus steal you from me.

When this terrible idea came to me, I relaxed a little and fell asleep. Then I got up. It was night and the rain was drumming on my window, so I decided to come to your grave and tell you everything.

I decided it was time for me to weep and mourn and be inconsolable.

I decided you were dead and that I'd go on with my life without you, without the hospital and without our stories, of which we've only told little bits.

You remember.

When I left you it was 7.00 p.m., the last of the shadows were disappearing from the horizon, and I went to your house for the pictures. On my way I stopped at a shop and bought a bag of bread and a little halva thinking I'd have the halva for dinner with a glass of tea.

I took the bag and set off, and there, about fifty metres from your house, I saw her. She was wearing a long black dress, her head was covered with a black scarf, and she had a suitcase in her hand as though she was travelling.

She stood, the suitcase in her hand, and didn't turn, as if she was a photograph. When I got closer, she turned her head in my direction.

"Good evening," she said.

"Good evening," I answered.

"Do you know the house of Elias El Roumi?"

"Elias who?"

"Elias El Roumi," she said.

"There's no-one called Elias in the camp," I said.

"Yes," she said. "Elias El Roumi."

"So far as I know, there's no-one by that name."

"Where are you from?" she asked me.

"From here, from the camp," I said.

"From which village?"

"From El Ghabsiyyeh," I said.

"I could tell by your accent," she said.

"But I don't speak the Ghabsiyyeh dialect."

"Yes, you do," she said. "You speak it without knowing."

"Perhaps," I said. "That would be my grandmother's influence."

"Tell me," she said, "where his house is. I want to deliver a letter from his wife."

I said I didn't know and told her she might be mistaken; this was Shatila camp.

"I know, I know," she said. "I've come to Shatila from far away. His wife in Ein El Zeitoun gave me a letter for him and I have to deliver it and go back because it's night now and I'm a stranger here and know no-one."

"I'm afraid I can't help you, madame."

I continued towards your house.

I heard her voice behind me, so I went back to her.

"What did you say?"

"Where are the people of the camp?" she said. "Can't we ask one of them? Where's the headman?"

I told her people didn't leave their houses in the evening.

"Why?"

"Because they're afraid."

"Afraid?"

"Yes, afraid. Things aren't too good, as you can see."

"What am I supposed to do now?"

"I don't know."

"I have to deliver the letter and go back. If you could give it to him, I could leave it with you and go."

"But I don't know the man."

"Ask about him."

"I assure you, madame, there's no-one by that name in the camp. The camp's small and I'm a doctor. I know everyone."

"What's your name, sir?"

"Khaleel. Dr Khaleel Ayoub," I said.

"Please, doctor. Help me."

"I'm at your service."

"It seems I'm going to spend the night here. Take me to one of the hotels in the camp."

"You want a hotel in a refugee camp? Out of the question. You can go into town. Beirut's full of hotels."

"I don't want to go into town," she said. "I don't have time. I want a hotel here."

"I swear there are none. I don't know what to say."

"Can't I spend the night here?"

"Of course," I said, "but where? Where? You can sleep in my house, if you like."

"You're married?"

"No."

"You live with your mother?"

"No."

"Sleep in the house of a bachelor who lives alone? Impossible!"

"No. You misunderstood me. I'll take you to my house and go back to the hospital. I'm a doctor, as I told you. I'll take you there and go."

"Agreed," she said.

And she set off.

She walked ahead of me to the house. The truth is I didn't want to take her to my house; I had it in mind that your house was closer. I'd take her to your house, collect the pictures and go, and she could sleep there.

She walked ahead of me as though she knew the way to my house, and when we arrived she stopped in front of the door. I got out my keys and opened it. We went in. It was dark and there was a smell of mould. I struck a match because the camp's electricity was off, and lit a paraffin lamp. Then I saw her. She was sitting on the sofa, her case next to her, her head in her hands, and the slope of her shoulders extended like a shadow that danced on the floor of the room.

"Please make yourself at home," I said. "I'm going. Good night."

"Where are you going?" she asked.

"To the hospital," I said.

"But I'm hungry," she said.

I put the bag I was carrying on the table and said, "Please help yourself."

She opened the bag and saw the bread and halva.

"After all that distance you're going to feed me halva? No. I'll make dinner. Where's the kitchen?"

I picked up the paraffin lamp and led her to the kitchen.

"I hate the smell of paraffin," she said. "Don't you have any candles in the house?"

"Yes, yes," I said, and I went to the bedroom and looked in the drawer for the pair of candles I'd hidden there in case the paraffin ran out. I lit the candles and put one in the kitchen and one in the sitting room.

She opened her case and pulled out a plastic bag.

"Wait," she said.

I sat in the sitting room and waited for her, thinking the situation over. No, I had nothing in mind: the woman was wearing a long black dress that covered her from head to toe, and her face was half hidden by her scarf. I could say I didn't see her. So how?

No, master, I had nothing in mind.

Then I saw her with a towel tied around her waist. She started cleaning the house. I tried to help her, but she waved me off. In a matter of minutes – I swear it was minutes, not more – everything was sparkling clean. She was like a magician: she went around the house upending things and cleaning them, and the smell of perfumed soap emanated from every corner.

She said she'd make the food now.

"There's nothing in the house. Do you want me to go out and buy things?"

"There's no need," she said. "I've got everything with me."

I was in the sitting room waiting for the food when I saw her come out of the kitchen and ask me to go in and bathe.

"You go in and bathe. I've got everything ready for you, and you're not clean."

I picked up the pot of hot water she'd got ready for me in the kitchen and went into the bathroom. When I came out she was standing in the living room waiting for me. Then she disappeared for a few minutes into the bathroom and came out again with her hair hanging down loose to her shoulders. Black hair, brown skin, large green eyes, a small oval mouth, wheat-coloured face, finely moulded hands and long, thin fingers.

Beyond description, master.

I never saw a woman so beautiful, or with such presence – it was as though she'd drawn a circle around me from which I couldn't escape.

The strange thing is, I didn't ask her who she was or what she wanted, for at that moment I realised the letter wasn't real but a pretext. Even so, I didn't ask. I was like one possessed, like one revolving in the circle of the Sufi ceremony of remembrance, as though all the language I knew was the repetition of the words, "God! God!"

We sat down at the table, across which she offered me a dish of fried fish.

I couldn't smell oil, so how had she'd fried the fish?

There was red mullet, sea bass and black bream – and I saw *taratur* sauce and parsley.

"Do you have any arak?" she asked.

"Of course," I said.

I fetched the bottle of local arak and poured two glasses, added water and offered her one.

"Where's the ice?" she asked.

"Where am I supposed to find ice?" I said. "The electricity's off, as you can see."

"On Jebel El Sheikh," she said and smiled. "He who drinks arak should know where to get ice."

She said she didn't drink arak without ice.

I drank though. I drank my glass and hers and poured myself several more and wallowed in fish, *taratur* and arak.

She ate slowly, watching me.

"Good health, good health!" she said.

"Drink!" I said.

"No. I don't like arak."

And I drank, master, till my pores opened and my sinews loosened up. I drank till I felt that my soul had come back to me.

She got up, took the dishes into the kitchen, came back with two glasses of mint tea and took aniseed cake out of her case.

"Eat some of this," she said. "There's a saying of the Prophet's that goes, 'If you eat fish, eat something sweet afterwards. The one is made for the other.'"

I ate, but I wasn't satisfied. Then I opened my brown bag and brought out the halva and ate it all.

I swear, master, all I remember is her arm around me and me being with her and around her and in her. I was revolving, and leavening and eating honeycomb such as I'd never tasted in my life.

How can I explain how she was – her breasts, her waist, the slope of her thighs, her knees and the water that sprang from inside her; her whispers and her kisses and her tongue. And it was her, not me. I smelled her and drank her. I drank her drop by drop and she drank me drop by drop. I'd stop and start, rise like waves and descend with the waves, and never end. The waves were in my guts and the waves renewed themselves and began anew, and I was above the wave and inside it and beneath it, and she was the wave and the sea and the shore.

I didn't sleep at all.

I didn't speak. No, I spoke – and she put her hand on my lips and silenced me and took me . . . Then how can I . . . Brown-skinned, not white, her eyes green, not honey-coloured, her hair long, not short . . . I don't know.

That woman who came from I know not where and stood like a photograph in front of your house, whose head was covered with a black scarf, and who then entered my house and took off her scarf so I saw her hair was done up in a bun at the back of her head and thought she must be past sixty, and who then came out of the bathroom and was changed . . .

Her hair was long, and she was brown-skinned, with green eyes.

We finished eating the fish and she became white-skinned, her eyes large and black, her black hair hanging all the way to her knees.

We drank tea and her body became full, with two small, sleepy eyes and a wheaten complexion, and she took me.

She started to shimmer and change as though she was a thousand women.

Now I understand. I want to weep, master. Please forgive me. I didn't . . . I swear I didn't . . .

The light rose over us. She was lying on the bed, her eyes enigmatic. I got up and put on my clothes. I said to her, "A few minutes. A few minutes and I'll be back. I have a patient I have to check on in the hospital and then I'll be back."

She closed her eyes and whispered, "I know, I know," and held out her arms as though calling me to her.

"No," I said. "I'm going to the hospital for a moment and then I'll buy you *kunafa* with cheese for breakfast and come back."

I left her and went to the hospital, and there at the door I saw Nurse Zeinab. She hugged me, wept on my shoulder and grasped my hand to take me to your room, where you were waiting to be washed for burial.

I pulled my hand from hers and said I'd be back in a moment.

I left the hospital and ran to the *kunafa*-seller and asked for two platters. The man looked at me with astonished eyes.

"Condolences," he said.

"Thank you," I said and snatched the platters from his hand and ran towards the house, imagining her brown arms and wide eyes and her full lips and her whispers.

I entered the house and she wasn't there.

She wasn't in the bed, or in the bedroom, or in the sitting room, or in the bathroom. The bed was made and everything was in its place.

The kitchen was clean, the smell of mould filled the house, and the bag of bread and halva was in its place on the table, untouched.

I thought of the suitcase.

I raced through the house, I looked under the bed, I opened the drawers, and I searched in everything and for everything.

I left the house without closing the door behind me and ran through the streets of the camp, peering into the faces of the women, not daring to ask. What should I ask?

I stopped in front of the halva-seller's shop.

The shopkeeper asked me, "What time is the funeral?"

"Now," I said.

"How can it be now? Aren't you going to wait for the noon prayer?"

"Yes, we are. What's the time?" I asked him.

"Eight a.m.," he answered.

I asked about Elias. "Do you know a man who lives here in the camp and is called Elias El Roumi?"

"An *Elias* – a *Christian* – here in this camp? Are you nuts, brother? God bless you, they say you were very concerned for the man. You'll have a great reward, I'm sure. Go and rest now, then come back for the burial."

I went back to the hospital. I saw Dr Amjad wiping away his tears and there were men everywhere, and an uproar of lamentation. Amjad said they'd finished washing you, that the procession would start from the hospital, that there was no need to take you to your house.

I left them.

"Where are you going?" asked Amjad.

"I'll be back," I said.

I left them and ran through the streets of the camp. I peered into all the faces, then went back to my house and looked for her in the bedroom, the kitchen, the bathroom, the sitting room.

I sat on the chair in front of the table with the bag of bread and halva. I opened the bag and ate a loaf with some halva, then went to the funeral.

I didn't go back to the hospital after the funeral.

Nurse Zeinab told me that Mme Widad was coming to the hospital in the afternoon and would inform me of the decision to transfer me to Hamshari Hospital in Ein El Hilweh camp because it'd been decided to close Galilee Hospital. Nurse Zeinab said she'd refused a transfer to Tyre: she preferred to stay here, even without work, because anyway she was just waiting for the visa from her son.

I said, "Fine," and didn't go to the hospital.

I wanted nothing except to find the woman.

Why had she taken me to my house and fed me fish?

I'm in love.

I burn like a lover and I die like a lover.

Three days I was alive in death.

Three days before I despaired of death.

And today, father, I was lying on my bed and I saw her phantom image and I went up to her, and she waved me away.

Once upon a time I saw, as a dreamer sees, that I was on your bed. I was in your room lying on your bed and the pictures were swinging on the walls around me, and I saw her. She came out of the wall and approached me. I tried to embrace her and she retreated, then flattened herself against the wall. I looked at the picture for a while. It was my wife, who'd been in my bed – what was my wife doing inside the picture? What was this woman whose name I didn't know doing inside the picture of Naheeleh?

I woke with a terrified start and wept.

I didn't weep for Shams as I've wept for you and for this woman.

I didn't weep for my father as I've wept for you and for her.

I didn't weep for my mother as I've wept for you and for her.

I didn't weep for my grandmother as I've wept for you and for her.

I left my house barefoot and ran to your grave.

I'm standing here. The night covers me, the March rain washes me, and I tell you, "Master, this isn't how stories end. No."

I stand. The rain forms ropes that extend from the sky to the ground. My feet sink into the mud. I stretch out my hand, I grasp the ropes of the rain, and I walk and walk and walk . . .